Mrs. Leith-Adams

Winstowe

A Novel

Mrs. Leith-Adams

Winstowe
A Novel

ISBN/EAN: 9783337007539

Printed in Europe, USA, Canada, Australia, Japan

Cover: Foto ©Andreas Hilbeck / pixelio.de

More available books at **www.hansebooks.com**

A Novel.

By MRS. LEITH-ADAMS.

"For as gold is tried by fire,
So a heart must be tried by pain!"
ADELAIDE ANNE PROCTER.

NEW YORK:
HARPER & BROTHERS, PUBLISHERS,
FRANKLIN SQUARE.
1877.

TO

THE MEMORY

OF

A FRIENDSHIP.

WINSTOWE.

CHAPTER I.

THE MASTER OF WINSTOWE ASKS FOR A CHRISTMAS PRESENT.

THE snow was falling fast. The sky looked so dark, you wondered how such fine white fleecy flakes could come showering down from it. Already each ivy leaf had caught as many of the pretty crystals as it could well hold, and the roof of the old cathedral was spread with a deep white covering, as even and compact as the "sugaring" on a bride-cake.

A short, hale-looking man of sixty or thereabouts was trotting briskly along under a large green umbrella, and making all haste to reach the shelter of the cathedral porch. But at the gate he had a regular hand-to-hand encounter with this said umbrella; for the wind whisked round the corner of Long Lane as if it were in a very bad temper indeed, and wrestled hard to get the green umbrella altogether, or, failing that, to turn it inside out for spite. But its owner was as determined as the wind, every bit, and stuck manfully to his property, though the snow came loyally to the assistance of its companion the wind, and blew into his eyes so that he was pretty well blinded.

At last, however, the porch was reached in safety, and the umbrella, ignominiously furled, became at once perfectly helpless.

From within the cathedral sweet voices sounded, for it was the hour of evening prayer, and our wayfarer listened intently, his hands folded on the knobby handle of the umbrella, and his chin on his hands. Now and then he cast a rueful glance at the snow still drifting along the ground, and swirling by the entrance of the porch.

We will take his portrait, if you please, for he was by no means an ordinary kind of personage, and we shall have to hear a great deal about him before this story is done. He was, as I have said before, short in stature, also somewhat stout, and had a face like a rosy-cheeked apple for all the world, and perhaps the roundest mouth, and the most kindly, gentle, beaming eyes, that ever adorned a human countenance. Not even his spectacles could hide or diminish the look of universal kindliness which beamed upon every created thing, animate and inanimate, from David Earle's eyes.

The elderly marriageable female world of Weaverton (that fine old cathedral town lying in the gentle slope of a valley, picturesquely spanned by a double tier of railway arches) considered Mr. Earle, the owner of many-gabled Winstowe, in the light of a great social failure. All his kind-heartedness, instead of being, as it ought to have been, concentrated upon some fair being who would gladly shed the brightest rays of affection upon his life, and disseminate the same in his home, was diffused over the whole human race in general, and too often broke out into what the neighborhood in general was pleased to term "eccentricities."

Winstowe, whose red gables could be seen peeping through the beech-trees that clustered against a hill to the right of the cathedral town, was a perfect nest of comfort, in which this incorrigible bachelor made merry after his own fashion; and where he battened in a serene content that naturally aggravated those ladies of his acquaintance who held the doctrine that a man's "home" could never be complete without a wife.

Perhaps David Earle would hardly have so successfully repelled all matrimonial advances on the part of the many *vieilles filles* of Weaverton and its neighborhood but for the protection he enjoyed in the person and temper of Mrs. Timmins, his housekeeper and general manager. She was a female, sharp of tongue, before whose majestic proportions and coffee-colored "front" the bravest lady would turn pale, when, bent on some truly Christian errand, and discreetly chaperoned by a friend, she ventured to invade the castle of the ogre.

"It's a sin—a positive sin, my dears," said Mrs. Bunting, the local doctor's wife, to her three charming, but, alas! no longer young, daughters, as they one day filed past Winstowe, "to think that such a place as that has no lady at the head of it! Why, the poor man can't know what the meaning of the word *home* is! Winstowe's about as old as any county house in this part of Cheshire; and David Earle, though he makes so little show with his money, is just as rich as he can be. His uncle, Stanley Earle, the banker, left him a fortune, and I'll be bound he'll leave it all to some hospital for incurables, or some such rubbish."

But the fire-light glinted cheerily from the wide old-fashioned windows, in spite of all Mrs. Bunting's lamentations, and the furry, white Pomeranian looked out, and curled his tail still tighter over his back, as he rudely barked at the passers-by; no doubt, in his own way, he was saying derisively,

"We're vastly comfortable in here, thank you,

and don't want you, or any one else, to be setting us all to rights, and turning the place upside down."

So, with a withering reference to the state of household management that allowed of "heathen dogs sitting on crimson-leather chairs, like Christians," Mrs. Bunting sailed out of the avenue, and Winstowe, its master, and the Pomeranian were left in peace and quietude.

But we have wandered far from the cathedral porch, where Mr. Earle is still held a prisoner by the drifting snow. A louder burst of melody from the choristers' voices within tells that the Gloria is being sung, and then there is a silence, broken at length by a voice close to Mr. Earle's elbow.

"They're a-readin' now, sir."

Mr. Earle gave a start, and turned quickly round. Then his eyes fell on a bundle of ragged clothes huddled together in the corner. He took off his spectacles, wiped them carefully with a bandanna handkerchief, and put them on again.

"Bless me!—why—it's a boy!"

He touched the bundle with the ferule of the green umbrella, and it got up and stood before him.

Yes, it was a boy—a boy with a little, pinched, wizened face, and large wistful eyes, that looked both sad and hungry, and as if they were quite used to being both. In his hands he held a flower-pot, containing a plant, which he had tried to shelter by drawing round it the flap of his tattered jacket; his little feet were bare, and blue with cold, and curled up every now and then, as if shrinking from contact with the floor.

"Dear, dear!" said the old gentleman, looking up and down, and down and up, the small figure that stood before him, "how ve-ry extraordinary! What a queer boy!"

"Hush!" said the lad, holding up his hand, with a solemn look in his eyes, "they're singin' again—we mustna' talk." And the glorious song of the Virgin Mother pealed through the cathedral aisles.

"God bless my soul!" muttered Mr. Earle—"never saw such a queer boy before!"

The child listened intently, his eyes fixed on the closed door that was a barrier between himself and the sweet voices of the singers; and David Earle watched the child, and noted the features, worn with want and poverty, yet perfect in beauty of outline, and the golden, tendril-like hair that might have been the pride of a mother's heart, but was now all matted and tangled. The chanting ceased, and the boy turned to go. He shivered as he looked out at the snow, still falling fast and thick. Mr. Earle touched him again with the umbrella.

"Don't go yet—it snows too much."

"I'm agoin' home, sir—I've got to go," said the small wiry voice, and the flower-pot was held closer up against the ragged jacket in preparation for an encounter with the wind.

"Bless me!" said Mr. Earle, "doesn't look as if he'd got a home! What's your name, boy?"

"Willie."

"Well then, Willie, tell your mother she ought to be ashamed of herself—no, don't say that—say you'd no business out such weather as this, and that I said so."

"Ain't got no mother," said the boy, ungrammatically. "I'm Mother Dutton's boy, I am."

"And who may Mother Dutton be?" asked Mr. Earle; for his tender old heart ached over this fragile creature, this waif and stray, that the wind and snow had drifted to his feet in the old cathedral porch.

"She's the person I belong to, she is," said the child; "but she's not my mother—my mother's *theer*," and he pointed to a distant corner of the grave-yard, now one vast white sheet of snow, covering the quiet sleepers even as the righteousness of Christ spreads a pure garment over sin-soiled souls.

"Poor boy! poor boy!" said Mr. Earle, and the snow must have got into his spectacles again, for they required another polish with the bandanna.

"What's that for?" and he touched the precious plant.

"It's for Jimmy," and the child drew his old coat closer round it.

"Who's Jimmy?—your brother, eh?"

"No, he's not my brother—I ain't got no one 'cept myself. Jim's ill, he is—he can't walk. I say," continued the boy, while his companion looked at him in amazement, "do ye like to hear 'em singin' in theer?" and he jerked his head towards the oak doors of the church.

"Of course, of course," said the old man, and then muttered to himself, "Of *all* the queer boys I ever saw! Bless my soul!"

"I'm glad you like it," said Willie, coming a step nearer to his companion's knee. "I come here every day of an afternoon; and sometimes in summer, you know, they keep the door open, and then you can speer in and see them. They're all dressed in white—oh, they look fine, I can tell you!"

"Do you think it must be nice to be one of those boys, to sing in this big church, and be dressed in white?"

The child almost dropped his precious plant.

"O—h!" he said, a long emphatic exclamation of wordless ecstasy.

"Bless my soul!" cried Mr. Earle, "I never *did* see such a queer boy! Where do you live, child?"

"Over yonder in the town—Jim lives there, too, he does."

"Well, the snow doesn't fall so fast now: I'm going home with you. You must show me the way."

The boy smiled.

"You'll see Jim, and he'll see you, and I reckon he'll be pleased above a bit."

They set off together, the child's bare feet wading along in the snow, sinking in so deep sometimes that Mr. Earle started forward, expecting him to disappear altogether, flower-pot and all. From the boy's own account, he seemed to be a sort of "waif and stray," belonging to no one in particular, but of whom Mother Dutton "took care," such care as it was. The one object of Willie's love seemed to be Jim, the sick boy, for whom the dejected-looking plant was destined.

"Where are we going to?" said the old gentleman, as they turned down a street leading to the lowest and least-civilized part of Weaverton.

"To Wapping's Court, sir—that's where I live."

Down another street, and then another, each one narrower than the last, and then into a dark covered way, called a court, where the air felt heavy and close, even on that cold day. This led into a square yard, upon which entered many wretched dwellings. Willie pointed to a half-open door.

"That's where I live, sir—Jim's in there."

"Umph!" said Mr. Earle. "Queer place this!"

It certainly was a queer place. The child entered, beckoning his companion to follow.

A low room, with a window whose broken panes were stuffed with dirty rags, a few red cinders in the grate, and before it, seated in a little wooden chair, his hands stretched out to catch the warmth of the feeble fire, a boy about Willie's own age. His eyes lighted up as he saw his playmate.

Mr. Earle looked at this child with tender, pitying eyes, for his poor form was twisted in cruel fashion, and his face had that melancholy expression peculiar to the deformed.

"Jim," said Willie, kneeling by the hunch-back's chair, "I've brought it at last—ain't it a beauty?" and he produced the plant from its hiding-place, and gave it into the long bony hands eagerly held out to receive it.

"It's grand!" said the sick boy; "we must put it in the window where the sun can shine atop of it."

"Umph!" growled David Earle, "don't see how the sun's to get in *there*," and he pointed with the green umbrella to the patched and dirty window.

Thus reminded of the stranger's presence, Willie, still kneeling by his little friend, said, quickly,

"Jim, there's a gentleman, a good, kind gentleman, come to see you."

But with the sensitiveness that is so marked a characteristic of the physically afflicted, Jim covered his face, and would not look up.

"Poor fellow!" said Mr. Earle, and laid a kindly hand upon the child's shoulder, "poor little fellow!"

He looked up, still half afraid.

"*You* won't laugh at me, will you, sir?"

Mr. Earle was quite staggered.

"Bless me," he said, "here's another queer boy! There's a pair of 'em! Laugh at you! No, not I, indeed."

"Willie don't laugh at me, you know," said the child, with a confiding look up at the stranger's face. "He's very good to me, is Willie, but the others laugh and ca' me names, even when they see how bad the pain is."

"Is it often bad?" asked Mr. Earle.

The child sighed heavily, and nodded his head.

"It's worst at nights."

"And what do you do for it?"

"Willie sings out of his book—don't you, Willie?—very soft and easy, you know, for fear we'd wake mother."

"And what is the book, my boy?"

On one side of the fireplace was a narrow shelf, with a bit of colored calico nailed before it by way of curtain. Willie went to this shelf and brought out a book, which he placed in Mr. Earle's hand. It was a small plainly bound hymn-book, much worn, and on the fly-leaf was written, in faded ink, "May."

"Was this your mother's?" said Mr. Earle.

"Yes," answered the boy, holding out his hand for his treasure to be given back.

"And so you sing out of that book?"

"Yes, sir."

"Sing now; I want to hear you."

Willie squatted down by Jim's little chair, and opened the book at a place already well-fingered by much use. In a clear voice he sung the evening hymn,

"Glory to thee, my God, this night,
  For all the blessings of the light;
Keep me, O keep me, King of kings,
  Beneath thine own almighty wings."

When the last verse was finished, he looked up timidly into Mr. Earle's face: that gentleman was leaning both hands on the handle of the green umbrella, and looking very thoughtful.

"Where's this Mother Dutton who takes care of you?" he said, presently, without any comment on the singing of the hymn.

"She ain't at home of a day—she goes out selling oranges; she's Jim's mother, please, sir."

Mr. Earle pointed to the book in Willie's hand.

"You can read, I see."

"Oh yes, sir; I was learned at the Dame's school, in Jennings Street, and I kind of took to it, and read to myself of an evening; and then Bob Smithson took to helping me. He's a gradely scholar, is Bob, sir."

"Bob gave me Mouser," said Jim.

Something black in the corner of the hearth got up and rubbed its sides lovingly against Jim's legs, as if conscious of being named. This redoubtable beast was "Mouser," a cat, the object of whose existence apparently consisted in showing how much bone and how little flesh it was possible to display, and yet call itself a cat. It arched its sharp back, and, setting its ragged tail on end, sprung up upon its master's knee.

"Ain't it a beauty?" said Jim, appealing to the visitor.

Mr. Earle felt dubious, and took refuge in silence. At that moment a voice, the very reverse of that which Shakspeare assures us to be "an excellent thing in woman," made itself obtrusively audible in Wapping's Court.

"Now, 'Arry! Drat the child! can't you find nothin' better to do nor be flinging your nasty snowballs at a body like that?" and a sound followed as of one having his head cuffed.

"That's Mother Dutton," said Willie, with rather a rueful countenance.

A stout, buxom woman, with very short petticoats, and the upper part of her person vested in a man's coat, entered as he spoke. Her bonnet was violently tilted up behind, and appeared to have met with much ill-usage during its earthly career, and her face seemed to have been hardly more fortunate, for the prismatic hues of a lingering black eye adorned it. A basket containing a few oranges hung on her arm, and a small and disconsolate boy, apparently the identical individual who had flung the snowball, and suffered in consequence, followed her into the room.

"And what may *you* be pleased to want?" she said to Mr. Earle, with an emphasis on the pronoun not overrespectful or polite.

"You've not got a very comfortable place

here," said the old gentleman, with great truth, but small diplomacy.

"I know that well enough without your telling," was the rejoinder, and flop went the basket down upon the table with such energy that the golden oranges bobbed about like apples in a game of snatch-apple; "worse luck to them as makes it so!"

"Dear me!" said Mr. Earle, troubled at having raised such a storm. "I beg your pardon, I'm sure; I meant no offence."

"Where none's meant, none's taken, as the saying is," replied Mother Dutton, quickly mollified by the kindly words and beaming face of her strange visitor. "P'raps you'll be seated, sir?"

"Is your husband living, my good woman?" he asked, taking no notice of this suggestion, perhaps because of the untrustworthy appearance of the two chairs the room contained.

"Ay, he's livin', worse luck! I wish he weren't."

"Now, my good woman, don't say that," said Mr. Earle, coming a step nearer to her in his earnestness; "you don't mean it, you know."

She pondered for a moment, and turned a bruised orange with the injured side downward; then she looked up at her visitor.

"Well, sir, maybe I don't."

"Of course not—of course not, even if he's a bad husband to you."

But the woman, womanlike, took up the cudgels for the man she had just been wishing dead.

"He's not a bad husband when he's not in drink, and that's about as much as a body can say for *any* man, I reckon."

"Well," said Mr. Earle, smiling, "I hope he isn't often drunk, at all events."

"Oftener than not, sir, and then we're hard put to it, so we are; for twopence a week won't keep a woman and three children, stretch it how you will, and that's all he gi' me last Saturday was a week."

"Poor woman!" said Mr. Earle. "Such weather, too, to be out all day with that heavy basket!"

"And trade bad too, sir. I reckon it's too cold for folks to set their teeth of a edge and give their insides the chills with eating oranges, which aren't a baking sort of thing like apples, as can be warmed up. I've a mind to try them sort next time."

"See if that will buy you a good stock in trade," said Mr. Earle, slipping something into her hand.

Now Mother Dutton thought it was sixpence, but as the light fell on it as it lay in her open palm, she saw it had a little, round, yellow, shining face.

"God bless you, sir, this day!" she cried out, while the two boys looked on, astonished at the shower of gold that had fallen on the household.

"Stay, stay, my good woman," said Mr. Earle. "We mustn't have all the gifts one side. It's coming near Christmas-time, you know, and it's right for every one to have a Christmas present in his hand for his neighbor, if only to remind us all of the gift God gave to us. So now, Mrs. Dutton, I want *you* to give *me* a Christmas present."

Jim hugged Mouser closer to him—so tightly, indeed, that Mouser didn't like it, and mewed a piteous "mew." Who could tell, thought Jim, but the strange gentleman might be seized with a burning desire to possess that inestimable animal?

"What would the likes of me have to give a gentleman like yoursel'?" said Mother Dutton, extracting a shabby purse from some inscrutable and mysterious recess of her garments, and carefully placing therein the welcome Christmas windfall.

"Why," said Mr. Earle, laying his hand on Willie's shoulder, "*I want you to give me this boy!*"

<hr>

CHAPTER II.
AND GETS IT.

"His mother was but a young bit of a thing. She come here one night when it was cold enough to freeze yer marrer, and the snow were as deep as now, or deeper. She stood shakin' and shiverin' at the door·way there, and axed for to be taken in for the night, and set on her way towards High-town in the mornin'. Well, sir, you see, my man he was away on the tramp for a job just then, and the poor lass weren't in a way to be properly out in such weather, so I made shift to take the two childer—we had two little 'uns then as is since gone to a better place—into my own bed, and let the stranger lie in theirs. Well, sir, next day she couldn't hardly lift her 'and to her yed, as the saying goes, and afore night that there boy was born, and how could I turn the poor critter out then?"

It was as though, at this stage of the story Mrs. Dutton told to David Earle, her worldly wisdom reared its head retrospectively, and she had to fling herself upon it and wrestle with it, and get the better of it.

"How *could* I, sir, turn the poor critter out?" she repeated emphatically, rubbing the hair of her youngest-born all the wrong way, till his eyes watered, and grew as red as any ferret's. "How *could* I go for to do such a thing?"

"True, true," replied her impatient hearer. "And so you kept the poor thing till she was better, of course?"

But when was a female of Mother Dutton's kind ever hurried in the recital of her experiences?

"As I was just going to say, my man he came home next day after that. He were sober, but he were short—ready to take one up all roads. But, mind you, he's not a bad man when he's out o' liquor; so I says to him, 'Ben,' says I, 'there's a gal and a babbie, a little new-born, innercent babbie, lying in the childer's bed.' 'Lawk-a-days!' says he, and stare he did, I warrant. 'That's a rum go!' says he. 'Well, it is,' says I. 'But we'll make shift somehow, if you're willin'?' 'Oh, I'm willin',' says he; and so we did make shift, for, you see, she was a delicate kind of a critter, that girl was, and somehow I couldn't abear for to send her into the House."

"Yes, yes, I see," said Mr. Earle, somewhat troubled, too, at the estimation in which the charitable institutions of the country were held by the very class for whose benefit they were supposed to exist. "And so you kept the poor thing, and your husband agreed to it?"

"Ay, we kep' her; but it wasn't fer long.

Three nights after, Ben come home; and just as he'd begun to be a bit tetchy at lying four in a bed, she took very bad—all of a suddint, as you may say, sir; and quite queer in the head she was, and kep' callin' out, 'Oh, my babbie! oh, my babbie!' all the night long, till I was fair mithered; and I gets up and scrawls to her —for we was all in the dark, and I couldn't lay my hand on the matches—and 'Don't cry like that, lass,' I says; 'we'll take care of the babbie, and you too. Don't fash yoursel', but go to sleep and rest yer poor yed.' 'What have yer laid me in a cold, damp ditch for?' she says, and her big eyes seemed alive in the dark, like a cat's, and her teeth chattered with cold, though I had her wrapped up in my shawl, and the little 'un cosy beside of her. 'Don't talk about ditches,' says I, 'but hold the young 'un close up to yer boosom, and get to sleep a bit. Stay,' says I, 'I'll try and strike a light.' 'No, no,' says she, ketchin' hold of me, and her hand as cold as if she a cops already, 'I see the light comin'—it's comin' fast,' says she — 'the beautiful shinin' light! Oh, dear Lord Jesus!' Then she seem-ed to be falling asleep, and I crep' back to the bed, and slithered mysel' in, without awakin' of Ben or the childer. But in the morning she was lying dead, with the babbie crying for the suck, and shoving its face up agin the cold bress' as could never give it ony more."

At this stage of the story Mother Dutton seemed to lose command over her voice, and cov-ered her emotion by rubbing up the small boy's hair again—fortunately, though, it was the right way this time.

"*Inasmuch as ye have done it unto one of the least of these my brethren, ye have done it unto* Me!" murmured David Earle to himself.

"Beg pardon, sir, what was you a-sayin' of?" she asked, with the quick suspicion of her class, as she failed to catch the softly spoken words.

"I was only repeating the words of Him who came into the world on the first of all Christmas-days. I was only feeling very sure that you will have a blessing on you and yours for your good-ness to that poor wanderer."

"Well, sir, I'll be glad enough to see the blessin' when it comes, but it ain't come our way at present," she said, wiping her eyes with her apron in a jerky, defiant kind of manner. "Why, the inquisition itself were a dreadful piece of work, and set Ben off on the drink aw-ful, so it did!"

Mr. Earle was puzzled, and she saw that he was, and hastened to enlighten his mind.

"They sat upon her, you see—them gentle-men, I mean, as the queen pays to go and look after sudden corpses, and all such like—the crowners they call them, I think, sir."

"Oh! yes," he said, smiling, "I understand now—there was an inquest."

"That's the word. I'm a real bad 'un for words, never havin' had much of an edification in early days. Well, sir, they put the inquess in the papers, and one of the gentlemen he put a kind of notice of how she come, and how she died, and how we found a book, with 'Mary' wrote in beautiful; but, Lord bless you, sir, no one never took no notice, and never no more than nothin' did we ever hear who she was, or where she come from. She was a born leddy, ony way, and sich also was the few poor clothes she had upon her, which we buried her in, hav-ing nothing else handy. I reckon she was some poor critter as had lost her 'usbin', or as had fell in wi' a bad 'un, and got clear of 'im. There's a many bad 'usbins in the world," added Mrs. Dutton, reflectively.

"Then she had a wedding-ring on?" said Mr. Earle, with a little sigh of relief.

"No, she hadn't got no ring on her," replied Mother Dutton; "but people—'specially female people—gets druv in a mort o' ways; and I'm not one to think harm of ony poor creetur till I've some call to do so. 'Tain't no manner of reason for to call a woman wuss than her neigh-bors just because—"

The good woman tossed her head so that her bonnet fell off, and took up an uncertain posi-tion on her back, held there by the strings, of which one was black and the other a dingy red, and bore no sort of family resemblance to each other.

"*I've* never the shadder of a ring to my name, and yet I'm Dutton's lawful wedded wife, and have my marriage lines safe at the bottom of that old metal teapot up behind you on the shelf, together with a solid silver spoon as be-longed to my mother before me. I've never brought myself to 'put that away,' no matter what straits we've been in; for, 'Martha,' says she to me upon her dying bed, 'them as is born with a silver spoon, as the saying is, should stick to it!' And stick to it I have, though at times Ben has longed after it so that I've had to hide it in my shoe or slip it down the back of my gownd, and neither of these is comfortable places for a hard lump of a thing like a spoon. But, as I was sayin', my weddin'-ring went long enough ago to get bread for me and the childer, when Ben was on one of his worstest sprees; but lor! I don't make no account of that. When childer's bellies is empty, and they're tellin' you so every blessed minute, it's only natur' to do what you can to put a cruss inside of 'em. It's only what mother said upon her dying bed as kep' the spoon weer it is."

"And you have reared this boy as your own?" asked Mr. Earle, hoping to stem this torrent of personal reminiscences.

"Oh yes; he's had part and parcel with us reg'lur, as you may say—bread and, maybe, drippin' one time, and nought but bread another, and whiles again no bread nor no drippin' nei-ther. He's been a good boy, as boys go, though perhaps that ain't saying much, and I've made shift to give him a power of schooling at the Dame's round in the next court. It stood me a penny a week when I could ill spare it, but, says I to mysel', edification's everythink in these days; and when times looked so bad it seemed as if mother's spoon would be forced to go, I'd say to mysel', well, if it must, it must; better for learning than drink, any day. He's throve well, has Willie, sir, though I say it as shouldn't, as the saying is."

You see, the fact of the case was this: Mother Dutton had passed her word, a quarter of an hour or so ago, to give David Earle the strange Christmas present he had asked for, and now she was beginning to repent of her bargain; she had grown fonder of the boy than she knew.

Which of us ever know how fond we are of a thing until Fate begins to try to draw it from our hold? *Then* our fingers close tightly enough upon it, and its value in our past possession of it increases like something looked at through a magnifying-glass.

"What will you do with the boy (if I may make so bold), if so be I *do* give him to yer?" she asked, looking anxiously at her visitor's round beaming face, and casting a glance of valuation at his attire, including the green-cotton umbrella.

"Well," said Mr. Earle, "first of all I should get him a new suit of clothes, then put him to a good school—the cathedral school, most likely; then, when he's big enough, I should have him made into a chorister—"

"O—h!" cried the two lads, in the extremity of their amazement.

"Mew!" cried poor Mouser, whom Jim was squeezing in a grip of extra tightness in his excitement and delight.

"Come, come!" continued Mr. Earle, anxiously, "you're not going to try to cry off your bargain, my good woman?"

"Well, sir, I don't know as I am, but I'd like to speak to my man about the matter. You see, Willie's useful in a mort of ways since he's grown some size; he's fust rate to mind the child here, and I can't think what Jim there will be doing of without him. You kinder took me suddint and by surprise, and I answered hasty. I've bin a deal upset just of late, sir, what with one thing and another, and Christmas is a bad time, a sorry bad time, sir, for them as has men who drinks."

Mr. Earle looked very grave at this.

"Let us hope," he said, feelingly, "that your husband will keep out of trouble this Christmas. Do you think he would take the pledge?"

"Take the pledge! Oh yes, sir, he'd *take* anything, but keeping of it's quite another matter. He'd never keep nothing, not even mother's spoon, if I hadn't hid it reg'lar when he began his games. Why, I bought this little 'un a new hat, for the crown of the other was gone, and the brim in bits, and, Lord bless you, sir, he took and pawned it that day—was a week last Saturday! Then the child hisself was contrary over the matter, and drove me, so he did; for when I got it took out o' pawn, he went a-walking by the canal side, along with another varmint like hisself, and began for to ketch fish with it. Who ever heard the like, to ketch jacky-sharps in a bran-new 'at! He brought it home a reg'lar smudge, and with no shape left about it."

Mrs. Dutton began to whimper over the ruined grace of the youngster's hat, but David Earle readily recognized the true source of these tears. She was grieving over the thought of parting with Willie, though no power of persuasion would have induced her to say so. The relation of the little domestic incident regarding the hat had led Mr. Earle to the conclusion that her "man" either was now, or very lately had been, on the "spree," and therefore he looked upon the wife's suggestion as to holding a consultation with him to be a mere feint, for the purpose of giving a sop to her own half-roused repentance in the matter of parting with Willie.

"Well, now, look here," he said, raising his umbrella in one hand, so as to be all ready to emphasize a word or two, if necessary, by bringing it down upon the red-bricked floor, "what do you say to putting it to the boy's own choice? Let me hear what his own feeling is. Will you agree to that?"

"Well, maybe, sir, that's as good a way as any. You see, Ben, he's bin drinking a good sup of late, and his brains gets as addled as a six-weeks'-old egg when he soaks 'em in liquor all day, and goes to his bed of a night like a log—though to be sure a log's good for fire-wood, and a drunken man's good for nought; so, to say 'a log' is to say what's too good."

"Now, my boy," said the old gentleman, cutting short off this new pathway into which the good woman's eloquence had strayed, "would you like to come and belong to me, and go to school, and be a chorister, and who knows what all, some of these days?"

Willie looked at the kindly face beaming upon him like a cheerful sort of sun upon a poor sickly, ill-grown plant. There was nothing to awaken distrust *there*. Why, surely no man or woman living could be found to distrust the master of Winstowe? But the boy's eyes turned away from those that shone upon him through Mr. Earle's spectacles, and rested on the helpless form of poor little Jim, his crippled foster-brother. His mouth twitched and trembled a moment, then he turned again to his would-be friend.

"Please, sir, could you take Jim too?"

David Earle was nonplussed.

"Bless my heart!" he cried, and down came the umbrella ferule on the bricks, "what a queer boy!"

Willie twisted and turned his thin hands one in the other, and looked appealingly up into his face. Jim bent his shaggy head down lower and lower, and cuddled Mouser closer to his breast. As to Mother Dutton, she had given up all pretence of putting a brave face on matters, and was weeping undisguisedly, wiping away the tears as they fell with the ends of the twisted bonnet-strings.

"I can't take Jim, too," at last said Mr. Earle; "but you shall come and see him as often as you like, and bring him plants with lovely flowers growing on their branches,"

"But I'm feart he'll be lonesome when I'm not by," cried the child, torn in two by his wish to go and his longing to stay, and the utter impossibility of doing both these things. "*Won't* you be lonesome, Jim—dear Jim? Oh, do say if you'll be lonesome!"

Jim's face was hidden in the furry coat of the black kitten, and his voice had rather a muffled sound in consequence; but the words themselves were as brave as the spirit that dictated them, even though that spirit was shrined in a poor crippled frame.

"I'll get along reet enough. Go with the gentleman, Willie, and just come and see me and Mouser—as—oft—as—ye—can."

Then Willie flung himself down by the little chair, and the two children fell a-weeping together. And this was how David Earle got the Christmas present he asked for. What he did with it, we must leave for future chapters to tell.

CHAPTER III.

WHAT HE DOES WITH IT.

It is quite true that the joys and sorrows of childhood are as keenly felt at the time as those of riper years, but in sketching the history of a life it needs not to linger too minutely upon early days. Suffice it, then, to say that David Earle was not a man to do anything by halves, and that a trust once undertaken by him was sure of complete and faithful fulfilment.

One short year after that day, so eventful and all-important a one to Willie, when Mother Dutton gave the Christmas present she was asked for, a stranger would have taken it for granted that the boy was the son of the owner of Winstowe. I pass over the storm of gossip that buzzed about the old cathedral town—the astonishment of the dean and the dean's lady, the indignation of Mrs. Bunting, her train of daughters, and Weaverton in general, at the eccentricity of Mr. Earle—"positively taking a boy out of the gutter, and openly adopting him as the heir of a fine old property, that had passed from father to son for goodness knows how long!"

To Mrs. Timmins "master's" word was law; to Mr. Briggs Mrs. Timmins's word was law; and Pompey, the Pomeranian, always did exactly what the other two did; so the allegiance of the Winstowe household was tendered at once to the little stranger, and on the very first occasion of Willie coming to spend a half-holiday at *home* (for he was by this time a scholar at the cathedral grammar-school, and a chorister as well), Mrs. Timmins announced the fact of his arrival to her master in these terms:

"*Master* William has arrived, sir."

It was enough; Briggs followed suit, and Pompey sat down by the child's chair and laid his fluffy white head upon his knees.

Certainly there is no small truth in the saying that "fine feathers make fine birds," and our friend Willie was now a very different sort of individual from the ragged, barefoot boy who had taken shelter in the cathedral porch that snowy day on which our story first opened. Not only so, but the atmosphere in which he now found himself appeared to be strangely congenial to him; he took to a better state of things as though "to the manner born," and, as Mr. Briggs sagaciously observed, "it shooted him to be a gentleman just as if it was clothes he'd been measured for."

All little vulgarities of speech, all roughness of manner, fell off with wonderful rapidity, and by the time he had run the gantlet of the local grammar-school, and drifted into the ranks of one of our best public schools, no one could discover, or be led to surmise, that his earliest years had been spent in so humble a social stratum; indeed, the peculiar refinement of his face and manner was often the subject of remark.

You may be sure those humble friends who had so nobly out of their own poverty found bed and board for the little waif and stray were not forgotten by Willie's generous benefactor. Mrs. Dutton had long since become the proprietor of quite a flourishing grocery store; and little Jim, whose deformity was less a cause of helplessness as he grew older, a day-boarder at the cathedral school. With that sharpness of intellect so often found in the deformed, he quickly distanced boys of his own age, and became such a "scholard" that his mother's opinion as to the value of "edification" grew more confirmed than ever.

At the outset of these changes there had been some little exercising of mind on the part of Mr. Earle as to Willie's surname. He had delicately inquired of Mother Dutton if the boy had ever been baptized, and to this query (most gently put) the good woman answered with some show of indignation and a redundance of negatives:

"I'm not one to neglect nothing. I always had all my children done for both worlds—they was every individual one vaccinated by the parish doctor, and christened by the parish parson. I was brought up respectable myself, and I brings them up the same."

"And it is very creditable to you, my good woman," said Mr. Earle, soothingly, "very creditable, indeed; but, you see, the point I want to understand is this—by what name was the boy you have given me baptized, and in what name was his birth registered?"

"Well, sir, he were christened William—just short, and no more—for, says I, poor children have enough burdens to carry without a name as long as yer arm; and for another name—you see, sir, he come in the snow, and in the snow we tuk him, so we called him 'Snow,' and William Snow's his name, fast and sure, and so it's wrote in the parish book."

But of course this conversation took place a long while ago now, for five times the leaves have budded out upon the grand old elm-trees in the cathedral close; five times they have lived in the fulness of beauty through the golden summer sunshine; five times they have fallen to the ground, and been covered up by the beautiful white snow—that heaven-cast pall that covers the dead year—since Willie left Wapping's Court, and became as a son to the master of Winstowe.

The only one in that group upon whom the interest of our story centres, who seemed to have gone down, instead of up, hill during these five years, was "Ben," Mrs. Dutton's "man." At the best of time he had never worked to maintain his family, except by fits and starts, which eccentric and jerky efforts invariably ended in a "bout of spree," as he called it, and the consequent hiding of his wife's mother's silver spoon in those uncomfortable places of which we wot. Prosperity seemed to make things worse with him, instead of better.

When Mr. Earle gave his wife the stock in trade and the first year's rent of the smart grocer's shop, in a respectable street of the populous cathedral city, Ben expressed his supreme content at the condition of affairs, more especially at the shop being a concern that would just "stand still i' the street, and keep itsel'." He took the pledge, too, subsequent to a long talk with Mr. Earle: then he broke it, met that gentleman in the street, and hiccoughed out an assertion that he had "had for to giv' up the temp'rance dodge, for it didn't noways agree with his constitootion."

This outbreak lasted for a month: dreadful sounds issued at intervals from the back regions of the grocery establishment, and Mrs. Dutton appeared behind the counter with a black eye.

Once Ben met Willie as he was returning to school from a happy afternoon at Winstowe, and the half-drunken man asked the lad for money, reminding him that all his luck in life was owing to what he, Benjamin Dutton, had done for the poor castaway mother and her babe. Willie went penniless to school that afternoon; but he never said a word about what had happened, you may be sure, and shortly afterward it was decided that he should go to that public school of which I have before spoken.

It is summer now, when we take up the regular thread of our story again; the leaves of the quaking ash upon the lawn at Winstowe rustle and tremble, and show their pretty silvery linings in the gentle breeze, that is sweet with the perfume of the crimson, white, and palest golden roses of which David Earle is so proud. Little banksia roses, like golden buttons, dot the gable that looks into the garden, and the jasmine pushes milk-white, starry blossoms through the open window of the study, where the master sits in such deep thought, and with so sad a look upon his usually genial face, that you feel sure neither the rustle of the boughs outside, nor the pretty flowerets peeping in at his window, are noticed by him, or give him any pleasure.

On the desk at which he sits (a piece of furniture whose recesses in the way of pigeon-holes and drawers are quite confusing to an ordinary mind) lies an open letter—a letter written on that thin paper that tells us the missive comes from a foreign land, and from those that seem doubly, trebly dear because they are so far away.

Above the fireplace of this cosy room hangs a picture. It is that of a young and lovely woman—lovely, not so much from small and perfect features as from the sweet and gentle expression that smiles upon you as you look upon her face. The soft yet earnest hazel eyes, the smiling mouth, the sunny hair falling in careless ringlets on her shoulders ; all the beauty that he so well remembered, all the beauty that he should never see again, spoke with touching power to the old man's heart as he laid down the letter that told him of her death, and gazed at her pictured face. His only sister's child, early orphaned, tenderly reared and watched over as his own, Lilian, in the days of her bright, beautiful girlhood, had been as a sunbeam about the old house, as a sunbeam in the heart of its master. He had so long looked upon her as a child, that when Vere Selwyn, captain in the Indian army, asked his permission to offer her his hand and heart, all he could find to say was—"That child! my little Lillie!" And it was only when they reminded him that his "little Lillie" was eighteen years of age that the possibility of such a thing as her marriage dawned upon his mind.

"But she'd never go all by herself to such an outlandish place as India!" said David Earle. Captain Selwyn flushed up at that, and suggested that a woman who had a husband by her side could hardly be said to be "all by herself." After all, it was Lilian herself who settled the matter; she clung about his arm, and said, so low he had to bend down to catch the words,

"I shall always love you, dear Uncle David—always ; but, please, I think that I must go with —Vere!"

And she went; like a true woman, she left all to follow the man she loved. This was many years ago now—years during which her letters had been the one great pleasure of the old man's life.

There had been news of a baby boy born to Lilian, a little blossom that early drooped and died ; and two years later of another, a girl this time, with the mother's eyes, too, so Vere said.

Like many a delicate woman, Lilian stood the enervating Indian climate better than others apparently more robust, and had always written home cheerfully, telling how "Lilian the younger" grew and prospered, and what a "great girl she would be when mother should bring her to England to see Uncle David."

But mother would never bring her now! Death, in swift and sudden form, had snatched Vere Selwyn from the loving arms that could not hold him back, and, weakened by sorrow and anxiety, Lilian herself had fallen an easy prey to the "pestilence that walketh in darkness."

Ever close together, hand to hand and heart to heart in life, in death the husband and the wife were not divided.

A friend, the wife of a brother-officer, had hurried to Lilian in the first hour of her trouble; had aided and supported the poor stricken wife in tending her dying husband; had stayed with her when all was over, and nursed her through the illness that so rapidly followed, supporting in her arms to the last the fragile form in which had dwelt a soul so brave and gentle.

I almost think that it is in military life alone that such devoted friendships as this that I am telling of exist; not because hearts are not as true, affections as warm, elsewhere, but because people in the same regiment are thrown together, and obliged to be dependent one on the other, in lands far distant from all family ties, as no other people can be. I for one can look back and say, Can any friendships be so close and true, and ride so triumphantly over all minor difficulties when once the hour of sorrow comes, as the close bond of union between the members of the same regiment?

To this true friend, then, had Lilian, dying, committed her last wishes about the child, orphaned in a strange land. The little one was to be sent, by the first opportunity that offered, to the dear old home at Winstowe, to the loving care of him who had so well watched over the mother's childish years.

And this opportunity had come almost immediately. The wife of a sergeant in a line regiment was returning home with her husband, he having completed his "time," and this woman, in every way trustworthy, was willing to take charge of the little Lilian.

"Even now," thought Uncle David, wiping away the tears that had stolen down his cheek, "they may be on their way."

He rung the bell sharply, and Briggs so promptly answered the call that it was impossible to suppose he had come from any very distant region ; indeed, to tell the truth, he and Mrs. Timmins had had a long confabulation as to the reason of a black seal upon "master's letter from foreign parts," and they had both been restlessly wandering about the hall, and in and out of the pantry, anxiously waiting the sound of the bell.

"Briggs," said Mr. Earle, in a somewhat unsteady voice, "I have had bad news, very bad news from India—"

"That's what we was respectfully afraid of," said Briggs, keeping his hold on the handle of the door, and giving a look over his shoulder in the direction of the hall.

"Tell Mrs. Timmins I want her immediately."

But there was no need for any one to "tell" Mrs. Timmins, for she broke past Briggs, and cried to her master,

"Oh, sir! what is it? Is it bad news of Miss Lilian?" The master's face—the black-sealed letter—answered her.

I have said that now "it was the time of roses," and that those lovely flowers lifted their perfumed blossoms to the sunshine, and gave out their sweet breath in the Winstowe gardens. Surely it must have been the summer holiday. Where, then, was William Snow?

Our hero, by this time a tall, slender, blue-eyed fellow of thirteen, had the excellent gift of making friends, and even in these days had won the heart of the mother of one of his schoolmates, a boy whose home was close to the college. So it came about that David Earle received a letter from this lady, asking for Willie to go and spend the summer holidays, with herself and her son, at a sea-coast village, where boating and bathing would make the time pass pleasantly enough.

It was a great disappointment to Jim when he found that the holidays would pass without bringing Willie to Winstowe. Jim's heart was a universe, of which Willie was the sun. No change in the circumstances of either could alter or lessen the mighty love he bore him; a love that had in it the humble faithfulness of a dog's attachment to its master. No one knew what the pain of parting with Willie, just a year ago now, had been to the crippled boy. He had lain awake at nights counting the days until the Christmas holidays; and when at last he saw Willie (changed strangely, too, even during that short four months' of public-school life) rush through the shop and into the little parlor at the back, Jim couldn't find one word of welcome. Even the face of his foster-brother seemed all blurred and indistinct, seen through the hot tears of gladness that rose and fell.

"Why, Jim!" said Willie, holding the long, thin hands in his—"why, Jim! are you crying because I'm come home again?"

"No, no; it's because I'm glad. Oh, more glad than any one can think or know!" And Mouser, by this time an obese and majestic cat, rubbed his fat sides against Willie's legs, and purred almost as loud as the tea-kettle sung, to show that he, too, wished to offer a welcome, as far as his humble capabilities would allow.

But there was to be no such happy meeting this summer-time, and a cruel jealousy ached in Jim's heart. These fine friends had taken the sun from his sky. He was jealous *of* Willie, and *for* Willie, after the fashion of an absorbing love. When rumors of the little child coming all the way from India to find a home at Winstowe reached his ears, he harbored hard, unkindly thoughts of the stranger, just as if she had been a little cuckoo coming to push the rightful owner out of the nest.

Presently the leaves turned brown and fell, and the garden at Winstowe was strewed with their little shrivelled bodies. The evenings began to close in early. People were glad to gather round the fire, shut the windows close, and listen to the cold wind whistling round the corners and swaying the bare branches of the poor naked trees, from the safe, snug shelter of their "ain ingle nook." Then first one and then another began to speak of "Christmas-day" coming near, and the cathedral choir practised carols, until the boys were all as hoarse as if they each and all had chronic bronchitis.

The biggest turkey in the Winstowe farm-yard strutted about with a happy unconsciousness of his approaching end, and grew daily more impertinent and tyrannical to his fellows, by reason of being uplifted at the flattering notice bestowed upon him by Mrs. Timmins.

She, for her part, was absorbed in the preparation of mince-meat, and often smiled knowingly over her work, and remarked jocosely to Briggs, that "Master Willie would find a bonnier Christmas-pie awaiting him than any *she* could make."

And so at last, on Christmas-eve, as the sweet cathedral bells were chiming, and the dying sunlight was glinting on the snow that had fallen just in time to "whiten Christmas," Willie came home.

"Uncle David," as the boy had learned to call his benefactor, was a prisoner to his room, a sharp attack of gout threatening to spoil his Christmas enjoyment; but not even pain could quite drive away the happy, beaming look from his round old face, at the sight of the tall, fair-haired, handsome lad, the sightly young tree that his own hand raised.

There seemed to be also some secret source of satisfaction and amusement tickling his fancy; and when he said, "There now, my boy, go down to my study and get your tea; you need it, I'm sure, after such a journey," he chuckled to himself, as if he was enjoying the flavor of some exquisite joke.

CHAPTER IV.

WILL MAKES A PROMISE.

I DON'T suppose it would be possible for a room to be more cosy, bright, and comfortable than the study at Winstowe. There stood "the master's" special easy-chair, just by the fireside —a chair that was actually more restful than a sofa. At the side of this stood the desk of which we have before spoken, and near the long, low window, with its deep, softly cushioned seat, stood a round table. Crimson curtains shut off the recess of this window in the winter evenings, and on the woolly hearth-rug, before the fire, Pompey usually took up his position, blinking at the fire with his knowing eyes, and, no doubt, indulging in scornful wonder as to how unhappy dogs existed who had no soft rugs to lie upon, and whose tails hung ignominiously down, instead of curling tightly over their backs like his.

We left our young hero on his way, at Uncle David's bidding, to this same pleasant parlor, and truly very pleasant it looked as Willie came in.

Tea was set on the round table; the crimson curtains were drawn; Pompey was in his usual place, and had even more than his usual air of self-complacency. But what on earth was that strange object in Uncle David's chair?

It was a doll.

Now Willie had heard of "second childhood;" but even supposing Uncle David, Mrs. Timmins, or Briggs himself had attained to this venerable condition, could it be possible a doll, and such a doll too, with one eye missing and its wig all awry, could be the result?

Just as he was going to lift the object up and examine it, there was a stirring of the crimson curtains, a little hand appeared pushing them gently aside, and a little lady stepped out from the dark recess. She held out her hand, and said, with perfect self-possession,

"How do you do, boy?"

"So the doll is yours?" said Willie, trying with boy-like pride to look as if he wasn't at all astonished, and rather expected half a dozen more little girls to step out from behind the crimson curtains.

"Yes, it's mine," said the child, fondling the one-eyed creature, and vainly trying to pull its scalp into place.

"I'm glad you've come," she continued, giving a sigh of evident relief; "I've been waiting in there ever so long. Uncle David said I was to —till you came in, you know, and then I was to come and say, 'How do you do?'"

Willie's blue eyes were round and large with astonishment, not so much at her being there (though that was strange enough), as at her gentle, self-possessed manner.

"I'm to make tea for you," the elf continued. "Please lift me on that chair, and then you can ring the bell for them to bring the tea."

He lifted the dainty, fairy figure in his arms, noticing, as he did so, that her dress was black, as also was the simple band that tied back the glory of her golden hair. Then he took his seat beside her. Mrs. Timmins, coming in with hot cakes and a tiny silver teapot, well fitted for such little hands as the tea-maker's, laughed at his serious, puzzled face, and told him *this* was the "Christmas pie" her master had written to say would be ready for him. Then she asked him "how he liked it?"

"Oh! I like it very much—I think it a very pretty pie," said Willie; and they all three laughed, till the old man heard them all the way up-stairs, and laughed himself to think how happy their voices sounded.

"This little lady's name is Miss Lilian," said Mrs. Timmins, "and she's to be a little sister for you, Master William."

"Oh!" said Will, eying the small creature, who was gravely pouring out the tea, and popping in the lumps of sugar with her own rosy fingers instead of the legitimate sugar-tongs. Then they were alone again, and, after the manner of children meeting for the first time, less shy and constrained in consequence.

"I'm six and a half," volunteered the lady, with charming candor. "How old are you, boy?"

"Thirteen," said Willie, helping first his companion and then himself bountifully to Mrs. Timmins's delicious marmalade.

The child looked grave. Thirteen seemed a great age. Perhaps, resting on the dignity of his years, this big boy would not care to play with her?

"Uncle David said you was to be my big brother, and always take care of me," she said, rather wistfully, her great violet eyes suddenly becoming "bright with unshed tears."

"Well, and so I will, you know," said Will, cordially, but (as became his advanced age) with a certain air of patronage, too.

"Then I think you had better kiss me," was the unexpected rejoinder; and she laid down her bread and marmalade, carefully wiped her rosy bit of a mouth upon a ridiculous handkerchief that hung at her side, and waited patiently for Willie to carry the suggestion into action.

He got up, stood beside her, and, bending down, softly kissed the little smiling mouth. And thus the compact was sealed. Lilian was now quite happy: she invoked his aid to mend poor dolly's dilapidations, and prattled away as if she had been in truth his little sister always.

That night, when Lilian had gone to bed, and Will sat beside Uncle David's fire, the old man told him all the story of how the orphan child came to Winstowe. As he listened, the boy's heart was drawn towards this little one, who, like himself, had in the world no friend save David Earle—no home save the dear old house that was now so brightened by her sweet presence.

Later on in the evening he stood looking up at the picture over the study fireplace. Yes, the child was very like the mother—the child's eyes were darker, and the brows more clearly defined; but the exquisite sweetness of the mouth was the same in both; and the trustful smile told in each alike of a nature that "knew no guile."

The next day was Christmas-day. The sun shone brightly, but the air was frosty, and it was only in places here and there that the snow melted.

Uncle David came down to dinner, and then took up his place in the big easy-chair. The children had been to service at the cathedral, and joined in the glad hymn that bids the whole Christian world rejoice, because the Lord of Life and Glory has come upon the earth. They had walked home hand-in-hand, all the crisp, clear air filled with the music of the glad, gay bells. Every face was arrayed in Christmas smiles, and many a kindly glance followed the two figures that contrasted so well together; the tall, lithe lad, his crisp brown locks clustering close about his square brow, his bright blue eyes and cheery smile so "good to look upon," and the little creature at his side, stepping out bravely, her glistening hair showing fairer for its contrast to her black frock. Every now and then she glanced up into her tall companion's face, as if to be quite sure he approved of her ceaseless chatter.

Well, after dinner was over, as I said before, Uncle David ensconced himself by the study fire. Lilian sat beside his knee upon a low stool, nursing the doll, whom all Willie's ingenuity had not succeeded in restoring to anything like respectability.

"I'll buy her a new dolly," Uncle David had once said.

But the child hugged the disfigured one closer to the bosom of her dress.

"No, thank you. I couldn't have a new one. This dolly would be sorry, and think I didn't love her any more."

It was but a trifle, and yet it told of a tenderly loving and faithful nature. And it is just such natures that are marked out for the keenest suffering. They suffer through their very faithfulness; and where the love of a lesser nature would cease to be, their love lives on,' through pain and misconstruction, and the faults and unkindness of the loved one.

Leaving the uncle and niece mightily contented with each other, Will set off to pay a Christmas visit to the old friends towards whom his heart never changed. He had heard of the black-silk dress given to Mother Dutton by Mr. Earle as a Christmas gift, and thought how pleasant it would be to see her arrayed in all her grandeur. In the old - fashioned days of which I write, a silk dress was a thing to make a woman of that class proud for the rest of her life — a thing to give her a certain standing among her neighbors, and to be watched over, and worn on high days and holidays, as a sort of heirloom, much as a fine lady wears her family diamonds.

With a bright face and brisk step William Snow stepped along the high-road that led from Winstowe to the town. It was at least a three-mile walk, but not a bit too long to please an active lad like our hero. He whistled as he went, and kept his hands snug and warm in his pockets.

But once in the parlor behind the closed shop, he saw that his old friends were having anything but "a merry Christmas." No one was at home but Mrs. Dutton and the boy Harry, now grown a strapping fellow. There was no grand black-silk dress to be seen; indeed, the only adornment the poor woman's person displayed was the questionable one of a black eye.

As soon as she saw Will, Mrs. Dutton, to use her own expression, "gave up all of a lump." She sat down on a chair, put her apron to her eyes, and burst out crying.

Of what use was it for Will to ask questions? Don't we all know, when we see a home look desolate, a wife miserable, and showing the cruel marks of a cowardly hand, that the devil of drink has entered into and possessed the man who owns both home and wife? Don't we know that the children listen for the sound of his staggering step, and when they hear it, shrink into corners, or fly to the shelter of the streets, from the home that is no home except in name?

Too well Will read the signs before him.

"Where is Jim?" he said, anxiously, sitting down by the weeping woman, and taking her hand in his as tenderly as though it had been the soft white palm of some great lady, and he the lover that worshipped at her feet. Mrs. Dutton only rocked herself to and fro, and moaned out something he could not understand.

"Jim's gone after father," said Harry, his lip trembling; "he'll come for Jim sometimes when he won't for no other of us. He come 'ome two days ago, and beat mother dreadful: he'd have beat me too, but I made off, I did!"

The faintest trace of a grin illuminated his young countenance as he made this last remark.

"And he's took mother's spoon this time, true and fast," sobbed Mrs. Dutton, finding her tongue at last. "We'll never have no luck no more! never no more!"

"Don't say that," said Will, patting the hand he held; "we'll get the spoon back, never fear."

"He's disgraced me in front of my neighbors, so he has!" cried the disconsolate woman. "He come and took every farthing out of the till, and then he got mad-drunk—drunk as any beast—though I don't rightly know as beasts *do* get drunk, and perhaps I'm miscalling of 'em behind their backs. Home he come, did Ben; and I'd no more money for to give him; and when I tellit him so, he—he—"

"Hush!" said Will, "don't speak about it, dear; it don't make it any better, you know, and it hurts you to remember it."

A sudden thought seemed to come over her.

"You'd best go home, Master Willie," she said, rising as she spoke, and giving her face a scrub with her apron; "Ben might come in any blessed moment as ever is, and he's taken agen you awful, 'as Ben! It sounds bad to be saying of it, I know, lookin' at all the dear good gentleman 'as owns you 'as done for us this past years; but it's true, for all that. Ben's taken agen you most awful!"

The woman seemed so earnest—she trembled so as' she spoke, and was so possessed by the fear of her husband coming home while Will was there—that the boy felt the truest kindness was to go. He pressed into her unwilling hand the golden guinea that had been his Christmas-gift from Mr. Earle that morning, and then he took his way home.

All the bright anticipations with which he had set out had vanished away. He had looked to find peace and plenty, and a happy though humble home: he had found only sorrow and desolation and tearful reproaches. And this sad state of things did not come from grinding poverty, or from sickness or suffering — none of these sources of misery were there; it was drink, drink only, that with its blighting breath breathed a curse upon the home that should have been so happy. As Will made his way through the crowded streets, he saw more than one reeling figure making an uncertain progress along the pavement. These had been *keeping Christmas!* One, more drunken than the rest, with a ghastly remembrance of some teaching of his boyhood, yelled out the sacred words of a Christmas-hymn, ending the line with a burst of drunken laughter and vile oaths.

We all of us see such sights and hear such sounds in the streets of England's great cities; but do we call to mind that to each reeling figure, each muddled brain, in which all evil passions rise and foam as filthy scum, pertains a home? Do we realize that the drunken, maddened wretch goes there at last, to bring the curse of his presence upon the unhappy ones who share that home?

Hardly, I think. Surely, if it were so the rich would set a brighter and better example to the poor. The only shadow on the happy Christmas-day spent by our Winstowe friends was Will's account of the state of things at Mother Dutton's.

"And indeed, sir," said Briggs, when his master was undressing that night, "I'm not one to be bringing scandal into the house of those you see fit to give a helping hand to, but Tuesday last it was just a week, I saw Mr. Dutton that drunk he didn't rightly know which end of himself was uppermost."

"I'm sorry—I'm very sorry, Briggs," said his

master — "most of all for the poor woman's sake."

"He'd be sorry for a thieving blackguard of a rat as was caught in a trap, master would!" was Briggs's comment to Mrs. Timmins afterward; "and I wasn't going for to tell him how the man bellowed out after me, and called the master himself names as I wouldn't demean my lips to be repeating, least of all in the presence of a lady, Mrs. Timmins. 'Who's bin and stole the boy away?' cries he—'the boy whose friends might have turned up, and offered a reward any day, and me and my missus bin made a gentleman and lady of!' It's a deal for a respectable man to have to put up with, to be mocked at like that, but I can bear a deal for master! I don't know as even a dead cat or a rotten egg would seem too much to put up with for *him!*"

The day after Christmas-day a thaw set in. The snow all vanished, as though the wand of some enchanter had been waved over the landscape, and the wind moaned and wailed as only a thaw wind seems to know how to do.

This was quickly followed by that uncomfortable kind of weather called a "black frost."—uncomfortable, that is, to all but the young and hearty, whose energy is yet undamped, and whose blood flows too quickly for its stream to turn sluggish, because the thermometer stands below freezing.

The canal that ran through the town, down by the cathedral close, and then under the bridge that led to the great iron gates of Winstowe, was frozen so hard that not the most anxious mother could conjure up a fear lest it would not "bear" properly, and on New-year's-day the surface of the ice was all alive with dark restless figures, gliding here and there, tumbling down and getting up again as though coming an awful bump on the hard ice was rather a pleasant thing than otherwise!

To Lilian's great delight, Will was allowed to take her to see the skating. What a little darling she looked in a close hood lined and edged with delicate white fur, and her tiny hands nestling in a snowy muff! Pompey walked after the two, stalking along in his accustomed manner, as though he was above being on speaking terms with any other specimen of the canine species.

They went to that part of the canal that ran by Moss Lane, just below the cathedral, and after watching the fun for some time, began to feel rather cold, or, rather, Willie began to fear Lilian did so. Just then they met the dean's wife, a gentle, motherly woman, with whom Mr. Earle was a great favorite, and who accepted his eccentricities (Will among the number) as part of himself. She insisted on the two companions coming to the Deanery. There they warmed themselves by the bright fire, and had some tea and sweet cake. The good lady seemed hardly able to part with Lilian, whose sweet face peeped out from the furry hood like some fair flower from its velvety calyx.

The Deanery was a childless home, but a mother's heart and a mother's yearning had their place in the bosom of its gentle mistress.

"I think we had better go now," said Will, standing, cap in hand, in the shimmer of the fire-light. The boy looked so bright and brave and good, that the Dean's wife gave a sigh to think no such "braw laddie" called her mother!

So they went their way, and found the afternoon had changed rapidly while they had lingered by the cheery fire, eating cake.

The "gloaming" had come quickly and stolen all the brightness from the day.

"Are you tired, dear?" said Will, as they mounted a hilly bit of road, and he fancied the tiny feet beside him dragged.

"No, I'm not tired," said the child; "but it's very dark—and there's a black man, Willie—oh, I'm frightened!" and she dropped the pretty, snow-white muff, and caught the boy's hand with both her own.

"No, no, there's no one," he began.

But as he spoke, a dark figure made its way over the bank at the road-side, and a man leaped into the road and stood right in their pathway.

CHAPTER V.
"AND KEEPS IT."

THE intruder was Ben Dutton.

He was not drunk in the fullest acceptation of the word. He was sodden and sullen from the effects of being what he called "on the drink" for close upon a fortnight.

Pallid of face, unsteady of speech, wild, haggard, his eyes blood-shot, his lips swollen, Ben was just in that mental and physical state when a man hovers on the brink of the "horrors," and in which the lust of drink is upon him in all its irresistible and maddening force.

"Not so fast, young master—not so fast!" he said, fiercely, as Will tried to push on, leading the trembling Lilian. "I've not dodged yer day and night, I've not watched for yer, my young cock-sparrow so long, to let yer gi' me the go-by now!"

"Oh, Ben, Ben!" said Willie, appealingly, "what have I ever done to you that you should speak like that? Let me pass and take this child home."

"No, I woan't let thee pass!" roared the man, "not wi'out toll. I want money, and money I'll have. Shell out and make no more ado! Ain't yer 'shamed to see the man as picked yer out of the streets wanting a drop and nought in his pocket to get it wi', and yersel' rolling in money like ony gentleman born?"

"If you were in want, Ben," said Will, the color rushing to his face, "I'd work willingly to help you; I'd give my last shilling to help you and the mother that was so good to me, but I *won't* give you money to buy the drink that's a curse to yourself and those belonging to you."

What a contrast were the two!

The boy, with his clear, frank, fearless eyes, his proud, determined bearing—and the slouching, dogged, drink-soaked man, degraded to a level lower than that of the "beasts that perish!"

"Set a man on a 'norse," sneered Ben, "and we all know where he'll ride to. It's the devil of pride you've took up on the crupper to ride along with yer, and now yer won't give a hand to him as picked yer from the gutter!"

Willie's face flamed at this reiterated charge of a base ingratitude.

"It is not true—you know it is not true!" he cried, fast losing his calmness in the strait in which he found himself. "I would do anything that is right, but I've thought about it, Ben, and it is *not* right to give the money that is not mine, but my master's, for you to spend it in drink. I was wrong ever to do so; but I was only a little fellow, and knew no better. Now neither you nor any one shall force me to do what I know to be wrong."

"We'll see about that!" yelled the half-mad drunkard; and then followed such a volley of oaths that Will, beside himself, pushed the frightened child (who was by this time sobbing aloud) past Ben, and, hurriedly telling her to run on towards Winstowe, turned to face his antagonist.

Lilian did as she was told. Yet she could not resist, in her terror and her love, looking back now and then at the two dark figures seen so distinctly on the brow of the hill against the now ruddy western sky. Once she cried out, and started a step or two backward. It seemed to her as if the man raised a threatening hand to Will. She could hear his loud and angry voice raised, as if in wild, ungovernable rage. The child would not stir a step homeward after that. If "Willie" was to be killed by the bad man who had come through the hedge, he should kill her too. Full of all tender, loving thoughts, she made a slow approach again towards the two figures in the road, but in a moment more the two had parted, and Will was coming towards her.

Seeing this, she ran to meet him, her fair hair streaming out behind, her rosy lips parted in eagerness; but as she ran, she saw, to her renewed terror, that the man lifted up his arm on high, and shook his clenched fist at the boy's retreating figure. This sight made her fly the faster to his side. She caught his hand, and urged him on with all her tiny strength. And as they hurried on, looking up in his face, she saw that tears were streaming from his eyes, and heard him sob aloud in the bitterness of his shame and pain.

Mrs. Timmins, with her pocket-handkerchief tied over her cap, for fear of the cold wind, was looking out anxiously for their return. She caught up Lilian, and carried her into the warm, fire-lit kitchen, while Will hastened to the study and told the story of their long delay.

"You should have told me about this man taking money from you when it first happened," said Uncle David, looking up with a troubled face.

"I know I should, sir," returned the lad, frankly, "but I was ashamed."

"Well, well, let it be the last concealment between us. My boy, you must never keep things from me: you are my son—my dear and trusted son—the child of my adoption. Shame and fear should have no place between the father and his child. I must see to this matter. Perhaps it would be well to send the poor misguided man away from his bad companions, and give him a chance in some distant country. We must see what can be done."

But, alas! David Earle was pondering on the best way of nailing up the stable door, and the horse was already stolen.

After tea Lilian came to see them, but the child was pale and tired; she was very silent, and, hushing dolly off to sleep upon the rug, hushed her tired self to rest too.

"God bless the little lass!" said Uncle David, bending over the figure lying at his feet.

"Let me carry her up to bed," said Will to Mrs. Timmins, who came to say it was "Miss Lilian's bed-time." Very quietly he raised the little sleeping figure in his strong young arms, and bore her tenderly up the broad, old-fashioned staircase, Mrs. Timmins following with the candle.

Winstowe was three stories in height, and irregularly built. The rooms were large, but low. They were lighted by lattice-paned windows, and in many of the upper parts of the house the ceilings sloped oddly here and there, following the turnings of the gabled roof.

The study, with which we are already so well acquainted; a charming old-fashioned drawing-room, with glass doors opening on to the lawn, and deep window-seats at intervals, and a long, oak-panelled dining-room, were the principal apartments on the ground-floor. The comfortable kitchens, the cool stone-floored dairy, ran out from these in somewhat straggling fashion. Above came the guest-chamber, the master's room, and a sitting-room, large and light, owned by Mrs. Timmins, but much invaded by Lilian by reason of its multitudinous cupboards, in which the child took great delight.

Briggs slept near his master, so as to be handy when that arch-enemy, the gout, saw fit to assail his venerable joints.

The uppermost part of the house was approached by a staircase whose rail was of carved oak, black with age, and which, in all sorts of odd places, broke out into little elfish, goblin faces. This was, no doubt, some quaint fancy of the original owner of Winstowe, one Geoffrey Earle, said to have fought and died in the cause of the unhappy house of Stuart.

Mount we, then, the staircase where the goblin faces grin at us as we pass.

A large room ran the whole length of the house, and faced the front. This was the bower of the faithful Timmins. Behind it were two other rooms, long since apportioned out to "Master William." One—the smallest—was his bedroom; the other, a strange, irregularly shaped kind of place, he called his "grub-room."

The term was a suitable one. Litter, consequent on amateur carpentering, fishing, painting, and what not, made it the depot of all possible odds-and-ends.

It had a wonderful window—half in the wall, half in the gable of the roof—and in front of this were slender, twisted iron stanchions, a safeguard against burglars. This window opened widely on the inner side, and many a moan had Will made over the bars that stood between him and various delightful wanderings up and down the tempting hills and valleys made by the sharp angles of the red-tiled gables.

Lilian shared Mrs. Timmins's airy chamber, a tiny white bed standing by the larger one, and looking like a kitten nestling to its mother's side.

At the lodge, a pretty little cottage-like erection at Winstowe gates, lived the gardener and his wife. The wife came up every day to help in the housework, for David Earle, among his other eccentricities, had a rooted objection to giddy young maid-servants idling about his establishment; so Briggs was butler and footman and valet all in one, while Mrs. Timmins combined the offices of housekeeper, cook, and general overseer.

Now, Mrs. Timmins, though quite as trustworthy as her own master (indeed, more so, as not being subject to what Mr. Briggs called "wrong-headed fancies"), was by no means perfect as to temper. Briggs had become so used to her occasional fits of irritability that it was opined he rather liked them, as affording a certain variety in the somewhat monotonous round of daily life at Winstowe. Be this as it may, he was just now himself the cause of an aggravated attack, for he had committed the imprudence of asking and obtaining from his master a fortnight's holiday, without consulting her beforehand. The master had, with equal inconsiderateness, had a rather sharp attack of gout during his faithful henchman's absence.

Very carefully Mrs. Timmins had nursed her master, taking up her temporary abode in a small sleeping-room near his own, and ready, at the mildest tinkle of the bell that rung at the head of his bed, to be up and doing. All the same, she considered the combination of circumstances vexatious, though had any one else ventured to make the remark, that person would have been visited with her sorest displeasure.

Thus it came about that no one slept just now in the topmost story of the house, save the two children. Hither, then, Will carried his helpless little companion on the night of that unhappy day when Ben Dutton had met them and so terrified poor Lilian that she had grown sleepy and weary from the exhaustion that followed.

He laid her gently down upon the white bed, and kissed her sleeping face; then stole gingerly back to the study, where he and Mr. Earle sat over the fire, talking of the evil fortunes of the Dutton family. They heard Mrs. Timmins come down after undressing the sleepy child (who was with difficulty roused to put her dimpled hands together and say the nightly "Our Father" that ever hallowed her slumbers), and, nearly two hours later, retire to her temporary resting-place. Then Will helped his still lame companion up the stairs, and with a fond "God bless you!" from Uncle David, and a cheery "Good-night, sir!" in return, they parted at the bedroom door.

Tired and weary as he was, Will could not rest. Every now and then he heard the boughs of the trees in the garden crack in the cold, frosty air. The big clock down-stairs told the hours of the night. He counted out twelve, and thought he would listen for one; but before that came he had fallen asleep.

Not, however, that that improved matters much, for in a vivid and distressing dream he seemed once more to face Ben Dutton, fiercer and more drink-maddened than he had been in reality.

The boy tossed and tumbled, and muttered in his sleep. Now the dream grew more distinct, and filled him with a still more terrible dread. Close and ever closer to his own, the bloated, sodden features seemed to come; he felt the hot, fetid breath from those swollen lips scorching his cheek, the cold, clammy hands gathered round his throat, striving to press his life out in their cruel grasp. He strove to throw the phantom off, and, in one mighty effort, awaked.

Stay, though. Was it all a dream? His breath seemed to come with painful effort. Hot and stifling, the air of his room scorched him as he lay. One instant and he was on his feet, reeling with the sudden shock, but promptly in possession of his presence of mind. God of heaven! the floor felt hot to his naked feet—a red glare illumined the panes of his window—he could hear a faint, rustling, rushing sound. Could it—oh, could it be the sound of flames!

As he stood there, dizzy, horror-struck, yet rallying his shaken powers to think what it might be best to do, he seemed for one short awful moment to see a mocking vision—it could *only* be a vision, he thought, a phantom from the dream-land he had just left—but it took the form of the bloated face, the jeering, mocking face, of Ben Dutton pressed against the window, gloating over his agony and terror! It was there but for an instant; then the red light gleamed brighter, only to fade before a volume of dark smoke that rolled upward from below.

One thought only filled Will's breast—"Lilian! Lilian!"

He had groped about, and found his shoes, hastily thrown on his coat and trousers, and now rushed out into the landing that separated the rooms.

Where the goblin staircase had been was a chasm filled with black and acrid smoke! As he peered into its depths, an angry tongue of flame leaped up into his face, and curling round the slender column of the carved rail, cracked and shrivelled its dark, shining surface, lapping the elfish faces, that seemed to gibe and mow in weird mockery. He listened intently for a moment. Not a sound!—no human voice, no hurrying footstep, broke the awful stillness; nothing stirred save the faintly rustling flame, the curling smoke, that blinded his eyes and stifled his breath.

With a cry such as the hunted hare gives as the cruel, eager mouths of the dogs close about her, Will burst open the door of Lilian's room and rushed in. She lay as softly sleeping as though the tender silver moonlight shone upon her bed and caught the glint of her golden hair, and not the red glare of the flames that lapped against the narrow panes of her casement window. Cry after cry rang from the boy's lips as he looked upon that awful sight. He tore a blanket from the little bed, wrapped her, all sleeping as she was, in its sheltering folds, and bore her to the window. Then he tore at the fastening. Air! air!—only to get the sweet, fresh air of heaven to blow upon that death-white face, that now, he saw, was still in a stupor deeper than any slumber.

Surely he could get the window open, and drag her through? But oh! what then? A moment's thought told him no foothold existed at that side by which he might bear her to the ground in safety. Yet again he tried to pull the casement back, but the frame had warped with the long snow: why, he remembered now hearing Mrs. Timmins say only that morning that she must send for the carpenter to open it.

He looked down. Lilian had stirred, and opened her great violet eyes. He knelt beside her, held her close and fast, and tried by every loving, soothing word to calm her wild affright.

"Oh! the fire! the fire!" she moaned, hiding her face upon his arm. "It is so hot in here—we shall be burned all up! Oh, take me to Uncle David, Willie dear!"

As he raised her in his arms, and bore her to

what he thought might be the less intolerable heat of his own room, he caught sight of the yawning abyss which but a short while back had been the burning staircase. Cunningly devised scroll, quaint figures, goblin faces—all were gone! The stairs themselves had fallen in, and the up-curling smoke seemed to come from un-fathomed depths of lurid heat.

Will put his hand beneath the poor child's head, and, as he bore her past this gulf, pressed the dear face close against his breast.

It might come—that dreadful death—but she should not see that tossing, raging sea of fire and flame. Not yet! not yet!

At the door of his own room he started back. It was filled with the overpowering stench of burning wood, and in one place the carpet had curled up, as if it were a living thing and felt the flame. Little bright tongues forced themselves a passage in between the boards.

Help would come—was coming! God would not desert his children! So Will thought, as steadily, and like the sound of some vast rising tide, the murmur of voices and the tramp of many feet were heard more and more above the hissing of the flames, the crackle of the burning timber, and the whistle of the keen wind, that unhappily had risen into strength since mid-night. Only to preserve her, only to shield his tender charge from flame, and smoke, and sti-fling heat, until that help should come!

With the wisdom often born of dire necessi-ty he staggered with his burden into the room where all his boyish treasures lay in the confu-sion that boys love. Here, at all events, the floor was not scorching to the touch; and though the glare of the flames, that all seemed to come from below, lighted up the little chamber with the brilliancy of a summer's day, the window was not dimmed with rolling masses of smoke, like those of the other two. The heat from the burning staircase was insufferable, and increased with every moment.

Lilian gasped for breath, and clung more closely to his breast.

"Listen, dear," he said, speaking calmly, striving to keep her fears in check; "let me go for a moment; I will not leave you. Do you hear?"

Yes, she heard, and the little hands unclasped themselves from about his neck. Then he shut the door. Full well, ah, me! too well, he knew that on that side escape was not. If help came, it must be from without. No living man could cross that sea of fire, that widened every moment at their feet. The door shut, Will dragged the table close to the slanting window in the roof. Then he lifted Lilian up, and followed, carrying the blanket that in her fear she had thrown off. They were stifling, these poor children, stifling like rats in a hole!

Will knew the iron stanchions were across the window—he knew he could not make his way out upon the roof; but iron bars cannot keep out the blessed air of heaven. Moments were precious; Lilian's breath began to come and go in hurried gasps, her great, frightened eyes looked up at him imploringly.

"Stand aside a moment," he said, setting his teeth, and giving a strong pull to the window, swollen and stiff like the other. The force of its opening almost threw him backward; but,

oh, the blessed, sweet relief of the cold, frosty air blowing in upon them!

"Take fast hold of the bars, Lillie, darling," he said, putting her where she could get most air. "Squeeze your face in between them—there, that's right. Now we will pull the blanket round behind us; it will help to keep off the heat.

"Kiss me," said the poor child, and turned her face from the welcome breeze to meet his. Thus they waited. He had done all he could; there was nothing else but waiting for it now.

"Where is Uncle David?" asked Lilian, a moment later, with a sob.

What answer could he make?

And below them the sound of voices, and of feet hurrying to and fro, grew ever louder, like a rising, raging sea.

CHAPTER VI.

FAREWELL TO THE "AULD HOUSE!"

MEANWHILE outside the leaping flames light up the night with a lurid, awful glow—light up a sea of white and anxious faces turned upward towards the blazing pile that was once the ven-erable Manor House, Winstowe Hall.

See! the fire has nearly caught the western gable, and the red tongues of flame wrap them-selves about the old ivy that clothes its every nook and corner, shrivelling each spreading branch that has borne unharmed the heats and frosts of a hundred summers and winters.

The fire had got so far ahead before it was discovered that the lower part of the house will be gutted before long, and the beams give way.

May God Almighty help any that are yet left unrescued from that awful furnace! See how it seethes, and glows, and riots, and thrusts derisive tongues of flames up to the sky, where the clouds are scudding and hurrying along before the wind, as though they hastened to fly from the sight of devastation beneath!

"Water! water!" is the cry from every lip; but the tanks are frozen at the mills, the ponds by the orchard-gate are almost solid ice, and the canal is covered with the thick coating that yester-day bore crowds of happy, thoughtless pleasure-seekers! Crash! crash! goes the ice as men break wildly through it with iron crow-bars, and the hose of the engines, like thirsty serpents, suck up the water from beneath. But all this takes time, and fire, like the tide, waits for no man.

Who can realize the value of a moment, until he stands before a flaming dwelling of which each window begins to belch forth smoke and flame, and hears a whisper pass along the crowd, like an electric shock, that a human creature is in the midst of that burning fiery furnace?

In the front of that heaving, pushing, ever-gathering crowd is one awful figure, that is the centre of every man and woman's interest, the object of sympathy and pity to every heart.

It is that of an old man; his white hair—his pallid face—his look of anguish as he gazes at the flaming building, once his home—his voice raised now and again in a hoarse, wordless cry, as with some added impulse the flames leap higher and higher—all, seen in the vivid, glowing light, form a picture such as none are ever likely to forget! A dozen strong hands hold him back, a dozen voices plead with him to yield to what must be—to let younger and stronger men brave the dangers of the falling beams and blazing floors, from which he himself has been with difficulty rescued. See! he has fallen forward on his knees, and vainly those about him try to raise him up! He stretches forth his trembling hands to the heaven that is all aglow with the blaze of his burning home; he calls out in a voice whose sound of agony dominates the din surging round about him; he cries that there shall be no limit—none—to the rewards that he will shower upon that man who rescues those two children that are yet beneath that burning roof—who are left, as he in his wild agony supposes, without help from any! Once there is a cry that at the upper window something is seen to move, and the crowd sways and ebbs and heaves; women sob aloud, and cry out to incite the men, who clamber, cat-like, up the tall slender ladder reared against the wall, to greater effort.

Here and there a woman faints and falls, and the crowd has to be held back lest she be trampled underfoot. But of all this tumult that awful figure, ever in the front rank, takes no heed. His eyes are strained up, up to the windows highest of all — the windows of those rooms in which he knows his darlings but a few short hours ago lay safely sleeping. The thought maddens him.

"A thousand pounds!" he cries—"a thousand pounds to him who saves my children!"

No one could make him understand that no promise of reward was needed to spur on men brave and true and valiant as any soldiers that face their enemy upon the battle-field, and fight even to the death for victory. Where can there be a fiercer enemy than the fire-fiend? Where can there be braver soldiers than our firemen?

But David Earle is driven by cruel fear beyond the power of reasoning. Even as he cries, and far above the echo of his words, two dark figures, their bright, brazen helmets catching the glimmer of the flames, are seen scaling the walls, here passing through a sheet of fire, there lost in the billowing, acrid smoke.

Hiss! goes the friendly jet of water. Guided by the watchful hands below, it plays upon the points where most difficulty has to be encountered. The skilled fireman, crow-bar in hand, has made for the little window in the roof, the only part upon which the fire has not yet got a firm hold. See! he beckons his comrade. Now the two are out of sight.

One moment—short in reality, but that seems interminable, measured by suspense, and then— A sound like the rising of a rushing tide, a sound that swells into a roar, and rising, swells and swells until it grows into a ringing, deafening English cheer!

For high above the peoples' heads the dark figures with the shining helmets have come to sight again, and held in the arms, clasped to the breast of the foremost, is a little, white-robed figure. A ripple of golden hair falls across the sheltering arm; and see! behind these two, creeping stealthily and warily down towards the eaves of the gabled roof, is the second fireman, guiding by the hand a figure that they all know,

the boy that David Earle took from their midst, and made as his own son.

Still, clear, and cold breaks the wintry daylight over the scene of the fire at Winstowe. A ghastly framework of charred and blackened beams, a heap of strangely mingled *débris* smoking and smouldering, and now and again emitting fitful flames, are all that remains of what was yesterday so fair a home.

And a mile away, upon the slope of a lonely field, a man lies upon his face—dead! He has lain there through all the bitter frost of that long winter's night, and sunk from the fatal stupor of drunkenness into the sleep of death. That cold and stiffened form is all that remains on earth of the drink - maddened incendiary, Benjamin Dutton.

The day after New-year's-day was the date on which the leave of absence of the faithful Briggs expired. He duly arrived at the station, which was situated in the centre of the town, and on alighting on the platform, and searching for his very modest amount of luggage, it struck him that he was more than usually honored by the general notice. His holiday had been spent in London, among well-to-do friends, and for an instant a thought darted across his mind to the effect that it was possible the provincial mind discerned some new and striking elegance in his appearance. But no; the notice bestowed upon him was more suggestive of curiosity than admiration. At last a porter approached him, relieved a feeling of slight embarrassment by critically examining the condition of his own right-hand thumb-nail, and then stolidly observed,

"I say, yer place is burned down."

Briggs sat down upon his box, which providentially happened to be near.

"It's a fact," continued the man, finding that curious delight in astonishing and shocking a fellow-creature which is inherent in the human breast. "They say as how it was set alight to by one Dutton, a drunken sweep of a chap—"

"I know," gasped Briggs, holding on to the sides of the box, and staring, open-mouthed, at the speaker.

"It's a bad job, for Winstowe 'All was a fine old place. Anyhow, he's dead."

"*Who's* dead?" shouted Briggs, springing up so rapidly that the porter stepped back with promptitude.

"Him as set it alight, of course."

Briggs sunk upon the box once more, and drawing forth a crimson and yellow handkerchief, like one of M. Dumas' heroes, he "wiped his humid brow."

"Is every one saved belonging to the house?" he mustered courage to ask. Several voices answered at once in the affirmative, for a crowd had by this time gathered round, and information as to the fire poured forth with extraordinary volubility. "Ah!" said Briggs, "if I'd pitched that there Dutton into the canal the evening as he gave me a dose of his imperence, it would have saved a sight of trouble, *I* see."

By this time he had recovered his calmness. Subsequently, however, the sight of the blackened ruins of the house that had sheltered him for half a lifetime overset him again, and he finally staggered into the lodge parlor, looking more like the portly Briggs's ghost than his corporeal presence. There he found Mrs. Timmins, her hands and arms swathed in cotton-wool, and her eyelashes and eyebrows burned off. The only portion of her that was really presentable was her wig, for the old one had been burned, and the gardener's wife had procured a new one in the town.

"Where's master?" said Briggs, looking at his old fellow-servant as though she were the remains of some curious extinct animal. Mrs. Timmins melted into tears, and answered through them.

"Master's at the Deanery, and so's Master William, and so's Miss Lilian; and, oh! Briggs, ain't it dreadful that ever you and me should live to see this day?"

"Where's the plate-basket?" said Briggs, who only seemed capable of giving utterance to two or three words at a time.

"Burned up," said Mrs. Timmins.

"Where's master's chair?" continued Briggs.

"Burned up," said Mrs. Timmins.

"After this, the deluge," is perhaps the best definition I can give of the poor man's state of mind.

"What's the good of wasting thoughts on things as couldn't feel, nor yet suffer," said Mrs. Timmins, reproachfully, "when all we ought to do is to return thanks where thanks is due that living creatures is safe and sound? Why, I myself was carried out without my senses, and master was rolled up in his own bedclothes like a winding-sheet, and the poor children were fetched out through the blazin' roof; and then to be thinkin' of plate-baskets, and chairs, and such like — shame upon you, Samuel Briggs, this day!"

"What's come of the miserable century?" asked the reproved one, callous to all hard words in the extremity of his astonishment.

"What! Dutton?" chimed in the gardener's wife. "Oh! he was found lying dead upon his face — dead-drunk, as the sayin' is, and truly dead in this case, as was well deserved."

"Matthew Hale met him that same night," continued Mrs. Timmins, in a feeble voice, "and so full of liquor that he looked more like mad than sane; and 'Where are you off to?' says Matthew, thinking, by the look of him, he was primed to do himself an injury. 'I'm going for to smoke rats in a hole,' says he, very fierce, and snarling like a dog over a bone."

Briggs struck his forehead with his clenched hand.

"It's all come of me not chucking him in the canal!" he wailed and lamented; "and then, when the misfortune come, no one never had the thought to save the plate-basket and master's chair! This is the first holiday as ever I took since being in master's service, and *it shall be the last!*"

He took this vow so solemnly, and looked so awful the while, that the women shuddered, and Mrs. Timmins expressed an opinion that if she had not a cup of the very strongest tea, with one spoonful of brandy therein, she should, in all probability, "lose her senses," by which alarming term she meant to intimate that she should faint.

"The inquisitors will sit upon Dutton," remarked Briggs (he prided himself upon the flowery nature of his language at all times), "and all things will be brought to light imperceptively; that is, 'without favor or affection,' as the law hath it."

Then he set off to the Deanery to see his master.

"What a knowledgeable person Mr. Briggs is!" said the gardener's wife, glancing through the little ivy-framed casement at that gentleman's departing figure.

"He's a very clever man is Mr. Briggs," sighed Mrs. Timmins.

For, in spite of hard words and occasional disputes, there was a sort of chronic courtship carried on between this venerable pair; and only for certain doubts and misgivings as to him "gettin' his head up too high," or, in other words, wishing to rule, instead of be ruled, Mrs. Timmins would have changed her name to that of Briggs many years ago.

The meeting between master and man was perhaps one that would seem strange to people in these days, when class is set against class — employé against employer — masters against servants — servants against masters; but in the time of which this story treats, some thirty years ago, things were different. People did not change their servants every six months; servants did not try to ape their betters, spend all their money on dress, and save nothing for sickness or old age; they served for love as well as for wages, and the interest of their masters ranked before their own. Often a lifetime was spent in the same service, and friendship real and true existed between master and man, mistress and maid.

Thus it came about that when Briggs saw the dapper form of his master come out from the Deanery drawing-room to meet him in the hall, Briggs's heart "rose up so full," as he afterward expressed it, that it "choked him off," and the tears came rolling down his cheeks.

The master, on his part, was scarcely less affected; and indeed the only really cheerful person present was Pompey, who, having fortunately escaped harm in the conflagration, was now a guest at the Deanery by special invitation from the dean's wife.

"I'm so took up, sir, with the thought that no one should have been there to look after the plate-basket and your chair," said Briggs, when he could find his voice, and bring himself to stop shaking his master's hand, "that I can't never, I know, forgive myself for being habsent so unconditionally."

"I am thankful to have escaped with my life, and the life of those dear to me," said David Earle, bowing his white head before the thought of God's infinite mercy to him. "It was a marvel, Briggs, that of all of us no life was missing. They say the house must have been set on fire in at least three places. That wretched man even clambered on to the roof by the branches of the pear-tree at the gable-end. They were all torn down by his weight. To think of those dear children sleeping in their beds, helpless and unsuspecting, and a madman prowling round about them!"

"It all come of drink, sir," said Briggs, shaking his head slowly from side to side; "there's a terrible mort of things comes of drink in this 'ere world! A man as takes to drink is like one as sets off running down a hill; he goes faster and faster, and don't never know what kind of a pit he'll jump into at the bottom. It was a deep hole as Dutton got himself into, and no mistake; and I'm glad he's departed, sir; for a trial would have 'arrowed you most awful, *I* know, let alone Master William, as the defunct was good to once, after a fashion, before his 'art was reg'lar case-hardened and 'eadymized, as you may say, by liquor."

"Well, well," said his master, restraining a dawning smile at his retainer's wordy eloquence, "we won't speak or think hardly of the poor man now. *'Forgive us our trespasses as we forgive them that trespass against us,'* that's the prayer we offer, and we must live up to it as far as we can. Now about our plans for the present. I have been talking matters over with my good friend the dean, and come to the conclusion it would be well for us to leave this part of the world for a time. I think it would do me good to travel abroad a little; our poor Timmins will be all the better for a holiday with her friends in Manchester, and you—"

A look of intense anxiety had lengthened Briggs's countenance while Mr. Earle was speaking, and here his impatience got the better of his respect, and he broke in agitatedly,

"I really couldn't be left behind, sir. Since ever I lived in your service I never left you till now, and you've bin and near got burned alive while I was away! How can I tell what might happen to you in foreign lands—"

"My good fellow," said his master, soothingly, "I never thought of leaving you behind. I am looking forward to you being my factotum, my right hand—"

"Right hand, or left hand, or teetotum, or what you will, sir, so as I may go," cried Briggs.

Lilian just then flew down-stairs, caught him by the hand, and began dancing about like a mad thing.

Briggs did not consider this a respectful or proper proceeding in the master's presence; but the child was wild with joy, and beyond all restraint. Suddenly, however, her mood changed; she heaved a deep sigh, and looked sorrowfully in his face.

"Poor dolly's all burned up!" she said, and her violet eyes grew dewy.

"That's a bad job," said Briggs, and as he spoke the thought of the picture that hung over the study fireplace came sadly to his mind.

They could buy a new "dolly," but the fair pictured face of that Lilian who died in a far-off land must live now only in the memory of the heart that had so tenderly loved her.

"Where's Master William, please, sir? if I don't take too much upon myself by asking," said Briggs, when, after receiving various orders about things that needed arranging promptly, Mr. Earle was about to rejoin the dean and his wife.

"Master William is in his right place, Briggs —trying to be of some comfort to the widow of that unhappy man."

And truly she stood in great need of comfort. "She had only got rid of a bad husband," you may be ready to say. True, but women are so strangely and curiously constituted that they will forgive, ay, and forget—forget as though it had never been—all the wrong done them by a hus-

band, once death has stepped in between the past and the present. It is as though the memory lost all power of retaining the black shadows of the past, while, by their shining, the bright spots ever remain clear and distinct.

Mother Dutton, wringing her hands, rocking herself to and fro by the side of that awful thing covered with a sheet, that had once been Ben— her "man," her husband—forgot the hard words, the harder blows, the squandered money, the drunken ways, that had made her life a thorny path indeed. At the sight of Willie, the boy whom their humble roof had sheltered in his birth, one memory only seemed to arise in her mind:

"Dear, dear! how good Ben was when he come home and found a gal and a babbie in the childer's bed! 'We'll shift,' says I, 'if you're willin'.' 'Oh, I'm willin',' says he, and we lay four in a bed for nights and nights, and never a grumble out of him. Oh, he were a good man, were Ben, at heart! If there'd never bin no such thing as that dratted liquor, we'd have lived real 'appy, 'im and me!"

But Jim's face was drawn and white, and his grief a wordless, tearless one. He, too, had much in the past to forget, much to forgive. Yet his own wrongs were easily blotted out. But oh, bitter, bitter truth! the dead man had tried to injure "Master Willie"—had died with murder in his heart—murder that aimed at a life dearer, far dearer, to Jim than his own!

At the first sight of the dear bright face, the tall, slender figure of the object of a love that was almost worship, Jim fell upon his knees, covered his face with his hands, and cowered down till he grovelled at the feet of his foster-brother. He clasped his arms about the boy's knees, he raised his white, pleading face to Willie's troubled, pitiful gaze, and when he found a voice wherewith to speak, implored pardon for the man who lay dead in the home his sin had rendered so wretched.

"He was mad—mad with the drink; he didn't know what he was doing, father didn't," sobbed Jim, in the extremity of his distress.

"I know, I know," answered Will, sobbing too. "O Jim, dear Jim, never think I don't forgive him!"

To those who looked upon this strange and touching scene the sight was one not easily forgotten—the poor cripple falling prone at the feet of the one his dead father had tried to slay; the shame, the agony, the cruel pain of the father's evil life and awful death, pressing down to earth his innocent child!

You may be sure the "fire at Winstowe Hall," with every possible particular that did happen, and endless particulars that did *not* happen, not only filled the papers of that day, but formed the ceaseless topic of conversation among high and low for weeks to come. Only for weeks, though. The world hasn't patience to linger long on *any* subject, however exciting and interesting. Some other matter of astonishment, or horror, or virtuous indignation, rises up and jostles the worn-out theme aside; its day is over, it falls like a dead leaf to the ground, and the wind drifts it into some out-of-the-way corner.

And so it shortly came about that a fire-damp explosion in some coal-pits near the town absorbed men's interest, and the fire at Winstowe was forgotten. David Earle had gone to "foreign parts," accompanied by Briggs, the "little lady" (as people were wont to call Lilian), and Mrs. Timmins, who, after all, obstinately refused to be left behind. (Perhaps from a fear that Briggs might "get his head up too high" if he went about without her gentle hand to "keep him under.") Will was at school again; Pompey had taken up his abode with Mrs. Dutton, whose grocery establishment flourished mightily, now that there was no one to make periodical onslaughts upon the till; and Jim was rapidly approaching to that most honorable position, "head boy" in the cathedral school.

And thus for a time we must leave our *dramatis personæ*. With these younger members of our company the time of life's "early spring" is passing rapidly away; before them stretches the path of life, with all its ups and downs, its light and shade, its perils and its joys. Presently we shall again take up their story, and follow them through the realities of life, that seem, to the inexperienced eye of hopeful youth, flooded with the rosy light of happiness, but that, once encountered, practically prove to be checkered paths, winding as much through shadowy gloom as through golden sunshine.

CHAPTER VII.

WIG AND GOWN.

I wonder does any one love the City of London as well as I do?

The West End, with all its brilliant shops, aristocratic places of resort, gayly dressed ladies, and courtly men, is not half so interesting to me as the great, noisy, bustling, busy City.

When "town" goes "out of town," and all the squares and streets of palaces are shut up, because fashion is dead for the time being; when all the blinds are drawn, and the houses look like sleeping giants with closed eyelids; when it is easy to cross Regent Street, and the Row is a desert; then, my friend, the City wears its accustomed face; its streets are not one whit emptier to the eye of the casual observer; *it* doesn't close its eyes and go to sleep, bless you! Why, how would all the money be made if it did? People don't stop eating and drinking because they go "out of town;" and sea-side "costumes," and dainty plumed hats for the "holiday" time, cost as much as aërial bonnets for the Row; so husbands and fathers must see that the City mill keeps grinding on, or the supply of corn would stop, and then— Well, I don't know *what* then!

"The Deluge," I suppose, and the suicide of milliners and *modistes* by the score. So the City buzzes on, the hive is as noisy as ever, and the bees work hard through August's baking heat and September's enervating, foggy, humid warmth.

Yes, I love the City!

True, even the sunbeams seem to get a little dusty as they pass through its dingy atmosphere; the leaves, that come out so bravely spring after spring, become somewhat smutty very early in life; and the sparrows, that seem to me more knowing and wide-awake than sparrows elsewhere, have more soot than could be wished upon their feather coats. But the hum. and the stir, and the hurry of busy, active life all around —the people rushing about here and there, with an air of the deepest importance and thought—I like all that. It is like a tonic to lazy, pleasure-seeking West-Enders, and seems to impress one with the fact that there are thousands close to us who *work* to *live*, and who have something more important to think of than where they shall go, or how they shall amuse themselves through the hours that seem so long to the idle.

But well as I like the City in its working dress, with its hands toil-stained, and its feet hurrying hither and thither in the pursuit of wealth, I love it best of all upon a Sunday. For then the busy City is at rest—a rest well earned by a week's toil; and the soft, sweet, happy voices of the bells, such as those of St. Botolph's and Cripplegate Church, sing to it in its dreamy quiet. The people that one meets seem to have put on Sunday faces with their Sunday clothes. Now, by this I don't mean sanctimonious faces "long drawn out;" Puritanical greetings to the Day of the Lord, that seem to say, "God's day of rest has come round again, and *I'm very sorry for it*, and mean to look as miserable as I can;" but joyful faces, that gladly smile a welcome to the weekly time of rest from labor. Sunday is a day for the active man to take breath, and raise his tired thoughts to the things of God and heaven; a time for the working-man to begin the day with hearty prayer and praise, and then go forth and breathe the fresh air of heaven, and rejoice in the beauty of God's creation; not a time when we should close all innocent places of amusement, all means of cultivation of mind to the masses of our people, *and only leave the public-house and the gin-palace open.*

However, I am wandering in reprehensible fashion from the thread of my narrative. *Allons donc!* turn we again to the City streets. How delightful are those green spots here and there to be found in the heart of a wilderness of streets and buildings! They look like little bits of country that have lost their way among the crowded thoroughfares, and, finding themselves hemmed in by brick and mortar, have just settled down and made the best of it, determined to grow their greenest and look their very best, if only to let the City see they won't be trifled with.

One of the prettiest, and, I should think, one of the oldest, of these emerald isles is to be found just under the walls of St. Botolph's Church, Bishopsgate Street. Not only does this particular oasis boast of trees, and miniature lake, and dripping fountain, but bright-plumaged ducks of curious breed swim about, and stand upon their heads in the water, after the droll manner of their kind; and a couple of peacocks sun their tails in whatever sunshine they can find, and make the best of it when there isn't any.

Here, then, loitering among the small and very juvenile crowd that ever stands in gaping admiration of these ducks and peacocks, we find an old friend; a young man, pale and earnest of face, and deformed about the back and shoulders sufficiently to call forth at times a pitiful glance from some passer-by, but yet wearing an air of perfect peace and content any one might well envy, and dressed in good substantial broadcloth, that tells of a respectable and well-to-do position in life.

Things have gone well with Mother Dutton's son since last we saw him, twelve years ago, in the cathedral town: those long fingers of his write a beautifully neat and clear hand; it is like copper-plate, and the head that guides the willing hand is as clear and business-like as the writing; and so it comes about that sundry of his fellow barristers-at-law envy Mr. William Snow, of the Inner Temple, his clerk, James Dutton.

Now, it is a delightful thing to think that in this world of ours, so teeming with sin, and sorrow, and pain, and weary men and women plodding on with tear-dimmed eyes and faltering feet, now and again one comes across a person who is thoroughly, perfectly happy. And at the time when we take up the thread of this story, and find Jim in the heart of the great City, as busy and active a bee as any in that busy hive, I think that we may safely say few more happy and contented creatures paced its endless labyrinth of streets, or lived and moved amidst the whir and hum of its thousand voices. Indeed, Jim would have been puzzled, I think, to know what to wish for, had some genius appeared and offered to grant it, after the pleasant fashion of the good spirits in the "Arabian Nights' Entertainment."

He was working *for* William Snow. What more could his heart desire? He had all the City to wander about in at leisure times, and surely no nobleman that ever owned park and pleasance had half the curious sights to see that Jim found *there*. Why, there was not a Sunday that he went on his accustomed wanderings through the quiet streets that he did not light on something new and interesting—some quaint old house, with curious half-defaced shields and arms carved in stone—some fresh nook of greenest verdure hiding away in the corner of a hitherto unknown court or quadrangle—some tiny half-starved street Arab, whose story interested the tender-hearted, simple-minded man, as no romance, however wild and stirring, could have done.

Then where could Jim have slaked his thirst for music as in the City? Why, his Sundays were days of a supreme enjoyment, that seemed at times something quite awful to himself, as opposed in the bitterness of recollection to the want and misery of his early years.

"Who could have ever thought that *I* should come to *this?*" he would ponder to himself, as he stole into the great cathedral, or wandered in the lovely cloisters of Westminster Abbey, or lingered in some old City church, where the hymns that Willie used to sing to him in past days rose sweet and soft, and caused the passers-by to linger near the door.

It is Sunday evening now, when we find him watching the crowd gathered round the gardens by St. Botolph's, whose sweet bells have finished chiming more than an hour ago. Jim has been wandering in his dreamy way here and there about the streets, and is thinking of making his way home: he smiles at a tiny morsel of a girl who is clapping her hands to try to frighten the peacocks, and who smiles back at him again, and then he goes slowly down Bishopsgate Street.

He cannot pass the quaint old church of St. Ethelburga. Evening service is almost over, and the soft rise and fall of a plaintive litany draw Jim to the door, as the magnet draws the steel. It is not the first time he has been there: he knows that within those venerable walls the poor are made as welcome as the rich. He goes softly in, and, sitting down near the door, covers his eyes with his hand, and listens to the chanting:

> "By the thorns that mocking crowned Thee,
>   By the bloody sweat that brake
>   From Thy brow in bitter anguish,
>   Save us, for Thy mercies' sake!
>
> "By Thy limbs outstretched and wounded,
>   By the cleft the spear did make,
>   By the Blood and by the Water,
>   Save us, for Thy mercies' sake!
>
> "In the time of tears and laughter,
>   When we sleep and when we wake,
>   Rising, resting, coming, going,
>   Save us, for Thy mercies' sake!"

Ay! that is the religion men and women want. No gloomy Puritanism, that would rob life of all sweetness and joy; no terrified thoughts of God and eternity, put off to the hour when death's dark wings begin to hide the light of earth; none of these—but a living reality, that hallows not only the sorrow but the joy of life; that sustains us in the hour of a tearful parting, and sanctifies the joy of a happy meeting; a religion that is the staff we lean upon at every step of our daily life!

Now the benediction has been given, the last chanted Amen rises and falls, and the little church rapidly empties. People stand aside and make way for our friend Jim, and he, fully recognizing the truth that his affliction is turned into a passport to men's hearts, is grateful for their kindly thought.

He strolls on, past the cross-crowned cathedral, up Holborn, through the arch and across the causeway of Staples' Inn, where, in the gardens below, are creepers and trees in which he takes an interest. It is now early summer, and every time he passes by he finds the Virginian creepers have stretched out fresh, pinky-green arms, and the fig-trees, trained against the walls, have grown thicker of foliage and of a fuller green. He leans on the balustrade a moment or two to notice all this, and then loiters on to St. Clement's with its belt of trees, just to see how their leaves are getting on. Satisfied on this point, he goes through Temple Bar and turns down Temple Lane, where one or two quaint old dwellings bulge out across the street, and are supported by pillars. Very soon he is among the courts, and there is the little fountain sparkling merrily in the evening light, as if it were trying to make believe to be a country fountain. Lower down, a lovely glimpse of the Temple Gardens, now dressed in a green garment too freshly put on to be smoke-stained or dust-laden, seems to his eyes a perfect picture.

But Jim does not linger long; the evening is beginning to close in, and the office-boy (who is at this moment balancing himself perilously out of the second-floor window, and grinning with delight at the risk he is running of tipping over on to the flags below) will have the tea all ready. So through an archway, above which is written up "Elm Court," Jim turns, passes through a paved square, with lawyers' and barristers' chambers on all sides, and then up a somewhat dismal entry, and so into Fig-tree Court.

There is no trace of even the most infantile fig-tree to be seen anywhere, but perhaps in remote ages some such tree may here have flourished, and given the court a name. Neither do clean windows appear to be the fashion; certainly the cleanest are those appertaining to a set of chambers that bear upon the door-post this announcement for the public benefit:

MR. WILLIAM SNOW.
MR. FREDERICK BOULTBEE.

As Jim approaches this dwelling, the rough head of the boy before mentioned gives a sudden lurch and then disappears.

"I was a-watching for you, sir," says this active member of the legal household, appearing at the top of the steep, narrow door-step.

"You can watch for me, I should think, Beams, without tilting yourself out of window in that ridiculous manner. You'll come down upon the flags the shortest way some day, *I* know."

At this gloomy prophecy a radiant smile dawns upon the countenance of Abraham Beams.

Abraham had been early apprenticed to life, having commenced his career as a public character at the age of five, when he "earned his own bread" by following the trade of "baby-tenter," a profession that employed many youthful inhabitants of London City before the days of school-boards and compulsory education.

Mothers who went out charing, selling oranges, or washing, brought their babies to the house of the "tenter," and these innocents were so arranged that the juvenile care-taker could best attend to their wants. Each infant was supplied with a feeding-bottle, and, as a rule, they sucked themselves to sleep; but sometimes a baby would suffer from inward uneasiness or nightmare, and then the baby-tenter had a bad time of it, staggering about under the weight of a child hardly less heavy than himself, or rocking the weeping creature until his own little back ached fit to crack.

Nowadays Abraham, or "Beams," as he was called in his business capacity, rejoiced in the change of being Mr. Snow's office-boy.

"It's better than baby-tenting," he confided to Jim, with a grin. "Them hinnercents was forever chokin' theirselves with the noses of the feeders, if I took a bi orf of them; and as to a chance of seeing a street row, or watchin' of Mr. Punch, or follerin' a chap as was bein' run in by a bobby—why, I might as well have lived in the country, where, by all accounts, there's naught to be seen, and lookin' out of winder ain't called for."

"Well, well," said that important personage, Mr. Dutton, "I'm glad you like the place; but mind what you're about, Beams, and when you run messages for the master, don't you be looking at sights by the way, or you'll come to grief, I warn you."

And really Beams was a very good boy, as London boys go; true, he would make a rush out of chambers sometimes, to go and stare at a certain archway, which had for him a strange fascination. Above it was written, in corpulent letters, that themselves looked like a row of well-

fed judges at the least—"Samuel Coplethwaite, Law Wig-maker." But, then, these proceedings on the part of Beams arose, as it were, out of his awe and reverence for that mighty engine, the law, of which he himself was one of the very smallest and most insignificant wheels. To his youthful mind a barrister in wig and gown was even a more terrible personage than the head of the police himself; and therefore it is no wonder that the man who was, as it were, admitted into the very innermost recesses of the art of making barristers and judges seemed a delightful sort of "mystery man" to Beams.

Of all the inhabitants of Fig-tree Court only two were more than migratory. The majority lived in grand West-end lodgings, or in the suburbs, and only came to chambers for the working hours of the day.

A man of the name of Twigg, however, owning the upper rooms next door, made his home there; and William Snow—partly because he liked the City itself, party because he wished to make his way as independently as might be—also lived in Fig-tree Court. He occupied the upper part of the house. The lower rooms were those of Mr. Boultbee, a conscientious, plodding man, whose pupil William had been. His family residence was in Dorset Square, then a more fashionable locality than it is at present. William was a favorite with Mrs. Boultbee, and popular to an almost trying degree with her offspring. They would peep at him through the banisters of the nursery landing, and cry out, "Mr. No! Mr. No! come up and see what we've dot!" or, after dinner, descend to dessert, climb on "Mr. No's" knee, and request promptly to be fed with raisins.

There was one child—a girl with long locks flowing down her shoulders, locks with a sheen of gold on their ripples—who quickly discovered her power over the heart of "Mr. No," and traded on it accordingly. Perhaps, had Mrs. Boultbee known that her favorite's fondness for this "sweet Ella" was but a reflected light, she would not have prided herself so much upon her darling's conquest.

She was one of those women whose whole natures are saturated with motherhood. She was in all respects an excellent wife, but I am not sure that even "dear Fred" had not his highest value in her eyes from being the "papa" of her children, and the bread-winner who enjoyed the privilege of working his brains to provide those sweet innocents with food and raiment. Her gamut of approval ran high or low, exactly in accordance as this or that person showed a just and true appreciation of "the children." Early in her acquaintance with our hero she confided to her husband the high estimation she had formed of William Snow's character, in consequence of his attention and kindness to the olive branches that "round their table grew"—"Especially Ella," added Mrs. Boultbee, "who adores him."

Would the fond mother have been equally pleased had she known that Ella's little dancing figure, floating locks, and violet eyes, brought back a dear, dear memory to his mind—that his thoughts flew back to an evening long ago, when "Uncle David's Chissmiss-pie" came like a fairy vision from the recesses of the crimson curtains?

It chanced, on this particular Sunday upon

which we have followed Jim in his City wanderings, that William Snow was at Dorset Square. On the previous evening he had been some distance into the country with Mr. Boultbee, and had returned home with him to spend the Sunday—a not very unusual occurrence. It also chanced that the late post on Saturday night brought a letter to Fig-tree Court for W. Snow, Esq.—a letter that the trusty clerk turned over and over, and then laid gently down upon his master's desk.

"That's from home," he thought to himself: "it's Mr. Earle's writing—all jerky, and the tops of the capitals flying off as if they were in a high wind. Master will be glad to get that, I know. He said he might be home late to-morrow night; I hope he may, and then he'll get it all the sooner. There was some talk of the old gentleman and Miss Lilian coming to London for a month or so; perhaps this is to say they're coming at once: if it is, how pleased he'll be!"

So now, when Beams was sent to bed, Jim sat patiently in the dusky gloom, waiting for the sound of the quick step on the stones below— the step he knew so well, and that was sweeter than the sweetest music to his ear. Presently the moon rose, and through the wide-opened window he watched her silver light creep over the high roofs opposite. "It's getting late," he thought; "he won't come to-night."

But just then came the sound of footsteps down below. Jim caught up the letter, and hurried to meet his master at the door.

If he had only known—if Jim had only guessed that in his hand he held a dagger destined to stab the heart of one he would have gladly died to serve, how would the smile have died upon his lips, the glad light faded from his eyes!

* * *

CHAPTER VIII.

JIM KNOWS ALL ABOUT IT.

WE have all heard of that estimable bird, the phœnix, which enjoyed the privilege of being able to rise from its own ashes in all the vigor of restored youth. Perhaps in these days the only wand that can accomplish such a feat is a golden one. Certainly wealth wields a powerful arm, and brings about marvellous effects. Winstowe, by the magic of this golden wand, acquired the power of the phœnix, and arose from its ashes, not, indeed, itself, but a younger, more modern, and far finer edifice than the old-fashioned dwelling-house destroyed by the vindictive hand of Ben Dutton.

This new and more pretentious Winstowe had no diamond-paned casements, no quaint gables; all modern comfort and luxury adorned its rooms; and now, when twelve years have gone by since that memorable New-year's-night, the tender, healing hand of time has to a great extent restored the damaged beauty and luxuriance of the ivy and the banksia roses; indeed, the gardens have become a local celebrity, and in the season for those gorgeous flowers no place for miles round can rival Mr. David Earle's rhododendrons.

And what changes has time brought to the old man himself? Not very many, nor yet very noticeable ones. He is not quite so upright as he was, and the hair, that was fast turning gray when we saw him last, is now of snowy whiteness. He still retains that beaming expression of benevolence—nay, more than retains, for God has added many happy days to his life, and "blessed the work of his hands exceedingly."

Lilian has grown up under his eyes, into the flower of perfect womanly grace and beauty. Her hair has darkened. Her eyes have grown deeper, and full of a more subtle tenderness. He watches her lithe, willowy figure in and out among the flowers in the garden, and thinks to himself that no sweeter sight could be given for his eyes to dwell upon; he calls her, and she turns upon him a radiant look of fondness, hastening to his side with the alacrity of love. Yes, she is very "fair to see," this child whom he has reared as his own, whose mind he has enriched with every cultivated taste, and trained to all highest appreciation of the beautiful in art and nature.

Lilian is no ordinary woman; no pretty doll, fitted to be a man's toy, but never his companion. She can think and feel, and clothe her thoughts in fair words and true. The keys to the literature of other countries besides her own have been put into her hand. Uncle David has spared no cost upon her education; he had given up what is more valuable in his eyes a thousand times than any gold—the sweetness of her presence during the last two years of her training— in order that she may reap the advantages of foreign schools. Now she is repaying all his care by the companionship that has made their life together so complete during the past year. Yet, stay! as Lilian stands upon the broad terrace walk, her soft, gray dress gently wafted backward by the breeze that is laden with the breath of the summer roses—a crimson blossom stolen from their number nestling in her breast— is there no deeper joy, no shy, sweet, secret gladness in her dreamy eyes and on her parted lips? Is there not some new-found source of happiness, some gentle stirring in the depths of her woman's heart, the heart that has been hitherto but a folded bud?

Has Uncle David reared and tended this fair, sweet flower, but for some other hand to gather it and inhale its fragrance? Have dreams of a closer, dearer, fonder love begun to stir the slumbering heart of the maiden? Is that heart learning that lesson, so exquisitely sweet to the timid pupil, how to beat a little quicker at the sound of a footfall? Is the hand that wanders among the roses, touching delicately their perfumed petals, learning to thrill and tremble at the touch of another, ever hot to clasp and loath to let it go? Is Lilian learning the old, old story of the love that could brighten even the hearts that mourned a lost paradise?

But to return to our retrospect of the past years.

Not only had David Earle seen the little maid, the "Christmas-pie" of the olden days, grow up into all the beauty and the grace that may best adorn a gentlewoman, but William, the son of his adoption, the boy to whom he had given a love truer and more unselfish than that which many a parent lavishes upon his children, he, too, had grown and prospered.

Since last we saw him, striving to comfort and console in their sorrow those who had been the friends of his earliest days, William Snow has passed through all those various stages of life that carry the boy of twelve on to the man of four-and-twenty. At fourteen he had attained to that unpleasant phase of a boy's existence when, no matter what exertions his tailor may make, his trousers and the sleeves of his coats look too short; when he does nothing but ask questions upon every conceivable subject under the sun, and oversets and damages pretty nearly every article of a fragile and breakable nature with which he comes in contact.

His holidays, at this period of his life, were one long hostile engagement with Mr. Briggs and Mrs. Timmins. Even Lilian fled to her governess on more than one occasion, shedding bitter tears, and telling piteous tales of Willie's ravages (generally committed in the interests of scientific investigation) upon her most cherished toys.

Secreting gunpowder in unhallowed places—letting it off at inconvenient and unsuitable times—going fishing in the secluded parts of the canal, falling in head foremost, and coming home as wet as if he had been himself a fish newly caught—these and many other similar enormities was our hero guilty of.

Then a further stage was reached. He grew more awkward and less boisterous; a sort of dirty smear upon his upper lip refused to be washed off, and told of an incipient mustache; Briggs caught him twisting himself into impossible attitudes in the effort to part his hair behind; he fidgeted over the state of his hands induced by much cricketing; and thought Mrs. Dutton ridiculous when she wept for joy to see him grown so tall and "gradely," and called him her "dear boy." Lilian, too, then a romping, laughing, mischief-loving child of nine, offended his fastidiousness; he affected the society of the Miss M'Tavishes, mature young ladies of seven and eight and twenty, on a visit at the Deanery. They thought him a "handsome boy," and made him fetch and carry like a retriever. Lilian pouted over this desertion. She was found on one occasion by Mrs. Timmins crumpled up in a corner, damp and limp with much weeping, and had to be carried to the "housekeeper's room," and comforted with barley-sugar.

Oxford soon changed our hero into a "regular young man," as Briggs expressed it; and after a brilliant career at Alma Mater, he duly went up to London to "eat his dinners." This phrase cost Briggs many an hour's puzzling reflection, and he was, when hard pressed by Mrs. Timmins, obliged to confess his ignorance as to its meaning.

Then William was "called" to the Bar, and Mrs. Dutton being informed that he wore a "wig and gown," failed to see in that fact a matter for congratulation.

"Poor *dear* boy!" she said, with grave concern, to the delighted Lilian, "whatever's bin and 'appened to his lovely 'ed of 'air, as he's got to wear a wig so young?"

However, Mrs. Dutton's fears were groundless. William's brown, curly locks were as thick and luxuriant as of yore; neither had the man lost the bright winning glance of the boy. The blue eyes had deepened, but they looked out from beneath the square intellectual brow with the same frank, fearless expression as ever. You felt, as you met them, that their owner had passed through life so far unscathed; that the manliness that declared itself in the tall, well-built frame and the genial smile, was of the truest, highest stamp—the manliness that is founded upon purity and truth.

From all the coarse temptations life could offer, William Snow had ever had the best shield any man *can* have. He loved one woman so dearly, so passionately, so entirely, that for her sake he held all other women sacred. As for the sin that drags so many a young head beneath the waters of ruin, social and moral, Ben Dutton had been to him what the unfortunate Helots were made to be to the Spartan youths. His earliest years had been darkened by the misery that ever travels in the train of drunkenness, and hence he shunned, as he might some deadly pestilence, even the slightest approach to it. Not only so, but he had more than once put forth a hand to strive to rescue others from its toils.

Yet there was no more popular fellow among his compeers. Every one liked Snow. If here and there some brother "limb of the law" thought him a trifle "strait-laced," the natural solution was that some "country daisy" occupied his heart, and blinded his eyes to the attractions of the "fair and free" of far-famed London town. And how the man did work! He worked with that unflagging energy, that tireless zeal, that only work that is the outcome of a powerful motive can possess. The mainspring is strong—*ergo*, the machinery knows no flagging.

People used to say that he was destined to falsify the popular notion that at the Bar a man can never make his way until he is gray-haired. He seemed determined to show the world a successful Q. C. with a curly brown pate under his legal wig.

Then, when the vacation time came, he would run down to Winstowe, inspect all the endless improvements David Earle was making in the property, and slake his heart's thirst at two wells of light, soft violet eyes that were his stars, and ever shone a bright welcome upon his coming. How proud was Lilian of her "big brother!" What happy times they had, wandering about on the long terrace walks, listening to the mellow cathedral chimes as they ushered in each passing hour! Fair to Will's eyes, pleasant to his ear, the lovely face, the soft, melodious voice of his old playmate; but something beyond all this deepened his pleasure in her society—she was companionable to him.

That is a charm "time cannot stale." Yet few women value it as highly as they should. A man may (and often does) weary of a pretty face when it is always opposite to him; but a woman who has so cultivated her mind and heart as to be a true companion to him, has a jewel in her possession that no lapse of years can dim; and this jewel Lilian possessed.

Those long, happy "talks," as the girl called them, were sweet memories for William to carry back with him to Fig-tree Court. In his leisure hours he lingered on the thought of them. But how had all this come about? When did the reign of those "mature sirens," the Miss M'Tavishes, cease? Quickly enough; for that reign was not theirs, but the inevitable one of vanity that occurs in every boy's life, and passes with amazing rapidity, once the boy fairly becomes the man.

Behold our hero, then, attained to the years of manhood, returning for the "Long" to Winstowe. There he finds not the child Lilian—not the merry, romping puss whose tomboy ways had once jarred upon his rising sense of fastidious refinement — but a maiden, sweet and fair and gentle; somewhat timid, too, at their first meeting after several years of separation.

At once his heart opened and took her in, a tenant for life, "to have and to hold," alike through dark days and bright, when smiles dimpled her cheek, and when tears bedewed her eyes. He loved her in her fair young beauty, in the freshness of her maiden bloom; he would hold her just as dear if the beauty and the bloom faded. The casket was beautiful, and he loved its beauty; but the jewel it held was dearer by far, and to wear it shining on his breast through life was the one hope round which all other hopes circled.

Yet never a word had William spoken, save such as might be justified by the old compact made in the study twelve years ago. He who aimed at being an eloquent "pleader" had failed to plead his own cause. And why? Two motives combined to hold him back—two motives made him shrink from disturbing the sisterly love which Lilian gave him. And these motives were strong enough to make him bind down the impulses of his heart, keep a watch over his looks, his words, his actions, "hold passion in a leash," and neither by word nor sign let the girl see how tenderly he loved her. All the strength and passion of a nature whose intensity had never been squandered upon less worthy objects, and whose earnestness of purpose doomed his love to be either the keenest joy or the keenest pain of his life, was centred on her. Yet was he silent. And the motives that held him so? First and foremost, the weight of his indebtedness to Mr. Earle, and the knowledge that Lilian would be his benefactor's heiress.

"She has seen little or nothing of the world as yet. Is it a generous return for all *his* goodness to me, to try to win her heart in all the inexperience of her secluded life with him? If he had wished that she should ever be my wife, would he not have shown me his heart in the matter already?"

Thus would William ponder. Yet even in thought the words "*my wife*" seemed so sweet, so full of exquisite possibilities of happiness, that he lingered upon them, muttering softly to himself,

"My wife! my wife! Oh, my darling! little harm should come to you, God helping me, if once my arms had the right to hold you close and fast!"

But I have said there was a second motive which held him back.

And it was this:

His own nameless, unknown origin!

Would what was dark ever be made light? Would what was now obscure be made clear? Should he know one day who he was, and whence he came?

Even so, might not knowledge be as bitter as ignorance? Would it but show him a social gulf across whose wide expanse he could not dare stretch out his hand to clasp Lilian's?

Darker thoughts still crossed his mind in these sad self-communings.

Could it be that there was shame in the story of his birth? Was he but a base-born bantling, after all?

Yet against this searing thought a passionate protest would arise in his heart; a protest so intense as to seem like a spirit-cry from the woman who bore him, and gave her life for his.

He had no right to the name of Snow beyond that of a strange chance; this he knew well. To the wife he might one day win, and to the children she might bear him, he had no other name to give, save a name that was in reality none!

Uncle David had at one time urged his adopted son to take the name of Earle. But Will quietly yet firmly refused. To his proud and sensitive nature the idea of merging the name given to him, as to a "waif and stray," in that of an old ancestral family was repugnant beyond all words.

"To shelter my unknown parentage under what is the birthright and heritage of others, would be a *lâcheté* in my eyes; the falsity of the position would drag me down!" he had said, with head erect and fearless eyes looking the truth boldly in the face. So Uncle David let "the boy" have his way.

In spite, however, of all stern resolves and proud humility, William Snow had his weak moments. In these he not only built castles, but also lived in them. That name, the name received from his godfather Nature, should by hard, untiring energy be made great and famous —should be made a fit offering at last to be laid at Lilian's little feet.

Now and again a rough touch would show our hero how tender was the wound he bore in the very heart of his life; how sensitively he could suffer from any chance word unwittingly aimed at his unknown parentage.

Once, in a gay company of men of his own profession, the charms of a reigning beauty were under discussion.

One young fiery spirit chose to take Will's "faint praise" amiss.

"I tell you what it is, you're a regular iceberg!" cried this gallant "limb of the law." "Your name describes you well—I swear it does! Doesn't the immortal What's-his-name say something somewhere about some one being 'cold as *snow?*'"

The speaker was the *esprit fort* of the occasion; a thoughtless youngster, but good-hearted to the core. The hot color fled to William's cheek and brow; he bit his lips savagely, and yet the hasty, passionate nature, generally so nobly curbed, got the better of him for once, and he answered the idle jest in words repented of as soon as spoken.

The crestfallen wit was astounded at the effect of his harmless fun, and only when the young barrister had left the room was it made clear to him by others how he had unwittingly "touched a raw."

How *do* these things get known? Heaven only knows, and yet it is so. How does the world learn that the maternal grandfather of that pleasant fellow you met at a certain Richmond dinner was clothed in a neat and unassuming suit of dark gray at his country's expense, and toiled beneath the hot sunshine of a distant colony for his country's benefit? It is hard to say; yet you will not know him long before some one will tell you of the fact "in confidence," and beg of you not to speak of our convict establishments in his presence. Such secrets are like moles, they burrow in the earth, and seem to be forgotten; but in some unexpected place they cast up a hillock, and their presence is declared. Thus the thought of the mystery that overhung his birth weighed upon our hero's mind, and held him back from striving to win the prize that his heart so longed for. Yet "in time," he said to himself, he would teach Lilian to love him, even as he loved her. He would work with such untiring energy as should give his name so high a place in his profession that men would cease to remember the cloud upon his birth; he would attain such eminence as should enable him to raise the woman he wedded to a social standing enviable in the eyes of others. Then he would go to David Earle, and say,

"I have built upon the grand foundation you gave me—the education that was so costly, and so generously given; I have made a name that is worthy of your goodness to me, and I love our child Lilian as none other can."

But William knew that this sweet fruition of his hopes was yet a long way off.

Perhaps there is no profession so disheartening in its early stages as that of the Bar, though to an ambitious man few offer so grand and glorious a career, once the steep hill is climbed and the summit gained. If a young barrister is so fortunate as to possess among his relatives or family friends a solicitor of influence and position, "cases" may be put in his way, and the drudgery of the first few years of his career lightened considerably; for the solicitor, after all, must act the part of "jackal to the lion," he must supply the stepping-stone upon which the other may firmly plant his foot.

In these days, that grim and useless social barrier which custom gradually built up between the members of the Bar and the solicitors who were so essential to them is to a great extent broken down. Twenty years ago rules existed prohibiting a barrister on circuit from travelling in a public conveyance, lest he might chance to have an attorney for fellow-passenger, and forbidding him to stay at a hotel, for the same reason; hence friendships between men belonging severally to these two branches of the law were rare, and the Bar, and what may well be styled its *brother-in-law*, were parallel lines; they ran side by side, yet never touched. All this burdensome and needless etiquette is nowadays much less stringent, though in other particulars things legal have become more rigid. Thus in former days no examination was needed before a young fellow could be "called;" he "ate his dinners" (generally very good ones, too) for the three needful terms, and then became a fully fledged barrister, often making but a feeble flutter with his scantily feathered pinions, and coming eventually, with an ignominious flutter, to the ground. Nowadays the candidate for wig and gown must, if he has not passed an examination at one of our universities, submit to one before becoming a member of an Inn of Court; and at the end of three years' studentship all alike must pass another examination before being admitted into the ranks of the Bar.

The result of this change of system is, that there are now fewer abortive careers than formerly among the members of the Bar. The stricter rule sifts the ranks more quickly, and the worthless are promptly rejected.

Even to the man whose zeal never flagged, those first years of apparently fruitless toil were disheartening; to be dependent on another, no matter how near and dear that other may be, is ever galling to a manly spirit, and therefore, by every available means—by extra work, essay-writing, reviewing, and such-like mental toil, did William Snow strive after self-help.

David Earle saw and appreciated this longing for independence, and therefore forbore to render burdensome a generosity that would willingly have put every comfort, and even luxury, in the power of one dearer than a son. He had taken the poor waif and stray to his heart and home, not to stunt and dwarf a nature naturally grand and noble by foolish indulgence, but to train up a great and good man for the battle of life; and I think David Earle was succeeding very well.

Seeing and acknowledging the difficulties to be surmounted before reaching success in his career at the Bar, William was yet nothing daunted. Like the Alpine climber who fixes his eyes upon the glittering summit bright with the gleam of the sunlight, grasps his alpenstock, and, heedless of all obstacles, makes bravely for the goal of his desires, so he toiled, and plodded on, certain in his heart of success at last.

A man can hardly have a stronger rope to pull him on in life than one formed of the twofold cord of ambition and love. Without ambition, he is like a spiritless horse starting for a race; without love, he lacks the softest shining jewel in the crown of a hard-won success.

And now, as William Snow looked back over the past year, he was able to say to himself, "I have done well." By dint of "rising early and late taking rest," of steady persevering toil in the many by-ways where time may be coined into money by a willing hand, he had managed to be almost—almost, but not quite—indebted to his own exertions for his own living. To answer "cases for opinion," to spend hours in drawing "pleadings" or "conveyances," may be irksome, and not very profitable, but, like many another humble path of perseverance, such labor leads to higher things. Among other good fortune that had already come to our hero was, first the notice, and then the friendship, of a man in his own profession who had distanced pretty nearly all the men of his day; but we shall come to this presently, and must confine ourselves just now to following our hero on his homeward way from Dorset Square to that same Fig-tree Court in which no fig-tree grew.

A pleasant evening among pleasant people— people who like us, and whom we like, is as refreshing to the spirit as fresh air to the body. We are all the creatures of atmosphere, mental as well as physical; and I suppose there are few who have not known at one time or other of their lives that awful weariness and lassitude that is the result of living among those with whom we have nothing in common, and who turn everything we say wrong side out, and put a wrong construction on everything we do. Naturally the reverse of this picture holds good;

and a certain buoyancy of feeling and lightness of heart are the sweet echoes left lingering about us by congenial companionship.

Yes; life has a trick of taking its reflections from ourselves; and the man who to-night steps quickly along the quiet city streets, that will wake up to such bustling life to-morrow, carries a light and hopeful heart in his bosom. Another week's work is before him, and he is glad of it; he is ready to meet his work with a smile —the best greeting man or woman can give to the task God has given them to do.

The Temple Cloisters look really quite Moorish in the moonlight, that, like charity, ever "covers a multitude of sins;" the Gardens at the bottom of the lane look actually beautiful, and he thinks, as he glances that way, how delightful it would be to wander up and down along the walks with Lilian by his side. He thinks how the moonlight would glimmer on the ripples of her hair, and shine in her grave, sweet eyes— Well, well! even the legal mind is open to the weakness of a day-dream now and then, and legal hands may sometimes deign to fashion an airy castle in the Spanish main.

There is that faithful fellow Jim on the lookout, and holding something in his hand. It is a letter.

"From home, sir," says Jim, radiant.

William is up the stairs two at a time, letter in hand.

"What, Jim!" he says, entering the front room, a chamber devoted to the interest of the profession, "no light? What a lazy fellow you are! Hurry, hurry, my man, and let us see what the good folks at home have to say."

He flings his gloves and hat down upon the table, and as Jim sets the gas flaring miles too high in his zeal, William opens the Winstowe letter.

Jim has left the room; everything is very silent, so silent that at last the clerk ventures to open the door very softly and look in. The open letter has fluttered to the floor; William's arm rests upon the desk, and one hand covers his eyes. He does not stir when the door opens, and Jim timidly advances to his side.

"Master! master!" he says, trembling.

But there is no reply, and Jim draws nearer still, laying his long thin hand upon his master's arm.

Then the master looks up at the troubled, loving face of his old playmate. And as he does so, Jim gives a sudden cry and clasps his hands together. Ay, Jim, thy faithful, loving heart is learning the lesson most of us have to learn some day or other—that, love as fondly, as truly as we may, our love cannot always shield the heart we hold so dear from sorrow.

"Here's fine news, grand news!" said William, in a voice that sounded hardly like his own. "My people are coming up to town; and, Jim, Miss Lilian's going to be married!"

Without a word the clerk turned and left the room, closing the door softly, as though some one slept and must not be disturbed. Then he stole on tiptoe up to his room on the topmost floor, and there, without light, save the faint gleam of the moonlight, sat and watched and waited; and not only watched and waited, but prayed too—prayed, in an agony of supplication that brought out the sweat like beads upon his pallid brow, for God's comfort to fall upon the stricken heart, as the dew of heaven upon a trampled, bruised, and drooping flower.

With the intuition that is ever born of a great love, Jim had read his master's heart long since.

CHAPTER IX.

GUY TREMLETT.

Mrs. Masher was the "laundress" who "did" for Mr. Twigg, and Mr. Twigg was William Snow's next-door neighbor in Fig-tree Court. Perpetual war raged between Mrs. Masher and Abraham Beams: sometimes hostilities were active, sometimes passive; occasionally projectiles were hurled, and sorrow dire and deep was the portion of Beams, that young person invariably proving to be the aggressor. Mrs. Masher wore a rusty brown front, and the remainder of her *coiffure* was composed of a brown-silk skull-cap. Hence such remarks as "Yer back 'air's a-coming down!" or a polite request for a "lock of them lovely curls!" were fraught with keenest satire, and enraged her to an extent that at times rendered her speechless, and capable only of shaking her fist at the enemy. Mrs. Masher was a Scotchwoman, whom some wave of fortune, or rather misfortune, had landed high and dry in the City of London. She had strong national proclivities, and a strong national brogue; denounced English people as a "lump o' Sabbath-breakers," and bemoaned her fate in dwelling thus "in Kedar's tents." Even the exquisite softness and brightness of a day in June did not soften or delight Mrs. Masher; besides, her enemy, the Mordecai whose prosperity vexed her soul, was singing at his work,

"All pee-pul that on earth dew dwell,
    Sing—toe—the—Lord—wi' cheerful vice—"

He brushed hard as he sung, and the lively friction imparted a delightful *tremolo* to his voice. But here Beams caught sight of the enemy, "taking the top of the dirt off the back window," as he described it. Intuitively recognizing that she by no means appreciated his strain, the aggrieved singer proceeded to justify himself.

"I learned that there at Cripplegut Church—it's a fine toon as you'll hear in a day's march."

"Church, indeed!" replied the old woman, giving her head a disdainful toss, and leaning out of the open window, the better to fling her words down below; "if ye gang to the church of a mornin', it's my opinion ye play at godless games a' the lave o' the day. In my country the vera doggies dinna wag their tails o' the Sabbath-day!"

"And don't the old women wag their tongues neither? That must be a fine country for to live in, that must! But what if I do handle a marble now and again of a Sunday arternoon?— it's better nor countin' over all the savin's you've got hid away in that there old storkin' up yer chimbley at 'ome."

This was an old sore, and Mrs. Masher bestowed several flowers of speech upon Beams by way of reply.

"Just keep yer tongue to yerself!" bawled the incorrigible one, setting his arms akimbo, and desisting from his work. "I'm not to be spoke to so free, *I* can tell you, Mrs. Masher!

We've got the quality a-comin' to our place to-morrow. Just you wait till you see the shoot I'll be bursting out, and you'll be proud to let folks think as you knows me!"

"Hear t'im!" cried the exasperated female; "he'll drive me fair daft one of these days, I know! Stay a wee, my young billy! I'll be reporting ye to Mr. Dutton one of these days yet, and maybe then ye'll dance on the other leg!"

"Oh! yer will, will yer?" cried Beams, going through the preliminary movements of a pugilistic encounter. Then he suddenly changed his tactics, drew nearer to the window, and put up his hand to his mouth, so as to impart something of a confidential air to their interview: "I say, yer gownd's a-gaping open behind like a sleepy man's mug—'tain't of no manner of consekens, yer know. It don't signify what *you* dresses yerself in, there's no quality comes to *your* place, and Mr. Dutton and me, we're used to it, we are! You're allers made up of odds and ends as don't fit, *you* are!"

But patience has its limits, and Mrs. Masher's was exhausted. She turned quickly round, and catching up a wet scrubbing-brush that lay upon the window-sill, let fly at the boy's head. At that moment the clerk turned into the court, and beheld Beams shedding bitter tears, and wiping them away with the corner of his black apron.

"It's that Mrs. Masher, sir; she's allers a-molestin' of me, and preventin' of me doing my lawful work. She's hit me a horful blow this time, and a nice sight I'll be presentin' of to the quality to-morrer!"

Now there was this peculiarity about Abraham Beams. No matter what row he got into himself, or led others into, he invariably came out as the aggrieved party; a peculiarity I have met with in various other people, to my no small discomfort. It is well to give such persons a wide berth, for they persistently get into every conceivable scrape, and, in some snaky fashion or other, contrive to throw upon you the blame of their misfortunes. However, in this case Beams had fortunately received but slight injury, and was able to put in a very presentable appearance on the all-important morrow.

If yesterday had been bright and lovely, surely to-day was its twin sister. Never had the Temple fountain sparkled more brightly; never had the City sparrows chirped so loudly, and enjoyed themselves so thoroughly. And Fig-tree Court put on quite a rakish and festive appearance. Plants in pots adorned the window-sill of Mr. Snow's front room; a large bouquet graced the table; and men in white aprons, with trays full of covered dishes on their heads, ran in and out, nearly colliding more than once, with bewigged and begowned barristers, who bustled along, with eyes glued to the briefs in their hands, and pulled up sharp and sudden, just in time to prevent themselves from going headlong into the trays of delicacies and their bearers.

Beams appeared clothed from head to heel in a resplendent new "shoot," and passed Mrs. Masher as though she were a person of whom he had once heard, but of whom his recollection was but dim. The only face that seemed hardly in keeping with the general festivity was that of the cripple clerk.

"If he don't cheer up, I'll have to tie a black ribbing on the cat's tail, so as she may keep him company. He looks as if he was a-preparin' of hisself to go to a walkin' funeral, so he does! It's a sin and a shame for a man to be goin' about like that, and such meats and sweets, to say nothin' of drinks, before his very eyes!"

Thus Beams to his friend the boy who "did" for Mr. Coplethwaite, the wig-maker. But Jim's depression rather increased as the morning wore on, and once or twice, when alone in the little room that was his own special den, he might have been seen twining those long, thin hands of his together, like one who was striving to give himself courage for some trying ordeal.

Just as two o'clock chimed from the hall clock hard by, the group of expected visitors entered the court. Mr. Twigg saw them from the front window of his chambers; Mrs. Masher's brown front appeared over the dirty blind of an upper room; and Beams flew down-stairs to usher them up with so much energy that he slipped on the soles of his new boots, and landed most ungracefully in the court at their feet. Upon seeing this occurrence, a smile lighted up the countenance of Mrs. Masher, for the first and only time that day. Beams was up again in a moment, though, and preceded the visitors in splendid style up the narrow stairway, flinging open the second-floor room, so as to dazzle them at once with the full glory of the preparations for their entertainment.

If the day was fair, and soft, and bright, she too was like the day, this happy, smiling maiden of the dewy violet eyes and nut-brown hair. She had a smile for Beams; a kindly hand held out to the shrinking figure of the clerk, whose pale face filled her gentle heart with pitiful thoughts of city toil, and sunless days in the dull, endless streets; and for Willie, her dear "big brother," she showed the same steadfast love as ever, and a pretty interest in his home, and all the odd management of his household matters.

It was as if the sunshine had got inside the dingy room, and was shining on the court below, Will thought, as Lilian sat by the open window, leaned her arm upon the ledge, and looked out curiously at the tall buildings on every side. Even Mrs. Masher, catching a glance of the pretty face, the shining locks, crowned with a bonnet of delicate silver-gray and pale-pink roses, thought that, after all, Beams was right, and his master's visitors "quality" of the highest order.

But talk of sunshine in the court or out of it, what could beat old David Earle's face, as he looked at every detail of the place where "his boy" worked? What could equal his delight at the quaint newness of everything about him? They had had a rare time of it getting him along the City streets, I can tell you; first it was one thing, then another, that caught his fancy. Now he stood rooted before a shop window; now made an unexpected dive after some shoeless and almost garmentless street Arab, to give him a penny. But, though a trial to others, the old man had never enjoyed himself so much for many a day. He had paid a visit now and then to the great metropolis of England, but he had never been into its *heart* before. The fashionable whirl of West-end life wearied him, and only for Lilian's sake, and to give her pleasure, did he mingle in the crowded Row, or drive in the parks. But this quaint, old-fashioned, busy, bustling city!—he would have liked to ferret out each interesting nook and corner, and visit each time-honored building, round which historical associations grew as thickly as the ivy about Winstowe. As to the Temple—the queer old houses bulging over the streets—the grand hall with its massive iron gates—the Temple Church with its marvellously green church-yard, dotted here and there with tombstones ancient as itself—the courts with their strangely undescriptive names—these were all delightful in his eyes.

"And to see you look so well, my boy, too!" he said, laying a hand on either of William's shoulders, and holding him thus, while his eyes beamed with love and pride through his spectacles. "But I tell you what it is—this life of brain-work takes it out of a man. Yes, it does. You look well enough, but older—older—older, my dear boy, since I saw you last."

Yes; there were lines round William's firm-set lips and on his brow that some hand had lately planted—lines that three months ago were not there.

Lilian, who had drawn quietly aside to the little room, Jim's "den," and was speaking softly to him of his home, and of Harry's progress at the cathedral school, heard through the open door the old man's words, and read their echo in the sudden change that passed across the face of the clerk, the sudden welling-up of pity and tenderest reverential love in the deep-set eyes that turned towards his master.

"How devoted he is to Will!" she thought, noting this look; but it seemed strange that the next moment the earnest, searching eyes were turned upon herself, and in their glance she read reproach. "He must think I don't feel the same interest in Will *now*," she thought, and the soft rosy color flew to her cheek at the remembrance of all that little word "now" meant. She moved quickly to William's side, and looked searchingly in his face.

"Uncle is right—you *do* look older; and not only that, but tired and weary. You are working too hard, sir," she added, laughing, "and not taking care of yourself; come now, confess!"

It was hard work to meet calmly the scrutiny of those innocent eyes; hard work to make his voice *quite* steady as he answered,

"You and Uncle David would make a regular milksop of me, Lilian, if you had your way."

Neither words nor manner was as gently courteous as usual; and a surprised, wounded look, like that of a grieved child, came into Lilian's eyes and trembled round her lips. She tried to laugh it off.

"See, Mr. Dutton has shut his room door, and is, I know, making believe to be very busy, so that he mayn't have to witness against you."

But even as the words passed her lips the subject passed from her mind like an image that ceases to be reflected in a mirror. A glad light, shy and sweet, shone in her eyes, her lips parted in happy expectation, and she turned away from the window.

"Mister Trimblit!" shouted Beams, throwing open the door, and excelling himself in grandeur of air and manner; but as the new-comer entered Beams so far forgot his manners as to stand gaping at the assembled company, until his master sharply requested him to relieve them of his presence. This reprimand he resented (with crying injustice!) upon Mrs. Masher. He made un-

becoming and aggravating gestures at that sorely tried woman from the shelter at the yard door, varying the proceedings by pointing to the room above, and turning up the whites of his eyes, to intimate that the entertainment was of a description defying words, and that he pitied Mrs. Masher for belonging to such a vulgar establishment as that of the respectable Twigg.

Meanwhile Lilian, with Guy Tremlett by her side, and William and Uncle David near, thought what a fair world this world of ours could look when seen through love-lit eyes. Her merry laughter rung out, and trilled more blithely than the twittering of the jubilant sparrows by the fountain edge.

Jim heard it, as he bent over a mass of papers and made marginal notes here and there with an inkless pen. Beams heard it down below, and thought the "quality" was enjoying itself in grand style; and Mrs. Masher heard it, and thought what a fine thing it was to be young and beautiful, and a lady, and to have a handsome lover, and silks and satins to wear.

"If she'd a face like a stale apple, and hands as hard as horn, and had to scrub and clean all day long for that blessed Twigg, she wouldn't laugh like that," thought Mrs. Masher; for Mrs. Masher's ways were not "ways of pleasantness," nor yet of peace. She had a drunken old husband who beat her when she didn't take her wages home, and spent them in beer when she did. If she bought herself "a tidy bit o' clothes," he straightway pawned the same; neither could the laws of the country give her any protection, for the law held that a man had a right to "do what he would with his own," and his wife was his own, and so was the money earned by his wife's toil. We know better now, but in those days the law on such matters pressed cruelly on women in the lower grades of life.

But I am neglecting a very important personage in my story, namely, the hero of all Lilian's dreams—the man who has intensified to her eyes the glory and beauty of the world, the desirableness of life, the sweetness of sympathy and tenderness. I, however, must sketch Guy Tremlett very faithfully, not looking upon him through the love-blinded eyes that follow him with a happy pride, nor yet with the simple faith of old David Earle, whose guileless nature sees all men even as he would have them. I must judge him not with the jealous exacting of the man who loves Lilian too intensely to be able to judge her lover fairly: I must ignore the hot vindictiveness that lurks in the eyes of the cripple clerk, as he passes down the stairs with a photograph on his heart, taken instantaneously by a glance at the dark, handsome face bending down to Lilian, and listening to every word she utters as though the old fable were a truth, and each word a pearl. All these would draw the picture too light or too dark.

If you come to think of it, there are perhaps very few of us who are ever really fairly valued, fairly judged. Love covers our defects, or even turns flaws into beauties; hatred and prejudice paint in the shadows very black indeed, and blur all the lights. Those who differ from us widely misconstrue us, and refuse to see extenuating circumstances for our errors; in turn, we misconstrue others, and so the world wags.

After all, God only can estimate and judge

unerringly—a thought that should, I think, make us shrink more than we do from judging and condemning others.

There is a powerful and mysterious attribute which certain people possess, a power of attracting and interesting those with whom they are thrown in contact, even against their will.

Such people linger in your thoughts after you have quitted their society; this or that little trick of manner or speech remains indelibly graven upon your memory; you are disposed to believe all that is most delightful of such a one, and to resent a chance word of disparagement from others.

This power of charm, or call it what you will, Guy Tremlett possessed to an intense degree. His life had been neither pure nor true; yet there was no wrong of which he was at any time guilty, but that that wrong appeared, in the eyes of those who knew him, as more excusable in him than it would be in any one else.

"Dear Guy has been a little wild, as young men will be!" said that handsome, languid lady, his indulgent mother; "but now he is going to marry, and settle down steadily, as well becomes one who will have some day to fill the responsible position of a county landed proprietor."

Mrs. Tremlett gave these confidences to her intimate friends; and the friends on their side looked sympathetic, and murmured affectionate approbation at "dear Guy's" very proper conduct.

Certainly of "wild oats" he had sown a goodly crop. Could it be possible that the soil had become so deteriorated that wholesome verdure could find no nourishment, and even when planted must droop and die?

Mrs. Bernard Tremlett, of Tremlett Court, hoped better things. Even now she was expected up in town, and her house in Lowndes Street was in that state of resurrection, chronically entered into by London houses in the season, that betokens the return of the occupants.

Mr. Earle and his niece were installed in a charming but somewhat squeezed-up residence in Park Lane. The rent, however, was large enough to satisfy any one; and if the frontage gave you the idea that the houses on either side had swelled out, and forced it into the background, what matter; since from the balconied windows Lilian could look upon the park all freshly green, and dotted here and there with glowing islands of blossom, massed flowering plants, now in their first brilliant summer beauty.

It was a most fortunate and delightful circumstance in Mrs. Bernard Tremlett's eyes, that "dear Guy" had gone down to that old cathedral town, among the Cheshire hills and vales, and paid a visit to the Deanery. The dean's wife had been her own "school-friend" in days gone by; and it was a most fortunate circumstance that Guy had there met Lilian, lost his heart, pleaded his cause, and plighted his troth as he and she wandered about the Winstowe gardens, sweet with the perfume of spring.

In those happy yet uncertain days—days when love and hope played hide-and-seek in her grave, sweet eyes—Lilian's heart was as bright as any spring flower, and love its perfume. Then came that one strange evening—an evening that must forever (so she thought) stand out in bright relief from her whole life, when they lingered later than usual among the hyacinths and lilies. A soft, white knitted scarf rested on her bright hair and framed her face, and Guy bethought him of an exquisite Madonna in an old Italian church that he had chanced to visit. His rich, mellow voice, one of his many gifts, pleaded eloquently. The quiet gladness and serenity of the Madonna face stirred and grew troubled: the violet eyes drooped; the fair cheek flushed and paled; the little hand he held grew cold, and trembled in his clasp.

Their lips met at last, and then Guy led her into the room where David Earle was poring over "the boy's" last letter. If he had only known—if the old man had only known that the blessing he so gladly gave to the happiness of Guy Tremlett tore the heart out of "his boy's" life! that the morrow's letter, written in all the first rush of sympathy with his darling's happiness, was the knell of hopes that had hitherto been the mainspring of life's energy to the one dearer to him than a son!

But he did not know, and the sympathy he, in his ignorance, claimed from Lilian's "brother" was neither withheld nor yet doled out in stinted measure.

Listening to Guy Tremlett as he went from one subject to another, equally *au fait* at all; watching the play of his clear-cut varying features, the softness and brilliancy of his eyes, dark and deep as those of one in whose veins runs Southern blood; noticing the perfect finish of manner, the air of exceeding refinement pervading the whole man, William Snow said to himself,

"What wonder? It would have been strange indeed had Lilian resisted that marvellous charm of manner, which even I feel the power of, I who—"

But here, even in his thought, he paused. An ugly word was to follow—an ugly word to think, still worse to utter—"*distrust.*"

Yes; William distrusted this brilliant, charming, winning man. He hated himself for his distrust. He was one to judge himself pitilessly, to arraign himself at the bar, and let conscience speak out as his accuser; and he feared that distrust was born of jealousy and pain, and his own dead yet still infinitely dear hopes.

When lunch was over, a stroll in the Temple Gardens was proposed. So you see William's day-dream of sauntering with Lilian in that green and lovely spot was realized—as many of our airy castles are realized—with a difference. In those fond fancies Guy Tremlett had had no part. But now it was *he*, not William, who strolled along at her side, and looked with loving eyes upon her happy face. Behind came Uncle David and "his boy"—the old man's heart full of pride as he leaned upon Will's arm, and fancied him a thousand times more clever, and a thousand times more celebrated, than he really was.

After wandering in the gardens for a time, our *parti carré* made their way in the same order to the entrance of Temple Lane, where the Winstowe carriage, with the staid and respectable roan mare, awaited them.

"You'll dine with us to-night, Will?" said Mr. Earle, eagerly, as they passed under the pillars at the head of the lane.

"I hardly think I can to-night. You see I've had to set aside some work already to-day, and I must work late; but I'll come up during the evening if I possibly can."

Guy Tremlett had stopped a moment to speak to some passing friend, and Lilian came up to William's side, slipped her little hand beneath his arm, and whispered with a pretty insistence,

"Do come, dear Willie—*you shall hear Guy sing!*"

Poor child! she had, according to her own estimation, no greater bribe to offer. William dropped his arm, so that her hand fell to her side. He was sorry for the pettish action the moment it was done, but had no time for reparation. Uncle David handed Lilian into the carriage; the coachman tried to make the roan look as if she were very anxious to start, and Guy, with a graceful word of apology for keeping them, himself sprang in.

William stood bareheaded as they drove off; then he turned homeward, and for the first time in his life thought the Temple, and the fountain, and the gardens, and the whole city itself dull and dreary.

Perhaps our friend Beams was the only inmate of Fig-tree Court to whom the day's festivities had given unalloyed and unmitigated satisfaction. Towards evening he divested himself of the resplendent "shoot." He had done a hard day's work, had Beams, of which "putting to rights," after the departure of the company, had been the most satisfactory portion; for sundry and manifold fragments of delicacies, such as the *ci-devant* "baby-tenter" seldom tasted, supported him through the Herculean labor, and enabled him to "put up with," as he phrased it, the irritable condition of Mr. Dutton's temper.

"He was that full of haggravation, I wonder I didn't break the dishes and stand upon the bits! He shut hisself up in that there little room, and when I took a squint at him through the pane o' glass in the door, there he was a-talkin' to hisself like anything, a-wagging of his 'ed, and a-twistin' his 'ands frightful. It was the most horfullest sight as ever I see!"

This was a confidence given by Beams to Mrs. Masher later in the day; for the old "laundress" was devoured with curiosity as to the fine company that had been at Mr. Snow's, and so she was trying to be amiable to her late enemy.

"When folk crack like that, Mr. Beams, t'ain't theirsels they be holdin' converse wi', but worse manner of things—auld Hornie, and sic like."

"Lor!" cried the boy, with a countenance of extreme dismay, "how horful!"

Then he recovered himself. To call him "Mr." Beams was to flatter him in the most delicate manner possible; so he smiled upon Mrs. Masher approvingly.

"You'd a fine sight o' quality at your place to-day. That young lady, she's like a flower, she is!" said Mrs. Masher, with her head sentimentally on one side, and her hands thoughtfully rubbing her elbows.

"You was like a flower yerself, yer know, one of these days!" said Beams, with an impudent grin.

"Hech! hech! hear t'im!" chuckled the old woman, by no means displeased.

"I'll show yer somethink, Mrs. Masher, if yer'll promise faithful to stan' still and keep yer 'ands orf of it."

She nodded. Then he drew forth stealthily and cautiously three half-crowns, laid them in a row along his dirty palm, and held them out before her.

"Dinna tell me," she cried, relapsing, as usual in any excitement, into the Doric vernacular—"*dinna* be telling me they gie'd a chiel like you a' that siller! A bawbee or twa would be mair than enoo; but three great siller bits!"

She held up her hands, she turned up her eyes, her claw-like fingers shut and opened as if they grasped ghostly coins.

Beams fixed his eyes unwinkingly upon her face, and dropped each individual half-crown into his trousers-pocket with grave deliberation.

"The old gent he giv' me two on 'em; the young lady she giv' me one; t'other gent he didn't giv' me nothink," he said, with fat and sleek content in the sum total.

Then he drew one "bit o' siller" out, so that only a tiny arch of its shining rim appeared, and an abominable leer dawned upon his countenance.

"Wouldn't yer like to have one of them there to put in the old stor—"

But Beams never finished the sentence. Mrs. Masher made a dash at him; he ducked to avoid her fist, and then sped off like a young lapwing, siller and all.

———◆———

CHAPTER X.

THE CORAL PIN.

"It was very pretty of you to come and see me like this, child."

Mrs. Tremlett lay back in a luxurious lounge near the carefully shaded window of the Lowndes Street drawing-room. By her side, holding her slender hand, stood Lilian Selwyn.

Mrs. Tremlett was still a comparatively young woman. She married at seventeen, and when Guy was a tall stripling of thirteen, he looked more like her younger brother than her son. Now, as you noted the beautiful outline of a face that had once been a celebrity, you felt that it was more faded, more worn than it ought to be. The dark, almost Oriental eyes had a strange, dull languor in their shadowy depths, and about the lips was a certain coarseness that repelled you as something altogether alien to the noble brow and classically formed head.

Between mother and son there was a strong resemblance, but Guy's heavy mustache, the only hirsute adornment of his face, hid the feature that tells most clearly of the mind and character. Therefore was the son more faultlessly handsome than the mother.

Only the day previous the mistress of Tremlett Court, Berkshire, had arrived in town, and Lilian, blushing somewhat at her own boldness, had begged of Guy to take her the very next day to Lowndes Street.

"My mother is never visible until afternoon," Guy had answered, pleased at the girl's prompt thoughtfulness. "I will come for you, my darling, at three, and support you in your first meeting with the lady mother."

Lilian was no vain coquette, but she looked anxiously in her pier-glass when she was dressed for that trying ordeal. She pressed her little hands one in the other, and in her earnestness said out aloud,

"Oh, I hope—I *hope* she will like me!"

How her heart fluttered as Guy opened the door of his mother's house with his latch-key! How her breath failed her as she mounted the broad stairs, an object of intense but respectful interest to the two grand footmen whose severe and laborious duty it was to lounge about the hall and attend to visitors! When Guy had his hand on the drawing-room door, poor Lilian laid a trembling touch upon his arm, and, turning, he saw a poor little white face looking piteously up at him.

"Do you think she will like me, Guy, dear Guy?"

"Do I *think* so? Why, who could help liking you, Lilian?"

It was the best answer he could possibly have made. It brought the wild-rose bloom back again, and seldom had Lilian looked so lovely as when Guy Tremlett led her to his mother's side.

"How foolish I was to be so frightened!" thought the girl to herself as, ten minutes later, she knelt by Mrs. Tremlett's knee, her hand nestled in one that clasped it lovingly. On her part, the elder woman seemed as fascinated by the girl's fair beauty and gentle ways as her son. Her dark eyes lingered on every detail of that innocent face, with what looked like a yearning, nay, a grateful fondness. For in Lilian Selwyn the mother saw not only her son's future wife, but—or so she fondly hoped—his savior.

What a strange world this would be if we could read the thoughts of others! I think Guy read his mother's look clearly enough. I am sure he loved sweet Lilian well enough to fancy himself safe from all baneful influences for evermore, guarded by the shield of her purity and truth. The dark side of his character was in abeyance, nor could he look forward and imagine a time when temptation would be once more irresistible. He loved her to the highest standard of which he was capable; but even this, measured by the love that William bore her, became dwarfed, and "of the earth, earthy."

The exquisite delicacy of Lilian's beauty attracted Guy Tremlett as a rare flower might have done, and its varying character was such that his eyes were never tired of dwelling on the changeful expression of her face. He thought so much of this wonderful charm in her, of this winning trick of look and manner, that he forgot to think of or to value the cultivated mind, the chastened and most womanly character of which these beauties were but the outward expression.

His mother more justly divined and valued the pure jewel that her son had won.

"She is one who will not only win, but try to keep, a man's love," thought Mrs. Tremlett, watching the wistful violet eyes that followed Guy as he left the room.

Thinking such thoughts as these, jealousy slept, and something rose up in Mrs. Tremlett's heart that was almost a prayer, yet not quite; for in this woman's life, as yet, there had been no helpful creed, no God-fearing aspirations, no reliance on any power higher than that of her own will.

That which we have not ourselves, we cannot give to others; therefore Mrs. Tremlett had never, in the days gone by, taught her boy to kneel beside her knee, and fold his hands, and lisp God's name with lips that knew no guile. Nor yet, as time went on, and he grew tall and strong, and passed away from her immediate companionship, had she taught him obedience to any higher law than that of his own pleasure and advantage. Through all her life, as maid, wife, and widow, she had herself lived for no nobler aim. How, then, could she give her son any truer rule of life?

Yet she loved him—loved him with an intensity of love that was the one thing good and real and true in her life. There had been, long years ago, in the freshness of her girlhood, another bright ray in the moral gloom of her nature— a love that had uprisen in spite of herself, like some little way-side flower in an arid desert. With relentless hand she had uprooted this blossom, and sold herself to Bernard Tremlett, a man with the passions and the cruelty of a wild beast, but—the owner of Tremlett Court, and revenues many a duke envied him.

Bernard Tremlett's name had borne as black a reputation as any man's well could; but when he married, society kindly forgot all his failings, or saw them through a golden haze that softened their black outlines. His early death, which occurred about a year after the birth of the heir to Tremlett Court, still further assisted in blotting from men's minds his many social sins; and if ever his wife's lips uttered a sincere thanksgiving, you may be sure it was when kindly fate freed her from a loathsome chain, and yet left her in the full enjoyment of the wealth which, to her sensuous nature, was a necessity.

Suitors innumerable beset the handsome young widow. It was said that one needy duchess, mother of a future needy duke, actually knelt at her feet, and with bitter tears pleaded the cause of her enamored son. But to all alike Mrs. Tremlett turned a deaf ear, and in time it became an understood thing that the case was hopeless—of course only until such time as the young heir should be of marriageable years; *then* the campaign might be opened again. This time the generals were mothers with daughters to marry, instead of mothers with sons, as heretofore. However, the second siege seemed as hopeless as the former one.

Reared in a ruinous indulgence that shrunk from the unpleasantness of fault-finding, Guy Tremlett very early in a wild career showed a firm determination to avoid the snares spread for his entanglement in legal bonds. He had as yet steered clear of any public scandal or open dishonor.

And why? Because his mother's hand was ever ready, ever open to lay a golden salve upon the wounds of those whose resentment might have been harmful to him; because she permitted her son to make her the confidante of his troubles, and, without the courage to reprove, shielded him from all the consequences of wrong-doing.

But she was getting tired of this sort of thing. Her man of business began to look grave at the sums of money that had melted away, like dew in the sunshine, before Guy's wild career. She fancied that on one or two occasions old friends had looked coldly on her son. This worried her; and though she turned to consolations that for the time being deadened the pain at her heart, the worry asserted its power again and again.

"Guy has sown his wild oats—plentifully too," she pondered to herself; "he must settle down, and be a respectable member of society now."

As she thought of the "wild oats," and the cost of their worthless harvest, did the thought never enter Mrs. Tremlett's heart that her own hand had aided in sowing the seeds thereof?

Even had it ever done so, she was one to make no sign. To her proud, self-reliant nature penitence was almost an impossible evolution.

And now all was well. Fate had been kind; and the gentle, violet-eyed woman whom Guy had led, trembling and blushing, to her side was to redeem her darling from all harm.

She did not think of this as another mother might have done—as fearing a moral death or God's anger for her child; she thought of it only as social ruin, the loss of social position and of the esteem of men, that might follow an evil course too long persisted in.

And now, having thus far dissected Mrs. Tremlett's character, we can better solve the yearning look in those dark, weary eyes that lingered on the girl's face. Yes, weary; for, in the end, there is nothing that becomes the root of such hopeless, rayless weariness as a life of complete self-indulgence. Sorrow and pain and suffering bring sadness; they may rob life of its sunlight for a time; but only a life absorbed in self, a life that knows no higher law than the gratification of the will, can look upon the world, and all that is in it, with hopelessly weary eyes; can find no pleasure in the beauties of earth and sky, no sweetness in the perfume of the flowers that God's hand has set in the path of the sad as well as in that of the happy.

It was this very weariness, this strange brooding gloom, that, as time went on, drew Lilian nearer and nearer to the mother of the man she loved. At times this depression was varied by a fitful excitement of look and manner, a buoyant gayety that had seemingly no cause. This disappeared, to be succeeded by even deeper gloom; and all these strange uncertainties of conditions were accounted for by the plea of "delicate health." Yet Lilian slowly but surely drifted into a conviction that some hidden, deep cause of sorrow lay in Mrs. Tremlett's life—some grief that called for a double tenderness, a double watchful care, on the part of the woman whom her son had honored with his love.

"She must stand to me in the place of my own dear mother now, Guy," said the girl one day, about a month after Mrs. Tremlett's arrival in London. "It is the happiest thing that she has learned to love me so quickly. The very happiest thing that could have come about, I think."

Lilian was standing by her lover's side; his arm was round her, and her hand toyed with the scarf-pin that he wore. It was a pretty toy—the smiling face of Hebe, carved in coral of that most costly kind that is whiter than the purest marble, and of a more exquisitely delicate hue.

"I can only just remember mamma," she went on, speaking very softly, as we are apt to do when we take upon our lips the name of the sainted dead. "And, you know, in that dreadful fire at Winstowe, long ago, the beautiful picture of her was burned; still I can call to mind what she was like, and just how her face used to look as she bent down above me when I was kneeling by her side. Oh, she was so dear and good! It was she, you know, who carried me in her arms to kiss papa when he was dying. I remember him lying there, all white and still. Nothing about him looked alive except his eyes. They were closed when first she took me in, and then bright—oh, Guy! as bright as stars—when he opened them and looked at me. He said 'Good-bye, little thing!' I felt mamma shake and tremble. She held me close, but she did not cry." The girl's voice faltered, and her eyes grew misty with tears.

"Hush, hush, dear!" said Guy, tenderly, thinking that even in grief her beauty took a new and rarer loveliness. "Do not talk of those days; it only makes you sad, my darling." .

But she persisted.

"Nay," she said. "You must let me speak to you, Guy, of all that is in my heart. Those days are always there, you know, like something hidden away. It seems, too, as if I had thought of them more, and dwelt upon them more, lately—since I had you, I mean—and more than ever since I have known your mother, and she has been so good to me. When she was ill yesterday, and sent for me to her room, she looked so pale and worn that I quite forgot I had ever been afraid of her; and, Guy, when I came away I kissed her, and whispered, 'Good-bye, dear mother.' I hope you don't think she was angry? It was so long since I had said 'mother' to any one, you know; and I thought, as I said it, how glad *she* would be—my own dear mother, I mean—if she could know how you both love me, and how—"

But here Lilian stopped, and gave a low cry.

"O Guy! Guy! why do you wear a thing like that?"

She had gone on toying with the coral pin, and, as she spoke, at last had turned it gently round, and there, in place of the lovely, smiling Hebe, was a grinning skull. The image and sign of death suddenly faced her as she spoke with thankful gladness of a new, bright, happy life.

CHAPTER XI.

TANGLED THREADS.

I AM always glad when the thread of my story takes me back to City haunts, even though the days are not all so bright as the last one on which we visited Fig-tree Court.

They have been bright enough, though, since last we were there on that day in early summer, when William Snow wandered in the Temple Gardens, and watched Lilian and her lover going on before, and Guy bending down towards the sweet face that was as smiling as the day.

Intense and long-continued hot weather throughout the first weeks of July had somewhat stolen the bloom from Lilian's cheek, and driven Mrs. Tremlett away from town altogether.

"Such sunshine is bearable when you can lie under the shade of impenetrable trees, and hear the running of the river, as you can in the gardens in the court. Here, where the water-carts are the only rivers, and the long streets of houses let the air get stagnant between them— bah!" said Mrs. Tremlett, shrugging her graceful shoulders, "it is insufferable!"

"I, too, shall be glad to get back to the country," said Lilian, listening to these murmurings, "and it must be twice as trying for you, who are so often suffering—"

"Suffering? Oh, you mean when I have the vapors, child! That's when Ponsonby here provokes me with her stupidity: if it weren't for Ponsonby I should never be ill at all."

Ponsonby, a woman who has been in Mrs. Tremlett's service for years, and who has a stolid-looking face, a yellow complexion that never varies, and heavy black brows, makes no sign. The bestowal of these gentle compliments apparently causes no emotion in her breast. She goes on quietly with the work of braiding back the plentiful silver-lined hair of her mistress, and does not even raise her eyes from the task her hands achieve so skilfully.

Not then; but afterward, when Lilian and Mrs. Tremlett are busily discussing the merits of some etchings that David Earle has unearthed from the depths of a little out-of-the-way City shop, Ponsonby gives a long, searching look at the younger woman's face, and her sluggish mind rouses into something like speculation as she does so—speculation that is cruelly unjust to Lilian, though pretty correct in its estimation of the part that is being played by Mrs. Tremlett, and the motives that influence her.

So the house in Lowndes Street is left again empty; and very soon David Earle and his niece are to return to Winstowe.

Uncle David had most thoroughly enjoyed his visit to London. And he had managed to enjoy it in his own way.

Now, I suppose most of us have, at one time or other, experienced the weariness and bitterness of soul induced by kind but unwise persons insisting upon us enjoying ourselves in *their* way? Well, just at first Mrs. Tremlett endeavored to make David Earle "take his pastime" in *her* way, but it wouldn't do. His genial, old-fashioned courtesy made him as difficult to hold as an eel, and so he slipped through her fingers.

He "gang'd his ain gait," as our Northern neighbors say; and a very pleasant "gait" it was, too, though as completely *inconvenable* as most of his proceedings in life.

He would get away by himself during the hours that Lilian, chaperoned by her future mother-in-law, and squired by her lover, drove here and there and everywhere. He, David Earle, the owner of Winstowe, and of some yearly thousands, would be placidly content with his feet on the knife-board of a City "bus," entering into quaint converse with his chance companions.

He explored for himself, and to his own exceeding satisfaction, as many odd nooks and corners of the City as Jim Dutton himself.

But the Temple and its immediate neighborhood were ever the most attractive to him. All its grandeur, all its venerable buildings, and its legal atmosphere, seemed in some sort part and parcel of his "boy's" fame and glory. Nothing could exceed the dear old man's indignation when, on one occasion, he lost himself in a maze of innumerable "courts" and "lanes," and applying to a policeman as to the direction in which the chambers of Mr. Snow of the Inner Temple lay, received a reply that betrayed utter ignorance of that gentleman's existence.

"Party from the country," grinned Policeman No. 47 to a colleague, jerking his thumb over his shoulder at the departing figure of David Earle. But the old man was in happy ignorance of this disrespectful pantomime.

On more than one occasion he provided exquisite amusement for Her Majesty's liege subjects inhabiting "ye vaste towne of London," and on still more occasions he fell a grievous prey to the extortions of the same. He gathered together such a collection of objects of "bigotry and virtue," as Mrs. Malaprop would say, as necessitated two large packing-cases being made for their safe conveyance to Winstowe.

Especially did David Earle delight in visiting the City churches; and finding that St. Giles's, Cripplegate, was almost entirely filled with school-children taken from the poorest and lowest classes, he on one occasion changed half a sovereign into pennies, took up his post behind the church door, and pressed a "copper" into each little dirty palm, as the children came out from the afternoon service.

You should have seen the row of happy, smiling faces coming out into the church-yard! The children formed into groups under the trees that make it, even now, look almost like a church-yard in the country. Each child clutched his or her penny, and mentally made vast investments in sweet-stuff of wonderful succulence.

For long afterward it was a happy memory among the St. Giles's school-children—that Sunday afternoon when the old gentleman gave them all a penny, and two to little Sammy Hindle, the boy who walked by the aid of a crutch.

I think this "double dole" was given for Jim's sake; for Jim was a rare favorite with David Earle.

Beams thought a general collection of odd half-pence ought to be made for his benefit, for it was he who told the gentleman about the school-children at St. Giles's, and the beautiful bells, whose music makes all Cripplegate sweet on Sundays.

Indeed, I am afraid Beams was a sad scamp, and one who always had an eye to "number one."

Here we find him again, one July day that is not hot and sunshine-laden, as the days have been of late, but dull and dank, and full of oppressive, enervating warmth; a kind of day when London is the last place any one would wish to sojourn in, and compared with which a November fog is cheerful and inspiriting.

But Beams is not enervated; Beams is not depressed.

Even when Beams senior beats him, and he goes about with a plaster-patch over one eye, he looks impudently at the world with the other. He is of what may be called an elastic temperament, so that whatever pressure may temporarily be brought to bear upon him, the instant that pressure is removed, up he springs, and is the same happy-go-lucky, impertinent creature as before. Of late, to all these endearing characteristics has been added a certain increase of self-importance, a mysterious dignity which gives him somewhat the appearance of the fabled frog who swelled himself to emulate the ox, and by his ambition met a deplorable fate.

The fact was, Beams was in possession of a secret, and, like him of old who learned the objectionable length of King Midas's ears, he longed to tell the same to some discreet confidant. After due deliberation, he had come to the conclusion to honor Mrs. Masher by this confidence. So on this misty, dull, uncomfortable day, of which mention has been already made, Beams sought the society of that estimable woman in the "kitchen" that pertained to Mr. Twigg. Through the grimy window of that beetle-haunted apartment a glimpse of Fig-tree Court could be commanded.

"Guid preserve us a' this day!" cried Mrs. Masher, in reply to a confidential communication from Beams. He, having uttered it, stood staring at her with eyes unnaturally widely opened.

"Ain't it *just*?" said Beams, with a grin. "He keeps the most horfullest hours! It's truth I'm telling yer—every word reg'lar gospel. Mr. Dutton's bin and took to bad ways—him as master thinks so much on!"

Mrs. Masher sat down plump on a crazy-looking chair, and stared in her turn at Beams.

"I'm 'specting to see 'im comin' 'ome some of these here nights that screwy as he can't get up the stairs. He'll sit there groaning, like Coplethwaite's missis the time as she went to her sister's weddin', don't yer mind?"

Mrs. Masher nodded.

"Well, he'll be like that, will Mr. Dutton. I'll be dodgin' about the harchway, yer see. I've had the toothache shockin' this month back, and can't sleep a bit of a night, so I'll be kind of handy to 'elp him up to that room of his among the chimbleys. He won't be after reporting of me *then*, Mrs. Masher, for a hod game of pitch and torse, or a ride on the step of Her Majesty's carridge-wan, to get a peep at the birds as is caged inside! He'll be *werry* amiable will Mr. Dutton, after that little adwenture!"

"Hear t' 'im!" said Mrs. Masher. "He's a sharp one, he is!"

Beams winked, and his companion munched her nut-cracker jaws, and snapped her shrivelled fingers together, in keen appreciation of his humor.

"I'm glad you've come in to see me, Mr. Beams," she said, when these demonstrations were over; "you've made yourself scarce enough this while back now, and I'd a mind to think you were bearing malice for the little fallin's-out we've had now and again."

"No, no," said Beams, with an air of ineffable condescension, "it's not that; but I've bin seein' a deal of 'igh life, and it gets into a chap's 'ed sometimes, spite of hisself. 'Tain't *your* fault, Mrs. Masher, as Twigg isn't in 'igh life, and can't helewate his belongin's like my master does his'n—you must just put up with it, as the catechism tells yer to."

"Ay, ay," replied the old woman, "I reckon they make a deal on yer, and many a bit o' siller comes your way; don't it, now?"

She had sidled up to him with insinuating fondness, and her face took a hungry look as she mouthed out the word "siller." That curious compound of Sabbatarianism and covetousness, so often to be found in the Scotch character, was not wanting in Mrs. Masher.

Beams elevated his eyebrows, as if to intimate that a steady flow of cash ran into his coffers from the pocket of the "quality," as represented by Mr. David Earle in his frequent visits to Fig-tree Court.

"And what do yer do wi' it?—wi' the siller, I mean?" asked Masher, munching more and more, as though she chewed the cud of some delightful fancies.

"Mother's bin and invested it for me, mother has."

"In the counsels, or the fun's, or some o' that ilk?" (sidling nearer still).

"No, no; them sort o' things is never safe, Mrs. Masher. Why, don't you know folks goes and puts their savin's in 'em, and then cuts their throats, 'cause the money drops through 'em, like as if ye'd put it in a bag with a reg'lar hole a-bottom? Mother's a knowledgeable woman, mother is, and she's bin and sewed the 'siller,' as ye call it, in a nold glove, and hid it by, in a place as no one but her and me knows on."

But here Beams suddenly made a rush for the door. The figure of Mr. Earle had passed into Fig-tree Court. Mrs. Masher, with a hasty wipe of her apron over face and hands in case of smuts, followed suit, and, standing on Mr. Twigg's doorstep, began to execute a series of reverences that gave her the appearance of a dancing doll in a barrel-organ. Beams, meanwhile, after pulling at the front lock of his carroty poll as though he wished to uproot it altogether, made vehement signs to the old "laundress" to "cut her lucky."

To these signs Mrs. Masher was, however, both deaf and blind.

"Dear me!" said Mr. Earle, "dear me! my good woman, are you one of my—of Mr. Snow's household?"

"Which she's not, sir," put in Beams, promptly; "she's the old woman as does for Twigg— Mr. Septimis Twigg, of the Middle Temple, I should say," he added, remembering that the mention of that worthy man in such curt fashion might appear a liberty in the eyes of his visitor.

But Masher was not willing thus to have her light put under a bushel. She took a step or two nearer Mr. Earle, and never once glanced at Beams, whose face was undergoing a series of threatening contortions.

"I'm a poor auld bodie, sir, as waits on Mr. Twigg; but I knows Mr. Snow, and a finer gentleman to my mind aren't to be found in all the Temple, nor yet a more kindlier spoken one neither."

Mr. Earle's hand slid into his trousers-pocket, and there was a gleam of silver in Mrs. Masher's shrivelled palm.

"Now may the Lord A'mighty's blessing gang along wi' ye, sir!" she cried, almost weeping for joy at the good luck that had befallen her.

Mr. Earle passed on quickly up the stairs that led to "his boy's" rooms.

But not so Beams.

That worthy lingered behind, and craning his body round the door-post, the while his legs were half-way up the stairs, put his hand to his mouth in the old confidential way, and in a blood-curdling whisper besought her to "go home, and put that there ill-begotten gain in the old storkin' up the chimbley!"

Then he fled precipitately from her wrath—presented himself all breathless before Mr. Earle, and informed him that "Master" was out "along with Mr. Dutton, and they'd gone to 'Mr. Pettinggrew's,' and took such a sight of papers with them, he didn't think they'd be back this hour."

The old man sat down to wait for their coming. He fingered the blue business-like-looking papers; he looked at "the boy's" pen—that wonderful pen that doubtless wrote marvellous "pleaders" that took every court by storm, and rendered the jury an almost useless and uncalled-for body of men. He was not irritated by this waiting; on the contrary, he rather enjoyed it.

Sitting in that room, and before that desk, he almost seemed to be a sharer in his boy's fame and reputation. He began to ponder over the last few weeks, the time of his stay in London. As he pondered, one shadow seemed over all his quiet enjoyment, his simple, almost boyish pleasure in the sights that he had seen, the people he had met, above all in the actual sight of William's success. And the shadow was this:

A sort of half-acknowledged fear that the boy's heart was not as closely his as it once had been: a dread that the cares and the ambitions of life had somewhat dimmed the memory of past days—those happy days at Winstowe. Nay, even towards Lilian—Will's foster-sister, the flower whose growth and sweet unfolding he and "the boy" had watched together with a ceaseless love and pride and tenderness—even towards her there seemed to be some change. Will hardly entered into her happiness, her shy yet full and sweet content in her betrothal, as Uncle David had fancied he would do.

Thinking thus, the old man grew half jealous of the ambition that could wean the boy ever so little away from the home that had sheltered him—from the heart that had loved him so well. So deep in thought had he become that he started when the clerk, laden with papers, opened the door. Jim started too, for Beams had sped on some unholy errand, and left the visitor's arrival to reveal itself.

"You hardly look as well as one could wish to see you," said Mr. Earle, shaking hands, after his invariable custom, with the hunchback.

"Thank you, sir, but I am as well as usual—a little tired, perhaps, with the heavy press of business we have had of late—a little tired, sir—nothing more."

He drew a handkerchief from his pocket as he spoke, and passed it across his forehead, where the sweat stood out thickly.

Mr. Earle saw that his hand was worn and thin, and that the knuckles stood prominently out, like that of one weakened by recent illness.

Jim said that his master would be in shortly: he had remained with Mr. Pelham Pettigrew to consult over some "case for opinion."

"Dear, dear!—but there's no saying what your master will come to, Jim. Pelham Pettigrew—ah! well, well, he's near the top of the legal tree."

"Yes," said Jim, "Master William has never taken a back step; it's been all going steadily on, and steadily up."

"And you like the city life?"

"I like anywhere where he is—I like any work that's done for him."

The pale, eager face lighted up, the long thin hands took their old trick of clasping each other.

"Ay, ay, I know the love you bear my boy—the love you always have borne him."

Jim moved closer, and spoke with strange and ever-increasing earnestness and passion:

"Hasn't it been so from the first? Wasn't he all I had? Wasn't it him that used to sing to me in the old days when I suffered pain that no one else knew? Didn't I watch him as he grew so strong and beautiful, and look for his coming till I couldn't sleep at night for the joy of its being near? Oh! what a happy time it used to be when I saw him come into the little room, the old smile on his face, and his hand held out to me as if he were my playmate still, and not one who might well have turned his back upon me!"

Startled by this strange outburst, David Earle looked wonderingly at the speaker. He noted that the keen, deep-set eyes, encircled by dark shadows, like the eyes of one who sleeps little, and that ill, were looking, not at him, but out into the court that yet they did not see—dwelling in imagination on a picture-memory of the days when he and the man now his master were boys together.

Something misty obscured David Earle's vision as he noted these things, and he remarked that the murky City air was apt to dim one's spectacles. Then he took his off, polished them on his handkerchief, and put them on again. During this proceeding the dark eyes of the clerk were bent upon him with an eager, questioning look; he came still nearer, and leaned his hand upon the desk.

"To love any one as I love my master means that you would do anything—*anything* for his sake; that you would watch, and wait, and wrestle with fate, to overcome and thwart those who would rob his life of one happy hour; that you would care for nothing only to see him content; that you would pray as I do—as I pray night and day—that God may yet 'grant him his heart's desire,' and 'fulfil all his mind.'"

The passion with which Jim uttered these words so astonished and excited Mr. Earle that he could only look in silent amazement at the agitated face and trembling hands that told how truly from the heart they came.

"When you love any one with devotion, you can *see* and *know;* your love gives you eyes and ears different from those of others."

"But," said Mr. Earle, recovering his powers of speech, "you speak as though my boy were threatened by some calamity, or some enemy. Surely you cannot mean that?"

"No, no," said Jim, troubled, and as though regretting his hasty admission—"no; it is only my love—my love, you know—that makes me speak like that. It is only that to see him suffer, to see him grieve, would be a dreadful pain to me. I would rather be torn in pieces—"

"Suffer?—grieve? God forbid!" interrupted his hearer, beginning to realize that, like most deformed persons, Jim was of that supersensitive and exalted temperament to which all things appear in an intense and fervent light; whose hate is deadly, and whose love is a passionate sentiment, that becomes the very core of a life, the necessary limitation of which results in concentration.

"Yes, yes, that is what I say too—God forbid! God forbid that his heart's desire should not be fulfilled! Mr. Earle, if any one had told me years ago that I should ever come to this—that I should ever have been thought worthy to work for him, and to be always with him—I should never have believed what that person said—never!"

He said these words with a pleading, loving humility that, coupled with his pathetic countenance and afflicted frame, had something in it infinitely touching.

Mr. Earle felt it so, and was about to speak some encouraging and comforting words, when, all at once, a change, sudden as that brought about by the touch of a finger on a sensitive-plant, came over Jim Dutton.

The impassioned man of the moment before disappeared, and became the matter-of-fact business clerk—the servant who heard his master's quick step upon the stair, and fell back naturally into his social place. He glided quickly and silently into the little inner room, where, in company with innumerable papers, a desk, and a stool made exceptionally high on account of his deformity, it was his wont and duty to spend many hours each day.

The door of this room closed softly on his retreating figure, as that of the outer chamber opened and William Snow came in.

CHAPTER XII.

"WOMANLY PAST QUESTION."

Two months have passed since last we saw our hero: has that time brought any changes to him?

There are seasons in the lives of all of us when time becomes, as it were, compressed, and a day does the work of years. To look back upon even the past week may seem like looking back into a vista of time, because in those few short days the whole current of our life has changed.

It was so with William Snow.

He had been like a man running a race, striving to reach a certain goal—a prize ever in his sight as the motive for energy and endurance. Suddenly the prize was lost, taken by the hand of another, and he had been learning the lesson of striving still, though the precious, longed-for guerdon was before him no more.

A hard lesson that.

No wonder there are lines about the finely chiselled lips, lines on the square, broad brow, that were not there when the summer was young, and hope was looking forward with expectancy to become one day fruition.

Oh, the day-dreams he had dreamed! the airy castles he had built! Which of us can bear to sit amidst the ruins of such fond fancies—to weep over the beautiful folly of the things that "might have been," and now shall never be? Which of us, I say, can pass through such deep waters, and be the same men or women as before our weary feet waded through the torrent?

If I have so far sketched William Snow's character aright, you will know that useless, helpless repining would be to him an impossibility. The boy that stood in the upper room at Winstowe, amidst the lurid light of the flames that lapped against the window like mocking tongues, and could so command his thoughts as to recognize and act promptly upon the wisest course for life, was not likely to grow into a man whose firmness would desert him in the time of trial.

It was, perhaps, strange, yet certainly true, that the thought of another hand gathering the fair flower of Lilian's love had never hitherto crossed William's mind. Perhaps he had hoped, unconsciously to himself, that she read *somewhat* of his heart's history, in spite of his endeavor to blind her eyes to its nature.

I think we often, all of us, fancy others can read what is so prominent and clear to ourselves, only because it is a part of ourselves; and about this Lilian of mine there was an exquisite maidenliness that (so William thought) might have led her to appear to ignore any love save that that was plainly and unmistakably set forth.

In the first bitterness of the pain with which he learned the fact of her betrothal to Guy Tremlett, William was ready to blame and cavil at the motives that had led him to refrain from teaching her gentle heart to turn with a new and closer tenderness to the brother of her adoption. When calmer thought and more dispassionate self-review were a possibility, he once more recognized the fact that, if an error at all, this forbearance had been an error on the right side. He even allowed to his own heart that for Lilian it might be well that she should have been kept in ignorance of the love of a man having no fitting name to offer her.

He knew full well that in unequal marriages these two rules hold good—a man raises a woman to his own higher level; a woman sinks to the lower level of the man. How, then, could he fail to feel that in the face of a possible revelation that might one day come, it was better that he should stand alone?

Then there was that other darker possibility—

Yes, think of it as he might, the wisdom of the resolve that had cost him so dear only showed more clearly.

Uncle David's simple soul could not grasp the idea of the value the world sets upon a man's birth; he was wont to dwell delightedly upon the story of "the boy's" early years, and took it for granted that others looked upon matters in the same light.

That William should bear with faultless equanimity the loss of the woman he so passionately loved would have been superhuman; indeed, we have already seen how far from perfect had his conduct to Lilian been.

It was the consciousness of his irritable and, as he felt, most cruelly unjust manner to her when too sorely tried, that was one of the many reasons that had caused him to hold aloof from the house in Park Lane, and absent himself far oftener than Uncle David or Lilian herself liked.

At this time of his life William was most thoroughly dissatisfied with himself. We are all dissatisfied with ourselves when we fall far short of our own standard, and it is not a state of feeling that tends to make us agreeable either to ourselves or to others.

For nothing did William take himself more ruthlessly to task than for that secret distrust of Guy Tremlett, which, strive against it as he might, grew steadily.

"I am jealous of the fellow, and I call jealousy distrust. I am a brute!" Thus he judged himself.

Meanwhile, others judged him differently. His more than father, as we have already seen, accused the worldly career in which he had so successfully embarked of weaning his heart from the old home and the old ties. Lilian—yes, what did Lilian think of her "big brother?"

There was a pain at the girl's heart even amidst all the rosy glamour of her own love-story, an aching regret that the dear companion of her childish days seemed drifting—how or why, or from what cause, she could not tell—strangely far away from the old companionship and confidence.

Besides this, her passionate, absorbing love for Guy gave her a marvellously unerring intuition as to the mind of others towards him, and she felt—felt with bitter pain—that her friend and brother did not appreciate the worth of the idol at whose feet she worshipped.

It will be needless to tell any woman that in consequence of this misgiving she clung with greater tenderness to the ideal of which Guy was the embodiment. Her recognition of this want of appreciation on William's part widened the rift that his own undisciplined pain had already made between them, and it really would have been hard to say what Uncle David would have felt, could he have realized the estrangement that existed between his children. Fortunately he did not do so.

His very first words, on William entering the room where we have kept the old man too long waiting, showed how far such knowledge was from his mind:

"I'm a delegate, my boy—a delegate from the court of 'Queen Lilian,' and I intend to have my request granted, too."

Unfortunately, however, for the carrying-out of this resolve, the delegate met with stronger opposition than he had anticipated; indeed, he had to return to Queen Lilian's court with the news that William could not by any possibility present himself in Park Lane that evening, by reason of the fact that he was going to dine with Pelham Pettigrew, Esq., the eminent Queen's Counsel.

"You see, my dear, I couldn't very well say anything in the way of urging the boy to throw over his engagement. We know what a good friend Mr. Pettigrew has been to him. The acquaintance of such a man is an immense benefit to Will—an im-mense benefit!" added Uncle David, emphatically.

For Lilian's face expressed extremest dissatisfaction as she heard of the high and distinguished social honor that had been bestowed upon her old playmate.

"It seems to me William is *always* engaged to dine with some one else just when we want him," she said, giving her pretty head the least toss in the world. "Last time it was those people in Dorset Square."

"Ah, yes, the Boultbees — charming people. I called, you know, and there is a child so like—"

"I have no doubt *all* William's friends are charming, Uncle David," interrupted Lilian;

"but that is no reason why he should forget his oldest and best."

"God bless me, child!" cried the old man, "don't say that! You don't understand—women never *do* understand—"

"No," said Lilian, "they only *feel*."

Then she left the room.

Now we, who have the privilege of reading people's thoughts, know that David Earle had himself harbored the very same misgivings as Lilian had now clothed in words, and presented before him.

But many of us think things that we shrink from hearing spoken.

And then Uncle David felt that there was some allowance to be made for the girl; it was only natural she should be a little irritable at this time, for suddenly, and without a word of warning, some two or three days back, Guy had left town. There had been none of those fond and lingering words of farewell that soften the pain of parting, and cheer the lonely heart to look back upon. True, a few lines written at the club to which he belonged had reached her, but only after Guy had gone.

The letter contained no further news than the simple fact that urgent business called him North for a day or two.

"Can anything have happened to trouble him? Is he keeping some sorrow from me? Dear Guy! how I wish he had told me all about it!"

She thought thus anxiously about her lover, because the letter that told her of his departure seemed as if written by an unsteady hand. It was quite unlike his usual writing.

"Can he be ill? Has he gone down to Tremlett Court for fear I should be distressed?" she pondered.

Then she kissed the little note, carried it in the bosom of her gown all day, and placed it beneath her pillow at night.

She wrote to Mrs. Tremlett, too—such a dear, tender, anxious letter! She identified herself with the mother of the man she loved. She spoke of their two hearts as one, by reason of the love they both bore him; she besought her to write and say if "Guy, dear Guy!" was at the Court; to say if he was ill, or troubled in any way? "You must make him understand," wrote the pen of this sweet writer, "that our love should be even more to each of us if any sorrow comes than when everything goes well. You must make him understand, dear mother, that he can *always* trust me fully, and that there can be no sorrow unbearable to me, except the finding he will not let me share his whole life always—the evil as the good!"

I have said Mrs. Tremlett was a woman without a conscience, and who knew not the fear of God; but as she read these lines a misty softness crept over the heavy eyes that were little given to tears, her hot, dry lips twitched for a moment, and her hand clenched on the arm of the couch on which she lay.

For a moment—a moment only—she looked across the wide gulf that separated her own soul from the pure, true, loving heart that had dictated those words of tender faith and trust—looked and recognized its vastness.

And the spirit of regret looked into the vista of the past years, and sighed.

But Mrs. Tremlett's mood quickly changed.

She tore at the bell by her side till its peal echoed through Tremlett Court; and when Ponsonby hurried into the shaded room, her mistress stood before her like some wild animal brought to bay. Her eyes flashed with a baneful light, her lips worked with uncontrollable passion, and in her clenched hand Lilian's letter was all crushed and torn.

Ponsonby quietly turned the key in the door, pressed her mistress firmly back upon the couch she had quitted, flung wide the window, and then set herself to try to unloose the convulsive grasp of the cold fingers. She bathed the distorted face with cold water, opened the black-velvet robe at the throat and chest, so that the working muscles might have perfect freedom, and, drawing the beautiful head upon her breast, the woman kissed the pale cheek of her mistress with a passion of tenderness and pity.

Gradually the hysterical attack passed off. The fight for breath ceased. The clenched hands grew placid, and Lilian's letter fluttered to the ground.

Then the maid bent down to her mistress's ear, and in a voice so unlike her generally measured tones that I doubt if any member of the household would have recognized it, asked, for the first time, a question:

"Mistress, is it—Master Guy?"

"Yes—yes—he has broken his promise! The girl thinks he is here—fancies he is ill—curses on her folly! Could she not keep him from harm? Love-sick fool! Guy—my boy!—I know—I know— Oh, my God! it is the old story!"

It does not need that men should fear the great Creator of the universe, to call upon his name in the hour of their sorrow!

CHAPTER XIII.

PELHAM PETTIGREW, Q.C.

A SMALL man of an immense presence, and a grand manner that gave him all the social effect of a very big man indeed.

Such was Pelham Pettigrew, Q.C.

Though in person, as I have already said, somewhat diminutive, his iron-gray hair stood up upon his crown in such fashion as added at least four inches to his height.

This was the more remarkable because you would naturally have supposed that the wig, so often worn, would by this time have quelled in it so ambitious a spirit.

Like himself, however, his hair was self-assertive. It grew upward from the top of his ears, and formed a peak so pronounced as to be quite a salient feature in his personality. Dark eyebrows, a good deal raised in the centre as if in perpetual astonishment at any one seeing fit to differ from him, added to Mr. Pettigrew's consequential demeanor, and the eyes beneath were keener and more penetrating than could be pleasant to the feelings of a witness conscious of a gentle inclination towards perjury.

In startling contrast to his appearance, Mr. Pettigrew's voice was mellow and musical always, and could be on occasion deep and thrilling. It would "tremble with suppressed emotion" during the pathetic portion of some elo-

quent "pleader" to an extent that touched to tenderest pity the heart of each individual intelligent member of the jury, and filled the hearts of all opponents with a cold and chill foreboding. We have heard of the maid whose "face was her fortune," and of Pelham Pettigrew we may say that his voice was, or rather had been, his fortune.

For this fortune was long since a grand reality. One of his foibles was to speak of himself as though trembling on the verge of bankruptcy. He would offer a friend a "shake-down" at Hazlecroft, his shooting-box at the foot of the Cheviot Hills, and the "shake-down" would prove to be a room furnished with every known luxury. He would speak of Hazlecroft itself as a "little box," and invite a guest to "pot-luck," or a "chop or so, and a glass of Allsopp." The "little box" was an abode rich with carved artistic furniture, priceless paintings, china calculated to drive a Belgravian dowager mad with envy, and was perfumed with flowers from January to December.

"I like plenty of flowers about me," the great Q.C. would say, flipping lightly with his finger and thumb the petals of blossoms that cost a small fortune, "they cultivate the eye, and a poesy or two can't ruin any one."

As to the "pot-luck," it was a kind of "luck" a man would gladly look forward to a repetition of seven days in the week; and wives declared that when their liege lords paid a visit to the house near the Cheviot Hills, they were wont to look with disfavor upon the best efforts of the family cook for weeks to come.

Speaking of the ladies reminds me to record the fact that Pelham Pettigrew was ever the most devoted slave of the gentler sex. His manner to women recalled the days of Sir Charles Grandison, so devoted, so courtly, so chivalrous was the homage he laid at their feet. In fact, he would do anything for them—anything except marry one of them.

On this point no man, or woman either, could remember a shadow of indecision on his part. Even the most skilful manœuvrer in the matrimonial field never gave a thought as to the best method of attacking the invulnerable tower of his jealously guarded liberty. Ladies were content to receive and enjoy the hospitalities of Hazlecroft, discreetly chaperoned by their husbands, brothers, and fathers, without an *arrière-pensée*, either for themselves or their belongings, as to the possibility of the courtly master taking to himself a wife.

It was *bien entendu* that Pelham Pettigrew was "not a marrying man," and among his legal brethren a delicious anecdote illustrating his anti-matrimonial proclivities had long since become current coin.

Mr. Pettigrew's chambers consisted of three rooms *en suite*, in a certain gloomy court. The rooms themselves, however, had an air of fallen grandeur quite oppressive in its solemnity. The chimney-piece over the fireplace of the principal one was curiously ornamented with intricate designs in marble, apparently representing the funeral urns of various departed inmates, all joined together by wreaths of fruits and flowers; here and there female forms, clad in diaphanous robes, were blowing lustily on various wind instruments as though trumpeting forth to an admiring world the fame of those defunct pleaders whose ashes were supposed to rest peacefully in the above-mentioned urns.

The doors of this room were of solid mahogany; none of your paltry veneer, or clever "graining," false as the bloom of Ninon on a woman's cheek, but real, substantial, respectable mahogany, that would close with a deep and sonorous clang.

Well, by one of these doors, the middle one, leading from the outer to the inner room, there hung a tale—or, rather, a man—for on a massive peg in that same door, and by means of his own silk neckerchief, a melancholy clerk belonging to Pelham Pettigrew in the earlier days of his career did hang himself by the neck until he was dead. Such an occurrence was naturally unpleasant to the owner of the chambers.

We are told in the "Ingoldsby Legends" that

"To see a man swing
At the end of a string"

gave a certain young nobleman a weird and gloomy satisfaction; but, perhaps, had the affair taken place in his own particular dwelling, that young nobleman would have changed his mind.

At all events, Pelham Pettigrew was not a little disgusted at the inconsiderate behavior of his clerk in thus making his very disagreeable exit from life on another man's premises. The only satisfaction the great man gathered from the subsequent inquiry was the bringing to light of the reason that had impelled that unfortunate one to put an end to his own existence.

"Suicide while in an unsound state of mind, caused by 'domestic troubles.'"

That was the verdict with regard to the motive of the act.

In fact, the clerk's wife had made things so insufferable to the clerk that he had fled from his sorrows after a most effectual manner.

"Quite—quite!" said Pelham Pettigrew as he heard the verdict, and the first smile that had crossed his face for some time curled in a sneer about his lips.

Of course the vacant clerkship must be filled; and, in spite of any superstitious terror that might have been supposed to act as a deterrent, the applicants for the post were numerous.

Mr. Pettigrew selected the man whose appearance and manner best pleased him; then, fixing his keen eye on the unhappy being, he thus put "the question" to him,

"Are you a married man?"

"No, sir," said the clerk; then he grew all over a moist, pink hue, and, twisting his hat in his hot hands, hazarded a confession:

"But I—I—hope to be—soon, sir."

"Ah! hum! very well; then, under the circumstances of such being the prospect before you, I must ask you to give me your solemn word of honor, before entering my employment, that *when* you find it necessary to hang yourself, *you will not do it on my premises.*"

The man left the august presence of the "rising man of the day" with his hair standing on end, and his eyes wider open than ever they had been before; but he was of a dauntless nature, this City clerk, and he did not shrink either from the possible fact that the ghost of the suicide might see fit to suspend his intangible self behind the mahogany door, and creak and sway about in the dimness of the eventide, or yet from the eccentricities of the ghost's former master.

Also, it must be supposed that all wives are not equally aggravating, for though the new clerk married in due course, he had never apparently had occasion to make away with himself, since, at the time our story first crosses the line of Mr. Pelham Pettigrew's life, he was still in that gentleman's service, having been promoted to the position of head and confidential clerk, with a subordinate under him.

From what root the tree of Mr. Pettigrew's hatred of legal fetters had grown, it is not our province to inquire, since he is not our hero, but only one of the wheels—a powerful one, I grant you, though—in the machinery of our story.

I shall by no means take upon myself to say that his life had been an immaculate one; but, be this as it may, a fastidious refinement was never lacking in his demeanor to the women of his own social world. In the presence of such women his conversation was always *raffiné* to perfection, and, though brilliant, never trenched ever so slightly upon broadness of expression. On the other hand, among society exclusively masculine, the order of things was reversed, and the dainty viands on the festal board were not more highly seasoned than the conversation of the host.

Yet, as a proof of the marvellous powers of adaptation this man possessed, it may be told of him here that if he saw (with that quick intuition that had been the pilot of his professional career) a dislike in any man to stories smacking of the *coulisses*, and the world that is called "half," he at once became the brilliantly intellectual man of culture—the wit whose humor was as refined as it was trenchant.

Hence it came about that various people had various and often opposite impressions of him, impressions to which each adhered with pugnacious obstinacy.

Unlike many men in his profession, Pelham Pettigrew was ever ready to lend a hand to young and struggling members of it in whom he saw what he called "incipient greatness."

Very early, in a chance acquaintance with William Snow, the man who had already surmounted difficulties and climbed the ladder of fame took a warm interest in the man whose foot was but newly set upon the lowest rung. "A fine young fellow that," said Mr. Pettigrew to a brother light of the law, "plenty of good stuff here," and he tapped his own crested head; "it only *wants sorting*, and time will do that."

"It's a devilish odd thing, you know," continued Mr. Pettigrew, after a moment of reflective silence; "but the first time I saw the young fellow, gad, sir! his face seemed familiar to me. 'Mine own familiar friend,' you know, and all that kind of thing; associations of a forgotten past—eh? Bless my soul, what odd chords there are in human nature! I'm d—d if I know which of *my* chords that fellow has something to say to; but it's one of them, at all events—quite, quite!"

When Uncle David was first told of the distinguished notice bestowed upon his "boy" by the eminent man of law, he was perhaps less impressed by the fact than might have been expected by those who did not understand the perfect simplicity of his nature.

You see, to him it seemed only natural that any one with the slightest penetration should recognize the brilliant parts of that young aspirant to fame, William Snow, Esq., of the Inner Temple.

Still, Uncle David saw the advantages that must accrue to the boy he loved from the great man's friendship, and, feeling this, could be resigned to the fate that took William on the evening alluded to in our last chapter to the rooms in St. James's Street, rather than to the house in Park Lane.

Perhaps William would have found the epicurean "pot-luck" provided for him on this occasion by Mr. Pettigrew, as "funeral baked meats," could he have known how sad and lonely a heart had Lilian as she sat by the open window and looked out into the dusty street, where carriage after carriage rolled by, carrying a fair and gayly bedecked freight to one or other fashionable gathering.

Opposite to her was Uncle David. The evening paper had fallen upon his knee, for the close, drowsy evening had lulled him to "sleep the sleep of the just." A gentle snore now and then told of the completeness of his repose.

Lilian pressed her hand upon the bosom of her dress, and the crackling of paper, as she did so, told of the whereabouts of that hurried letter—the few unsteady lines that Guy's hand had traced before his sudden flight from town..

How soon should she hear again? Would Mrs. Tremlett write quickly? If Guy was ill, would they let her go to him? Why was William unable to come this one evening—this particular evening on which she had determined to carry out a certain resolve?

Now the resolve was this:

She would tell him all the misgivings that were tearing at her heart; perhaps she would show him that letter. Uncle David said there was no cause for anxiety. But love has its intuitions—she was sure, *quite* sure, something was wrong with Guy; and William was wise, wiser than most people, and would do anything she asked him.

Now, this was a peculiarity of Lilian's feeling towards her old playmate; she knew instinctively that his kindness and his willingness to help her were a bank upon which she could never draw a check that would be refused payment. I am afraid she was not very grateful for this fact, but just took it as a matter of course, after the fashion of a woman who thoroughly idolizes a man, and is ready to sacrifice every one else to his welfare. This sort of selfishness is often engendered, even in the sweetest natures, by a great love.

"I wish I had written to William myself, instead of letting Uncle David go and ask him. He would have thrown over this Mr. Pettigrew if he had known I was in any trouble," thought Lilian.

And she was right, too; but then William did not know; he was not even aware of Guy Tremlett's absence. I am not sure that, if he had known of that fact, Mr. Pettigrew's "potluck" would have been partaken of. An evening like the evenings of old, just those three together—Uncle David and his two adopted children—might have proved a temptation hard to resist.

You see, William had spent several evenings at the house in Park Lane, and had not experienced any very exquisite enjoyment in the same. With all his love for Uncle David, he did *not* relish talking over the politics of the day with him in one drawing-room, while Guy and Lilian enjoyed themselves in the other. True, Tremlett had one of those sweet, mellow tenor voices that are to the hearing what the perfume of flowers is to the scent; but when you love a woman with an intensity and tenderness that are only the stronger for being held down, it requires more magnanimity than William possessed to listen complacently to another man singing lovesongs to her in a liquid voice, and to catch now and then a glimpse of her violet eyes, almost tearful with admiration and love. At all events, William did not enjoy himself on these occasions.

Lilian pitied him, in that she felt he did not fully appreciate either Guy or Guy's singing. She was sorry for this: sorry for *him*, be it understood, because he lost so much. But, for all these regrets, her confidence in his helpfulness never failed.

So, sitting by the open window in the summer dusk, on that still evening when not a breath of air stirred sufficiently to sway the long arms of the Virginian creeper hanging from the balcony above, Lilian made up her mind to write to him at once.

She stepped softly, and without awaking Uncle David, across the room, opened the door, and stole up-stairs. A few hasty lines were soon written, and then—clearly proving herself a "country cousin" by the proceeding—she tied on her bonnet, threw a black-lace shawl over her shoulders, and set off to the pillar-post at the corner of the next street but one. It was now getting late, and the street lamps were lighted; but with the bravery of innocence she stepped lightly along, never noticing a too-pronounced stare that followed her now and then. There was no possible reason why Lilian should not have sent a servant to post this letter; but there are certain conditions of suspense, anxiety, and unrest, when it is a relief to do *anything*, and Lilian was in this condition now.

The letter, duly addressed to Fig-tree Court, was dropped into the pillar, and she gave a little sigh of relief to think it was one stage on its journey. Then she turned homeward, but stopped suddenly at the sight of a familiar figure.

There could be no mistaking William's hunchback clerk. Jim Dutton was by his affliction easily distinguished from his fellows.

He was walking slowly along: his eager eyes looked out from beneath his bushy eyebrows with the expression of a man who is on the alert, seeking something that he fancies he may come upon any moment, and that he is determined shall not evade him.

He gave a start, and stood still, as he saw Miss Lilian. Then such a look of guilt came across his face that he seemed to shrink and cower, and made as though he would have gladly hidden himself away.

"Why, Jim," said the girl, coming up to his side, "this is very far away from home for you to be wandering! Did you fancy Mr. Snow was with us to-night? Is he wanted for some business or other?"

"No, Miss Lilian," said Jim, taking off his hat, and holding it in his hand while he spoke, "I've wandered mostly all about the City, and seen all it's got to show, and so now I've taken to seeing the west of the town, just to get a bit of fresh air, you know, after business is done. It's best to see as—much—as—you—can—"

But the words came haltingly, and he kept his eyes averted from her face, twirling and twisting the hat in his restless hands.

"Well, since you are here, you can walk as far as our gate with me. I hardly think I ought to have come out at all, but I wanted to post a letter—"

"She is out on the same errand as myself," thought Jim, walking by her side.

But Jim was wrong. Had Lilian known the quest that *he* was pursuing, she would have forgotten her tiny strength, and, in the might of her hot, indignant wrath, tried to hurl him from her where he stood. As it was, she thanked him for his escort, and, with the sweet and gentle courtesy to those beneath her learned from Uncle David, held out her hand in a kindly "good-night."

But Jim dared not touch it. Something seemed to rise up in his throat and choke him. He made believe not to see the outstretched hand, and, still bareheaded, stood silent at the gate until the door was opened by an astonished footman, and the young mistress admitted.

Then Jim pulled his hat over his eyes, and set off at a rate that made people turn and stare to think a man could be so mad as walk at such a pace on a sultry summer's night.

Meanwhile, William Snow was partaking of Mr. Pettigrew's hospitality; dining for the first time *tête-à-tête* with the great man.

But here I must give some description of the town abode in which the eminent barrister was wont to say he "roughed it."

The rooms were all *en suite ;* a dining-room, two drawing-rooms, with bed and bath room beyond all. The small amount of color visible in the three reception - rooms was of a pale sea-green, eminently calculated to throw up in high-relief the gems of art that graced the walls. An utter absence of looking - glass in the arrangement of the whole suite told at once the sex of the occupant. The selection of pictures displayed admirable taste, as far as judgment went, for of each "school" the representatives were perfect of their kind. The overhanging rocks and deep shadows of Salvator Rosa, the faint soft blue skies of Canaletto, the graceful figures and fairy foliage of Watteau, all were there.

At one end of the drawing-room, a Venus rising from the foam of the sea represented the school of Etty ; and, though one might well wish the goddess had not forgotten to make her toilet before quitting the shelter of the spray, it was a gem in its way.

With perfect fitness — born, I fear, more of artistic taste than reverence—quite apart from the rest, in a sort of alcove shaded by curtains of crimson velvet, was an exquisite creation from the master-hand of Carlo Dolce. The chastened beauty of the Mother of God, full of a holy purity, setting forth the highest and divinest type of womanhood, thus kept apart from all the more earthly beauty surrounding her, was very striking.

It was a custom with Pelham Pettigrew that the latest addition to his unique collection should occupy for a time an easel so placed that the most advantageous light fell upon it. It was thus exposed to his own scrutiny and to the comments and criticisms of his friends, and in due time relegated to a suitable position among the rest, to make way for some new favorite.

When William Snow entered the outer drawing-room on the evening of which we are now speaking, he found his host attired in as faultless an evening costume as though all the judges on the bench were his expected guests. He was lounging back in a marvellously easy chair before this easel, newly adorned by a De Hooghe, in which the glow of the western sun seemed actually *hot*, as it poured through a window at the back of the quaint Dutch room, where a woman in a high cap was sweeping the floor.

In his hand Mr. Pettigrew held a focus-tube, and through this he was ecstatically gazing at the beauties of his latest acquisition.

Have I neglected to mention that the one physical beauty he possessed was the perfection of his hands and feet? Well, let me make up for the omission now, and call the reader's notice to the foot that is outstretched before him. It is clothed in a small dress-shoe, tied with a broad black ribbon, and arched over an instep, pride in which is one of the great man's weaknesses.

A Rembrandt, dark and mysterious, and apparently consisting of a shadowy plume, and a pair of wild, sad eyes, had been the reigning favorite until to-day. Now Mr. Pettigrew was as much absorbed in the perfections of the Dutch school as though no other style of art had ever possessed any charm for him.

The deposed Rembrandt hung behind the dining-room door, a monument of the instability of the favor of the great.

Mr. Pettigrew turned round as William passed through the heavy velvet *portières* that divided each room from those on either side of it, removing his eye from the tube of observation to do so.

"Ah! how do?" he said, laconically, nodding his head, and extending a white and delicate hand for his guest's benefit. "Ever seen a better picture than that, eh?" and again he stared down the tin tunnel.

William, as in duty bound, took his stand behind his host's chair, the better to view the idol of the hour, and expressed his admiration of it.

"Art, sir—true art that!" said the fortunate owner of the industrious and thrifty female in the high cap. "You know *the* peculiarity of De Hooghe's pictures, of course ?"

But William didn't know anything about it, and stated the fact.

"Bless my heart!" said Mr. Pettigrew, turning round in his chair, and putting the speaking-trumpet-like spy-glass into his hand, "I thought every one knew that! Look at it attentively, and you'll see that the light seems to come from *within* the picture. What a glow, eh!—what a clear warmth about it! Why, gad! I can almost see the motes dancing in the sunbeam that comes through the upper pane of that window!"

It was truly a triumph of art, and William said so.

"De Hooghe is like the 'contented man' in Tupper's Proverbial What's-his-name—(awful proser that man Tupper !)—' carries his sunshine with him,' likes to be independent of climate. Don't talk to me about Pre-Raphaelites—all nonsense ! Give me the detail of the Dutch painters ! —it's a detail true to nature. Nature doesn't make her details unnaturally prominent, like those pre - what - do - you - call - 'em fellows. The brick in the wall is there in nature, and the bit of golden lichen is on the brick, but they are softened and toned down by more important matters, not staring you out of countenance—"

Here (perhaps fortunately, for the Q.C. was beginning to canter briskly on a favorite hobby) the silky - voiced, light - footed major - domo announced that dinner was served.

William had been asked to take "pot-luck" on this occasion, but owing to the bill of fare beginning with oysters dressed in some new and wonderfully appetizing manner, and these being the "advance guard" of an army of rare and curious dishes, the repast extended to a late hour, and it was past 10 P.M. before the dining-room door closed softly on the retreating servant.

Then host and guest were left to easy chat "across the walnuts and the wine," the first represented by rare and costly conserves and fruits, the last by Château Lafitte and "'34" port—an old - fashioned drink much favored by Pelham Pettigrew.

The talk had turned upon a certain light of the law, one Pitchford Bland, and the host was giving his opinion on the subject with explicit candor.

"The best trait about the man is that he knows a good bit of coloring when he sees it. A man like myself, who is fond of having a daub or two about him to look at out of business hours, likes the help of a friend to get hold of anything worth having. But when you've said *that* of Pitchford Bland, you've said all. Such a name, too—*Bland!*—for a man who goes through life like a porcupine, and makes you feel as if you'd stroked the quills the wrong way ! He thinks his 'mission' is to crush the foibles of others, and so he treads on every man's corns, till he makes himself about as welcome as a pin in the seat of your chair, or a cinder in your mince-meat."

"People with a mission to set other people right are always a 'noosance generally,' as Artemus Ward has it," said William. "He was a shrewd fellow that, and knew human nature. If you set about not tolerating other people's little failings, it ends in other people not tolerating you."

"' That's a fact,' to quote from our cousins across the herring - pond again," returned the host.

"Yet Bland has pushed his way well professionally—"

"Ah !" interrupted Mr. Pettigrew, "the very essence of the law is treading on people's corns, and showing up their weaknesses, so Bland takes to it like a duck to water. But look at his family—"

"I only knew him in his public life," said William, "and that very slightly."

"But to know a man rightly you must take the two together—the public career and the private life," replied this shrewd dissector of humanity; "and I can tell you Pitchford Bland's son, a fine young chap too, to look at, has gone to the dogs—to—the—dogs !"

Here he raised his glass, held it between himself and the light of the shaded lamp, and shook his head as if he were reading the fate of Bland junior in the ruby wine.

"The father was a tyrant at home. A fanatical Puritan—scowled at the smell of good cavendish—never let the lad bring home a friend, and preached like any old rural dean. That's the way to train up a hypocrite ! There was a hard reckoning to pay in the end. Women and wine, sir, the old story !—and debts all about the place. Bland roared and raved like a mad bull; and the mother—well, after the fashion of mothers, she sold all she could call her own, and tried to help the young rascal out of the mire. A d—d nasty mire it was too, for the lad got into some drunken gambling row with young Tremlett, a son of Bernard Tremlett, as big an old— God bless my soul, Snow ! what's the matter ?"

———————

CHAPTER XIV.

"GOD GUARD THEE, MY BELOVED ! GOD GUARD THEE !"

"GOD bless my soul !" cried Pelham Pettigrew again, rubbing up the iron - gray crest on the top of his head till it formed a spiky peak, and staring, open-eyed, at Snow across the table, "what have I said ? What is young Tremlett to you ?"

"Tremlett is nothing to me," replied his companion, speaking in that quiet, measured tone that is the surest sign of suddenly enforced self-control—"nothing to me personally; but he is going to marry a woman in whom I am deeply —whom I have known all my life. She is the niece of my adopted father, Mr. Earle, of Winstowe, and naturally I feel the same interest in her as if she were my sister. It is for her sake I am pained at—"

"Yes, yes, I see," interrupted Mr. Pettigrew, "the same interest as if she were a sister—quite, quite !"

It was another of this gentleman's peculiarities that when any one asserted a fact to him, he seemed to set that fact before his "mind's eye," wrestle with himself mentally in argument upon it, and settle himself ruthlessly with that short, decided monosyllable, "quite."

"You know my history," went on William Snow, a dark flush stealing slowly up to his brow; "you know how friendless in the world—"

"Yes, yes, I remember you told me all about it—capital old fellow Earle must be !"

Mr. Pettigrew was, however, only affecting jocularity because he saw that his guest had hardly recovered from the shock his words had caused.

His bright gray eyes gave a quick, penetrating glance at the face of the man who seemed to have suddenly grown years older; and the result of his scrutiny was the humming of a tune under his breath, and a certain nodding of the head, that apparently answered an argument within himself.

"Rum—tum—tee—rum—tum—tee; it's a queer world, Snow; here you go up and here you go down, and all that sort of thing, eh ? Well, well, you've gone ' up ' steadily, my boy, and you'll get to the top of the tree before long."

"I was saying," continued William, "that,

being so much indebted to Mr. Earle, I naturally feel a deep interest in what must so nearly concern him as the character of the man his niece is going to marry."

"Just so," nodded his companion—"just so—to say nothing of the girl herself."

"To say nothing of the girl herself," was echoed in a voice that faltered ever so slightly, yet enough to tell the story of William's secret to a man who had learned to gauge the current of every life by the very smallest straws floating on the surface.

"Do you think Mr. Earle knows that young Tremlett is not exactly an immaculate being, and winks at it? Tremlett Court is a fine old place, and the fellow's got good blood in his veins—good, I mean, as far as coming over with the Conqueror, and all that lot. As to quality, I should think his blood was half alcohol, even as a 'puling infant!' Ha! ha! few men could lift an elbow so high or so often as old Bernard Tremlett. Chip of the old block, this youngster."

It was with difficulty William had remained silent throughout this speech.

"If you knew Mr. Earle, you would be as certain of his ignorance as I am. He is one of those guileless souls who never harbor a hard thought of any human being; and when the evil in them is so thrust before his face that he must look at it, he mourns over the wrong as if it was his own doing, and pities the sinner with all his tender heart."

"Capital! capital!" cried the delighted host. "Eden before the fall transplanted to the nineteenth century! Gad! but I should like to have the old gentleman in court, and let him hear a cause I'm just now concerned in. By Jove, sir, his eyes would start out of his head before it was over!"

This idea tickled the Q. C.'s fancy so exquisitely that he rubbed his topknot up a little stiffer, like a bird pluming its feathers complacently.

All in a moment he grew thoughtful.

"This is a serious business, Snow, a serious business. What will you do in the matter, eh?"

This was just the question that had been surging in William's heart for the last half-hour. What should he do?

And he could find no more satisfactory answer to give to the question than this:

"I cannot tell; I must think."

"Turn it over. Think it out dispassionately. Make up your mind what to say to the old gentleman. Quite, quite."

But he fathomed every motive that rendered this so difficult a task. He read the man's heart as though it were an open book. Dispassionately! Ah me! how could that be, when he loved this woman, betrothed to a man unworthy of her—loved her with every fibre of his being? Would he not have counted it the dearest bliss life could offer to see those trusting eyes looking up into his face, as he had seen them looking into Guy Tremlett's? It is at all times easier to human nature to act rightly than to feel rightly. Had he not already had to take shame to himself for one fierce instant's joy, as he learned the truth that would dash the cup of happiness from Lilian's lips if she too gained knowledge of it? Any happiness or benefit that comes to us by the death or misfortune of another must ever be a flawed gem, a wilted flower; and yet, for one moment, William Snow had rejoiced in his rival's sin?

Only for a moment, though. Love that is pure and true can never batten in the mire of mean and petty jealousy. Has not our laureate set this truth to exquisite melody, when he sings,

"Love took up the harp of Life, and smote on all the chords with might;
Smote the chord of *Self*, that, *trembling*, *passed in music out of sight*."

High and true and pure and tender as William's love for Lilian had ever been, it was now being "tried by fire," and purged from every lingering taint of self.

The reaction from that shaft of unworthy thought—that one passing thought of triumph in another's degradation—prompted his next words.

"Guy Tremlett may have sown his wild oats like many another man, and now better things may be looked for from him. A man has a powerful motive for reform when a true woman loves him, and Lilian—Miss Selwyn is one to possess a strong influence over those with whom she is thrown. For her sake, and for the sake of the old man who idolizes her, I trust in God Guy Tremlett may prove better than our thoughts of him."

Pelham Pettigrew enjoyed the spectacle of the younger man's enthusiasm without sharing in his hopefulness. He appreciated and admired the generosity that underlay his hot words, without in the least changing his opinion of anything that bore the name of Tremlett.

"Any one (except the devil, of course) *may* reform; but drink and gambling are two bad dogs to bite a man—dogs whose fangs poison the blood, and leave a nasty taint behind. However, my dear sir, we should always let hope tell a flattering tale, if she will, and try to look as if we believed it."

This man of the world had a heart that at times yielded to the influence of a generous kindliness, of which he almost denied the existence to himself.

"You'll be able to get out of town for a bit now, Snow," he said, puffing the smoke of his cigar high in the air, and looking critically at a Joshua Reynolds that hung beside the mantelshelf, as if he saw it for the first time, and was mentally valuing it with a view to purchase. "Come up to my little box near the Cheviots and rough it there for a week or two. I intend to run up on Friday—come with me? The journey's a mere nothing. You throw yourself into the train at Euston, read the paper, take a nap, and there you are!"

He spoke of doing all this as though it were some acrobatic feat, and waved his hand in an imaginary greeting to the "North countrie." The proposal sounded in William's ears like a suggested escape from a labyrinth of perplexities. Perhaps he would have been a good deal startled, had he known how plainly Pelham Pettigrew read this state of mind on his part.

Happily ignorant of this fact, he accepted the welcome offer of change of scene and place. How gladly would he escape from meeting a pair of violet eyes that were the last things he cared to look upon, with the knowledge of Guy Tremlett's sins rankling in his mind!

He took leave of his jolly host, pledged himself to meet him on the following Friday, and proceed to Hazlecroft, there to "rough it" in most approved fashion. As the sound of the closing door below told of his young friend's departure, Pelham Pettigrew had a mental wrestle with himself again.

"A sister—just so—quite, quite!"

He rubbed his hands, and chuckled over the result. Then he rung the bell, ordered the obsequious major-domo to light some dozen or so wax-candles in various sconces and massive candelabra in the inner drawing-room, seated himself once more before the reigning favorite, wiped some imaginary specks of dust from the housewife's dress with his cambric handkerchief, smiled, and nodded, and hummed a tune, ordered the lights to be put out, and went to bed. Meanwhile William Snow paced the streets, that were almost as busy and noisy at this late hour as in the bustling day. In his heart he carried a fresh burden, and that no light one.

To learn evil of one who has cruelly wronged us brings with the knowledge a certain guilty sensation of harboring revenge. How much more, then, is this so when the wrong has been done unwittingly!

The man who had taken his heart's darling from him was unworthy of the prize that he had won. This one searing thought seemed burned in upon his brain, and a great self-distrust welled up within his heart—a fear lest he should think the worst of Guy, and be ready to cast suspicion upon his reformation, in that he, William Snow, loved Lilian so dearly. But by one of those painful yet salutary mental processes by which a man or woman may wade through a great evil to a great good, by the time he reached the familiar neighborhood of the Temple, it had come to this: self and love had wrestled for the mastery, and love had won. His own disappointed love became a lesser pain than Lilian's possible suffering. He could, honestly to himself, and in harmony with his conscience, earnestly pray, not that the woman he loved might be his, but that the man she loved might prove worthy of her.

"Oh, my God, save her from sorrow!"

That was the prayer which rose from the man's heart, as, thinking only of Lilian's happiness, he learned the lesson of putting aside every passionate longing, every tender craving born of love. Yet he was glad to think of getting away from the place that held Lilian; glad to escape the temptation to suspicious distrust that seeing her lover at her side might lead to; glad, too, if the truth were told, to get away from the old familiar rooms and courts and streets for a time. The places that are haunted by the sad-eyed ghosts of dead day-dreams are always dreary to us, for when we most try to forget, then most persistently do these regretful spirits watch us with their dreamy eyes. Perhaps few of us can say truthfully—

"....though memory calls
Dead dreams from out their silent grave,
Obtruding through uplifted palls
Reproachful faces—*I am brave!*"

For my own part, I think a dead day-dream one of the most unpleasant ghosts that can meet us on the way. Not a ghost, however, either of dreams or men, and yet a figure that made William start in surprise, greeted his eyes on passing through the archway that led to Fig-tree Court.

"Why, Beams, what on earth brings you out of bed at this time of night?" said his master, as that worthy rose reluctantly from his lair near the entrance to the inner court.

Beams took off his hat, and scratched his head.

"It's the toothache, sir, as I've had shockin' bad, last We'n'sdy was a week. I can't sleep a mossel for the pain of it."

"But to come out of your warm bed is a bad way to make it better: go home directly. I am astonished your mother—"

"Please, sir," said Beams, grinning ever so slightly, "mother's a little overtook with liquor this evenin', and father's bin and laid her comfortable up agin the fender; and the groanin' of me was so 'orrid with this here tooth of mine, he said I'd best bolt for fear of disturbin' of her in her sleep."

This story, made up of a patchwork of truth and lies, left little to be said; so with a strict caution to Beams to go straight home, Mr. Snow passed on towards his own door.

Surely the members of his household were possessed that night by a wish to follow the example of that unpleasant personage, the Wandering Jew.

Fully half an hour after he had come in, he heard the passage door opened by a latch-key, and, looking over the stair-rail, saw Jim creeping up to his room, with such a guilty, shrinking look upon his face as might have rested there had his hand been red with the blood of some murdered enemy.

"These are late hours to keep, Jim," said his master, as the ungainly figure of the clerk reached the landing where he stood.

"Yes, sir," said Jim, volunteering no explanation of his strange night wandering. He was secure from any fear of his master putting a bad construction on his proceedings by reason of the perfect trust that existed between them—a trust that had its root in the days of old, when master and man were playmates, and the elder boy sung to soothe the sufferings of the little cripple, his comrade.

Feeling small inclination to sleep, William drew the shaded reading-lamp near to his elbow, and set to work to strive to drown unpleasant thought in the pages of a book just then taking the world by storm, though it did but tell the varying fortunes of an humble individual, one Amos Barton.

Yet not even the charm of the most charming writer that has ever won men's hearts, and led them on to even higher ground in aims and purposes of life, could chase away from his haunted eyes the vision of the dear face he loved—could hide from his mental sight two grave, sweet eyes, raised in loving, trusting homage to an idol that was but of clay.

Should he see them one day heavy with weeping, dim with sleepless nights of weary watching?

Blame himself as he would for this never-resting distrust of Guy Tremlett, this conviction that he was acting a part, and that one day the real man would declare himself, William could not overmaster such feelings, try as he would. He remembered some one once saying of a similar case, "Once a gambler, always a gambler."

Yet he had, or thought he had, one tower of strength and hope in remembering that Guy's mother showed such affection to her son's betrothed, as told how gladly she welcomed the idea of his marriage.

No woman (so William reasoned) could lend a hand to leading a sister woman into all the degradation that is the lot of her who is mated to a man at once intemperate and impure.

An almost indissoluble marriage exists between these two evils, as he well knew; and he dared not even picture to himself the thought of Lilian linked to such a one. Could it be possible that she who had been reared like some delicate flower—sheltered from the very breath of evil—guarded, fostered, kept apart from aught that could assail the fair beauty of her mind—trained to be the sweet appreciative companion of the man who should one day win her love—could *this* woman be reserved for such a fate? *this* flower destined to be trampled in the mire?

Thus he pondered. The light had fallen on a page, unturned for close upon an hour, when the door slowly opened, and Jim, still fully dressed, crept into the room.

CHAPTER XV.

"NOW WHAT MY LOVE IS, PROOF HATH MADE YOU KNOW."

As William Snow sat by his desk, the end of the room farthest from the round disk of light thrown by the lamp was almost in darkness. For some seconds after the stealthy opening of the door recorded at the close of our last chapter, he looked curiously into the gloom before he recognized the untimely intruder.

"Why, Dutton," he said at last, "what is the matter? Are you ill?"

Jim came slowly up to his master's side. His hands were closely pressed together, his eyes were full of pain, that yet seemed half a fierce, triumphant joy.

For a moment, looking at his pallid, troubled face, a fear darted through William's mind that his faithful servitor had been led into some wrong-doing, and was about to disclose its nature in the hope of finding in his old playmate a helping hand. But this surmise passed quickly away. Jim's eyes were sunken and unnaturally bright, but they did not shrink from meeting his master's. They had the pleading, pathetic expression you may see in the eyes of a dog who fears he has forfeited the smile and the approval of the master whom he loves. Every line in the sensitive face of the cripple was deepened, and the involuntary working of the muscles round the mouth told of a state of high nervous tension—a mental condition that, if long sustained, ends in madness; and to which only morbidly sensitive temperaments are liable.

Under such conditions the focus of the mental vision is deranged; all things are distorted; one fixed idea dominates the rest; the mind is, as it were, color-blind, and sees all things, not as they are, but as the false medium through which they are seen renders them. For weeks and months past, one absorbing, one intense passion had filled the poor cripple's breast, one chimera had been the Alpha and Omega of his thoughts. These thoughts were born of love and hatred. Love of the man to whom his whole life was one devotion; hatred of the man who had taken from the object of this idolatrous love his "heart's desire."

Guy Tremlett little thought that whenever he set foot in the chambers in Fig-tree Court, he encountered a man who harbored towards him a passionate hatred, who dogged his footsteps in the hours when a man is least on his guard, and who read in the face of William Snow a distrust of him hardly acknowledged to his own heart, and yet legible to the quick clairvoyance of love as though written in an open book. Guided by this strange, electric knowledge, Jim had divined the existence of hidden evil, and, with a bloodhound's tenacity, had set himself to track and bring it home.

All the happy, innocent City wanderings were long since given up by the City clerk. A new and beautiful peacock had been lately added to the collection in the little green island in Bishopsgate Street, but Jim did not know it. The sweet chimes of St. Botolph's, the music of the bells of old St. Giles's, had not fallen on his ear for many a day. Jim dared not take a heart full of hatred and revenge into the very presence of God. Once he had gone softly at eventide into the Church of St. Ethelburga, but this time no sweet Litany rose and fell. A stern-faced old man was preaching to a crowded congregation on the sins of hatred and vengeance.

"Vengeance is mine—I will repay, saith the Lord," thundered the rich, ringing voice of the venerable priest, and Jim stole quickly out into the night with his burden of hatred in his heart.

Night by night, when the day's work was done, the clerk took his way westward. Now on this pretence, and now on that, he frequented those parts of fashionable London where men of Guy Tremlett's stamp are wont to seek for pleasure and amusement. Long and patiently he waited for the reward of his perseverance, and, like most things doggedly pursued, it came at last.

One night Guy left the house in Park Lane, and on the way to Lowndes Street met a congenial spirit, one who had been in the days that were past the companion of many a night's debauch.

It would be an awful thing to think that men can strengthen the hands of the devil by cruel and unholy aspirations; yet, if such a thing were possible, I should think Jim's longings for the triumph of the tempter, as he watched and divined the meaning of this interview, were vehement enough to warrant such a thought.

And the tempter and Jim had their way. Not even the remembrance of the sweet face that had been lifted to his for a good-night kiss but a few moments before—not even the lingering touch of little clinging hands, the pressure of pure lips that trembled beneath his own—could quench in Guy's soul the lust of again tasting the fruit of the tree of evil. Of late the places that knew him of old had known him no more: the new excitement of winning Lilian's love, the exquisite pleasure of watching her whole heart yield to his power and turn to him like a blossom wooed by the sun, had filled his time and thoughts; but now—

He had not ceased to love her—he had not even begun to feel the promise that Mrs. Tremlett had drawn from him press irksomely upon his liberty of action; but the novelty was gone from the situation of being an accepted lover. The ghoul of *ennui* began to brood over his soul, and in this evil hour, just when the soil was ready, opportunity became the handmaid of desire.

There was a feeble protest, a weak resistance, and then Guy Tremlett's arm was linked in that of his former friend. Behind them, at a safe distance, his face eager and triumphant, his eyes peering forward to keep the two figures in sight, came Jim Dutton.

He had not very far to follow.

Only as far as the neighborhood of the Haymarket—only to the door of a hell, fitly so called, for devils frequented it, and led the weak and unwary to destruction. The portal that might well have had inscribed above it Dante's line,

 "Lasciate ogni speranza, voi ch' entrate,"

opened at some recognized signal, and then closed.

And the man who stood outside laughed aloud—laughed so that passers-by thought some poor lunatic who ought to be held in close restraint was wandering at large. It was, however, no business of theirs, and so they passed on.

Thus had Jim's hands garnered in the bitter grain, and now he was about to lay the harvest at his master's feet. He went up to William's side, and stood where the light of the lamp fell upon his face. After a moment's silence, in a low yet steadfast voice, he told the story of his westward wanderings, and the reward that had at last been given to his patient labor. The story ended thus:

"They went in together; and two hours later *he* came out alone—*drunk!*"

Why would not his master speak?

He had looked to have seen joy and hope kindle in the face that had grown so old and worn in but a few months' time.

He had thought to have heard something like the words of a master of old, "Well done, thou good and faithful servant, enter thou into the joy of thy lord!" But William was silent. His eyes were shaded with his hand, and as Jim watched and waited breathlessly for some faint sign of approval, a tear fell upon the open book upon the desk.

If we love any one very dearly, no pain can be so intolerable as that of seeing some misfortune threatening to overwhelm them, and yet feeling utterly powerless to avert the coming evil day.

"My God! what can I do for her?"

Was *this* what Jim had looked for? Was *this* his reward?

There was no joy, no triumph, only pity in William's face, as he turned at last to look at the man who had scented the trail and run the prey to earth.

"Jim, my poor fellow, what suffering all this must have been to you, knowing as you did that it would be such pain to me! I read all the motives that have led you to keep the suspicion from me until you were sure. And now you are trying by perfect candor to place me in a position to help—"

What is the pain of stern reproof from lips that we love compared to that of unmerited praise? Jim could not bear it.

He sunk down gradually, slowly, upon his knees, grasping with his long hands the edge of the desk: fearful in his humility, strong in his love, he looked up piteously into his master's face, and laid bare the motives of the past weeks.

"It is not true," he said, with passionate pleading in his voice and in his working lips; "I have not thought these thoughts you speak of; I have not acted from these motives that you give me credit for: I thought you would be glad—I was glad myself—until to-night—"

"*Glad*—until to-night?" echoed his listener.

"Yes, until I met her—Miss Lilian—watching for him, following him as I was, perhaps, who knows? She held her hand out to me, and I—I could not take it. I looked at her face, and felt as if I had—murdered some one; I had; I have carried a hell in my heart; I would have been glad if some one had told me he was dead. I have heard it said that in God's sight it is as bad to think these things as to do them; and I am a murderer—in God's sight! O master, I was so glad—I laughed aloud for joy when that door closed upon him! His beautiful face had come into your life like a curse, and stolen from you what you loved. How could I wish him anything but evil when I knew—when I saw—"

Was this wild-eyed man, who poured forth such a torrent of hot words, but the awful personification of that one sinful moment when William had triumphed in Pelham Pettigrew's denouncing of the man Lilian loved?

Our own sins are apt to look heinous in our eyes when developed in others; they are then presented to us in all their deformity; and thus, though the evil spirit had been cast forth as soon as its presence had declared itself, William could pardon the wrong towards which he himself had been tempted.

And as Jim crouched almost at his feet, borne down by the agony of his dreaded displeasure, he bent down and laid a hand upon his shoulder.

"You have been sadly wrong, and wronged me in your thoughts; but, Jim, dear old fellow! I know you have done it all, and felt it all, for love of me and for my sake."

At that moment the distance of years, the barriers of caste, all ceased to exist; they were once again the playmates of the old boyish days, once again in the old, happy times, whose memory hallowed the present and blotted out from it all that needed pardon.

CHAPTER XVI.

A SKETCH IN WATER-COLORS.

PERHAPS it would be a difficult matter to come across a human being who took a more generally cheerful view of life than our amiable young friend Abraham Beams. On the particular morning succeeding the evening that was such an eventful one to each of our *dramatis personæ*, this natural cheerfulness of disposition was so increased as to become quite riotous. He lost no opportunity of giving vent to private ebullitions of a delight that kept his countenance perpetually lighted up with a grin; he stood on his head, turned cart-wheels, and otherwise misbehaved himself in intervals snatched from his morning's work.

Masher, looking through the kitchen-window, and beholding him in an inverted position in the little dark den behind the house in Fig-tree Court that was dignified by the name of yard, felt certain that some important event had taken place, and went about her usual avocations, bursting with curiosity as to what it might be. "He's flittin' here and there like any spunkie," she muttered to herself. In due time the old woman's curiosity was gratified, for Beams, taking advantage of his master and his master's clerk both being out, launched himself, like an arrow from a bow, into Mr. Twigg's premises, running against Masher and nearly capsizing her into the fireplace. "Can't you look where you're going to?" she grumbled, setting herself straight, and restoring her head-gear to its lost equilibrium. "What do you go upsetting folks like that for?—as if you was an enjine or some such wild beastie!"

"Cos I'm that upset myself as I can't see nothink nor nobody," replied the incorrigible one. Then he put his mouth close to her ear, as if a dozen eager listeners were at hand, and jerked his thumb over his shoulder in the direction of his master's room. "*He's* bin and got cotched this time, Mrs. Masher. Lor, ain't it splendid?—cotched like a rat in a trap! *I* see'd him shirkin' in like a shadder, and I knew he'd come right agin' the master. 'Get along, my hinnercent,' says I to mysel', and get along he did too: and flop! I throws myself down to have my laugh out with my head in the gutter. I reckon they went at it 'ammer and tongs, just for all the world like Coplethwaite and his missus when she comes 'ome off the square, you know."

"Well now, Mr. Beams, I really shouldn't have thought it, unless a gentleman like you had told me with his ain tongue. Mr. Dutton, he do look so quiet and douce, such a personable kind of a man," said Mrs. Masher, shaking her head reflectively over the depravity of human nature.

"It's allers them kind as is the wust," replied Beams, with the precocious and awful knowledge of evil peculiar to the London boy. "When a chap turns the white of his hyes up, don't you never go for to put no confidence in him, Mrs. Masher. Why, bless you! Mr. Dutton's like a saint this morning, and master's like that there saint's twin-brother; but *I* know the game as is up, and I'm glad he's cotched. Master 'll be for thinkin' a little more of them as keeps theirselves respectable now. I shouldn't much wonder if he rose my wages, just as a kind o' relief to his feelin's."

This soothing idea caused Mrs. Masher's fingers to itch, and she was about to make some observation expressive of her admiration of one so young having such a proper regard for the coin of the realm, when Beams was reduced to the ignominious necessity of rushing wildly forth in answer to Mr. Dutton's peremptory call.

Perhaps Beams's idea of the clerk looking like a saint was a little far-fetched, but he certainly looked like a man who had gone through some painful and severe mental struggle, and been decidedly worsted in the encounter.

This worn and weary appearance on his part was by Beams attributed to the after-effects of what he called "being on the spree," a judgment that is, I think, a fair sample of the construction put by the vulgar and uneducated on the conduct and demeanor of their betters.

And truly a very storm of self-reproach and remorse had passed over the sensitive soul that animated Jim's poor deformed body! How clearly, looking back, was he able rightly to estimate the motives that had led him to seek out and glory in the shame and sin of Guy Tremlett!

How little had he, in his pettiness of soul, understood that a keener pain might come to the master he loved than even Lilian's loss! That to see her in sorrow and suffering would be worse, far worse, to bear than to learn that another than himself was chosen to make her happy!

He had thought to see some lifting-up of the cloud that had rested on the face that was his life and light, ever since the night on which that letter from Winstowe had awaited his coming, and now it was but deepened. If a dead hope had haunted William Snow's dreams—if a tender regret had made his eyes sad and his heart weary in those weaker moments that come to all of us, as memory tells the tale of some sweet "might have been" and that now shall never be —he had, at all events, felt that with the woman he so passionately loved all was well; that to her dear eyes life had taken brighter and more tender hues, even though to him a shadow seemed brooding over all things.

But now that the words of Pelham Pettigrew had been verified by the knowledge gained by poor faithful Jim, he was enduring that greatest of all agonies, apprehension of evil coming upon some head that we would fain, God knows how tenderly, shield from ill.

If act or word of his could have wrested Lilian's lover from the power of temptation, could have set him by her side, free from the trammels of degrading vice, and worthy of her love, the man she deemed him, not the weak wretch he really was, William would have thanked God. He could have been content to bid God bless her with the man she loved, and pass upon his own way, in loneliness perhaps, but yet rejoicing in the knowledge of her full content. In the first bitterness of learning Guy's unworthiness, he had found some comfort in the admission made by a man of the world, a man who read human nature like an open book—"he *may* reform."

Of course, like all men who are capable of that intense and concentrated love that makes the world for them hold but one woman, William set his darling up upon a pedestal above the head of every other, no matter how beautiful or how gifted. That a man should look into *a* woman's eyes, and read there the sweet story of the love she bore him—that a man should press with his own, lips that kissed him back, and going straightway from that loving presence, should fall into the lust of drink, and lower himself beneath the "beasts that perish," no doubt did happen, and would happen; but that any man should look into *that* woman's eyes, hear *that* woman's lips murmur words of love, and then fall so low!

There lay the wonder of it.

All through the night that followed the hearing of Jim's story of those West-end wanderings, William lay sleeplessly pondering upon some possible way of shielding Lilian from the sorrow that seemed about to fall upon her.

All petty jealousy, all selfish longings, died before the might of his pity. Again and again his memory recalled her as the little dainty maiden of the old childish days, the fairy with the streaming locks, stealing from the shelter of the crimson curtains, putting up her innocent face to his, and saying, with a gentle dignity, "Then I think that you had better kiss me."

One other little incident, too, he recalled—the poor broken doll that she was so tender over, the firm refusal that she gave to the suggestion of a new one, lest the old favorite should fancy that she "did not love it any more!"

As the child is father of the man, so is the girl mother to the woman; and, thinking over the past, William realized that Lilian was of that type of woman who will cling to and weep over the shattered idol, and stifle the cries called forth by his cruelty upon the breast of him whose hand deals the blow.

Therefore he knew that in learning (if such bitter knowledge ever came to her) the fact of Guy's unworthiness, she would suffer more intensely than another woman might have done.

And when, weary from a restless night full of unquiet tossings, he went down to his sitting-room, there upon his desk lay Lilian's letter.

It was as though her little hand were stretched out to him for help. It was like a cry from her heart to his—to the brother of her childhood, the boy who had saved her from the cruel flames, and would save her now if he could.

If he had seen her once again a little blue-eyed lass no higher than his knee, and seen her feet nearing the edge of some terrible precipice, his heart could not have been more full of loving fear, his arm more ready to clasp her in a strong and sheltering hold.

The helplessness of love has in it a terrible pathos.

As William read the short letter before him, he recognized that even though actual sorrow had not yet come to Lilian, its shadow was upon her.

"Would he come and see her—soon, if possible? She was very troubled about something, and was sure that he could help her."

Was he sure himself?

Of the will—yes; of the power—no.

For a moment he leaned his head upon his hand, and covered his eyes from the familiar objects all around. Every thought was half a prayer.

One resolution was easily taken. He would write a line to Pelham Pettigrew, and renounce all intention of that pleasant "roughing it" at the little box near the Cheviot Hills.

Twenty-four hours ago this plan would have had certain attractions for him; the attraction that complete change has for all of us when we get beset with a tangle of thoughts and self-reviewing from which there seems no escape. We are glad to break through the cobwebs, and try to forget them for a time.

But now he could not leave London as long as Lilian was in it.

Such thoughts forming the warp of William's reflections, you may be sure the woof was made of vain repetitions of the oft-put question, Should he tell Uncle David the real state of the case? Should he let him see clearly the character of the man to whom his child's hand was pledged? But here, again, resolution was beset by uncertainty.

If he had not loved Lilian as his own soul, if he had not distrusted himself in every motive that seemed to prompt him to such a course, I doubt not but he would have laid the whole matter bare before the man to whom he owed every advantage he possessed.

I am not even prepared to deny that had he done so he would have taken the wisest course; but to a man of highly sensitive and honorable feelings such a course was fraught with exceeding humiliation, and only to be had recourse to as a last resource.

He would have felt himself steeped in unutterable meanness when laying Guy's unworthiness before Lilian's natural guardian. The man who stood in the way of the realization of his own hopes, the satisfying of his own love, was sacred to him, as the life of a sleeping foe might have been. And, then, even what Jim's eager eyes spied out might have been but a solitary fall; a stumble made by feet that were yet striving to go up, not down hill.

To watch and wait, and to soothe, if possible, these new fears that had sprung up in Lilian's breast, these were the called-for actions of the present. For the future—*au jour le jour!*

She was watching for him through the misty downfall of the summer rain—rain that fell gratefully on the dusty leaves of the trees, and on the soiled flower-faces of the clustered blossoms in the park.

As he entered the room she came forward from the window, and then he saw how a few hours of unaccustomed anxiety had drawn dark shadows round her eyes, and stolen the bloom from her cheek.

"Uncle David is up-stairs in the inner drawing-room writing letters; run up and speak to him, and then come back here. I waited here for you; I thought you would have come sooner."

As she said this both her hands rested in his, and he felt how chill and cold they were.

"I could not get off from the court earlier; indeed, it was with great difficulty I came at all," he answered, holding them in that firm, friendly clasp by which a man's hand can always give to a troubled woman such a sense of help, such an assurance of protection and comfort.

Then he hurried to Uncle David, who, between delight and surprise, was moved to offer to desert his letter-writing in honor of such an unusual event as a visit from "the boy" at that hour. But William resolutely refused to allow of such a sacrifice.

"I am going to have a chat with Lilian downstairs," he said, with an indifferent air.

"Yes, yes," answered the old man, pulling down his spectacles, which, in the excitement of the arrival, he had pushed up to the top of his head, "go and have a chat with the child: cheer her up, that's a good fellow—she's a bit down-hearted. You know, it's the old story,

"'The village seems asleep or dead
When Lubin is away.'

Lubin went away deuced suddenly too, some days ago—sent for about some business at Tremlett Court, I tell her. You see, the old lady is a sad invalid, up one day, down another, regular case of the bucket and the well—eh? Guy must have been busy, too, to find no time to write the child a line since he got there. It made me sad to see her little pale, anxious face at breakfast this morning. She listened for the postman's rat-tat, and when it came, and there was nothing but one of Briggs's long-winded epistles for me, she couldn't taste another bit. I saw it all, though she chattered hard to try to hide her disappointment. Well, well, 'love is a little teaser,' so they say. We'll have you falling in love some of these days—eh, Will?—and sighing like a furnace; putting out all the fires when you come to Winstowe—eh, eh?"

The old man was delighted with his own joke. He chuckled delightedly over it, like a child over an apple that some good stroke of fortune has made him the proud possessor of; also, after the manner of ancient jokers, he must needs reiterate the point of it ("Sighing like a furnace—a furnace—eh?") and chuckle anew.

He was too much engrossed in the pleasantry of his own idea to notice that William hardly seemed to enter into the spirit of the thing, and, perhaps fortunately, his attention was drawn to a letter lying before him. It was written in a tall, attenuated hand, and besprinkled with capitals in all sorts of unexpected places.

"Here's a precious epistle!" he said, smiling in the most radiant manner, and taking the letter in his hand. "I've no doubt our faithful Briggs has spent many hours over its production, and read it aloud to Timmins with a regular flourish of trumpets. Now just listen to this:

"RESPECTED SIR,—Things at Winstowe are progressing as well as can be expected. It requires a good deal of circumlocution—"

"I'm really very sorry," interrupted William, "but I am rather pressed for time this afternoon, and—"

"Quite so," said Uncle David, laying down the letter; "I forgot the child is waiting for you down-stairs—what an old fool I am! By-the-way" (just as he was leaving the room), "it's all right about you coming down to Winstowe for Christmas, of course? Guy's coming too, and we'll have a 'right merrie time,' please God. Did I tell you the wedding's to come off early in spring—eh?"

And with this last pleasant piece of information William at last got away.

Perhaps he went down-stairs and across the hall more slowly than if he had been left in ignorance of it.

The most patient woman is impatient in what concerns a man she loves, and Lilian had performed quite a cantata of the movement vulgarly called the "Devil's tattoo" during William's interview with Uncle David.

She met him quickly in the middle of the room as he came in, with that eager, confiding manner you may always notice in a woman towards a man of whose unfailing sympathy she is assured. I think, too, that it may be taken as an invariable fact, that once let a woman be passionately devoted to a man, she will smilingly and gracefully sacrifice her friends and relations, male and female, to what she conceives to be his interests; also, that she secretly entertains a conviction that the said friends and relatives are highly honored by being made useful at the shrine of the idol she herself blindly worships.

Surely, too, love sharpens a woman's wits as the whetstone sharpens the steel; for, under the influence of a "grande passion," even a stupid woman will develop an amount of astuteness foreign to her nature. How much more, then, will love make powerful in expedient the brain of a highly educated, intelligent woman such as my heroine! It has been said that she felt and suffered from the estrangement that had crept in of late between herself and her old playmate; that she recognized with a loving woman's quick perception the fact that William did not appreciate Guy in a proper manner, and that she resented this as only a loving woman could.

Well, her aim and end now were to do away with this absurd prejudice—to smooth out with her little white hand every trace of constraint between the two men. Her motive for wishing to do this was because she had had her own anxieties on Guy's account of late, and had arrived at the conclusion that he wanted help in some difficulty or other, and that the hand she herself most trusted could best aid him.

But naturally a little cloud of coldness had arisen between herself and her adopted brother; on her side arising from an all-womanly resentment of his misjudgment of her lover, and on his from bitter pain—from the aching of a heart that had hardly known the depths of its own tenderness until Guy, and Guy's love, had taken his darling from him.

This coldness, then, was the outwork to be first undermined, and then, when they were once more the boy and girl who had knelt together in the midst of the fire and commended each other to God, Lilian would plead for William's friendship to be given to her lover.

Her lover, so beautiful, so winning, so resistless in every charm of look and manner—the man who had kissed her lips as she wandered among the flowers in the garden at Winstowe!

"And what is it that is troubling her?" said William, looking anxiously at the girl's face, a picture of which all the colors seemed to have faded and grown faint.

"I have been anxious; I have had troubled thoughts; I will tell you all about it presently. But first of all, I want to show you something— a little present I have got for you. Will you like it, I wonder?"

Upon a carved book-stand was something covered with a sheet of tissue-paper, and as she spoke Lilian drew the screen away. Then she stood silently watching William's face, as he bent over what was thus revealed. She could, however, only see his profile.

A good thing, maybe.

Had she met his eyes just then, more stories than one would have been told. The present was a sketch in water-colors, and the best specimen of art ever achieved by the artist's fingers.

It represented a cathedral porch; each quaint sculpture upon the archway was tipped with snow that looked as light and feathery as if but newly fallen. Inside the outer door-way, seated on a bench of dark oak that ran down either side, was the figure of an old man. His face was turned towards a strange little mortal standing at his knee—a boy in ragged clothes, a flower-pot and plant in one arm, and holding up a hand, as if to bespeak attention to sounds seeming to his simple mind sweet as the angel-voices of heaven.

This picture was called "Listening to the Choristers."

"I did it as a surprise for you; I thought you would like it," said Lilian, in a rather timid voice; for William still looked silently at her effort of genius, and for the first time the thought smote her that he might be angry at such a record of his childhood.

Uncle David and his niece, you see, were not rich in the lore called knowledge of the world, and the suspicion that William's origin might be held as a disgrace to the now rising man had never entered the mind of either. Again and again, in days gone by, had Lilian sat by Mrs. Timmins's knee, and listened to the ever new story of "Master William's" coming to Winstowe. Briggs would interlard the narrative with marvellous new-coined words, and remind Mrs. Timmins of some interesting particular overlooked, while all three would feel that no "strange story" was ever written in a book by pen of mortal man so beautiful as the history of the boy David Earle found in the snow, and took to be even as his own son.

"I painted the old man's face from a daguerreotype of Uncle David; but, you see, I was afraid to try to paint *your* face, because I can't remember what sort of a little boy you were; so I put you with your back to the audience, and only the golden hair, all tangled, as they said it was then, hanging over your jacket."

Still silence, broken at last by a very frightened, pitiful voice:

"Do you like it, William? I thought—indeed, I did—you would be sure to like it......"

———◆———

CHAPTER XVII.

"I FANCIED THAT YOU DID NOT LIKE HIM."

At length the mist that had grown up between William Snow's eyes and the picture so cunningly drawn by Lilian's hand cleared away.

After those long moments of silent conflict with memories of the past, he was sure of himself.

He dared not have trusted his voice sooner. Now he turned and took her hand in his.

"I *do* like it, Lillie; I shall prize it all my life: it came upon me rather suddenly, you know, and brought a flood of strange thoughts—"

"Yes," she said, drawing a deep breath of relief, "I know; it was the same with Uncle David. I would not let him see it until it was quite finished; then I tied my handkerchief over his dear old eyes, and led him into the room, and set him on a chair right before it. Then, presto! I drew the handkerchief away, and there it was! I wish you'd seen how pleased he was. He set off talking of those old times: he said, 'God bless the boy! how he held up his little hand for me to listen to the singing! He carried the scrubby plant as if it had been a perfect treasure; his poor bare feet sunk in the snow at every step!' Then, Willie, when he had said that,

Uncle David took his big red handkerchief out, and took his spectacles off and wiped them, 'to see the better,' so he said, but I knew he was just ready to cry for joy to think how great and clever you had grown to be."

"He thinks me, dear old man! a thousand times more clever than I am," said her listener, smiling at the story of his benefactor's fond remembrance of the little waif and stray.

"And Jim, too," the girl went on; "Uncle David told me, for the twentieth time, about the hymns you used to sing to ease his pain, and about the black kitten; such a wretched-looking little creature as it must have been! He said he saw the same devotion to you in poor Jim now, as when you were boys together."

William moved away from the table. How her innocent words tortured him! Had not that very devotion led the faithful cripple to hunt down the man she loved, to triumph in his fall, to gloat over his degradation?

"You have painted the picture very cleverly. I hardly thought you were such an artist," he said, taking refuge in commonplaces, as most of us do when hard-pressed.

"Uncle David said Guy ought to be proud of such a clever little wife."

This was her graceful fashion of introducing the name ever in her thoughts.

Even as she spoke it, tender stealing shafts of rosy color stained her cheek; for in her heart she questioned if she were not over-bold in speaking thus.

Taking his courage "by both hands," as our Gallic neighbors have it, William here took the initiative. He noted the pretty virginal flush with which she spoke her lover's name, and thought to give her confidence.

"And is it about Guy that you are troubled, Lilian?" he said, taking her hand, and drawing her to a place by his side.

"What made you think so? Did any one tell you anything? Do you know where he is gone?"

This time it was the white flag, not the red, that ran up to the signal.

"I know nothing of where he is. Uncle David told me he had left town suddenly, and so I concluded that this was what troubled you, dear."

She drew a long, deep breath of relief, and, looking bravely in his face, spoke out her heart, keeping nothing back.

"Willie, you and I ought to have no reserves from each other, ought we? You know in all the world there is no one I would sooner go to for help in trouble, no one I would trust so wholly, as my dear 'big brother.'"

He pressed the hand he held by way of reply, having, truth to say, no words ready just then.

"And so I wrote to you, because I knew you to be so clever and so kind, and always able to know just what is the best thing for any one to do."

"Dear Lilian, that is rather comprehensive praise."

"No matter" (with the familiar shake of the little head—the pretty tyranny of a spoiled child), "I think it true, and Uncle David thinks it true. I think it was very brave of me to write to you about Guy, because, do you know that I have had a strange, unhappy sort of feeling—a foolish feeling—that you—did—not—like—him?"

It was such an astonishing idea that any one should "not like" Guy, that it made her open her eyes very wide indeed; and when she had said the last words, her lips remained a little apart as if in eager expectation of indignant denial from the accused. But no denial came.

William rose, walked to the window, and stood there looking out at things he did not see.

He had been quite unprepared for this form of attack.

"It is true—it is *true!*" said Lilian, in a pitiable, trembling voice, clasping her hands tightly together, a fashion she had in any moment of excited feeling. "There is nothing so hard as when people we like won't like each other!"

"'Don't like' is too strong a term to use, Lilian," said William, returning from his contemplation of the dripping trees in the park, and the dripping people in the street; "I have seen very little of—of Mr. Tremlett, and really feel to know—"

"Yes, that is *just* it!" she interrupted, with a brilliant smile, "you don't understand Guy. Then, you see, because you don't, your manner is constrained to him; not like your manner to other people one bit. *He* said you were jealous, but that was a foolish notion, as I told him."

"Very foolish."

"People aren't jealous of their sisters and brothers, you know."

"Certainly not."

"So I told him." Lilian had left her seat, and was busying herself in putting the silver-paper cover over the water-color sketch. After smoothing it very carefully and deliberately down at each separate corner, she came and stood by William's side. "I think I am rather like Briggs this morning," she said, smiling, yet unable to prevent a quiver of the lip at the same time; "there seems to be a great deal of 'circumlocution' needed for me to come to what I want to say."

"Not because you have any want of confidence in me, surely? Lilian, never let me think your *trust* could fail me."

"Indeed it never could; but there are some things that are hard to speak about: they seem to choke you just when you want to begin."

"Never mind, then, trying to do such unpleasant things, dear, but tell me all about these troubled thoughts: sometimes there is quite a simple remedy for things that we worry about in our own minds."

"Well, I will tell you—they have been about Guy." Here the poor child looked as though she fancied William might find in this fact a subject of surprise—a proceeding on his part that would have been something like being astonished at the needle of the compass pointing to the north. "I have fancied, only lately, but fancied more and more, that there is something—that he has troubles—some sorrow hidden from me." She was silent for a moment, and the little hands pressing each other so closely began to shake and tremble. Then she gathered courage and went on: "I cannot bear to think it, and yet the thought grows and grows—"

"Tell me, dear Lilian, all the reasons that you have for fancying these things. You know there is nothing I would not do for you—and Guy."

It was the first time he had ever spoken of her lover by his Christian-name; an exquisite delicacy of perception had prompted him to do so, and his reward was the happy look that came over her face as the dear name passed his lips. Womanlike, upon that one short syllable she built an edifice at once, and in her "mind's eye" saw those two side by side, even as she would fain have had them—husband and brother, the two best-beloved in her true heart.

That little word opened the floodgates of her speech. She told the story of her anxieties and fears as fearlessly as any child might have done; she told him of the strange, moody absence of mind that now and again would come over Guy, and, like a cloud across the sun, dim all the gladness of her day; how he would be restless and ill at ease; and if she seemed to notice this, or tried to offer any sympathy, he would leave her abruptly. "And then the time seems so long till I see him again!" she said, sighing, and with a weary look that had never been on Lilian's face before, and made his heart ache to see.

Naturally, Guy's sudden departure, and the few hasty lines that had told her nothing beyond the fact of his departure, and had said nothing of his destination or the time of his possible return, had roused into greater intensity all her fears and misgivings. One night of sleepless thought following another had traced those purple shadows round her eyes, had stolen the tender rose from her cheek, and the sweet peacefulness from her smile.

There had always been a peculiarly childlike character about this girl, reared so exceptionally. It was as though in the close companionship with Uncle David, something of his own guilelessness and simplicity had reacted upon her, and made her even younger than her years; but now it was an older Lilian, a woman with a woman's hopes and fears, and trembling love, that stood before her old playmate, and looked into his face with earnest, questioning eyes.

"You, who are so clever, when you get to know Guy better, will soon find out if there is any trouble weighing on him, anything that he keeps from me, in his fear lest I should suffer in knowing it; and perhaps you might be able to say—to bring it in somehow or other—that, having known me from the time I was quite a little girl, you can tell, and are sure, it would be best to keep nothing from me. You can say that I can be strong to bear anything that he and I share with each other. It is his love that makes him so thoughtful for me, and so afraid of giving me any pain; but you could make him see that it is the worst pain of all to think he will not let me share whatever there may be at any time to trouble him."

If the pathway to perfect immunity from every taint of selfishness had been to William Snow a pathway of thorns, a pathway of stumbling and toil and weariness, at last the end was gained!

For looking on her as she thus laid bare to him the beautiful truth and sanctity of her love, the womanly, tender faithfulness of her devotion to the man to whom her troth was plighted, even the faint memory of his own hopes and dreams died away.

And yet he did not love her less. It was himself he loved less: her more.

"I dare say," she continued, with a far-away

look in her eyes, "that all this seems strange to you: I mean that you very likely think my mountains of anxieties only mole-hills, after all; but it is so, when everything belonging to any one belongs to one's self. I am not being very eloquent, or very grammatical either, I am afraid," she added, smiling; "but you may love some one very much yourself some day, William."

"I may."

"And then you will understand."

"Perhaps I shall."

"No, there is no perhaps about it. You will feel then how everything that hurts them, hurts you far more than if it came to yourself."

Poor little troubled face, looking into his! Poor little restless hands, on which shone the diamonds that were Guy's pledge and gift!

Be sure he soothed and comforted her fears as far as he was able; be sure he cast away for ever and for aye the faintest shadow of jealous thought of the man she loved; be sure he promised to win his confidence, and made her happy by the kind words he said. Indeed, she began to look more like the merry Lilian of old, and began building airy castles of the happy Christmas they should have at Winstowe, when all at once the sound of rapid wheels that stopped outside made her start to the window.

"It is Guy!" she said, crossing the room quickly. Then, with a pretty maidenly timidity, she stood there with shining eyes, and smiling, trembling lips, and hands ready to be outstretched to meet him.

One moment's delay, and then the door opened, and Guy Tremlett came in.

<hr>

CHAPTER XVIII.

OUT IN THE COLD.

There can be no doubt that, on the occasion of sudden and unlooked-for meetings and partings, the proprieties and *convenances* of life are apt to be somewhat hardly used.

If you know a certain interview is before you, you can make up your mind to a certain line of action; but if you are taken unawares, and if you are not a very cold-hearted person indeed, you are pretty sure to act upon the impulse of the moment, be that impulse what it may. It was thus with Lilian.

At sight of Guy, the object of so much anxious thought and loving fear—Guy safe and well once more before her—she forgot everything but the one mighty fact of his return—forgot the presence of any other save themselves. They had been parted, they were united once again. She threw herself into his arms with a glad and happy cry—"Oh, Guy, I have been so miserable about you!"

She spoke of her sorrow in the past tense; she "had been" miserable, but he was with her again, his arms were round her, her face was half hidden upon his breast—sorrow was a thing past. As to William, she had for the moment forgotten his existence. He, however, looking on, hoped that Guy Tremlett was not equally oblivious, and that to the fact of his presence was due the coldness of the kiss laid on Lilian's brow.

"I have been so anxious about you!" she said again, tears of joy trembling in her glad eyes.

"So it seems," he answered, putting her aside, and shaking hands with William as he spoke, "or you would not have written to my mother in the way you did. Any one would think I was a boy in leading-strings, Lillie, and obliged to give an account of my comings and goings."

But the surprise and dismay in her face checked him, and he added, more gently, "Men hate that sort of thing, Lilian."

"What sort of thing?" the girl thought, looking at the scowl upon his brow—looking into the dark eyes that could be so soft and winning, but that now had in their depths such a strange anger.

Loving thoughts and tender fears—were these, then, the things men hated?

"Oh, Guy, I was unhappy! You left without a word of good-bye. I had nothing to look back upon, nothing to think of. It is dreadful, people going, and never saying good-bye! I fancied you must be ill, and were afraid to tell me so. Of course, I wrote to Mrs. Tremlett. Who else is there I should be likely to write to? who else could care—"

"A pretty pleader, isn't she, Snow?" put in Guy, struck with the fair beauty of her earnest face. "I'll back a woman to beat all you fellows of the wig and gown—that is, when she pleads her own cause."

If the irritable reproof of a moment before had jarred painfully on William's ear, still more so did this idle jesting.

For to be terribly in earnest was one of the girl's strongest characteristics; and he who knew her so well, knew how real and deep had been the suffering of the last few days.

Uncle David, bustling into the room in a perfectly radiant state of delight at Guy's return, caught the last words.

"Yes, yes," he said, shaking hands with him as though he had been to the North Pole on a dangerous voyage of discovery, and just returned to the bosom of his family, "she's a little witch, is the child Lilian. Never argue with her, my boy—never argue with her; you'll get the worst of it."

In the excess of his delight at the turn of affairs in general, he pinched Lilian's little pink ear.

William began to feel a certain degree of that unpleasant sensation called being "out in the cold." These people seemed, in truth, to form a happy trio, well able to do without him; so he did what most men do when they are either bored themselves or in fear of boring others; he pulled out his watch, and glancing at the time, said he must take his leave and return to the City.

"City!" said Uncle David—"a most delightful place that City! I'll go down with you, my dear boy; there's a fellow in—let me see—yes, Wardour Street, who really wants looking after. He's getting some charming old tapestry into ship-shape for the corridor at Winstowe."

"I *know*," said Lilian, shaking her head mischievously, "that if Uncle David stays in London much longer, we shall have to get an extra goods-train to convey all his packages home."

Turning quickly towards her in mock anger at this speech, his coat-skirts caught the flimsy silver paper that covered the sketch. It fluttered to the ground, leaving "Listening to the Choristers" fully displayed.

The old man took William by the arm, and drew him opposite to it.

"Not bad, eh?" he said, chuckling in exceeding content; "the child never let me see it, not a glimpse, sir, till it was done. Don't the snow look just as if a bit of it might come tumbling down any moment? And isn't my umbrella a capital portrait? Timmins destroyed that umbrella in secret—I know she did—had a sort of *auto-da-fé* in the back garden, eh?"

All this banter was a cloak to hide the stirring of his dear, old, tender heart at the sight of that small figure in the tattered jacket.

"What a little, cold, starved chap you were, eh, Will?"

Not a whit more cold and starved than he felt at heart now, William might have answered; but beyond a few commonplace words of approbation of the skill displayed by the painter of the sketch in water-colors, he could find very little to say, indeed.

He fought against the feeling of annoyance that Guy Tremlett should be present when this picture was discussed. He hated himself for the meanness of what he was ready to condemn as a false and petty pride, an unworthy shame in the humbleness of his own origin; and yet, struggle as he would, the feeling got the better of him, and it was with a sensation of intense relief he found himself out in the soft, dank mist that had now succeeded to the rain.

"You had really better not come with me, sir," he said to Uncle David, as they stood at the open door—"it will be even worse than this in the City."

"All right, all right," said Uncle David, mysteriously, and with a benevolent wink in the direction of the breakfast-room door; "they'll think I'm gone. Don't you see, eh? Lovers like to be left to themselves—don't you see? You don't know much about it yet; but all in good time, eh? all in good time!"

Then William donned his mackintosh, and set forth on his way eastward.

Out in the drizzling fog, going to his work again. Yes, that was, after all, the proper place for such as he. Had not her own little hand drawn the picture that was the only genealogical tree he was ever likely to possess? Had not her own hand penned the record of the social gulf that lay between them? Guy Tremlett, with his long line of ancestry, his grand old family manor, his lands and wealth inherited from father to son for generation after generation, was on a level with this woman. If William's footsteps seemed to fall to the rhythm of those noble words—

"The rank is but the guinea's stamp,
The man's the gowd for a' that;"

if words still more apposite rose to his mind—"Refinement of thought and feeling are links that set at defiance all the barriers of caste and class: an educated and intelligent mind is a bridge that spans the widest social gulf"—he put both suggestions manfully aside.

He knew full well that, true as are such high and noble sentiments in the abstract, in practice they are lamentably apt to break down, and at all times form a firmer and surer ground for friendship than for love.

Guy Tremlett was too truly of the blood of "Vere de Vere" to sneer at humble birth or defective social position in another. For, after all, it is your mongrels and *parvenus* that fall into such petty sins; it is those who are conscious of a painful uncertainty in their own social standing that are so chronically and unpleasantly alarmed for their own dignity. But Guy's silent ignoring of the topic ever welcome to simple Uncle David; the taking it for granted that in such a matter as the fortunes of a little waif and stray, a homeless atom, owning neither kith nor kin, he could have no part or lot—this quiet ignoring of facts so far beneath his stand-point as to be invisible had hurt William Snow cruelly, even while he despised himself for the feeling.

How mean even the best of us are occasionally in our thoughts! How we criticise others, and yet wince at hearing of the least criticism passed upon ourselves! We do it secretly, of course; but still we do it, and feel that so-and-so has not displayed the delicacy we should have expected in giving utterance to this or that remark. Also, we compare ourselves with another, and would blush a right celestial rosy red if Dr. Slade's "spirit pencils" could write down our thoughts in black and white and place them before us; for the mental scale that holds our neighbor is energetically kicking the beam, and we ourselves are seated, complacently smiling, in the corresponding one that drops heavily earthward.

"I am worthy."
"He is not worthy:"

this was the form of verb William Snow was unconsciously conjugating as he paced the damp, sticky pavements, and ran against people at the corners of streets, because his mind was too busy to look properly after his body.

All at once he awoke to the real nature of the train of thought into which a wounded *amour propre* had drifted him. He anathematized himself mentally as a prig of the first water, and called up the vision of a dear, troubled face, and two trustful violet eyes, tear-laden, raised in pretty, earnest pleading to his own.

He had promised to do all he could to win Guy's confidence and friendship, and his own "confounded selfishness" (so ran his thoughts) had made him false to the spirit of that promise even in the first half-hour after quitting the girl's presence.

She had forbidden him to take the picture home to-day: it was to be properly framed, and then Jim the faithful was to be despatched to Park Lane to fetch it.

Well, he would hang it up right over his writing-desk, just between the windows, so that whenever he looked up from his work it would remind him who and what he was, and that he might aspire to be her slave, and in some sort her guardian and her brother too; but nothing nearer and more dear. It would remind him, too, how far better fate had ordered things for him than his own undisciplined, passionate heart could have done.

Meanwhile, he must see that his promise was fulfilled. He had made a boyish promise to Lilian Selwyn "long years ago" "to take care of her always," and that promise had been well redeemed — tried, indeed, "by fire." Let him see, then, that this second promise was as fully kept, in spite of the fiery trial of disappointed hopes, and the painful death of tender dreamings that should never become realities.

It was tiresome to have to go through all this argument with the monster self again; for as he listened to the story of Lilian's fears and anxieties about her lover, he had attained the platform of a high and noble disinterestedness; but that sharp reproof, that sneer at a heart that loved, perhaps "not wisely," but certainly "too well;" the idle, jesting tone that Guy had taken when Lilian spoke of her anxiety about him—these had hurt William Snow more than all the rest; not because he thought them intentionally cruel, but because they showed such an utter incapability of understanding aright the woman he loved.

And now, thinking it all over, William called to mind that Guy Tremlett had offered no explanation of his sudden and mysterious departure. He had found fault with Lilian for writing to Tremlett Court; he had not said that he had been there.

He looked ill and worn; more so than a man at his age ought to do. Was the knowledge Jim had gained the key to the whole matter? Had Guy Tremlett sought safety from temptation in flight?

"So few fellows would go to the devil if there was not some willing hand near to give them a push down hill!" thought William, looking back upon various experiences of his London life.

William Snow was no prig, no milksop, no Pharisee. If he had held aloof from the coarser temptations of life, it was because the love of one woman had been ever fresh and green in his heart, like that plant that keeps the water of a fountain bright and clear.

Failing these influences, failing the training of a simple-minded, God-fearing man, what was there to prevent him from having been as many of the men he saw about him?

The really pure and generous-minded are the last to cast a stone at others, and the first to hold out a hand to their weaker brethren. It is the questionable and the self-righteous who gather their garments about them, lest they should come in contact with the sad and the fallen. He turned distastefully from the thought of Guy's unworthiness, with no puritanical self-righteousness, but rather as seeing in him the future husband of a woman who was in his own loving estimation "far above rubies."

"I will let Pelham Pettigrew know that I cannot take a run northward just yet," he thought, as he turned into the Temple Cloisters. "I declare I feel as if I'd just been standing god-father to some one! Lilian's face was as solemn as a little judge when she made me 'promise and vow' to be that fellow's friend."

At the door of the chambers in Fig-tree Court stood Beams the jocund. His hair was rumpled up all over his head, and his eyes so wildly opened, it would not have surprised one to hear that he had seen a ghost.

"Please, sir, Mr. Pettingroo's bin 'ere; he says he wants to see you most pertickler."

"Oh, all right," said his master, passing on.

But Beams hadn't "said his say." He hurried a step or two, so as to come along-side his master, pulled the forelock of his hair in lieu of a cap, grinned, and ventured on the remark,

"Please, sir, he'd got his wig and gownd on."

"Had he? I dare say he came out of court. By-the-way, Beams," William added, as if the idea had just occurred to his mind, "I hope the toothache's all right again?"

I am happy to have to record that Beams blushed.

But, "Oh yes, thank you, sir," was what he said, and then he shook his head, and scratched his head, and finally snapped every individual joint on each hand after a fashion peculiarly his own when in any distress of mind.

"I won't never go for to deceive him no more," muttered Beams to himself; "there ain't no sort of credit in deceivin' a chap as is so easy took in. I really do think as the devil hisself can't be no wuss a pusson than Abrim Beams."

Mrs. Masher had seen the short interview between Beams and his master, and her mind reverted to the old subject of worldly gain.

"*Has* he rose yer wages?" she asked, softly, craning herself round Twigg's door-post to put the question.

Beams turned up his eyes till nothing but the whites were visible, and gently patted his pockets. Then, without a word, he swiftly departed, leaving the avaricious Masher munching her lantern jaws over the flavor of imaginary "siller."

As anxious to see Mr. Pettigrew as Mr. Pettigrew could be to see him, William hastened to the City chambers occupied by that great man. Mounting a flight of stairs, he entered a small square vestibule, having on either side doors, upon which were painted in white letters the names of eminent legal lights, each of which luminaries appeared to possess a knocker for his own separate and particular use.

After William had given a modest rap to the one that was labelled "Mr. Pelham Pettigrew, Q.C.," the door was cautiously opened about a quarter of a yard, and a tall, pale-faced young man, with spectacles and a squint, looked forth. He gazed with one eye down the staircase, and with the other into the visitor's face.

"Is Mr. Pettigrew in?" asked Mr. Snow.

"Yes, he *is* in, but he's engaged—a consultation, in fact," replied the other, mysteriously.

Now, William knew that a consultation with an eminent person like his friend the Q.C. was an important and solemn occasion, and one not to be lightly interrupted.

He was therefore about to say he would call again, and take his departure, when suddenly an inner door was flung impetuously open, and, with gown flung back and wig awry, the object of his inquiries stood revealed.

The pale young man with the defective vision shrunk back into a small chamber wherein he spent the main portion of his life, and bit the nib off a newly made pen in his embarrassment.

"Ha, Snow! thought it was you—come in; never mind what Mudge there says. As it's *you*, I'll break through business rules—ha! ha!"

By this time they were in the inner room, and Mr. Pettigrew had flung himself into an easy-chair, and resumed the occupation which Mr. Mudge had dignified by the name of a "consultation."

His legs crossed, his dapper little boots elevated in the air, his white hand curved into a focus tube, his head as well as his wig on one side, the great Q.C. was truly holding a "consultation;" but the "case" on which it was convened was one containing an exquisite female head by Greuze.

"There's a dainty little lady! Shouldn't mind meeting her 'coming through the rye'—eh?" said he, focusing the other eye by way of variety.

"Look at her lips—they seem to breathe! By Jove! I feel Shakspearian as I look at them. 'One kiss!—rubies unparagoned,' etc."

The picture-dealer, taking all these compliments to himself, bowed and smiled obsequiously.

"The light's wrong," suddenly cried Mr. Pettigrew, jumping up; "here, Mudge—Mudge!"

The depressed Mudge presented himself without delay, and tried to look as straight as he possibly could.

"Wheel that desk aside—there now, help Mr. Nathan to lift the case on to the table. Capital! Now, Snow, what do you say to that, eh?"

At this moment a violent knocking took place at the outer door.

"Mudge," said his master, mysteriously, "I can't see any one. Important consultation. Mind now, if it's that Breach of Promise again, kick him down-stairs."

"Yes, sir," said the long-suffering Mudge; and Mr. Pettigrew concentrated his attention on the picture.

"What a smile—eh, Snow? After all, there's *nothing* like a Greuze."

The day of De Hooghe and Rembrandt was past; the thrifty housewife and her broom would "go to the wall" (literally), and this dreamy, pensive girl would smile and blush, "first favorite" among Pelham's art beauties.

There was something in the pensive violet eyes of that pictured face, something in the sweetness of the delicate mouth, that touched a chord in William Snow's heart. It was just one of those chance likenesses that we often come across in art or in life: a glance, a smile that is a reflection of something graven on our hearts—something that seems familiar to us, and that we look at with a tenderness that is like borrowed light.

"You like it, Snow?" questioned Mr. Pettigrew, glancing up at the young lawyer's face—"seen some one like it once—eh?"

"It is a lovely picture; and you are right. I *have* seen some one like it."

"Rum-tum-ti-tay!" hummed the Q.C. to himself, regarding with affectionate eyes his own faultless boot, with its wonderful arched instep.

"Name your figure." This last observation was made to the insinuating Mr. Nathan, who thought it the correct thing to bow and smile each time he caught the eye of either of the two gentlemen, and consequently went through a good deal of exercise in that way.

Mr. Nathan rubbed his hands gently together, and named a figure.

Mr. Pettigrew pushed back his wig with an impetuous movement till the iron-gray crest liberated itself and stood defiantly on end.

"What!" he said, turning his piercing gray eyes upon the dealer, as though he were a mendacious witness who had just perjured himself. "*What* did you say?"

"Well, sir," replied Nathan, shivering, but still smiling bravely, "to *you*, being a customer, and so kind in saying a good word—"

"When I've been done myself, sir, I like to have a haul in another man's being done too—that's why I recommend your daubs," put in the intended victim.

This was of course a joke, so Nathan was bound to laugh; but his merriment sounded hollow, and his unwholesome complexion took a duller tinge as he named a slightly smaller sum than before.

"We can do it at that figure for *you*, sir," he said, cringingly, "because, you see, your name—"

"Yes, yes; I know. You can tell any lie, palm off any worthless daub upon a poor devil by telling him I gave four figures for its twin brother!—ha! ha! very good. 'What's in a name?'—a good deal's in a name. I'll give you a fair price for this bit of color, and my name into the bargain!"

Here he named a sum little more than half what had been Mr. Nathan's original proposal, and, without giving the dealer time to make a single objection, touched a hand-gong on the table at his elbow.

Mr. Mudge appeared, check-book in hand; his master wrote out a check for the amount, and bowed Mr. Nathan into the passage.

Then Mr. Pettigrew fell into raptures over his new acquisition.

"We'll take it with us to Hazlecroft. Mudge there is a capital hand at packing. I know the very nook where it shall hang. A perfect light, and just—"

"I'm really sorry," interrupted William, "but I find I can't get away from town just now."

Mr. Pettigrew's wig, which had been hanging down his back, here fell off. He stooped, raised it, and set it on a wig-stand, where it roosted nightly like a gigantic bird.

Then he looked his companion gravely in the face.

"Business, eh?"

William was a bad hand at subterfuge: a hot flush mounted to his brow as he answered,

"No; but I have made a promise that necessitates my remaining in town for the present."

The keen reader of human nature saw that this resolve was unassailable.

> "'This rock shall fly
> From its firm base as soon as I,'"

he said, laughing. "That's it—eh, Snow?"

"The quotation is an apt one," said William.

"But the trip is only postponed?"

"I hope so."

"Well, then, I sha'n't go myself. There's plenty to do here, if I choose to do it; and we'll wait till the pheasants are in trim to be touched up."

So this was decided upon, and William took his departure.

"So she's like that, is she?" muttered Pelham, looking intently at the soft, smiling face of the picture. "Then she's a devilish pretty woman. He takes the same interest in her as if she was 'a sister,' and makes her a promise that must needs keep him in town."

Then he chuckled to himself, and repeated the words as if arguing with an invisible opponent,

"A sister, a sister—quite, quite!"

Then he touched the gong for Mudge.

"Has that confounded Breach of Promise been?"

"Yes, sir."

"Did you—no, of course you didn't. Well, if he calls again, say I'm at home, and at liberty. The consultation is at an end—clients can be admitted."

CHAPTER XIX.

ON THE EDGE OF THE STORM.

THERE are times and seasons in the lives of most men, and most women, when perplexities and uncertainties gather round the mind, as mosquitoes hover round the traveller in the American woods. Like those noisy insects, too, each *pro* and *con*, each reason for, and each objection to, some particular line of conduct, lifts up a little irritating buzzing on its own account, and swells the general din.

It was thus with William Snow.

The knowledge of Guy Tremlett's wrong-doing seemed to oppress him as though it were a blot upon his own conscience. Lilian's confidence and trust in himself seemed outraged by this knowledge; a great dread of what the future might have in store for her was ever before his eyes; he wished that through some other than himself David Earle might learn the true character and past life of the man to whom he was about to intrust his darling's happiness. Then a sudden passionate longing that this might come about would lead him to bitter self-distrust lest any unacknowledged joy in the thought of Lilian, free Lilian, "not another's," but his to woo and win, might color his anxiety.

To a generous mind the position was a torturing one.

"If I had not learned to love her so well, the way would have been clear enough," he thought.

To keep watch and ward over himself as well as others, and to strive to fulfil his promise to Lilian in the matter of winning Guy's friendship, seemed the only things to be done at the present time. The future held unpleasant possibilities, and was best left alone. But, of course, no one ever *did* leave a thing alone because no good could be done by mentally dissecting it, and Mr. Snow was no exception to the rule.

Jim, watching his master with eyes rendered doubly sharp by self-reproach, noted how the bright, buoyant youthfulness that had been once so marked a characteristic both in look and manner had altogether died out.

From having been a man who looked even younger than his years, William Snow began to look like one whose youth had passed away, and carried with it some of life's sweetest illusions.

Now that Jim had learned to recognize the greatness of a nature more noble than his own, he would have gladly toiled all over London to save Guy Tremlett from harm. The strange fascination of tracking the man whom he believed to be his master's enemy—the spell that had led him, even after having gained knowledge enough for his purpose, to wander westward again and again, and make, if possible, "assurance doubly sure," had died away: the poor faithful heart had recognized the truth that forgiveness, not approval, had been the reward of all his unwearied search after evil. After the morbid fashion of temperaments such as his, he magnified his own vileness, until in his own eyes he walked the earth with the brand of Cain upon his brow. Day by day his cheek grew more hollow, his eyes more deeply sunken beneath their shaggy brows. Beams heard him muttering to himself oftener than ever, and on reporting this fact to Masher, received an unhesitating assurance that constant intercourse with "the deil" was the cause of this peculiarity; also, that the cadaverous appearance of the clerk was the result of this Satanic possession.

Firmly believing all these statements, Beams began to "make tracks" if he chanced to encounter Mr. Dutton after dusk.

The sketch in water-colors had duly arrived in Fig-tree Court, and now hung just above William's writing-table.

No heavenly faced Madonna ever drew more adoring looks from devout Catholic than that simple picture from Jim.

If it served to remind William Snow from whence he had risen—if it set before him, in plain unvarnished fact, the wide social difference between himself and Lilian Selwyn—to Jim it was the dearest record of the tie that bound master and servant in one common bond.

I doubt much if there is any barrier of restraint that will resist a persevering, patient, determined effort to overcome it; at all events, opportunity must be wanting if the siege is unsuccessful.

William set himself to win Guy Tremlett; he overcame whatever aversion had once existed in his own mind towards him; he went to Park Lane at such times as he knew Guy would be there; he tried to stifle all remembrance of Jim's nightly wanderings and their results, and to silence the clamor of his own misgivings.

Was it not reward enough to see the happiness written on Lilian's face, as she watched the growth of a better understanding between the two men? All the soft, bright color returned to her cheek, smiles dimpled round her lips, and her eyes lost their dreamy sadness. She always felt so safe herself with William in every trouble and difficulty, that she was sure Guy would be safe in his hands too.

Whatever had been wrong, whatever had been troubling Guy, seemed to her to have passed away; and it spoke volumes for the delicate calibre of this girl's mind that no petty feminine curiosity mingled in her anxiety about him. "Perhaps," she thought, "Guy has told William all about it, and William has made it all right."

But the thought never entered her mind of questioning William, and she was content to let "it" stand for an unknown source of restless dissatisfaction.

Some very pleasant evenings were spent during this time in the house in Park Lane, and people would loiter in the street outside to catch the soft, sweet rise and fall of Guy's voice, as he sung the tender refrain of some Neapolitan serenade, or rendered with exquisite passion and pathos the sterner music of Beethoven and Mozart.

Uncle David would testify his enjoyment of the music by gently beating time upon the arm of his chair; and sometimes Lilian's fingers trembled with delight so that she could hardly play the accompanying chords, and found the notes but little help, because her eyes grew too misty to see them.

And William, seeing her happiness, rejoiced in it with an honest sympathy that he thanked God for having made possible to him.

Just when the sky seemed so cloudless, just when Lilian's heart knew nothing but peace and love and fond content, the shadow of coming sorrow arose.

Not to her eyes; no, thank God! William saw those dear eyes were still unclouded by any suspicion of the truth.

It came about in this way:

Guy was expected to dinner, and did not come. So the trio that had once formed the home-circle of Winstowe dined together, Lilian's face a trifle grave, because of the empty chair beside her.

Late in the evening, while the soft summer gloaming still asserted its sway, and Lilian, having refused to let prosaic lamp-light shut out the dreamy dusk, nestled at Uncle David's knee, Guy came in.

The scent of a cigar in the wide balcony outside told of William's whereabouts; but Guy had not been many minutes in the room before the cigar was flung into the masses of the Virginian creeper below, and with a grave anxiety upon his face, which was fortunately not very clearly visible in the faint, fading light, William entered the room and took his stand by Lilian's side.

The girl was sitting on a low chair, her hands folded on her knee, and Guy, standing before her, was speaking rapidly, and in a higher voice than was usual for so polished a man of society. He was recounting his evening's enjoyment; he had met a friend, a "capital fellow," and this friend had insisted upon him going to dine with him at the Wellington.

"He's a capital fellow, is Hetherington; used to be in the Guards. I haven't seen him since he and I spent a month at Monaco, two years ago. A jolly month, too! There are worse places than Monaco, I can tell you, Lillie, for a fellow to amuse himself in—"

Here the thought of the figure Uncle David would cut at that prince of gambling haunts overcame Guy altogether. He laughed long and loud; but as no one knew what was the source of his merriment, no one joined in it.

"Well, well, if you met an old friend, I suppose the child must forgive you for deserting us, eh?" said Uncle David, laying a hand on the girl's shoulder.

"Lilian's struck mum to-night, I think; and Snow here hasn't much to say either; it's like coming to a Quaker's meeting after—"

But, heated by wine as Guy Tremlett was, he stopped short here.

The gathering he had left was, perhaps, not exactly one to be minutely described in the presence of Lilian Selwyn.

A man's friends could not feel any very great satisfaction in knowing he frequented the Wellington, which was a sort of outside planet, revolving in a wider orbit than the large military clubs and their civilian congeners.

The Wellington was open later (or rather earlier) than any other club in town; and more money changed hands there in one night than in all the others put together during a week.

Admission to its roll was easy; and its rules were so elastic that it required a man to be a very heinous offender indeed to overstretch their limits.

Certain men, well advanced in years, mostly ex-defenders of their country, and of either a very shabby or very flashy appearance, were regular *habitués* at this club, and these worthy men *never got drunk.* Indeed, their sobriety was edifying in the extreme.

The fact was, they were always sober, in order to make the best of men who were generally drunk.

To this latter class belonged Hetherington, the "capital fellow" whom Guy had met that afternoon, and with whom he had dined at this club; subsequently a game or two at écarté had been played, to a running accompaniment of "brandy-and-soda," and so fast and furious had been the "pace," that, considering all things, it was marvellous Guy had ever appeared in Park Lane at all.

However, as we have seen, he arrived in their midst, and now William's mind was exercised as to the best and most prompt means of getting him out of Lilian's presence. For every moment his hilarity became more pronounced, his voice louder, his words more inexpedient.

A less perfectly simple and unsuspecting creature than Uncle David would have guessed the truth at once; a less perfectly innocent woman than Lilian would have readily seen through that wild elation of spirits.

As it was, her lover's noisy merriment depressed her, though she could hardly have told why. She could not have given a reason for shrinking from the sight of his perfect physical beauty, heightened as it was by a flush upon his face, and a strange brightness in his dark flashing eyes: yet she was glad when William said good-night, and proposed that Guy should walk part of the way home with him; and she was glad when Guy, after one quick, questioning look at the other's face, assented to this suggestion.

Once out in the street, William slipped his arm beneath his companion's. Not, however, that Guy needed any guidance; he was not drunk, only on the pleasant road to that Avernus.

"I promised those fellows, you know, to go back to the Wellington," said Guy.

William stopped a moment to strike a vesuvian, and light a cigar.

"I wouldn't go back, Tremlett, if I were you," he said, very deliberately, and once more taking Guy's arm.

"Why not?" returned the other, sharply. "D—n it, Snow, you're not coming the Puritan, I hope, and going to preach. I won't stand—"

"Still," continued William, as quietly as before, "I wouldn't go, if I were you."

"What the devil do you mean? Why shouldn't I please myself?"

"For Lilian's sake, I think."

William looked straight ahead as he said this, carefully avoiding even a glance at his companion.

If he had watched the man, to see how his words told, defiance would have arisen like a giant in his might, would have gleamed in the depths of the dark eyes, and been written in every line of mouth and brow.

Presently they came to the turning of Clarges Street, where Guy had rooms.

"Good - night," he said, holding out a hot, feverish hand to the other's grasp.

Then he sauntered slowly away, and William heard him humming softly the refrain of a certain barcarole,

"Te voglio ben assai, ma tu non pensai di me."

It was one that Lilian loved, and one that her lover used to sing to her more often than any other.

Then William knew that the battle was won, and that the "capital fellows" at the Wellington would see Guy Tremlett no more that night.

Hitherto his energies had been concentrated on the difficulties of the hour; the peril of Guy appearing in the presence of Uncle David and his child when the old failing had gained supremacy over him, had, for the time being, put aside all other thoughts. Once, however, alone in the quiet of his own home, other fears, other perplexities, crowded in upon his mind.

This last unpleasant adventure had rendered his position still more difficult than before. That Guy loved Lilian, he had no doubt—the words "for her sake" had been a silken cord strong enough to keep him back from further wrong; but he was weak—weak in resolve.

The spell of the gambler's delight in the wild excitement of play still swayed his soul.

And as he thought these things, a bitter sorrow filled his heart—sorrow for the gentle, loving woman who trusted him, and yet whom he was so powerless to shield.

"I saved her from the fire that would have burned her body; I cannot save her from the fire of pain that would consume her heart! Oh, my God! comfort her in the sorrow that is coming—that must come!"

For he saw no escape.

It was suffering—keen, cruel suffering—for the girl, either way.

To learn her lover's unworthiness, to feel his shame as her own, perhaps to have to tear her heart from his; or, on the other hand, to become his wife.

William Snow drew a long, deep, shuddering breath, as he thought of his darling passing through the ordeal of a martyrdom such as that would be.

For he knew how Lilian would meet such a fate; he knew how far more keenly than another woman she would suffer in her husband's wrongdoing; he knew that, once Guy's *wife*, she would cling to him through the evil as through the good; that she would hide her pain even from the eyes that watched over her most tenderly; that she would make no sign, and thus in silence and steadfast endurance that gentle and all-womanly heart would break!

"Better the pain of knowing the truth *now*, better the wrench of giving back her troth-plight *now*, than a life in the future lived 'to such a bitter end.'"

Thus pondered the man who loved Lilian Selwyn as his own soul.

And yet, just because he so loved her, was the task of unveiling the unworthiness of the man she loved better than himself unspeakably distasteful to him.

"I will go and speak quietly to Uncle David to-morrow," was William's resolve as he went to bed that night.

"I will wait until one more day's reflection has helped me to weigh well the words that I shall say," was his decision when that morrow came.

He kept away from Park Lane.

How should he meet those grave, sweet eyes? how should he hold that trustful hand in his, knowing the task that he had set himself to do?

I can safely say that, at this time, the thought of Lilian free from the tie that now bound her to Guy Tremlett, the thought of that little hand once more unadorned by the diamonds that were his love-gage, held no hopeful thought, however secret, for William Snow.

The truth that no hatred is more deadly than that which rages in the heart of a woman towards the being who has hunted down or injured the man whose name she bears, is also true, in a lesser degree, of the resentment she will lavish on the enemy of her lover.

William therefore knew full well that to bring Guy's sins to the knowledge of Uncle David was to put a barrier of aversion between his own and Lilian's heart—a barrier so strong that years of patient kindness might hardly suffice to break it down.

Twice only had he met Mrs. Tremlett during her stay in town. But the twice had been enough to create in his mind a dislike to the handsome mistress of Tremlett Court—a dislike that, at the time, had seemed unreasonable to himself.

He understood it better now.

That woman with the dark, weary eyes, and the set, determined, sullen mouth, knew all the secrets of her son's life: she clung to Lilian as the possible instrument of his salvation.

If she had been a different woman, William might have made some appeal to her better feelings, and laid before her the pitifulness of sacrificing one so pure and trustful; but his own clear, penetrating sense of the fitness of things told him that to appeal to *that* woman would be like dashing one's self against a rock.

There were two things in life that Mrs. Tremlett loved—herself and her son.

Herself first, or she would not have trained him up in indolent and ruinous indulgence, because to correct the boy would have been disagreeable, and an effort; him next, because he was in some sort a reflection of herself.

At one time a mad jealousy of the girl Guy loved had torn her very soul. Hitherto the creatures of his fancy, the victims of his evil passions, had been passing influences that could not clash with her own supreme reign; but a wife was another thing altogether. You could never gauge the irresistible power those low - voiced, soft-eyed, fragile-looking women manage to gain over a man.

Yet the mother — misguided, undisciplined, even in the best feelings of her nature — beat down this jealous fiend that would have possessed her, because she realized that in marriage lay the only hope of her darling's social redemption.

It may seem horrible to say that a secret joy ran riot in her heart as she watched Guy's devotion to his new toy, and thought of the suffering that must inevitably one day be the lot of the violet-eyed child whose innocent mind could not grasp the idea of what the life of such a man as Guy had been: and yet such was the case.

Ponsonby, that strange, colorless, silent woman, who was like the shadow of her imperious mistress, now and again heard Mrs. Tremlett laugh to herself, and wondered what thoughts had power to cause such solitary and weird rejoicing.

It was the possible complications of the future that amused Mrs. Tremlett thus.

Yet she would have cast out of her path by any means, lawful or unlawful, whatever obstacle had now come in the way of Guy's marriage.

Tremlett Court, that vast domain for which, in the days of her youth and beauty, she had sold herself into a horrible bondage, must have an heir; it would have been unbearable to her pride of heart that those broad lands should pass away into the hands of people who were strangers and aliens to herself; and if Guy died childless, such would be the case.

Lilian therefore had a certain value in her eyes as the possible mother of the heir to Tremlett Court.

She would gladly have had the marriage hurried on at once: the sooner Guy was in possession of his new toy, the sooner he would tire of it, and begin once more to return to the old confidential habits of allegiance to his mother. When an heir to the ancient house of Tremlett was born, she, the mother who had reared Guy so successfully, would take the management of the child; it would be easy to set aside a mother who would be little more than a child herself; besides, Guy and his wife should live at the Court—on that she was determined.

But in these two particulars—the hasty marriage, and the permanent home of the young couple with herself—Mrs. Tremlett found an unexpected and quite immovable obstacle in David Earle. His gentle, genial, simple manners had led her, early in their acquaintance, to rate his firmness of character and perspicuity very low—in fact, to "write him down" in the tablets of her mind much under the same uncomplimentary title as that which Dogberry so hotly aspired to. But for once Mrs. Tremlett was deceived: Uncle David's placid manner, his simple, straightforward reasoning, was like a feather-bed to a bullet as opposed to her own imperious will.

"Let the young folks get to know a little of each other," he said, smiling as genially as though he were saying the thing of all others Mrs. Tremlett most delighted to hear; "the acquaintance has been a short one, dear madam, and they have much to learn—much to learn. Marriage is a long journey, and it's well to start with some knowledge of your travelling companion. When the spring comes round again, we'll talk about setting the cathedral bells going, but not yet—not yet."

"I shall soon talk the old man round," said the mother, confidentially, to the son.

And she talked a good deal, but she did not alter David Earle's determination. His father and mother (so he told his secretly wrathful but outwardly calm listener) had been plighted to each other five long years, and not thought it too long. He would not part with his little lass until after another Christmas had come round. When the spring flowers were out in bloom again, then Guy should take his bride from Winstowe.

On this ensued a discussion as to the whereabouts of the new home.

"They will always be welcome at Winstowe, and at Tremlett Court too, I am sure; but let them have a 'bield o' their ain—ain—ain,' as our Scotch neighbors say—a nest where none other but themselves claim a permanent place. Man and wife are best left to themselves, dear madam," said Uncle David, still with the same radiant countenance, and as innocent as the daisies on his own lawn of all the plotting and scheming of the woman before him.

A cutting sarcasm that unrolled itself like a serpent from beneath the lady's tongue, and was intended to strike home—a sneer at his long bachelor life and necessarily scant experience of matrimony—glanced off harmlessly, met, as it was, with a sudden sad look upon the gentle face, a reverential drooping of the head.

"I had my days of hope once, dear lady; but God saw fit to lay them to rest in a girl's grave, and they never waked to life again."

For once the woman of the world repented her of hard words aimed at so true a heart. She left town without carrying the day in either one point or the other on which her heart was set, and Ponsonby had a bad time of it when mistress and maid settled down at the Court.

Guy, however, had proved more pliant to her will than David Earle; for though he had, to her intense though hidden indignation, yielded in the matter of an immediate marriage, and sided with the enemy in the question of Lilian and himself living under the ancestral roof, a promise had been wrung from him by passionate entreaty, combined with certain threats never meant to be carried out, and Guy had pledged himself to avoid the sin that had so "easily beset him" in the past. How he kept this pledge, and the net of perplexities that his unfaithfulness had woven about William, we already know. From these perplexities had now, however, been born a determination, and William had resolved to carry that determination out. Yet he shrunk from the task before him, as from some ordeal of physical pain.

He could bear to see the woman he loved shrink from him as from her lover's detractor; but the thought of her suffering—the suffering that was inevitable, and from which he could not shield her—that thought unmanned him.

Pondering gravely on these things, and finding small comfort in his own thoughts, William Snow was giving a very divided attention to a review over which his pen was oftener poised than doing much active work, when a light knock at the room door was followed by the entrance of Guy Tremlett.

Paler than usual, and with an unsteadiness about the lips that not even the heavy mustache could wholly conceal, he came in in his usual indolent fashion; but in his dark eyes was a strange, unwonted expression, a look of appeal that smote William to the heart, and for the moment gave him an unpleasant sensation of guilt.

CHAPTER XX.

BOUND DOWN.

WHEN you are mentally engaged in arguing yourself into a conviction that it is your plain and positive duty to put an unpleasant spoke in some individual's wheel of life, nothing can be more trying or less welcome than that individual's sudden and unexpected appearance. There is a disagreeable suggestion of electro-biology, psychic force, and other objectionable and mysterious agencies about it, that is the reverse of agreeable.

Has some subtle intuition of the evil plotting in your mind drawn him with irresistible power to your presence, to try the spell of eye and hand and voice, and thus unnerve your arm to strike the meditated blow? Does he want to set your tongue stammering and your voice failing, when you would try to speak the words that shall do him hurt?

Looking at Guy's altered face, noting the trembling of the hand that had for a moment held his own cordially as though it were that of a trusted friend, William was conscious of a sudden flash of thanksgiving in that, as yet, he was innocent of having carried his resolves into action.

"Faultlessly perfect in every detail of dress, faultlessly refined in manner and voice, faultlessly handsome in physical beauty, dowered with a subtle, winning charm which few men, and still fewer women, could resist—"

Thus did William Snow take mental stock of the man who lounged in a chair opposite to him —the man who loved Lilian, and whom Lilian loved.

"And if so, what wonder?" was the ultimatum of his thoughts. "What wonder? since even I, knowing as I do his hidden inner life, and resenting his foulness for her sake—if even I feel the power of his influence, and rejoice, in spite of myself, at having as yet said no word to injure him."

"I say, what a cadaverous-looking fellow that clerk of yours is, Snow!" said Guy, pulling out his cigar-case (a pretty trifle embroidered by Lilian's hand), preparatory to "lighting up," as he called it. "When I asked him if you were at home, as I overtook him in the outer court, he looked at me as though he rather thought I was concealing a dagger, Spanish fashion, in my waistcoat, with intent to do you 'grievous bodily harm;' he's quite a Quasimodo in modern life, and only wants little Esmeralda and the goat to be perfect. I beg your pardon, old fellow," he added, hastily, with a sudden remembrance of having heard the story of the hunchback clerk from Lilian and Uncle David. "He's an old chum or something, isn't he?"

"Yes," replied William. "We were boys together, and he has followed my fortunes; indeed, I don't think there could be any turn of fortune or misfortune in which he would not follow me, if I would let him."

"Ah, yes, I understand the kind of thing you mean; my mother has a maid, a woman like a sphinx, who would cheerfully be burned in her service, if such a sacrifice were called for." Here the speaker rose from his seat, and absently laying down his just-lighted cigar, and leaving it to smoulder on the mantel-shelf, strolled to the opposite side of the room, where the wall was formed of books piled in tiers one above another.

He made believe to examine the titles of one or two of these volumes, then came back to his old place, rested his arm on the corner of William's desk, and shaded his eyes with his hand.

"I'm not intruding upon business hours, I hope, eh, Snow?"

"No, certainly not; my day's work is nearly done—a pretty stiff one, too, it has been. The pace is always fast and furious as the long vac. draws near; but I must not complain: many men as young as I am in the law have to grumble at having no business at all to get through; not even such as preparing cases for other people."

"Well, I'm glad I'm not *de trop*—"

Then Guy was silent a moment, and gave a quick, questioning glance at his companion.

"Have you any guess, Snow, as to what brought me here in this unceremonious fashion?"

"Not the faintest."

"Well—I've come to 'make a clean breast of it.' You did me a good turn last night; I was a beast, Snow, a beast, to be led by Hetherington; but I tell you what it is, you fellows who have ruled your lives in a straight line don't know how hard temptation pulls—"

"Temptation comes to us all, my dear fellow, one way or the other: after all, it is the influences that surround a man that make him what he is. I, for one, dare not place myself upon a higher level than another, just because he yields to what I have never had to resist."

"You're a right good fellow, and I want to tell you 'the truth, the whole truth, and nothing but the truth.'"

William Snow rose, and stood looking out into the gardens that were already growing dusk and shadowy in the fading light.

He was agitated beyond all power of concealment; his voice sounded full of pain and dread.

"You had better think twice before you make a confidant of me, Tremlett: I am not the man —there are reasons—"

People said that Mr. Snow, of the Inner Temple, promised to be gifted with exceptional eloquence one day, but certainly the talent of fluency failed him now.

"I know there are reasons. I am not blind," began Guy; but he was interrupted.

"For God's sake, tell me what you mean!"

"I mean that I know we both love the same woman."

Silence, broken only by the deep breathing of the man who stands by the window with folded arms and set lips.

"If you have guessed my secret, you should respect it. I will not deny the truth of what you say. I had thought the knowledge of it known only to myself and one other."

"Not Lilian?"

"No, thank God, not Lilian."

"Snow," said Guy, earnestly, lifting his dark eyes, full of pleading and regret to the other's face, "I sometimes wish that I had never met, had never known, that poor child. If Lilian and I had never met, she would have come to love you in time; it would be a much better fate for her to become your wife than mine."

"Was it true that she would have loved me in the end?" thought his listener; and a little pang, that contracted his heart at the thought, told him his love was not yet purged of all taint of self.

It was the strangest thing to William Snow to listen to the pathos of Guy's words.

Hitherto he had thought of this man as a mere idol of society, a creature who had no thoughts, no aspirations, no regrets beyond the mere satisfying of his animal instincts; now he was learning the lesson life teaches many of us—namely, that, however fallen, however degraded a human creature may be, still beneath the slime and mire on the surface is to be found the trace of good, the faint, lingering reflection of the great truth—that *in his own image* God created man.

He recognized the possibilities for good that were latent in Guy's faulty nature, but which had been dwarfed and warped by evil training and bad companionship. It was as though from behind the mask of the man he was, looked forth for a moment the man he might have been.

"You say I should respect your secret," at length continued Guy. "I do respect it; and, more than that, the knowledge of it makes me come to you with more perfect trust. I know that, *for Lilian's sake*, you will—"

It was surely something very like a sob that broke William's voice as he hurriedly gave a hot assurance of his willingness to hold out a hand to this man who was the accepted lover of the woman he loved.

"I'm a man of many friends, Snow, and yet among them all there isn't one who would not sooner give me a push downward than a pull upward. I've had my own way all my life, and my own way has been a bad one; no one ever said a faithful word of warning to me. I have gone blindly on from bad to worse; even my—"

But here he was suddenly silent, and bit his lip as a man who feels he has uttered a word too much. For how could he speak against the woman who bore him?

Yet William knew that the wanting word was "mother"—knew, in one flash of thought, that his own estimate of that heavy-eyed, sullen-lipped woman had hit very near the mark—knew that Guy Tremlett had been worse, a thousand times worse, than motherless.

"I fancied, when — when Lilian was my promised wife—"

"Do not hesitate to speak plainly," said William, "from any idea of giving me pain. Whatever my foolish hopes and dreams may once have been, you must remember they had not much solid foundation to go upon. Even had she—had Lilian never known and never loved you, there are social distinctions that would have stood between us. I dare say at times my fancy has overstepped them, but in my saner moments I have always recognized their existence."

A glance at the picture hanging between the windows—the picture, drawn by Lilian's hand, of the little tattered wanderer in the snow—the picture of which Guy Tremlett knew the strange, pitiful story—gave significance to his words—words spoken with the quiet and noble dignity of a pride that scorned to shrink from the plain, unvarnished utterance of a truth, however bitter.

Silence was the most fitting tribute to this nobility of candor, and, feeling this intuitively,

Guy let the subject drop, and passed on to his own personal experiences, past and present—his own fears and anxieties for the future.

It was a dark story to listen to, this laying bare of a life's wrong-doing, and at first William shrunk from hearing it with an acuteness of pain that almost betrayed him into irritable intolerance.

As Guy went on—as he spoke of the struggles and longings towards a better and purer life that had arisen in his heart—as he told of self-abasement in the presence of Lilian's innocent truth, of the loathing of past degrading influences when compared with her sweet, womanly refinement, all the generosity of William's nature was aroused. He began to feel as though his hand clasped that of one who was sinking in the deep waters of sin, and who might be saved by the firm, helpful hold of one stronger than himself—saved *for her*, and in the end made worthy of her love.

"It is strange you should have come to me and told me all this, Tremlett," said William, feeling, as he looked back upon the resolves of the last two days, as if they were phantoms seen through the mist of many years of existence.

"I am the creature of impulse; I came on the impulse of a moment's repentance," answered Guy. "My whole life has been without ballast, and without aim or end, and you are the only man I have ever known whom I felt to be stronger and better than myself. I disliked you once because I was forced to feel this."

William smiled.

"Perhaps our aversion was mutual."

"And yet you are too generous, I know, to have been jealous of me."

"Few men are above jealousy; still I hardly think I should have felt as I did, had I been convinced you were worthy of the dearest, sweetest, truest woman that ever drew breath."

"By Heaven, you're right there!" broke in Guy; "I am not worthy to kiss the ground her little foot has pressed! I know it in my better moments, Snow; but when the raging devil gets hold of me—that horrible, irresistible craving for the old excitements, that eats into a man's very heart—I forget; and then others try to get hold of me and lead me on. Once already in my life I have been mad—mad with drink—"

For a moment his voice failed, and his listener, gleaning more and more the bitter truth of what influences were at work urging on the mother to sacrifice Lilian to the chance of her son's salvation, could find just then few words to answer.

"I must tell you," went on the poor fellow, after a moment's struggle with himself; "it will do me good to have it all out; and for her sake you will help me to make the future more worthy of her, and of myself. It was down at the Court; no one, not even the servants, ever knew; no one but my—mother—and that shadowy creature, Ponsonby: they gave out that I had the fever, and in one of the upper rooms, shut off by double doors—a room where tradition says a mad Tremlett died by his own hand, the two women nursed me through it. Think of it, what it must have been! Two women alone, hearing the ravings of a poor mad wretch—striving with their poor strength to hold down hands that would have torn—"

The sweat stood out in beads upon his brow; his eyes looked as full of fear as though he saw before him the dreadful scenes he was describing re-enacted in some weird, mental fantasy; his lips worked nervously, yet seemed losing the power of coherent speech.

"Hush!" said William, authoritatively, "say no more of these past troubles; let the dead past lie, Tremlett; cast it behind you; resolve to look steadily onward. No man ever yet retrieved a past that he suffered himself to dwell upon."

"'It is never too late to mend,' eh?—that's what you mean?" put in the other, with a faint smile. "Well, I thought so too once; but there's a devil within one stronger than I thought."

"There's a God above one, stronger than man or devil either."

The simple, manly expression of dependence on a higher aid than that of any mere human strength sounded strangely in the ears of one whom no hand had ever yet led even one single step heavenward; to whom no tongue had ever spoken of the high and holy influences that can mould man's life after the divine pattern of the God-man, Christ.

There is ground too sacred to be intruded upon in the pages of a story such as this. We who know what the training of William Snow's life had been, and the simple, faithful, God-fearing life of the man who had been to him more than ever father was to son, may well imagine how the precious herbs of healing garnered up in boyish years, and held sacred still in the days of manhood, were opened out in all the sweetness of their heavenly balm and consolation.

Honest, manly, straightforward words of warning were spoken; encouragement and sympathy, such as one human heart can bestow upon another in time of need, were given freely; and Guy, with that elastic rebound from depression which was a characteristic of his impulsive nature, began to take a more cheerful view of life and its possibilities.

"Well, now you know all, and what a weak fellow I am, what do you think of me taking a run in Charley Bolton's yacht for a couple of months?"

"I think you could do nothing better," said William, decidedly; "you look as if a brisk seabreeze would do you all the good in the world."

"So it will. I shall come back as fresh as a rose—*start fresh*, you know—turn over a new leaf, and all that sort of thing."

"God send it may be so, for your own sake, Tremlett, and *for hers!* By-the-way, the poor child will hardly like your going—"

As he spoke he had a vision of the dear eyes he loved growing suddenly misty with tears, of a childlike mouth trembling with the knowledge of Guy's intended absence.

"If I tell her it is for my good that I should go, and if you endorse the bill (your word is a sort of complete gospel to Lilian), she will rest content, though her dear little face will grow sad over it, I dare say; she is such a loving darling!"

"She is a woman 'in whom there is no guile,' and whose nature is pure and true as crystal: she will be faithful to you through 'evil report and good report.' May God help you to spare her from sorrow!"

"Amen to that! My dear Snow, there never was a fellow so full of good intentions as I am! When I first learned to love that girl, and found she loved me, I would have defied the devil himself to lead me into the old bad ways! I promised my mother not to touch a bit of painted pasteboard, not to lift my elbow—in fact, to be a respectable member of society; and then I broke the promise, and when the bout was over, cut away from the sight of Lillie's face, for fear her eyes should drag the truth from me."

"I'm glad Mrs. Tremlett is so anxious—" began his listener, with a sudden qualm of self-reproach for past harsh judgment.

"Oh, my mother would pawn the Tremlett diamonds to see me settled down in life! You see, if there's no heir to Tremlett Court—"

William started up, crossed the room rapidly, opened the door, and looked out into the passage.

"What is it?—what's the matter?" said Guy.

"I thought I heard some one—it might have been some one wanting me."

"It might have been a ghost!" laughed the other. "Why, you're as white as a sheet, Snow!"

The room had grown dusky while the two men were talking, and now Guy could see the pale face of his companion distinct against the gloom.

"I am rather done up," said William. "I have had a stiffish time of it lately;" and he passed his hand wearily across his brow.

"And I've been bothering you with all my nonsense! Well, I don't think you'd mind, if you knew what a relief it is to have told some one all about it. It will make things ever so much easier, to know you're hoping that I shall jog along straight. I shall write to you while I'm away, and at Christmas we shall foregather at the old place."

"At Winstowe?"

"Yes. What a jolly place it is! far the most comfortable wigwam I know. Why, there's a chair in the smoking-room that beats any chair I know into fits—not excepting, mind you, the Wellington, or any other club in town; it's a regular Sleepy Hollow!"

How strangely the man's sensuous, self-indulgent nature came out even in a trifle like this! The pleasure of the passing hour was the ruling passion—if anything so paltry deserves the name—of Guy Tremlett's life. To walk along life's way, and gather the flowers as he passed; to revel in their perfume and their beauty, and then to cast them aside, and seek fresh blossoms to replace them—this was his idea of happiness!

"Unstable as water, thou shalt not excel."

The old vivid description of a vacillating, undisciplined man came into William's mind as he looked at the handsome head thrown back against the crimson-covered chair, just where the faint lingering light caught the glossy rippled hair and soft dark eyes. Guy's serious fit was over; like a child "tired of being good," he began to weary of what he graphically designated to himself "sober yarns."

"What sort of fellow is this Bolton, with whom you are going on this cruise?" asked William, searching about for matches, and turning the gasalier towards him, ready for lighting.

"Oh! steady as old Time without his scythe, and nothing to amuse himself with but his hourglass; smokes like a chimney, and warranted free from any other vice. Charley's idea of perfect bliss is to lie on his back on the deck of the *Sea-star*, as tight a little vessel as ever put to sea, and gaze at the stars through a cloud of A 1 cavendish."

Here, the matches having been found, the gas suddenly flared up, and displayed Mr. Tremlett in the act of stifling a prolonged yawn.

"You're not coming up to Park Lane to-night, then?" he said, recovering himself, pitching the long-since-discarded cigar out of the window, and lighting another.

William touched a formidable pile of papers that lay upon the desk, still to be copied out.

"This doesn't look much like going anywhere."

"Well, no," said Guy, "confound it! What a d—d infernal nuisance it must be to have to do what you don't like!"

Guy Tremlett, you see, was of that peculiar class of men, not very rare in the higher ranks of society, who, in the presence of the gentler sex of their own class, are the perfection of refinement and "good form," *jusqu'au bout des ongles;* but whose polish is, after all, but veneer; for, once away from the restraint of conventional proprieties, it drops from them like a mask, and the true man stands revealed.

The lips beneath Guy's heavy mustache, the lips that could murmur sweet words of tenderness in Lilian's ear, that could troll the refrain of a passionate Southern love-song in tones of "linked sweetness long drawn out," could also tell the broadest and foulest "good thing" at the mess-table or in the club-room, and could utter the deepest oaths, and soil themselves with the coarsest *double-entendre*, when fitting occasion offered. Some of the most charming men of society have this "reverse side" to their characters; a peculiarity which suggests the well-known saying about the "cloud with a silver lining;" only in this case the electro-plate is *outside*, and the lining is the shady part of the affair.

"By Jove! there's that uncanny familiar of yours doing sentry below there," said Guy, glancing through the open window.

Yes, Jim was wandering aimlessly about Fig-tree Court, too restless to set to any work, too beset with vain imaginings as to what the long interview in his master's room might mean, to do anything but roam here and there like a goblin shadow.

Was some fresh trouble coming to the man whom he loved with a love "passing the love of women?" On what errand had that soft-voiced man, the "gentleman" who haunted places of evil repute, and came out into the streets drunk, come to the quiet court in the City?

How Jim hated—yes, in spite of the experience of the past—*hated* his smooth words, and the gleam of the big diamond on his long white hand! How he loathed each particular sign of wealth and prosperity in the man who had stolen the light from his master's life! It was all very fine for the white-headed old priest in the little church—that hallowed spot of rest in the restless, bustling City—to cry aloud against those who harbored vengeance in their hearts; but what did *he* know about it, after all? Had *he* ever loved any one as Jim loved the old playmate whose voice had soothed his pain in the days long past? Had *he* ever seen some alien hand lay cruel hold upon the fairest flower that grew in a man's pathway, tear it up, and fling it, withered and dying, at his feet?

More than once during the last few weeks Jim had stolen of a Sunday evening into the little church; he had listened to the rise and fall of the litanies, and the voices of the choristers chanting sweet antiphons of praise; but the old spirit of humility and faith was no longer in the heart of the listener, and so the holy sounds found there no echo.

"If you were a different fellow, Snow, I should fancy you were glad to get me out of the way," said Guy, with an uneasy laugh, as he was about to go. "As it is, I know you will be true as steel."

His hearer flushed hotly for a moment, then, looking him straight in the eyes, he said, sternly,

"I have always been true to you, *and to myself*, Tremlett—God forbid I should ever be otherwise!—but, since you have given me your confidence, it is best that I should guard against even a shadow of distrust. I shall start next week for the North, and spend some time with my friend, Pelham Pettigrew. When you and I 'foregather,' as you say, at Winstowe, we will travel there together."

Before the grander, greater nature, the lesser one felt some shame.

"I was only jesting," said Guy, flipping the ashes from the end of his cigar—*pour se donner de contenance*. "I trust you fully, Snow: I have proved it by the confidences I have given to you to-night."

"You have; they and you are safe with me, Tremlett."

Then the two men shook hands and parted.

"Good-night," said Guy, as he passed the figure of the clerk standing outside the door below.

Jim's distorted form cast a weird shadow on the flagged court; his deep-set eyes looked up at the speaker's face, his hand touched his hat in respectful salutation, but by no single word did he return the greeting. He would wish his master's enemy no manner of good thing, not even a "good-night."

Softly whistling to himself, Guy Tremlett crossed the court, and passed along the cloisters out of sight.

Then Jim crept softly up the stairs.

The door of his master's room was unlatched: he pushed it softly open, and took a step or two in.

But he stopped, hesitated a moment, and stole away as silently as he had come.

William Snow's arms rested on the paper-strewn desk, his hands were clasped across his brow; he was too deep in thought to hear the light footfall of his faithful servant.

"I knew it! I knew it!" moaned Jim, safe in the refuge of his little room under the leads.

Meanwhile, in the light room below, William let bitter thoughts and ponderings have their way.

It had come to this.

Whatever came or went, he could do no more than stand by and commend his darling to God's keeping.

Guy Tremlett had given him a sacred trust; he had sought his counsel; as a weak and tempted man, he had stretched forth his hand to him for help; henceforth his tongue could utter no single word against one who had so trusted him—he was "bound down!"

CHAPTER XXI.

"OVER THE HILLS AND FAR AWAY."

OF all the seasons of the year, I love the autumn best.

It is by no means the most popular of the four seasons; spring has it, I think, in the way of being a general favorite, perhaps because the hopefulness it typifies is such a powerful element in the human heart.

Summer too, with its glorious high noon of beauty, queens it right royally in the hearts of the children of men; and winter, with its long fireside evenings, and its Christmas and New-year's rejoicings, does not lack for votaries. In truth, I have met with only very few who chime in with my love for autumn.

It seems to many a sad season. "*Summer is ended*," is the burden of its song, and not all the beauty of the ripened grain, not all the dower of golden sheaves, not

"All sweet, holy thoughts supplied
By seed-time and by harvest-tide,"

can shut their eyes to the fact that the beauty of autumn is the beauty of something that says "passing away," and the brightness of its glowing colors are the death-robes of a dying year.

Well, well! *à chacun sa fantaisie*. *I* love the autumn best.

Is it, perhaps, because an English autumn seems to me as the faint reflection of the glorious Canadian "fall;" and so I love it, as we love some friend because in him we trace a chance likeness to one whom we have loved and lost?

Is it because the crisp, invigorating air, the rustle of the fallen leaves beneath my feet, and the faint, dawning tint of yellow or rose here and there among the trees call back the memories of a far-off land? because they bring back to me the gorgeous funeral pyres of the dying year in the glorious Western World—burning crimson, vivid flame-color, towering pyramids of burnished green and delicate golden brown, and over all this beautiful painted world the sunshine of a Canadian sky, and the soft plaintive chant of the American robin?

Is not the pictured memory a fair one? We are all more or less the children of association, *nous autres*, and a voice that finds an echo in past happy years is apt to be dear with a dearness other than its own.

Granted, then, that autumn hath charms—that after the heat, and the glow, and the languor of summer, it is refreshing to see the fern fronds begin to put on their yellow-brown jackets; and the hedge-berries grow ripe and red —where, with us, is she seen so fair as in the heart of the heather-clad hills?

At early morning a faint white mist, the veil of the virgin day as she comes forth to meet her bridegroom the sun, lies softly on the purple slopes, purple with a thousand, thousand tiny blossoms rich and ripe.

The shadows chase each other, wraith-like, over the hill-sides, and play a phantom game of hide-and-seek in every dell and fern-decked cranny in the rocks; herds of patient sheep stand ankle-deep in cool, sweet pasturage, and have no disturbing dreams of weary trampings on a dusty road that leads to the butcher's knife at last.

Birds toy with the ripening hips and haws, and sway themselves upside-down on lithe, slender branches, twittering wonderful stories to each other of all the brave delights that they have known during the summer that is drawing to its close.

The soft, round, compact bodies of the grouse push in and out of the knots and knolls of fragrant heather, and their pretty feathers make a soft *frou-frou* as they dart about in happy dalliance. Fortunately no one is there to hint that the twelfth is ominously near; so their content is undisturbed by visions of themselves and their companions, tied by the legs, hanging heads downward in the London poultry-shops, with blood-stained feathers, and poor dim, sightless eyes.

The grasses are all heavy with seed; the heather is in its fullest bloom; and as the sun rises higher and higher in the cloud-flecked sky, the uplands in the distance grow brown and purple, while here and there a turnip-field in bloom gleams like a sheet of gold.

Let us mount the steep hill-side, and from an eyrie in the craggy rocks glance round at the world below.

The sun now slopes towards the west; the birds have done swaying on the branches, and are gone to roost; the little grouse are nestled away securely in cosy nooks best known to themselves; and nature is very still. You can hear the sharp, imperious bark of the colly, as he flings himself off in mad pursuit after some rebellious sheep who objects to being penned in the fold, and rashly ventures on an independent ramble on her own account. Very quickly are her ambitious ideas quelled, and the colly brings her home to the flock in such haste, that in the swiftness of her flight she now and again leaps off all fours, and clears the heather as if she were a chamois.

We are so high up upon the hills now that all below us looks like some toy-picture; the sheep grow into little gray specks, and the cottages here and there are mere flecks of white against the green and brown and purple earth.

Higher still are the graceful firs, whose spire-like heads tower one above another, their slender stems clustering like ship-masts in a dock; while in between each the golden sunlight filters down, and turns their bark to silver on one side and ebony on the other.

Our feet sink in the various mosses covered with a million tiny spears, or bells, or cups, each bearing, in most exquisitely beautiful array, "seed after its kind."

Higher still, the mosses grow more thickly, lichens of strange, fantastic form clothe the rocks, bunches of pretty mountain plants hang from their niches, and ferns push slender roots into imperceptible crevices, and wave graceful fronds in the breeze that grows, with every upward step we take, more keen and chill. Our eyes, outstripping our feet, gaze upward to the hill-tops, and there, motionless upon a towering crag, is the form of that giant bird whose dauntless eye fears not to meet the gaze of the sun.

How grand he looks, as with folded wings, and head raised in contemplation of the sky that is now stained with delicate opal tints, he dominates the world of God's silent, everlasting hills!

But a careless step has dislodged a heavy

stone; it rolls down the steep incline, and at the sound the kingly bird sways slightly forward, poising for flight; then he floats with a soft whir of outspread wings upon the ocean of the air, and at each powerful stroke of those mighty pinions grows less and less as he leaves us far behind. The mellow sunlight, lingering as if the earth were too fair to leave, streams from beneath a solitary cloud-bar on the horizon, and catches the edge of the golden eagle's wings, and thus, light-tipped, he floats away, and soon becomes a speck in the distance.

A fair sight, this still, grand mountain world, this monarch of the hills, in his solitary state and his beautiful flight, to eyes jaded by the glare of a city summer, and wearied by watching the brightest lights die out from life, and hope, and love.

Truly our story has taken a flight as bold as that of the eagle! We dropped the thread of our narrative in the crowded, busy courts in the heart of England—among toiling men, and the hurrying to and fro of those who "rise early, and late take rest," in order that they may win the day in the race for wealth and fame—and we find it again in the heart of the lovely Cheviot Hills.

We have been looking through our hero's eyes; for here, alone with the grandeur of nature, we find William Snow.

He had done as the eccentric Q.C. suggested, and come to "rough it" at the shooting-box that stands on the purple moorland, in the shadow of the hills.

The "roughing it" is, after all, smooth sailing enough—almost too smooth and too luxurious a life to please him; so he has taken advantage of his host going over to visit distant friends, to ramble at his own sweet will among the pasture lands, and up the steep hill-sides, that have to him all the sweet, bright freshness of a new world.

And if there is any "balm in Gilead" for a heart troubled and storm-tossed on a sea of perplexities and doubts and fears, is it not to be found in the quiet study of nature? Have not the trees voices, and the mountains counsel? Does not the stillness of the evening landscape speak of peace and patient endurance; and the tiny blossom on the crag tell us of the Heavenly Father's care that is ever over his creatures?

"He paints the wayside flower,
He lights the evening star;"

and in the thoughtful contemplation of his perfect works is borne in upon our souls what should be the reality of our trust in him.

Perhaps most of us, when beset with perplexities, and overshadowed by a cloud of anxious thoughts, have known the infinite relief and rest of leaving far behind those scenes amidst which we have suffered, and feared, and hoped, and prayed for guidance?

It often happens that to set a thing far away is to be able to look at it dispassionately, to see it through a clearer and truer medium, to gain the power of weighing ourselves and others more correctly. It was so with William Snow.

Guy safely off on that delicious cruise which was to be the turning of "the new leaf;" Lilian and Uncle David (together with those innumerable packing-cases, the results of the latter's many wanderings into London shops), seen on their way to Winstowe; and he turned with hearty pleasure to the thought of bracing winds and long mountain wanderings, new scenes and new faces, and, at all events for a time, freedom from the tension that sooner or later tells upon the nerves of the strongest of us.

To be an ever-watchful spy upon one's self, to weigh every action, to produce every word, to think each moment, as the hours roll by, "Is this wisest? is this best?" is to wear out slowly and surely the very springs of life. It is like the torturing, ceaselessly falling drop of water that at last crashes upon the brain of the unhappy sufferer with all the force of a sledge-hammer; for freedom of feeling is as precious to human nature as freedom of body, and as needful to health in the long run.

It was therefore with a long-drawn breath of relief that William felt the Northern train glide out of smoky, densely crowded London, and knew that a week or two of complete change and relaxation was before him.

By some legerdemain between the guard and Mr. Pettigrew, our two travellers had a first-class (smoking) compartment to themselves, and certainly the figure of the Q.C. opposite to him was enough to cheer the spirits of even a more lachrymose individual than William Snow.

A natty little velvet travelling-cap covered his head; a large and most superfine cigar sent up its cloud of perfumed smoke from between his lips; his small, beautifully shod feet were crossed in a position at once becoming and comfortable, while papers of all sorts and kind, comic and serious, illustrated and plain, covered the whole space of that particular side of the carriage.

Comfort, entire and supreme, was the fact that seemed to exhale from his whole being, and before the genial and perfectly unalloyed content of his presence wearing anxieties and troublous thoughts fled as bats from sunshine.

"M'Glashan—that's my game-keeper—sends me capital accounts of the birds," said Mr. Pettigrew, holding his cigar gracefully between two taper fingers as he spoke; "we shall make good bags, no doubt, and by the time M'Glashan has multiplied the birds slain by three, and sent the result to the local paper, our prowess will charm the county."

But when the travellers reached Hazlecroft it wanted still five days to the magic twelfth; so peace reigned on the heathery billows of the hills, and the grouse took their pastime gloriously.

Hence it came about that William could wander in whatsoever fashion he pleased, "over the hills and far away," an occupation he preferred to any other; and in these solitary rambles— these quiet communings with nature—things that had seemed dim grew clear.

For he was no love-sick fool, to turn a coward's shrinking glance on life because the woman whom he loved could not walk along the pathway by his side. Life held other possibilities of well-doing than the realizing of the heart's sweet dreams; and to let the cords of life slip from a nerveless hand because God had seen fit to take from him the fulfilment of *all* his longings, would have seemed, to his vigorous and manly nature, the act of an unfaithful soldier taking to flight because the day seemed going against him.

To be loyal to himself, to prove himself worthy of the advantages showered upon him by the generous hand of his adopted father, to watch over Lilian as a brother might—all these seemed energetic motives to fill his life, and save him from that slothful, languid depression which is ever the stamp of a feeble mind.

Our feet may stumble, our eyes may be blinded by tears for a season—nay, we may fall prone at God's feet in an agonized supplication that the bitter cup may pass from us; but, if we are true men and true women, we shall stagger to our feet again, once the storm of pain has swept by, and face life bravely—not as we would have it, but as God has set it before us.

One thing William Snow never did. He never dealt uncandidly with himself; never tried to twist and turn the truth, or was so false to himself as to fancy, even for a moment, the possibility of setting aside Lilian Selwyn by placing a less high ideal on the throne where she had reigned so long and so entirely.

Neither did he make fond and foolish vows that all his life he would "love no other." He took the present as it was, and left the future alone.

He loved her—more, revered her as all that was highest, holiest, best in womanhood. This being so, he could not unlove her in a day, nor ever, though time might change the manner of his love; and once he saw her Guy's loved and happy wife, he could thank God, and go on his own way contentedly enough, knowing that it was well with her.

He knew, too, that, as far as his own individual suffering was concerned, the worst was over now. The wrench that had torn the very fibres of his heart was past. He had grown used to thinking of Lilian as Guy's, not his; and it was strange, too, how the man who had trusted him, the man who had bound him down by that entire confidence, which is the strongest chain with which one human being can grapple the heart of another, had gained his interest—I had almost said affection. How often did he think of the expression of pain in Guy's dark eyes as he uttered the words—

"My whole life has been without ballast, without aim or end; and you are the only man I have ever known whom I felt at once to be stronger and better than myself."

Those who look to us for help so easily become dear by virtue of their very weakness.

Already the fresh breezes of the hills, the outdoor life, the rest from all sedentary occupation, had enabled William to throw off the lassitude that is born of mental strain. He had carried with him the thought of Lilian's face as he had seen it last, still sad with the shadow of the parting with her lover. Like very many last looks, William's had been taken at that most matter-of-fact place, a railway-station. Just as the train that bore Uncle David and Lilian away left the platform, he had walked along-side the moving carriages, and as he stood bareheaded, she smiled and waved her hand, and then the great crawling iron serpent had passed on, and he was left standing there alone, and all the sunshine seemed to have died away from the great city.

To follow all these lines of retrospection, we have left William Snow a long time wandering among the hills; not, however, that I think there is any chance he should weary of their varied beauty.

Now, as he turns homeward, the sun sinks towards the western horizon; its level rays no longer gild the hill-tops, or filter through the pines. Here and there a bat, like some tiny fantastic shadow, circles round, and the piercing cry of the plover seems to mourn over the day that is dying and has been so fair.

In the distance is seen the waste and bleak mountain ridge called Carter Fells, a desolate upland, of which strange and eerie tales are told by the superstitious. Its farthermost boundary, the Reidsmuir, as it is called, was once the scene of cruel and bloody conflict between the Scottish clans and their English oppressors, and something awful and sinister seems still to pervade its bleak and lonely outline: this is now seen in sharp relief against a sky where faint opal tints, like sweet memories of past days, still linger.

The river Jed takes its rise amidst these wild moorlands, and one of its smaller tributaries forms in its passage wonderful foam-flecked cascades, that leap and fall, and foam, and sing a sweet monotonous song to the listening hills.

In this fair vale of Liddesdale, nature is ever beautiful, and sometimes awful, in her grandeur.

Now the mellow dying sunlight, the "everlasting hills," dark and solemn in the distance, the sheen of the falling water, and below, stretching out like a panorama, the verdant valleys, the rich and teeming fields, the purpled stretches of heather—all were beautiful; all spoke peace and rest, and trust in the Almighty hand who had made the world so fair, to the weary, jaded heart of the man worn by the turmoil of life, and torn and sore from conflict of thought and feeling. William had wandered farther than he supposed, and as he reached the gates of Hazlecroft, eight o'clock chimed from the clock in the hall.

"I fear I am late. Has your master returned?" he said to Mudford, the major-domo, who had accompanied them in their flight northward, and now went about his various duties with supreme contempt for even the very best the country could do to make itself agreeable plainly written on his features.

"No, sir, he has not," replied that dignitary, with as mournful an air as though he considered his master's safe return from a ten miles' ride improbable, to say the least of it. "My master often *is* late when he visits Ardreggan, the seat of Sir George Plaistow."

CHAPTER XXII.

SOME ADVICE ON THE TREATMENT OF A SKELETON.

"I RODE a devil of a pace home," said Pelham Pettigrew, as, nearer nine than eight P.M. on this same evening, he entered the dining-room at Hazlecroft. The little man was "*tiré à quatre épingles*," and looked as fresh and buoyant as though a ride of twenty miles over by no means faultless roads were a mere bagatelle in the way of exertion.

"I'm heartily glad you were, like myself, somewhat late," said William, as they sat down to table. "I wandered farther over the hills than I intended."

"They're not bad hills in their way; but, mind you, they're a vast deal pleasanter now than in winter, when the snow turns them into big sugar-loaves, and the wind whistles down their crevices like all the fiends of hell let loose."

"I can fancy it being enough to cut a man in bits, and scatter the pieces."

"Just so. They say that a certain carrier, a wag in his way, being once asked his opinion of the climate on old Carter Fell there, expressed his 'opeenion' that 'the deil himsel' wadna bide there, else he war' *tethered*.' Ha! ha! good notion that!"

At this moment Mudford the immaculate discovered a surreptitious smile lurking round the mouth of a young footman, a "country lout" (to use his own expression), "who would as like as not get into his livery hind-side before, unless his betters looked after him."

Now, to laugh at a joke that was the property of his master and his master's friends alone, was in the eye of Mudford a social sin of dark and heinous dye; so he glared upon the offending menial in so savage a manner that the lad dropped a dish with an awful crash.

It was peculiarly characteristic of Mr. Pettigrew that he wholly ignored the confusion consequent upon this calamity, and hummed a tune softly to himself as he gazed with much apparent interest at a Claude on the opposite wall, while the delinquent, more scarlet than any peony that ever bloomed in the Hazlecroft gardens, cleared away the *débris* under the stony eye of Mudford.

He was ready to foam at the mouth with suppressed rage, Mudford was, and marched off the unhappy sinner at last, as though to instant execution.

"The devil was one too many for that poor fellow!" said the host, with a quietly-amused smile.

"I hardly wonder at it," said William, laughing. "'A tethered devil' is a most original idea, and perhaps he's 'one of those gentle ones that would use the devil himself with courtesy.' By-the-way, I saw a golden eagle this evening —rather a rare sight, isn't it?"

"You didn't want to shoot it, I hope?" put in Mr. Pettigrew, leaning eagerly forward; "you didn't swear because you hadn't your gun with you, and couldn't bring him down head first from his perch?"

"No, certainly not," replied William, emphatically. "I never saw a finer sight than that he gave me when he spread his pinions and sailed off towards Carter Fells.

"That's right—that's right. There are some men who can't see a beautiful creature of God's creation without wanting to kill it. I hate that sort of thing myself."

"But how about the birds on the twelfth?" asked William, dryly.

"Ah! just so—quite, quite!" said the other, with a twinkle in his eye; "but then your grouse is such an edible beast: a most delicious dish, sir, well served, and with crumbs brown to a turn. The eagle, on the other hand, is a noble sight, seen in the freedom of our glorious hills, and one that becomes rarer every year. Did the grand old fellow make you ready to quote Py-

thagoras, and, with Malvolio, hazard that 'perchance the soul of your grandam might inhabit a bird?'"

"It might have occurred to me, had I ever been able to indulge in such a luxury as a grandsire, or a grandam either; but as it is, unhappily I cannot even mount one step towards either."

"Ah! yes, just so; I forgot. Let me tell you, however, men don't always look upon their grandfathers as blessings. Gad, sir, I've known men who would a deuced deal sooner be without such an appendage. If a man has 'made his way,' he don't care to hark back to somebody's blacking, or somebody else's pills. I knew one man—ha! ha! I can't help laughing when I think of him —a millionnaire, a man who could have bought up half Lombard Street, and he used to confide to every one that he 'didn't know his own grandfather,' he'd 'made his way,' he 'wasn't ashamed of it,' and all that sort of thing; but, God bless you! he knew his grandfather a precious lot more than he wished for. The old chap had bought a giant dust-heap, and made a fortune out of it: 'Dusty Dick,' we used to call him. So you see a grandfather may have his drawbacks; and, upon my soul, Snow, I think you get on remarkably well without one."

Then, with ready tact, Pelham Pettigrew changed the current of the conversation.

"I've promised that we'll dine with Plaistow on Thursday. You'll be pleased with Ardreggan; it's one of the oldest places in the Lowlands, and its owner is a character—a ripe old sinner, ready for the devil's gathering. I'm the only man in the county that hasn't quarrelled with him—I *won't* quarrel with him! Why, he saves me from the approach of *ennui* when I'm up here; and I say that I owe that man a debt of gratitude, sir: a man who prevents a country life becoming monotonous should be looked upon as 'a jewel of great price.'"

"He would hardly plume himself on being valued in such fashion, I should think," suggested William.

"Ah, perhaps not. I don't know, though; he prides himself on having no consideration for any human being under the sun except himself— revels in it, glories in it; and his wife's face sets the seal of truth upon his boasting. It must have taken years—*years* of repression," went on Mr. Pettigrew, reflectively, "to wash out the life and hope from a woman's whole nature so completely."

"Poor woman!" put in his hearer.

"Ah! you may well say that! She's like a lantern with the candle put out: 'A still gray life and apathetic end'—that's about it; but it's a stillness that has succeeded to a storm, I fancy. A woman doesn't give up all hope of happiness without a struggle for it: they've the tenacity of limpets in sticking to the hope of better things!"

"What a brute the man must be!" broke in William, hotly.

"Quite, quite! But what can one do, my dear sir? These things *are*, and always will be: matrimony is a lottery, and one that, thank God, I never took a ticket in. You'll be amused with Sir George—gad! you can't help yourself. He's the most selfish old beast in existence, and his own hobby-horse. He brings out his own character—mounts and gallops about before your eyes!"

"And the wife looks on ?"

"Oh, there's a pair of them to look on : a sort of humble companion—a woman without a name, who never looks at you, and watches my lady as a dog watches its master. She's been at Ardreggan for long years, indeed, ever since— Ahem! I'm treading on the bony heels of the family skeleton ; he's a hidden skeleton, too, the worst kind of all, is he of Ardreggan. It's a bad plan, Snow, to keep a family connection of that kind always locked up : better fetch him out now and again, dust his bones, see that he's all right and tight, and shut him up again. That's the way ; take a peep at him occasionally, and then you won't fancy him worse than he is. If he's always shut up, you'll fancy you see him gnashing his confounded jaws, and mowing at you in the dark."

"Yes ; it's best to look everything in the face, even a skeleton !" said William.

"Just so — quite," added his host (without, however, going on to particularize the Ardreggan skeleton), "and I assure you you'll find Plaistow a study—a *rara avis*, in fact."

"Happily rare, I should think ; a specimen one would gladly number among some fossil and extinct species."

"Ha! ha! very true," laughed Mr. Pettigrew ; "but, bless you! we must take the world as we find it. After all, men, and women too, have their types in the animal world. I've got an elderly maiden cousin so like a lop-eared rabbit, that I always feel as if she might sit up and wash her face with her paws ; and I know a man so marvellously like a bird of prey, that to see him peck at his food with the sharp beak that adorns his ornithological countenance, instead of eating it like a Christian, would hardly surprise me ; my friend of Ardreggan has his quadrupedal congener in the grizzly bear. There's not a doubt of it, that these resemblances correspond with certain characteristics."

"I dare say they do," put in William. "I know a man with eyes exactly like a St. Bernard, and in faithfulness and fidelity he is certainly that creature's equal."

As he spoke, Jim's deep-set eyes, with their grave earnestness of purpose, came before him.

"I can imagine it : my rabbity cousin is positively brainless, and has been steadily imposed upon ever since she was a child in arms. As to the vulture I told you of, he's the very double of the man in the Bible—he 'ravishes the poor when he gets him into his net.' A precious big net it is, too—ha! ha! — small mesh, the very deuce and all to get out of. Some people would tell you that's a very good description of the law, eh ? and, by gad! they'd be right — 'the deuce and all to get out of'—quite, quite !"

"You would hardly like to hear an outsider express that opinion, though," suggested William.

"No, no. 'Honor among thieves,' my dear fellow — 'honor among thieves.' If a man speaks against my honorable profession, I pitch him out o' window, and then argue the point calmly with him."

Here Mr. Pettigrew rose from table, rung the bell, and summoned Mudford.

"Mudford, place the lights."

Mudford, with ready comprehension of his master's ways, brought in two massive sconces holding wax-candles ; these he placed on either side a small picture that rested on a console which was placed directly opposite the oval dinner-table, by this time cleared of all more substantial viands than fruits and wines.

Softly smiling, pensive of eyes, childlike in sweetness and purity, the Greuze face came out in bright relief against its dark background.

"A pleasant addition to our party, eh, Snow ?" suggested the delighted host ; "fair to the eye, a dainty woman and a *silent* one. Ha! ha! that's a great recommendation !"

William slightly moved his chair, so as to command a better view of the picture. As he did so, his clear, gray eyes took a softer tone ; it was like another glimpse of the face that he had lost sight of at the railway-station.

"So Miss—Miss Selwyn is like my Greuze, is she?" said his companion. "You must introduce me. I like pretty women ; particularly when they're not fools, and a woman with that face isn't likely to be a fool."

"No ; Lilian is hardly that."

"Not blue, though, I hope ? Not of aspiring masculine proclivities? If so, I retract the request for an introduction."

"No, no," said William, smiling ; "she is a most womanly woman."

"That's right — that's right. Why the devil can't women be content to be as God made them ? 'Sweet girl - graduates with their golden hair' may sound very well in poetry ; but I would rather see the golden hair without the mortarboards, any day. By-the-way, what's Tremlett doing? and when is that marriage to come off?"

"Tremlett is off on a yachting cruise with Bolton of the Enniskillens. He will be home before Christmas, and the marriage is to take place early in spring."

"Ah! he's busy making 'stepping-stones of his dead self to higher things!' Well, I hope, for the sake of the Greuze face, the footing will be a sure and safe one. And the old Arcadian —the ancient Strephon—the man who 'thinketh no evil,' has he left town and gone to his native wilds ?"

"Yes ; he and his niece went down into Cheshire last week."

"After parting with her lover ?"

"After parting with her lover," echoed William, firmly, as he carefully deprived the kernel of a walnut of its delicate brown covering.

"I wonder they didn't try to persuade you to go down with them."

"They did ; but I preferred coming up here with you. I hope to go to Winstowe for Christmas ; I never miss hearing the Christmas hymn sung at the old cathedral, where I was once myself a chorister."

"And Tremlett will be back by that time ?"

"Yes ; he will join me in town, and we shall run down together."

Pelham Pettigrew turned his back upon the Greuze, and spoke no more of Winstowe and its inmates.

CHAPTER XXIII.

ARDREGGAN.

ARDREGGAN, the seat of Sir George Plaistow, Baronet, bore on one of its time-darkened stones the date 1104.

Tradition said that one Sir Ronald Cummyne Plaistow, a "wicked laird" of those ancient times, was credited with the practice of magic. At once a tyrant and a sorcerer, he is described as a fiend in human form, guilty of every conceivable cruelty, and carrying out his fell designs by the aid of incantations. It is said that during his lifetime hardly a night passed without the piercing, wailing cry of the "kelpie" (a sort of family banshee who haunted the burn that trickled through the Ardreggan grounds) being heard by terrified travellers.

This "kelpie" was supposed to foretell any evil about to befall the Plaistow family, and his custom was to sit crouched upon a certain stone that rose from the bed of the river, and there, rocking his misshapen body to and fro, utter that prolonged and pitiful wail peculiar to banshees in general. One would have thought that, in the reign of the wicked Ronald, the poor kelpie must have cried himself hoarse; for one misfortune upon another befell the family at that time, of which the cruel murder of the eldest son, the presumptive heir to Ardreggan, was the last and crowning one.

The second son, "fair-haired Geordie," as he was nicknamed, succeeded to the lands and title at his father's death, and then the kelpie had a quieter time of it; indeed, for many generations the Plaistow lairds were tolerably fair specimens of humanity. One, however, had the misfortune to be hanged for treason over his own gate-way, and gave the banshee a good deal of trouble in keening over him.

We must not forget to chronicle the existence of a second ghostly retainer at Ardreggan. It had been one of bold Sir Ronald's foibles to cast a certain sheriff who had offended him into a dungeon beneath the castle, and there to leave him to die the fearful death of starvation. The ghost of this unhappy man very properly tried to make himself as unpleasant as possible to the future lairds of the castle, and on a still evening he might be heard scratching against the wall of the place that had been his living tomb.

My own opinion is that rats had a good deal to do with this legend; but as nothing speaks more emphatically in support of the respectability of any family than the possession of a ghost, the Plaistows naturally clung to the popular conviction on the matter.

Certainly the dark spells and wicked practices of the ribald Sir Ronald seemed to have left a weird and grievous trace in and around the square, massive towers of Ardreggan.

Dark woods, mostly of pine, formed a belt about the house, and ran down here and there to the banks of the trickling, whispering burnie, whose shallow stream divided at the "kelpie stane," formed a steep full of foaming water, and then, uniting once more, and gaining depth and power, hissed and boiled and seethed through a natural bridge formed by overhanging rocks.

Narrow windows dimly lighted the vast chambers of Ardreggan : and the entrance-hall was thickly hung with deer-antlers, that cast fantastic shadows like gigantic elks upon the wall of a winter evening, when logs blazed upon the open hearth.

Modernized, and made comfortable by all the luxury of the nineteenth century, still about this Lowland castle lingered a spirit of uncanniness that refused to be exorcised. Year by year, during the reign of its present possessor, fewer and fewer carriage-wheels have rolled up the noble avenue of firs that leads to the entrance-hall ; rarer and rarer have grown the sounds of hoofs pawing at the door ; for Sir George Plaistow has quarrelled with the majority of his county neighbors, and his timid, shrinking wife has let first one acquaintance and then another drop, until a passing call is an event, and puts her and her "companion," Miss Pheemie, into a flutter of excitement.

We have all heard of the "man without a shadow." Well, Sir George was "a man without a conscience"—a godless man, who never entered the walls of the kirk, or bent his stubborn knee to the Almighty Being who gave him life. He was a man who owned no duty to any one save himself, and only recognized *that* duty in the way of pandering to every instinct of his lower nature ; and his existence was one long effort to make life comfortable to himself, no matter how uncomfortable he might render it to those about him in the process. He scoffed at the idea of a life after death, and in his creedless soul knew of no other and no higher good than to make the best of this world—that is to say, trample on all that crossed his will.

Early in life, Sir George had married a woman well-dowered with worldly goods, but dowered not at all with strength of mind or character —a woman who trembled and shook when he cursed and swore, and fled from the sound of his voice when he roared in anger, or yelled out defiance to those who dared to thwart his will.

Few did, for he gave them little chance—least of all his wife.

Yet in his eyes she had been guilty of a flagrant sin. She *had* had a daughter, and she had *not* had a son.

True, this was the only instance in which the Lady Jane had crossed the imperious will that ruled and crushed her life. Nevertheless, Sir George resented it as unpardonable.

"For what else did I burden myself with a wife?" he had shouted, in the ungovernable passion of his rage.

And then Lady Jane had not even the grace to die. Nothing in her husband's eyes would "so have become her life as the leaving of it ;" for then he could have married again, and retrieved, perhaps, that appalling domestic blunder of there being no heir to Ardreggan.

But she lived on ; yet not with much love of life in her dwarfed and stunted heart. Physically, she had by this time become an utterly colorless old woman. Her hair was bleached, yet not of that lustrous silvery white that is so beautiful a crown to age. The color of her eyes seemed to have been washed out by years of secret weeping (Sir George did not permit tears in his presence) ; and so timid had she become, by reason of a lifetime's repression—a weary, hopeless pilgrimage of more than forty years' duration—that she spoke with a nervous, hesitating utterance that had all the effect of a natural impediment of speech.

Yet time had been when she had fondly loved the young laird of Ardreggan ; when she had gloried in his prowess over moor and field ; and when he had seemed all that was bravest and best, bestriding his gallant gray as though man and horse were one, and doffing his cap to her as he passed. She had loved him too well in those by-gone days to remember the fact of her own wealth, for the wealth of the love she gave him seemed more precious than all the gems of Golconda. She was but a blue-eyed, fair-haired lassie, who could sing like a linnet all such simple songs as "Logie o' Buchan," and the soft, sweet "Land o' the Leal;" but all the music died out of her life full soon, and she sung no more.

Ah me! what a pitiful, ghastly, sad-eyed train of shades, could we but see them, would be the dead day-dreams of many a woman's heart!

She sets out on the journey of her married life, that unknown land on which her maiden feet venture so tremblingly, carrying fond fancies in her heart, like sweetest flowers; but soon the pretty blossoms lie scattered on the ground withered and dead, and she passes on her way with empty hands: it may be, by God's pitiful mercy, to do her duty well and bravely to the end; it may be to fall and falter, and become a scorn and a by-word to those whose feet are set in safer paths.

It is given to so few men to understand the needs of a woman's nature; to realize how easily the tolls of life are paid, if the little coin of sympathy be plentiful; to learn the truth that a feeble hand can grasp the thorns upon life's roses bravely enough, if only a strong clasp closes about it now and again; to realize that a weary head may toil, and think, and plan, yet never know discouragement, if only there is a broad breast on which it may lean awhile, and be cheered by a loving word!

These are little things, perhaps, but they make the sum of a woman's life; and if they fail her, if the shadow of a patient sorrow broods above her, then—oh, shameful, pitiful truth!—it is in those of her own sex who are happier that she finds her bitterest enemies.

Men are never as pitiless as are women to each other; they are open enemies, at least, and do not point the tiny barbed arrow that pierces the very marrow of the heart, and is flung under cover of some honeyed phrase.

After the manner of their kind, the matrons round about Ardreggan discussed the state of domestic matters in that gloomy abode, and came to various conclusions highly satisfactory to the speakers. If "they" were in Lady Jane Plaistow's place, "things would be very different;" doubtless she was a poor "feckless" sort of woman, who must be a trial to her husband— "men hate that kind of thing"—and so on. Of course, Lady Jane did not know of these comments (happily we none of us know the comments our friends make upon us in our absence), but even had she known, I think she was past caring for such trifles.

Long, long years ago, the one flower that had given sweetness and perfume to her life had been torn from her arms, leaving a void whose aching no hand save that of death could ever still! For, say what we may, there is no sorrow on earth like a mother's sorrow; no cry so bitter and so prolonged as the voice of Rachel weeping because her children "are not!"

The widow, bowed to the earth with grief, yet lets time soothe her pain, and years teach her to love some other than the one for whom she shed such bitter tears; but where—oh, where in all the world shall a mother replace the child of her love?

If you force a woman's sympathies out of their natural channels, those sympathies will centre with concentrated passion in some one object that attracts them. Lady Jane, unloved as a wife, and taught to be unloving by years of cruel suffering, clung with an intensity of fondness to the little daughter who had been so unwelcome an arrival at Ardreggan, and became more an object of distaste to its master as years went on, and each one added to the probability of her being an only child. Still a tiny lassie, and naturally fearless—as children always are until unkindness teaches them the nature of dread—this little one, early in her sad life, learned to fly from the sound of her father's voice, and to tremble at the echo of his footstep; but a refuge was seldom wanting, for in a distant wing of the house Miss Pheemie, the child's governess and most willing drudge, was sure to be found, and the little flying figure would leap into her arms to be held safe and close.

"I *hate* papa!—I *hate* him, I say!" sobbed the baby-girl one day, when he had come upon her unawares, and hounded her out of his presence with scant courtesy.

"Hush!" said Miss Pheemie, glancing round the room as though she feared the very walls had ears, "you must never, *never* say that to mamma. Will you remember, May, my darling?"

"But why?" questioned the culprit, with great grave eyes upon poor Miss Pheemie's face. "It's *true*, you know?"

"Because it would pain her so much, my dear," said the governess, falteringly.

"Then I *nebber* will," quoth May, crimson in the face with the energy of her asseveration.

And she kept her word.

Time passed on, and the fair-haired child grew into a fair-haired maiden. She inherited her mother's Northern beauty, but had in her nature (perhaps in compliment to her sire) what is generally called "a spice o' the deil."

She had an opinion of her own, and was given to stick to it; also, she possessed good mental powers, and devoured the volumes in the Ardreggan library with a hungry zest for knowledge remarkable in so young a woman.

At the age of seventeen this wilful, winsome, charming lassie went upon a visit to some English friends, and there met Arthur Mallinger, the man who was destined to be the one dominant influence in her life.

Now, it would be highly romantic if I could say this dark-eyed lover, who rose upon the horizon of the girl's life like a star, was a prince or nobleman in disguise, filling *par fantaisie* the post of tutor to the delicate, backward son of the house in which Sir George Plaistow's daughter enjoyed an amount of liberty Ardreggan had never yielded, and rejoiced in her freedom like the simple child she still was.

But I fear me the young tutor's genealogical tree was a shrub of the most stunted dimensions —if, indeed, such a plant existed at all. He was one of those by no means rare things, a born gentleman—a man whose every thought and feeling was as refined as though he could carry back his descent satisfactorily to the days of the Conqueror. He had "made his own way," as the saying goes, by dint of sheer hard work, and attained even his present humble position at a cost of self-denial and study that would have discouraged a less persevering nature. Nor was he without hopes of a still more ambitious character.

He knew he had literary powers of no mean order; and in those days competition was not at the high pressure it is now, when Darwin's theory of the "struggle for existence" is so aptly exemplified by us slaves of the pen.

How Arthur Mallinger ever dared to love the high-born lady who seemed as far above him as though she were some "bright particular star," I cannot say, and must admit that nothing could have been more unwise or more unfitting; but what would you? Love, that laughs at bolts and bars, occasionally takes a run up, or down, as the case may be, very steep social ladders indeed.

At all events, the little winged god did so conduct himself in this case; and not only did the young tutor love this said "star," but it gradually dawned upon him that that same luminary was pleased to shed upon his life its very softest, brightest beams, and so—

Well, I hardly know how it came about.

I think the pain of parting showed, at last, how close two hearts had grown to each other, and one of those chance *tête-à-têtes*, which are always coming about just when they shouldn't, ended in another edition of the well-known story that has been told in such exquisite words by England's sweetest, truest poetess:

"Softened, quickened to adore her, on his knee he fell before her,
And she whispered low in triumph, 'It shall be as I have sworn.
Very rich he is in virtues, very noble—noble, certes:
And I shall not blush in knowing that men call him lowly-born.'"

When it came to "Good-bye," May looked up into her lover's face and said, with simple earnestness,

"I shall never change to you; I shall be always the same, Arthur, come what may."

And to a nature such as May's, faulty and unwise at times, yet ever real and earnest, these words had all the solemnity of a vow. Then he kissed her on the lips that gave that loving pledge, and so sealed their truth.

Are not the lives of all of us open to that sudden and startling change of color caused by some new influence unexpectedly crossing our path? We look back a few months—or, it may be, but a few weeks or days—and we can hardly recognize, in what we are, what we once were!

Perhaps the change is a sad one; we have lost something—the clasp of a hand, the sound of a voice, and life holds for us an awful silence that is *felt* even beneath the current of our outward daily life.

Or one has grown so dear that our very sorrows are gilded by that one's sympathy, as clouds are turned to gold by the sun; to our happy eyes, the "valleys sing for joy," and the "hills skip like rams;" nature seems more lovely because our hearts are more open to impressions of her loveliness; the past is sweet to linger upon; the present is silver; the future golden.

This was the story of the girl whose tale I am now telling. Let no one grudge her this short gleam of sunshine, for it was the last that ever shone upon her earthly life.

As she journeyed homeward, the magic of her lover's kiss still lingering on her lips, the world seemed fairer than ever it had done before. Even Ardreggan, gloomy and frowning as it was, looked lovely in her eyes, and in the plenitude of her joy, she could, I am sure, have kissed her hand to the kelpie himself, had that worthy been sitting on his "stane!" People said he came soon enough after this, and night by night he wailed and cried till the sheep huddled together in the fold, and the men and maids of the Ardreggan household cowered round the "ingle," and refused to go about the house alone.

For Arthur Mallinger wrote to Sir George; wrote humbly, as became him, but still bravely, as became him, too. He told the story of the unpremeditated avowal of his love without extenuating and without falsifying, asking for nothing in the present, only praying for the boon of hope in the future, should he win his way.

The day on which this letter arrived at Ardreggan was a memorable one in the domestic annals.

A petty nature is incapable of appreciating greatness in another. Sir George Plaistow, therefore, could not recognize the nobility that scorned deception, and conscious of an impulsive error, laid that error bare.

He tore the tutor's letter to atoms when but half read, and then Lady Jane and poor Miss Pheemie came in for the brunt of the storm. The air was dark with curses, and the women, white and trembling, clung together as terrified animals huddle up to each other in a tempest.

All but May herself.

She stood pale, silent, and tearless, listening to a string of epithets hurled at her love, of which "low-born whelp" was about the sweetest and most courteous. Each term of reproach aimed at the man she loved hit her like a lash, and she writhed beneath it; but she spoke no word, and her silence so exasperated her father that he raised his arm and struck her down where she stood.

After a storm comes a calm.

Days and weeks of silent misery followed this outbreak.

Miss Pheemie's eyes and nose entered into a friendly rivalry as to which should become the reddest. My lady, to quote the old housekeeper, a retainer of many years' standing, "gaed like a ghaist;" and the girl herself, tearless and dumb, would sit gazing out into the night through the diamond-paned casement of the old school-room, or crouch by the fire and watch its burning embers, as though, in their fantastic shapes, she could recall the brightness of those few sweet days when she had known a joy that had been too quickly overcast.

All correspondence was of course forbidden with the presuming suitor; but by some agency, that was forever a mystery, the sorrowing girl received a few hurriedly penned lines from one of his relatives.

He was ill—seriously ill. The hard mental strain of the last few weeks, coming upon a frame already weakened by over-study, had proved more than nature could bear. He had had to leave his situation, and take refuge with the only relatives he appeared to possess.

They were people in humble enough position in life, but rich in love for the boy who had raised himself above them all by his "knowledge," as they were pleased to term his self-earned education.

"I can't bear to see the child so steadfast, Pheemie," said poor Lady Jane one evening to that faithful friend; "sorrow that has nae outward mark eats the heart out."

It was a late autumn night, and the bare arms of the trees beat against the casements as though they shrank from the blast and demanded admission, while the wind shrieked like half a dozen kelpies at least, and the burn, swollen by heavy rains, roared and tumbled with the sound of a distant sea.

"Mother," said May, gliding into the fire-lit room like a spirit, her great eyes bright with some intense feeling, her hands clasped upon her breast—"mother, I am going to my room; the noise of the wind has made my head heavy; father is out at the bailie's, so he will not miss me. Kiss me, and bless me too, that I may sleep the better."

Then the mother clasped her, and kissed her, and blessed her, with tears, the girl kneeling by her knee, and holding her about the neck, and Miss Pheemie stole away to the window, and wept quietly to herself. When the morning came, the nest was empty, the bird had flown.

A letter lay open on the table—a letter that Sir George tore to atoms and then trampled on the bits—a letter that was photographed upon the mother's heart in one instant's sight!

"I would not have gone to him, dearest mother, but he is ill, perhaps dying, and I am his promised wife. Father will never forgive me, and I shall never come back any more; but I stole your blessing last night to take with me!"

That was all.

Then Sir George Plaistow did as we have already heard Pelham Pettigrew describe: he shut up the family skeleton, and turned the key upon it.

He not only forbade his wife ever opening a letter from her child on pain of being instantly turned out of her home, but forbade every mention of, or allusion to, such a creature as their disobedient daughter.

Henceforth and forever Ardreggan was a childless house—childless by his will. Not even the smallest girlish trinket had May taken with her; her room was left just as though she might be expected to return at any moment; only the bed had been unpressed by her slight form, and her simplest dress and cloak were missing.

By whose connivance she left the castle that grusome night, when the fir-trees bent almost to the earth before the blast, and the rain drove pitilessly along instead of falling downward, no one ever knew.

That part of the letter which contained the address from which she had received the news of her lover's danger was torn off; but even had it been found, there was no one to pursue the fugitive, for had she been brought back, Sir George would have spurned her with his foot, and cast her out pitilessly. In these days of terror, he held those two weak women in such bondage of fear that they stole about the vast rooms and crept up and down the wide stairs like frightened ghosts, and spoke under their breath.

He would have turned Miss Pheemie away, but for fear that she should seek out the child, and perhaps help her and comfort her, if help and comfort were needed. He watched his wife, and the woman that was her faithful shadow, by night and day, locking their rooms at night, and, to the best of his power, preventing them from conversing together out of his presence.

Miss Pheemie, lying awake and shivering in her bed, could hear him go from his own room, that opened into his wife's, and there pace up and down the floor, raving and cursing in such fashion as now and again forced a low wail from the unhappy woman at whose head his words were hurled. Then he would lock the outer door, set the inner one open so as to command the slightest movement Lady Jane might make, and presently silence would reign. But Miss Pheemie knew—how well she knew!—that the mother was lying in the darkness, not weeping, for she dared not weep lest he should hear her, but open-eyed, keeping an awful vigil of pain, and praying to the good God who watches over all for the child she had once carried beneath her heart and suckled at her breast.

At length Sir George found keeping guard both monotonous and wearisome. He therefore announced to his slaves that in a fortnight's time they must be prepared to start on a long Continental tour; that they would sojourn for a time in such cities or countries as it might fall in with his royal will and pleasure to abide in, and that Ardreggan would meanwhile be shut up, and left to the care of certain trusty servants. The rest of the household were to be dismissed.

In one week from the day in which Sir George Plaistow made this determination known to his wife, her hair, until then fair and abundant as in the days of her girlhood, turned to a lustreless gray, and two deep lines, lines graven by the hand of a cruel anguish, marred the beauty of her mouth.

And so for three long years—years that seemed like a whole weary lifetime to Lady Jane and her companion—these three wandered about in foreign lands. Now they rested in some Italian city; now sailed up the Nile; now spent a winter in the lovely climate of Malta; now pushed far into Spain.

But in all places, and everywhere alike, Lady Jane,

"Bearing a life-long hunger in her heart,"

saw no beauty in earth or sky. Quiet, submissive, and uncomplaining, she lived her life day by day; but no one ever saw her smile.

You see, the breaking of a human heart is a long and troublesome process; though there are few things more certain when it is once set well *en train*.

Be sure, the two women, whenever a happy chance gave them half an hour together, spoke with tenderest, fond regret of their lost darling; be sure they recounted to each other many a little story of her baby days, each refreshing the memory of the other in this particular or that; be sure they wearied themselves with conjectures as to where she was and how she fared, and wondered if the love that she had given up all for was so "leal and true" that she "counted the world well lost," and, as Arthur Mallinger's wife, was utterly content with that little world bounded by the walls of the home that was hers and his.

It is often thus. We weary ourselves with conjectures about some absent loved one; what is he doing, we think, even now—this very moment, while we are dwelling on the thought of him? Is it well with him? Has he good friends about him, and trne? Has he found some to fill our place, and to love him as we loved?

And all the while our darling is in God's safe-keeping, and the sorrows and the pains and the partings of earth can hurt him never more!

CHAPTER XXIV.

AN AUTO-DA-FÉ.

It was considered by the superstitious peasantry round Ardreggan a very sinister and unlucky omen that, almost immediately after the departure of the family to foreign lands, and the strange disappearance of the young daughter of the house, a flock of herons came and settled in the little wood on the western side of the estate.

Through this wood the burn took its troublous way, and there the kelpie held high court. The melancholy cries of these herons and the rustle of their dark wings certainly added to the weird desolation of the deserted house; but perhaps the kelpie was glad they came there, as the mournful noise of their unmelodious voices may have given him a good excuse to take a little rest, nod in pleasant slumber on his stony seat, and dream of what things kelpies best may love.

It was reported, too, that a white owl, an owl of abnormal and gigantic size, had been seen by more than one individual resting upon the window-sill of the room that had been Miss Plaistow's; also that it fluttered its snowy wings against the glass, and, staring in with marvellous great monstrous eyes, did cause to fall into a swoon a maid-servant chancing to come into the chamber.

"There can be nae doot," said the village oracle, "sawing the air with his hand," to give due emphasis to his words—"there can be nae doot ava that the deil's gotten himsel' a muckle further ben the hoose of Ardreggan than he has a richt to be in ony respectable hoose; and it's my opeenion that the auld Sir Ronald maks o'er free, and does na' lie as still i' his grave as a man who had his senses aboot him when livin' ought to ha'e the breedin' to do when dead. A bodie might overlook an unco' deal done by a puir ignorant speerit that kens nae better ways, but what's the good o' quality, leevin' or deed, if they have na' gotten nae manners ava?"

Thus the uncanny reputation of Ardreggan rather increased than lessened.

Three times the snow fell, and made the firs lovelier than in their fairest spring or summer dress; three times the roses on the southern wall budded and bloomed, and shed their petals like perfumed tears, because there was no hand to gather them. And still Ardreggan was like a sleeping giant: all its lower windows were closed and barred, and but one solitary spiral column of blue smoke ascended from its countless stacks of chimneys.

Then, all at once there was a "stirring among the dry bones."

Windows were unbarred, and set as wide open as their old-fashioned sashes would allow of.

The gardener, one Colin M'Dougall, set to work to bring about something like order in his own department, and retrieve the laziness of the three past years. Nature, too, did *her* best in the way of helping on the general festivity.

She hung a bright-green tassel on the end of every spray upon the larch-trees; she touched the buds of the beeches and limes with faint rosy pink, so that, seen from a distance, the woods seemed to be blushing beneath the glance of the sun that grew warmer every day; and the birds sung in soft, imperfect twitterings, earth's sweet orchestra tuning up for the gala summer-time that was coming.

In the midst of all this dawn of spring, the wanderers came home—Sir George, Miss Pheemie, and Lady Jane, "the mistress," as she was styled by her own household. Oh God, what a weary, white-faced woman!

Colin M'Dougall, standing barebeaded at the big gates to see the carriage pass, forgot to don his bonnet again, and, *planté là*, did thoughtfully scratch his carroty poll instead.

This operation finished, Colin shook his head gravely from side to side, looked into the crown of his bonnet, turned it round, and finally put it on, muttering to himself as he went along,

"And 'Colin,' says she — 'My lady,' says I —'Colin,' says she, 'will ye gether me a rose or twa, and a bit little young bud? They're ower high for me to reach up the wa'.' That was jist her way; she was a fine saft-spoken leddy to the lowest as weel's the best, and what's come of her ava, God save us a'! The mistress is turned crazy wearyin' for the sight of her, that's certain; and the maister—d—n the maister!" said Colin, with a sudden *accès* of anger, slapping one hand vehemently on his thigh. But he repented him of his wrath, and added, under his breath, "The Lord forgie me for an untenty deevil's-buckie!"

Colin was not far wrong in thinking the mistress was in very bad case indeed.

What is a worse pain, my friends, among the many life brings, than the coming back to a place once made lovely by the presence of one we loved, and now a desert in our eyes, even though beautiful itself, because the sunshine to us is cold, and the song of the birds a mockery, for lack of

"The touch of a vanished hand,
And the sound of a voice that is still?"

Does not the familiar room where stands the vacant chair strike us dumb with its emptiness? Does not our ear ache with the sense of silence for want of one dear voice, though there are many others to bid us welcome?

Sir George, looking at his wife's face as the carriage rolled down the avenue, read her heart like an open book. Miss Pheemie, opposite the two, cast down her eyes, and the end of her poor little nose grew burning red.

She longed—this poor, faded, faithful creature —to stretch out her hand and clasp that other that worked and twitched in nervous pain; but the eye of the tyrant was on her, and she was held back by fear.

Now, it had been Sir George Plaistow's orders that whatever letters might arrive at Ardreggan during his absence should *not be forwarded.*

They were to be placed in a certain drawer in the black oak press in his study.

His factor would, of course, keep him in full knowledge as to how the estate was going on; if the farmers and laborers paid their rent regularly; the means that were promptly used to enforce a sense of this duty upon them if neglected, etc.

This was all the home information he cared to have. These orders had been given, and most emphatically given, in the presence of Lady Jane and of Miss Pheemie.

They had dared to make no remonstrance, though my lady shivered as her lord spoke, and Miss Pheemie gave the least little bit in the world of a sniff, which she cunningly merged in a cough as Sir George turned slightly towards the part of the room in which she stood.

"If you offend him, he will send you away from me, Pheemie, and I have *no one* but you."

Thus had my lady once spoken, and the faithful Pheemie had kissed the thin, white hand and the faded cheek of the speaker with hot assurances of fidelity.

"I will never leave you—never!" She trembled as she spoke, and her little forlorn curls trembled too; she was but a feeble, frightened-looking woman, was Miss Pheemie, but her heart was "golden ore."

You see, the Bible character of Ruth has its faithful prototypes even now, for hearts still beat whose beautiful spirit of faithfulness might be clothed in the words that were God-inspired of old:

"Entreat me not to leave thee, or to return from following after thee; for whither thou goest, I will go."

And so Miss Pheemie "set a watch upon the door of her lips," and guarded against offending the master of Ardreggan with a constant self-watchfulness that was a quiet martyrdom.

To those who are rich in friends, and who wander from home for a time, a goodly pile of letters will accumulate during absence; but few and far between were the missives in the Ardreggan post-bag.

Lady Jane, "the daughter of a hundred earls," had been an orphan heiress, and was singularly without near relatives; those she had taking only a tepid sort of interest in her welfare, on the ground that, with her beauty and her dower, she ought to have "done better for herself;" that meant, she ought to have married a man of higher social status than a baronet, even though he *did* date back his pedigree to the year 1100.

Her husband had quarrelled with all his own people early in life. Naturally, therefore, under these combined circumstances their joint correspondence was limited; and now, after these three years of wandering, only some official county circulars, and a small, very small, number of private letters lay in the drawer of the black oak press.

Most of these private letters—indeed all save one—were in the same handwriting, and all bore the postal date of the year immediately following that in which the family went abroad.

Sir George took up, turned over, and critically examined the outside of each of these epistles.

Then he rung the bell.

"Why the devil is there no fire?" he shouted at the servant who answered his summons.

"The housekeeper thought, Sir George, that as the day was—" began the man.

"Don't tell me what anybody thought. Light the fire!"

Laid with pine knots in true Scotch fashion, the fire soon blazed and roared up the ample chimney.

Then the master issued another mandate: her ladyship's maid ran up to the morning room, and a moment later her ladyship herself, closely followed by the shadowy Pheemie, came into the room.

Intense fear was written on the faces of the two women.

One thought had been dominant in the minds of both ever since they had entered Ardreggan.

"Oh, Pheemie! the letters, the letters!" Lady Jane had moaned, wringing her hands in the piteous suffering of suspense; "there surely *must* be one lying there in the black oak press. My darling *must* have written! What *can* we do? Dare you steal down softly? He might not notice you—perhaps he is gone to look at the dogs."

But Sir George was not gone to look at the dogs.

Even as they spoke, the women heard the sound of the "study" bell, and very shortly afterward the summons to the master's presence reached them.

At once, when but half-way across the room, where the fire blazed and crackled so merrily, the mother's eyes fell upon the packet of letters lying on the table, and with a quick, glad cry she started forward.

Was she about to hear again the sound of a voice that had been silent all these long and weary years!

A strong arm held her back; a cruel hand closed upon those precious letters, and kept them from her reach. Then she fell upon her knees beside her husband, and clung about him sobbing—not with tears; grief such as hers—anguish such as hers—has no tears; but with the long-drawn gasps of one who fights against some cold and deadly flood.

"For God's sake in heaven, George, give me those letters! It is May's hand—we shall know where she is—they will tell us all about her. Oh, husband, forgive the child now! I have been silent—I have mourned—I have prayed—I have wrestled with my pain in obedience to your will; but now—now— Oh, my God, have mercy on me, and soften his heart!"

Sir George was silent. Slowly and deliberately he turned over the letters, looking now at this one, now at that. Even the massive beard and mustache that shaded his handsome mouth could not conceal the whiteness of his lips—white with the pallor of passion.

"Remember, husband," pleaded the voice of the poor woman, whose mother-love made her strong and brave as the animal that fights for its young—"remember how, long ago, when she was quite a tiny thing, the child wept because you hurt your hand, and brought her little handkerchief to tie up the wound! Think of those days, husband, and—forgive—her! And—have—pity—upon—me!"

Tearless sobs broke her voice, as with strained and starting eyes she saw him make one step nearer to the blazing pine wood; saw, and with a shriek that echoed through the room sprung to her feet and clung about him!

Too late!

Just where the fire was hottest the packet fell. Once in the flames, the papers burst from the envelopes that held them, and the letters curled and writhed like living, suffering things, turning at last to a bundle of spark-starred, blackened films —all that was left of a murdered voice!

But the foul deed had not been done in silence.

Strong as he was, it had taken all Sir George Plaistow's strength to hold back the shrieking, maddened woman, who fought to get at the burning papers—fought with a strength marvellous in one so frail, and which roused to more deadly frenzy the anger of the man whose will she strove —how vainly, poor fond fool!—to cross!

As for Miss Pheemie, she had slipped from her chair to the ground, and, hiding her face in her hands, shuddered in terrified silence; while frightened servants gathered about the door, and, quickly comprehending the cause of those piercing cries that had penetrated even to the remotest corner of the house, would doubtless have joined heartily in the spirit of that curse which Colin had already uttered.

* * *

CHAPTER XXV.

"OH, THESE ARE VOICES OF THE PAST...."

OUR last two chapters have been glancing back over a space of more than twenty years, but now we shall get on to level ground again; not, however, before I have said a few words as to Mr. Pelham Pettigrew's acquaintance with the inmates of Ardreggan.

There was nothing the great man of law more disliked than the idea that any human being should presume to suppose that his heart was softer and more feeling than he himself chose to make it out to be.

He would therefore boast of his intimacy at kelpie-haunted Ardreggan, and his marvellous friendliness with the head of that mansion; avow his determination *not* to quarrel with the man whom everybody else fell out with as a matter of course, and say, in his didactic way, "He can't quarrel with me, sir! he can't do it!"

Thus far Pelham Pettigrew spoke the truth, but only part of it.

The whole truth was this:

Poor, faded, down-beaten Lady Jane—that silent, patient, suffering woman—appealed to his pity more powerfully than he would have liked to acknowledge; for if it is a man's pet foible to try to make himself out to be as utterly heartless as a thorough man of the world ought to be, he will stick to the coveted reputation through thick and thin, and utterly eschew the notion of there being even one chink in the steel plates of his armor.

Yet it was not difficult for any one of ordinary penetration, who heard Pelham Pettigrew speak of Lady Plaistow, to discover that a manly and true sympathy and friendship for her had a large place in his heart.

And what wonder?

If it is pitiful to see a woman hopeless and broken down in youth, while the body is tolera-

bly well able to endure the fretting of the spirit within, and energy and patience can face bravely all depressing influences, how much more infinitely sad it is to see that same woman, shorn of all youth and beauty, her strength of mind, as of body, stolen from her by the approach of age, *still* striving, *still* enduring, with none of the consolations a loved and cherished wife carries with her to gild the vale of years!

Children and children's children are around a happy woman as the evening of her life draws on; and their pleasant voices seem like sweet echoes of her own youth, while the grandchild is almost dearer than was the child, because it borrows a reflected value from the memories of her own early, happy motherhood.

By her side is one whose arm has shielded her from every blast of the wind of heaven,

"Lest it should visit her cheek too roughly."

Together they have climbed life's hill, together now they "toddle down;" for the love with which they started on their journey years ago has gathered to itself a threefold cord of friendship, trust, and sweet companionship.

This is one guise in which old age may come to a happy woman.

Another case may be that of one whose declining years are made beautiful by *memory;* who awaits in faith and hope the time when God shall call her to join those dear ones whom she has

"Loved long since, and lost awhile."

The sweetness of her life lies in the thoughts of the years that are past: she can sympathize in the happiness of others, yet never envy them.

"I would not give my memories for all another's joy."

That is the language of her heart, and its echo is heard in the calmer, quiet helpfulness of her voice, and seen in the grave, sweet peace of her eyes. She has that which the world can "neither give nor take away," a secret and abiding fountain of content which none may share, and which makes the desert of her life "rejoice and blossom as the rose."

Contrast these two cases that I have thus tried to sketch with the life of such a woman as the Lady Jane. A life of repression, of struggle, of stumbling; of hands stretched blindly forth only to grasp the air; of scalding tears pressed back to their fountain of pain, for fear their indulgence may weaken her for the battle that is still to come; and because—pitifullest reason of all—there is no one to grieve at the sight, let the tears rain down ever so thickly!

In all the desert of this life, fancy one only flower, and then *that* gathered, and cast to the winds by the cruel hand of fate.

Granted, then, that the cast-iron case in which it pleased Mr. Pettigrew to keep his heart had in it one or two chinks, what wonder that pity for the Lady Jane crept in and nestled there?

The consummate tact, the exquisitely keen knowledge of his fellow-beings, which were such remarkable characteristics of the man of law, enabled him to avoid misunderstandings with the irascible and pugilistic Sir George; and he on his part (you see the very worst people have some capability of good in them) had actually grown to like Pelham Pettigrew. That is to say, he liked him as much as it was his nature to like anything that was not himself.

In the presence of this, his one sole friend and companion, it was curious to see a faint, shadowy reflection of the deferential courtesy with which that friend ever treated Lady Jane make itself visible in his own demeanor.

Very early in Mr. Pettigrew's acquaintance with Lady Plaistow, a chance interview with the silent, timid woman had raised for his eyes a corner of the domestic curtain; and as the skilled naturalist will describe the whole fossil skeleton of an animal from one fragment of bone that to the eye of the ignorant would be unsuggestive of anything more interesting than a dust-bin, so from this one glimpse of the state of affairs did the clever mental anatomist form a correct and exhaustive estimate of her life and trials.

It happened thus:

Finding her, on one occasion, alone in the dreary dining-room, with its long array of narrow windows and dark panelled walls, and struck with the white desolation of her face, Pelham Pettigrew, in that marvellously sweet voice of which we have before spoken, addressed to her a few gentle words of kindliness—expressed a fear that she was suffering—a sympathizing sorrow in this suffering, whatever it might be.

For a moment the poor lady looked at him with an eager wonder in her colorless eyes, a look like that you may meet in the eyes of a person who suddenly hears an old and well-remembered melody that has long been strange to his ears; then she covered her face with hands that shook as though with ague, and spoke in a voice "holding tears in its tones."

"Do not speak to me like that! Oh, anything but that! I cannot bear—" "sympathy," she was about to say.

Here, however, Miss Pheemie glided in with her noiseless step, and rapidly passing her arm round the shoulders of her friend, looked at Mr. Pettigrew with what there is every reason to suppose she meant for a fierce and withering glance, but which, in reality, only gave her the air of an enraged mouse.

"My dear, my dear!" she crooned over Lady Jane, "what is it?"

"Nothing; it is not his fault. I am weak and tired this morning; that is all."

But no doubt Miss Pheemie eventually learned just how things had been, for ever afterward she made a sort of fetich of Mr. Pettigrew, getting quite a pale salmon color whenever she met him, and casting shy, adoring glances at him when she thought no one was looking.

They say that "the way to the mother's heart lies through the child," and in like fashion the way to Miss Pheemie's heart lay through that faded, wretched woman, who was at once her mistress and her most dear charge.

That Mr. Pettigrew and his friend, a stranger to them, should dine at Ardreggan, was, it may well be supposed, an event in the quiet, monotonous life led by the two women who composed its household. Of course, when I call their existence monotonous, I purposely overlook the variety afforded by divers outbreaks of temper on the part of Sir George, and the howlings and stampings and cursings of that potentate when any trifling matter overset the balance of his content.

I overlook these trifles for this reason: even variety becomes monotonous when constantly indulged in, and, like Mark Twain's cow, descending matutinally upon the breakfast-table, these fits of ungovernable rage became part and parcel of the Ardreggan routine. Miss Pheemie's virgin breast was quite in a flutter as the all-important Friday grew to evening, and the hour when the guests might be expected drew near.

She had been made supremely happy by the gift of a bit of almost priceless lace from Lady Jane that morning, and with this cobwebby structure gathered about her thin throat, and fastened with an amethyst brooch of ancient setting, seemed in her own eyes almost *too* gorgeously caparisoned—too manifestly set forth in her best, to try to dazzle the eyes of the man whom she "delighted to honor." Mr. Pettigrew's unknown friend was, in her estimation, a sort of moon shining in the reflected light of the sun.

The domestic atmosphere of Ardreggan had been cleared the day previous by a severe storm. Lady Jane had, in consequence, retired shaking to bed at night, and now, having been benefited by repose, appeared in the "long drawing-room" —as the state guest-chamber was styled—certainly a shadowy, worn, and faded woman, but having about her a peculiar air of high-breeding and refinement. She displayed a certain grace, too, in the wearing of an old-fashioned brocaded dress, and marvellous airy folds of lace, that looked as though woven in some fairy loom, were crossed and recrossed over her bosom. Her gray hair was folded back under a kerchief, also of the finest lace, and something like the very faintest smile played round her lips.

For Sir George was in a good humor—there could be no doubt about that. He had only cursed the butler once since he came down from his room *en grande tenue*, and was now standing in the rampant fashion Englishmen are addicted to upon the hearth-rug before the open grate, where a small pine-wood fire was pleasant enough in the freshness of the autumn night.

The abomination of gas was naturally unknown in the Ardreggan drawing-rooms. Old-fashioned sconces on the walls held waxen lights; tapestry curtains shaded the long row of windows that ran down one side of the room, each one casting a square of pale gloaming on the polished oak floor; for the blinds were still undrawn, and one star and a crescent moon hung in a cloudless sky.

Low down in the valley, and following the course of the tumbling burn, lay close a faint white mist. The harsh, rasping note of the corn-crake, and mournful cries from the heronry in the wood that stood blackly out in the dimness, mingled with the sound of the falling water, while above towered the massive pile of the castle, a soft flood of light shining like a welcome from its many windows.

It was thus that William Snow first saw Ardreggan.

"What a grand old place!" he said, enthusiastically, to his companion.

But Pelham Pettigrew's attention was at that moment taken up in turning his high dog-cart and spirited bays so cleverly into the avenue as to round the corner without leaving an inch to spare; so his reply was a sort of sound between a grunt and a growl.

Another moment or two, and they swung

round to the hall doors, the sound of the wheels making little Miss Pheemie's heart beat at least six times a minute over its usual rate.

She puts up her shrivelled hand to the all-important tucker, and gives the edge a little pinch here and there, to make it sit more jauntily; she looks at my lady, calm, pale, shadowy, and for once peaceful; at Sir George, smiling, actually smiling, as he rubs his hands and watches the door, anticipating the entrance of his guests.

He has not long to wait.

The Scotch servant announces "Mr. Pettigrew and Mr. Snow" (turning the *o* into an *a*, of course, as he utters this last), and the cherished idol of Miss Pheemie's simple heart, followed by his friend, enters the room.

The faultless evening-dress, the diamond studs, plain as the plainest setting can make them, the little high-arched shoes tied with broad black ribbons, the brilliant smile and genial greeting of Pelham Pettigrew to his host and hostess, are almost overpowering to Miss Pheemie. She gives quite a little gasp, and is too much engrossed in offering up mental incense at the shrine of all this magnificence to notice the mistress of the house. Her ladyship has risen, and stands with her hand in that of Pelham Pettigrew; but her eyes, suddenly dilated with an expression half wistful, half fearful, and wholly and most marvellously strange, look eagerly beyond to where William Snow stands beside her husband, answering his warm and hearty greeting.

The stranger is presented to the hostess. For an instant he touches her hand—a hand whose deathly, lifeless cold strikes thrillingly to his. And she is silent; this strange, marble woman, whose face is set and still, and yet whose eyes burn with a wondrous intensity, and hold his own by some irresistible power.

She sinks back into her seat, and as she grasps the arms of the chair, he can see the livid veins stand out on the transparent hands that seem to clutch at some support, as though all things around her grew indistinct—as though she

"Moved among a world of ghosts,
And felt herself the shadow of a dream."

"Surely," thought William to himself, "this poor lady is mad, as well as sad."

She seemed to hang upon the sound of every commonplace word that issued from his lips as though each held a verdict of life or death; yet still she maintained the same strange silence, and at last, just as he turned with a smile to answer some timid utterance of Miss Pheemie's, a cry rung through the room—an awful, pitiful, yearning cry—that might have come from the weird lips of the kelpie himself, and my lady, who had risen from her chair, and stretched out her arms as though to touch some phantom visible to her eyes alone, fell forward, and lay lifeless at the feet of the stranger guest.

<hr>

CHAPTER XXVI.

"LINKS OF A BROKEN CHAIN."

Sir George pulled at the bell-rope till it came down with a run, and then ran round the room with it in his hand.

This was Sir George Plaistow's "way" of showing his sympathy with his wife in the sudden seizure that had struck her down as though a bullet had pierced her heart.

Sir George did not offer a silent sympathy either, but his flow of speech was somehow cut short by a sharp glance from Pelham Pettigrew's keen, gray eyes.

They had bent over the crumpled-up heap of brocade and lace, and a dead, white face and lifeless hands, that lay upon the floor, and had raised her up and laid her on the couch—

The semblance of a dead woman!

Miss Pheemie, crouching on the floor beside her, chafed the limp fingers, and though distraught with terror, yet did not fail to cast more than one glance of dread at the master of the house. He, still grasping the deposed bell-rope, and looking as though he were about to apply it lash-wise to the world in general, stood silent (thanks to the presence of his imperious guest), but glowering at the motionless form of his wife.

"She'll soon be all right again; it is the—the weather—the—the fire—" stammered and gasped Miss Pheemie, looking at the closed eyes and drawn mouth that seemed as though light and life were fled forever.

But Pelham Pettigrew, being an eminently practical man, took the law into his own hands, ordered the servants about as though they belonged to him, and at last, seeing a flutter of returning life passing across the face that lay back upon Miss Pheemie's arm, he took still more upon himself.

He went round to William Snow's side, and motioned him to retire into the shade of the tapestry-draped windows.

"She will not like to see a stranger near her when she comes to herself," he said, confidentially. This matter settled to his satisfaction, the active, dapper little man actually pressed Sir George into the service, and made that august individual hold a wineglassful of strong brandy-and-water until such time as he, Pelham Pettigrew, saw that her ladyship was capable of swallowing the same.

This feat accomplished, he fully acquiesced in her faintly expressed wish of retiring to her room, gave her the support of his arm to the foot of the stairs, and then, by some magic of manner, obliged Sir George to take his place and aid his wife's feeble steps as far as the door of her chamber. Miss Pheemie and the lady's maid followed; the former, appalled out of all self-possession by the turn of things in general and Mr. Pettigrew's daring conduct in particular.

"Pheemie, Pheemie!" said Lady Jane, when the two women were left alone, "I think I have been dreaming. I must be *mad!*" and she held her two hands across her brow, and closed her eyes wearily.

But there are phantoms that even darkness cannot shut out. Miss Pheemie knelt by the bed on which the stricken woman lay, and laid her cheek down upon the pillow by that death-like face.

"Do not think of it, my dear," she said, "do not think of it. It was some fancy—some strange fancy."

"No," said my lady, sitting up, and pushing back the gray hair that had fallen about her in confusion—"no, it was no fancy, Pheemie."

Then she stretched out her arms, as if to some dear vision hovering near, and sobbed out wildly,

"Oh, my darling, some one spoke to me with your voice, and looked at me with your eyes!"

"I know, I know!" replied the other, trembling. "It is so sometimes; one sees strange likenesses; one might be deceived."

But Lady Jane is not listening.

On either thin cheek some strong and passionate emotion has painted a hot pink spot; her hands are cold and dank as they lie in Miss Pheemie's clasp, and they are not still, but writhe and turn and twist, as though some bodily pain racked their owner.

"Let me move the lamp away," says poor Miss Pheemie, after long and troubled silence. "You must try to rest. Shut your eyes, dear, and then perhaps you'll fall into a doze."

She takes the lamp away, and draws the heavy curtains of the bed, that is large enough and gloomy enough for a family hearse. Then Miss Pheemie retires to the deep embrasure of the window, lamp and all, and gives herself up to terrible forebodings as to what will be the conduct of the master of the house when his guests shall have departed, and, warmed with ample draughts of generous wine, he shall seek the bosom of his family, and there deliver himself of what he is wont to call "a line of his mind."

Of course, for Miss Pheemie to defy any human being was a thing impossible; therefore she brooded over the vengeance that should presently fall upon the devoted heads of herself and Lady Jane, until she nodded in her chair and dozed, to dream she was pursued by an enormous scarlet serpent having the head of Sir George Plaistow (which vision was doubtless a *rechauffé* of the unfortunate bell-rope). Then the good lady waked with a jerk, and became presently conscious of a voice speaking in strange, disjointed sentences, of now and then a sob—not the sob of a woman's quiet weeping, but a dry, tearless catching of the breath.

Then once more came those wild, half-incoherent adjurations, addressed apparently to some phantom presence; something infinitely dear, and to be called upon by every loving name fondness could suggest, yet something that evaded the speaker, like Undine as she sank into the sea, and the little sobbing waves cried, "Lebewohl!"

Lady Jane's life-long self-restraint, her powers of self-repression, had snapped at last. One moment of a trial too keen had made the fetters yield; memories that were buried deep down, with the earth pressed hard upon their deathwhite faces, stirred and rose, and confronted the tortured mind in ghastly, weird array; a voice from the dead years that lay behind her had cried out; eyes with the same clear radiance, the same half-sad, half-triumphant candor as those that had looked up into her face by the fire-light long ago and pleaded for a blessing, had looked into hers to-night; and, as she was held silent and motionless by their spell, a smile, the very turn and trick of which was graven on the innermost tablet of her heart, passed across the face before her.

Rest? Sleep?

Ah, no, dear, faithful Pheemie, not to-night!

Draw the curtain aside, and look upon the Lady Jane as she mutters and moans and weeps; cast your arms about her as you may, you cannot lull the pain of that mother-heart. Her eyes do not look at you—do not see you. They are gazing at what you cannot see.

Fear is stilled before the storm of anguish that has broken over her life. She would not cringe or shrink, though the voice that has been the knell of all her life's joy were to ring ever so loudly in her ears. Curses, however deep, could not drive the hot color from her cheeks. For a lifetime nature has been trampled underfoot, and now is the hour of its retribution.

As Miss Pheemie stands trembling by the bed, my lady, all dishevelled as she is, her costly laces and the robe of trailing, rustling brocade looking strangely, weirdly out of keeping with the awful ghastliness of her face, rises and stands for a moment, with one hand clinging to the curtain. Then she takes a faltering step or two across the room.

"Oh, come back, my dear!" cries poor Miss Pheemie, feeling, in her sore perplexity, as though the very foundations of the earth were moving, and all the proprieties of life dissolving, to "leave not a wrack behind."

But some strong purpose, some stern, unalterable resolve, is written in my lady's eyes; an almost superhuman exaltation of feeling has, for the time being, so changed the features that are usually expressive only of sadness and submission, that Miss Pheemie, dreading she knows not what, sinks upon her knees and grasps a fold of my lady's dress.

"Let me go! I must go! Do not touch me, Pheemie. The child has called me!"

Miss Pheemie's hand falls as if paralyzed from its hold, and the next sound that breaks the silence is the soft rustle of a silken train upon the polished floor.

Like a sleep-walker, seeing nothing as she passes on her way, Lady Jane glides down the wide stair, and in her wake, a trembling, feeble shadow, creeps Miss Pheemie.

"I hate snivelling; why, when first—ahem! —I mean some years ago—my wife and Miss Pheemie there used to snivel together: I caught them at it one day, and, confound it, Pettigrew, I raised the devil's din!"

"I do not doubt it," said that gentleman, dryly.

Sir George Plaistow, you see, was entertaining his guests by favoring them with a few of his ideas upon domestic government, and at the same time, in his usual candid fashion, he was edifying the servants who were waiting at table. Sir George had no sense of delicacy on such points; no uncomfortable feeling of refinement chained his tongue in the presence of his inferiors, though he *could* trace his lineage back to 1104.

"Sit down to dinner with me, with red eyes and swollen noses!—not if I know it! So, as I said before, I raised the devil's din."

William Snow was apparently absorbed in contemplating every minutest detail of the pattern on his plate. Therefore, though this genial remark was addressed to the world at large, it was left for Mr. Pettigrew to reply,

"Ah! just so."

There was evidently something wrong. As a rule he had a ready answer for Sir George; a quelling one, that had the damping effect upon that gentleman's egotistical assertions of water upon fire. Perhaps the vacant place had all the effect of a Banquo at the feast; perhaps the thought of a dead white face, and the echo of a bitter cry, haunted Mr. Pettigrew? Other perplexities may also have beset him; he was absent, and apparently at times deaf, even to the host's loudest roar, or most blatant boast of prowess in the hunting-field or on the moor.

Every now and again he gave a sharp yet furtive glance at William sitting opposite; and once he muttered to himself the characteristic words,

"Quite, quite!" evidently thus answering some mental suggestion of his own.

The result of this preoccupation on the part of the principal guest of the evening was a rampant, unrestrained freedom on the part of the host.

He so enraged and maddened William Snow by his comments on Lady Plaistow's sudden illness, that at last he made a slight effort at repression on his own account.

"I trust Lady Plaistow may be able to join us again during the evening?"

Sir George was about to say he'd "be d—d if she did;" but bethought himself that Mr. Pettigrew might not be so harmless as he looked, and peradventure rouse up to some sudden vehemence. He therefore merged this intended remark in a shower of abuse at the butler, who had, so he said, served them with the wrong wine. This poor scape-goat of his master's ill-conditioned temper stood meekly enough to receive a torrent of such language as few men would lavish on a hound that had bitten them; and William, meanwhile, made vehement mental resolves never to put his legs under Sir George Plaistow's mahogany again, or eat the salt that closes a man's mouth.

Mr. Pettigrew looked calmly and patiently on: he pitied the butler; but having state reasons of his own for wishing Sir George to "gang his ain gate," and let off the steam of irritation as much as possible, he did not see fit to succor the distressed one.

Everything comes to an end, and so at last the hail-storm of his master's anger ceased to batter the head of the butler, and wine of a different seal was opened, and pronounced "A 1," by Mr. Pettigrew. The host drank a generous glass, rubbed his hands, smiled, and dashed into a story of the hunting-field. It was a veteran story, that ought to have been ashamed to show its face, after having been told for the last forty years, and was now unearthed for the especial benefit of Mr. Snow.

"You've *heard* the story of the pug that ran from Scarsfoot to Abberdingy—eh, Pettigrew?" quoth the host, by way of preface.

"Yes, oh yes, I've heard it; it's a capital story: you'll be delighted with it, Snow—it's as good as a run with the hounds on a clear, frosty morning to hear Sir George tell it."

Mr. Pettigrew did not mention the fact that he had heard the story about twenty times, and considered it in the light of an unmitigated bore. He would have liked to have had an audible chuckle over "letting in Snow" for the infliction; but that indulgence being forbidden by the *convenances* of society, he was obliged to content himself by drinking a Lilliputian wineglassful of raw whiskey, one of a brotherhood that, at this stage of the entertainment, were handed round in true Scotch fashion.

Inspired either by this libation, or by some spirit of mischief, the offspring of his own private surmises, Pelham Pettigrew now began to eke on and encourage his host in caracoling right royally upon the hobby of his own achievements in the hunting-field, and showing off the paces of that venerable steed, the fifty-times-told adventure of the run from Scarsfoot to Abberdingy.

> "Over hill, over dale,
> Thorough bush, thorough brier,
> Over park, over pale,
> Through flood—"

No, not "through fire," so I cannot finish the rhyme, but through everything else did they in imagination rattle the poor fox of forty years back, whose wraith ought surely to have been left to rest in peace ere this.

Sir George grew more and more excited as his story progressed: he shouted "tally-ho!" so that the echo of his voice reached the kitchen below, and the domestics expressed an opinion that master was "unco daft the night." He waved his arm as he described a country yokel going up wind and doing his best to throw out the run; he screamed words of encouragement to the field, when poor pug, trying hard to save his brush, slipped back and doubled round the edge of the Scarsfoot wood; he yelled as he was driven out into the open once again, and the ladies of the kennel gave tongue loud and clear. Now one of the riders is left "doubled up" in a ditch; another has come to grief over a sunken fence; the pace is fast and furious; Reynard, a little red-brown spot in the distance, glides on with swift yet scarce-seen motion; the hounds, running so well together you might cover them with your handkerchief, sail compactly after him; while the master of the hounds and the narrator of the story are the only riders in sight. Now a high fence, falling on the other side to a deep trench, tries the mettle of both horses and riders. Up! soh! they're safely landed — no, the master is down — "by gad, sir, a regular crumpler!"

But at this point of his story Sir George himself went a mental "crumpler" of such astounding force that he was struck dumb by it, and for that night at least the story of the run from Scarsfoot to Abberdingy was doomed to be an unfinished tale.

He had heard the door, which was directly behind him, open softly; he had breathed a deep breath that boded no ultimate good to the intruder; but he had forborne to turn round, for fear of spoiling the point of his story.

Just as the last words we have recorded passed his lips, there was a rustle of silk on the dark oak floor, and he sat staring at the apparition of his wife as though he hardly believed but that he saw a vision.

"She *dare* not! she *dare* not!" he thought to himself, during those few terrible moments of silence.

But apparently Sir George Plaistow for once underrates the daring of his long-submissive wife.

Lady Jane is pale as one of the shrouded dead —pale with the dull, gray pallor of old age, not the delicate whiteness of youth; the blood that had mantled fever-hot in her cheeks through the past hours of mental struggle has now suddenly curdled round her heart; her gray hair falls in disorder on her shoulders; and her eyes, bright with a terrible eagerness, grow to the face of William Snow.

Her strength seems about to fail her; she clings to Miss Phœmie's hand, and yet seems to draw that terrified woman after her.

Appalled by the enormity of his wife's conduct, Sir George is still silent.

His eyes follow her slowly moving figure as though she were some basilisk, the sight of which has turned him to stone.

Pelham Pettigrew has risen from his chair instinctively as that strange pair enter the room, and William would doubtless have followed his example, but that some undefined feeling chains him where he sits, watching the slow approach of that dishevelled, wild-eyed woman, whose white lips seem about to speak words meant for his ear alone.

Fear has died out in the heart of Lady Jane; dread of her tyrant can find no place in the heart that travails with a mother's passionate yearning. She does not even *see* her husband, or once meet the glare of his indignant eyes.

She sees *no one*—no one save the man with the clear, dark-lashed gray eyes and the square brow—the man at whose smile and at whose voice the dead-and-buried pangs and hopes of the past have started into life, and are clutching at her heart, and tearing open anew the scarce-healed wounds that have hardly yet ceased to bleed.

Close up to William's side she comes, and lays her hand upon his shoulder. She bends down until her eyes are on a level with his own, and then, in a voice scarce louder than a whisper, but that yet penetrates to every distant corner of the room, she speaks.

"Tell me," she says, "in the name of the dear Christ who loved his mother, and pitied her pain—who are you that look at me with my darling's eyes, and speak to me with my darling's voice—my darling whom I—lost—so—many—weary—years—ago?"

*　　*　　*　　*　　*　　*

————◆————

CHAPTER XXVII.

TRÄUMBILDER.

"How *dare* the fellow be related to us? It's a d—d impertinent liberty!"

"Reflect, my dear sir, that he cannot help himself."

"Picked out of the gutter—"

"Whose fault was it that he ever got into the gutter?"

"A beggarly lawyer— Hi!—here!—stop!— Pettigrew, don't do that! I beg your pardon, old fellow; I forgot whom I was talking to!"

"Don't forget again," said Mr. Pettigrew, returning from the door of Sir George Plaistow's study, which he had already reached, preparatory to leaving the room.

"How confoundedly peppery you are with a fellow!" grumbled the baronet, as his companion once more lounged comfortably in an easy-chair.

"I never allow a word against my honorable profession to be spoken in my presence," returned the other, with an air of incomparable grandeur, and making a movement as though he were hitching an imaginary gown over his shoulders.

"Well, I've said I won't do it again: I can't do more than that, can I?"

"Yes; you can stick to it."

"Well, well; don't be so mighty full of your con— Bless my soul, Pettigrew! can't you see I'm driven to death with all this fuss and upset? If you'd let me do as I wanted to do, and go down myself to that old buffer, what do you call him—?"

"And frighten him to death, eh, with your rough Northern manners? blow the roof off his house, and the windows out of it? No, no; I'm not such a fool as that, Plaistow."

"How the devil do I know that the fellow you've got hold of to investigate the matter won't go and idle his time hanging about this cathedral town, and run up the deuce of a bill for me at the best hotel in the place?"

"Simply because I am in the habit of putting any business that comes in my way into the hands of *gentlemen;* besides, I thought you said just now that you looked upon it in the light of a—ahem!—a liberty, in fact, that my young friend Snow—"

"If he's my grandson, his name isn't Snow," broke in the baronet, vehemently.

"Just so. Well, then, we'll start upon the hypothesis that he *is* your grandson, and call him—Mallinger—"

"D—n it, Pettigrew!" roared the other, "do you know, no one has dared to name that—that —person to me these five-and-twenty years back! I—I—won't stand it! I—I—won't listen to it!"

"As you like; but it appears to me that this interesting affair cannot possibly be looked into without that name being mentioned to you many hundreds of times."

"A low, beggarly fellow! A man who taught reading, writing, and arithmetic for the clothes on his back!" bellowed Sir George, bouncing up from his seat and beginning to perambulate his study as a bear paces its den.

"My dear sir," said Pelham Pettigrew, holding up his faultless hand, "bear in mind you are speaking of the dead."

"I'm glad of it! I'm glad the beggar's dead! No, no—I say, Pettigrew, I take my oath I won't say another word! Sit down again, there's a good soul! You're the only friend I have in the world; I do assure you you are!"

"Probably."

Sir George looked sharply at the speaker; even his tough hide felt the sting of that one quietly uttered word; but it was no use entertaining any idea of resentment against a man who looked as calm and polite as it was possible for man *to* look, and who was quietly striking a vesuvian and lighting a cigar.

"Well, well, you think it's all conclusive, eh, Pettigrew? You're a sharp fellow, you know—"

"Thanks."

"I mean it; I'd stake my life on your opinion any day. Now just tell me the plain truth—you think there's no doubt about the matter?"

"I think there is not only no doubt, but no shadow of a doubt. The half-effaced name of the publisher on the old hymn-book being that of a Jedburgh man, and the discovery of the marriage register at Liverpool—the marriage between your daughter, Mary Desborough Plaistow, and Arthur Mallinger, are, to *my* mind, conclusive facts."

Sir George winced at the conjunction of those two names.

"And allow me to tell you," continued Pelham Pettigrew, "if I had been a marrying man—which I rejoice to say I am *not*—and if I had had a son, I should have considered myself a fortunate—a *most* fortunate man, had that son been such a man as William—ahem!—Mallinger."

Again Sir George started and breathed hard; but he continued silent, and so his companion went on,

"Of course, a fine gem is never the worse for a good setting; and to turn out to be a scion of an ancient house such as yours is no ordinary luck for any man."

Here he "bowed foo' low," like the Laird o' Cockpen, and with perhaps a more courtly grace than that worthy; but what Mr. Pettigrew was thinking to himself all the while was this:

"I wouldn't be related to you, you old brute, for twenty thousand a year, and the privilege of tracing myself back to the patriarch Noah himself, and skipping the Flood!"

Fortunately, however, none of us have the power of reading another's thoughts, and at his companion's well-turned compliment Sir George plumed himself like an overgrown bantam.

"The fact is, Pettigrew," he said, after a long silence, "there's a great deal in this business to—swallow" (here he gave a gulp, as though some bitter pill were sticking in his gullet); "but I'd swallow a d—d deal more to 'do' that beast Lumsden!"

Now the obnoxious Lumsden was the man to whom Ardreggan would go, in the event of Sir George dying without an heir. The baronetcy would become extinct, unless—

Yes, that "unless" was the cat in the bag—the secret motive that, as it were, underlay all the man's blustering, like a vein of satisfaction.

For the law of the land decrees that the royal hand can recreate a title in the person of a baronet's grandson, he being the son of that baronet's daughter.

Perhaps in the whole course of his previous life Sir George Plaistow had never opened so many books as in the comparatively short time that had now elapsed since that eventful night on which my lady glided into the Ardreggan guest-chamber, and solemnly adjured the man then passing under the name of William Snow to tell her, "for the dear Christ's sake," who and what he was?

Every family history that lay upon the shelves of the Ardreggan library had been ransacked for a precedent; the man's whole nature was concentrated in the longing to gratify what had been the passion of his life—the longing to have an heir to his name and lands, and to "do" the obnoxious Lumsden.

Under the prompt and energetic management of Pelham Pettigrew, the search into the circumstances of William's birth, and the finding of some trace of his unfortunate parents, had prospered mightily.

It was Mr. Pettigrew himself who had deciphered the faint character of a publisher's name upon that old hymn-book which William treasured as his dearest possession, and from whose pages, in the days now long gone by, he had sung to Jim in the sleepless hours of his pain.

Miss Pheemie, seeing this little volume, and recognizing it as her own gift to the girl who had been dear to her as her own life, fell into an ecstasy of tears, and "kissed the book" with a devotion that suggested to Mr. Pettigrew scenes familiar to him in his legal capacity.

The searching of every parish register within a wide radius of the cathedral town whither May had wandered, and where she had given her own life for that of her babe, had been also Mr. Pettigrew's idea; and the finding of the record of her marriage to the despised tutor had filled his soul with a self-satisfaction, under the influence of which he seemed to expand before the eyes of the beholders.

Another proof of William's relationship to the Plaistow family was to be found in the Ardreggan picture-gallery; for if a close resemblance might be traced in the features of that laird who was hanged above his own gate-way for treason to those of the present representative of his line, a still stronger likeness came out—a reflection in the vast mirror of time—between our hero and a certain Hugh Plaistow, who, deserting the Puritan principles of his house, died gloriously at the age of twenty-four fighting for the cause of the Young Pretender.

There was the same fearless candor of expression, the same square brow, the same clear-cut mouth and chin; even the brown locks had the same ripple in their thick, closely shorn masses; and the honest, outlooking eyes the same blue-gray tint.

"I know now," said Pelham Pettigrew, "what made me feel as if the lad's face was familiar to me, when I first met him at old Bland's chambers."

William was not, perhaps, exactly a "lad;" but, you see, to Mr. Pettigrew's eight-and-forty years, twenty-five seemed an infantile age for a member of the Bar.

Of course, during the time of which we are now writing, a perfect turbillon of gossip and chatter gathered about Ardreggan and its affairs: mysterious paragraphs appeared, no one could tell how, in the daily papers; villagers and servants—those ever active scavengers of gossip regarding their betters—told marvellously strange tales of the doings at the "great hoose"—told how the master of Hazelcroft, and the gentleman who had come up north with him, spent hours and hours closeted with Sir George; how a telegram had been despatched to London, and resulted in the arrival of a grave man of law, followed by another of the same species.

And first one of the surrounding families called, and then others followed their example.

Let your friends fall away ever so much, a little active curiosity will gather them about you again, like a flock of eagles round a carcass.

Only do something bad enough, or good enough, to render yourself an object of public interest, and your acquaintances will rally round you with touching promptitude, and with amiable avidity pry into every possible detail of the state of affairs.

Miss Pheemie, having some time ago reached the utmost climax of astonishment possible to the human mind, had calmed down into a chronic state of amaze, taken her Sunday go-to-meeting dress into every afternoon wear, and set herself to receive the visits of excited and chattering matrons, and young ladies deeply interested in the romantic story of a new-found heir to the broad lands of Ardreggan, kelpie-stane, kelpie, ghost, and all!

For no one could see my lady.

Thus far in my story I have had to chronicle much suffering, much sadness, but not, I think, even one transient gleam of sunshine, in the life of Lady Jane.

Well, she was happy now.

Happy in a visionary world of her own; a world in which there was no place for pain or parting; a world of happy dreams; a world peopled with phantoms that were the creatures of her own imagining.

The fetters that had bound her life, the bondage of fear that had driven the light from her eyes and the peace from her heart, were broken.

She no longer shrunk and shivered at the sound of her husband's voice; no longer lay awake through the still watches of the night, keeping a vigil of desolation.

And tables were turned nowadays, for Sir George, instead of being the cause of fear, became the subject of it.

Yes, he was afraid of his wife; afraid of being left alone with her even for a moment. Tyranny and cowardice go ever hand-in-hand: the man who blusters and curses his way through life "in piping times of peace" is the first to cower like a beaten hound when the day of trial comes.

Sir George Plaistow had an inordinate dread of mad people, and his wife was mad — at least that was the way *he* put it. Others would have shrunk from using that word of terror to the harmless, gentle woman who lived in a shadowy, lovely world of her own.

May, her own little child; May, with her golden locks floating out far behind as she danced in the fire-light, her shadow flitting mistily across the polished floor; May, her hands filled with roses from the garden on the terrace; May, with her arm about the colly's neck, and her shining tresses mingling with his shaggy coat — these and a thousand other dear, fond memories take shape and form, keeping the mother company through her lonely yet contented days.

For hours she sits by the casement, her hands softly folded in her lap, watching what no other eyes can see.

She speaks tender words that hold all a mother's foolish fondness, and strings of baby-names such as a woman lavishes upon the child whose little velvet-soft hand "toys with the circle of her breast."

She clasps her arms about a shadow-child in sweet content, thinking they zone her heart's lost darling; and, lulling "baby May" to rest, she croons broken snatches of songs that her lips have not lilted since the days of her girlhood, more than forty years ago.

When first it became a recognized fact that some fine chain in the machinery of her brain had given way under the pressure of intense mental exaltation — in a word, when the doctors said (veiling their verdict in a cover of delicate phrases) that Lady Jane Plaistow was — mad, Sir George hastened to suggest that Miss Pheemie should, at once and forever, appropriate the room leading through his wife's that had been his; and expressed his wish to migrate to the western wing of the house.

"She is used to her, you see; women understand each other's ways; it's the best arrangement that can possibly be made," said the domestic bully, eagerly; and poor Miss Pheemie, in a paroxysm of gratitude for what would have seemed to any less loving heart a somewhat questionable piece of generosity, took his hand in hers and kissed it, murmuring, as she did so, "God bless you, Sir George! She and I will never be parted; I will be very faithful to the trust you have given me!"

I think it was the only blessing Sir George had ever had bestowed upon him in his life, and, in consequence, it sat somewhat uncomfortably upon him, like an "uneasy crown."

There are other and more important threads of my story soon to be up-gathered — interests that will take me from the gloomy grandeur of Ardreggan, and those two faded women who inhabit the eastern wing of the castle; but before I travel south again, I must depict one scene within the chamber that once saw May glide softly in, and claim the mother's kiss and blessing that were that mother's last gifts.

Autumn has grown old since the day on which we first came north with Pelham Pettigrew and our hero. The ferns are no longer radiant in golden livery, but lie battered down upon the chill earth; the heather has lost its purple bloom, the fallen leaves lie ankle-deep upon the ground, withered and dead.

But within all is brightness and comfort; and the glow of fire-light fills the room where once Miss Pheemie reigned over one little subject — a golden-haired, rebellious lassie, with a rose-bud mouth that could be *mutine* and winning both at once.

This room is now set apart as my lady's sitting-room, and a tender thoughtfulness for her has made it beautiful.

Just now it is the time of the gloaming: that tender, dreamy half-light that gives a shadowy picturesqueness even to the most commonplace chamber.

The rich, red, leaping fire-light flickers on the walls, kisses the flowers that make the air sweet with their perfume, casts dancing shadows in the distant corners, and even lends a little of its glow and color to the cheek of the woman who is lying back in a low lounge. At her side is the man whose story we have thus far told, and whom we have seen so often in the heart of the big city on the other side of the Tweed.

Lady Jane holds William's hand in both her own, now and again lovingly stroking it with fingers that seem to him each day thinner and more fragile.

"May told me you were coming; she was here last night. I like you to come; it is from being always with her that you have grown so like her. Put your head down nearer to me: I want to see your eyes; yes, they are the same."

William does as she bids him, and then he bends down over the little worn hands and kisses them lovingly.

She laughs — a low, happy laugh, almost like a child's — and touches the thick, brown locks caressingly.

"I am now happy!" she says; "but I dreamed once that I had lost May."

There is a sudden trouble in the poor faded eyes, a restless movement of the hands he holds; but it is gone very quickly, this passing cloud of confused recollection; and she is once more smiling up into his face, and telling him what "May" said and did when she was there last.

"She brought those flowers," says my lady, pointing to a group of roses. "Did you help her to gather them for me?"

Strange, disjointed, changing, shadowy, are the images that cross the disk of her thoughts; but always happy, always loving, God be thanked; and with all the dark, sad past blotted out forever. Does it seem hard that this should be so? that now that the reality of joy had come, the failing brain could not grasp its tangibility? Are we ready to mourn, and say, "How sad that it should come *too late?*"

The answer to regret lies in this:

So many things in life *seem* too late. Yet it is only seeming.

For in the time to come, *God's own time,* earth's pains and partings, earth's lonelinesses and desolations, will seem but shadows, and we shall know that in his ordering of the lives of men there can be no "too late!"

CHAPTER XXVIII.

HAD HE FORGOTTEN?

WAVES of changeful fate have circled, and eddied, and swirled about the centre figure of our story with mighty power and restless turmoil.

Standing within this turbillion of change, no longer owning the same name, of different position, different prospects, altered life, how fares it with our hero?

Doubtless in time he would have leisure to put this question to himself; at present a misty sense of unreality was over everything about him, himself included.

The change from the obscure position of an exceedingly humble member of the Bar to that of finding himself the centre of interest, not only to those immediately around him, but in some sort to the world at large, was a startling one.

It is here needful that I should impress upon my reader the fact that such proofs of William Snow's identity with the child of Arthur Mallinger and May his wife, as were convincing enough to Sir George Plaistow, Mr. Pettigrew, and David Earle, would by no means suffice to establish this identity in the eye of the law, nor yet satisfy "that beast Lumsden" (to quote our friend, the baronet), as to the propriety of Ardreggan eventually slipping from his unwilling hands.

Perhaps never had the tact, energy, and enterprise of Pelham Pettigrew shone with so steady —nay, almost so blinding—a lustre as now.

Solely to his determined and persevering efforts was to be attributed the happy fact that a lawsuit between Sir George Plaistow and the abominated Lumsden did *not* adorn the family records; for in less skilful hands, and under the management of a less clear head, there can be no doubt that, once Sir George Plaistow should be gathered to his fathers, the country might have been edified, and lawyers and counsel greatly enriched, by a "case" such as convulsed society some years ago. Doubtless, also, during the said case, endless witnesses would have been requested to inform the public "if they would be surprised to hear" a variety of contradictory and idiotic statements. As it was, no such "case" was ever brought before the law-courts of our enlightened country, though the unregenerate Lumsden more than once threatened such a proceeding as an ultimate yet certain result.

At this time the newspapers fairly bristled with advertisements, entreating any person or persons who might have any knowledge of a certain "Arthur Mallinger and May his wife" to come forward and lay such information at the feet of Mr. Pelham Pettigrew, Q.C. It will be easy for any of us to imagine the distress of mind with which William awaited the results of these appeals flung, as it were, to the "wide, wide world."

Nothing so weighed upon his heart as the thought of that poor mother whose life had been so short, and yet long enough to hold so much pain—that loving and faithful life that had been given for his—that wilful, yet all womanly woman who had loved, "not wisely, but too well," and whose sorrow God's hand had stilled at last. We are told that the blood of murdered Abel "cried from the ground," and truly, in these days of search and uncertainty, the cry of a murdered voice sounded in the ears of the man whose hand had given May's unopened letters to the flames, for Sir George Plaistow would have given half his lands now to hold that little packet safe and sound.

The expression of Pelham Pettigrew's countenance, as the fate of those letters was explained to him, had made Sir George wince as a blow might have done; nay, it was, I think, a worse hurt than any blow could have been, for the man clung more and more helplessly to the only friend he had, and would willingly have lied about the letters had he dared. But his confession was dragged from him by that relentless eye and voice which had long since made Pelham Pettigrew a terror to the witnesses on "the other side."

There were one or two questions which it was considered needful to put to Lady Jane, in the hope that recollection might still hold some faint reflection of what concerned the past, even though the present was but a confused mass of images, melting the one into the other in the mirror of her mind. Pelham Pettigrew, ushered in by Miss Pheemie, and followed by a most unwilling visitor in the person of Sir George himself, therefore paid a visit to the room in the eastern wing of the castle.

As they entered, my lady rose to receive them, bending low in courteous salutation, with all that perfect grace that was the one charm she had preserved throughout the troubled years of her life. She did not offer to give her hand to either; but held some freshly gathered flowers very tenderly, as though she were guarding them for some one dear to her; and now and again she glanced wistfully at the door.

"You are welcome," she said, speaking without a trace of that shy timidity that had been so painfully evident in the past, "but I cannot ask you to stay long. I am expecting my daughter: she has sent me these flowers, you see—it is they who tell me to expect her: she will be here very shortly now, I think; she will kneel here by my knee—we shall kiss each other—we shall like to be alone together."

Sir George had backed gradually out of the room as his wife spoke.

As to Pelham Pettigrew, if ever that astute man of law was in danger of utterly disgracing his reputation as a hardened worldling, I think it was at this moment.

"It is no use—no use at all!" he muttered to Miss Pheemie. Then he turned to leave the room.

Not, however, without one backward look.

Lady Jane was sitting by the fire, gazing dreamily at the flowers now lying on her lap; she touched them tenderly one by one, and spoke softly words that to the ears of others held no meaning.

"She is quite, *quite* happy!" whispered Miss Pheemie, following Mr. Pettigrew out into the corridor.

But he cannot have heard; for he never even looked at her, by way of reply. Then he passed on—for the first and only time in his life guilty of discourtesy to a woman.

It may perhaps be as well that at this stage of my story I should anticipate a little, and say that the numerous and constantly recurring advertisements of which we have before spoken, appealing to those who could give any information respecting William's parents, at length resulted in the appearance at Mr. Pettigrew's chambers in the City of a certain Thomas Mallinger, no other than the son of those relatives beneath whose roof the broken-down tutor had taken refuge.

It appeared that at the time of Arthur Mallinger's illness, the worthy couple, Thomas's father and mother, were bound for Australia, being possessed by an idea that in that golden land men ran up the ladder of success with a hop, skip, and jump, and sat complacently at the top for the remainder of their lives.

The illness of the boy who was dear to them as a son, though in actual relationship only a nephew, put off, though it did not ultimately stand in the way of, their emigration to the other side of the world.

Mary Plaistow was married from their house, at that gloomy little church among the Liverpool docks whence Pelham Pettigrew had succeeded in dragging forth the record of the event, and shortly after the marriage Arthur's relatives set sail for the country that was the haven of their desires.

Poor May's letters reached that distant land at long intervals, and the story told by each succeeding one was sadder than the one before. With natural pride she forbore to speak of the grinding poverty that haunted her home like a gaunt-eyed spectre; forbore to tell of all the privation she, so luxuriously nurtured, had to endure. She never told the pitiful story of long months of struggling to "keep the wolf from the door;" of letters penned in hope to those who should have aided her — letters replied to only by unbroken silence.

With weary, aching head, Arthur Mallinger strove to coin money from an already over-strained brain; his tired fingers plied pen and pencil, yet never thought the task a hard one, because it was done for May.

And she, hiding her own anxieties and suffering from his eyes as best she could, strove to cheer him on, and never once by look or word led him to fear that she repented casting in her lot with his.

Indeed, how should she; seeing that her life, however troubled outwardly, had the full completeness that is ever born of a love that knows no changefulness, and never faileth?

At last to these two came that terrible day when the man's head and hands could toil no more. He who had so passionately, if so unwisely, loved her, lay dying.

What, think you, was the burden on his heart of knowing what her helplessness and desolation would be in the future?

She, a delicately nurtured girl, would be left, lacking even the shelter his poor efforts might have won for her, to face the weakness and the pains of motherhood—alone!

"May, I shall write to Lady Plaistow myself," he said one day, when the hand of sickness was very sore upon him.

And May, white and wan, brought the pen and paper.

But the poor, feeble hand refused to trace the words; the poor, dim eyes were growing sightless.

"Oh, my darling!" the man cried, in his bitter pain, as the pen dropped from his hold, "oh, my love, what suffering I have brought upon you! What sorrow has come upon you for my sake! What will become of you, my own—when I am gone?"

In a moment she had flung herself upon her knees beside his bed, and with her arms about his wasted form, and her words broken by kisses showered upon his sunken cheeks and pallid lips, sobbed out how "gladly, gladly, gladly" she would wade through that sea of sorrow again; how more than twice tenfold she counted all the trouble overbalanced by the sweetness of that love that he had borne her through it all!

Even dread of the future could find no place in her mind just then; for all lesser shadows were hidden by the great black cloud of anguish that brooded over her soul, as she realized that her husband was going from her.

Death is often merciful at last, and hushes the dying to sleep right tenderly.

And so, in the end, to Arthur Mallinger the King of Terrors came in gentle guise enough, for the images that floated before his failing senses were those only of a happy past, and, with his head upon the breast of the woman who had been faithful "even unto death," his spirit passed away.

All the money that could be spared by those good people in Australia was sent at once to Mary Mallinger, when they received the news of her husband's death; but perhaps Australia is *not* just the country from which one would select to have urgently needed help sent to one, and the only result of this generosity was the return of both letter and enclosure through the Dead-letter Office, some months afterward.

But before this, one more letter—the last they ever received—came from the young widow. Things with her had gone on from bad to worse, as might naturally have been expected.

She had parted with everything, even with that little golden circlet to the possession of which a woman clings with a loving tenacity.

By such means she had managed to pay for the bare necessities of life. She had written, not once, but many times, to Ardreggan, beseeching her father and mother for help and forgiveness, and telling them of her widowed state, and of the time of trial that was now so fast approaching.

No notice had been taken of these pitiful appeals; even a letter to Miss Phœmie — dear, good Phœmie, who never in her life denied "the child" a single thing she had it in her power to give—was unanswered like the rest.

May was in despair.

The lodging-house keeper began to urge her to quit the room, or rather attic, for which she could now hardly manage to pay, even by working closely at her needle, and counselled her to apply for admission to one of those lying-in hospitals of which there are several in Liverpool.

But the pride of the girl's birth and breeding rose in hot protest against this suggestion, and, in what seemed to her a happy moment of inspiration, she bethought her of an old servant who had left Ardreggan to marry an Englishman. May happily remembered the name of the cathedral town where this woman had gone to live.

Yes; she would go there at once. Indeed, what choice had she?

To make her way to Ardreggan was not to be thought of. Not that she feared for herself; but full well she knew that to appear before her father would be to bring terrible anger and suffering upon the head of that mother who had kissed and blessed her in the glinting fire-light on the night that she had left her home, to follow the fortunes of the one that had grown dearer than all others.

So the worn and weary creature set out on what proved to be her last journey. She took the ferry across the Mersey, that, in spite of a lead-colored sky, looked bright and full of life and bustle, with its countless ships and busy steamers. On the Cheshire side of the river May travelled by train as far as her slender stock of money would allow; then she made up her mind to walk the rest of the way to Weaverton. All things seemed to combine against her. Heavy snow had fallen during the latter part of her journey; a bitter wind now arose, and made fine sport whirling the flakes here and there; and against this wind and snow, she, a delicate, suffering creature, with the first pangs of motherhood even now turning her cheek whiter than the snow around her, made her weary way, until the sweet chimes of the old cathedral bells fell through the snow - thickened air, and the lights of the town glimmered here and there, and seemed like friendly guides beckoning to cheer her on.

With the few coins she had still remaining May dared not go to an inn. She made up her mind to inquire at the door of some humble dwelling for High-town, the part of Weaverton in which the old servant lived.

Thus the poor, homeless, heart-broken woman came to Mother Dutton's, with what result we who have read this story already know. I have taken advantage of an author's privilege, and told the story of Arthur Mallinger's wife in its entirety at this stage of my tale; but it must be borne in mind by the reader that only piece by piece, and bit by bit, was the knowledge of it all laid before the man most deeply interested in every detail.

Ah! how sadly William thought of that short and troubled life that had at last been given for his own!

The only relic he possessed of that poor young mother was the hymn-book taken from the pocket of her dress by Mother Dutton's hands, and shown to David Earle when first he asked for that Christmas present which had proved so onerous a gift.

It may well be imagined that the marvellous events of this period of William's life created intense excitement in those various people who had been hitherto most *lie* with him; from Beams, the jocund, who shot, like an arrow from a bow, into "Twigg's" kitchen, and shouted at Mrs. Masher that his master "had got hisself into the papers, and was agoing to be made king of the Calibin Islands," to Mother Dutton, who, as she expressed it, "got her head turned wrong side afore," when she was informed by Mr. Briggs that Master William had turned out to be a lord, and would "eventuate into a dook" one of these days.

And Jim?

Well, he heard the story of his master's greatness with very mingled feelings. No honor, no glory, no rank, however high, no wealth, however unlimited, could seem to his devoted heart to form too bright a crown for fate to lay at his old playmate's feet; nor did he do the grand and noble nature of his master such injustice as to think, even for a moment, that prosperity could change his heart towards those who had been the friends of his early days; but Jim, with that subtle intuition of sympathy that was love-given, knew that rank, and wealth, and all the good things fortune could bestow, lacked for William just the one thing that would have made them most precious. Nor was Jim far wrong; for in these days, when fortune seemed bent upon showering her best and richest gifts upon his pathway, now and again a passionate protest would arise in William's heart, in that these good gifts had not come sooner in the day. *Now* he stood upon an equal, or rather upon a higher, social platform than the woman he loved: and yet it availed him nothing.

Doubtless the fair ones of the social world in which he now must take his stand would generously show every inclination to make life pleasant to him: mothers would smile, and daughters simper; indeed, already Sir George Plaistow had speculated upon the matrimonial prospects of his grandson, and thrown out a hint or two, each one of which had fallen to the ground, as dead a weight as that "dead leaf" of which the laureate so musically tells us.

Sir George had at this time yet to learn that William was not one to be shouted or yelled at, or cursed into this line of conduct or that; but he recognized the fact fully in process of time, which must, I am sure, have been a piece of most wholesome discipline for the old tyrant.

You see, the fact was this: our hero's heart was a shrine in which reigned supreme a woman with steadfast eyes, and a low, sweet voice, and a rare grace all her own. This being so, all other women, were they ever so fair, ever so charming, ever so wise, seemed but as shadows in his sight.

The bitterest misgivings of his mind centred in the fear that Guy Tremlett better loved the beauty than he understood the golden nature of the woman who was his promised wife.

Once this loving fear dispelled, and half the sting of her loss would be taken away.

For he knew Lilian was not of those women who, finding the highest happiness fail them, are content to batten in the lower.

"Fall lower, yet be happy,"

could never, he knew, be said of her. Faithful she would ever be, and of unfailing courage; dauntless in her power of keenest suffering, beyond what another woman could be, wrapped in the armor of indifference; but all the peace and joy would die out of those gentle eyes, and only patience linger in their sad and tender depths.

"Are you forgetting us among all those grand folks you belong to now?" she had asked in one of her latest letters—letters written half at her own, half at Uncle David's dictation.

Was he forgetting? Had he forgotten? In all the excitement and turmoil of the last eventful weeks, had there been an hour in which she had been cheated of that deep indwelling in his thoughts which had been her heritage so long?

Ah, no! for as the still depths of the ocean are untroubled by the fiercest storm that lashes the surface, so the under-current of William's inner life was all unruffled and unchanged.

In this same letter are some few sentences that set him thinking gravely:

"I think Uncle David is just a little jealous of your new relations; he has a wistful look when speaking of you that makes me fancy this: you know he is getting very old now, and he is not so well and strong either as he was. The visits of those lawyers, and the excitement of the whole thing, have tried him a good deal, and I think, dear William, he will be glad when you can run down and see us.

"I, too, shall be glad when that time comes. You always smooth things out for me, you know, and just now they are a little crumpled."

"Something in Tremlett's letters has set the dear heart worrying," said William to himself, as he folded the closely written sheet. Then he bethought him of the fact that a long letter, sent to catch Guy at the *poste restante*, Naples, had never been answered, though more than ample time for a reply had elapsed.

The result of these reflections was that he journeyed south next day, and, just as the evening was closing in, drove up the avenue to Winstowe.

The good folks there had not expected him; but Mrs. Timmins, hearing wheels upon the gravel sweep, was so certain as to who the arrival would prove to be that she precipitated herself towards the study, and ran violently against Briggs, hurrying in the same direction.

"Oh, sir, if you please, there's a fly coming up the avenue! It's Master William, sir, I know!" cried Mrs. Timmins.

David Earle rose and looked so agitated that Lilian sprung up from her low seat by the fire and threw her arms about his neck.

Meanwhile, Briggs hastily pulled on his livery coat, that had been laid aside in the retirement of the pantry, and wildly argued with himself as to whether he should address Master William as "my lord" at once, or whether such a proceeding might be considered premature? He made a plunge for the door, shot himself out on to the step, and then stood bowing like a Chinese mandarin, and staring at William so intently that he forgot to look after the luggage or abuse the cab-driver.

"He don't look a bit changed," thought Briggs. "He's just the same, just as haffable as if he weren't nobody at all!"

For William had shaken hands heartily with the old servant, and then rushed forward, leaving fly and luggage to their fate.

A little timid, a little paler than her wont, Lilian came forward to meet him; two hands were held out to him, two grave, sweet eyes were raised to his.

Thus he sees again the woman he loves, thus he holds her little hands in his, and, changed to all the world, unchanged to her, reads the stirring of some new trouble in her eyes.

"Uncle David is in the study; I would not let him come out to you here; he is greatly agitated," says Lilian, leading William to the door of the room.

Then William Mallinger, the boy to whom David Earle had stretched forth a helping hand in the old, old days that were past—the boy whom he had loved and tended as his own son—went into the presence of his benefactor.

Uncle David would fain have given him a bright and joyous welcome, fain have given expression to all the loving thoughts and wishes that filled his heart; but as he stands and looks upon the face of "his boy," greater now in the estimation of the world, but the same, the very same, to him, the old man's greeting finds no utterance but tears.

<hr>

CHAPTER XXIX.

A WILL OF HIS OWN.

It may well be imagined that the days seemed only too short for Uncle David and his children to talk over all the strange events of the past two months.

A delightful excitement and flutter pervaded the Winstowe household.

The dean and the dean's wife called upon the hero of the day, and many other county magnates also paid their respects to the man who had been once a "waif and stray," and was now a "nine days' wonder." But no one was so "upset" (to use his own phrase) as Briggs.

Within the memory of man or woman (in the person of Mrs. Timmins) the dinner-table of Mr. David Earle had never been so ill-waited upon as now; for so irresistible a fascination had the hero of the "Ardreggan romance" for the eyes of Briggs, that that worthy went through the duties of his office somewhat after the fashion of the despairing lover of old, who tried the hazardous experiment of "finding his way without his eyes."

Briggs "tended the light" of his optics so perpetually upon "Master William," that Lilian derived a fund of amusement from watching the endless domestic calamities that resulted from his preoccupied condition of mind; and Mrs. Timmins rated him soundly over broken glasses and cracked teacups.

"Lord have mercy! to think of such an eventnation coming out of master's fads and fancies!" Briggs would say each evening as he took his ease by the kitchen fire after the labors of the day. At last Mrs. Timmins could stand it no longer.

"Can't you think of something *fresh* to say, Briggs? I'm tired of that," cried the good woman, with great irritation of manner.

"No, I can't; and, what's more, I don't want to," replied Briggs, shaking his head. "It's enough for a man to think of all the days of his life: and then to see *him* looking just the same, just as haffable and identical as hever!"

"Why, you don't suppose that dooks, and marquises, and such like folk have two heads, like Farmer Crabtree's calf that was the town's talk for months, do you? There's not so much difference between rich and poor as all *that* comes to, Briggs, when you look into things," said Mrs. Timmins. "And as to Master William's haffableness, it's what's to be looked for in all real quality, for it's only your half-and-half gentlebodies that trample other people down, and try to stand upon the heads of those that God Almighty made."

"Oh, I know the ways of the quality as well as you, Mrs. Timmins! I've been among the best ever since I cleaned the boots and the knives at Sir Barnaby Diggs's, when only a boy of seven, and earned eighteen-pence every blessed Saturday night that ever circulated round; and I will say Miss Lilian's young man is a real gentleman, and free with his money—" added Briggs, giving a gentle pat to his breeches pocket.

"Free with his money, and free with his tongue too!" said Mrs. Timmins, viciously. "I hate your whited sepulchres, walking like a tomcat upon eggs in the drawing-room, and cursing, when his man brought the wrong horse, like— like nothing any Christian woman that goes to church on Sundays, and minds her manners on week-days, ought to hear. Get out!"

This last vehement adjuration, apparently addressed to some intangible being only visible to Mrs. Timmins's own eyes, made Briggs feel as if cold water were being poured down his back, and he wisely said no more as to Mr. Guy Tremlett's generosity.

One of the first visits William paid after his arrival at Winstowe was to the grocer's shop in High Street; and though Mrs. Dutton did not on this occasion "lose her senses," she was in that state of trembling agitation which, with females of her kind, necessitates a constant "settling" of head-gear, and in this case resulted in her smart cap falling off altogether.

Harry, now grown a fine tall fellow, with incipient ideas of matrimony, was the *esprit fort* of the business, and with a pen perpetually sticking in his curly locks, and a most business-like white apron about his person, rendered the lives of the two errand-boys employed by Mrs. Dutton a burden to them by what they were pleased to term his "nagging." Jim had been home for a short holiday, and received that domestic incense usually offered up at the family shrine to the boy who has "bettered himself."

· When the day's work was done, and Harry had superintended the putting-up of the shop-shutters, and despatched the boys home with "a flea in their ears," then Mrs. Dutton and her sons sat round the cosy fire in the parlor behind the shop, and talked over, with an interest that knew no flagging, the early days of William Snow, the child that had drifted into their midst, and whose story now claimed the attention of the world.

From constant repetition, Mrs. Dutton's accounts of her interviews with Pelham Pettigrew's man of business had, unlike the rolling stone, gathered much moss—that is, they had become more and more elaborate, always showing an irresistible tendency to stray into the story of "mother's silver spoon," an article of domestic utility which must have been a constant stumbling-block to that much-enduring investigator, the man of law whom Sir George Plaistow wrongfully suspected of nefarious and dishonest trifling.

Perhaps never in Mrs. Dutton's previous life had she been so triumphantly, so perfectly happy, as during that period when she had been called upon to give all the information she could as to her foster-child's birth and early days. She was one of those gracious, portly matrons who delight in hearing themselves talk, and find a sweet and soothing pleasure in entering into every possible detail of their once personal experience; and it was found that the only way to glean what information it was really needful she should give was to let her wander on through a perfect maze of domestic incidents, and then set to work to winnow the wheat from the chaff.

Having already recounted every particular of these interesting interviews to every neighbor she possessed, Jim, on his arrival at home, was doubly welcome in the capacity of a fresh audience; and with a patience that did him infinite credit, he listened for hours at a stretch to things he knew by heart already.

On the occasion of William's first visit, Mrs. Dutton was, however, provided with a new topic of conversation, and a new source of surprise— one so delightful that, for the time being, it drove "mother's silver spoon" completely off the ground. For then she learned how abundantly that "blessing," which David Earle had foretold as the certain guerdon of her charity to the little one cast destitute and motherless upon her care, was to fall upon her now.

A farm — a glorious place among the bonnie Cheshire Hills — a place with fields, and cows, and cocks and hens, and a house "fit for a queen," all complete — was to be made over to Martha Dutton, widow, and to her heirs forever.

"To think," she said, as the tears ran hot and fast adown her face — "to think such luck should come to me and mine, and poor Ben not here to see it! Oh! Master William, if it hadn't a bin for the drink, what a man he would have been! What a nater he had!—that is, out o' liquor; and even at his worst, when he'd drunk the shoes off the children's feet, and didn't know no more than a child unborn which end he stood upon, he wasn't like a many; he'd just give yer a black eye, or something simple of that sort; none of yer wiciousness; none of yer kickings, and stampin' on yer with his boots on; nothing of that sort; everything simple and plain, and just what ony man might be expected to do, bein' in liquor. 'Twas only the drink,

Master William—sir, I should say, now ye're a living lord—that set him on to burn the house about yer yed that weary night; he never meant it, didn't Ben, no more than nothink! Ah, dear! but he'd 'ave bin a proud man this day, would Ben!"

Doubtless, had "Ben" lived, he would long since have brought his Martha's "gray hairs with sorrow to the grave;" but Ben was dead, and "distance lent enchantment to the view" of his failings. A husband's memory is often, I think, dearer than the reality has been; and a woman who has been "naggetted" to the very verge of dissolution will speak with tearful tenderness of those "happy days" when *he* was by her side.

Blessed and merciful veil that falls over the errors of the dead! May your memory and mine, dear reader, be looked upon through such a tender, sacred covering! and as those who love us speak of what we were, may they forget to call to mind how far, far better and more true we might have been!

"Come, come," said William, taking her hand in his, "you must not think of things to make you sad to-day, mother; I want you to be happy and cheery. Why, I declare you're cut out for the mistress of a farm-yard! I fancy I see you carrying a mighty big dish of barley, and calling all the fowls and chickens about you."

"I fancy I sees myself," said Mother Dutton, half laughing, half still tearful; "and may God Almighty bless your faithful heart, Master William, that don't mind callin' the old woman—mother—still—for—all—it's not—what—might—be—looked for—in—sich!" sobbed out the good woman. That one word "mother" had gone straight to her heart, and pierced it through and through. "When he said that word, I 'ad to get up mortial sharp, and let on as I heard the shop-bell a-ringing (which it often do, after hours), for fear I'd be like Joseph when he saw little Benjamin, and fall upon his neck and hug him, which wouldn't 'ave bin my place, considerin' as he's all among the 'ighest in the land, and not to be reproached without respect which is his doo."

Such was Mother Dutton's graphic account of this interview to a neighbor subsequently, or rather, I should say, *one* account; for surely it is needless to state that now, more than ever, Mrs. Dutton became a heroine among her friends and acquaintances.

Thanks to the straightforward principles upon which the grocery business had been managed, and doubtless owing somewhat also to curly-pated Harry's energy and talent in the matter of book-keeping, the shop in High Street had turned out a most profitable investment; and now that the business was to be disposed of, liberal offers were not wanting.

It seemed, in truth, that the evening of Mother Dutton's days was to be passed in peaceful comfort—in fact, in a sort of clover, as sweet and pleasant as that in which (eventually) her own cows stood nearly fetlock-deep, chewing the cud of happy vaccine fancies.

The only shadow that was wont to fall athwart the bright disk of the good woman's content was an all-womanly and most unwise regret that "poor Ben" was not beside her, to be "a proud man that day."

William Mallinger had now been nearly a fortnight at Winstowe, and during the whole of that period he had lived in a perfect hailstorm of letters bearing the Ardreggan arms (wild-boar rampant, surmounting the motto, "*I spare none*"), and written by the baronet, his grandfather, to urge more and more vehemently his return to the ancestral halls.

These letters, in the eyes of Briggs, were missives of solemn and awful import; and he bore each as it arrived upon a silver salver, held out at arm's-length, as though he were uncertain whether it might not blow up at any moment.

"Bless me!" said Uncle David, looking over the top of his spectacles at about the thirteenth of Sir George Plaistow's epistles, "what an impatient old fellow this grandfather of yours is, Will!"

The fact was. that, had the master of Ardreggan had his own way, he would never have let his grandson out of his sight.

A life's wish, long thwarted, was at last gratified; he could talk of nothing else than the royal prerogative that was to be obtained, *coûte que coûte*, and brought to bear upon the title that otherwise would become extinct as the breath left his own body. Naturally his zest and enjoyment in this project were at times dashed by the exceedingly unpleasant reflection that the one needful condition for its fulfilment was his own decease; but in spite of this drawback, the topic of his plans and designs was an endless one, and, failing any better audience, they were poured into the ears of poor Miss Pheemie, who on one occasion fell into peaceful slumber during the process, and was roused from her maiden dreams by a shower of invectives more powerful than pleasant.

To have William back again, to walk with his grandson over the Ardreggan lands before the eyes of the Ardreggan tenants, were now the longings that possessed the mind of the baronet. All his life he had had his own way, and now he could not get it; and the safety-valve of abusing his wife was denied to him.

Under these circumstances, I rather think the household in general had a bad time of it, and were inclined to look forward to the possible day when "George Desborough Plaistow, Baronet," should "sleep with his forefathers," and William his grandson should reign in his stead, as a millennium greatly to be desired.

"Why can't the boy give up these people down South, and stick to his own flesh and blood?" roared Sir George.

Miss Pheemie, winking and blinking, and trembling before him, quavered out a suggestion that "those people had been so good to Mr. Mallinger."

"Well, d—n it all, ain't I willing to pay anything they like for the boy's cost, and let him have done with the lot?"

This refined and gentlemanly proposition struck Miss Pheemie dumb at the time, but resulted in her writing a most piteous little letter to William—a letter which for the first time caused the fact to dawn upon his mind that the poor lady possessed a surname! For the primly written epistle was signed "Pheemie Blunt."

"Ha! ha!" laughed Pelham Pettigrew, when William happened to mention this letter on the occasion of their next meeting—"poor *Blunt's* been worn down to a *sharp* point by that old— Excuse me, my dear fellow, I really forgot I was speaking of your—ha! ha!—your respected grandsire: but it's true about Blunt, you know —worn so sharp, she's almost worn away altogether—eh? Gad! I never saw such a ghostly creature! But it's a plucky one is Blunt, mind you that; and whatever would have become of—"

But here Mr. Pettigrew abruptly changed the subject. He always avoided speaking of the Lady Jane if possible.

William wrote to his grandfather, and firmly and respectfully expressed his inability to go North again just at present. He promised, however, to do so as soon as his own affairs in town should be brought to something like an orderly wind-up, but these matters would, he said, in all probability keep him in England well over Christmas.

Now that his grandson should give up being what he chose to style "a beggarly lawyer," was the baronet's most urgent desire; and about this time it dawned upon his mind that there was a quiet but strong vein of determination in the character of his intended heir that would brook no violent restraint, and was better met by a wise moderation.

"He's got his mother's eyes, and could look at me as she did the day I thonged with my tongue that cur she married. We're a plucky race, we Plaistows!" thought the baronet; and maybe one repentant, pitiful sigh rose from his heart at the memory of the dead white face and dauntless eyes of the girl whom he had felled to the ground as she stood before him, silent and tearless, yet unconquered. "If I want to make the lad bend to my will, I'd better manage him a bit, or he'll take the bit between his teeth and bolt, as *she* did."

It was, perhaps, late in the day for the man to learn a little self-discipline, but an old proverb tells us that all things are "better late than never;" and the time was to come in the future when Sir George should consider other people occasionally, instead of only trampling upon them if they chanced to stand in his way.

However, he had not as yet reached this pitch of perfection, though launched upon the road that led to it. The first outward symptom of the healthy change beginning to work lay in the fact that he forbore to tear William's letter into shreds, a proceeding Miss Pheemie was quite prepared for: indeed, the omission of this performance, and the utterance of a few considerate words as to the "boy" being detained by business, sent her to her room in a gasping state of astonishment.

Then she recovered herself, and then stole softly along the corridor to the western room.

"My dear! my dear!" she said, "oh, my poor dear!" And Miss Pheemie's tears fell thick and fast on my lady's hands as she clasped them and kissed them.

"Don't, Pheemie!" said Lady Jane, freeing her hand from the other's clasp, and holding up a warning finger. "Hush! you will wake the child."

A white shawl was laid across the couch by which she sat, and in her fond fancy it covered the sleeping shadow-child, "Baby May!"

"If he had only been kinder—a little sooner!" sobbed Miss Pheemie.

7

"Hush, Pheemie!" said Lady Jane, "you must not cry; there is some one who will be angry if you cry."

She held Miss Pheemie close, as if to shield her from harm; and, haunted by the phantom of past fear, glanced timidly about the room, peering with eager, wistful eyes into each shadowy corner.

"*Who* is it that will be angry, Pheemie?" she whispered at last, putting up her hand wearily to the head that could harbor none other than disjointed thoughts.

"No one, no one!" said Miss Pheemie.

"I am glad of that," sighed my lady. "I have strange fancies sometimes; I'm afraid—but I don't know what I'm afraid of. Listen! May is sobbing in her sleep! Hush, my bonnie, bonnie bird! Mother will hold you in her arms, and then you will not cry any more!"

CHAPTER XXX.

"BY THE FIRE-LIGHT."

GUY TREMLETT made a perfect photograph. Some people when photographed look as if they had lost all their relations, and not one among the number had left them a decent legacy; others, as if they had just made a feeble joke, and wished to encourage their friends to laugh at it by simpering idiotically. Indeed, it is only clear-cut, faultless features that can stand the test of photography with anything like a cheering result.

In Guy's case, I am not sure that the pictured face was not even more winning than the real one: there was a repose about the former that the latter somewhat lacked; the dark eyes gained in steadfastness, and the mouth, at rest, was wholly hidden by the sweeping fall of the mustache.

A girl, looking at that picture with love-laden eyes, might dream the rosiest day-dreams, and fancy the original a hundred times better and more true than in reality he was; indeed, it would take me many chapters to write down the story of all the day-dreams that had already been offered up at the shrine of that "fetich" that, shut up in a crimson-velvet case, lay upon the *prie-dieu* in Lilian Selwyn's room.

Her love was a part of her religion; her religion was a part of her daily life; hence the union of the two interwoven threads. To hold her lover in the sanctuary of her heart; to commend him to God's keeping every day that dawned, and every night that fell; to think of him when he was far away with more intensity of tenderness, more anxious, loving thoughtfulness than when he was by her side—this was Lilian's way of loving.

An old-fashioned way, perhaps, and lacking in that element of expediency that seems to be the fashion of the day; by no means a "safe" way either, for where much is staked much is apt to be lost. A girl who can look with complacency upon "the spoils of love" in the shape of a variety of pretty *cadeaux*, that are the offerings of as many swains, runs little chance of breaking her heart; she is always ready to answer to the warning voice of caution, and "nobly give up" the man whose worldly prospects turn out less satisfactory than she at first supposed them to be; she takes refuge under the cloak of the wishes of her friends, and wisely says nothing of how completely her own inclinations chime in with theirs.

She is a very sensible person, this girl, and makes her "book" with as much acumen as the keenest sporting character who adorns the turf; she is the pride and comfort of her family circle, and teaches those "young ideas," her more juvenile sisters, how to shoot at the matrimonial target so as to hit the *gold;* and she is never guilty of the sin of idolatry towards any human being except herself.

I don't think this type of woman often breaks a man's heart; but she often does what is worse—shakes to its very foundations his trust and reverence for womanhood, and shatters his belief in love's reality.

On the other hand, by way of complete contrast, there is the girl who sets up an idol in her heart, clothes it in all the beauteous attributes a woman's fancy can evolve, and when the bitter day of knowledge dawns at last, and shows the idol to be but clay, still wraps the mantle of her love around it, to hide all blemishes from every eye save her own.

If immunity from suffering is the best and highest aim in life, then those who know how to love not "too well," but "wisely," and whose moderate and well-regulated affections, and total independence of sympathy, keep them safely in the beaten path of respectable content—if this be so, then assuredly the least sensitive people have the best of it; but it may be that a broken, erring heart laid at God's feet is a surer stepping-stone to heaven than any "want-begotten rest!"

Capability for suffering often denotes predestination to it; and as the rose that is crushed will give out its sweetest perfume, in like manner that human soul whose life-agony has been an utter lack of sympathy will become more exquisitely tender in the power of giving sympathy to others.

Do you think that the last few months of William's life had been passed through, and yet left him just the man he was before?

Do you think his own pain had not taught him how to sympathize more perfectly in that of another?

Coming upon Lilian sitting solitary by the fire-light, and seeing in her hand the pictured face of the man she loved, I tell you that not one single pang of passing petty jealousy stirred his heart. Pity, that is said to be "akin to love," can only claim affinity with the love that is grand and great and true; for that love which is mean and selfish, and rotten with covetousness, is pitiless, not pitiful.

"Are you thinking of the 'crumples' that I was to straighten out for you, child?"

Lilian did not hide Guy's likeness in her pocket, as if she were ashamed of being caught looking at it. There was no taint of prudery or unreality in the girl's nature. She laid the photograph down upon her knee, and looked up wistfully into William's face.

Pray do not suppose she had been damply and limply weeping over her lover's photograph. She was not one of those gushing individuals who ardently embrace every possible opportunity of shedding copious tears. With her, to weep was a rare thing and a painful one; nor did she find in it the easy relief that some women indulge in at the cost of great discomfort to their friends. She was no love-sick, moon-struck, lackadaisical girl, gazing with pathetic imbecility at the picture in her hand, but an anxious, loving woman, whose heart was aching sorely for lack of knowledge if it were well with Guy.

William had drawn a chair to the fire, and as he sat down within the circle of the flickering light, Lilian saw that he held a letter in his hand.

"Is that from—" She drew a long breath, and stopped.

"From Guy?" he put in, promptly. "No, it's one of Pelham Pettigrew's characteristic epistles, and must take me up to town to-morrow night at latest. But I don't want to talk of my own affairs just now, Lilian. My sister wrote to me before I came that she was glad I was coming, because there were some worries that needed to be smoothed out; and now I have been here very nearly a fortnight, and she has told me of none of these unpleasant things."

What a helpful face it was that looked down upon her with candid, steadfast eyes!

That a woman should infinitely trust one man, yet love another with blind and passionate tenderness, is by no means a rare thing.

"Well, what is it, child?" said William, as the girl was still silent.

He saw her hands clasp themselves tightly in the old fashion, and, so clasped, fall upon her lap, where lay the open photograph of that perfect face, to which the flicker of the fire-light seemed to lend a changeful look of life.

"It is—that it is so hard—waiting."

How well he recognized the ring of suppressed pain in her voice!

"For Guy's coming back? It cannot be long now, Lilian, and it was best he should go. You know you are always in his thoughts, as he in yours; and when you see him come home, looking strong and well, and all the better for the sea-breeze and the—"

"It isn't *that*, William—you mistake me. I know it was right he should go. Who could see and *feel* so well as I could how different he looked from what I longed to see him? It isn't that —it's this—this silence—"

"What do you mean?" asked her listener, sharply. "Silence! Hasn't he written?"

"It is a long, long time now; and oh, how hard it is—to me!"

The little tress-crowned head drooped; the hands held each other tighter and closer.

"My poor child! Why did you not tell me before?"

"There has been so much to talk about, so much to hear; and I thought—I hoped *any* day might put an end to it all, you know. The foreign posts are so uncertain; the letters may have got mislaid."

"What does Uncle David think about it?"

"He doesn't know: he has been so excited and upset by all this about you; and he is getting very old now, Will; he can't stand things as he used to do. I wrote to Mrs. Tremlett some time since, and Ponsonby sent me a few lines, just saying that her mistress was laid up with one of her most severe attacks and couldn't write; but that she sent her love, and to say there had been no news from 'Master Guy' for nearly three weeks."

"Three weeks!" echoed William, appalled. "Is it so long as that since *you* heard, Lilian?"

"Yes; rather more. The last letter I got was from Malta. Guy had met an old friend there—some one in the Artillery, and they had dined together at the mess, and finished the evening at the club: he said Captain Bolton was too lazy to go; but I dare say the other two didn't mind his absence: old friends like to talk over old times by themselves, don't they? They were glad to get away from the mess and have a nice long chat at the club, no doubt."

"No doubt."

Will's voice sounded so odd that she turned quickly round to look at him; but his eyes were shaded by his hand, as though from the fire-light.

"And, after all, it's foolish, isn't it, for me to be worrying myself as I have been doing, when the last accounts were so good? And besides, of course, I know Guy's silence doesn't mean that he—forgets."

"I would stake my life on that," said William, earnestly.

"Yes, I know. Why, there are a hundred things that may account for his not writing. Perhaps he wants to give me a surprise, you know, and just walk in. I know all this, of course, and yet I can't help worrying; and when the post comes and there is no letter, it seems like an age to look forward to the next day."

Oh! sad, sweet eyes, gazing dreamily at the fire—dear eyes that he would have given his life gladly to save from the shedding of one tear! How terrible sometimes is the helplessness of love!

He watches her, keeping silence because he dare not speak.

But his thoughts are bitter, and his hand clenches and crushes Pelham Pettigrew's letter out of all form and shape.

"I saved her from the fire that would have burned her body; shall I have to stand by and watch a crueller fire consume her heart? Stand by—*helpless?* Oh, my God, spare her! save her from sorrow, even though I never look upon her face again!"

Such thoughts as these surging through a man's brain chain his tongue to silence—a silence that was in this case broken by Lilian herself.

"When Milton wrote these words, '*They also serve who only stand and wait*,' I think his great heart must have felt how hard such passive serving was—how much harder than any active work. Perhaps he meant waiting for the light—God's light—that should one day come to him in the gloom of his patient blindness."

"You will let me know at once when you hear from Guy?" said William, changing the subject abruptly. He could not bear to hear Lilian speak in that way; he could not bear to think that her power of sweet, true thought was doomed to a life-long repression. Upon that intellectual platform he and she—Will and Lilian—might stand side by side.

But there Guy Tremlett could never come.

And therefore, since he dared not set one added barrier between those who were plighted to go hand-in-hand through life, Will would not answer to the electric current of the girl's thoughts.

"Of course I will let you know," she answered to his question, looking round at him with gentle surprise.

In the olden days, the days of those long talks as they paced up and down the terrace walks, no thought of hers had ever been uttered without finding a swift echo and response in his.

"Perhaps he has grown too clever now to care to talk to me about books," the girl thought, and she thought this half sadly.

For even to herself the thought had never yet taken form that a part of her intellectual nature would be ever a sealed book to Guy Tremlett—she was too faithful to harbor such an idea; yet she missed William's appreciation, and he saw that she did so; he saw the slight quiver of the lips that answered his inapposite question, and the wistful look in the eyes that were turned upon him with something almost like reproach.

Yet neither sign met with even the faintest outward recognition.

"I will be true to you, and to myself," he had said to Guy—to the man who had trusted him and looked to him for help, and he would be faithful even "in small things."

Yet, as he turned away from Lilian's look of pained surprise, the thought of all that "might have been," and *was not*, came upon him; the fulness of sympathy, the electric, swift answering of thought to thought—

> "....heart and thought and mind,
> Linked with each other; soaring far above
> The meaner passion of a lesser love!"

The thought of these things that could not be, and would have made his life one "golden day" into which could have come no sorrow that should be unbearable save that of losing her, came to him with the bitterness of death.

"Bats in the twilight, eh?" said Uncle David, coming into the room with his bandanna hanging gracefully over his shoulders, having slid thither from its place on his head—a station it usually occupied during the "forty winks" he indulged in every afternoon.

"Yes, bats indeed!" said Lilian, laughing. "I shall blink dreadfully when Briggs brings the candles in, I know. Since when has it become the fashion for elderly gentlemen to wear their pocket-handkerchiefs tippet-wise?" she went on, drawing the old man down upon a lounge, and restoring the bandanna to his pocket.

Then she put a stool beside his knee, and there took her place, well knowing he best liked to have her thus near him.

"William is going to leave us to-morrow, Uncle David."

"To leave us?" echoed David Earle, with quick jealousy. "Going back to Ardreggan—eh, my boy? Well, well, they've a claim upon you now—of course, of course."

"No one has, or ever can have, any claim upon me that can equal yours," said William. "But a letter from Mr. Pettigrew tells me I am needed up in town. As to Ardreggan, I shall not go back there until after Christmas."

"Ah, yes. I remember you said so before," replied the old man, well pleased. "We'll have a 'right merrie time,' please God, this Christmas.

> "'Come with all good-will and cheer—
> Call around us all the dear,'

That's an old-fashioned rhyme, but a good one. Do you hear, little one?" he went on, pinching Lilian's ear—"' *all the dear!*' They'll be home again by that time, eh? It wouldn't do to have the play of 'Hamlet' with Hamlet left out. No, no. Our prince will be back again by then—all the better for his voyage, too, I'll be bound."

The girl laid her head down against his knee, so that he could not see her face.

"Shy—eh? Well, well, girls are like that, I believe—eh, Will? You don't know much about it, though. Well, well, all in good time —all in good time. He'll be bringing home a bonnie bride to that grand castle of his up in the North one of these days—won't he, little one?"

"I wonder what she will be like," said Lilian, suddenly lifting her head and looking full into William's face.

."Time will show," he said, quietly. "Perhaps she'll never exist at all; perhaps I shall be like Uncle David."

Then the two men drifted into other subjects; but Lilian was silent. She was pondering on the qualifications that it would be necessary for William's wife to possess.

"If she isn't very nice and .very clever, and if she doesn't take as much care of him as I shall of Guy, I shall *hate* her!" was the conclusion she finally arrived at.

———◆———

CHAPTER XXXI.

IN A FOG!

THE whole city of London lay smothered beneath a pall of fog.

Not a fog that seemed to be any relation at all, however distant, to a country mist, that is white and fair, and melts at last into gentle dew; but a fog that looked red in the distance and yellow close to you—a fog that got into your eyes, and up your nose, and down your throat, and that held all the heavy, grimy smoke in its dank embrace, and would not let it go. .

Men and horses moving about in the streets acquired a ghostly indecision of outline, and loomed shapeless masses through the darkness. Gas-lights flaring here and there only seemed to make the fog look more dense outside their own radius, and everything and everybody was stickily damp to the touch, and smuttily and unpleasantly adhesive.

Over the heart of the city the fog was densest, and all business was being conducted by gaslight; the Temple fountain could not. sparkle one bit, no matter what exertions it might make, and the peacocks in the oasis near St. Botolph's were under a total eclipse, and lost heart to such an extent that they could not even pluck up courage to preen their draggled feathers, but just wandered about disconsolate. The ducks, however, managed to keep up their spirits by perpetually standing on their heads in the pond, and derisively presenting the tips of their tails to the fog.

The weather affected people's brains and tempers as well as their throats, and Septimus Twigg did that morning so rate and abuse the unhappy Masher that she shed copious tears, and, in so doing, smeared her countenance with such a mixt-ure of fog and smuts that her best friends would hardly have known her.

"I wish I vos with Dinah,
I do! I do!"

rung out the cheery voice of Beams from the inmost recesses of the fog; and shortly afterward the damp and shining countenance of that ornament to society rose like a sun upon the gloom of Mrs. Masher's night.

"Don't I just vish I vos with Dinah, or with any other respectable young 'ooman as lived in a decent climate, that's all! Why, 'ere's a day to give a chap the liver kimplaint for the rest of his nat'ral life! What, you're down on yer luck, are yer, Mrs. Masher?" went on Beams, setting his arms akimbo, and screwing up one side of his face sympathetically. "'As the fog got into yer witals? or 'ave yer found as some evil-minded bloke's bin stealin' of a hod coin or two out of that there old storkin' as 'angs in yer chim—"

"Hould yer noise!" cried Mrs. Masher, giving her face a last wipe with her apron, and thereby designing a long, black smear right across the bridge of her nose; "I'm in no humor for any of your imperence, my young spunkie. It's enough to have to put up with Twigg, let alone a fog as you might cut with a knife, and fry in rashers."

"O—h!" replied Beams, with a prolonged and irritating whistle, "Twigg 'as bin misbehavin' of 'isself, 'as he? I wouldn't stand it, not if I was you. Why don't yer try to better yerself? I'm agoing to better myself, I am ; for my master he's givin' up business, sold the connection and fixtures, including 'is wig and gown, to some other cove, I reckon, and I ain't going to stay with that other cove. I'm going into the civil service."

"Hear 't 'im!" cried Mrs. Masher, greatly aggravated, "talking as if he was a born gentleman!"

"Wait till yer see!" continued Beams. "I've got my name put down for the shoeblack brigade: if yer keeps a civil tongue in yer 'ed, and gets plenty of custom—that's what I call civil service, that is; and sha'n't I look a cure in the uniform, neither! Why, yer eyes 'ull be dazzled when yer pass me in the street those days!"

"And so yer master's goin' to give up business?" said Masher. "Well, I never! and, as I hear, he's turned out to be a lord! Bless us all! and whatever's going to become of Mr. Dutton?"

"He's goin' clerk to Mr. Pettingroo—'im as looks if his 'air was a flying orf his 'ed, and 'as to sleep in his wig."

"Sleep in his wig! Lor, Mr. Beams—" began Masher ; but what other dark secrets of Mr. Pettigrew's life might have been divulged by that worthy will never be known, for Mr. Dutton's voice, calling peremptorily for the boy's appearance, obliged Beams to plunge into a fogbath which under happier atmospheric conditions represented Fig-tree Court.

Here he only just saved himself from running foul of what looked like a tall white ghost, but was only his master in a light mackintosh.

How strange it was to William Mallinger to be once more in the old City home! Ardregan—the breezy hills, the strange, eventful weeks spent on the other side the Tweed—might have been a dream, for any reality they now possessed for him. Even when Mr. Boultbee plunged out of his chamber like a spider darting out of its web, and wrung his hand till the wrist ached, hailing questions upon him in a perfect shower, even then he felt as if he were only William Snow, coming back to the toil of work and to long hours in the familiar room where Lilian's water-color sketch hung over the desk between the windows, and as if Boultbee were an amiable lunatic suffering from harmless but unfounded delusions.

"Any letters to-day?" said William, as he reached the room where Jim's thoughtful care had made all things as comfortable as possible.

Yes, there were three or four: a pompous-looking missive from Sir George, and kindly words of congratulation and sympathy from various friends, but no thin, foreign envelope—no answer to that letter sent to Naples long ago—no word, no news of Guy Tremlett. Mr. Boultbee, with affectionate cordiality, had accompanied William up-stairs and sat by, garrulously rambling on about "Mrs. B." and the "small fry," as he styled the olive-branches, while his hearer lunched.

Hitherto the worthy man had simmered through life in a state of comfortable mediocrity—a man much respected by his friends, but not distinguished in any way from the common herd, or likely to be; hence it may well be supposed he revelled in the reflected importance now cast upon him by the fact of the hero of the "Plaistow romance" having been once his pupil. It was delightful to Mr. Boultbee to say to astonished and interested acquaintances that the newly discovered grandson of Sir George Plaistow, Bart., of Ardreggan Castle, Roxburghshire, had been "really, you know, a tame cat at our house—came and went as he liked, my dear sir—always a knife and fork ready, and all that sort of thing." To say this gave Frederick Boultbee of Fig-tree Court intense satisfaction, and to sit by and hear him say it delighted the soul of his spouse.

Under these circumstances he was now determined to make the most of his interview with William, and return to the bosom of his family laden with exquisitely interesting particulars of the changes that had overturned the even tenor of his old pupil's life.

And all the time William's mind was dwelling on the memory of rippling, nut-brown hair on which the fire-light glinted, the memory of a downcast face, and two white hands clasping each other close. All the time the accents of a soft, low voice lingered on his ear—a voice that said how hard it was to bear this "waiting!" He had hoped, all through his long, cold railway journey south, that a letter from Guy might be waiting him in town, and that the evening post might carry a few cheery lines to Winstowe—good news of the "absent, unforgotten"—news that would break the chain of suspense now holding Lilian's heart in "durance vile"—news, perhaps, of her lover's swift return.

"I must run across to Pelham Pettigrew's now," said William, rising from his repast, and devoutly wishing Boultbee would leave him in peace to have a few words with Jim.

But he reckoned without his host, or rather without his visitor.

How infinitely delightful to have a friend who could speak of "running across" to that brilliant constellation, Mr. Pettigrew, Q.C., as if he were just an ordinary sort of fellow! How cheerfully Boultbee groped his way across the court, affectionately slipping his arm under William's and suddenly discovering that, by a remarkable coincidence, he had a business appointment that took him in the same direction!

It must take an immense store of inward satisfaction to enable a man to see anything *couleur de rose* through the medium of a London fog; but to Boultbee, jauntily stepping along by the side of Sir George Plaistow's grandson, the earth could not have seemed fairer though the sun had been shining in a cloudless sky, and each particular lamp-post had been a tree in which sung birds innumerable.

"How pleased Elinor will be to hear that I have seen you!" he said, even at Mr. Pettigrew's very door still lingering over a fond farewell. "And you will come and see us soon—*very* soon?" he added, turning back as if suddenly inspired with a fresh idea.

William promised an early visit to Dorset Square, and then, fearing a further relapse on the part of his friend, hurriedly attacked Mr. Pettigrew's knocker.

"So here you are! that's right! that's right!" cried Mudge's master, as Mudge, squinting more horribly than usual in consequence of the fog getting into his eyes, ushered our hero into the chamber immortalized by the story of the suspended clerk.

"Here's weather to cheer a man's heart! I tell you what it is, 'our dear own native land' is the deuce of a hand at this sort of thing!"—and Pelham Pettigrew stirred up the fire with such energy that he stirred half of it into the ash-pan. "And how's Strephon, eh! how's the venerable gentleman who believes in everybody! Quite well? That's well. I'm glad you went to see Strephon. Old friends are like old wine—the best of all. The old boy's deucedly jealous of Strephon—deucedly; but you're right—'stick to those who nobly stuck to you.' I rather think that's a quotation, but I don't quite know where it's from."

"Yourself, I think, sir," said William, smiling.

"Has a sound of me, eh? Quite! quite! But, seriously, my dear fellow, you must run up to Ardreggan again before long, or 'the Philistine will be upon thee, Samson,' and no mistake about it! Why, Plaistow hasn't been up in town for years, and he writes me word to 'keep an eye open' about a house in the West End for spring or thereabouts. Not much good to keep an eye open, or a mouth either, eh? this beastly weather: I've swallowed enough fog to-day to ruin any man's constitution. I say, it's a rum go, all this business, after all," added Mr. Pettigrew, with a quick glance at his companion, "but delightful, quite! Charming idea, too—Snow melts away, and leaves Mallinger. By gad, sir, how the old boy roared when I first called you Mallinger!"

This remembrance seemed to afford Mr. Pettigrew the most unfeigned delight. He rubbed his hands over it, and then rumpled up his hair, which the fog had rendered limper and more reposeful than was its wont. Then he whistled through his teeth in a manner peculiarly his own, and, putting his head slightly on one side, critically regarded a snuffbox lately purchased from the urbane Mr. Nathan, and having on the lid an exquisite miniature of Marie Antoinette.

"Not bad, eh? No wonder the world went mad about that face! Fancy cutting off such a head, when so many ugly women are allowed to wear their head-pieces unmolested through a long lifetime. Inconsistent thing, human nature. Hum!—ha! By-the-way, when you left Ardreggan, was Lady Jane in the same condition as before? No change, eh?"

"None," said William, sadly, watching Mr. Pettigrew as he carefully dusted the lid of the snuffbox, and placed it in a more advantageous light. "Her state is, to tell you the truth, a subject I can hardly bear to think of. It has often been hard to me to hold myself in—"

"Ah, yes; just so; Vesuvius—and so on. Quite. But, my dear fellow, one must *not* allow one's eruptive tendencies to get the upper hand. A man of the world—men of the world, like you and me—should learn to keep ourselves cool. Confound the old curmudgeon! What the devil did he mean by burning those letters? Mallinger, upon my soul, I beg your pardon; I—I apologize; but, as I was saying, one must keep a cool head—"

"Pray don't apologize to *me* for using strong language in the matter," returned William, hastily. "When I think of what that woman must have suffered; when I think of what I would have done to try to make the close of her life happy, if only—"

"Ah, there's 'the pity of it'—'Oh, the pity of it!' as the Moor puts it. Of course, we men of the world—men of the law—who see and know the dark side of life; *we* look at it calmly and dispassionately. D—n it, Mallinger, I'm haunted by the woman's face; I can't get it out of my mind! It's monstrous; it's— Light those candles, can't you?" shouted Mr. Pettigrew at the alarmed Mudge, who here presented himself with a message from some urgent client. "Do you think one lamp has any chance at all of keeping this infernal fog out of the room? No, I'll see no one. I'm busy—engaged on most important business. No one has any business to be out on such a day. Tell him I say so, whoever he is. No one but a fool *would* be out. There, shut the door."

Mudge disappeared in a crestfallen and depressed condition, and doubtless framed some soothingly courteous message for the unwelcome visitor.

"You see how people pester me!" said Mr. Pettigrew, waving his hands as though he were swimming through a river of interruptions. "I never try to give half an hour's calm and quiet consideration to a thing, that Mudge doesn't appear with that church-yard face of his—"

"I'm afraid poor Dutton will—" began William.

"Have a bad time of it, eh?" put in the other, quickly. "Not a bit of it! Mr. Dutton has the gift of *intuition*, sir, or I mistake, and he'll get to understand me in a week. He'll recognize the fact that my 'bark is worse than my bite.' Mudge, there, is a machine, a mere machine; Dutton is an intelligence—there's the difference. Not but what Mudge is a most worthy fellow," continued his master, "a most worthy fellow. He has behaved admirably; he has married while in my employ, borne all attendant trials with fortitude, and *not* hanged himself as his predecessor did. That fact alone says volumes for Mudge—quite, quite!"

You see, not even the fog, that seemed to grow denser every moment, if that were possible, could damp Mr. Pelham Pettigrew's lively energies to-day. He was apparently possessed by the very demon of restless activity; he was in and out of his chair like any Jack-in-the-box; he looked out into the "Cimmerian gloom" of the fog one minute to anathematize it, and in the next breath he declared the state of the weather admirably suited to insure those who desired such a boon an hour or two's peaceful confabulation.

The fact was, he was fencing with time, and putting off "the evil day" like the veriest coward that ever shrunk from giving pain to another, instead of acting like the case-hardened man of the world he would fain persuade himself and others to suppose him.

"And you had a comfortable run up from Weaverton, eh?"

"Well, it might have been warmer with advantage."

"Ah, just so. I hope you *insisted* upon the porters giving you a fresh hot foot-warmer at every station; I *always* do."

Mr. Pettigrew did not add that the porters had good reason to wish he might travel daily by rail during the cold weather.

"And you left Strephon—ha! ha! good old Strephon!—quite well?"

"Yes, thanks."

A pause, during which Mr. Pettigrew once more violently assaults the fire. Then he falls back in a breathless condition, and looks deprecatingly at the dank, dirty mist that is creeping up against the window as if the cheery fire-light had some attraction for it.

If you and I, dear reader, had been looking in at that window too, we should have seen William Mallinger start up at some words spoken by his companion; seen him take up his stand upon the rug, lean one arm upon the mantel-shelf, and so set himself to listen to a story just as a man might set himself to bear some pain he knew must be faced and endured.

You and I know that story well. We have already followed a widowed girl's weary footsteps—followed them, in pain and desolation, "even unto the end." We have traced Mary Mallinger to the old cathedral town—seen the lights glimmering in the distance, as if to cheer her on—heard the sweet cathedral chimes dropping notes of melody through the snow-laden air, and falling on her ear like friendly voices telling of peace and rest. We know how God's peace came to her broken heart at last, and how when morning came she lay dead, with her baby at her breast. But to William—to her son—the tale was new.

Lower and lower sunk his head as Pelham Pettigrew went on, softening each detail, suggesting every possible comfort with a tenderness and delicacy a woman might hardly have attained to. Closer and closer over his eyes William pressed a hand that trembled and grew chill as death; but vain was all his manhood, all his resolution to keep back the tears that rose and fell at thought of that weary, faithful, loving woman—the mother who bore him beneath her heart through that terrible journey, and gave her life at last for his!

I shudder to think of what would have been the fate of Mudge, had the interview that lasted—not until the light had faded, for there was none to fade—but until the big bell of the Middle Hall clock chimed out the hour of eight, been interrupted by any inadvertence on his part. But Mudge was wise in his generation, and only over his prostrate body would any client, however eager, have penetrated to Pelham Pettigrew's inner chamber. He stole about a-tiptoe; and when an unlucky copying-clerk in a corner of the outer room overset a folio, he turned upon him so threatening and wrathful a countenance that that unhappy one shrunk into himself till the top of his head was all that was visible above the collar of his coat.

Mudge could read the signs of the times, for all that his master had described him as "a mere machine," and, looking on the dial of his master's face, there descried "what o'clock it was;" in other words, recognized the fact that to interrupt the conference at present going on would be to incur vast and unknown penalties.

To have tied up the knocker in his pocket-handkerchief would have been a relief to Mudge, though no one could be more acutely sensible of the incongruity of such a proceeding in bachelor chambers. He passed the long half-hours of William Mallinger's visit to his master in ceaseless dread of hearing this said knocker plied by some impatient hand, and in his anxious excitement did so sternly and unceasingly watch and spy upon the junior clerk that that functionary gave as many nervous twitches and jerks as though he were a confirmed sufferer from the disease called St. Vitus's dance, and gladly flung himself down-stairs with precipitation when Mr. Pettigrew, opening the door of his sanctum, called out to have a hansom sent for without delay.

"You will come to my rooms and dine with me—eh?" said Mr. Pettigrew, as he and William stood awaiting the emancipated one; "pot-luck, you know—take what you can get, and be thankful."

Mr. Pettigrew had got a disagreeable duty over, and was buoyant accordingly. The worn, grave face of his companion was not, however, lost upon him, and with good, kindly commonsense he felt that a solitary evening would be the worst possible thing for William to face with the sad story, but now heard, by way of subject for meditation.

"By-the-way," said Mr. Pettigrew, as he wrapped a scarf about his throat and carefully drew his coat-collar up to his ear, "how's the girl with the Greuze face getting on? Tremlett's back, I see, so I suppose it's all *couleur de rose*—eh? I passed him in Piccadilly yesterday."

CHAPTER XXXII.

HELPLESS!

THAT much-abused individual "the clerk of the weather" was tired, perhaps, of seeing London "under a cloud." Anyway, he sought out a brisk young westerly wind, and set him to drive away the vast murky curtain that hung over the City, and disperse it with as little delay as possible.

The sun had gone to bed some hours ago, or no doubt he would now have taken a peep from behind a cloud and with a parting smile said good-night.

However, in his absence the stars did their best, and twinkled faintly here and there in the still misty sky, as though they were just as glad as everybody else that the cold, dank, dirty fog had been rolled away, and the gas-lamps had now a chance of being something better than mere blurs of hazy light, struggling beacons in a sea of fog.

"This is something like!" said Pelham Pettigrew, as he and William reached the street. Bang! bang! went the doors of the hansom as the junior clerk sprung out, and, with a touch of his hat to Mr. Pettigrew, disappeared up the stairs.

That gentleman, with his own inimitable bow, made way for his intended guest to enter the vehicle first.

But William had evidently no intention of taking advantage of this politeness.

"You must excuse me to-night, sir," he said, holding out his hand in adieu; "I cannot dine with you. I shall see you to-morrow, of course; but just now there is something I must see to."

Pelham Pettigrew was too perfectly polished a gentleman to pry into any man's affairs, even those of his nearest friend; and in another moment or two he was being whirled along towards St. James's Street, all the superfluous energy of the cab-driver, pent up by the fog during the day, finding vent in a pace that caused more than one member of the metropolitan police to turn an anxious glance upon his progress.

"Gad! it's something to do with the Greuze girl, I'll swear!" muttered Mr. Pettigrew. "I don't think he knew Tremlett was back till I told him. Has that scion of a virtuous house been shaking the ivories again, or looking at himself too often in the bottom of a glass? Gad! now I think of it, Mallinger never opened his lips after I said Tremlett was back. What the devil has the fellow gone and fallen in love with the wrong woman for? No, no; I don't mean that—the Greuze girl is a good sort, or I'm a Dutchman. Why has the right woman fallen in love with the wrong man? That's it; quite! quite!"

He said these last two words so loudly that the cabby opened the little trap-door in the roof, and politely requested to know "if the gentleman spoke?"

"Not to you, sir, certainly. Shut that confounded door, and don't let the draught in upon the crown of my head again," was the unexpected answer.

"All right, sir!" said cabby, grinning delightedly, and telegraphing to a friend in the same line of business that he'd got a "rum customer" inside.

Meanwhile, William hurried along the streets—hurried along hardly conscious of what was around him, of the people he passed, or the objects he saw; conscious only of this one fact—Guy Tremlett was back. Pelham Pettigrew had passed him "in Piccadilly yesterday." Guy was here—in London, and down at Winstowe, Lilian was wearing her heart out because she had no news of him.

What did it mean?

Had Guy planned some pretty surprise for his darling? Had he dreamed of seeing those sweet, true eyes dilate with a sudden, unlooked-for joy, and then hide their shy passionate gladness on his breast?

Should he find that Guy had already started for Winstowe? Was Lilian even now clasped in her lover's arms, and able to smile at the doubts and fears of the past? God send it so! God send that it was well with that gentle heart! God send that smiles were on her lips, and if tears dimmed her eyes, that they were but the dew of a too happy content!

"There's a swell as has somethin' on 'is mind!" said one street-Arab to another, as William hurried along somewhat recklessly as regarded his fellow-passengers.

"Vot," replied the other, keenly interested, "'im in the white night-gownd?"

"Just," said the first speaker, nodding; "he near upset me. I wouldn't wonder if he's agoing to destroy hisself; a deal of swells destroys theirselves when they 'as something on their minds—"

It is always the way, my friends: in our hours of keenest suffering, our times of deadliest mental conflict, we afford satisfaction and amusement to other people. Just as the time-honored sport afforded by the cockchafer, as he whirs and buzzes when comfortably spitted upon a pin, charms the mind of the boy who looks on, so your sorrows or mine provide our servants and acquaintances with the most piquant interests and the most delightful speculations.

"Is your master at home? I hear he has come back," asked William, eagerly, of Guy's servant at the door of the rooms in Clarges Street.

"My master returned four days ago, sir. I believe he is at home at present. May I ask you to step in?"

Four days ago!

The man's slow, London drawl, his impassive countenance and smooth manner, irritated William beyond endurance. Everything about the man irritated him — his sleek appearance, his noiseless footsteps, even his faultless attire. Which shows how unreasonable anxiety may make the best of us.

"Tremlett!" cried William, as he entered the luxurious room that rivalled in comfort even that far-famed haven of delight, the "Wellington."

Then he stopped short, and said no more: neither did Guy rise to greet him. The servant closed the door, and left the two men together.

"Tremlett! In God's name, what is the matter? Have you been ill?"

William might well ask that question. The lamp, hanging from the ceiling by gilt chains, and shaded with an opaque disk, cast a full glow upon Guy's face and figure—a face changed and marred almost out of all recognition; a figure strangely shrunken, and crouching over the fire.

Still Guy did not rise. He only held out a hand to his visitor, and looked at him with dark sunken eyes that seemed to be full of suspicion and fear. The hand William touched was cold and clammy, and shook in his hold.

A small table stood by the fire, and on it a glass and a bottle of cognac.

All this William took in at a glance; not overlooking a long stain upon the table top, as though an unsteady hand had tried to pour the liquor from the bottle to the glass.

At last, in answer to the former question, earnestly repeated, and as William drew a chair to his side, Guy spoke.

"Yes, I have been ill—I am ill now—very ill. I am dying, Snow—of want of sleep."

He stretched out his hand towards the half-filled glass.

But William firmly yet quietly took possession of both glass and bottle, and deposited them upon a distant table. Guy's eager, glittering eyes hungrily followed the poison so fatally loved, but he made no remonstrance.

"What has come of Bolton, Tremlett?" asked William, returning to his place by the fire.

"Bolton?—Charley?" he said, putting his hand up to his forehead as if to recall his thoughts from some absorbing subject that they persistently wandered to. "Oh! I don't know what's come of Charley. I never saw him, you know, after that night at Malta."

"That night at Malta?" echoed his companion. "Do you mean to say he *left* you there?"

"No," said Guy, a sudden flash of cunning triumph lighting up his worn face, "I left him."

Then he laughed softly to himself; holding out his hands to the fire all the while, and never once meeting William's eyes.

"You left him? Well, and where did you go to?"

"I put myself on board the home mail, and got to Paris *via* Marseilles. We had a lively time of it at Malta — a glorious time, by Jove! They're a jolly lot of fellows, I can tell you, there."

"Yes, yes," said his listener, impatiently; "but I don't want to hear about the jolly fellows or any other kind of fellows. I want to hear about yourself. Do you know," he added, emphatically, and compelling the shifting eyes of the other to meet his by sheer force of will, "that Lilian is breaking her heart about you?"

What a marvellous change came over the man's face as he spoke! The eager, unholy light died out of the dark eyes, the muscles round the mouth twitched and worked, the restless hands fell down between his knees.

"Poor—little—Lillie!—poor—little—girl!" he said, softly, and with exquisitely pitiful lovingness; then in a moment the gentle mood was past, and he sprung to his feet, and began tearing at the bell like a madman.

"Tremlett! Guy!" cried William, vainly striving to draw him back into his chair. "What is it? For God's sake, tell me what it is!"

But Guy took no heed. He never even once glanced at William — he did not seem to hear his voice.

His eyes, filled with unutterable fear, were fixed on one corner of the room, and when the frightened servant opened the door in answer to the peal that rung through the house, he pointed to the same spot, and with a volley of awful oaths asked the man how he dared permit strangers to enter that room?

"There is no one, sir," stammered the valet. "I have let no one in but Mr. Snow."

"Liar! cheat! devil!" shrieked his master. "Look there, there, *there*—in the corner, watching me with his red eyes—gibing at me, mocking at me! Turn him out! Do you hear?—turn him out!"

The wretched man's voice rose to a perfect yell, and throwing up his arms above his head as if in utter despair, he fell back in William's hold, the sweat pouring off his face in great drops of cold moisture, his cries dying away in hoarse, gasping sobs.

"Wheel the sofa to the fire. Help me to lay him down—do as I tell you—there is nothing to fear."

These orders, promptly uttered, seemed to bring back the scattered senses of the servant, who had displayed unmistakable signs of a longing for flight.

Between them they laid Guy Tremlett on the couch, William carefully seeing to its being so placed that the dreaded corner was out of sight.

"He's gone now," whispered the sick man, tightly grasping William's hand. "It's cruel—cruel to watch me like this—night and day, day and night—here, and there, and everywhere. He has made up his mind I sha'n't sleep, and I haven't slept for so long. O God! if I could only sleep!"

He began to look about uneasily, and William quickly divined what was the object of his quest; for as his glance fell on the glass and bottle the old hungry gleam flared in his eyes. Only momentarily though, for with a madman's cunning he tried to hide the longing that possessed him.

"You had better let me try to sleep," he said, closing his eyes and motioning to the valet to leave the room.

"No one can sleep when he is being watched; you had better leave me alone—both of you; but don't go far away, Snow," he added with sudden, pathetic pleading. "I told you, you know, that you were the only friend I had, and it was true—true—true! I should be all right if I could only sleep, but I can't. How can I, when *he* haunts me day and night!"

"Who haunts you?" asked William, quietly.

"I don't know who he is," returned Guy, trembling as if with ague, in his terrible dread of the phantom called up by his drink-maddened brain. "Yesterday I thought I would outwit him; I went out; I walked along the streets, and looked in at the shop-windows; but he was too cunning for me. When I got to Regent Street there was a crowd, and there he was, a head and shoulders taller than the rest, with the same grin upon his face, just as I had seen him in my room at Meurice's, and on the steamer as I crossed— But he is gone now," he added, with a deep sigh of relief, "and if you will both go away, I think I can sleep a little."

"You will have a much better chance of getting to sleep if you are in your bed," said William, firmly; and the weaker will bowing before the stronger, ten minutes later Guy Tremlett was in his bed, the cognac safely under lock and key, and a dainty ivory razor-case, that usually lay on the dressing-table, safe in William Mallinger's pocket.

"There are certain things to be seen to at once, and either you or I must go for further help," he said to the valet. "Are you afraid to remain with your master? I will be back in half an hour at most, and I think this quiet fit will last longer than that."

Quaking in every limb, and with an ash-colored face, the man besought that such a task might not be set him.

"Bah!" said William, with all a brave man's contempt for cowardice, and turned away to write a few hurried lines in pencil.

"Take the first hansom you can get. Give the man a double fare to drive like the devil, and take this paper to my chambers in Fig-tree Court, Temple. Wait for my clerk, and come back at the same pace."

With a celerity that certainly left nothing to be desired the man disappeared, and William took his place by the window. Every now and then a moan or a muttered curse came from the restless figure in the bed. In the street below an endless string of cabs and carriages passing to and fro told of the restless tide of life surging through the city; of men and women hurrying here and there in the pursuit of an evening's pleasure, their hearts perhaps filled with joyous anticipations of the coming Christmas-tide, of happy promised meetings, of misunderstandings swept away by the hand of the holy season that softens all resentment; and meanwhile, high above their heads, in that chamber where the light is lowered to give those weary, aching, burning eyes a chance of rest, life and death are entering on a desperate battle, and with bowed head and aching heart a man is wrestling with the awful pain that comes to each and all of us when some terrible storm of grief threatens the one creature we hold unutterably dear, and we know that we are helpless—wholly, pitifully helpless—alike to shield or to comfort.

⁂

CHAPTER XXXIII.

JIM'S EXPIATION.

To hate a person with blind, unreasoning hatred; to pursue him with unrelenting resentment, and then—to see him lie helpless and unconscious; to watch the restless hands forever moving to and fro in an aimless search of what they know not; to listen to meaningless words, babbled by lips that can no more give us scorn for scorn; to meet the eyes that see, yet see not, having no recognition for us in their fever-bright gaze—

What an experience!

Our own hatred and resentment are made to feel unutterably small beside the might and the power of God's hand. Before such a spectacle bitterness dies out, hatred fades away, resentment can no longer hold the citadel of the soul.

Watching, tending, praying by Guy Tremlett's bed, Jim passed through just such an experience as this.

The man whom he had tracked and hunted down, the man in whose weak yielding to evil he had triumphed with an unholy joy, lay doing grievous battle with death.

Perhaps only those who have seen such a case can fully realize the horrors that a sick-bed like that of Guy Tremlett presents. Foul and mocking phantoms, ghosts of a degraded past, rise up before the maddened brain; vile words and dreadful oaths are uttered by parched and blackened lips, and sound in the ear of the watcher like the ravings of some devil. Now and again an overwhelming terror takes possession of the sick man: he shrieks at the wild creations of his own mind, or shudders as he fancies that the most loathsome creatures are crawling over his shaking limbs.

And ever and always he is consumed by that awful lust of drink that has been his undoing; while even in the midst of all his madness he has cunning enough to try to induce those about him to leave him, in order that he may gratify this morbid craving, or carry into action the wild impulse that is ever leading him to attempt the destruction of his own life.

Looking on Guy Tremlett thus, in all the wreck of his beauty, in all the miserable ruin of his youth, truly it would have been a hardened heart that should have refused to him the tribute of a sorrowful pity.

To Jim, the man whose morbid vehemence of character had led him to hate what stood in the way of his master's happiness, the sight of that poor, struggling frame, the sight of his enemy laid low, was fraught with a bitterness of remorse, proportionate in its vehemence to the passionate resentment that had been the root of the wrong committed.

Never had the sense of his own wrong-doing come home so bitterly to Jim as now. Never had the sin of that one swift shaft of thought that had darted through his heart, as he saw the evil counsellor tempt the weak and erring man—that one *hope* that evil would win the day, seemed so black.

Well and wisely had William counted on Jim being a good and faithful nurse by that bedside. The grave, soft-voiced doctors who came and went, and glanced at the restless figure on the bed, and then at each other significantly, said that such an attendant was invaluable both to the patient and to themselves. Strangely enough, too, Jim's voice seemed to have more power, his touch more control, over Guy than those of any other. No woman could have been more tender; indeed, no woman could have fitly watched and tended such a case, for no woman's ear could have endured to listen to the ravings of that unconscious sufferer.

Jim seemed to be incapable of weariness. His eyes dwelt ceaselessly on that poor, changed face—the face that women had found so fair, and which was now bereft of all its beauty: at one time pallid with the gray hues of a terrible exhaustion, and dank with the cold dews of a deathly weakness; at another, flushed and livid with the raging heat of fever, while the parched lips were blackened with a thirst that nothing could slake.

William had promptly telegraphed to Tremlett Court, and now dreaded, even while he longed, for Mrs. Tremlett's arrival.

"It was the only thing to do, and yet—how will she bear it?" he said to Pelham Pettigrew, as the two men stood looking out into the street that was quiet with the hush of Sunday. Here and there people passed on their way to church; bells rung from many a steeple; the winter sunshine glinted bright and clear upon happy faces and gay dresses.

Christmas was coming; why should not the world be glad?

Yes, Christmas was coming; the Christmas they had planned that all should spend at Winstowe; the Christmas that Uncle David had said should be a "right merrie time," when "the prince" should be with his own again, and the old cathedral chimes should ring out a joyous peal.

It was coming, this promised "merrie time," and Guy, their "prince," lay dying, and Lilian was kneeling in her own accustomed place, and praying for her lover's safe return. Praying, not knowing of the awful cloud that was hanging over her head.

For what could they do?

How could they let her come to Guy's bedside? How could they let her see that struggling madman held down by sheer brute force because else he would have laid violent hands upon his own poor miserable remnant of a life?

How could they let those curses, those cries, those moans of pain, fall upon her innocent ears, to haunt her with their dreadful meaning all the days of her life to come?

What do you think were the thoughts of William Mallinger—the man who loved her as his own soul—the man who would have gladly given his own life for that of the man she loved, all this while?

"What can we do?" he had said, looking into Pelham Pettigrew's face.

And the other had answered "Nothing," and turned away, because, if he had not done so, he might have acted in anything but such a manner as would have been consistent in a man who prided himself upon invariably "keeping a cool head."

"If Strephon knew, he'd be sure to let it out, eh?" Mr. Pettigrew said on one occasion, when things looked very bad indeed. "He's not quite a Macchiavelli, isn't Strephon—eh!"

And William shook his head, smiling faintly at the idea of any *finesse* being possible on the part of Uncle David.

"There is nothing for it but to hope things may mend. Things often *do* mend just when they seem the worst. The darkest what's-his-name, you know, my dear fellow, is just before the other thing—quite, quite!" But Mr. Pettigrew did not utter his favorite asseveration with his wonted energy and crispness. His mental wrestle with himself was not this time altogether satisfactory.

"My future clerk is about the best sick-nurse I ever saw," he continued, giving himself a sort of shake together, like a man who gets out of an unpleasant subject that he has been mentally wading in. "If I were *in extremis*, hanged if I wouldn't sooner have that fellow to see me than any female 'ministering angel' that ever did her best 'when pain and anguish,' wringing my manly brow, might render her services a necessity."

"He is wonderful," said William. "It must have been an inspiration that led me to send for him. Even at his worst, poor Tremlett seems to be controlled by Jim's voice."

"Ah! hum!" said Mr. Pettigrew, pulling out his cigar-case, preparatory to departing. "I wish his worst weren't quite so bad, eh? It's just the —very—*dooce*, Mallinger, that's what it is."

Then he took his way down Clarges Street, the

most dapper, prosperous-looking, best-dressed man in town, but carrying such a troubled heart in his breast as was a disgrace to "a thorough man of the world," bound to look on life calmly and dispassionately.

As each night closed in, a fresh acerbation of fever added to the sufferings of the patient and the difficulties of his attendants. After some hours this would wear itself out, and then a state supervened that was one of insensibility, yet could not be called sleep—a condition in which each heavy breath Guy drew sounded strangely in the hush of the early morning hours. William, worn with anxiety and loss of rest, would then doze in his chair, and the valet would creep down to his own peculiar den below stairs. But Jim's eyes were ever watchful; not a stir, not a moan of the sufferer escaped him; and as, even in unconsciousness, the poor fever-baked lips parted thirstily, he would wet them with a feather dipped in iced water, and then, firmly holding the hot and restless hands, sit as motionless as a statue hour after hour, seeming not to know what weariness meant.

Once or twice when his master urged him to take some rest, Jim only shook his head and turned back silently to his "labor of love."

Yes, of love! For from repentance had grown up a strange fondness for the object of his care.

To wrong any one grievously, and then to take up the work of expiation towards him, is often to learn a lesson of love.

Prejudice, that has before blinded us, drops from our eyes; the wrong that irritated us may still be there, but we look upon it with more of the spirit of our Divine Master's infinite pitifulness, and, so looking, see the influences that have made that being what he is. We plead to ourselves on his behalf the extenuating circumstances that resentment has hitherto hidden from us; we realize that we have judged our fellow-man as though we ourselves stood on some grander and more elevated platform; and what we have seen fit to designate as "just resentment" now unmasks itself to our clearer vision, and we know it for the spirit of the Pharisee of old.

Just as the third night of watching was closing in, Mrs. Tremlett came.

The doctors had paid their second daily visit, looked more gravely at each other and at William than they had ever done yet; and Pelham Pettigrew, who had "looked in" *en route* to his club, was standing on the rug à *l'Anglaise*, whistling very softly by way of accompaniment to his own thoughts, apparently not over-pleasant ones.

For William, after seeing the great "medicine-men" to their neat broughams, had come back into the room, flung himself down in poor Guy's special chair, and had groaned, rather than spoken the words,

"God help her! what can I do?"

"Poor little girl!" echoed Pelham Pettigrew, and then, as I have said, he set to whistling softly to himself.

At the sound of wheels stopping outside, William started to his feet.

"It is Mrs. Tremlett!" he said, hesitating a moment what to do; for at that moment a wild cry came from the inner room—the cry as of a man pursued by some fiend, and appealing for help to those about him.

Mr. Pettigrew hastily closed the farther door,

and as he did so Guy's mother entered by the nearer one. She was followed by Ponsonby, impassive and inscrutable as ever.

"Where is my son?" said Mrs. Tremlett, going straight up to William and laying her hand upon his arm.

A long veil of black lace was thrown back from her dead-white face—a face from whose fierce questioning a man might well have shrunk.

"Your son is very ill, dear lady," said William, gently taking her hand. She gave him no time to say more.

"Take me to him."

Hastily, yet with perfect calmness, throwing off her cloak and removing the bonnet and veil from her head, she stood before them in all the glory of her statue-like beauty—a beauty grander than that of any girl could have been, and pitiful beyond all power of words, from the intense restrained passion and anguish of dread that were written in every feature.

"I have been ill—I could not come before. Ponsonby did not give me the telegram until this morning. Fool! dolt! coward!" she added, turning to the silent woman behind her, and still speaking in the same unnaturally calm and concentrated voice.

But each separate and particular epithet thus aimed at her devoted head might have been the tenderest and sweetest of a lover's whispers, for any impression it made on Ponsonby.

She was intent on folding her mistress's cloak, and smoothing out the long folds of the veil that during that journey of agonized suspense had been closely drawn over her face.

"Who is with him?" asked Mrs. Tremlett, stopping short, as William was about to open the door of the bedroom. "Is that baby-faced fool—that toy he has a fancy for—tending his sick-bed?"

Before her hard, cruel words could be answered, a volley of curses, not only "deep," but also "loud," became audible, and with a bitter resentment beating in his heart, William, writhing under an irritation that he hated himself for afterward, gave her back sneer for sneer.

"Could any girl tend *such* a sick-bed, madam?"

How mean, how pitiful he felt himself to be the instant the taunt had passed his lips!

"No," she said, with a smile that haunted him for nights and days to come, "you are right; it is only a mother that can never know what fear is!"

He knew the inference was all untrue; he knew that if his darling had been Guy Tremlett's *wife*, no horror of sight or sound could have driven her from his side; he knew that she would have stifled his cries upon her breast, and striven to slake the thirst of his parched lips with the kisses of her pure, sweet mouth; but already he had spoken "unadvisedly with his lips," and the shame of that thought held him silent.

Assuredly Mrs. Tremlett's power over herself was a marvel.

Most women would have cried out, or sobbed, or in some way faltered, at sight of that fearful figure on the bed; for truly, the starting eyes, the working mouth, the restless heaving of the chest, that had become bared during a struggle with those who strove, almost vainly, to restrain him, made Guy Tremlett a sight to appall the strongest heart.

But with no outward sign of emotion beyond a shade of still deeper pallor on her set face, his mother walked firmly to the bedside, and taking in her own the hot hand that tore and plucked at the coverlet, held it closely against her breast, the while her eyes strove with craving, yearning love to read one sign of recognition in his face. Vain quest!

After one startled glance at what evidently touched no chord of memory in his poor bewildered brain, with a piercing cry Guy cowered down among the bedclothes, and called piteously for help, crying out that a fiend was in pursuit of him, and that a frightful precipice stood right in his pathway.

"For God's sake, come away! He will be calmer soon. This frenzy will pass. Let me take you into the next room," pleaded William.

But she stood her ground firmly, and her voice, though low, was steady as she answered him.

"Can't you see that you would do more good by helping to hold my son than by thinking of me, who want none of your sympathy? There!" she went on, vehemently, "he will hurt himself —don't you see?"

There was truth in what she said, and, recognizing the utter hopelessness of inducing her to leave the room, William gave all his attention to aiding Jim and the frightened valet in their trying task.

"He is dying for want of sleep," said Mrs. Tremlett. "Have they tried *everything?* Have they *given up* trying opium?"

She knew the symptoms and the treatment by heart, so there was nothing for it but to treat her with perfect candor.

"Yes; the largest doses failed. We are to try to keep up the strength now. But it is so difficult to make him take the strong beef-essence and turtle-soup: he seems to revolt against it, poor fellow!" said William, and was going on to explain the details of the doctor's orders, when he was interrupted by pitiful entreaties from the sick man for "Brandy! brandy! only a little brandy!"

Hoping to deceive him by a show of compliance, Jim held a cupful of strong beef-tea to his lips, and the next moment the cup and its contents were dashed to the other side of the room amidst a storm of curses that at length subsided into maudlin weeping.

"He will be quieter now," said Jim, timidly stealing round to Mrs. Tremlett's side and touching her dress.

"I do not know who you are," she said, turning her heavy, haggard eyes upon him, "but you are very good to my son. May God reward you for it!"

Poor Jim! Her words carried a sting she knew not of, and his head drooped low upon his breast as he listened.

Low mutterings and plaintive moanings came from the sufferer now. He lay back upon the pillows Jim's hand had smoothed so tenderly, and slowly from side to side ceaselessly moved his weary, aching head. His eyes were closed, and the long, dark lashes, that gave an almost womanly softness to his beauty, lay upon his sunken cheeks. The fever-spots were dying away, and a gray, livid pallor that began to gather round the mouth told that the reign of exhaustion was setting in.

"We must try to get him to take some of the soup," whispered Jim, still softly stroking the sleeve of Mrs. Tremlett's dress. "Will you raise his head upon your arm while I see what I can do to coax him to swallow it?"

The suffering woman seemed to lay aside all her defiant pride to this grave-eyed, strange, deformed being, whose beautiful soul ennobled his fragile body, like some rare jewel shining in a casket all unworthy of it; and William saw a slight quiver round her mouth, a faint mist of tears soften the hard anguish of her eyes, as she turned towards Jim and listened eagerly to his words.

"She has found a better comforter than I can be," he thought, watching the two. Then he left the room, having first dismissed the too-willing valet, and ordered him to prepare some refreshment for Mrs. Tremlett. Meanwhile, our friend Pelham Pettigrew had found himself *tête-à-tête* with the sphinx-like Ponsonby, and been about as cheerful and as much at ease as a patient who awaits his "turn" in a dentist's parlor.

"An automaton, my dear fellow!" he said to William, with a deep sigh of relief, as Ponsonby disappeared under the escort of the valet, to be shown to a room on an upper floor appropriated to her mistress's use. "She might as well be deaf, dumb, maimed, halt, and blind, for any practical use she makes of her senses. She never raised her eyes once the whole time, give you my word. Gad! when the other one called her a fool, and a dolt, and various other sweetmeats, she looked for all the world like Aunt Sally in a shower of sticks! Give you my word, she'd no more expression in her face than Aunt Sally." The little man appeared so much more excited than the occasion seemed to demand, that William was somewhat puzzled; but the riddle solved itself promptly.

Mr. Pettigrew stole a-tiptoe to the doors on either side of the room, and ascertained that they were closely shut; then he came back to his place on the hearth-rug, and tipped William gently on the shoulder to bespeak his close attention.

"I say, you know that woman's an opium-drinker; she's been at it all her life, sir; she'll die in a mad-house, see if she doesn't. Gad! Mallinger, I'm never mistaken in a matter like that."

"Who! Ponsonby?" returned the other, incredulously.

"Phew!—Ponsonby? No; Ponsonby's mistress. The maid knows all about it, though, bless you, it's the business of *her* life to hide it. Gad! they're a queer pair. The thing grows interesting—a psychological study, in fact— quite! quite!"

Which of us that has ever watched beside a sick-bed does not know the chill dankness that ever makes itself felt as the night-lamp begins to burn with a sickly glimmer, and through the drawn blinds a cold gray light steals in, and tells us that the night is passing away and the day-dawn is near at hand?

The night that has seemed so long; the hours

that have passed so slowly! They are gone; and we are one day nearer—what?

To the time when our darling shall smile upon us once more with the old smile, look at us once again with eyes that are like those of a child waking to the joys of renewed life and hope; or to the time when there is nothing more to do, save to fold the dead hands meekly over the still breast, and commend the soul of the loved one to God's keeping.

"He is much quieter—much," said Mrs. Tremlett: "the worst is over; we must be patient. When he wakes from this sleep, he will know us all again."

She spoke half to herself, half to Jim, and looked inquiringly into the face that was pale and weary enough, you may be sure, after such long vigil.

But Jim did not echo her words, and William turned away as though to avoid meeting her gaze.

No one answered her. The fire flickered, and a little bubbling flame made a soft, fluttering noise.

No other sound, save the stirring in the streets outside that told of the birth of another busy day in the great city, broke the quiet of the room.

For the sick man seemed at last to have sunk to rest, or what was the semblance of it.

Now and then a faint moan came from his lips; and once, as William bent over him, he fancied he caught the sound of a well-loved name.

The dark eyes, once so beautiful, now glazed and dim, were but half covered by the heavy lids, and as the searching day-dawn fell upon his face, it looked gray against the white pillow.

"His breathing is less oppressed: it was like this before—that other time—at the Court, you know," said the mother, continuing that pitiful monologue of hope that was harder to listen to than any sobs or cries.

"He took the turn for the better then, just as the morning broke: Ponsonby can tell you it was like that. I remember a bird beginning to sing under the window, just as Guy called me to him and I saw that he knew me: it will be like that now. Yes; you will see; I shall be right; he will wake presently, and put out his hand and pull me down to him, and he will say ' Mother,' just as he did before."

Would *no one* answer her?

She looked from one to the other, something of proud, imperious dissatisfaction mingling in her anxious love; but they were silent, both Jim and his master, and each avoided looking at the other.

The figure on the bed lay very still; the deep, labored breathing grew less noisy, and each breath was drawn at a longer interval.

"You see he is sleeping *quite* quietly now: I told you how it would be."

There was a subdued triumph in her voice as she spoke, but something in William's face, as he drew nearer to her side, must have startled her, for she bent over Guy with a sound like a sob, though her eyes were still dry and tearless.

She laid her cheek down close to his and kissed him softly; then, with a troubled, fearful look she caught hold of William's arm.

"He feels *so* cold," she whispered, trembling; "put something over him; it is the morning air: he must not get chilled: give me the eiderdown coverlet—"

Jim had sunk upon his knees and bowed his head upon his hands; but as she spoke he lifted up his face, and meeting *his* look, Guy's mother, with a bitter, wailing cry, fell forward across the bed where her son lay dead!

CHAPTER XXXIV.

BRED IN THE BONE.

To keep Lilian in ignorance of her lover's condition had appeared to be the only possible course of action. There had been nothing for it but to await the issue of events, hoping, almost against hope, that in time the shattered nerves would rally and the over-balanced mind recover itself. Then the woman who so dearly loved Guy Tremlett might be told of his illness, and permitted to take her place at his bedside.

Throughout those four days and nights, during which curses and cries of fear and pain had rendered the sick-room a very Gehenna, the thought of Lilian, patiently waiting, wearily longing for news of the absent one, was ever present to William's mind, a ceaseless undercurrent of pitiful thought.

And yet, as I have said, there had seemed no other way than that of keeping her in ignorance.

But now, looking on the quiet face of Lilian's dead love, what had seemed, while he lived, inevitable, assumed the aspect of a crime.

Guy, lying dead, became a murdered part of a woman's life. The horror of having to break to that woman the cruel tidings of his death oppressed William as no personal trials of his own could have had the power to do.

All had been done for the best; yet how, in God's name, should he lead Lilian to see the truth of this?

Could he blacken the character of the dead? Must he not rather, if mortal tact and cunning could achieve such a task, spare her the pang that is a thousand times worse than the death of those we hold dear—the knowledge of their unworthiness?

It seemed to be taken as a matter of course by every one that *he* should be the one to go down to Winstowe, and tell, as best he might, to Lilian and Uncle David the story of Guy Tremlett's death.

"You must just make the best of it," said Pelham Pettigrew, balancing himself, in his perplexity, alternately on his heels and his toes; "it's a deuced bad business, that's what it is—a *deuced* bad business; and the girl had better never know that he died of—ahem!—his own indiscretions. What an idiot that Bolton was to let him bolt, eh? I tell you what it is, my dear fellow, if all the people who *ought* to be in Earlswood were sent there, gad! the half of England wouldn't be big enough to allow of the necessary extension of premises."

Mr. Pettigrew whistled softly for a moment, after his usual fashion; then, suddenly remembering what lay only two rooms off, pulled himself up with a round turn and broached a new subject.

"Our friend Strephon will be easily hoodwinked, worthy soul, and you must call the cause of death—anything you please, in fact. The pharmacopœia offers a wide range; disease is a plant of many ramifications. When do you start?"

"To-night," said William, passing his hand wearily across his brow; "there is no time to lose: these things get into the papers, no one knows how."

He was no coward; and yet the thought of meeting a woman's eyes, and hearing a woman's voice, blanched his cheek, and made him set his teeth hard together.

If Lilian reproached him with the seeming treachery that had kept her from her lover's side, what should he say?

Could he tell her that not one ray of recognition would have shone in the dark eyes she loved, had she been ever so near? Could he tell her that horrible curses would have rung in her ears, and their echoes haunted her to her dying day? Could he tell her that Guy—her beautiful love—had died as much by his own hand as though that hand had been raised in violence against himself?

Ah! no. The memory of her dead love should never be blackened by him. It should be left to her in its beauty and completeness, let her misjudge him as she might.

Would she fall at his feet like one dead? Would she break forth into an "exceeding bitter cry" when he told her that Guy would never come to her again? or would a dumb anguish turn her face to stone, and quench the light of her eyes?

"How would it be? how would it be?" he asked himself over and over again, chafing madly against what was before him; yet rejoicing that he—he who loved her so tenderly—was the one to bear the news.

But all these thoughts, and others akin to them, could but be an undercurrent; outwardly there had been nothing but turmoil and anxiety.

Mrs. Tremlett had awakened from that first merciful unconsciousness to a raving, ungovernable grief that appalled even the seasoned mind of Ponsonby.

It was with difficulty the poor distraught mother could be induced to quit the room where all that remained of her idol lay; indeed, this object was only attained by means of that strange influence Jim seemed to have over her, and, led by his hand, she at length quitted the chamber of death.

By what subtle link of sympathy the undisciplined, imperious woman was drawn towards the poor hunchback, who may say? We see these marvellous elective affinities around us; we are ourselves the puppets of their power, but we cannot explain upon what electric chains of attraction they depend.

Certainly without Jim they would have been hard put to it, Ponsonby and all, to manage Mrs. Tremlett. It was only when she had sunk into a profound state of quietude, which that inscrutable female saw fit to call "sleep," that William dare let Guy's faithful nurse return to Figtree Court, there to seek that rest of which the need was at last making itself sorely felt.

"My clerk that is to be is looking confoundedly ill," said Pelham Pettigrew, as he and William stood on the step of the house in Clarges Street, from whence Jim had just driven off. "The what-you-may-call-it is too sharp for the

scabbard, eh?—inclined to wear itself through at the edges. I think we'd best give Dutton a run in the country—a good long run, you know—turn him out to grass, in fact, before he begins work again, eh?"

"Indeed, I think he has earned his rest well," said William. "May God bless him for as true a heart as ever beat!"

The hand of death oft restores the beauty marred in life. It was thus with Guy Tremlett. The lines graven by sin and weak indulgence were now smoothed away. The long black lashes lay upon the marble cheek; the slender, long-fingered hands were folded, and the heavy mustache hid the mouth—that one feature that death ever mars so cruelly. Guy looked like some fair statue, or one that slept a dreamless sleep.

Oh! what are the dreams of those quiet sleepers that we call the dead?

Can we look on their still and changeless faces, and not wonder whither the restless spirit has fled?

What is the judgment it has by this time encountered? In what balance has its good and its evil been weighed?

Be sure that mercy is dealt out more pitifully by God than man: be sure that he who "watches the world with larger eyes than ours," knowing each influence that has been brought to bear upon the erring soul, looks in his infinite mercy on the perfect righteousness of our great High-priest in heaven, and by the pleading of his sinless life—pardons!

Was there nothing to extenuate the sins of Guy Tremlett's life?

Read on, and then judge him hardly if you can.

They had thought Mrs. Tremlett safely wrapped in the torpor that comes to mind and body when both are worn out.

But the effect of the drug that had been her bane through life was either weakened or destroyed by the excitement of her ungovernable grief. She had risen from the bed where Ponsonby believed her chained by the power of opium for hours to come, and startled William, busy over some preparations for his journey, by passing through the outer room and making her way once more to that wherein her son lay. Dishevelled by sleep, her dark silver-lined hair fell in wild disorder about her shoulders; in her eyes gleamed a light not far removed from that of madness; her lips, white as her cheek, were drawn tightly over her teeth in the tension of agony.

She had slept—and forgotten!

She had awakened—and remembered!

And the sting of recollection had goaded her into frenzy, the drug that she had taken adding to the fever that consumed her.

William hastily followed her, and at the foot of Guy's bed she turned upon him like a fury, grasping the rail for support. To her distorted imagination it seemed that this man, strong in the uprightness of his life, mocked and scorned her poor ruined, murdered boy—her darling—who lay dead in the flower of his youth and beauty.

With all a woman's misguided, cruel injustice she resented that which existed only in her own imagination.

"Do not dare to blame the boy!" she cried,

wildly, looking at William with hot, burning eyes that had not yet known the softening of a tear. "Do not dare to blame him! What chance did he ever have? Do you hear me, you immaculate creature who have never known temptation—what chance did he have? How *dare* you scorn him!"

"I never scorned him," he answered, quietly. "Madam, if you think so, you do me a most grievous wrong."

"Do not lie to me!" she cried, still more vehemently. "I know the truth: you all scorned him, my beautiful Guy, my poor dead darling! All but the hunchback: *he* was good to him. God reward him for it all!"

Her voice had become less shrill; she had crouched down at the bedside, and her hand touched lovingly the dark locks that lay upon the pillow—the silken, curling locks that had been once pressed against her breast as her innocent baby boy nestled in her arms!

William hoped her mad excitement had worn itself out; he hoped that tender memories were rising up, and that their spell would bring tears to soften the dull, murky shining of her eyes.

He came nearer to her; he strove to comfort her as best he might: he would have taken her hand but that she spurned him from her.

"I hate you!" she hissed through her set teeth; "I have always hated you! Your goodness is loathsome in my eyes—do you hear me? —loathsome! As the old man who picked you out of the street told me of it, I hated you—as I do now. After all, in what are you so much better than my poor dead boy? He had no chance, I tell you—no chance—no chance—no chance!"

When would the sound of that weary refrain cease to haunt William Mallinger's ears? When would the sight of that heart-broken woman, swaying herself to and fro in the abandonment of a helpless, godless sorrow, fade from his memory?

She went on speaking—half, as it seemed, to herself, half to him.

"His father drank—drank night and day; and I drank too—not as *he* did—not with vile boon-companions, men his very grooms would have scorned to herd with, but secretly—"

She laughed to herself—a low, soft laugh that it chilled his blood to hear.

"No one found it out but Ponsonby: she used to cry and kneel to me to give it up; but it was rest—rest—rest! Ah God!" she sighed, and stretched her arms upward wearily, "all my life has been one longing for rest! Do you wonder that I drank? Do you scorn *me too?* Ah! you do not know—no one knows—what a woman's life is, tied to a man like Bernard Tremlett—a monster, whose greatest pride was to humiliate and degrade his most unhappy wife. If I had not found *something* to deaden my pain and daze my brain, something to give me forgetfulness, I should have done some worse thing. I tell you the very milk my baby sucked from my breasts was poisoned—his whole life was poisoned! As a boy I put the glass to his lips, and laughed to see him drink. Oh, my bonnie boy—my beauty! how fair he was! Then he grew wild and wayward, and I would not control him: it was too much trouble, and I always hated trouble—"

Her listener tried to stem the current of these bitter recollections, but in vain; he might as well have striven to stem Niagara with his hand!

"Guy was cruel to me sometimes, but he did not mean it. See!" she said, with a sudden *accès* of excitement, pushing back the heavy tresses from her brow, and laying bare a scar, deep and darkly marked upon the delicate skin —"his hand did that. I came in one night and saw him standing before me, with a full glass in his hand. I went forward to take it from him, and as I moved towards him he flung the glass in my face! It cut to the bone: I shall carry the scar to my grave."

Her breast heaved and labored with tearless sobs—sobs terrible to see as to hear.

"Oh! Guy, my darling, how could you be so cruel, when I loved you all the while so well!"

Then the old refrain of her grief came once again, that awful, wailing lament, full of a passionate despair.

"He had no chance—no chance! That baby-faced girl might have saved him if she would. My curses upon her coward heart! but, oh! I am glad she did not take you *quite* from me, Guy! I always hated her, though I kissed her, and she blushed and smiled, and thought I loved her for your sake!"

William shuddered as he listened: it was as though some one suddenly had shown to him a precipice near which his darling's feet had wandered, and from which God's hand had held her back.

"He would have tired of her—in time," said Mrs. Tremlett, "and turned to me again. If there had been an heir, I could have—"

Her words stung him beyond all endurance, and in his pain he uttered a sudden exclamation of impatience.

"Ah!" she laughed, "that stings you, does it? You wanted her yourself. Do you think I did not *see?* Do you think I did not *know?* But she did not love you; she loved my son. Guy, with all his sins, was dearer to her than you! She will *hate* you now, if you blacken his memory to her—I tell you she will hate you: but you will not dare! you will not dare!" she cried, her voice rising almost to a shriek. She clung to his arm with shaking, trembling hands. How awful was the contrast between the torrent of her wild, impassioned words and the quiet of the still figure on the bed! The vehemence of life!—the silence of the grave!

But as she stood by William's side and held his arm, a sudden, startling change came over her face—and his.

For looking towards the door, that opened stealthily as though to admit some ghostly visitant, they saw Lilian Selwyn, herself wellnigh as pallid as the "sheeted dead," come slowly towards the bed, and behind her was the tender, troubled face of Uncle David.

The poor child held her hands out before her, as one who is blind and needs must feel her way; her bonnet and veil had been hastily put aside, and the long travelling cloak she wore fell in heavy folds almost to her feet; her eyes, glancing from William as she passed, as though from some pitiable thing they could not bear to rest upon, grew to the quiet beauty of the dead face from which the sheet had fallen back.

Then she sunk upon her knees beside the bed,

and laid her colorless cheek against the dark locks that rested on the pillow.

"I did not know," they heard her murmur to the ear that could not hear; "I would have come to you—they did not tell me— Oh, Guy! my love! my love!"

CHAPTER XXXV.

MUDFORD IS MYSTIFIED.

THAT Christmas which was to have been, according to Uncle David, such a "right merrie time," and to which he had looked forward with such content, had come and gone.

Surely he could never forget those anxious, weary days!

When, after invariable custom, the cathedral "waits" came to Winstowe, they had to be quickly silenced and dismissed, because his darling, his precious child, Lilian, lay prostrate with nervous fever.

Now there are few things harder to bear than a sorrowful, desolate Christmas.

When all the world is rejoicing at the coming of the Incarnate God—when the "day-spring from on high" visits the earth, and breathes over all the spirit of peace and love—it seems as if our own sadness shows darker by contrast; and as the sight of the vacant chair makes our hearts ache and our eyes grow dim, our desolation seems all the more intolerable because holy Christmas is a season whose very name calls upon us to "rejoice and be glad."

Alone, Uncle David went to the cathedral on Christmas morning; he went to entreat a Christmas gift at the hand of the Lord, even the gift of renewed health and strength for his child; and many a pitying look was cast upon the old man as, with bowed head and troubled face, he made his way up the long aisle, and knelt at the altar to receive the sacramental pledges of the Saviour's love.

Those who felt so deeply for the venerable master of Winstowe knew how sorely he missed the girl who had been wont to kneel at his side; and as the congregation dispersed, even those who knew him best held aloof. For how could they give him a "Christmas greeting?"

Lilian lay, weak and white, in the pretty room that in summer-time looked out into a perfect nest of roses.

She was suffering from the effects of a severe shock to the nervous system, so said the doctor. He was haunted by the sad little face upon the pillow, and the great eyes full of pain; for Lilian Selwyn was one of those women who interest every one coming within the sphere of their influence, much as a perfumed flower attracts by the sweet atmosphere that surrounds it.

At the actual time of Guy's death there had been an unreality about everything that helped to sustain her; but now she had time to realize his loss—now she had time *to think*.

Thoughts, memories, and regrets all circled round and centred in one crowning sorrow—the theft that some one had been guilty of in robbing her of Guy's last words.

Naturally enough, she resented upon William the wrong thus done to her; and perhaps no more fortunate thing could have come about

than the fact that urgent law business detained him either in London or at Ardreggan during the time of her illness. What he suffered meanwhile no one but himself knew; yet he was convinced of the wisdom of his absence, for he had read too plainly the resentment that filled her heart towards him, and he knew that his presence could be but a source of irritation that must tend to retard her recovery.

He used to feel at this time as though, if that daily line from Winstowe had been delayed but for one post, he should have gone mad. Happily the envelope stamped with the Weaverton postmark made its appearance as regularly as the sun rose, and often (so often that he would like to have kissed Mrs. Timmins for her thoughtfulness) there were two of these missives—one from Uncle David, and one from that most worthy woman. Indeed, on more than one occasion he was guilty of the folly of pressing to his lips the not over well written epistle of the Winstowe housekeeper; and I am inclined to think there was a certain subtle undercurrent of sympathy and understanding between Mrs. Timmins and "Master William," and that it was this vein of sympathy that made her letters so precious in his eyes.

As for the good woman herself, she was at all times possessed by the conviction that the only way in which to "minister to a mind diseased" was to supply the body with every possible nourishment, and she must have boiled down whole cows into beef-jelly during the weeks her young mistress lay sick.

As for Briggs, he put on a deeply mourning countenance from the very time of Mr. Tremlett's death; indeed, Briggs considered himself so thoroughly part and parcel of the family he served, that naturally, when sorrow overwhelmed them, he was crushed too; and he now took to such a habit of shaking his head portentously as he sat on one side the kitchen fire of an evening, that Mrs. Timmins was driven to ask him, in her most withering and sarcastic manner, "if he meant to shake it off altogether?" adding, with a spiteful jerk of her own head, that there was "as good fish in the sea as ever came out of it, and the best weren't caught either," and that, for her part, she "thought the Lord knew best who to take and who to leave."

"But some folks might as well have eyes in the backs of their heads for all the use they make of those they have to look straight afore them," said Mrs. Timmins, lifting a saucepan off the fire with a jerk, and setting it down with a flop on the cross-bar. "When folks are ill, they're ill, and it's right enough to entreat the Lord for them; but when they're gone, they're gone, and it's just flying in God Almighty's face to make such a fuss over them. Why, look at King David: when his baby was dead, didn't he just get right up and wash his face, and behave himself like a sensible man that knew it was no manner of use carrying on when the Lord's will was made as plain as needs be? It's all very well, Briggs, but I've stood that long face of yours long enough, and I won't put up with it no more. I've no appetite for my victuals with you opposite me; and as to Miss Lilian, why, poor young lady! when she gets about again, the very sight of you a-waiting at table will be enough to throw her back as bad as ever!"

"Good Lord!" groaned Briggs to himself, as the irate old lady left the kitchen with a bit of a taste for the young mistress, "she's off in her tantrums, she is, and I'm going to have a reg'lar time of it! I must just try to pluck up a bit. But such a terribly mortality! such an orful eventuality! Lord bless us! cut off in the flower of his age, and *such a free gentleman with his money!*"

Briggs was so overcome at this last reflection that he drew forth a spotted handkerchief; but hearing the rustle of the tail of the enemy's dress round the corner of the passage, and not having time to get it back into his pocket, with admirable presence of mind he sat upon it, and postponed shedding a few quiet tears to the memory of the dead, until he should be safe in the seclusion of his pantry.

To use Mrs. Timmins's own words, the master wandered about in these anxious days "like a ghost as had no respectable home." To see his darling lying still and quiet, her sad eyes turned upon a pictured face whose dark eyes would never more meet hers in life, was a terrible pain to his tender heart.

He would steal in a-tiptoe twenty times a day, and just touch the bright hair on the pillow, or stroke the white cheek that had somehow lost its lovely roundness of contour; and Lilian always had a smile for him, but oh! such a faint, wan smile, that, meeting it, the old man would turn away, and, wandering out into the gardens, pace a weary "sentry go" up and down the terrace walks, where once in the dusky twilight, heavy with the perfume of a hundred flowers, Guy Tremlett had told the story of his love to a girl's willing ears, and stolen sweet kisses from her lips.

"Master," said Mrs. Timmins one day, when she came upon the old man sunk in sad thought, and resting his head upon his hand, "don't go for to give way so; she's coming round, is Miss Lilian: it's little by little, I know, but yet it's sure enough, though slow. Why, sir, a body couldn't help but come round when they're supplied constant with beef-tea like mine; it stands as firm as Gideon's rock when it's cold, and you can see the dish through it, it's that clear!"

"Ah! yes, yes, I know," sighed Mr. Earle; "you take good care of the child, Timmins—good care indeed; but I fear her trouble lies too deep for us to reach it. It's because she never saw him—because he died without a word. God of heaven! shall I ever forget her face as she knelt by his side and touched his hair with her tender white hands!" He paused a moment, overcome by the thought of what that awful, silent grief had been to witness; then he went on, speaking almost more to himself than to her, "If only Will had sent to let me know; who could have broken it to her so gently—who could have—"

"Beg pardon, sir," interrupted Mrs. Timmins, beginning to wipe imaginary dust from a table with her white-muslin apron, and trembling very much, "Master William's not one to do anything without a reason; he'd need to have a broad back to carry all the blame that's put upon him;" and here the good woman gave her head the peculiar toss that always made Briggs quail in his shoes. "I'll lay anything he'd good reason for what he did, sir, though I know I'm step-ping out of my place to say such a thing. Why, how could he tell the fever the poor young gentleman died of wasn't a catching one—a typhus, or something of that sort? There's never no knowing where you have a fever, sir, or what it might do with itself, or where it pokes its nasty nose into. There was an aunt of mine, a most respectable woman in the corn-chandlery business, and she knew a man that went to one of them fever hospitals to see a friend lying sick of a typhus, and when he came home, sir, he just went and dropped right down dead of an apoplexy in front of his wife's face! So you see there's no reckoning on these things, and to my mind Master William had a right to be careful," added the good woman, as if the remarkable case of infection she had just narrated settled the matter beyond dispute.

But though the ideas of Mrs. Timmins upon the subject of contagion might be, to say the least of it, open to controversy, she proved to be perfectly right as to the fact that her young mistress was "coming round."

Perhaps it tended to rouse the poor child from her lethargy of grief when news came to Winstowe of Mrs. Tremlett's dangerous illness; and, a little later on, of her sudden departure from the Court, accompanied by the faithful Ponsonby and a medical man, the destination of the travellers being only spoken of under the indefinite term of "abroad." Since her son died, Mrs. Tremlett had never penned one line to the girl who had been his destined wife; not the slightest notice had she taken of Lilian's pitiful, sympathizing letters, written with effort, and in the midst of pain and weakness. It seemed as if a pall of impenetrable silence was cast over the mother's sorrow —a sorrow deepened and intensified, as we know, by that bitterest of all ingredients, self-reproach.

While, at Winstowe, life went on in very quiet, monotonous fashion, the variations in a sick girl's cheek, or the fluctuations of her pulse forming the grand interest of each succeeding day, out in the world beyond, the "Ardreggan romance" formed the topic of universal interest.

Investigations conducted by learned men of law were followed with breathless interest by that insatiable monster known as "the public;" and when at last it was established beyond all manner of doubt, legal or otherwise, that William Snow, the boy that had drifted in the snow-storm of a winter long ago to David Earle's feet, was the grandson of Sir George Plaistow, of Ardreggan, County Roxburghshire, the public gave a sort of gasp of mingled astonishment and content, and then—turned to some other interesting case that chanced to crop up, and forgot all about the new-found heir and his romantic history. It is given to none of us to be *more* than a "nine days' wonder" to the world.

That correspondence of which mention has been made as existing between Mr. Pettigrew and his humble worshipper, Miss Phœmie, was kept up, as time went on and winter grew to early spring, with exemplary regularity. Week by week a missive indited in a hand that looked as though a feeble spider had dipped its legs in the ink and then crawled about on the paper, arrived at the Q.C.'s rooms in St. James's Street, and not a little exercised the curiosity of Mr. Pettigrew's factotum, Mudford. He, with that lively interest invariably taken by domestics, male and female, in the correspondence of their betters, was wont to turn over and over these unmistakably feminine epistles, speculating, as he did so, upon the possibility of there being anything matrimonial on the *tapis* — a turn of fate which he would have regarded in the light of a calamity, both for himself and his master. However, Mr. Pettigrew had one peculiarity which, it must be confessed, was rather hard on Mudford—he never *by any chance* left a letter lying about. Argus-eyed, as it is the manner of his class to be, after any chance of satisfying an innate and petty curiosity, it had never yet happened to Mudford to find more than an empty envelope on either desk or dressing-table. This circumstance placed him at a great disadvantage, when his brethren in livery told exquisitely delightful stories of the affairs of their employers; affairs of which they had gleaned a few fragments, and of which all deficiencies were easily filled up by those coarse suggestions that are the natural outcome of the vulgar mind.

Never had Mudford been more oppressed by a sense of the cruel injustice of his master's cautious habits than when in one week no fewer than three of the strange letters arrived one after the other, and this hailstorm of correspondence was followed by the delivery of two by the same post. Mudford remarked, too, that at this time his master was somewhat restless and uneasy, and that he walked up and down the room after dinner instead of going to the club for his rubber or game at billiards.

"Master's bin and committed hisself to matrimony, and the young woman's threatening breach of promise if he don't carry it out sharp," thought Mudford to himself.

The climax of affairs arrived when Mr. Pettigrew declared his intention of leaving town for a week, and added that he should not require Mudford to accompany him.

"Did you say I was *not* to accompany you, sir?" said that worthy, fidgeting with the handle of the door, and thinking his ears must have deceived him.

"You are getting a little deaf, Mudford, I see," replied his master, looking up from the latest edition of the *Globe*. "If the failing increases, I shall have to part with you. Nothing would induce me to keep a servant to whom I had to repeat my orders *twice*."

Mudford retreated with precipitation, and busied himself in preparing his master's things for the journey; but he shook his head as he communed with himself thus:

"He's going to try to get orf it, that's what it is. He's hoffered marriage by mistake. If it comes to a trial, he'd best make a friend of me, and not be so tarnation close. *I'd swear anything* for a suitable consideration."

In spite of the busy law-term having set in—in spite of the great Q.C.'s time meaning endless guineas, he was going to run up to Hazlecroft, and that promptly, too, for the day following that in which Mudford received orders to get everything in readiness he started, not even allowing his servant to go with him to the Euston.

Had he accompanied his master to that most dreary and dingy of all stations, he would have seen a neat, dark-green brougham drive up five minutes before the departure of the North train, and beheld a gentleman descend therefrom and join Mr. Pettigrew, who was pacing the platform, and smoking a tiny cigarette.

The two men greeted each other cordially, and then made their way to the spot where the train was waiting, and, as they did so, many an admiring female glance was turned upon Mr. Pettigrew's companion.

He was a handsome man, white-haired, dark-eyed, and gifted with a charming voice and smile, and a manner the very perfection of refinement. Apparently, too, his reputation was well known, for as he crossed the platform, one passenger nudged another, and whispered that that was "the great mad-doctor," thereby implying, not that Mr. Pettigrew's companion was a lunatic at large, but that he devoted his time and skill to the lunacies of other people.

However, had you listened to the conversation of the travellers on that long day's journey to the Cheviot Hills, you would not have supposed that such a thing as a disordered intellect existed among the human race. Certainly you would have felt it no small privilege to share in the brilliant wit, trenchant repartee, and keen intelligence evoked from the companionship of two thoroughly cultivated and clever men of the world.

On the other hand, the day following, which was the one fixed upon for the "great medicine-man" to have an interview with Lady Jane Plaistow, you would, had you again been a listener to the conversation, have imagined that no topic could be so all-important as that of the various diseases to which that delicate organ, the human brain, is subject, and no "case" of the kind so utterly absorbing in interest as that particular one under consideration.

It was William Mallinger who greeted Mr. Pettigrew and his friend on their arrival at Ardreggan; it was he who led the doctor to that chamber in the western wing, where the Lady Jane still lived her quiet, monotonous, phantom-haunted life.

Sir George, having gradually become conscious of the fact that people were only too ready to blame him for his wife's condition, and shrinking from the contempt of others, as all selfish natures invariably do, was now really anxious for her recovery, and quite forgot to fly out at poor Miss Pheemie, when, under the intolerable suspense of the new doctor's visit, she became feebly-hysterical, and sniffed to an extent that in former days would have insured her dismissal from the room, pursued by an anathema of the most fervent character. The fact was this: during the last few months the master of Ardreggan had been, for the first time in his life, taken out of himself; his pride, and, to a certain extent, his affection, had centred on his late-found heir, this grandson who treated him with every possible respect, and yet never yielded an inch of ground when he was convinced of having right on his side. The old man began to wish for William's good opinion; to cast uneasy glances at the square brow and steadfast eyes that reminded him of the girl whom he had "done to death" as surely as though he had driven a knife into her heart, and to wonder in what estimation her son held him.

The result of this change in the tone of Sir George Plaistow's thoughts and feelings was forcibly shown when Miss Pheemie timidly opened her mind to him, told him of certain changes noted by her watchful eyes in the mental condition of the Lady Jane, and ventured to suggest that Mr. Pelham Pettigrew should be consulted as to the wisdom of decoying a certain eminent alienist, a man of the highest reputation, up to the wilds of Roxburghshire, to give his opinion on the case.

Instead of throwing cold water on the scheme, no sooner did the baronet find that his grandson agreed with Miss Pheemie as to its advisability than he gave his gracious sanction to the same, and even went so far as to write a few lines to Mr. Pettigrew on the subject—a proceeding that caused that gentleman to indulge in such peals of laughter as made Mudge jump again upon his slippery horse-hair stool, and entertain ideas that his master was rehearsing for some startling "effect" in the course of an important trial just then looming like a legal cloud upon the horizon.

Of course the Ardreggan family doctor met the London F.R.C.P. in consultation, and, according to the strictest rules of medical etiquette, was the last to enter, and the first to leave the patient's presence.

Of course, also, the local Esculapius casually alluded to the said consultation for the remainder of his natural life, and his wife mentioned it at intervals to her friends for the same lengthened period.

After a protracted interview with Lady Plaistow, a verdict upon her case was given. And it was this:

A faint—a very faint hope—but still a hope existed that Lady Plaistow might be ultimately restored to reason. This hope lay in the effect which might result from total and entire change of scene—total and entire removal from all those surroundings and associations which were connected with a violent shock to the nervous system, that had supervened upon a weakly physical condition, the result of—

"Ha!—hem!" said the keen-sighted alienist, "it is impossible for me to say of what—but—a condition that has been, I should say—ahem! —*eminently* unsatisfactory for—in fact, some years—"

Miss Pheemie grew pink to the very tips of her ears; Mr. Pettigrew whistled softly through his teeth, and then carefully noted some little irregularity in the tie of his shoe; William set his lips in a hard, straight line, and looked out of the window; and Sir George cast an uneasy glance at the family doctor, who, on his part, presented a wooden countenance to the world in general.

These family doctors, you see, know so much —rather too much, in fact, sometimes—but, then, *en revanche*, no class of men are greater adepts at concealing what they know.

And so the verdict went forth.

Ardreggan was to be once more left to the tender mercies of the herons and the kelpie; and this last might laugh himself hoarse if he chose, or "keen" till he fell back on his "stane" in a fit, for there would be nobody of any consequence to listen to him.

And a *partie carrée*—Sir George, his wife, their grandson, and Miss Pheemie—were to set forth on a journey, first halting at Mentone, and then taking flight whither their own sweet wills might lead them.

"I'm glad you're going with them," said Pelham Pettigrew to William, as the two men returned from seeing the London doctor off on his homeward journey. "That old curmudgeon—I beg your pardon, I mean your grandfather—"

"Oh yes, I understood whom you meant," put in William, dryly.

"Well, well," returned Mr. Pettigrew, laughing heartily, "Sir George, then, let us say, seems on his good behavior while you are with him, and you will be able to watch any symptoms shown by Lady Jane, and judge when further change is needful."

"Surely it is my plainest duty to go with them," said William; "and as for her, God help her! the aim and end of my life will be to try to make some amends to her for what she has suffered in the past, if only—"

"Ah, yes, just so," echoed Mr. Pettigrew, "'if only'—that's just it; there are a good many 'if onlys' in a man's life—eh, Mallinger? But, you see, we men of the world—"

Here he was interrupted by a shout of laughter from his companion.

"What's the matter with the fellow? Deuce take it, Mallinger, what the devil do you mean?"

"Mean!" said William, still laughing as he spoke, "why, I mean that you're about the kindest-hearted and most generous-minded man living, and no more the cynical 'man of the world' you try to make yourself out to be—than—Uncle David is; and I can't very well say anything stronger than that."

"Well, no. I like Strephon; I'm glad I know Strephon: it's always a consolation, mind you, when a person comes up—or down, as the case may be—to the idea one has formed of him; and the excellent David is exactly—exactly—what I had fancied him—a man, my dear sir, so large-hearted towards the whole creation, so sensitively constituted, that he would catch a flea tenderly; afraid to hurt the beggar—eh, Mallinger? Quite, quite!"

Then they both laughed again, until Pelham Pettigrew pulled up short and sharp in his merriment, and said, with a comical glance,

"No, confound it, though! I'm not like Strephon. That won't do, you know. Still, I tell you what it is—I'm mixing myself up with family matters to such an extent that I'm becoming quite a domestic character: case of Darwinism, eh? Evolution, and all the rest of it. I shall find myself propelling a perambulator in St. James's Park some afternoon if this sort of thing goes on much longer."

The next day, Mr. Pettigrew and William returned to town together.

"You are going to run down and say adieu to Strephon, of course—eh?" said the former, as the two parted at Euston.

"Yes, on Friday," replied William, laconically.

But once safely ensconced in a hansom, and bowling along westward, Mr. Pettigrew shook his head reflectively.

There was some one else he knew to be said "good-bye" to besides Strephon—there was the girl with the Greuze face.

Ah, what a dead, white, hopeless face it was when Mr. Pettigrew saw it last!

"He'll have uphill work—uphill work!" he muttered. "It's a devil of a mess, take it altogether!"

CHAPTER XXXVI.

MISJUDGED.

MARCH had done all that could possibly be expected of it by way of deserving its proverbial reputation: it had "come in like a lion, and gone out like a lamb."

The pure white bells of the snow-drops, that had twinkled like stars against the brown earth in February, had been mercilessly beaten down by the wind, and then nipped by a bitter frost. The flame-colored and purple cups of the crocuses had fared no better; only the brave daffodils had nodded their golden heads at the blustering wind, as much as to say, "Do your worst, old fellow—*we* don't care!" and the little blue-eyed violets had escaped harm because they were so modest and retiring, and had hidden themselves cosily beneath the shelter of their leaves.

Now the changeful face of April was peeping at the world, and deep down in the bulbs where they had slept all winter, the hyacinths began to stir, thrusting up here and there through the moist soil pale-green shining cones, that told of a coming glory of white, or rose, or heaven-blue scented bells; while little bundles of crumpled-up feathery leaves, showing their soft edges, promised many-colored anemones, if only the sun would set to work to woo them out into the light with his bright beams.

In the hedges, every spray was hung with fresh green leaves, and every tree was musical with the happy chant of birds innumerable.

Lilian had ceased to be an invalid; her young and vigorous nature had asserted its elasticity, and with the coming of the first spring flowers her strength returned. But not the old light-hearted cheerfulness; *that* seemed gone forever.

True, she turned to her old employment; she sought the company of those best of all companions—books; she was not guilty of the folly of letting her mind lie fallow because her heart ached; she walked with Uncle David along the lanes about Winstowe, and drove him in her basket-carriage, that was drawn by the roundest and fattest gray pony in Weaverton or out of it. She did all these things, and many more, to show that she was striving to take a healthy interest in life again; but the old light was not shining in her eyes, nor the old smile so ready to part her lips.

There was much in the girl's life at this time on which, in such a story as this, I can but lightly touch, and yet which all tended together to make her the woman she ultimately became.

> "Many a blow and biting sculpture
> Polished well those stones elect,
> In their places now compacted
> By the Heavenly Architect,"

is not only true of Christ's Church on earth, but of the individual characters of men and women; the sharp chisel of sorrow is often the instrument by which the beautiful capabilities of a nature are developed, and its full power of sympathy for others called into life. But among the many lessons sorrow teaches there was yet one that Lilian did not learn. She did not attain to the great lesson of forgiveness; she did not rise so high above the level of undisciplined humanity as to pardon William for the seeming wrong that he had done to her—and Guy.

There is no wrong so hard to forgive as that done to one dear to us. An injury that strikes at ourselves alone may be forgotten and condoned with comparative ease; but the sin that touches the head we fain would shelter from the very wind of heaven—who does not know how it calls into being such a bitterness of resentment as blots out from before our eyes the beauty of forgiveness?

"I trusted him—and he failed me. I asked him to be Guy's friend; I told him all my heart; I thought him so true; and—he failed me!"

Is there any thought more bitter for the human heart to frame of one that has been both loved and trusted?

To lose a friend by death—what is the pain of *that*, compared with the loss of a friend by treachery?

Death leaves us the beautiful past—a picture for our eyes to dwell upon lingeringly, tenderly, hopefully, as we think of the eternal world beyond, where no parting is. Memories, sweet as dead flowers around whose faded petals the perfume still lingers, are ours, even when death has done its worst; but treachery strikes at the root, not only of what is, but of what has been. It slays our beautiful past, and stretches it bleeding at our feet.

For if falsehood and deceit have marred the soul that seemed to us one "pure and perfect chrysolite," how can we tell that the past was not mere seeming also?

We may, we must forgive; but we can never trust again.

Guy was dead, and Lilian had enshrined his beautiful memory in her heart: the world seemed all one desolation because he was no longer by her side, because she could watch for him no more, because the joy of expectancy was blotted from her life; the sun scarcely seemed to shine for her, because the light of those soft dark eyes was quenched in death.

Yet, in all her pain, Lilian had found a sweet though sad comfort in tender memories: she could dwell ceaselessly on the thought of all that Guy had been; she could recall the tender, passionate tones of his voice in the melodies they had both loved, the pain of their partings, and the gladness of their meetings. But William, the man whom she had loved and trusted with a friend's ungrudging confidence, he had been faithless, he had failed her, and the years of the past were for her henceforth as though they had never been.

He had robbed her of things infinitely precious; so precious that her whole life must be one long regret in that they were not hers.

He had robbed her of those last words, those last kisses, that lingering look as life fades into death, that are to all of us the consolations we most crave for in time of sorrow.

These things were hers by right of her position as Guy Tremlett's promised wife, and she had been robbed of her just inheritance.

Guy's mother, mad with grief, how could *she* be answerable for this cruel theft? Had not Lilian seen her led away by Ponsonby from the side of her dead son, babbling strange words that had no meaning? Had she not seen her set out on her journey to Tremlett Court, a dull-eyed, silent woman, dazed and torpid with a sorrow that seemed like the forerunner of death? What could *she* have done, poor soul?

But William, her brother, the friend to whom she had confided Guy's welfare, had he not robbed her of those four precious days and nights? He would not even tell her of her lover's last hours, or of those last words for knowledge of which her heart was thirsting.

"Guy was unconscious nearly the whole time." This was the tale they told her. It could not be true; he *must* have asked for her—his darling, whom he had held to his heart, and kissed so fondly ere he left her. He must have wondered that she did not come.

Even Jim was in the plot to keep her in ignorance of what she craved to know: Jim, so tender and so good to every one, was hard to her alone, and would tell her nothing. How long had she lived since that terrible moment when Uncle David, opening the *Evening News*, cried out to her, and caught her and held her close, while she read the record of Guy's illness? read how Guy Tremlett, Esq., of Tremlett Court, lay dangerously ill of typhoid fever at his chambers in Clarges Street?

How long had she lived since the day when she and Uncle David journeyed up to town, sitting hand-in-hand, like frightened children in the dark, and saying little to each other, because each read the other's heart so well, without the aid of words?

Ah God! how many of us can look back upon one day in our lives that seemed a year, upon one month in our lives that seemed an age, upon a few short weeks that seemed set back "a thousand years;" because in them the world about us was all changed, and a new-made grave became a landmark that made all outward measure of time an unreality!

In the weeks that had elapsed since Guy Tremlett's death, Lilian had lived—or so it seemed to her—a lifetime.

And this lifetime, measured not by duration, but by feeling, had set its mark upon her.

Never again would she be the same light-hearted girl as in the past.

Her beauty—that is, the mere external loveliness of youth and freshness—was dimmed by nights of weeping and days of weary, cankering regret. She was a woman who had lived, and loved, and suffered; her girlhood was past and gone.

And now William, the man whom Lilian could not bring herself to pardon for his misdeeds, was coming to Winstowe—coming to his old home after an absence that had been full of stirring and important events connected with that new life upon which he had now fully entered, but which had left him all unchanged in his love for the old cathedral town, for Winstowe, and the dear ones whose presence ever made his truest home, and ever would, let outward change do its utmost.

How would Lilian look? How would she greet him?

Would her eyes turn from him as from something they scorned to look upon—would they turn away as they had done the last time he saw her?

Or had time deadened the bitterness of the past, and would she trust him a little—just a very little again, as in the olden days?

When he arrived at Weaverton, Briggs was waiting on the platform to see to the luggage, and outside the station stood the basket-carriage and the fat gray pony; and seated in the carriage was Lilian, pale and changed, it is true, but better than he had expected to see her, for all that.

Her face showed very fair under the shade of her broad hat with its long, black, drooping feather, and her simple mourning-dress was only relieved by the little white driving gauntlets that held the reins so cleverly, and led the gray pony in "the way that he should go."

Now, William had formed many a picture in his mind of this meeting with Lilian; he had speculated on the idea of her taking up this or that ground in her demeanor towards him; but never once had it entered his mind to imagine what really came about.

For the girl greeted him with all the fastidious politeness due to an ordinary acquaintance, and was ready with all the conventional remarks such a position called for.

A hope that his journey from town had been pleasant; an allusion to the over-fed condition of the stout gray; an admiring notice of the fresh greenness of the hedges as they drove along— Heavens! what food were such-like hollow commonplaces to give a man who had been hungering and thirsting for the sight of her face and the sound of her voice; whose life was one long thought of her; whose anxiety for her while she lay sick had worn him as constant physical pain might have done!

He had not thought to find her so well; he ought to have been glad that fact so far exceeded fancy; and he was glad, after a certain fashion; but where, oh where were the dear old days of yore, whose very memory seemed drifting from him? Where were the days when a wistful glance or a close hand-clasp told him of his little sister's troubles?

He was paler by far than his companion, for all her recent illness, as the carriage rolled up the Winstowe avenue; and Uncle David, waving his handkerchief wildly from the doorstep, and then, in the exuberance of his delight, trotting down to meet them, and so obliging the driver to pull up, cried out,

"Surely you've been ill, my boy, and never told us! Why, bless my heart! those people in the North have taken very bad care of him, eh, Lill?"

But Lilian was flicking a fly from the pony's neck with her whip, and did not even look at William as Uncle David spoke.

"Master William's going to foreign parts, along with his mad grandmother," said Briggs, coming out from waiting at the late dinner, primed with news and complacent in its possession.

"Well, what if he is?" replied Mrs. Timmins, tartly, and utterly refusing the expected tribute of astonishment. "*What* if he is?"

"Oh, nothing if he is!" said Briggs, crestfallen and defeated. "Only I thought you'd like to know."

"Well, then, I don't like to know. There's a deal of fuss bin made over them as wasn't fit to hold a candle—"

"Don't speak ill of the dead, whatever you do, Mrs. Timmins!" interrupted Briggs, fervently, patting his breeches-pockets in a reflective and melancholy manner. "You know you think there's none of us, not even master himself, nor

—nor *me*, nor nobody, like Master William," growled Briggs, vaguely jealous.

"No," said Mrs. Timmins, "I don't *think* no such a thing, Briggs. I *know* it!"

Briggs sought refuge in his pantry.

Now, Mrs. Timmins was at all times devoured with jealousy of "Master William's" new relations. She would have heard, at any time, with serene content that sudden death had overtaken what she was pleased to style "the ruck of 'em;" and would have gladly credited any possible evil thing of any individual one, or of the whole collectively; therefore, that he should go with those interlopers to distant lands was to her intolerable.

She was the more aggravated about it, too, because she could not get her young mistress to agree with her in looking upon Master William's departure as a calamity; on the contrary, that young lady seemed to think the plan a truly admirable one. Lady Jane had always been to her an object of the deepest sympathy and pity, and this gleam of hope, this dawning "light at eventide," was to her mind something beautiful to think of.

"Besides, you must remember, Timmins," she said, with that quiet queenliness of demeanor that always routed Mrs. Timmins, "Mr. Mallinger does not belong to *us* now. Those who are his own flesh and blood naturally have the first claim upon him—and quite rightly too," added Miss Lilian, with her small head held high, and the train of her black dress making a soft ruff-ruff as she left the room.

"Mr. Mallinger!—his own flesh and blood! —him as saved her from the fire!—O Lord!" gasped Mrs. Timmins, sitting down promptly on the nearest chair, and untying her cap-strings with trembling hands. But, in spite of Mrs. Timmins, and in spite of the grief David Earle felt at parting with "his boy" (a grief he flattered himself he concealed admirably, but which was, as a matter of fact, most painfully apparent), the day upon which William Mallinger must once more set off to the North drew on apace.

Now, it was a part of Lilian's present tactics to avoid being alone at any time with him; and so cleverly had she carried out this resolve, and with such perfect womanly tact had she timed her goings out and her comings in, that only when driving in the phaeton, and with the groom well within ear-shot, had she and William as yet been *tête-à-tête* for a quarter of an hour.

It was utterly intolerable to him, this systematic avoidance of the old familiarity of intercourse—this "putting past," as our Scotch neighbors have it, of the old brotherly and sisterly terms; this doing away with the close companionship that had been so dear, and that had never seemed *so* dear as now that it was taken from him.

If the girl had been cold and distant; if she had treated him as though he were suffering under her displeasure; in fact, if she had treated him in any way save in the way she did, the barrier her hands had raised between them would have been less insurmountable.

Have not we all, at one time or other of our lives, taken refuge behind the impenetrable barrier that can be formed by extreme politeness? Can there be any entrenchment more complete, or more calculated to reduce the excluded one to despair?

How William smarted under the pleasant friendliness of Lilian's manner; how he hated the perfection with which she filled the post of hostess towards him; how he paced his room late at night instead of going to bed and to sleep like a sensible man; all these things may be imagined!

At last, indeed, pretty nearly at the very last, fate favored him so far that he succeeded in getting one quiet half-hour alone with this woman who was so dear to him, and yet who seemed drifting whither he knew not.

The rain beat against the windows; the wind seemed determined to try to do its best to uproot Uncle David's precious flowers; it was a day belonging to March, that had apparently been left behind and got into April by mistake; and for years to come, William never heard the rain pattering upon the panes in the same dreary fashion without calling to mind the memorable interview with Lilian Selwyn that ended in her saying to him, as she stood before him, with her steadfast, pitiless eyes looking into his face,

"Things can never be the same as they used to be between you and me. I am no hypocrite; I know the truth of it now; I trusted you, and you failed me. You know you—never—liked— him—"

It was a cruel, an unworthy taunt, but it went home; it made him wince as the stab of a knife might have done; it forced from his lips an unwilling cry.

"Lilian, you are hard—"

"You are *unjust*," he was going to say, but happily remembered in time that she might demand an explanation of wherein the injustice lay—an explanation that he could not give.

"I do not mean to be hard," she said, softening a little; "but you have robbed me of what you can never, *never* give me back......."

Silence, only broken by the splash of the rain against the windows. Now, nothing irritates an angry woman like silence.

"Have you nothing—*nothing* to say, nothing to plead as *some* excuse, Willie?"

Unconsciously to herself, the girl was urged by something in her own heart to take for him the part of extenuator. She was very angry, very indignant; but also very loath to part with her ideal of this adopted brother of hers. She had not known how high a place he held in her estimation until the depth of his fall made her realize it. She had loved Guy Tremlett—loved him as we love the bright, beautiful flowers, the song of birds, or the sunshine that warms the world into loveliness; but (though she would have been quick to resent the idea with hot, indignant passion), she had, unconsciously to herself, instinctively felt a certain want in his character—a want that she had supplemented by her perfect faith and trust in the adopted brother of her childhood. There was no smallest tinge of romance in her affection for William, but, nevertheless, he was a part of her life that she could ill brook to lose—something she had implicitly believed in. If Guy had been the brightness and beauty of her life, William had been the firm ground beneath her feet.

"Even Uncle David thinks it was wrong that you did not let me know—that you let him die, oh, my poor darling!—longing for me, thinking that I would not come! And now you are going to a new life, a happy life, and you do not think of how mine is full of regrets, and must be—always!"

Her hands, clasped in the old fashion, fell against her black dress; her head drooped; her voice was broken by tears.

"But, Lilian," said William, "after trusting me all your life, can't you trust me in this one thing more, and believe that I only—"

"I believe this," she interrupted, with a sudden scorn flashing from her eyes and making her lips tremble, "I believe that you were afraid for me—that you treated me as if I were a coward. Do you think I would have been afraid? Ah, you little know; but of course you could not know. I ought to remember that you could not know; you never cared for any one like that—"

A hot flush mounted to Will's brow as she spoke; hot words rose to his lips; he took one step nearer to her side.

Was he about to let go the cords by which he had bound passion down so long? Was he about to fling the truth, Guy's life, Guy's death, and his own hopeless love, at her feet?

Be this as it may, fate, in the person of Uncle David, interposed.

That worthy man had just returned from a visit to the Close, where the dean lay ill; he came beaming into the now dusky room, full of a lambent cheerfulness at having found his old friend somewhat better.

"What are you doing, children?" he said, in a playful sort of way, as he drew his chair to the fire and sat down. "Not quarrelling, surely?"

"Oh no," said Lilian, walking to the window and looking out at the drenched flowers; "we were only talking of old times."

Yes; they had been talking of the dead past—the dear dead past, that she had said could "never come back."

William did not see Lilian alone again before he left Winstowe.

They all went to the Weaverton Station together.

Uncle David and Lilian took their stand upon the platform to see the train start. The former was suspiciously shiny about the spectacles, and mendaciously cheerful in voice and manner; the latter grave and pale, as it was now her wont to be, but passing fair in the eyes that looked upon her with a tender yearning that her own were blind to.

There was a shriek from the engine, a jolt and a jar, and then the train glided by them.

Uncle David waved his hand; Lilian bent her graceful head and smiled; and William, bareheaded, looked upon her to the last.

"Good-bye—good-bye, my darling!" he muttered, softly. There was no one to hear him, as it chanced—no one to see the mist of tears that made the landscape he was passing through all blurred and indistinct to his sight!

CHAPTER XXXVII.

FIDELIS AD URNAM.

BELL FARM, that comfortable homestead among the Cheshire Hills, of which Mrs. Dutton was now the proud mistress, had been so called after one Josiah Bell, a worthy man and true, and much thought of by his neighbors. Unhappily, the son, who in the course of nature "reigned in his stead," was what is commonly called "a bad lot," and made ducks and drakes of the farm and its appurtenances.

When things grew to be very bad indeed with Josiah *fils*, he sold his patrimony, and William Mallinger became the owner of it, aided and abetted by Uncle David, who had been the first to hear of the fact that it was in the market.

Mrs. Dutton left the grocery establishment in High Street, universally regretted by everybody. She took weeks to find out all the exquisite details of the farm, and was perpetually discovering a fresh cupboard or a new drawer, and being enraptured thereby. She rapidly developed into a model farmer (or whatever is the feminine equivalent for that term), and grew plumper and rosier (if that were possible) than before.

Harry became a perfect specimen of a young agricultural magnate, and actually forgot to carry a pen about behind his ear: also, he harried the farm-manager, and badgered the farm-servants, and yet—how they all liked the curly-headed young fellow!

The neighboring farmers' daughters, too, fell in love with him, to a girl; and he sung in the choir of the little village church, and practised on a Saturday night until he was as hoarse as one of the blue-black crows that stalked about on the fresh-turned earth of his own farm.

All these particulars, and many more, may be imagined by those who know anything of the happy, healthy life led by farm households in the "North countrie."

Here I must not omit to chronicle the interesting fact that before leaving Weaverton Mrs. Dutton received a most eligible offer of marriage, and refused it in the following remarkable terms:

"When a woman has been wed, and knows what it is, and has come out of it all right and safe, she's a fool to have aught to do with it again; and if she brings a mort of trouble on hersel', she's got hersel' to blame; for how can she tell that, after havin' got out of the frying-pan, she bain't steppin' right clean into the fire?"

Perhaps the discomfited suitor experienced a certain grim satisfaction in hearing the deceased husband, into whose shoes he had thought to step, compared to that homely utensil, a frying-pan. Anyhow, he retreated from the field with precipitancy, and his "experience" being told to others, no man ever proposed to Widow Dutton again.

It may be said that the warm complexion of the good woman's matrimonial reminiscences was inconsistent with those tender, regretful yearnings towards "poor Ben" of which we have heard before; and the only excuse I can offer for this inconsistency is to beg the reader to bear in mind that she was of that sex which Mr. Briggs was pleased to speak of, in his moments of sublimest eloquence, as the "feminine persuasion."

When we pay our first visit to Bell Farm it is "the time of roses." Leafy June has done her best in the way of adorning the world with many-shaded foliage, and has beckoned to the roses, who have all rushed out to greet her, and are jostling each other in clusters at the windows, running after each other up the trellis-work by the doors, and turning standard trees into clumps of red and white blossoms that make the old-fashioned square flower-garden before the house sweeter than any lady's boudoir, and drive the bees mad, because, hurry and bustle and buzz as they may, they cannot rifle half the flowers of their nectar.

Just before the long, low, lattice-paned parlor-window stands a tall tree whose stem is bare half-way up; thence it branches out into a wealth of boughs that bear a thousand thousand pointed leaves that rustle in the very slightest breeze—indeed, a perfect baby of a wind that would not stir the leaves of any other tree, is enough to set the little green tongues of this shaking ash whispering and talking to each other.

Beneath the tree is a rude sort of garden-seat formed of gnarled roots and twisted branches, and here, with his dreamy sunken eyes full of far-away thoughts, and his weary head laid back upon a cushion, is our old friend Jim.

How changed he is since last we saw him, but six months ago, beside Guy Tremlett's death-bed! How worn and sharpened is each feature of the earnest face! How thin are the long hands listlessly folded on his knee!

"You see he's got a kind of a waste upon him, 'as our Jim," is Widow Dutton's account of her son's state. "Bein' down here among the cows and gilly-flowers and such-like, will soon set him up again," the good woman would add, cheerfully, giving a glance at the person addressed as though defying him or her to contradict this last statement.

But the "setting-up" process did not seem to be a very rapid one, and Harry began to get into a habit of watching his brother with round, frightened eyes for the space of ten minutes or so, and then making a bolt of it out into the garden or the farm-yard as if something were choking him.

"Naught but a fool would gape at a sick man," said Mrs. Dutton to her youngest born, impatiently, one night when Jim had dragged himself feebly up-stairs to bed, and she and Harry were left alone.

"The best of victuals won't do a body no manner of good, if you stares at 'em continual. Why can't you keep your eyes off Jim when you come in of an evening, lad? He'll be after fancying you think him—worse—than he—is," added the mother, bringing out the last few words with some apparent difficulty.

"It 'ud be hard to do that," said Harry, doggedly; and then he flung his arms down upon the white wooden table, and laid his head upon them, and fell to blubbering like a baby.

When William Mallinger went up to London from Winstowe, *en route* to Roxburghshire, he saw Jim at the old place in Fig-tree Court.

They had not met, this master and man, so strangely linked together by tender memories of past days, for several months, and at first William seemed hard-pressed to find a word to say to his old playmate. Then he laid his hand on Jim's shoulder.

"Jim, dear old fellow! what's wrong with you? Why have you never written to me, and told me—"

He could get no farther: the worn, white face, the short breath that came and went so hurriedly, the great bright eyes, that seemed to shine with an intenser lustre because of the dark circles that surrounded them, all these things struck him dumb with a dread that he could hardly bear to define, even in thought.

"It's sweating so much at nights, and the cough keeping me awake, that makes me weak in the days," said Jim, quietly.

Be sure no time was lost in getting the best medical opinion London could give; but, like most medical opinions, the verdict was what may be called "an open one."

Rest, country air, and plenty of good nourishing food *might* bring about a wonderful improvement; also they might not.

"I'm afraid Mr. Pettigrew won't have his new clerk for a long time to come," said Jim, smiling at his master—his master who could not smile back at him. "I sha'n't be fit for work for a long time, I fancy; look how my hand shakes; and it used to be so steady, too. You know, sir, you used to say there was no copying-clerk in all the Temple wrote such a good hand as I did."

So far, for convenience' sake, William had kept the chambers in Fig-tree Court, but now they were to be given up to a new tenant; and it was touching to see the pain with which the cripple clerk prepared to leave the place that had been to him a sort of home—the place that was, in his eyes, so dear, because there he had worked for William *Snow;* there he had watched for his coming, and looked after his comfort; there he had lived a life which, to his humble, loving heart, left nothing to be wished for.

And now it was all changed, and the old landmarks were to be swept away.

When it was decided that he should go down to Bell Farm for an indefinite period, Jim took to wandering about the old rooms, and toiling slowly along the City streets to visit his old haunts.

He took a peep at the ducks and peacocks in the little oasis by St. Botolph's: then he crossed over Bishopsgate Street, and made his way into the old City church that he had known and loved so long and so well.

There was no service going on just then; but the quiet of the place, and the soft gleam of the cross above the altar, all spoke of peace and rest and trust, as he knelt there alone, and heard the subdued murmur of the busy street outside, sounding like the far-off echo of that active life that was now to become to him only a memory.

The day following, Jim parted with his master. When I have said this, I have chronicled the deepest pain, the most cruel ordeal, that fate had ever called upon him to endure. That it was so bravely met, and nobly borne—that William, though deeply troubled and anxious about his old comrade, never once realized the fact that Jim knew he was taking an eternal farewell of the one creature dearest to him on earth—is only to say that Jim was true to himself, now as ever.

"*Lord! grant him his heart's desire, and fulfil all his mind!*"

It was the prayer that had been offered up,
incense-like, to heaven, by that faithful heart in
the past; it was the cry that rose from that wellnigh broken heart now, as the master, whom
he loved with a love "passing the love of wom-
en," bade him farewell with a hand-clasp that he
seemed hardly able to let go, and tried to cheer
him with hopeful prophecies of a happy meeting
in the future.

After coming to Bell Farm, Jim seemed for a
time to rally; but before the June roses decked
the garden so bountifully, he had given up wandering about the lanes and fields, and day by
day, if the weather was warm enough, he took
up his place on the garden-seat under the quaking ash, and listened to the whispering of those
countless little leaves above his head; to the
lowing of the kine in the distant fields, and the
warbling of the birds; listened to all these pleasant sounds, the while his thoughts were far
away.

Always centred, always dwelling upon one resolve.

And at last the time came for its fulfilment.

"I cannot manage to get up to-day, mother,"
Jim said, one sunny summer's morning, when
all nature seemed riotously glad; "I know it's a
pity not to get out into the garden such a day as
this; but, mother—come here close, and bend
your head down, while I whisper something in
your ear.... I don't think I shall ever get out
among all your pretty flowers again. There now,
don't cry so: you know you used to tell me how
the doctors said, when I was quite a little chap,
that I should never live; and see what a long
time God has let me stay with you, after all—"

He spoke with his arm about her neck, and
his face against her breast; he smiled softly, too,
as though to him

"Death, like a friend's voice from a distant field,
  Approaching through the darkness, called."

"If you cry so bitterly, mother, I cannot tell
you what I want to say; I cannot ask you to do
something for me that will make me very happy—"

"I'll do any mortal thing!" sobbed the poor
woman. "Oh, Jim, lad, there never was a
woman had so good a son as thou hast bin to
me! When I think of how thee used to turn
out in the cold bitter nights, and go a-seekin'
him as never should have needed no seekin' from
thee nor ony one—when I think—"

"Don't think," he broke in, tenderly, drawing
her apron from before her face—"don't think,
because it makes you cry; and then you can't
listen to what I have it on my mind to say."

"Say thee say, Jim, and never heed my
whimperin'," said Mrs. Dutton, trying to put a
brave face on matters, and being but feebly successful.

"Well," continued Jim, drawing a deep breath,
as one might who was embarking on a difficult
undertaking, "I want Harry, when he's done
with his work to-day, to put the black mare into
the hooded chaise and drive over to Winstowe.
The sun will be hot, I know, even by noon, but
the hood gives a nice shade. You see, I want
him to bring Miss Lilian back with him. I
want him to see her himself, and to tell her that

I am getting very near death—hush! dear; you
promised me you wouldn't cry—and to say that
I want to see her very much indeed—to speak to
her about—something—"

At another time, perhaps, Mrs. Dutton might
have been surprised at such a request from her
shy, reserved boy Jim; but now neither surprise
nor any other feeling could find place in her
heart; for a mother's overwhelming, all-absorb-
ing sorrow filled every niche and corner of it.

"She'll be sure to come?—you are sure of
that, mother, aren't you?—as sure as I am,
dear?" said Jim, peering eagerly into her face.

Yes, Mrs. Dutton was quite sure Miss Lilian
would come; and, quieted by this assurance,
Jim very soon sunk into that sleep of utter exhaustion that often so mercifully lulls the dying
in the last days of life.

Mother and son were quite right in their
conviction that Jim's message would bring Miss
Lilian quickly to his side.

Uncle David was out when Harry and the
black mare and the hooded chaise arrived at
Winstowe, after a hot drive of over twelve miles;
but Lilian did not even wait for his return. She
left a note explaining her sudden flight, and set
off with Harry as her charioteer, just as readily
as though the hooded chaise had been a grand
mail-phaeton, and the sad-eyed boy, her companion, some titled lord.

"Is it really so bad, Harry?" she said, in her
soft, low voice. "Is poor Jim going to leave
us?"

Harry was somewhat awed at finding himself
in for a *tête-à-tête* drive with the young lady
from Winstowe, and between his shyness and
the grief that was choking him, and the tears
that were blinding him so that he could hardly
see to guide the black mare aright, he was having a bad time of it.

"It's so bad, miss, that it can't very well be
worse—for us, I mean. As for Jim, he seems
that peaceful and content, I'm 'most ashamed to
let him see my sad face beside of him. It was
yesterday the minister of the church where I
sing on Sundays came to see him, and he had
the sacrament. His face seemed as if it was
shining with a light like what one might expect
to see upon an angel's. I daren't speak a word
to him, nor mother neither. It was like as if
he'd gone a little bit of the way to heaven, and
we were afeared to bring him back again."

Harry's self-consciousness had disappeared
before the great reality of his grief; and so, all
through that long drive, he chatted simply and
unrestrainedly to his companion, and forgot to
feel the least afraid of her. Indeed, he was almost sorry when Bell Farm was reached at last,
for the girl's kindly, gentle voice, and pitiful,
sweet face, brought the truest comfort, that of
sympathy, to his full heart.

I would not give much for any woman's refinement who cannot, when it comes to soothing
the pain of others, be it bodily or mental, forget
all the barriers of caste and class, and make others forget them too.

When Mrs. Dutton went softly into Jim's
room and told him that Miss Lilian had come,
such a happy, gladsome, thankful smile irradiated
his face, that for the moment a little stab of jealousy pricked the mother's heart; but such unworthy impulses are quickly set aside by a true

nature, and Mrs. Dutton, a moment after, could have kissed the gentle hand that slipped so naturally into that of her dying son, and thought no music could be sweeter than the quiet, sympathetic voice that inquired so tenderly into his condition.

"I must see Miss Lilian alone, please, mother," said Jim, when a few moments had elapsed. "Will you open the window?—wide, please, and then stay in the parlor till I send for you. Let no one disturb us, please, till then."

Mrs. Dutton opened the casement and hooked it as far back as it would go, giving a bunch of scented climbing roses a chance to push their way into the sick-room as she did so. Then she bent over her boy, kissed him in most loving fashion, and, loyal to his slightest wish, left the room and closed the door.

"Will you sit there, Miss Lilian — in that chair by the bed-head? It is a comfortable place, I know, and shaded from the sun."

She did not notice it at the time, but afterward, when in fancy she went over and over again through this strange interview, Lilian called to mind that as she so sat her face could easily be hidden from the sick man by the very slightest movement on her part; a piece of delicate consideration for her peculiarly characteristic of Jim.

I do not think she ever quite knew how Jim began that strange story, to which she listened as if she heard it in some wondrous dream. The soft, low murmur of the insects in the grass outside the window; the song of a robin on the bough of an apple-tree that stretched half-way across the open window; the hum-hum of a great golden-barred bee who took a fancy to the roses that had intruded their pink faces into the room; all these seemed part and parcel of what she heard—heard while her hands grew cold as death, and pressed each other closely in a tension of feeling that in a weaker-minded woman would have found vent in sobs and tears—heard with a shame that seemed to swallow up and hide away all power of astonishment—heard with that strange, mad fancy of having heard it all before, that most of us have experienced, and none of us can explain.

You and I, dear reader, know full well the story that Lilian Selwyn listened to—the true story of Guy Tremlett's life and death.

And of all this story Jim kept nothing back; yet he so exquisitely and tenderly softened in the telling of every detail that had power to sting the heart of the woman who listened, that it was only *afterward* that Lilian realized the full and terrible import of it all.

Least of all did Jim keep back one particular of what he looked upon as the great sin of his life—his hatred to Guy Tremlett for his master's sake, his thirst for revenge, and, worst of all, his longing for the fall of a tempted soul. As he spoke of that night of wandering, and of the man that he had "run to earth," and whose fall had filled his morbid mind with an unholy joy, a low, gasping sob from Lilian's white lips told how she suffered as she listened.

When he spoke of his master's stern rebuke—of his master's noble fidelity to the man Lilian held so dear, and to the sacredness of his memory in her eyes—a great amaze took possession of the girl; she looked back upon the past, and a thousand "trifles light as air" rose up as a

cloud of witnesses to the truth and reality of Jim's story.

Of that love, faithful, silent, and deep, that was the secret of William's life, Jim spoke with timid fear; but fear and timidity were at length cast aside, as he told of the grand nobility of purpose with which that love had risen far above the level of mere selfish passion, and had formed a shield and stay to the man who was preferred before himself.

"I have been so cruelly unjust! O God, forgive me! I have done my brother grievous wrong! I did not know, I could not tell; but surely—surely I might have trusted him a little more. Oh, Jim, what was *your* sin to mine? I heaped reproaches on his head; I taunted him with his faithlessness to me. Instead of being grateful, as I should have been, to the truest, noblest friend that ever any woman had, I sneered at his cowardice—"

"No, no; you never did, you could not!" cried Jim, raising himself upon his arm, and looking imploringly in her troubled face; "such words from you would break his heart!"

"I did—the very last thing before he went away."

She would not try to make out the wrong that William had suffered at her hands one shade less black than it was in reality: she could fall into error—this grave-eyed heroine of mine—like the very feeblest of her sex, but she could not be mean or petty; she could not acknowledge the wrong in a grudging spirit.

"If only any one had told me!" she moaned; "if I had only known! But I see it all now; I see how it was that it seemed best to keep me away; but, for all that, I shall be always sorry that I did not see him. Oh, poor Guy!—"

"You must not say that—you must not think that," said Jim, in great agitation; "you would not, if you knew—"

"Ah! do not tell me!" she cried, shuddering, and pressing her hands upon her eyes as if to shut out some terrible picture. "Perhaps you are right; perhaps it was best that I should only see him lying there so calm and beautiful!"

"It has been a daring thing of me, Miss Lilian, sending for you like this, and telling you what no one else would ever have done. I hardly think he would forgive me if he knew—my dear master whom I shall see no more on earth!"

She was frightened at the growing pallor of his face, and started to her feet.

"You are tired with so much talking. Let me get you something; let me call Mrs. Dutton. Is there nothing I can do?"

He pointed to a cordial standing on the table by the bed, and she poured it into a glass and held it to his lips, raising his head gently on her arm.

"You are not angry with me, dear lady, are you?" he asked, looking wistfully up into the sweet face bending over him.

For all answer she laid her lips a moment on the brow already cold with the chill dews of death.

"I am so glad—so glad and happy!" he whispered, as she laid him back upon the pillow. "I was so long making up my mind. I prayed —O God, how fervently I prayed!—for wisdom to see the right way. I think he showed me the light of his guidance at last. I could not bear to know that you judged *him* unfairly. He has been an idol to me, Miss Lilian. No one, I think, ever loved another as I loved my master; and in my heart I have always carried one prayer for him—'*Lord, grant him his heart's desire, and fulfil all his mind.*' Will you tell him that I thought of him, and how hard it was— No," he said, correcting himself, "don't say anything about the pain of dying without my hand in his. It will pain him too much; and he—has—had—pain—enough."

The last words were uttered with difficulty, and his breath came in short, sharp gasps.

"It is that strange fluttering at my heart again," he said, smiling to reassure her; "it always catches my breath like that, and then everything seems to go far away—to grow dim and distant—"

Then Lilian knew that the Angel of Death was hovering near, and for the time being all her own feelings, all the strange revelations but just heard, were put aside, and every thought concentrated on the dying man, he whose whole life had been—love.

Death is the great reality of life, and before its mighty import earth's sorrows and joys seem but "as a tale that is told."

"Is it all peace?" said Lilian, kneeling by the bed. "Is the light shining overhead clear and strong? Dear Jim, your master will be glad if I can tell him that his dear old playmate was happy—"

A less thoroughly real woman than Lilian would have fenced with death—would have murmured pretty falsities about "hoping Jim would be better soon," and "never giving up hope;" but thus to shirk the truth was not in the girl's nature.

"Tell him it was all peace—tell him that the Saviour was very near me—"

Sweetly a bird sung outside; all the faint, far-off sounds of life came through the open window; the sweet breath of the roses scented the room; and in the distance the green hills looked as if sleeping in the sunshine.

"*Peace I leave with you; my peace I give unto you.*"

Lilian hardly seemed to think the words, so much as to hear them whispered to her heart by some angel presence.

Utter prostration was painting a livid circle round Jim's lips, and quenching the light of his eyes.

"You will have to go soon," he said, speaking more feebly than he had done yet. "My master takes such good care of you, that I must try to follow his example," he went on, smiling; "and so I must not let you stay too long and tire yourself."

"I am not tired," she answered; "let me read to you a little before I go."

"Read me a hymn," said Jim, well pleased. "I know all the best of them by heart, but somehow to-day the words won't come when I want to recall them. Read me the 'King of Love.' Master William used to sing that to me often and often in the old days."

So she took the well-worn book, and found the hymn he spoke of, and then the rise and fall of her voice were added to all the murmuring echoes of that golden summer day.

As she came to the last verse, she paused a moment, unable to control the trembling of her voice; then read bravely on:

"In death's dark vale I fear no ill
  With thee, dear Lord, beside me;
Thy rod and staff my comfort still,
  Thy Cross before to guide me."

How peaceful everything seemed!

A cattle-bell tinkled softly in the distance, and from the turf outside the window a lark sprung upward and rose towards heaven, its rippling song trilling out sweet and clear against the sky, and ever rising higher and higher, nearer and nearer to the cloudless dome above, like some fair soul winging its way from earth, nearer and nearer to the gates of the Golden City.

And Jim lay so still, Lilian felt sure that he had fallen asleep.

She rose from her place by the window and bent over him a moment.

Then she gave a little cry, and Mrs. Dutton, waiting in the outer room, hurried in......

The Cross that had been Jim's guide through life had led him whither they could not follow.

CHAPTER XXXVIII.

TWO YEARS LATER.

Two years have passed away when we again take up the thread of our story—years that have been unmarked by any very startling or important changes in the lives of those in whom we take—or I would fain hope we take—some interest.

It often so happens that crushing sorrows, or events that strike at the very root of life, come upon us one after the other in quick succession for a time, and then a quiet "spell" of years follows, during which fate seems well content to leave us in outward peace at least, as though the capricious goddess, having done her worst, is content to nod at her wheel.

But though the outer life may be thus apparently smooth on the surface, it does not follow that powerful influences are not silently working in a steady undercurrent.

I must therefore "hark back" a little, and record the progress of events, and the various changes that time had brought about, both at Ardreggan and at Winstowe.

Mr. Pettigrew's friend, the eminent alienist, had not been wrong in his prognostications as to the case of Lady Plaistow; but the overwrought brain had taken longer than he had anticipated to recruit its powers, and months passed away before the fitful improvement in her condition became permanent. Hence it was winter again before the family returned from their long wandering to Ardreggan.

William and Miss Pheemie, comparing notes as to the dread of the effect that returning to the old familiar scenes might have upon their charge, found that each was oppressed by the same fears; but all these fears proved groundless, and during the following summer an event occurred which amply proved how much stronger, both physically and mentally, was the Lady Jane than any one had supposed.

As Sir George was returning from a ride, his horse took fright at a hay-cart rustling along with its sweet-scented load. The animal reared, then fell, in spite of the efforts of one of the best riders in Roxburghshire; and though Sir George managed to slip aside as the creature dropped, he received a severe kick in the side during the plunging that followed.

For weeks he lay a prisoner in his room, suffering great pain, and going through much vocal exercise in the way of cursing everybody; while, to the surprise of every one, my lady "rose to the occasion," took upon herself the post of head-nurse, and obliged William, by the power of her gentle persistency, to content himself with only a due share of the duties of the sick-room.

Mr. Pettigrew, paying a visit to the prostrate baronet, was amazed to see that his wife had established quite a supremacy in the sick-chamber, and—oh, marvel of marvels!—noted that Sir George seemed to value her ministrations, and became restless and irritable if she remained too long absent from his side.

"It is never too late—positively *never* too late to mend, eh?" said Mr. Pettigrew, with a droll glance at William. "Really, there seems *no* limit to time in the matter of a man learning to conduct himself *like* a man, and not like—I beg your pardon, my dear fellow—a brute! He's so tamed, is your respected grandfather, that, by gad! sir, *he'd feed out of your hand*. Remember Chaucer's lines, eh?—

>"'For he became the friendliest wight,
> The gentilest, and eke the most free;
> Dead were his gapes and his cruelte.
> His high port and his manner straunge,
> And eche of hem gan for a vertue chaunge.'

Quite, quite!"

But Mr. Pettigrew said nothing about Lady Jane. Men rarely speak of a woman in whom they are deeply interested, even to their best friends.

As to Miss Pheemie, her joys and sorrows were at all times apt to take the same form, namely, to "distil in gentle dew of tears;" and in these days of immeasurable content she wept for joy in the retirement of her chamber quite as often as she had subsided into a limp and damp solitude in the bitter past.

During the period of the baronet's confinement to his room she acted as his secretary, writing at his dictation long, and, as he fondly hoped, aggravating, letters, to that "beast Lumsden;" letters in which were enumerated and minutely described all the improvements in the Ardreggan estate that were being brought about under the skilful and energetic superintendence of "my grandson, William Mallinger," and, though feeling no doubt gratified by being so useful to the master of the house, poor Miss Pheemie was somewhat in the position of those who have "greatness thrust upon them," and are more or less mentally suffocated by the same.

Meanwhile, to Lady Jane's weary heart, the grandson in whom she felt such pride, the man with May's eyes and May's smile, was like "light at eventide." Very close grew the sympathy between the two. She was never tired of listening to the story of William's early life; of the poor little fellow whose bare, cold feet pattered through the snow; of "Uncle David" and all his countless goodnesses; of the fire at Winstowe, and frightened little Lilian asking Will to kiss her as the flames flared all around, and the hoarse roar of the crowd below sounded like a distant sea.

Even Briggs and Timmins figured in these narratives, and Widow Dutton and poor faithful Jim grew just as real to Lady Jane as though she had seen and known them all her life.

Of Lilian, William spoke with more reserve, and so it came about that the woman's quick wit read the man's heart better than he knew; and one day she laid her hands (those fair white hands that had survived the wreck of all her other beauty) upon her tall grandson's shoulder, and, looking up at him, said, almost timidly,

"Some day, Will, dear, perhaps I shall see Lilian?"

Now, strangely enough, Sir George Plaistow and Uncle David had up to this time remained strangers to each other personally, though of necessity a vast amount of correspondence and business had been transacted between them. I am inclined to think that some conspiracy existed between William and that sapient man of law, Pelham Pettigrew, on this point: assuredly the latter had been heard to deliver himself of an opinion to the effect that David Earle would not survive the sights and sounds consequent on one of the baronet's "tantrums."

"Strephon would never get over it, take my word for that!" said Mr. Pettigrew, his sides shaking with laughter; "the after-effects of such a moral douche would be to make the good man 'dwindle, peak, and pine.' Quite! quite!"

And so, when Lady Jane spoke of seeing Lilian, William felt, and no doubt looked, somewhat guilty; besides, it made his heart leap and throb to think of Lilian—here—Lilian in the house that would be one day his own.

Which of us has not felt the world go round at some chance word that seemed to embody an impossible dream of joy? William fenced with my lady's suggestion.

"Winstowe would be rather a long journey for you, 'little mother.'"

Now this was a pet name that he had evolved out of his own inner consciousness, and bestowed upon Lady Jane, to her great content.

"Nay," she said, smiling, "I meant something quite different from that, dear. I meant" (holding him closer, and laying her face against his shoulder) "that some day you might bring her here to me."

Lady Jane was a tiny old woman, a very fairy godmother, and so he had to stoop down low to kiss her faded cheek. Then he put her gently from him, and made no other answer to her words.

But she understood it all; and in her heart she wondered that a woman *could* be loved in vain by such a man.

And now we must turn our steps to Winstowe; we must once more wander within the sound of the sweet cathedral chimes.

Uncle David was getting a very old man. The "days of the years of his pilgrimage" were many. Hitherto his genial nature and active habits had almost blinded those about him to the lapse of time; so much so, indeed, that it seemed to come upon Lilian with a sort of pathetic surprise, when she first noticed how much sooner than of yore he became tired as they wandered about the lanes, and how much longer the afternoon "nap" grew to be.

The rosy color did not, however, forsake the

old man's cheek; and though the spectacles now-adays had to be very powerful ones, the eyes behind them were still bright and beaming as ever with that universal love for all created things, that ever had been "as a lamp to his feet" throughout his long life.

The dean, that life-friend of his, had been gathered to his fathers, and a new dean reigned in his stead—a most excellent man, but, nevertheless, always viewed by David Earle somewhat in the light of an interloper.

The removal of the old landmarks that have been about us for a lifetime is always a painful process; and perhaps nothing is more trying than to witness the breaking-up of a home where our welcome has ever been warm and true, and where we know the dear familiar faces we have loved so long will smile upon us no more.

The advance of years had also begun to make itself visible in the person of the faithful Briggs, and his master had insisted upon adding to the Winstowe establishment an assistant, in the person of a lad of great energy and intelligence, but whom Briggs saw fit to characterize as a "jackanapes." This page was, in reality, a most necessary and useful appendage to the establishment in consequence of the many infirmities that beset Briggs; but both he and Mrs. Timmins secretly rebelled at the innovation, as old and faithful servants generally do at such like domestic changes.

Altogether, I am inclined to think the "jackanapes" had a bad time of it, for when, according to custom, Briggs and Timmins fell out with each other, the unlucky page usually came in for hard words from both sides, and "sorrow his young brow shaded" to such an extent that he was wont to retire to the pantry, and there bewail himself until unearthed and driven forth by Briggs.

Timmins, that invaluable but irascible female, was but little altered since we saw her last. A coffee-colored "front" has the advantage of being impregnable to the attacks of time, and certainly her figure was as upright, and the toss of her head as full of direful import, as in the days when "baby Lilian" and "Master William" managed to get into various scrapes, that compassed the ruin or injury of some of those *lares* and *penates* she so rigorously guarded.

And Lilian, what of her?

We left her in the midst of one of those mental storms that sometimes occur in the life of a man or woman, and change the whole aspect of all around in the space of a single day, or even a single hour.

For the uprooting of preconceived ideas and beliefs leaves the mind in maddening confusion —a confusion that nothing but time and thought can reduce to order. Even then the order is a different one from that which prevailed before: things that have been to us realities upon which the very foundations of life rested, have resolved themselves into air; the past is taken from us; we know that it was but a chimera, a beautiful mirage that had no substance; and the present is desolate, because what we deemed most true can no more be our stay and comfort.

It was thus with Lilian, after that momentous interview with Jim.

Finding that his loving spirit had passed away, it was only natural, being what she was, that she should stay and try to comfort the bereaved mother—only natural she should put herself wholly aside for the time being, and be the one to go and meet poor unconscious Harry returning from his work, whistling as he came along with a hoe across his shoulder, and tell him tenderly, yet simply, of his brother's death.

This sort of quiet capability of doing just what is best to be done, and doing it in the wisest way, is a quality inherent in some women, and equally impossible to others; it is a gift best expressed by the word "helpfulness," and most assuredly a blessed quality to those who possess it, though women who make a science of their susceptibilities are apt to sneer at all such self-discipline as being "strong-minded."

Women who have been more thrown with the sterner sex than with their own are, I think, generally healthy-minded in such respects, and but little prone to indulging in that hysterical sensibility which is so abhorrent to the lords of the creation.

Lilian, from a child, had learned the lesson of self-control. To avoid tearful demonstrations in the presence of Uncle David, she would, as a wee lassie, screw up her little face and clench her tiny fists sooner than cry, when school-boy Will inflicted some horrible but unintentional injury upon her. As the "boy is no more father to the man" than the girl is mother to the woman, she had therefore grown into a woman whose intensity of feeling was well under control, and never strayed into the thorny and unpleasant paths of weak indulgence.

It was only when that summer day was past and gone, only in the "still watches of the night" that followed, that Lilian set herself to think out all the marvels of the strange, strange story that Jim had told her.

And it resolved itself into this:

Guy, the beautiful lover of her youth, the man whom she had loved and mourned, and enshrined in the temple of her memory, must be henceforth an intangible idea—a something that had been a creation of her own mind. She could not identify the Guy that had been so weak and sinful, with the dark-eyed lover who had been to her dearer than all others. It is so natural to us all to be very tender of the dead. Even a reproachful thought of them seems a *lâcheté*, a meanness for which we blush.

Swift-falling tears of pity over Guy's ruined, miserable life soon washed away even the very shadow of bitterness from Lilian's heart; and so instinctively did she shield his name from reproach, that she breathed no word to Uncle David of the pitiful truth.

She was very tender to his memory, but the idol was shattered.

Guy, whom she had "loved and lost," existed for her no more.

One sting rankled in and tore her heart, one pain never ceased to throb and ache—the consciousness of her miserable want of trust, her cruel injustice to William.

"I might have known, I might have known," she moaned, kneeling by her bed. "Why was I so blind—so mad? He was Guy's, poor Guy's best friend, and tried to save him for my sake, and for the love he bore me. Oh, noble, noble heart!"

You see, the pendulum was swinging to one extreme as high as it had swayed to the other.

Once convince a true woman that she has been unjust to a man who loves her, and she sets to work in passionate haste to make amends. Up, presto! she mounts the injured being on a pedestal, and forthwith prostrates herself in the dust.

"Some day I shall tell him that I know; that I honor him, revere him, and crave his pardon," said Lilian to herself.

But then, all at once, the remembrance uprose that "*I know*" meant more, far more, than the knowledge of Will's conduct to Guy, living and dead; it meant the knowledge of a strange secret.

And thinking thus, the rosy color flashed into the girl's cheek, and gave her back, for the moment, all the brightness of her beauty.

So it came about that the knowledge of the second secret held her silent on the first.

For when Will came to Winstowe, after his return from foreign lands, a shy restraint on her part reared itself up like a barrier between them, and was naturally misconstrued by him into a still cherished resentment of the past.

"She cannot forgive—she will never forgive!" he thought, wandering up and down the terrace walk, and consoling himself as best he might with a cigar.

When he fancied she was not noticing him, he would watch the dear face, and trace there every change that time and suffering had wrought.

"She looks older and graver, but the eyes have deepened in their steadfast earnestness, and the smile, though rarer, is even sweeter than it used to be." This was Will's conclusion, on the whole. And, in spite of all restraints and misunderstandings, that visit of his to Winstowe was "a real good time."

A truly intelligent woman must needs gain in charm, as time goes on and gives her the opportunity of cultivating and enlarging her mind; and pleasant indeed was the companionship between these two, albeit that a strange shadow of formality and restraint brooded over it all.

"I will tell him to-morrow: I will own how unjust I was, and ask him to forgive me," resolved Lilian, one night, when Will had been at Winstowe nearly a month.

But, alas! the morrow was ushered in by the arrival of a telegram summoning him to Ardreggan, in consequence of an accident to his grandfather.

How the girl missed him when he was gone! How empty and lonely the house seemed without the sound of his step! As to the garden, it was the very oddest thing possible not to see him pacing up and down before the long row of the drawing-room windows, and to miss the whiff of his cigar as he passed the one that was open.

It is the missing of these little commonplace things that are associated with one dear to us, that stabs the heart like a tiny dart, sharp and cruel.

I know the French tell us that "*Les absens ont toujours tort;*" but it is not an unvarying truth.

For, as Lilian now found, the absent are very difficult to banish from our minds, if we are conscious of having wronged them.

"I will write; I cannot wait until he comes again," she thought.

So she wrote a letter, not a very long one, and by no means as well put together as her letters generally were, but worth more than a king's ransom to the man who received it.

If you had only seen him read it—if you had only heard the deep, deep sigh of content, the fervent "Thank God!" that came from lips that quivered like a woman's, you would have known what the burden of her misconstruction had been.

Yet when Will read Lilian's letter again, and yet again, a chill struck to his heart; for, like a snake hidden in a basket of flowers, the same intangible restraint as had held them apart so long lurked in every sentence of the tale it told.

"She is not one to forgive grudgingly," he pondered, "nor to hold back from acknowledging herself in error. No, no; it must be—it can be nothing else: she has guessed; she is afraid I should misconstrue her candor. She loves him still, in spite of knowing him unworthy. I have heard that women are like that sometimes. Jim, dear Jim, my 'heart's desire' is not to be vouchsafed to me."

For Lilian had told him of the dying man's prayer.

From one chance or another, these two did not meet again for many months; and when they did, other guests were at Winstowe besides the heir of Ardreggan. No long *tête-à-tête* wanderings in the lanes and woods gave William happy memories to take away with him as a sweet solace in absence; there were no cosy talks over the study fire; no evening wanderings in the garden, the smoke of his cigar curling softly up in the still air, and Lilian, with a white "cloud" folded across her nut-brown hair, looking Madonna-like in the moonlight as she paced demurely by his side.

He had nothing of this sort to look back upon; and yet it was better than nothing to Will even to see her thus "in a crowd," on the principle, I suppose, that "a crust is better than no loaf at all to a hungry man."

The second summer since Jim died was now rapidly approaching. Upon his grave the violets had flung a heaven-blue pall, and in the hearts of those who had known and loved him his memory was as fresh and sweet as the scented flowers.

William was at Winstowe again, and had spent a day at Bell Farm, and set Widow Dutton's tongue going at double its usual rate for the next six weeks at least, by way of describing to everybody she could lay hold of how he looked, and what he said, also what *she* said, and all about the keen interest her visitor took in Harry's approaching marriage, and how he rallied that bridegroom expectant, until, to quote his mother's own words, "there weren't a bit of him, up to the tips of his lugs, as wasn't as red as ony pickling-cabbage in the garden."

Uncle David's old enemy, the gout, having caught him by the toe, held on so tight that he was a prisoner to his own room; but the old gentleman seemed rather to enjoy being an invalid, with his two adopted children to fuss after him. His "vagaries," as Briggs was pleased to style them, generally came out strong on these occasions, and his great delight at this time was to keep a certain stick within reach of his hand, and thump upon the floor of his room when he wished to summon any one to his presence.

Altogether, this particular visit was a very pleasant one to William.

You see, Lilian had to take upon herself the whole duties of hostess, in consequence of Uncle David's indisposition, and she filled them so well.

But business, that bugbear that is always ready to play marplot to any of our little enjoyments, called for William's presence at Ardreggan; and, though he delayed till "the eleventh hour," and Briggs became awe-struck, beyond the power of finding relief in words, by the number and size of the letters that arrived bearing the Plaistow crest, the last day of his stay at Winstowe dawned at last.

CHAPTER XXXIX.

AMONG THE PRIMROSES.

SUCH a day as it was, too!

One of those days when earth seems so fair that, as she lies dreaming in the sunshine, fanned by the blossom-scented wind, and lulled by the song of a thousand birds, it is hard to remember that such things as suffering, and death, and partings exist; or to realize that the sunshine that kisses the flowers so lovingly falls softly, too, on the grassy mounds that cover our dead, and are the landmarks time plants among us.

Lilian, looking a little paler than her wont, was wandering by William's side along the lanes that skirted the Winstowe grounds.

"Let us turn into the wood for half an hour," he said, as they came to a quaint, high stepping-stile, overlapped on either side by ferns. "I have nearly two hours yet," he continued, pulling out his watch, and taking a glance to see how what he truly felt to be "the enemy" progressed; "and Uncle David will not want you yet; he prolongs these afternoon naps now till they almost meet his bedtime."

"*Two hours.*"

The words hit the girl's heart like blows. Two hours—and what then?

Days, and weeks, and months, perhaps, during which she shall not see him. Has he, then, grown so dear?

Ah me! far dearer than aught else earth holds!

What was that love she once bore the man who first wooed her to the love she now bears this other?

Only as the shadow of a thing, when compared with its reality.

A girl's clinging, fond fancy: the spell of romance freshly flung over a young, untried, undisciplined nature. That was the shadow.

A woman's love, founded on a trustful reverence and a perfect faith; a love that, through all the changes and trials and sorrows of a lifetime, could never totter or swerve or fail, because it rested on that sure foundation. That was the reality.

They turned into the wood.

Have you ever wandered in the fair, fair woods that nestle among the Cheshire Hills, dear reader?

Are there such woods anywhere else, I wonder—woods where the sunshine filters through a screen of interlacing boughs and budding leaves, and shimmers down upon a carpet grounded in moss, and pied with groups of wild flowers, backed with ferns?

Just such a wood was this in which William wandered with the woman he loved, for part of those two precious hours that yet remained to him.

A tiny brook which ran through the centre trickled and tinkled along its shallow, pebbly bed, and a crowd of wild anemones grew so thickly on its banks that they seemed to be jostling each other which should get nearest to the stream, to peep at the reflection of a flower-face first.

Wild hyacinths, blue as the heaven that was seen in fitful gleams above the trees, rung their pretty bells in the soft west wind, and here and there an orchid, tall and stately, reared a spire of rose or purple blossoms from a sheath of leaves, spotted black and green.

Well, then, the primroses.

Why, no one knows what primroses are until he has seen them in the Cheshire lanes, and woods, and fields!

Not just a few scattered blossoms, mind you, but great masses of bloom covering the ground like a yellow carpet, running up the banks, and into all the nooks and corners, just as if a flood of golden flowers had been let loose, and this yellow sea was the result.

William had gathered a handful of these primroses, and set them round with their own leaves.

"You have no anemones, no hyacinths, nothing but primroses," said Lilian, evidently fighting against some spirit of nervous depression that would have held her silent, had she let it have its way.

"I will have no other flowers to-day—not one," said Will; then, after a pause, "Do you know what primroses mean, Lilian?"

"No—something pretty, I hope: they are so pretty themselves."

"They mean *hope*. Such a day as this would make a misanthrope hopeful, and so I am in a mind to gather only primroses, and let myself feel happy, and as full of hope as they. It is only a fancy of mine, child."

Now, since that strange restraint, of which I have already told, had grown up between these two, William had dropped the old familiar names that had been once forever on his tongue, and that one little word made Lilian catch her breath, and drove color from her cheek.

Joy does sometimes put on the mask of pain, you know.

And William, with that quick sensitiveness which was a failing of his, mistook the pallor of her cheek for a sign and signal of offence.

She had looked so happy as they came along the lane; nay, he had fancied he read a certain shy sweetness in the dear eyes as they met his—had fancied—

Heaven only knows what strange, fantastic thoughts had maddened him with their possible truth!

But now he put these phantoms from him with a stern hand.

For that one word, the old familiar word that had been, as it were, the first step across the barrier that held them apart, had sapped the soft, faint color from her cheek.

And so in silence they wandered on through the golden woods; but William gathered no more primroses, and spoke no more of the sweet meaning hidden in their delicate petals.

A wicket-gate led from the wood into the Winstowe grounds, and, as he held it open for her to pass through, a sudden idea flashed into his mind, and, on a sudden impulse, born of that idea, he spoke.

"Lilian, tell me, did Jim tell you anything else, anything more, besides that story of which you wrote to me?"

Her head drooped very low; but the little hat she wore left her face open to his gaze.

Whiter, whiter grew the cheek he looked upon: even the sweet lips lost their rosy color, as she answered him, in one word only,

"Yes."

He drew his breath hard; he saw it all now: she knew the secret of his life, and was afraid for him; she wanted to warn him of how hopeless his love was, and must be—her heart was buried in that dead man's grave.

They reached the house, and she would have gone up-stairs, but that he stood so that she could not pass.

"No, Lilian, do not go away from me; there is something I must say."

So she went into the drawing-room, where a bright fire burned cheerily, and Bijou, the canary, was singing fit to burst his little yellow body.

But something in the faces of those two as they came in must have frightened Bijou, for he cut his song off short, and after one little, plaintive, long-drawn note, kept silence.

"Can you not forgive me, Lilian?"

Was he not already forgiven? Had not the old bitterness died out long since? and now, what was shining in its place?

Great tears stood in Lilian's eyes, blurring the shimmering fire to her sight. He saw them as she turned and looked at him, saw the trembling of the slender hands that clasped each other so closely; but he did not see—oh! blind and senseless that he was—he did not see the love-light shining through the tears; he did not guess how dear her heart had learned to hold him—he did not know that if he had but laid his hand upon her shoulder, she would have clung about his neck.

And she, being a woman, could not speak, and he would not read the eloquence of her silence.

"It is I who have needed your forgiveness all along," she said, speaking hardly above her breath, "not you mine."

"I do not mean about your having misjudged me once, dear—that is past and done with; but I want you to forgive me for that other thing you say Jim told you—for having dared to love you—to love you as my very life, all these long, long years. Nay, you need not be afraid; you need not turn your face away from me. I read it all too clearly in the wood just now. You need not fear that I shall try to overstep the barrier you have placed between us."

Silence, during which Bijou ventured on another plaintive, questioning note.

"Nay," Will went on, coming nearer to her, as he saw that she was weeping, and gently taking in his own the hands that felt so cold and lifeless, "you must not fret like this; you must not pity me too much, just because I have been like a child that longed for the moon. Time teaches one to be something of a philosopher, Lillie dear; and yet I am grateful to you for your tender thoughts of me, and for those tears."

How fast, how fast they fell!

"Some day, when I have lived down, not the folly of loving you—it has never seemed to be folly—but the bitterness of it all, we shall meet on equal ground again, and be as we were in the old days at Winstowe—the days of Uncle David's wonderful Christmas-pie. Why, what a dainty little lass you were, stepping out from behind the crimson curtains! Do you remember it?—and how we punished Timmins's good marmalade?"

Did she remember? Did not her mental vision glance back across the plain of the years that were past, and see things in the clear, bright light of reality and truth?

"We needs must love the highest when we see it," but she had not known it for the "highest;" she had looked upon a mirage, and the phantom had hidden what was real. What had she loved? An ideal of her own creation, a shadow, a something that was not Guy Tremlett, but the visionary fancy of a maiden's dreaming.

What had she cast aside? The love of a true heart, the passionate devotion of a man great and good, a man by whose side a woman might walk safely through life's shade and sunshine, upborne by his loving arm in the time of sorrow, and finding sympathy in his smile in the day of gladness.

William Mallinger had so long learned to look upon his love for Lilian as a hopeless thing, a part of his life to be hidden away and held in check, that it was hard for him now to read the signs of the sweet face he loved otherwise than by the light of the past. A man who had known Lilian less well would have read her better.

"It is because I know you trust me, child, that I have no fear of you misinterpreting my conduct in the future, when I act up to the resolve of which I told you as we walked among the primroses just now. While there was a visible bar between us, and while you did not *know*, it was so much easier for me than it could ever be now."

This sentence, it must be confessed, was somewhat involved, and perhaps hardly as grammatical as might have been expected from a member of the Bar; but Lilian understood what he meant clearly enough, and he saw by the quiver of her lips that she did so.

"You see, I had my duty to do to *him*."

"To Guy?" she put in softly, yet without the least shrinking from the utterance of her dead lover's name.

"Yes, to Guy; and I trust, God helping me, I did it."

"Indeed, indeed you did."

The hands he held grew colder as she spoke: he touched them gently with his lips and let them fall.

"I am glad you can give me so much praise," he said, with a certain ring of bitterness in his voice, of which he was himself unconscious, but which thrilled to her very heart; "I shall like to look back upon to-day and think of it; I shall like to remember—"

A sob she could not restrain made him stop short, and leave his sentence unfinished.

When people "remember" a thing to take comfort from it, they are, *cela va sans dire*, lonely, and needing comfort.

He would be lonely, he would be thinking of her, and she—

Oh! if she were but beside his knee, her head

resting against his breast, her hand clasped in his; if nothing could part them any more; if he might never again be lonely, so long as God should give her life—

But, you see, he *would* take everything for granted; he *would* take his stand upon the old ground, and, being a woman, what could she do?

"But it will not always be like this," she said, *en revanche* for that inopportune sob; "some day you will care for some one else."

Silence, during which the fire had it all its own way, and laughed softly with little bubbling tongues of flame—at the exquisite folly of mortals, most probably.

At last he answered her.

"No, I shall never 'care for some one else,' child: there are 'women and women.' A man may love a woman, and forget, and love again; but there might be such a woman as, a man loving once, must love all his life, and would fulfil a higher destiny in so loving, utterly without hope, than in any lower content that he might grasp, *faute de mieux*."

He had taken her hand in his again, and felt it tremble.

"Gentle heart," he thought, "how she pities me!"

But I am not quite sure that Lilian was not pitying herself, too, just then.

"Don't you see," he said, making up his mind to bring the interview that tried her sensitive nature so sorely to a close, "that if a man has a certain ideal enshrined in his heart, an ideal that God has willed shall be to him unattainable, he does some woman a grievous wrong if he sets her in a lower place, when—all the while—"

But Lilian's strength was rapidly failing her: she twisted her hand from his hold, and turned her face away.

"I think I hear uncle stirring. I think I—had better—go—"

"No, no," he said, after listening intently for a moment; "the dear old man has not finished his nap yet: it is only your fancy, child. Listen to me while I say just one thing more: I do not want to recur to this subject again; it makes you suffer, and I cannot bear to see that. So I want you to understand that I shall never, as long as I live, speak of—of all this again."

This assurance on William's part appeared to overwhelm Lilian (with gratitude, no doubt) to such an extent that she had to sit down quickly on the couch by the fire—to conceal her joy, perhaps.

"I tell you this," went on the quiet, steadfast voice, "in order that you may have no fears, no misgivings; in order that you may be quite sure the pain of all this to-day will never happen again. I want you, in fact, to forget it all. Child, let it be as if it had never been."

How generous he was! how good, how noble, how kind!

Indeed, she was so touched by all this combination of good qualities on his part that she must needs weep over it!

"Hush, hush!" he said, troubled beyond all power of repression at the sight of her tears; "it is not worth such sorrowing over, dear, all this. You forget how used I am to it; and time, you know, soothes all pain, even such as mine."

It would have been hard, indeed, for him to have said anything more utterly unwise; but, on the other hand, he could hardly have said anything better calculated to call pride to the aid of love.

"I am glad of that," she said, with her small tress-crowned head held proudly enough; "that is a very good thing."

Then she set her little mouth in a hard, firm line, that told of a sudden *accès* of resolution: notwithstanding which noble emotion on her part, it took all her determination to prevent the set lips from parting in a piteous and altogether ignominious quiver as she pondered on the excellence of this same "good thing!"

"That is right," said William, with hypocritical cheerfulness; "don't let me go away carrying with me a self-reproachful memory of having hurt you so sadly, dear!"

"*Go away!*"

I do not know any combination of words, in the English language, more calculated to overset a woman's resolution.

They mean so much, those two small, insignificant parts of speech! They seem to call up a vision of distance by sea, or by land, or by both combined; and display it in its most appalling proportions to "the mind's eye;" they call up a sad-eyed ghost, whose name is "Absence," and who, like the "mither" of the unhappy heroine in "Auld Robin Gray," "looks in our face till our heart is like to break;" they suggest a horrible silence that is coming, and which we know, with prophetic dread, will make the ear ache with its intensity—a silence that will pervade the world about us, be that world ever so noisy, ever so full of turmoil.

These two words, so pregnant with coming sorrow, fell like lead upon Lilian's heart.

William would "go away;" the matter of which they had now spoken was to be henceforth a closed book; and, O triste consolation! she was to suffer no more in the hearing of his "most sade storie of love for a faire ladie."

On the mantel-shelf, already poor pretty blossoms growing limp and dejected, lay the primroses that he had gathered for her in the wood.

They had grown into life, sheltered by pale-green, velvet-soft leaves; they had pushed up their golden faces into the sunlight, to let the world see that spring had come at last, and summer was on its way; and now they lay a-dying, and "their day" was over.

Not quite, as we shall see; they had a message of hope to the world awhile ago, and perhaps a sweeter message still lay folded in their fading blossoms now.

William touched them gently as they lay.

"I shall never see primroses again, Lilian," he said, sighing, "without thinking of this afternoon."

She might have added, "Nor I;" but she heard the cuckoo-clock sing out the hour, and caught the sound of an ominous bustle and stirring in the direction of the stables, and these two sounds combined held her dumb.

"Bump! bump! bump!" went Uncle David's stick upon the floor above, and they knew that the "nap" was over, and that time had run on at an altogether ridiculous pace, considering that there ought to be sixty minutes in each hour.

"I had better go up to him, and then see that

all my things are brought down," said William, drawing a deep breath as he mentally stepped across the boundary that separates dream-land from every-day, matter-of-fact existence.

"I shall see you for a moment or two before I go, of course; but yet this is a sort of good-bye in its way, isn't it?" he asked, with—truth to tell—a rather feeble laugh at his own weak jesting. "Look at me, child, and let read my full pardon for all my faults in your eyes."

Such a sad face was turned to him! Such heavy, tired eyes were raised to his!

"What a brute I am to have pained you like this?" he muttered, impatiently, turning quickly from her, lest he should forget himself and all things else, save the irresistible longing to clasp her close to his breast, and kiss those weary eyes, and the little mouth that drooped so piti-fully.

But he quickly gained the mastery over his own will, and as he looked at her again, she thought—or perhaps the fire-light deceived her —fire-light *is* such an uncertain thing, you know—that a mist, as of tears, had come over the tender, steadfast gray eyes.

"Oh, listen to Uncle David's stick!" she said, hurriedly; and truly that instrument was per-forming an animated edition of the popular tune known as "the devil's tattoo." "You had bet-ter go at once—indeed, Willie, you had."

And so he went.

Well, it was all over; and, surely, as she had said before, "a very good thing too."

She would never bo troubled by hearing the story of his hopeless love again—never!

They would always now be as in the old, old days—the days of Uncle David's "Christmas-pie."

Lilian thought she would go to her room and bathe her eyes; they were sadly red, it must be owned, and it would never do to let Uncle David guess at this trouble between his children.

But human nerves are odd things to deal with: if you try them too sorely, they have a way of avenging themselves; so when the girl rose to her feet, something seemed to be the matter with the floor. It moved up and down in a most incomprehensible way, and, besides, her knees seemed to sympathize in the general *bouleversement*, and inclined to refuse her their wonted support; so she very wisely sat down again, but not before she had caught up the poor dying primroses. She held them in her open hands, and, bending low her white face above them, kissed them with a passionate *abandon*, as though they were living things that could read her heart.

Sobs shook her from head to foot, tears rained down upon the flowers she held; the strain of self-repression had been too long maintained, and now, having once broken through that band, emotion carried the day triumphantly. Sudden-ly, with a strange revulsion of feeling, she flung the flowers upon the ground.

Had he not said they were the emblems of hope? And did they not lie! lie! lie! false flowers that they were?—for what hope remain-ed to her, now that she should never more hear the sweet story of his love?

Without that melody, how could there be any music in her life for all the years to come? "Chime! chime! chime!" rung out the soft,

mellow voices of the old cathedral bells, and then—she never knew how it came about—but mingling with their lovely, gladsome music was the sound of a voice close, close beside her—a voice no longer calm, no longer telling of a hard, stern resolve, but full of passionate pleading, and vibrating with unutterable tenderness.

"Why did you kiss the poor dead flowers? Oh, child, don't be pitiless to me—tell me the truth, and quickly— Oh, my darling, do you know what all this looks like? do you know what I shall dare to think, if you let me? Am I dearer to you than I thought or dreamed? Has God given me my 'heart's desire' at last, as poor Jim prayed he might? Tell me, my darling, am I making a terrible mistake? Oh, my God, if you knew—if you knew what all these years have been, you would not keep me in suspense!"

He was kneeling by her; he had thrown one arm about her shoulders, and, with pleading eyes and lips passion-pale, bent towards her averted face.

"Ah, child," he said, "speak to me!—tell me, my love, my love! do you love me at last?"

Then she gave him her answer—a wordless one, but yet eloquent enough, I think; for the little trembling mouth sought his, and in the deep passionate content of that long, lingering kiss her story was told.

And "chime! chime! chime!" rung out the sweet cathedral bells.

Oh, happy, joyous bells, ring on, and tell the story of an answered prayer to one pure soul in heaven!

CHAPTER XL.

"AT EVEN-TIDE IT SHALL BE LIGHT."

UNCLE DAVID at all times delighted in the possession of a joke.

He worried it, so to speak; chuckled over it; enjoyed it as a child enjoys the possession of a toy; and was disappointed if those to whom he told it did not laugh as heartily at the seventh repetition as at the first.

And now he had got hold of a joke of which it appeared highly probable no one would ever hear the last.

Indeed, to the best of my belief, no one ever did.

He said that on a certain afternoon he, being kept a prisoner to his room by a "twinge" of the gout, fell into a doze, and, on awakening, heard voices in the drawing-room below, and tapped upon the floor with his stick, to signify that he was no longer in "the land of nod;" that William came up-stairs in answer to this summons, and was shortly by him despatched to fetch the *Saturday Review*, which lay upon the drawing-room table; that on this errand Will departed, and that he, David Earle, waited, with more than the patience of Job, a most un-conscionable time for his return, and waited in vain. That he again resorted to the service of his trusty staff, and played such a wild tattoo with the same that "*he broke it.*"

This was the joke, you see!

Well, it appeared to him that the people below stairs had become deaf, perhaps dumb too, to judge from their silence.

Therefore he rung the bell, which Timmins promptly answered, and as she was about to reply to his question regarding "Master William's" whereabouts, that defaulter appeared, and, leading Lilian up to Uncle David's side, and quite disregarding the presence of Timmins, put his arm about her shoulders, and, looking vastly proud and ridiculously happy, made the following astounding statement:

"Uncle David, this is to be my wife."

Mrs. Timmins no sooner heard these words than she so far forgot her manners in the presence of her betters as to give a little scream, and sit down with more force than elegance upon the nearest chair, shedding tears of joy; and her young mistress, instead of reproving this unseemly conduct, went to her side, and, kneeling down, clasped her arms about the old woman's neck and kissed her.

"I knew how it would be! I could have told you six months ago that Master William and Miss Lilian would make a match of it in the end," quoth Mrs. Timmins to the amazed Briggs at tea that evening.

"Why didn't you say so, then?" said Briggs, in an injured tone.

"Bah!" replied Timmins, "'tain't good for men to know too much!"

But Briggs was not aggravated.

He had a "hive of content" in his own reflection as to the state of affairs at Winstowe, present and to come.

"There'll be a weddin'," he thought to himself, complacently; "and ain't gentlemen just free with their money at such times!"

Then Briggs had to hurry off to Weaverton to send a telegram to Sir George Plaistow, Bart., informing that gentleman that "urgent business" would detain his grandson at Winstowe for some days.

"What the devil can the boy mean?" shouted the baronet at Miss Phœmie, whom ill fate had selected as the victim who should take the yellow envelope to his study.

"I'm sure I can't imagine," said Miss Phœmie, shaking very much.

"Phœmie, you're a fool! Go and send my lady here at once. *She's* got some sense," bawled Sir George.

In due course of time the old man obtained the fullest possible information as to "what the boy meant," and for days every one avoided the study as though some ravenous beast were chained up there.

Until Pelham Pettigrew arrived.

Then the "lion was bearded in his den," and the baronet gradually tamed by the matchless tact and winning tongue of his sole friend.

"Ah, yes," said Mr. Pettigrew, confidentially, to his cigarette, as he stood by the fire in the cosy Hazlecroft smoking-room that night, "the case of my young friend Mallinger is an admirable instance of the truth of the proverb—'*Tout vient à celui qui sait attendre.*' Quite, quite!"

Here I must take leave (reluctantly, indeed) of Mr. Pelham Pettigrew.

There are rumors that he will soon be Mr. Baron Pettigrew; but assuredly no titles, no honors, no reputation, can add to his worth as a man, or render the fact more patent than it already is to those who really know him, that under the mask of being a "case-hardened man of the world" he hides a heart as tenderly capable of feeling for others as that of David Earle himself.

Nor had his wonderful powers of penetration been at fault when he foretold the fate of Mrs. Tremlett.

Tremlett Court is desolate; its windows are closely barred; its lovely terraces and gardens neglected; its gates grow rusty on their hinges for lack of use.

And its unhappy mistress is the inmate of a private mad-house.

"Sorrow for her son's death drove her into a melancholy mania," said the world. "How sad!"

Then the world straightway went its way, and forgot that such a person as Mrs. Tremlett existed.

But there is one faithful attendant ever at the side of the poor lady, one creature who never forgets and never wearies.

Her mistress does not recognize Ponsonby: memory has ceased to link even one day to its fellow; and as to the past years, they are to her as though they had never been. Yet is the mad woman more easily controlled, more manageable in the hands of her old attendant, than in those of any other person.

And to Ponsonby this is reward enough.

Who cannot imagine the happiness of Uncle David in that of his children?

As he watches Lilian's happy face, and listens to her voice, singing as she goes about her household duties, or wanders among the roses that are now making the Winstowe garden fair with their countless blossoms, and sweet with their perfumed breath, it seems to David Earle as though the God whom he has served throughout a long lifetime has blessed him very bountifully, and "prospered the work of his hands" beyond all that it could have entered into his heart to conceive.

Has not the boy whom his hand rescued from the depths of poverty been to him more than ever son was to father?

And now, in his declining years, does not the very peace that "passeth all understanding" shine in his heart as the mellow western sunlight gilds an evening sky?

For it is well with those he loves; and though the time cannot be far distant when the "silver chord of life shall be loosed" and "the golden bowl be broken," when the "shadows shall fall upon the mountains," and the "spirit return to God who gave it," the evening of Uncle David's life is, in truth, a "golden sunset."

It is Sunday evening when we pay our last visit to Winstowe.

Lilian has been singing, and the last notes of that grand anthem, "Guide us, O thou great Jehovah!" have but just died away.

It is an old custom that Lilian should sing to Uncle David of a Sunday evening, and she is very, very careful in fulfilling every wish and fancy of his just now; for the time will shortly come when she must leave him. Not altogether; Will would never expect her to do that; but instinct tells the girl that once she is a wife, things will never again be quite the same; and very tender, very loving is she to Uncle David in these last few weeks of their being together as of old.

She has risen from the piano, and lingers a moment by his chair, touching softly the silver-white head, and asking if the music has pleased him.

"Yes, yes, my darling, but I am getting a little sleepy. I think I must try to take 'forty winks.'"

Which is a fiction on Uncle David's part, for it is not the time of day for his "forty winks."

However, the loving fable is successful, and with a smile Lillie passes on to where some one is sitting at the wide-open window.

This girl whom I have tried to put before you as by no means a "perfect woman," but yet all womanly and real even in her failings, knows nothing of that prudery and affectation which leads some women to endeavor to enhance their own value in the eyes of a lover by an assumed indifference.

Quite naturally she goes across the room to Will and slips her hand in his.

And he clasps it close, and draws her down beside him on the wide window-seat.

Her head droops against his shoulder, and her grave, sweet eyes look dreamily out into the evening, that is growing dusk with the coming of that soft, balmy darkness only felt in the calm of a summer's night. Every flower is giving out its sweetest perfume, and "robin's plaintive even-song" seems like the utterance of a pathetic joy, so passionately dear as to approach the very verge of pain.

And in the distance, against a sky where here and there faint stars begin to shimmer, the grand old towers of that cathedral, where once a little "waif and stray" sought shelter from cold and weariness, stand out in bold relief; while "chime! chime! chime!" ring out the soft, sweet voices of the bells, seeming like God's benediction on their happy love.

Hark! the last mellow tone has vibrated through the quiet night.

They listen, but the bells have "said their say"—for that time, at least.

Then Will speaks.

That is, if you can call "speaking" a whisper so low, that Bijou, sleeping with his little yellow ball of a head tucked under his wing just above them, never stirs a feather at the sound.

"Pet, they will ring for us soon—"

She creeps a little closer to him in the flower-scented gloaming, and steals her arm about his neck.

And he bends down to the face that lies against his breast, and lays his lips upon the little smiling mouth that is so eloquent in silence.

Meanwhile, that arch hypocrite, Uncle David, is *not* taking his "forty winks." His chair is at the far end of the long room, and looking down its vista, he can see a fair picture, of which the frame is the rose-wreathed window, and this picture is so full of content and joy to him in the beholding, that his eyes grow hazy with a tearful mist that is the very dew of thankfulness.

It is a pretty picture, too! So pretty that the climbing roses and the little milk-white, starry jasmine flowers push themselves in through the open window to enjoy it.

A girl with her head upon her lover's breast, and her hand clasped in his; an embodiment of the ideal of that dear solace God has given to man—"*Love: strong as death!*"

Thus, then, we take leave of Uncle David and the children of his adoption.

The old man's heart is bright with the radiance of earth that is called love, and the light of heaven that holds the twofold radiance of faith and hope; and of him it may be said, God's promise given of old has been indeed fulfilled, "*At even-tide it shall be light.*"

THE END.

CARING FOR NO MAN

A NOVEL

BY

LINN BOYD PORTER

BOSTON
WILLIAM F. GILL & COMPANY
300 WASHINGTON STREET
1875

TABLE · OF CONTENTS.

BOOK THE FIRST.

BOOK THE SECOND.

BOOK THE THIRD.

CARING FOR NO MAN.

CHAPTER I.

THE PEARL STREET HOUSE.

In a city bordering on the Atlantic seaboard of America—which, I say not — and which, it is no matter; in the month of December, in the year 1850; in an upper room of a strange looking, secluded old house on a quiet side avenue known as Pearl street; was sitting, at a large, old-fashioned desk, one wintry evening, a young man of the age of twenty-two years, writing.

Only twenty-two years! An age when many and the most of men are learning their first important lessons in responsibility; when they are fresh from the sweet influences of a home, where they have been jealously guarded from evil associations by a loving mother and sisters; when they are turning the opening pages of the book of Life, and marvelling at its wondrous and difficult problems; when they are feeling the first impulses of ambition, and planning to excel among their fellowmen, that they may reach some day the summit of that hill whose head towers far above them!

The young man who sits writing in that quiet room has had no such experience as this. The age of twenty-two finds him farther advanced in ex perience than many are at forty years. He has travelled far among men, has seen many strange countries, and has learned much from them. He has even written books which have made their mark in reading circles. The manuscript of his third work is that on which he wields his pen to-night. He is writing of Man, the creature he loves best to study, and which he has studied well. He has been with him on shipboard, in the lonely forest, in the villages and cities, and he is his favorite theme. But if there is one creature on earth of whom he knows nothing, that creature is — Woman.

He had a mother, you say? She died at his birth. A sister? None; nor any little playmate of the sweeter sex. He does not care for this, or even think of it, ever; he is only twenty-one, and there is time enough yet for that.

Perhaps so; who can tell, as to-night he sits in his room, writing? It is an old room, bearing the marks of age as well as the rest of the old house. A bright fire burns in the grate near him, and a bright light is cast over his desk by the lamp upon it. A tall book-case by his side holds volumes ranging in character from Shakespeare, Calvin and Paine, to The Hunter's Guide, and the Philosophy of Trout Fishing. Common articles of furniture are at hand, whose origin is of no recent date. Upon the walls are hanging, supported by pegs and hooks, a strange assortment of engravings, hunting knives, rifles, shot-guns, game-bags and other articles of a similar nature. Three doors open from the room. One of them leads into a large hall, from which stairs go down to the front door of the house. The second leads into a bed-room. The third door opens into a back room, filled with hammocks, oars, barrels, rubbish, and bits of iron, stone, cotton and wool.

While the young man is writing, the winter evening is cold outside of his room. The weather is boisterous, the wind howls dismally, and the snow is driven in angry masses against the lonely building. Inside of the room however, the air is pleasant and mild, seeming all the more so by contrast with the storm outside.

He knows nothing of the storm, of the cold, or of the snow! *He* is writing, and the line which runs straight from his active brain to the characters his rapid pen leaves upon the paper, admits of no foreign object's intervening. Sheet after sheet is covered and laid upon the pile before him, the pen is dipped again and again, the hours fly by unheeded. At last, when the echo of the midnight stroke is dying away from the city's clocks, the chapter is ended, the pen laid aside; and the young man moves back his chair from the desk, and looks at his watch.

"Twelve o'clock! Gracious!"

A very handsome young man he is, as he sits there with his head resting on one hand, watching the blaze that comes from the grate. Rather tall, good figure, erect bearing, firm mouth, high forehead, fine eyes, and above all, the heavy masses of dark, brown hair which are gathered away from his brows and hang about his neck, are enough to distinguish him anywhere. He is dressed in a hunting-frock, neckerchief, light pantaloons, and slippers. Yawning a little at the lateness of the hour, he sits musing over his evening's work.

"Another chapter for my new novel. A few more weeks, and it will be ready for the printer. It ought to be the best book yet, considering that I am getting more accustomed to the labor. How surprised I was when Jones & Co. came to offer me such a price for another book, relying wholly upon what I had previously written. Well, I told them they should not be disappointed, and I have tried to keep my word. If this story succeeds, I shall be obliged to put my price still higher next time, or they won't appreciate my value."

The young man smiled at the humor of the last idea. Then he grew sober again, and stirred the fire thoughtfully.

"How strange it all seems, to look back upon my life and see it all spread out before me like a map! What a curious map it has been! In some respects it has been a hard road that I have come over, but I would not give up one step of it for anything. It has given me independence that is of more value than I can estimate. What would I have been if I had been petted as some boys are? watched and tended for fear I should get injured or catch cold; if I had been sent to school by anxious friends till I was twenty-one, and passed my youthful days in manufacturing excuses to stay at home by the chimney corner; or taken a sudden fit to become a scholar, and filled my head with a mess of Greek and Latin nonsense; and come to be looked upon as an exemplification of how much a man can know and not show it! The idea is horrid, I am sure."

The speaker shrugged his shoulders disdainfully, and stirred the fire again.

"Wouldn't I have made a handsome prodigy for schoolmasters to gloat over, and show off to Committeemen on examination days; to be wondered at as a very smart boy while I spoke my piece at the Sunday School Concerts, and perhaps got my name in a newspaper next day; to be petted by old women, and patted on the head by young men. I thank my stars that I was delivered from such a fate. The idea is so absurd, though;" and the speaker curled his lip as he drew the distasteful picture in his imagination.

"How many fools there are in the world who think themselves fortunate that they were born rich, and can live without honest labor of any kind. How many fools of fathers (saving the disrespect) who carry their gray heads so proudly because they have money to leave to their graceless, spend-thrift sons. How many fools of mothers (though they mean well enough, GOD bless them!) who think their boys will be better off than their neighbors' because they can wear broadcloth instead of homespun, and never need to exert themselves from their cradles to their graves. But worst of all are the sisters" — he did not use the harsh term this time — "who spoil their brothers more than all the rest can, because they have more influence with the blockheads."

" But I? born miles from the habitations of men, cradled by a rough father in the cabin where my mother died in giving me birth; drinking in health from the fresh air of heaven, and learning the language of the wolf and panther almost before I could lisp a word of English; brought up as I was in that Southwestern wild, I would not exchange my boyhood for that of any prince; hearing the falling of trees beneath my father's axe, watching the young corn springing into life where wild beasts had roamed for centuries, playing with my pet foxes and bears as other children play with their mates, I was happy. And thou, O my mother, if it be permitted thee to look down upon me to-night; me for whose life thou gavest thy own; I thank thee yet that thou didst prefer the wild life of a poor hunter, whom thou didst love, to the luxurious living of thy proud father's house!"

He fell into a deep reverie, and was only aroused by hearing the clocks striking one. He arose and opened a window. The storm had ceased, and the cold stars were shining on him, serene and frigid. The snow was lying several feet deep about the yard, while the great trees were bending under the weight upon their branches.

"I must go down and clear the walk to the street," said the young man to himself. "It will be frozen before morning, and besides, a little exercise will do me good."

The slippers were drawn off and replaced by a pair of high-top boots. The frock was covered with an overcoat, from the pockets of which a pair of gloves were taken. A fur cap was placed upon his head, and taking a snow-shovel from the back room, he went down the front stairs.

The house was an old house, as

has been said before. It might have been a jail, from its barricades and locks. Every window was barred — every door was barricaded. When the young man bought the place, there was a great iron lock on every door, besides an iron bar and a chain. On every door there was an iron bar, lock and chain still. Undoing the chain, taking down the bar, and turning the lock, the young man opened the door and stepped out. On the street side of the door there was painted, in old black letters, the name of the owner: JAMES ALBERT ANDERSON.

CHAPTER II.

OUR LITTLE GIRL.

Winter clung to the earth this year of 1850-51, until people began almost to doubt whether there would be any spring at all. At last the snow melted down under the sun's rays, the little streams thawed out, the ponds became free from ice. Then, suddenly, the north-wind came down upon the scene, a cold snap set in, and directly everything was frozen over again. The poor suffered greatly from the chilly aspect of the weather, many of them having exhausted their supply of coal and being without funds to procure more. Children, where there parents could afford it, came in for new mittens, cloaks and boots; and it was really wonderful what an amount of trouble and expense, this well-meant visit of the North-wind brought in its path. The generous men of the city set about relieving what necessities of their poorer friends they could, and as usual, Albert Anderson was not backward in the work.

Still there were many cases that could not be reached, and the cold was not relished by the majority of the people.

In our worst misfortunes, however, we can generally discover some element of pleasure, and even out of this fearful cold weather that brought discomfort to hundreds, there were many who found a large share of enjoyment. The ice on all the bodies of water was several inches thick, and of a splendid smooth surface, making it a great attraction to lovers of skating. Every available skating ground near the city was crowded with young folks, taking their recreation there in the liveliest manner. One of the finest places of this sort was at the west end of the city, a short distance above Pearl street, and here the gayety of the scene struck Anderson, as he rode by one morning, on his way to transact some business in that section. Recreation of this kind had not been a common occurrence with him of late, but he had in past winters spent many hours upon the ice, and was a thorough master in the art of skating. A sudden desire to try his skates again came over him, and he determined to take the first spare hour he could well command, and come up to this place for a little practice. Towards evening of the following day the opportunity came, and he soon found himself gliding over the ice with the best of his companions.

The unaccustomed excitement brought the color brightly into the young man's face, and his eyes sparkled with a light they had not known for weeks. He grew decidedly handsome under the beautifying influence of the frosty air, and was looked upon with smiles by more than one of the fair sex who noticed him. But he knew little and cared less about the mysteries of the sport called flirtation, and never dreamed that his bright eyes and perfect figure were of interest to any other than himself. He had read some novels containing tales of love, but he had glanced over them as he might have done a detailed account of the condition of the planet Jupiter, as something which he did not understand, and never expected to need. His business through life had been for the most part with men, and he only thought of women as the beings who performed the duties of cooks and chambermaids. Many of his friends had taken some of these creatures for their wives. That might be all very well if they chose to do so. For himself, he preferred his boy Sam, and the neighboring restaurant. He acted the true gentleman whenever he met ladies, but it was the result of nature's breeding, and not of any acquired knowledge of forms and fashions. Sentimentalism was unknown to his nature, and even in his books he had avoided this field, in fear that from ignorance he should make some blunder. He had no guide in this matter but the writings of others, and these he never took to shape his own. He wrote only of what he knew, leaving other matters for the future to reveal. Up to this time, then, he had never drawn a girlish character, never having had an opportunity to study one. He never doubted that opportunity was yet to come, and come it did, though not precisely in the way he had pictured to himself.

The young man was clad on this day warmly and suitably for winter, and hardly comprehended that the mercury was in the twenties. He wore a thick suit with woolen underclothes, boots which came above the knee, fur gloves and hat, and a heavy, flannel-lined, black over-coat. Around his neck was a bright-colored Roman scarf, fastened with a large solitaire diamond pin. After skating for over an hour, he sought the shore, and just as he had seated himself on a bench and was about to unstrap his skates, his eye fell upon a little figure near him, between whose clothing and his own there existed the strongest possible contrast.

The figure was that of a little girl, clad in tattered shoes and stockings, a faded dress and hood, with a very old and thin shawl wrapped about her shoulders. Her hands were bare and red with cold. Over her neck was passed a small strap that supported a tin waiter on which lay a few sticks of candy and rolls of lozenges, explaining her business there on that freezing day. That the girl was suffering acutely from the cold was evident from her appearance, and the continual stamping she kept up to keep her feet from becoming entirely senseless. Her shoulders, too, were often shrugged and her shawl wrapped closer from the same reason. But in the blue eyes which peeped out from under the old hood there was not a sign of a disposition to falter till her day's work was completed. Cold the girl was certainly, and sadly she needed her supper and warm room, if she had any, but the candy must be sold first, for in it lay the money to buy her bread. The golden curls which were swept back from her face, were tangled and unkempt, but she had no thought of her appearance. A hard life, truly, but better honest labor than to beg in the streets. All this you could read in the sweet face of the girl, and Albert Anderson read part of it there as he glanced up from his seat before he took off his skates.

Always quick to notice distress in his fellow creatures, and always willing to relieve it when it was in his power, the young man determined instantly to inquire of the girl whether she was in need of anything, and to help her if he could. It was as natural for him to feel an interest in any one who was in trouble as it would have been to follow out his instincts in a more selfish direction. He, therefore, without giving a thought to anything but the impulse of the moment, was just about to call the girl, when she looked towards him, and seeing the movement came over to where he sat.

"Did you want some candy, sir?" she asked, as she came up.

"No, not particularly," replied the young man, "I wanted rather to ask you if it was not a little too cold for you to be out in your thin dress. It is nearly dark, too, and growing colder rapidly. You should not stay out after this time on any account. If you do, you may get a cold which will keep you in altogether."

The girl looked at the speaker suspiciously, hardly knowing how to receive such a strange speech. Then recollecting herself, she answered :

"I should like to go, sir, if my stock was disposed of. But I shall have to wait some time, I am afraid. Customers seem very scarce to-night."

The girl was turning away when the young man spoke again.

"Wait a minute," said Anderson, thinking of a new way to catch her attention. "How much is your candy worth — what you have left?" He took the tray up and lifted the strap from her shoulders gently as he said it.

"O, I don't know; about fifty cents I should think for the whole of it."

"Well, I will give you a dollar for it. There !" kicking the tray with his foot and sending the candy flying into the snow — where it became the plunder of a lot of urchins who rushed to the place — "that disposes of that trouble, and here is your money. Now sit down here a minute on this bench and let me talk to you."

Not knowing how to receive such an offer from such a well dressed gentleman, evidently far above her in life, the girl hesitated an instant, and then being reassured by the pleasant smile on the young man's face, sat down on the end of the bench farthest from him. It was getting quite dark and the couple were unnoticed by the skaters, who were intent on their own enjoyment. Anderson's first act was to take off his heavy overcoat and hand it to his companion.

"I am too warm, myself," he told her, "as I have been exercising so much, while I am sure you must be cold. Please put the coat around your shoulders while you sit here. I will not detain you long. I only wish to know whether there is not something that I can do to help you. I am young and have plenty of money. Speak out and don't be afraid. I only wish your good, and no one shall harm you."

The girl listened with surprise, and stared in unfeigned amazement at the young man. Why should he, a stranger, take such an interest in her, a poor candy girl? Still, the gentleman had a kind look, and had already helped her by buying her candy at a large price. She could at least answer him politely, and she proceeded to do so.

"Since you wish to know about

myself, sir, I can do no less than to answer you. I live in Cross Street, down by the water, with an old woman who boards me for what I can earn selling candy. I have been with her for nearly three years, and it is the only home I have. My father and mother have long been dead, and I must work at all seasons, or this old woman, who took me from an orphan asylum, will not give me anything to eat. That is my story, sir. I hope you will not think I am complaining, or finding fault, but as you asked me I could only tell you the truth."

"My poor girl," said Anderson, inpulsively, " Is this story indeed true? Well, you shall live so no longer at any rate. Come with me, and I will see that you are provided with a good home, from which you will never need to go out to sell candy again. You shall have plenty of warm dresses and go to a school. How would that suit you, my little girl?"

"Oh, sir, that would be very kind of you," said the girl, joyfully, "and I thank you for your offer, but can I be sure you will do all this for me? Excuse me, sir, but if I should leave Mrs. Jones, she would never take me back again, and then I don't know what I should do. Have you a wife, sir, or a mother to whom you would take me?"

The young man was a little perplexed.

"No," he answered, lightly, "I haven't a *wife*, nor,"—more soberly— "a *mother*. But I can find a home for you with some of my friends, if I pay for your board, which I am able and ready to do. As for your trusting me —where did you say you lived?"

"In Cross street, sir."

"Oh, yes, in Cross street. Do you remember the wharf they call Brown's

Wharf, near there, and the sign, 'J. A. Anderson, Broker.' Ah, you do. Well, that is my name, and here is one of my cards to prove it. Now there are my references, young lady," he added, laughingly. "You have the advantage of me in that particular, for your ingenuous face is recommendation enough for you anywhere. Come with me down to my house, now, and I will see what I can do."

The girl stood still again, half uncertain whether to trust so much to a stranger. The young man busied himself for a minute in removing the skates he had until now forgotten, and taking up his overcoat which she had laid down for him, he put it on and buttoned it tightly under his chin. Then he stepped to the girl's side and sat down close to her on the bench. He took her hand between his warm gloves and asked,

"What is your name?"

"Ella Hastings," she answered.

"And will not Ella Hastings trust a man who has offered to find her a home and friends, or will she rather go back to her old life, and suffer on from day to day selling candy in the cold?"

He bent down—they were all alone by this time—and looked into her face, awaiting her reply. She returned his glance timidly, hardly daring to answer. Just then a gust of wind came howling through the air, chilling the girl's frame, and almost freezing her blood. That was the decisive point. She rose and prepared to accompany her friend.

"Will you trust me, then, Ella?"

"I will trust you, Mr. Anderson." And they walked away together.

As they left the place the young man espied a little roll of something in the snow. He stopped to pick it up and opened it. It was only one of the rolls of lozengers from Ella's stock, which had escaped the sharp eyes of the boys who had scrambled for the remainder. Ten white wafery things rolled out into his hand. He saw what they were and laid them away in one of the pockets of his overcoat.

Where should he take the girl of whom he was now the self-constituted protector? This was the next thing to be decided. To take her to his solitary room in Pearl street was out of the question, as she would need to be under feminine charge. He thought over his list of lady acquaintances, which was not large at best, but there was none to whom he could go with confidence and ask them to take in this girl and give her a home. But he was not the man to give up at trifles. Neither would he look back after having undertaken a work. He had made the girl a promise, and it must be kept. There were plenty of institutions where she would be received—but that was not the thing. He had told her she should have a *home,* and she should have one, no matter at what trouble. Thus thought the young man, as he walked along with his ward. And she said not a word to distract his attention until he came upon an idea suddenly, and spoke first.

"I have been thinking, Ella, of the best place to take you for your presest home, and had nearly given up my hope of finding you a good one, when I remembered one lady who I am almost sure will accommodate you at my request. These omnibuses go near the place, and we will ride directly down there." He hailed the driver and the two entered the vehicle. "This lady," he continued, when they were seated, "lives in the block known as Giles's Row, on Jefferson street, and her name is Mrs. Haynes. I happen to own the block and she hires her tenement from me. She is a widow lady in moderate circumstances, and I think would prove a very pleasant person to get along with. I have hopes that she will board you until we can see what will be the best thing to do for you ultimately. Of course you will promise to give her as little trouble as possible and obey her in all reasonable things. You will do that, won't you, Ella?"

The girl looked her gratitude as she answered:

"Oh, Mr. Anderson, I will do anything that she asks me to do if she will take me and be kind to me. I will work for her from morning till night if she bids me. I will do anything for her or you, if I can be kept out of the streets!"

"I am glad to hear you say that," he answered, pressing the tangled curls back from her upturned face. "Only continue to meet the approbation of your friends, and you shall never be exposed to harm. I do not know what I would not be willing to do for you if you prove worthy."

They left the omnibus at a crossing, and walked through several short streets before he ascended the steps of Giles's Row. A ring at the bell brought to the door a pleasant-featured lady, about forty years of age, who saluted Mr. Anderson and his charge cordially, and bade them come into the house. It was Mrs. Haynes, herself.

"Step right into the sitting-room," said Mrs. Haynes, briskly. "There is a fire here, and we shall be all nice and comfortable. There, Mr. Anderson, you take that large rocking chair, and the little girl shall have the small one. What a cold day it has been, hasn't it? It seems as though the winter would never end. I hope you are well, Mr. Anderson, though it's a wonder you are not down sick abed before this. You work hard enough to kill most men. Why don't you get some one who can manage your business for a while? You look as if you needed a rest."

The young man was well used to the ways of his tenant, and paid not the slightest attention to her voluble discourse. He came at once to the object of his visit. The lady had glanced curiously at Ella when they entered, but was too well bred to ask questions about her. When she ceased speaking, Anderson said, abruptly:

"I come to ask a favor of you, Mrs. Haynes, which I am certain you will not refuse me. Yes," seeing her inquiring look towards Ella, "you are right, that's it exactly. It refers to our young friend here, Miss Ella Hastings, whom I have taken charge of, she being without lawful guardians or protectors. She has been living with an old woman in Cross street for three years, but her situation there was not suitable for a young girl like her. I want your assistance in my plan of doing something for her in the way of education and the like. Will you help me, Mrs. Haynes?"

The lady made a reply that was hardly a direct answer to his question. "Cross street!" she repeated with the least shade of repugnance in her tone. "You must know, Mr. Anderson, that it's a very bad neighborhood over there, where the lowest part of the city's people live."

Ella looked disturbed at her new-found protector as she heard this speech. But he stooped down and whispered something in her ear which brightened her face again. Then motioning to Mrs. Haynes to follow him he walked into the parlor with her and shut the door after them.

"Cross street is not, I acknowledge, the most aristocratic thoroughfare in the city," he began, when they were alone. "But I think we should not consign all of its inhabitants to perdition on that account. Among the worst of people are sometimes found treasures worth saving at any cost. Our little girl, here, I believe is one of these. I have resolved to save her from a life of misery, and it shall be done. She looks very different now in her faded clothes, from what she will in suitable garments, but you must perceive the beauty and grace hid even under her present garb. I wish you to take her and treat her as a daughter; do with her as you would with a daughter; advise her as you would a daughter; and if it is possible, as I am sure it will be after you have known her long, love her as a daughter. If you will do this, Mrs. Haynes, your kindness will never be forgotten. And your drawings on me for funds you need in the work shall be met with pleasure."

The worthy dame argued her point a little longer, but found all her arguments met with others unanswerable. And at last, being really of a kind heart and willing to do what she could for the girl, she consented to take her for a time at least. "While I keep her," said she, "I will do by her as by a daughter." With these arrangements, therefore, the matter was settled, and they went back to the sitting-room where Ella was awaiting them.

"My little girl," said Anderson, kindly, taking her hand in his own, "This is your new mother, Mrs.

Haynes. I must leave you with her now, but I shall call on you often and keep up my interest in you. Be a good girl and you will fare well with this lady. What is your age, Ella? "

"Fourteen years," she answered, while the tears came to her eyes as she thought of the debt she owed this man.

"Fourteen years?" he repeated. "I hardly thought you were so old as that."

Still, fourteen years was not very old. She was only a child, and he was to be her guardian. He thought of something like this as he bent down and kissed her gently on the forehead; then, as if a little ashamed of the act, he said "Good-by," and hastily left the house.

CHAPTER III.

THE MAN AND THE CHILD.

A visit was made on the following day to the house of Mrs. Jones, with whom Ella had been living, and after some conversation between Anderson and Mr. Jenkins, his legal adviser, a sum of money was paid to that lady, on condition that she release forever her rights to the young girl. Then taking Ella who had been half frightened to death by the earnestness of her protector and the strangeness of the legal proceedings, they stepped into their sleigh again and drove to the probate office. This they reached just in time to intercept the judge, who was on the point of leaving. He went back, at Anderson's request, and on becoming acquainted with the facts of the case and seeing the agreement signed by Mrs. Jones, made out the necessary papers of adoption and gave them to Anderson.

Ella signed her name, for she could write very well, having been taught at the asylum. And the young man said, as they rode to Giles's Row:

"These mean, my little girl, that no one can ever take you from me while we both live. Will that suit you, Ella?'

After leaving the girl with Mrs. Haynes, Anderson rode back to the lawyer's office, and in another hour several fresh clauses were added to his will, providing for the education and support of Ella Hastings Anderson, adopted daughter of James Albert Anderson, Broker, Commission Merchant and Author, until she should be of age, and leaving her twenty thousand dollars in her own right at that time.

"There we have it," said Mr. Jenkins, with a flourish of his pen. "To her and her heirs forever."

How strange that sounded for little Ella! "Her heirs forever." So thought Albert as he went away. And while alone in his room that night and after he retired to rest, those words rang in his ear like the burden of a song:

> "Her and her heirs forever,
> Her heirs forever."

Ella's education proceeded rapidly under the attention of the good Mrs. Haynes. She proved an apt scholar, and attacked her lessons with a sort of hunger, as if she had acquired an appetite from her long fasting. In reading, writing and the common branches, she worked on, determined to win the approval of the friends who had placed her in her present situation. Her foster-mother was herself an excellent teacher, and by every means in her power she strove to assist the girl in her pursuit of knowledge. It was only a pleasure, she said, to teach such a pupil; one who was so eager to learn and never tired of study; on the fertile soil of whose mind nothing failed to spring into life, and take deep root; who was so thankful for the attention shown her, and so fully appreciated the value of the information she received.

As to Ella, so long as her guardians were satisfied with her course, there was no more to be desired. While living with Mrs. Jones, Ella had accepted her fate as one from which she could not escape, but she had never put herself on a level with other girls in the neighborhood. There had seemed to be, somehow, a gulf between them, and with an instinctive feeling that they were in some sense below her, she had avoided them, and never mingled in their society. A more thoroughly independent spirit than found root in the young girl's breast could not be conceived. Now that she had accepted the offer of Anderson to receive an education and a home, she had a dim idea that if she did in every way as he wished, the debt would be lifted. His kind manner drove away the suspicion which came at first, that this was no more or less than that cold "charity" she had always been led to refuse. After the papers of adoption were made out, the last shadow was removed. Being now by law this dear friend's adopted daughter, with even his name given her for her own, no one could say she had not a right to all his favors. And in the enjoyment of such dreams as this the girl became very happy and contented.

Anderson could always find time at some period in the day to call in and see Ella. He would manifest the deepest interest in every thing which concerned her, and always inquire if there was not something more that she desired. His one anxiety was that she should never regret the day which brought them to the knowledge of each other. By consulting with Mrs. Haynes, he could learn what presents would be the most appreciated, and they were always forthcoming directly he found them out. There was a fine field for such work, for the girl had literally nothing when he found her, and her necessities were without number. An unlimited purse was placed at Mrs. Haynes's disposition, with the order:

"See that she lacks nothing which other girls of her age have, whose parents are in as good circumstances as I am. Make her understand that all she receives is hers by right, and encourage her to consider that I am best satisfied by her procuring whatever she wants, regardless of everything except that it is wanted."

Mrs. Haynes was a woman of excellent sense, taste and judgment. To this fact the young girl owed much. Had it not been for her prudence, Anderson would have loaded her with a superfluity of dresses and jewelry, in his fear lest that she should not have enough. More than once the good woman was obliged to reason with the young man, regarding his unneeded purchases. He would always listen with the closest attention to her protests, and then, forgetting them, go away and commit a similar error within a week.

As the spring ripened into summer, and the ice and snow gave place to warmth and sunshine, Anderson bethought himself of the secluded life of Ella, who had hitherto spent her days and evenings at her studies or other employments at her new mother's house. She must go out for rides into the country, and about the city, so that the fresh air could be enjoyed after her long confinement. The thankful girl received the proposition with delight, and declared that nothing would suit her better. So it happened one bright morning Albert drove up to Giles's Row in his open carriage, and taking his ward, drove away towards the suburbs.

For several hours they rode on, winding among the country roads, along the banks of ponds and streams, and under the shade of friendly trees. The pair kept up an animated conversation upon the subjects in their path, he telling many stories of the localities they passed, and she giving her own opinions and impressions in a frank way that won his heart. If he was more than usually affected, however, he never showed it by one look or action. He remained as dignified as ever, noting down everything that she said and did, intending to reproduce it all on the fictitious page when the right time should come. He was studying the girl closely, and with the view he had in mind, encouraged in every possible way her free, unrestrained manner and conversation.

CHAPTER IV.

NEITHER LITERATURE NOR LAW.

It is October, now, and Giles's Row is the scene of a corps of busy workers, for Ella is going away to a young ladies' school and must be fitted out with all the dresses and millinery that she can possibly find use for. These are the orders of Anderson, whose regard for his ward has taken the shape of prodigal liberality. The pleasant parlors of Mrs. Haynes's tenement have been turned into a place where sewing-women and bonnet-makers hold undisputed sway. The door-bell is jerked violently every hour by carrier boys, leaving bundles of dry goods, or additions to the already enormous stock of ladies' apparel. A carriage stands in readiness most of the time to convey the chief dressmaker to and from the store, at which she calls for "a yard and a half of this," and "another pattern like that, please," until the salesmen are half distracted at seeing her enter. Boot-makers are executing orders for boots, shoes, gaiters and slippers by the dozen, all to fit one little pair of feet, whose measure they have taken with scrupulous preciseness. Trunks, bags, satchels and valises have been selected from among the best that could be found. The perfumer has brought in his stock of oils and essences. The jeweler adds to the rings, bracelets and pins which he has before furnished. The countless trades that could supply anything that Ella needed were levied upon in great profusion. One would have thought an immense fair was in progress, instead of the mere fitting out of one girl, for the life of a boarding school.

At first Mrs. Haynes tried to reason with Anderson against this extravagance, saying that Ella could never find use for such a wardrobe in the quiet boarding school life to which she was going. But he replied that there should never be a possibility for the other girls to outshine her, upon occasions of festivity or public display. While she was occupied with the common routine of school life, she need dress only in common clothing. But at the parties or receptions to which she would be invited, she must be directed to omit nothing that would render her attractive. At last, finding that his heart was set upon it, the good lady made no more objections, but assisted as much as she was able in the work before them.

As for Ella, she had at first no other desire than that which had been uppermost since she had entered upon her new life — which was to do whatever best suited her friends, and she entered upon the preparations in this matter solely with that view. Yet it must be confessed that afterwards, when trying on some garment of peculiar elegance, or arranging her jewelry in the midst of the thoughtless criticisms of the modistes, a sense of their effect upon her beauty would come for a moment into her girlish head to a degree that amounted almost to vanity. The girl was really quite handsome, and sometimes she realized the fact, and felt happier for it. Still the evil seeds were very slow at taking root in her breast, and she continued as lovable as ever.

During the spring and summer which Ella had spent with her new friends, she had improved her time in a most praiseworthy manner, and was now quite as far advanced as most misses of her age. The rides which she took nearly every day kept her health in spite of her long hours of close study. She loved to have Anderson call in, and after finding how far she was advanced in a certain study, sit down with the text-book in his hands and ask her questions at random from its pages. Her memory was excellent and her calculating powers quick, and she seldom failed to pass a creditable examination. One day he said, in one of these lessons, "Do you know the difference between twenty-two and fourteen?" and she answered "Why, eight, of course; what

an easy question!" And he said, very soberly, "That is a great deal, is it not Ella?" And she replied, "I do not think it is, Mr. Anderson," wondering what he meant. She did not know he had referred to their ages, but he had, and was very glad to hear her answer as she did.

As the time approached when Ella should leave him, the young man thought seriously of moving his headquarters to Giles's Row, so that he might see more of her during the days that remained. This idea was, however, discarded as foolish, and he decided not to do so, lest it should reveal the fact that he thought more of Ella than he dared to own, even to himself. After she was gone he might go and board with Mrs. Haynes, where they could talk over the news from their girl together, without the change exciting any suspicion among the gossip-venders. But not now, on any account, should he give them the slightest cause upon which to found a story. His action in adopting his ward had been regarded as eccentric, merely, and was quoted as one more peculiarity in an always peculiar man. The young author was well known about the city and his reputation had travelled wherever his books were read. The newspapers joined with the crowd in commenting upon his latest freak, but even they could discover none but a right motive in the deed. As yet, the world was generally disposed to smile upon him, and treated his action in the good-humored way it has when dealing with its favorites.

The day of departure came at last, and wrapped in furs and warm garments, Ella bade good-bye to Mrs. Haynes with as light a heart as possible. She had come to love the lady as a mother, and was loved in return, as Anderson had requested, like a daughter. Now she was going away for many months among strangers, with new friends to make and new associations to form. Her heart almost failed her at the last moment, but when she remembered that the sorrow was not all on her side, that those she was leaving felt as sad as she, and that it was for her own good after all, she summoned courage and was the most cheerful of any of them. So cheerful, indeed, that they began to think she cared nothing about leaving them, until a tear that in some way escaped at the last moment rolled down her fair cheek, and betrayed her secret. Then Mrs. Haynes burst out into a real flood of tears, and had nearly brought Ella into a similar condition, when Anderson came in to ascertain the cause of the delay.

"Hush! Hush!" he exclaimed, reprovingly, as he saw what was the matter. "This will never no. Would you have our little girl go away remembering you with your face wet with tears the last time she saw it? She has need enough of smiles and encouragement now. After we are gone you may cry as much as you please. But, for goodness sake, dry your eyes for the present."

"How can I smile when my dear girl is going away?" said Mrs. Haynes. "You don't know how I love her or you wouldn't talk so."

"Who was it that thought Cross street such a very bad neighborhood, I wonder, only a few months ago?" said Albert, just loud enough to reach her ear alone. "I am glad you have altered your opinion since then; but," he added, louder, "don't inflict a shower-bath upon Miss Ella when she is going out in the cold air. She would not be comfortable covered with icicles, I fear." This was said in a droll way that brought a ringing laugh from Ella at the absurdity of the idea, and even caused Mrs. Haynes's face to grow brighter for the instant. Anderson seized the opportunity to utter a hasty farewell and hurry Ella into the carriage. Sam held the ribbons, and with a wave of handkerchiefs they were out of sight in a moment, and on their way to the depot.

"Mrs. Haynes is a foolish woman to act so silly just as you are going away," said Anderson. "But she has been a good friend to us, and you will not forget to write her letters very often. She will look anxiously for them. You must give her a full account of everything that is of interest to you, for she will be pleased with the very smallest matters that concern your happiness."

"I have promised her to write often," replied Ella, "and shall surely keep my word. But yourself, Mr. Anderson," she added, looking up into his face. "I can write to you, also, can I not? And you will answer me, won't you?"

The reply was so exactly as he could have wished, that the young man was nearly incapable of utterance for a moment. "Certainly you may write to me, too," he said, recovering himself. "I have taken too great an interest in my little girl while she has been near me to forget her when she is obliged to be away for a while. You must write often, and you must let me know at once whenever there is anything you want that your teachers cannot procure for you near the seminary."

"I do not think there can possibly be another thing that I shall want for a year, Mr. Anderson. I have been so well provided for now that I can hardly need more. You have been very kind to me, and you must believe I am truly grateful for all you have done."

Something came into his throat again, choking him for an instant, but he cleared his voice with a strong effort. It would not do to show his weakness now, when he had struggled so hard for these long weeks.

"Only be true to yourself, Ella," he replied. "Strive as you have done in the past to *excel* in all you do; study bravely and earnestly at your school; and never forget the friends you have left. I could ask no more."

They went aboard of the train together and soon left the city behind them. As they rode by the towns and villages in their path Anderson kept Ella interested by a descriptive recital of his visits to them at different times. All she saw was strange to the girl, unused to travel, and she kept up her watch from the car windows until darkness made a longer view impossible. The train would reach the place at which Ella was to stop about midnight, and it was decided that it would be useless to attempt to get so short a rest in a sleeping car. So they rode together — after the sun went down, after the brakemen lit the lamps, after the signal-lights could be seen at the crossings, after the red blaze in the stove grates sent out its heat into the car. The night became colder and colder, and at each opening of the doors, a gust of wind came rushing in. Ella spread out her largest shawl to keep in some degree the cold away, but it is not the easiest matter in the world to make one's self comfortable on a railroad when the weather is freezing without. See-

ing that Ella was far from warm, and knowing his own case to be quite similar, Albert Anderson determined upon a bold stroke of policy which he never understood how he dared carry out as he did.

"Let me arrange the shawl," said he, taking it up from the girl's lap. He placed his arm upon the back of the seat, where it served as a pillow for her tired head, and arranged the shawl in such a manner that it served as a covering for them both. "There, are you comfortable now?"

"Quite so," she replied, closing her eyes, and settling her curls upon their new cushion.

"You can go to sleep, then, if you choose. I will wake you in time to leave the train."

"But you will not get any sleep at all," she said, looking up an instant at the handsome face above her.

"Oh! I never sleep on the railroad. Don't think of me. I am quite satisfied as I am."

For once, at least, he told the truth. The young author was happy while reading his latest book, lying there soon with heavy breathing, that told of sound sleep. The young merchant was proud of such priceless merchandise as was now lying before his eyes. The young man began to acknowledge to himself, unwillingly at first, that he was inextricably in love! Ella was barely fifteen years of age, but when her school-days were over she would be much older, and then——! He would have given, had he followed the dictates of his feelings, all of his houses, lands, moneys and business to have been sure that that little golden head would never know another pillow, when he should choose to take it to himself.

But Albert Anderson seldom followed the dictates of his feelings ; so the men said who knew him best.

At twelve o'clock he roused the sleeper, though it cost him a throb of pain to break in upon such a sound slumber. They left the train, and were driven away over the country and up a long hill, in a coach sent from the seminary. On arriving, a pleasant featured Irish girl showed them to their rooms, with the explanation :

"The misthress said ye were to have these apartments, and she would see ye in the mornin'. The big room is for the gentleman and the little one for the young leddy. If ye want anything, ye can just be afther pullin' the bell rope."

"Perhaps you can render some assistance to Miss Ella," said Anderson, handing her a piece of silver. "She is in a strange place, you know, and not used to being alone."

"Indade I will, sur," said the kind-hearted Biddy. "It isn't the likes of me that 'ud refuse a shmall favor like that," and after bidding Anderson good-night, Ella went away with her new friend to her room.

When the morning came, the young man led his charge down stairs and introduced her to her new teacher, Miss Flint. He afterwards had a long interview with that lady, in which he explained his desire that Ella's life should be the happiest possible while she remained at the institution. Money, he said, was no object when considered as against her welfare. Miss Flint promised to do all in her power for the girl, and arrangements were made for the payment in advance of a certain sum quarterly during the school year. Before noon, Anderson had spoken personally with every attache of the seminary, and left with each a present of money, with the promise of more when he should come again, if they were good to his little girl. This measure can hardly be considered a wise one, but he felt that he could leave nothing undone which might make Ella's life happier, while separated from her only friends, by so many long miles.

At night he left her with a face that showed no sign of the sorrow he felt, giving a cheerful farewell, with many requests that she would write often. He did not kiss her, even once, which seemed strange to Miss Flint and the others who saw the parting. But he carried away a load upon his heart that neither of them knew or suspected. Through all the long night ride he had before he reached home he thought of but the one desire which now filled his breast, and though he strove like a giant to keep it down, it could not be done. He missed the golden head which had lain on that arm last night, and for the present there was nothing in heaven or earth that could drive this from his memory.

CHAPTER V.

A SCRIPTURE LESSON.

Ere Ella had been gone a month, Anderson found his new lonesomeness more than he could bear. He, therefore decided to make a visit to Texas and look over the old scenes where his earliest youth was passed. His personal effects were removed to the house in Giles's Row, and bidding good-by to his friends, and placing his business matters in the hands of Mr. Jenkins, the lawyer, he set out on the long and tiresome journey. Upon arriving at Catherine, the place of his nativity, he found his affairs in that section progressing favorably, and gave himself up to the pleasures of the frontier.

When he had been out about a month he found one day on his return from a ride, a large package of letters awaiting him. He took them into his room and commenced to examine their contents. Those from Harry Johnson, his chief clerk, and his other business friends were read first, and answers written to each. The former announced that all was well at the wharf, and that Anderson need be in no haste to return if he was enjoying himself among the forests. Mrs. Haynes's letter came next, containing plenty of good advice about keeping out of danger, and keeping in health, which admonitions the young man received with only a scornful smile. Then there was one letter more, with a double post-mark, forwarded per order; a little, dainty envelope of pink, with the initial "A" on the seal. He held it in his hand a long time, thinking of the writer whose name the law had changed to his own as his daughter, from which came her right to the initial "A." But "daughter" signified in some way "obedience." And it was sadly inappropriate in that way. He felt that it was she that was the mistress — mistress of his heart, his soul, his fortune. Then suddenly he tore open the envelope, and devoured the words inside as if he had been starving for them.

"*Dear Mr. Anderson:*—You will remember that I promised to write to you, when you left, and after sending Auntie a letter I will try and send a few words to you. I am enjoying myself very well here. I have studies enough to keep me busy nearly all the time. All of the teachers are very kind to me, and they say I am learning fast. I am sure I try to, for I appreciate the advantages I have here. There have been no entertainments as yet this winter, and so I have not needed my suits. There is nothing at all that I can think of which I require that has not already been provided for me. Please write me a letter soon, with all the news. Tell me about yourself and what you have been doing since I left you. I have been a little lonesome at times, but am getting over it. I have your picture hung in my room, where I can see it many times a day. That is better than nothing, you see, though I would like to see you, yourself. Good-bye ——.

ELLA H. ANDERSON."

That was all; but he kissed the name tenderly. And then, ordering a fresh horse, he hurried away for a gallop over the prairies where he could be alone by himself and think !

There is no truer proverb than that "time flies." Flying as usual, it brought to Anderson in Texas, the end of winter and the beginning of spring; the end of spring and another summer. When the hot days came and residence in the tropical climate began to be uncomfortable, the young man set out upon a Northern trip, visiting the States bounded by British America, and even extending his travels into the Canadas and the fur regions. As winter approached again he gave up his journeyings, and October found him back in his own city. Quietly he received the exclamations of delight with which his old friends welcomed him, and settling down into a steady-going existence, passed most of his time in writing and reading, with a proper amount of exercise. His publishers sent several letters, desiring to know when he would have another book completed, and he answered that if they would have patience he would furnish them one ere long that would far exceed in interest any he had before written. The newspapers threw out hints that the young author had finished his best days, and that nothing more need be expected from him. He kept as steadily at work, however, as if no earthly person was in the least interested in his concerns; seeming to care no more for the opinions of others, than for the flies that might buzz about his pages. He knew what he was doing, and that was enough for him. If he had written for money, he might have written more. But as it was, he preferred to wait until he knew his subject well.

Mrs. Haynes had planned to give him a little surprise on the occasion of his next seeing Ella, and to this end he was purposely misled as to the time when her school would finish. The girl herself was also in the plot, and it was arranged between them that Anderson should not know Ella was in the city until she presented herself to him in person. Mrs. Haynes had been moved to this deception by receiving photographs of Ella which showed a change she could hardly believe possible in so short a time — the change of a bud into a beautiful blossom — a girl into a woman. As Albert had not seen Ella for over a year, the great change would be all the more apparent to him, and Mrs. Haynes doubted whether he would even recognize his ward at first. Her doubts were communicated to Ella, and the plan suggested entered into with pleasure by the girl. When the school closed, she came alone to the city, and was met at the depot by her foster-mother. They drove to Giles's Row, and found by the servants that Anderson was in his library. Stopping a few moments to arrange her dress before the mirror, and after being pronounced by Mrs. Haynes, who was quite overwhelmed at sight of her, a perfect beauty, Miss Ella smilingly ascended the stairs, and knocked softly on the library door. Her heart beat fast as she thought of meeting her benefactor, but she strove to master her feelings, and succeeded to a surprising degree.

The young man was writing when he heard the knock. He sat in his dressing gown and slippers, in an arm chair, with his beautiful hair brushed smoothly from his thoughtful brow. He laid down his pen, and supposing his visitor to be Mrs. Haynes, looked up, and said simply:

"Come in."

Ella opened the door, and stepped tremblingly into the apartment. Discovering his mistake, the young man was on the point of explaining when she spoke, apologetically:

"I didn't know you were busy, sir; I only called——"

Her manner was well put on, and her carelessness well feigned, but with the first sound of her voice, he comprehended all. That form had been too much in his mind for him to be deceived when it came in substance before his eyes. If he had obeyed his first impulse he would have sprung to her side, and enveloped her in his embrace. It cost him one of those fierce struggles that he had been compelled so often to go through, to do otherwise. But he only said, rising to greet her, and smiling pleasantly:

"Very good, very good indeed! That was excellent, Miss Ella! I am sorry that I cannot pretend to be thoroughly deceived, that your plan might be carried to the end. But it is more natural for me to be frank, and I will be so with you. I am just as glad to see you, though, as I could possibly be. Sit down here and talk with me. I wish to know all about this little game, and who assisted you in plotting it."

Ella laughed heartily, and Mrs. Haynes came up to take her share of the blame. They were very merry over the failure of the plot, and Mrs. Haynes could not understand how Anderson had recognized Ella so easily. " I am sure *I* should not have known her," said she, "if I had not seen her picture. Don't you think she has changed wonderfully, Mr. Anderson?"

" She has changed, somewhat," he answered, trying to look unconcerned, "and of course I expected she would change—young ladies must grow older, I suppose, as well as the rest of us. Now look at me, for instance. Don't I look as though I was getting to be an old gentleman? Think of it! over twenty-three years of age! That is what you may call growing old, now, isn't it?"

Ella laughed again, and shook her head. "What nonsense! You getting old, indeed! I don't believe there is one man in a hundred at twenty-one that looks as young as you do."

"Ah, ha! How do you know so much about young men of twenty-one?" said Anderson with a mock-serious air. "You are pretty well posted, it seems to me."

Ella blushed a little, and said: "Well, I knew you when you were not much more than twenty-one; and you don't look any older than you did then, at any rate. There, now you see where I get my information."

This ingenious statement satisfied everybody, and brought the laugh around once more. A long time was spent in talking over affairs that had transpired since they had all been together last. Ella had changed as well in manners as appearance, and gratified her friends greatly. There was not left one trace of the Cross street life, and in the beautiful young woman, any man might have been proud to find a daughter. She was welcomed back to the old roof with an honest and heartfelt welcome. A new light came with her into the house —a beam of surpassing brightness, which was felt by every one she met. Always obliging and kind, unwilling to give the slightest pain, anxious to do anything that pleased her friends, she became endeared to them more and more. It had been a question whether she was to go back to Clare-mont for another year, but after as-certaining how far she was already advanced, her guardian decided that she had studied enough for the pre-sent. He wrote to Miss Flint that she would not attend the seminary for another year at least. Ella seconded this decision, as she really needed a rest, and was becoming so deeply at-tached to her friends as to dislike a separation.

Ella had returned quite a musician, and was provided at once with a piano of the best make. The large instru-ment seemed rather out of place in Mrs. Haynes's cosy parlors, where it took to itself the larger share of the rooms. But there was space enough left for the young guardian to sit and listen with pleasure to the music his ward brought from the keys with her white, ring-covered fingers. And there he did sit, many an hour, often pre-tending to read by the window, and always following the tunes she played, in his mind. When she practiced the hard lessons under the eye of her music teacher, Anderson's thoughts became as discordant as the piece in the unaccustomed hands.

He always envied the little German who leaned so closely over her shoulder, and turned the pages for her. Grave or gay, as the music might be, he followed it in his thoughts. It was as if the lily-fingers were playing on his heart strings, they responded so quickly to every touch. Yet he assumed an air of indifference, and was very careful that she should not discern the real state of his feelings. The man was in love, and what more need be said? But he had no intention of declaring his affection in words, or asking that it might be returned. He was satisfied for the present to see the flower growing daily more beautiful before his eyes, and to have it where he could care for it, and assist in its graceful development.

When the sleighing began to be enjoyable, they had rides together by the score. Nearly every day found them gliding merrily over the snow-crust, about the city and into the best suburban roads. (There is something about a sleigh-ride that unites two young people to each other more than any other pleasure in which they can participate.)(The knowledge that they two are alone together, enjoying the same exercise, braving the same cold, feeling the same exhilaration, wrapped in the same robe, is responsible, without doubt, for hundreds of marriages.) Something of its effect was felt by Anderson, as he rode out day after day with his ward. Something made him wish their relations were different— that she was, for instance, the daughter of some neighbor, so that his attentions might be naturally construed into expressions of affection which would be understood by everybody. As for Ella, she may have felt a little of this

after a time, but how much it is impossible to say. She was all goodness and grace to him, and the gratitude, which they say is akin to love, never lost its place in her heart. Perhaps the first actual move towards the hoped-for, change in their relations was made by Albert one evening, when they were riding along behind a quick-stepping pair, on an unfrequented road, some distance out. Their conversation had been quite animated, and losing his usual control of himself, the young man found that his arm had strayed around Ella's waist; and finding that she did not seem to notice the liberty, he was emboldened to broach the subject nearest his heart.

"I wish you would not continue to call me Mr. Anderson, now we have become so well acquainted," he said.

"Not call you 'Mr. Anderson'?" reiterated Ella, in a surprised tone, turning her rosy cheeks towards him. "What can I call you if not by your name?"

Her question was so very honest, that he wished for a moment he had not made the request; but it was too late to retract now, and he proceeded.

"When I was a little boy," he said, "I had a father who loved me with all his heart; who toiled all the day that he might amass a fortune for me; and who died happy in thinking that he had provided against my coming to want. He used to call me 'Albert'; and sometimes 'Bert' or 'Bertie.' After I lost him, I went to school for several years. There, the teachers called me 'Anderson,' or 'Master Anderson.' After I left school, the men in whose company I traveled; called me generally 'Mr. Anderson.' Now, every one call me by that name. I suppose it is right that they should, but I would be pleased if you, in memory of the days when one man loved me for myself alone, would drop the title and give me my plain, childhood's name again."

It would be folly to say that this speech did not awaken a new train of thoughts in the girl's mind—more than he intended it should do then. But she only answered, dutifully:

"I will call you whatever name you please, Mr. Anderson."

"Then call me Bert," he cried. "Always call me Bert. It will draw a line somehow between you and the rest of them, for you alone shall use that name. It will remind me of the time when some one loved me, and I shall think the more of you, Ella, I am sure."

She knew that he loved her now. Her heart told her that this was true. Woman-like she waited for his own time to reveal it by words, and in the interval she studied carefully her own feelings to discover if she loved him as she should in return.

It had been so strange, all through —their acquaintance. There were the pictures standing out in line so plainly. The little ragged candy girl, doubting if she ought to accept the friendship of the well-dressed young skater; the curious working of the law which took her from want and misery, and gave her to this man, and a loving home; the long months of school-life, where she had studied so hard to rise above the years when her mind was compelled to lay idle; the letters from her guardian and foster-mother, so good and true they had been to her; the return home, the gradual change of the guardian into the—could it be? Yes, that was it —the guardian into the lover! Not yet, to be sure, a declared lover; but she knew he was so as well as if he had made a formal declaration. And, knowing this, she was quite as happy as she could be.

The date of that ride commenced a new era for them both. Except when habit induced her to call him by his old name, she always spoke to him as Bert, when they were alone together. He had a sort of fear to have Mrs. Haynes know of the change that was going on in their attachment, and cautioned Ella to be careful in her presence. Unused to deceit in anything, she found some difficulty in this, but succeeded on the whole very well. (All women, even though wholly unskilled in the deceptive arts, find their powers wonderfully increased when love is the motive)

After this the rides began to mean something more than they had previously. The unfrequented roads were always sought, and the arm which had once stolen doubtfully about Ella's form was placed there as naturally as if it had always had the right. At home his library-room became her most common resort, and while he wrote, she would sit sewing or reading, each happy in the other's presence. Not a pledge had he made, or a word had he spoken about the future, but contenting himself with the delicious present, he allowed the hours and days to pass by, quite satisfied with his pleasant dream. She became no more a distant, shadowy thing, to be hoped for, and thought of as a possible possession of the distant, shadowy future. She was there, by him, near him, almost of him, a part of his existence, and he fondly believed, of his soul. He gave no thought to anything else about her, about himself, or about the future of both of them.

Mrs. Haynes complained that she was left alone so much, when Ella would say so often that Mr. Anderson wanted her to assist him in the library, and she must go up a little while. The witch even made a pretence of studying, and would carry up a book, to be assisted in her lessons. The book was often laid down on reaching his room, and only taken up again when she left it. Albert's writing, also, was sadly neglected, the pen being generally dropped at the sound of Ella's foot on the stairs. As she came in, he would place his chair near the grate, and draw up an ottoman for her, close to it. Then they would sit together and talk for hours, though neither could have told of what when they had finished. Her hand in his, or sometimes her head on his knee, with his fingers running through the tangled hair; or anon he would be stooping to snatch a kiss from her rosy cheeks. The only thing feared was the widow, whom neither would have wished to witness these acts, and who was constantly watched for by both. If she was heard approaching, it was wonderful how quick Ella was poring over a book, and Albert writing with amazing speed the most incomprehensible sentences upon his manuscript.

One day Mrs. Haynes was known to be confined to her bed by a violent headache, and it is to be feared that the young couple did not feel so sorry at the fact as they might have done. The library held forth attractions for them both that day, and being relieved of all fears of intruders, they passed the hours in the unalloyed pleasure of each other's sole society.

Feeling freer than usual, Ella abandoned the ottoman for Albert's knee, and her head soon lay upon his bosom, while they rocked slowly in the great arm-chair. The silence of nearly an hour was finally broken by Ella, who said, suddenly:

"Bert?"

"What is it, darling?"

"Do you believe the Bible, Bert?"

"Why, what a question! What put that into your pretty head?"

"Oh, I don't know. You never go to church with Auntie and I, and I have heard you speak as if you did not."

"Do you believe the Bible, Ella?" asked he, after a pause.

"Why, yes, I do. Of course I do."

"And why do you believe it, darling?"

"Why, because I have always been taught so, I suppose."

"Well, I have not been taught so. Now why should I believe it?"

"Didn't your father ever teach you from the Bible, when you were a boy?"

"Never."

"But you might go to church now and learn, mightn't you, Bert?"

"Yes, I suppose I might. But I do not like the doctrines they preach in most of the churches. So I stay away."

"What doctrines don't you like, Bert?"

"Nearly all of them. I went into a church some time ago in Texas, and heard the minister preach about the wickedness of Adam and Eve in picking the forbidden apple. Now, do you know, Ella, I should have done exactly as they did?"

"Why, Bert!"

"Yes, I should. I have always made it a point to examine and investigate into every new thing that I find until I understand it perfectly.

The more difficulty there is, the more anxious I am to make the discovery plain. The apple would have attracted me particularly, it being the only thing in the garden I was forbidden to touch, and I should not have waited even for the serpent to tempt me, as Eve did, before I had it in my possession."

"Oh, Bert, I am afraid it is wicked to talk so. You know how Adam and Eve were punished for their disobedience!"

"No, I do not, Ella. I do not *know* anything about it."

"But the Bible says so!"

"Well, as you please, darling. I shall not argue the question with you. I tried that to my satisfaction with the Texan minister. After the service was over, I obtained an introduction to him, and after a little conversation invited him to go out for a horseback ride with me next day. He accepted. While we were out, I recalled the Adam and Eve story, and after an hour I convinced him so thoroughly that it was untrue, that he resigned his position and gave up the ministry within a week. But one day before I came away, I met him looking awful shabby, and he said he could get no work and was very poor. He held his new principles well, but they didn't bring him in any money. I gave him a hundred dollars and left him. But I wished I had let him alone in the first place. He was satisfied then, and getting a good salary. I shall not attempt to influence any more men, I assure you."

Ella laughed at this story, and the conversation finished there. Its fruits did not, however. What Bert believed must be right, she thought. What he did was perfect. What he said must be true. He became her ideal in all things. She trusted him as she would have trusted only the man on whom her whole heart and love were set. He became her guiding star, and she knew no other in the wide, wide world. God forgive him, if he guide her wrongly! God forgive him, if he proves unfaithful to so great a trust! With the power he has obtained in her soul let him deal carefully. Her love may become wider and wider, and yet there is room in it for him only.

When they separated that evening, it was with lovers' embraces and lovers' kisses lingering on their lips. He walked with her to her door quietly, for the hour was very late. As they parted, he whispered softly in her ear:

"I believe one text in the Bible, darling."

"Which one, Bert?"

"*A new commandment give I unto you,*" he said, "*that ye LOVE one another!*"

With a last passionate kiss he was gone.

CHAPTER VI.

THE COMING STORM.

Great changes are the rule of life —coming swiftly in each other's train startling the unwary, and confirming the predictions of the looker into futurity. The passion of the hour does its work, and flies from us. As surely as it comes unexpectedly, so it departs without a shadow of warning. We daily witness results that would have been pronounced impossibilities yesterday. The human soul is prone to bind itself up in single things, and only learns after many a hard lesson the danger of leaning on the temporary fabrics raised by the chance of one day to fall by the chance of another. Bruised by falls and lame from frequent miss-steps we may come at last to a right conception of life, should we be permitted to survive our injuries. For our experiments are very dangerous, and often prove fatal to the inexperienced. Our strongest props give way, and our best hopes are shattered when we least expect it. Happy is he who has schooled himself to take every hour's tidings as they come, knowing that sorrow is useless, and that the pain we cause ourselves is the most difficult to bear of any. We cannot command the sun to shine brightly on us forever, but we can prepare for the storms which are sure to come, and wait in sheltered places till they are over.

Who would have believed that Albert Anderson, the man who hardly spoke to a woman from January to December, would give up his business, his time, his whole powers to devote himself to one of the sex? Yet so it had come to be. From morning until night, and hardly absent from his dreams, his adopted daughter was ever in his thoughts. He said to himself that it was only another Experiment he was trying, but an examination of his heart would have proved a denial. The fact that the situation was new to him only aided in the completeness with which he was overpowered, and caught in the meshes he had woven for himself. All was given up to the one aim of his life — the happiness of his adopted daughter.

Driven at last to the most ingenious of devices to procure her new delights, he concluded that the house in Giles's Row was not suitable for her to inhabit longer, and set about fitting up in elegant style the largest of the buildings he had recently erected on the site of his ancient rooms on Pearl street. For a time the occupation of selecting furniture and upholstery for the new home sufficed to occupy his mind and keep him satisfied. No luxury was at too great a cost, if she only smiled and praised it ever so little.

The young man was dimly conscious that the world took up his name in gossiping phrase, and held their own opinion of his conduct in giving up everything to an idol for which he had always affected to care nothing. But he seemed as if it were raised above the heads of the crowd, and could afford to let them have their way, knowing that they had no conception of the glory there was in the life he was leading. He would not have exchanged the fraction of one smile from his girl for the praises of all mankind. And so he went on, intoxicated with the fervor that filled him so completely, happy as he could be under the influence of the drug which locked his senses, Caring For No Man, whether they thought of him for good or for evil.

They left Giles's Row and entered their new home, where they found nothing omitted that could insure luxury and beauty. Servants attended to every wish, paintings delighted the eye, richness of fitting was everywhere noticeable, and nothing had been left out that could add to the impression of comfort and magnificence. A high tower, reaching above the summit of its surroundings, had been built and fitted up as a library and writing room for Albert, and here, without danger of molestation, he could receive his little visitor. Secure in their high nest they spent their hours on hours together, without a cloud to obscure their happiness.

Time went on, and with rides, books

and public amusements, the young couple were very happy together. Mrs. Haynes became neglected more than ever, only meeting the young people at the table, and even there they were not always to be found, often preferring to dine by themselves in the tower-room, to which their fare was sent in a dumb-waiter arranged for the purpose. Perfectly secure in their aerial castle, the very food they ate seemed to have a better taste. Albert thought the tea poured by Ella's white hands, acquired a new relish, and the toast passed by her was better than any he could taste elsewhere. Ella was pleased with the novelty of this style of living, and was satisfied if she could be away from the eyes of her foster-mother, whose notice she had begun to dislike. At last, Mrs. Haynes took occasion to remonstrate with the girl against being so much alone with Mr. Anderson. She met with a reply that only widened the breach previously formed between them.

"If Mr. Anderson does not know what is best for me," Ella said, with flashing eyes, "perhaps I had better send him to you for instruction. I think you are considerably overdoing your part in my education, Mrs. Haynes, when you try to prejudice me against one who thinks of nothing so much as my best welfare. I wonder what he would say, if he knew you talked in this way of him. I shouldn't want to be very near while you were telling him. Poor Mr. Anderson! He little thinks those who profess to be his friends are turning against him in this manner."

"Yes, Ella," rejoined Mrs. Haynes, "but think of the danger to which you expose yourself, by causing all sorts of reports to be circulated about the city. It is no light manner, my dear girl, to risk the loss of reputation, even though unjustly. People are already beginning to whisper about the lover-guardian! It is for your good I say this, believe me. It gives me much pain, and I would spare you the recital, did I not believe it my duty to warn you."

"Don't talk such nonsense to me, if you please," said Ella, sternly. "For what you have done for me I am truly thankful; but you must not take advantage of the affection you may have gained, to estrange me from my best friend. I wish the gossipping public would mind its business as well as poor Mr. Anderson. He never goes about talking of the sins of this one and that, and causing trouble. I can hear nothing of your fears, as I can only consider them insults to him. If it were only to me, I could overlook it. But you must not talk in that way of Mr. Anderson!"

Mrs. Haynes sighed. "My dear girl," she said, "you may some day see better than you can now the injustice you do me by this usage. You may one day remember what I have told you, and think of me kindly for it."

Ella was too excited to answer, and turned away, leaving Mrs. Haynes standing there, gazing after her with tears in her eyes. A few days later Anderson found a note lying on his desk, reading as follows:

Dear Mr. Anderson:— For reasons which I cannot at this time give you, I desire to leave your house for another home. You have been uniformly kind to me since I have been with you, and have my most affectionate regard. I propose, if it meets your convenience, to depart a week from to-day.

Yours etc., LAURA HAYNES.

Albert sat reading this communication, rather surprised at its contents, when Ella came into the room.

"Come here, pet," said he, in the lover-like tone he always used now, "What do you think of that letter?" Ella sat on his knee and glanced over the note, opening her blue eyes a little as she comprehended its meaning.

"Too bad, isn't it, pet?" said Anderson. "What shall we do without her? She has been with us so long, it will be difficult, I fear, to replace her. But we must induce her to stay, mustn't we? You shall try your arts of persuasion, and see who can resist them; eh, pet?"

"Oh, Bert," said Ella, hardly noticing what he was saying, "I am so glad she is going. It was more than I dared to hope."

"What!" said Anderson, with a look of the deepest wonder. "I thought you loved her better than any one else — better than me almost. Why, I have often been quite jealous of her, thinking she had the largest share of the love I so highly prize. What can have happened to separate you?"

"Don't ask me, Bert; don't ask me what it was. It is very foolish, I am sure, and I cannot bear to tell you so small a trouble. She is going now, and it will be over then. There, now, you foolish fellow, don't look so sober. It will be all right after she is gone."

"None of your troubles are too small in my eyes to demand notice," he replied tenderly. "But since you wish me not to inquire into this one, I will not." And here the matter was dropped.

At another time the young man might have felt some degree of sadness on account of the departure of the good woman who had been so thoughtful and kind to him and his ward. He did intend to have a farewell interview with her before she left, but Miss Ella managed to give him no time for it, by convincing him that she needed this or that, or could not bear to be left alone without him. So it happened that Mrs. Haynes was ready for her journey before he had an opportunity to say a parting word. He was coming up the steps with a whip in his hand, after tying his horses at the gate, preparatory to taking Ella for her evening ride, when he saw Mrs. Haynes coming down, with her traveling wrappings on, and a porter following her with the baggage.

"Why, really," he stammered, taking her hand, and feeling a sense of his neglect sending the blood to his cheeks, "I had not thought you left us to-day. I meant to have had a long conversation with you before you departed, but I—really—I have been so busy——"

He hesitated, knowing the falsity of such a statement, and looked down, still ho'ding the lady's hand in his own. At this moment Ella came to the door, looking so lovely in her light dress and ribbons that he drew a breath of surprise even in the midst of his vexation.

"Come, Bert," said Ella, putting her hand on his arm, and looking into his eyes with an expression there was no resisting. "Come, if you are going to ride with me. It is getting late, and I fear there is a shower coming up."

He was caught, entangled, thrown down, and his captor stood looking at him in calm triumph. But he was not quite so far gone yet as to forget every feeling of duty.

"Ella," he said, contracting his forehead, and trying to look stern, "Do you not see Mrs. Haynes? She is going to leave us. It is not right to behave in this manner toward your friend. Cannot you bid her good-by?"

Ella turned and recognized the lady with a haughty bow, though her lips quivered a little at the harshness of Anderson's tone.

"Good-by, Mrs. Haynes," she said. "Perhaps you will know better some day than to accuse—but then, it is no matter now. You are going, and what has passed between us is ended."

"Good-by, Ella," said Mrs. Haynes, trying hard to control herself. "I have nothing to add to what I have told you. May you be happy. Good-by."

The hack drove away, and Anderson, who had been a wondering spectator of the scenes just enacted, drove away also, with Ella, in an opposite direction. He said nothing for some time, and they came to an old road where they often drove among the pines, before the silence was broken by either.

"Ella," said he, then, placing his arm tenderly about her, as he was wont to do, "I was much grieved to see you behave so badly to Mrs. Haynes. Whatever she has done, it can be no excuse for such treatment. I am very sorry that you could not control yourself better."

"Oh, Bert!" cried the girl, hiding her tearful face on his shoulder. "How cruelly you speak to me! And it was all for your sake, all for your sake!"

"For my sake!" cried he, starting up. "How can that be?"

"I cannot tell you, Bert," she replied. "It is over now, and should never be called up again. The woman meant no harm, I am sure, but she did make me very angry. It was all for your sake, Bert, and I could not feel reconciled to her."

The tears had their effect, and he said no more, only brushing back her wet hair, and begging her to think no more of the matter. He was blinded by love, and every other sense was overpowered by this one.

The next day they drove to an artist's gallery and sat for pictures. Anderson had long desired to have a picture of himself and Ella taken together, and after some trouble had been experienced in overcoming the girl's bashfulness at being obliged to sit with him before the eye of the artist, a fine large copy was obtained. A painter afterwards transferred the likeness to canvass, and it was hung in the tower-room.

There is a handsome man of twenty-four, and a lovely woman of sixteen, Both of a clear blonde complexion, both with bright silken hair. Her eyes are of the bluest blue, his are hazel-gray. He sits in a large chair, upright, smiling, happy; seeming almost to say, "Look at my treasure." She, looking like a treasure indeed, sits on his knee, with one arm encircling his neck, and her head showering its gold over his own. Her beautiful dress sweeps over his feet, and one of his arms clasps her waist. Jewels shine forth from her fingers, bracelets of fine gold are upon her arms, a beaten chain is round her neck and hiding in her bosom. His broad collar is covered by the long hair that twines around his shoulders, sweeping back from his high, intellectual forehead. She looks a little shy—and much the prettier for it—but very happy. Painter never made so beautiful a scene, as that of James Albert Anderson, the author, and his beautiful, guileless ward, Ella.

His guileless ward, Ella! Guileless as the new-born babe, trusting him and loving him as her life. Believing him the essence of truth and honor. Seeing daily his great love for her, and realizing the debt she must always owe him.

He hangs the picture on the library wall. There it may hang forever, or drop away in a moment; but in his inmost heart it has been photographed deeper and more lasting, and there it will remain as a monument to him of the days when that pure girl sat on his knee, and wound her arms about his neck. When he bowed down to his idol, and worshipped her as the goddess of his existence. When he would cheerfully have placed his bare head between her and harm, and called on high heaven to strike him dead ere he should be the means of bringing sorrow to her door. When life was only dear for her sake, and a dreadful blank when she was absent for an hour.

How can I write what is to come! My pen lingers pleadingly in the path they trod so happily together, and almost refuses to record the opening of the dark, dark days fortune had laid out for them. Ah, Albert Anderson! you who held yourself so high, and were so sure of your theories in life; you were to be taught, through suffering you would not have believed possible, a greater lesson than any you had tried to teach!

From the day Mrs. Haynes left the Pearl street roof, the young couple became knit in a closer union than ever before. They were always together now, and each felt that the other was the dearest one on earth.

Only realizing that this girl was something very dear to him, that had become the chief figure in his daily life, Anderson lived on engrossed in the contemplation of his happiness, neglecting almost entirely all other affairs, trusting his business to Harry, and seeming as if locked in a dream. If he had given a thought to the prospect of an awakening, he might have struggled back to a sense of his manhood and his danger.

Ella, thrown at such an age into the exclusive society of her guardian, gave her whole love to him unquestioningly. What she was he had made her. What she was to be in life, lay in his hands to determine. What she had risen from was due to his kindness. A word against Albert was like a heart-thrust to her. If she ever uttered a prayer it was for him, and in her religion there was no other saviour.

It is the old, old story of blinded love. Of affection that was akin to worship on her part, of love that clouded every sense of right on his.

*　*　*　*　*　*　*

Were it not better the man had died with the mother who bore him, and been laid by her side in the shade of the Southwestern forests! Were it not better he had never found a place among men, and that no slab had ever marked his unknown grave! Were it not better the woman had dropped frozen, by the lake that day in January, and never known the comforts of her after life! Were it not well that it were thus and more, before they came to this!

For what is early death, but the passing of a little flower from its fellows, to bloom again — they say — in a better garden? What is the hunger of the child that has no bread, compared with the gnawing at the heart which comes of hopes unfulfilled and the bitterness of remorse? O ye who have suffered both, come in by hundreds and thousands, and bear me your testimony!

* * * * * * *

Realizing at last something of her true position, Ella prayed him one night that he would give her the legal right to be his, — his forever. She told him of her love and reminded him of the thousand expressions which betrayed his own. She begged him to marry her at once, that no danger of separation might come in view to distract her mind, and awaken her fears.

Cut to the heart he was as he listened to her earnest words. A heart must have been of stone, indeed, not to have felt sorrow at such a time. But he soothed her as best he could, and put off the answer she wanted by reasonings of his own. He knew his power over her and brought it to bear.

"My darling," he said, "I could never love you more than I do now, though you were made my wife a hundred times. There is not a husband in the world who is so bound up in his bride as I am in you. Our life has been one pleasant dream, Ella; be careful you do not hasten its end. What can we ask for more than we have — a beautiful home, everything at our call, and — above all — each other! If you loved as I do, you

was silenced. And yet he could not fail to see a look of melancholy which came, he thought, too often into her face, and at last, quite hid the old sunny smile. When he referred to it, and said it gave him pain to see it there, she found courage to speak once more of the matter that was preying on her mind.

"Oh, Bert!" she cried, sadly, "I am not happy, I *cannot* be happy while we live in this way!"

"I am sorry," he replied, looking very soberly at the girl, "to see that you continue to keep this subject on your mind. It is very foolish, Ella, and can do you nothing but harm. I wish — for my sake — you would try and be again the same pleasant, happy girl you used to be before you got these notions in your head."

She only answered by a look which showed the deepest sorrow, and hiding her head in her hands, the hot tears came running down like rain.

Once; oh! so little time ago! he would have sprung to take that head to his bosom, and felt his own heart wrung by every sob she uttered. Now he stood as quietly as if she had been miles away, and answered her mute appeal almost sternly.

"Ella! This will not do! You are jeopardizing both my happiness and your own by this conduct. When will you learn reason? If I was unkind to you, if I neglected you, if I did not give up my very life to you, there might be some cause for your

"And yet," said he, still apparently unmoved, "you will persist in making yourself miserable over nothing, when it takes all the sunshine from my life to have you do so. If you loved me, Ella, would you darken my days by your melancholly? Answer me that, before I can say more."

She could not answer him then, and she rose slowly, and went down stairs to her own room. All alone she battled with herself for many hours, and when the sun had long been set she crept again to the tower-room, and softly opened the door. Albert sat in his arm-chair — that chair in which they had passed so many hours together — with his head bowed on his breast, and covered with both hands. The stillness of death was upon the room, in which the pale moonlight shown, and Ella was struck with a dreadful feeling that she was guilty of a great wrong to Albert. She pushed open the door, and entered. She sat down in one corner of the room on an ottoman, and silently watched the still form in the chair for over an hour. But it never stirred so much as a hair's breadth. He did not know she was there, and feeling this, Ella hesitated to speak for fear of startling him.

God knows of what his thoughts were, that they wrapped him so completely in their meshes. But one little word he heard whispered through the stillness, pierced him like an arrow, and he gave a gasp as from a mortal wound.

"Bert!"

He did not answer. What had changed him so?

"Bert! dear Bert?"

Not one word! And yet he heard her plainly.

"I am sorry, Bert! Indeed I am!

Won't you take me to your love again, Bert? I shall die if you do not speak, Bert! Oh! say you forgive me, do!"

He never lifted his eyes, but he held out his hands towards her.

With a glad cry she ran towards him, and pillowed her head on his bosom, and they sat together without speaking until the moonlight faded and the sun shone in at the windows.

"It was a dreadful thing, my little girl," he repeated, firmly. "Once is too much of such an experience. Be very careful in future, I beg you, Ella. Life is too short to waste in this way. We are happy enough now; let us be satisfied."

CHAPTER VII.

PLOTS AND PLOTTERS.

An elegant house at the upper end of our city has been engaged by a stranger, and fitted up in the most elegant style. The stables hold the finest of horses and carriages, with attendants ready at a moment's notice to bring them out upon order. The great house itself has its multitude of servants, who spring instantly at every signal which denotes that their presence is required. The residents in the locality have been agog with wonder for some weeks, while dozens of workmen have been engaged in furnishing the honse, and have watched with the deepest interest the dark lady and gentleman who have taken possession, every time they have shown their faces outside the walls. The sound of carriage wheels coming to the side door is enough to cause scores of eyes to be bent upon the couple, while they enter and are driven away. Their return calls for a like demonstration, and the neighborhood is divided in its opinions. Some say the lady is very pretty, at any rate, while others declare they see nothing but recklessness in her face; some, (but these are the ladies,) that the gentleman is a perfect type of manly beauty; while others, (of the sterner sex,) say there is a look of dissipation too plainly to be seen for good looks to hold a place· on his countenance. That they are foreigners, no one attempts to dispute, and if they had been disposed to do so, the investigations set on foot would have soon proved their mistake. The servants of the dark gentleman and lady were interviewed by the servants of everybody else, and by their joint testimony it was found that not one of the former servants spoke English. As none of the other servants spoke the other languages, the amount of information elicited was inconsiderable, and the inquiring minds of the neighboring population were thrown into greater wonder than ever.

Had it not been for positive proof that the dark gentleman and lady spoke English, themselves, it is doubtful whether the neighbors would have been able to contain their wrought-up feelings. This crumb of comfort was vouchsafed them on the testimony of a young woman who had met the dark gentleman and lady on an unfrequented road towards dusk one evening, and being unobserved from her hastily sought hiding place by the roadside, had caught the sentence spoken by the dark gentleman to the dark lady, as the carriage swept by her, " But, my dear girl, " —— delivered in the plainest Anglo-Saxon. This information led the guessing minds of the vicinity into a new train, and various were the theories built upon it. But the dark couple went about their own business as quietly as if they were of no consequence to any one but themselves, and their servants continued to "jabber," as the neighbors said, in the unknown language of their native land.

It is to give the reader a pleasure that scores of the neighbors would have paid any price for, that he is allowed to take a look at the dark couple in their private parlors one evening in the early autumn. The dark gentleman sits loungingly in a great easy chair, dressed in the finest of garments, with gown, slippers and smoking-cap. He is dividing his attention between a fragrant cigar, an iced claret, and the dark lady — seeming to consider the three as about equal in value as contributors to his pleasure. For he passes his time about equally between them, flying from one to the other, as a butterfly might among the flowers — taking a few whiffs at his cigar, applying his lips for a minute to the claret, and then directing his attention to his companion for a few moments.

The dark lady reclines upon a sofa near by, with her long hair hanging about her waist, her form loosely dressed in costly materials, with one foot encased in a beaded slipper of value, the mate to which lies on the floor, as if it had been thrown there out of very *ennui*. She is regarding the dark gentleman attentively, and unless the light in her eyes is that of deep love, we must be much mistaken. He is taking a taste of the claret now, and she knows it will be her turn to call his attention next. Yes, he is going to speak. She is all attention, and casts her dark eyes full upon him.

"I say, Jennie, it has done me ever so much good to see the anxiety our friends about here have displayed to find out who we are. Funny, isn't it?"

"Yes, Fred," says the dark lady, smiling slightly. "I hope they will satisfy themselves. They work hard enough, at least."

The dark gentlemen takes another whiff at his cigar, and gets around to his companion again.

"You remember that man Anderson that I have told you of," he says. "Well, I saw him to-day riding out with the girl he has adopted. They say he loves her more than ever, and neglects everything else for her. They did look happy enough together, as they rode by me with their fine equipage. Damn him! I can ride in as fine a carriage, and live as well as he, now. Can't I, Jennie?"

A look answers him, and this time he forgets the cigar and claret.

"Once I was almost the dust before the feet of such as him. Now I am his equal, and he shall feel it, if we come together. The young devil! I wish I had my claws on his throat. I'd make him howl a little, the whelp that he is!"

The lady is evidently used to her companion's humor, for she only laughs quietly and nods her head.

"If he knew I was in the city now, and knew who I am, wouldn't he raise a noise about my head? But he can't do it, and there is no need for fear on that score. The sea is deep and covers its secrets well."

The lady shuddered a little as if his words made her cold to hear them. Then she smiled again, and waited for him to proceed.

"He has a young fellow in partnership with him, too, that I must see about. Quite a paragon of virtue and honesty, I understand. But I'll bring him to the ground with the rest, for presuming to have anything to do with such a chap as his master. I'll bring them all down together. What is money for but to make one man even with another? And I'll be even with Jim Anderson, or my name's not——"

"Very true," said the lady, looking up warningly. "But be a little careful what you say here, Fred. You may spoil all if you are rash. Who could tell but you might be overheard?"

"You are right, Jennie," acquiesced the gentleman, presently. "Right, I say, as you always are. You are worth your weight in gold."

"No more than that?" said the lady, frowningly. "Only my weight in gold, Fred?"

"Why, yes, of course, you are worth more than ten times that, my girl. But it is a common expression to denote an article of great value, and that is why I came to use it."

"If you really think I am worth so much, Fred," said the lady, "I wish you would devote more of your time to me. I am so lonesome lying here with nothing to do, while you sit over your cigars and wines. They seem almost as if they were my rivals."

"What nonsense!" said the gentleman, in reply. "Cigars and wines your rivals, indeed! Why, I cannot smoke you, and I cannot drink you. If I could, I would, I am sure. I should think you would be tired enough of me, and wish me away, instead of wanting so much of my society."

The lady gives an impatient shrug to her shoulders.

"What have I but you?" she says, somewhat sadly. "I want you all the time, Fred, and am only happy when you are near me."

Putting down the cigar he is raising to his lips, the dark gentleman suddenly wheels his easy chair about, and looks sharply at his companion. She returns his glance with a trustful, loving look, that he cannot mistake. Watching her attentively he says, as if he had just made a discovery:—

"D —d if I don't believe you do love me, girl. Come and sit in my lap. There! Are you happy now!"

"I am always so with you, Fred."

"You say you love me, Jennie. I am going to ask you to prove it. I wish you to assist me in a plan I am going to undertake. Will you do it?"

"I will do anything for you," says the lady, calmly. "What is it you would have?"

"My interests are your interests, are they not?" he queries, watchfully.

"Yes, Fred."

"And my friends are your friends?"

"Yes."

"And my ENEMIES," (she shudders at the venom he throws into the words) "are your ENEMIES?"

"Y-es."

"Then!" says he, with a face that makes her start and look up. "Then you shall help me overthrow them!"

"What can I do, Fred!" she replies, disturbed at the fury that has come over him.

"You? you can do everything. You can deceive and plot and bring ruin down on their heads. You can revenge me of the slights I had when I was poor. You can bring worse than death to their doors. And you shall do it."

"But how, Fred?"

"I'll tell you. You say you love me. Let me remind you that I was looked down upon once because of poverty. That I was pursued once by that man Anderson, and that he would have set the very dogs on my track if I had not been smart enough to evade him. That he would come with a gang of men and drag me to prison to-night, if he knew where I was. That he was looked up to, when I was despised. That——,but why go on. It is one story of hate between us, and I will be even with him for it."

"I understand, Fred."

"Ah! you do. I am glad of that. Now what I wish is that you shall influence his girl to fly from him and leave no trace. His soul is bound up in her, and her loss will be the hardest for him to bear. You can plan with your woman's tact how to get acquainted with her, and after that you will find it easy enough. Tell her of the scandal already afloat about her and her lover. Convince her that flight is her best recourse. Can you do this for me, Jennie?"

The lady had no choice of answers. She loved the dark gentleman, and had given up all to him. She knew what he expected her to say, and she said it, though with an inward sigh:

"Yes, Fred, I can and will."

"Bravo, girl! Well said! Do your part well, and I shall not forget it. While you deal with the girl I will try my hand with the warehouse boy. If I don't bring down that Anderson with his long, brown hair — what snaky hair it is — and his highflown ways, I am not the man I think I am. We will commence our work to-morrow, girl. And the sooner finished the better."

The next day found the dark gentleman, Mr. Fred Hawley, at Brown's Wharf, where he managed by false representations to ingratiate himself into the confidence of the unsuspecting Harry. Mr. Hawley appeared to be greatly interested in the details of the shipping and commission business, and told Harry that, being a stranger in the city, he had merely called to satisfy himself regarding the way such work was done. The young warehouseman received his visit very kindly and invited him to call often. They separated the best of friends, and from that day Mr. Hawley was a frequent visitor at the counting-room.

As Harry was striving to obtain an equal share in the business with Anderson, having been made partner, he had practised the greatest economy in his manner of living, with the intention of saving his share of the profits to go towards that object. Hawley soon discovered this, and in a way not calculated to excite suspicion, persuaded the young man to take rides with him after his fine horses, when his work would allow of his being spared. Becoming quite infatuated with his dashing companion, Harry gave up more and more of his time to him, and often passed whole days in his society, either upon the road or at his elegant residence. At the latter place he was introduced to Mrs. Hawley, who assisted her husband in his attempts to obtain a strong influence over the boy. From this woman's hands, in one of her most charming moments, Harry was induced to take a glass of wine, when he would have been angry at its offer by one of his own sex. As he became more and more pleased with his new acquaintances, he grew less interested in the warehouse business, and his work there was hurried over in a careless way.

"If Anderson chooses to take his whole time to himself and never come near the office," he reasoned, "why should not I have a good time as well?"

This proposition, on being mentioned to Hawley, was warmly seconded by that gentleman, and the young clerk kept on in the way he had first chosen, unmindful of the result. He began to feel uncomfortable in his common clothes, and to spend a good deal of money upon dress, so as to match his new associates. From the closest economy, he launched into the other extreme, and became one of the most fashionably dressed men of the city. The cigar he had never before touched, was often found between his boyish lips, and the breath of wine came far too often from his mouth. The dark gentleman could not have been better satisfied than he was with the result of his endeavors to draw Harry Johnson into dissipation; a better pupil could not have been found, or one who would have walked' more blindly into the snares set for his feet.

The dark lady had more trouble with her part of the work that was intended to humble in the dust young Albert Anderson. It was no easy matter to make the acquaintance of Ella, when she was given up nearly every hour in the twenty-four to her lover-guardian. Either in the house or in their daily drives he was with her constantly. And for a long time the dark lady's efforts were in vain.

But there came a time when the couple were at the theatre, and the dark lady sat next to Ella through the performance. In some carelessly spoken sentence, she commenced a conversation with the girl, alluding during its continuance to the fact that she was a stranger in the city, and had not a female friend to speak to within many miles. Ella was touched by her loneliness, and invited her to call at Pearl street, giving her the address, and receiving a plain card marked "Mrs. Fred Hawley," in return.

"I, too, have very little female society, Mrs. Hawley," said Ella, "and should be much pleased to have you call. I reside with my guardian, Mr. Anderson, and see very little company indeed. If you will come and spend a few hours at any time, I shall be very glad."

The dark lady exulted inwardly in her success, and begged an introduction to Mr. Anderson. The young man returned her bow and smile pleasantly, but gave the matter no thought, as his mind was elsewhere. It was enough for him to know she was a friend of Ella's. Her friends must be his friends, of course.

Agreeably to her invitation the dark lady began to call often at Pearl street, and little by little Ella became very much attached to her new friend. She had never had a confidante so nearly her own age (for the lady was very young) and gave her a place near her heart without a doubt of her truth. While the man was succeeding perfectly with his charge over Harry, the woman was accomplishing the deeper work she had undertaken with Ella. And Anderson dreamed on, without a shadow of suspicion of the plottings against him.

If the dark lady ever had a twinge of conscience over the baseness of the work she was doing (and who can say she did not?) she only threw her will upon it, and hid it out of sight. If she had known where it was all to end, she would have sooner plunged a knife in her bosom, than to have brought about what she did. But love was the motive for all her actions, and there at the mysterious house at the upper end of the city, as well as at the mansion on Pearl street,

and everywhere else on God's green earth, it is blind, blind, blind!

CHAPTER VIII.

THE DARK GENTLEMAN.

One evening as they sat together in the twilight Mr. Hawley asked : "Are you making any progress with the girl, lately, Jennie? It seems as if you were dreadful slow about it. How are you getting on?"

"Rather slowly, Fred, I'm afraid, but just as surely as can be. Indeed, I am often half afraid to go on at all, she seems so gentle and affectionate with me. She loves him so, too, Fred. Every thought of hers seems to be of him."

"Yes I suppose she does," said the dark gentleman, ironically, and with a contemptuous curl of his moustached lip. "Well, why shouldn't she? He has taken her out of the gutter and put her feet on velvet, so to speak. It's very natural she should love him, isn't it?"

"Yes, Fred. But I often think that sin is sometimes punished in kind in this world. And if any one should be so cruel as to take you from me — I would rather they took my life first. Indeed I would."

"Pshaw! pshaw! No danger of that, I guess," said the man, drawing the speaker towards him. "We have been too much each other's for us to be parted now. But the girl, does he love her as much as she loves him?"

"O, yes! He has given up everything for her. He is almost jealous of me, as the only one who comes there to take her from him for a minute."

"I wonder what he'll do when he finds her gone altogether," was the bitter reply. "Perhaps it will bring him down to a level with other men, to meet with a little sorrow. To make the blow the harder our plans must arrange for both to strike together. When he shall be partially stunned by young Johnson's loss, he shall be knocked complely senseless to find Ella gone. Harry is ready now at any time, and you must strike home with the girl as soon as it is practicable. The boy has been flattered and cajoled until he is an easy tool. He only wants the proposition formally made, and he will go as I would have him."

"I shall be glad when it is over," said the woman, drawing a slight sigh. "This continued deceit is wearing on me."

"Deceit, indeed!" exclaimed the man, with an incredulous look. "That sounds well from the mouth of a woman. Why, I thought it was the chief stock in trade of your sex."

"Fred," replied the woman, looking earnestly into his eyes, "did I ever deceive you, since we first met, or why do you talk in this way to me?"

"No," said he, looking rather abashed, "I'll give you credit for that; you never did."

"And did you ever deceive me, Fred? Ah, you cannot say no. It is your sex that is full of deceit, and not mine, I think."

"Come, now," said the man, a little ashamed, "if I ever deceived you, it was all out of my love. That was all you wanted, and that you have now. If you are not satisfied with me you can leave me at any time, you know. There is no tie that keeps you but your own free will. Is it not so?"

"Yes," answered the woman, wearily, "it is so. There is no tie between us but love. And yet how strong I feel that tie to be, Fred."

There was something in the woman's looks as she said this; something that recalled a day in the long past, when she was a girl in her own father's village; something that made him feel a momentary pang of remorse for the relation in which he stood to her now; something that told him how unworthy he was of the love of such a one as she; something that showed the shamelessness of the work he was making her perform against the young author and his ward; something that so pierced his heart with a sense of the baseness of the crime against her he was about to commit; that he sunk into a chair, and drew her head upon his shoulder; kissing her face with more real earnestness than he had done for many a long, long day.

She cried on his shoulder then, and *he* cried. For an hour they were to each other as in that distant day so long ago, and were for that brief space the better for it. Then he put her gently down, with one more kiss upon her lips, and went out into the dark night.

The clouds were gathering ominously in the heavens, and there was no moon or stars to be seen. A dark night for the dark gentleman to choose to go upon an errand of evil. He looked up at the sky, and the momentary good within his heart vanished. And in its place came resolutions darker than the clouds that gathered above his head.

"Poor girl," he said to himself, "she will take it hard at first, I fear. She is too sensible, though, to let it affect her long. This nonsense about love and affection is all in the imagination. She will know soon enough, I hope, to make the best of what cannot be helped."

There was a muttering in the thunder-clouds, and a flash of jagged lightning shot out of one of them. But it did not strike him to the earth, and he went on again.

"Why in the deuce it was ordained that I should take such a fancy to that young fellow's girl, I'm sure I don't know. However that may be, I must have her now. What is the good of money unless a man can have what he desires?"

Another peal and flash startled him, but he was unhurt, though it seemed as if the bolt must have passed very near him.

The dark gentleman walked on, until he came to a large building, which he entered and went up stairs. He struck a light, and drawing his chair to the window, waited.

He had not waited long when the door was opened and a young man came in. His dissipation was beginning to make ravages on his countenance, and his step betrayed his nervousness. It was Harry Johnson, of Brown's Wharf.

"Ah, my boy, is it you? Devilish glad I am to see you, Harry. I have been waiting here till I got awful lonesome."

"Yes, it's I," said Harry. "I told you I would come to-night, and I am here."

"So far, so good, then," replied the dark gentleman, laughing. "We will go right to business, and have it over in less than no time. By the way, Harry, I have a message for you. Jennie sends her best love and wants to know why you don't call on her oftener. "'Pon my soul, Harry, I shall be getting jealous of you, yet."

The dark gentleman twisted his moustache and smiled at the boy.

"Come," replied Harry, snappishly. "Don't be foolish, Fred. I want to see how we stand, and then will be time enough for your fun. It may be that there will be little use for it, after I find how deep in the mud I am."

"As you say, my dear boy," rejoined Hawley. "You *would* play with those fellows after I warned you over and over, and, of course, being your friend, I could not refuse to lend you a little money when you asked me. You will be more careful in future, I hope. Such a lesson as this should teach you something."

"You had not ought to have lent me so much, Fred, when you knew I was, — well — when, you know, that wine got into my head. But I don't mean to blame you. I only ask for a sight of the total sum I owe you, and I will see what can be done about it."

"I am afraid the sum is larger than you think, Harry," said the dark gentleman, pretending to look anxious. "I won't be hard on you though, whatever it may be. Here are the notes entire. You may add them up, if you like. I haven't looked them over since you gave them to me."

Harry took the notes and begun to count them over. His face grew longer as the figures rose, and after examining each one carefully and finding it undoubtedly correct, he counted them over once more, and then turned upon his companion with a look of dismay.

"How much do you make it, my boy?" said the dark gentleman, coolly, lighting a cigar, and commencing to smoke.

"Over two thousand dollars!" cried Harry, with a gasp. "Who would have believed it, Mr. Hawley? Over two thousand dollars!"

He was much excited, and his face grew red and white by turns.

"Well," said Mr. Hawley, elevating his feet upon the window-sill, and puffing out a cloud of cigar smoke. "It might be worse, Harry."

"I don't see how," said Harry, shaking his head. "I don't see how it could be worse than it is."

"Why," said Mr. Hawley, calmly, "if it was three thousand, now, or four thousand; wouldn't that be worse?"

"No," replied Harry, in despair. "For I am ruined as it is. Two thousand dollars is all I hold in the warehouse. I have worked three years to get it. Now I am put back where I came from then."

"And what do you intend to do?" asked Mr. Hawley, quietly.

"I see but one way," said Harry, sadly. "I can go and tell Mr. Anderson how I stand, what I have done, and that I wish my share in the business to be paid over. He will then get another partner, and I shall begin the world again."

He spoke with the calmness of despair, and appeared as one resigned to a fate from which there was no escape.

"And you see no other way?" said Hawley, putting down his cigar.

"None," was the reply.

"Then I will give you one," said the dark gentleman — and very dark indeed he was then, — "and if you are not a genuine fool you will take it. You owe this money to me. I can get along without it for a while. I am willing to help you out of this trouble, and will take one thousand down, and the other at your convenience. You can thus continue in business, and come out all right in the end, with a good lesson from your misfortune."

"But where am I to raise the thousand to pay you now?" said Harry, catching at the straw thrown towards him, like a drowning man.

"Not the least trouble about that," replied Hawley. "You can take that sum from the bank, crediting it against yourself, and replace it when you like. No one will notice it, for Anderson never looks at the books, and there will be no dishonesty about it, as the money will be repaid."

The dark gentleman leaned forward to mark the effect of his suggestion. Harry had caught at the gleam of hope thrown toward him, and was struggling with it, before he replied.

"You know, Mr. Hawley, said he at last, "that I would not do a really dishonest act for the world — especially to Mr. Anderson, who has been such a true friend to me. But if the way you propose can be carried out, I do not see why I cannot save myself yet. It is a bad matter all through, and must be settled some way at once."

"I am glad to see you take such a sensible view of the case," said Hawlew, grasping Harry's hand. "You will come out all right, and be the better for this youthful indiscretion. When will you draw the money for me? Make it at your convenience, you know, for I can wait, and don't want to hurry you."

"I will wait, I think, a little longer, until money is flush," replied Harry, knitting his brows thoughtfully. "Say in a month or two. I will be going now, I guess. I have a slight headache, and had better go to bed early to-night."

"Have a glass of wine before you go?" said Hawley, going towards the sideboard. "It will do you good if you don't feel just right."

"No, Fred," said the boy, putting

up his hand to stop him. "No more wine for me. I can't afford to pay so dearly for my wine as I did for the last again. I have done with it forever."

"Well," said Hawley, coolly. "As you like, my boy. I think a little does me good, but you have a right to your own opinion, I suppose. You will not refuse to send a message to Jennie though, will you? She always inquires whether you send any word. Really, I half believe the woman is in love with you, Harry. Well, you can have her, after I am gone. She is a jewel, my boy, and no mistake." The dark gentleman slapped his companion on the back familiarly, and laughed heartily at his confusion.

"Seems to me you are mighty happy when I am down," rejoined Harry, fretfully. "One would almost think you were glad of my misfortunes."

"Pshaw!" ejaculated Hawley. "Don't talk in that style to a man who has saved you from ruin and disgrace, as I have. If I were disposed, I could bring down a pretty muss about your ears. But come! Let's not think of that. I am going to stand by you, and some day when you are sorry for this, you'll do me justice. You are a little excited now, and I forgive you."

Do him justice, indeed! Perhaps the lad may do that yet. The rope is dangling ready noosed to go on his false neck were justice done him. He thinks of this and laughs inwardly.

The two men came down stairs and separated. Harry to go with aching temples to his room, wishing earnestly that he might awake from the dreadful dream into which he had been thrown. He feels that if it had not been for Fred Hawley's companionship, he might have been now an honest, upright man. He does not know that it was through Hawley that the gamblers were able to draw him into their net and fleece him of his money when his head was full of wine. But he does know that the dark gentleman did wrong in lending him such a large sum when he was incapable of appreciating its value. And feels that his protestations of friendship and esteem are not worth thinking of.

Yet he realizes that he is in this man's power, and must be careful in his actions toward him. He sees that only by slow steps can he hope to pick his way out of the net one night of drunkenness has thrown about him. He thinks of his life since he left Hillsdale, and wonders what his friends there would say were his position made known. If he had a thought of owning the truth to his partner, and relying on his mercy for aid, he gives it up, and resolves anew to do as the dark gentleman suggested. Tired out with thinking, he falls asleep, and dreams of dangers that are about him, until at last the morning wakes him, weary and dissatisfied.

Fred Hawley left the boy at the foot of the stairs, and walked to the mysterious house up town, where he found the dark lady sitting alone, waiting his return. He took his usual chair, and sat down by her side.

"I have seen the warehouse boy to-night," he said, "and he has consented to my proposal, as I knew he would. You must make quick work with the girl now. Then I will drop Anderson an anonymous letter, that will set him to looking over the books, and discover the lad's secret. The circle is narrowing around them and will soon close in about their heads. They shall learn a lesson they will not soon forget, before I have done with them."

"The girl will be ready for flight soon," replied the dark lady, sadly. "It is a shameful task you have given me, Fred, and I feel as if my sins must be revisited upon me for this deed I am about. Once through with this, I will never undertake another such mission. Even my love for you, great as it is, would not induce me to cast such a burden on a soul too full of sin already."

"I will never ask you to, Jennie," said the dark gentleman, with a secret meaning in his tone. "Remember, I promise you faithfully never to ask you to conspire against a living soul again."

"I shall be so glad if you will not, Fred," she replied. "There is no reason why we should not be happy together, and let others take care of themselves. After this is over, we will go away again, and live as we did before this hate got such a strong possession of your mind."

"Yes, Jennie, we will. But the best rule of life is to take the world as it comes, making the best of its ups and downs. It is a changeable world, anyhow, Jennie. That's what it is."

Several days after this the dark gentleman brought home a document, and read it over once to himself before he went to bed. It gave the mysterious house and furniture, with $10,000 in money to the dark lady, in remembrance of the giver's long love for her. And this was to pay for a broken heart! For it must break when he left her.

He took the dark lady in his arms when he had read the deed, and kissed her more than once upon her loving cheeck. And smoothing back her long, dark hair, and marking the beauty of her face, and feeling the pressure of her hand in his, he muttered between his teeth: "Poor girl. It's a changing world, Jennie. So it is!"

CHAPTER IX.

WRECKS AND RUIN.

James Albert Anderson was not the first man doomed to awake to terrible disappointment out of a dream of the fondest bliss. The blow came as hard upon him, however, it was so unexpected and unprepared for.

It was not until December snows again whitened the earth that the plans of the dark gentleman came to their fulfillment. One delay after another had interfered to postpone the final day of his revenge. At last it came, and he dropped the anonymous note to Anderson, advising him to examine his books at a certain date and see whether there was not a large sum unrightfully taken. The note was signed "A Friend," and bore the appearance of good faith and honesty. The young man received it with his usual mail at his residence, and read it over with an interest he had given to no other for months. Ella was sitting in another part of the room and he called her to come and see the letter.

"Come here a minute, Ella," said he. "This letter is about Harry — young Johnson, you know, down at the wharf. I am afraid there is some trouble there."

Ella came and sat down by his side while he read the letter over to her.

"What do you think of it?" said he.

"I think it's all a made-up story," she replied, frankly. "Or else some plot to ruin the poor boy. I'm sure he wouldn't do anything wrong, Bert. Do you think he would?"

Anderson kissed the sober face and answered:

"I can't tell, my pet, until I go and see about it. I made up my mind once never to trust another person, and it may be I have done wrong in breaking that resolution. Other men appearing as honest as Harry have deceived me, and he may be doing the same. I had not ought to have left everything to him so, but your sweet self has kept me from the wharf as well as from other places. I shall go down to-night and examine the books. If he is honest, all right. If he is not——"

"But if he is not, you won't be hard on the poor boy, will you, Bert?"

"No," replied Albert, smiling at her earnestness. "But you wouldn't have me continue in business with any one who had proved himself unworthy. That would be a ruinous rule to follow. If I find Harry has been taking advantage of my absence to defraud me, he must go, certainly."

The girl listened very soberly. "O, Bert; I don't believe you know how to forgive," she said.

He put back the golden curls that *would* fall over her face.

"I have forgiven you all your sins, haven't I? he said, lightly.

"And would you forgive me, whatever I did, Bert?"

Her manner touched him deeply. "How can you doubt it, my darling?" he replied. "Yes, I think I could forgive you — *anything*."

He could not understand then why she burst into tears, and laid her head on his shoulder, as if some one might tear her away else. He did not know why she clung so to his breast, nestling there as a frightened bird might

in the secure shade of a great tree. It was well he did not. That came too soon as it was.

All day she seemed strange, and the young lover was much troubled as he noticed it with his watchful eyes. He told her once he feared she was ill, and asked her to lie down for a rest. But she said no, she was quite well, and only wanted to be near him, and feel his arm about her. So he had the arm-chair brought to the grate, and made her sit in it, while he sat near reading and writing. Whenever he stopped a moment to observe her, he always found her gaze fixed on him so intently that it quite disturbed him. He kept on with his writing after that for a long time, knowing every minute that she had not taken her eyes from him once, but fearing to encounter them again, there was such a magnetism there. He had been often face to face with wild animals, and met their angry eyes with his own gaze. But this was so different, he knew not how to meet it. He decided to remain quiet, and at least not to disturb her by noticing her manner. Suddenly, after an hour of silence, she spoke. It seemed to him the strangest of all — that question that came from her sweet lips.

"Do you love me, Bert?"

He looked at her in amazement, and was for the time almost persuaded that she was delirious. But no, she was as sane as he, though very much in earnest.

"I say, Bert, do you love me?"

"Better than my life," he answered sincerely.

"Will you always love me?"

What did the girl mean?

"Yes, Ella, I shall always love you.

"Have I been a very bad girl to

you, Bert, since you took me to your home?"

"No, darling! No! You have been the best of girls."

"And will you never be sorry you took me in, that day you found me by the lake, Bert?"

"Surely not, Ella. It was the beginning of the brightest days of my life."

"So it was of mine, Bert; so it was of mine."

Filled with anguish he could not know, she let the tears come through the hands that hid her face. Anderson was inexpressibly pained at the sight and tried to comfort her. But she sobbed on for some time, seeming quite overcome with the violence of her feelings.

When she had become calmer, she went on with what she had to tell him.

"I am so glad you love me, Bert, and are not sorry you took me home. I wanted to hear you say so once more. I want you, besides, to never forget that I love you only; that I would give up my life if it would do you good; that I shall always love you, whatever you may come to think of me. There was never but one thing wanted to complete my happiness, and that you are persuaded is not for the best. I mean our marriage, Bert. I wanted that, so that no disgrace could ever come upon you as it might now. But I will not press it, after what you said before."

She paused a moment. The consequences of years might have been prevented had he granted the appeal that filled her loving heart. He might have stood upright again among men, and saved the suffering that was to come for both. The reply was half risen to his lips, but he shut it back. Should he give up his long-cherished theories for one weak moment's thought? He did not see the abyss before his feet, yawning impatiently for him, and Ella sighed, as she saw he made no answer, and continued:

"I am only a poor weak girl, Bert, but I think you have loved me or you would not have been so kind as you have. I have often thought how awful it would be to lose you, Bert, and can think if you love me as well, how you must feel when I am gone. But you will not forget me, then, will you? O! promise me you will not!"

"When you are gone, indeed!" said Anderson, rousing himself and going to her chair to kiss her sad face. "You must not talk in that way about dying, my little girl. I cannot spare you yet, and shall not let you go. You really are not well, and must go to bed and rest a while. Come, now, like a good girl. I insist that you lie down until you are better!"

He understood her speaking of going away to mean approaching death, and she did not dare to correct him. He assisted her to the couch, and after being assured that she needed nothing he could procure, he went back to his table. Pretty soon she called him, and asked that the curtains might be drawn away from the bed so that she could watch him at his work. He tried to persuade her that she had better go to sleep, but she persisted, and he drew away the curtains and sat down again.

How intently she watched him as he wrote page after page, and piled them one by one upon the mass before him! How she almost envied the table that he leaned upon, the paper he was confiding his thoughts to, and the pen through which he spoke. That pen was leaving a track that should delight thousands, for the young author had many admiring readers. What was she that she should stand in his way, when fame held the garland ready above his bright forehead? What was she that her name should be coupled with his by the scandal-mongers of the day? "When I am gone," she said, "he will be himself again. I have led him away from his duty. He will return to it then. I have brought him down to the level of other men. When I am gone he will rise again. He may not forget me — Heaven grant that! — but he will have before him a brilliant future that will much more than compensate for such a small loss as I am. I will go away, to work and earn my own bread, as I did before, and he will live on in luxury, blessing me perhaps, some day, in his heart, for leaving him free. O Bert! my soul, my life! may God bless you always!"

Albert wrote on, litttle dreaming of the thoughts in that young curly, golden head lying there on his pillow. On His pillow! He took up this last point, and held it in his mind. A fairer head was never laid on any pillow than that lying there on his. The love, the trust — that had been his; was it not worth a life to own them? How his pen wrote on, so fast and steadily, yet he hardly knew a word he was writing! His thoughts were not there.

It is a strange fact, but no less a true one, that the lines he penned that afternoon were never equalled by any others from his hand. Yet when he had finished he could have told hardly a word he had written.

There Ella lay, such a picture of beauty to his mind as never a painter produced. One white arm thrown over the snowy coverlid, the sweet face with those blue eyes turned always on him, and the clouds of hair —such hair, streaming about her neck and shoulders. What right had he to the possession of such a treasure?

None!

He thought of that, then. He thought of that dear girl whom he loved so well, and of the many evils that might come to her should he be taken by death. He half resolved that he would repent of his determination not to marry, and so far amend his wrong-doing. To-morrow he would speak to her on the subject. Ah! the fatal time men designate "to-morrow." A time that never came and never will. A time for the remedying of all evil, and the inaguration of all good. Oh! the fatal time!

Well! Let him think of it now, if he ever shall. For to-morrow she will be gone beyond the reach of his resolutions, his sympathies, and his love. Gone with the greatest secret a woman can have, that his rising fortunes may not be retarded by what she may thus prevent. Gone out of the greatest love a woman have, *which gives up all for its idol, even that idol itself!* She knew he loved her before all the world, and would stand by her side against all living. But if she remained, his shame would be brought home to him, and his prospects be forever blasted. Go she must. She was resolved.

When the evening came on, he left his writing and came and sat down by the bedside. He put one arm under her head and pushed back that wealth of gold with his hand.

"I'm going down to the wharf a short time, Ella," he said, softly. "I ought to see about Harry at once."

"You are going to see whether he has deceived you, Bert? And if he has you will never believe him again?"

"Never," said the young man, soberly. "He should have thought of all the consequences of his act, before he committed it."

"Yes," said Ella, musingly, "so — he — should."

"I still have hopes he is innocent, you know," said Anderson, not understanding her strange reply. "But if he is not, I shall be compelled to part with him. It is a rule I have always followed never to believe again in one who has deceived me."

What wonder that she should burst into tears again! It took away the last ray of hope from her heart. "After I am gone," she thought, "he will curse me, and drive me from his mind. It must be so."

What wonder either that she clung to him so when she gave him a parting kiss! And that she cried so when he left her side that he came back and asked her whether he had not better stay in with her instead of going out. He could postpone the visit to Harry until the morrow, and was really uneasy about her.

"No!" she said, "You must go, Bert. I am only a little excited, and will be all right soon. Forgive me if I have ever done you wrong or caused you pain. There now! Good-by. I feel better already."

What a story that was to tell when she raised to his the whitest face that ever served as the exponent of a living soul. But it was quite dark in the room, and he could not see this. He caught a long, deep kiss, and went away from the white face, to see it again, who can say in how many long, long years?

* * * * * * *

In half an hour more Anderson astonished Harry by appearing at the office and taking down the books. As he commenced to turn them over, the boy arose and started to leave the room.

"Where are you going, Harry?" said Anderson, quietly.

"Only to leave the room a moment, sir," replied Harry.

"I wish you to remain," said Anderson, in the same tone.

The boy looked up at his companion. "I told you I was going out for a moment, Mr. Anderson," he said.

"And *I* told you to remain," rejoined Anderson, in a louder tone. "I think I have a little matter to settle with you before you go. I am in earnest, and you had better not trifle with me."

"Mr. Anderson, please to recollect that I am your partner and not your slave!" said Harry, indignantly. "I shall go when I choose, and no one shall prevent me." He started for the door again."

"Stop!" cried Anderson, warningly. "I have a word to say with you first. Where is the money you have taken from the bank? I find a thousand dollars gone by these books. Speak, or it will be the worse for you!"

The young man was in a passion, and Harry saw a contest was not to be thought of. He gave up all hope at once, and answered, truthfully:

"I lost it at the gaming-table, Mr. Anderson. I——"

The young man waited to hear no more. He rained down a shower of abuse upon Harry's head that quite drove him to distraction. It seemed as if the months of love he had been through had been keeping back so much of hate, and that he had some premonition of the fact that those days were over, and the others must commence. Never before had Harry heard him use such language, and he was too stupefied to attempt a reply. Goaded at last to desperation, he watched his opportunity to dash out of the door and into the street.

In a minute more, Anderson left the warehouse and rode over to the office of Jacob Jenkins, Esq., attorney and counsellor at law, to lay the case before him, and ask his advice. He was hardly seated in the lawyer's room, when a cry went up in the streets that proclaimed the existence of the direst of destroyers, FIRE. A little later a breathless boy came running in to ask if Mr. Anderson was there, and to say that Brown's Wharf was burning and fast going down to ashes.

Brown's Wharf was built of perishable materials, and being partially filled with combustible merchandise, proved an easy prey to the flames. The forked tongues of fire ran over the old roof and ate the shingles as if they had been paper. They ran in and out of the windows, and closed around the bales and boxes piled up within the building. The light of the burning heap was seen upon the face of the sky for many miles. It gave light to more than one traveller, and more than one, too, that we know.

Anderson saw this part of his riches going down before his eyes, without emotion. Better so ten times over than the false faith of the man Fogg and the boy Harry. Was there no one he could trust? If not, then let the building burn and cover up the memory of these deceivers with its charred timbers and its white ashes.

The engines were brought to the place and after a time a feeble stream was playing upon the fire. Just at this point it was remarked the flames burned the brightest of any.

"There is no help for you I fear," the engineer remarked to Anderson, "The building must go down."

"Yes, it can't be saved now," said the young man. Then he added to himself: "Yet it could have been saved at the beginning by so little labor! Well, it's like the rest of our life. What is more dangerous in any sense than Playing with Fire?"

A call to man the brakes (for it was in the days of the old hand-engines), was answered by a hearty cheer from the crowd who had gathered, and scores of willing hands soon had all of the pumps working. At one of the engines a young lad was seen, flushed and excited, with his coat off, working in his shirt sleeves and urging on the others to greater exertions. There was a wild look about him that attracted the attention of his companions, and he seemed to labor with the strength of two men.

A dark gentleman, peering about through the cloud of smoke, found the lad and touched him on the shoulder.

"I am sorry to see this," he said. "You should not have let your anger carry you so far, my boy. It will go hard with you I am afraid, before this thing is over."

"What!" cried the lad, falling back. "Do you think I could be capable of such a crime as this?"

"You did not set the fire then?" questioned the gentleman in a tone of surprise.

"Never!" said the lad earnestly. "I swear to you, upon my soul to Heaven, I do not know how it caught!"

"A bad business, anyhow," said the gentleman, leading the boy away from the crowd. "I am afraid it will be charged to you, as I hear you had high words with Mr. Anderson to-night. Such things will count with a jury should you be taken."

The boy looked horrified. "What shall I do?" he said. "I am innocent, but how can I prove it?"

"Well, my lad, that is just the trouble. There is only one way —"

"And that —"

"Is flight. Come, I have stood your friend too long to give you up now. You shall be far enough away at sunrise to keep you safe until I can see whether you are suspected. Will you trust me?"

"Yes," said the boy, only thinking of the danger in which he stood. "I will go at once."

"Come with me, then," said the gentleman. He led the boy to a coach that stood near, made him get in and they drove away in the direction of the mysterious house.

Within an hour afterward the same dark gentleman walked on Commercial street, and watched the men putting the streams on to what remained of the great warehouse of J. A. Anderson & Co. Albert Anderson, himself, stood near, apparently the least interested of the spectators, except when he was questioned by the firemen or acquaintances. He had just ordered a supper prepared for the men who had labored to combat the flames, when the devil — I mean the dark gentleman — came up.

"Have they taken young Johnson, yet?" he asked Anderson.

"Taken him for what?" rejoined the young man, sternly.

"Why, for incendiarism, of course!" said the dark gentleman.

"For burning the warehouse, do you mean?" said Anderson, turning upon his questioner.

"Certainly," replied the dark gentleman.

"Who says he did it?" asked Anderson, giving the man a searching look.

"Why, I understand it to be a matter of no doubt. I supposed the officers were on the track of the young fellow. They say you had a quarrel with him in the early evening. But it may all be a mistake." The dark gentleman turned to go.

Anderson had been regarding the man steadily. A sudden dim remembrance seemed to connect him with himself.

"Hold!" he cried. "I have seen your face before."

"Very likely," said the other, coolly, "I have lived here some time."

What could the young man do? Certainly not follow his companion and arrest him by force as his first thought would have led him. So the dark gentleman escaped, and entering his carriage some way off, he laughed grimly, and said :

"Well, Mr. James Albert Anderson, I have been well revenged on you this night. Your trusted partner, your goods, and as you will yet learn, your lovely ward are gone. I will be her guardian, now, I guess. Only one thing more would I ask. And that is to see those tongues of flame lick up that dark brown hair of yours, and drink your ugly blood. Good-night, my dear fellow, good-night.

CHAPTER X.

LEFT ALONE.

The light of Brown's Wharf burning had lit up the sky and served as a brightener of its dark face to more than one traveller. The dark lady and Ella Anderson saw it as they rode away from the city, and though they knew their was a great fire in progress, neither thought for a moment of the possibility of its being Anderson's property that was being destroyed. Harry Johnson rode away with the dark gentleman, marking with an aching heart the red lines overhead. Later, the dark gentleman alone, was surprised at their brightness as he rode after his tired horses to an outward station. And later yet, Albert Anderson watched the heap of destruction that had been his property, and saw at last that there was no danger of a fresh out-burst of the flames. It had been feared all night that several adjacent warehouses would be burned, but the efforts of the firemen had saved them, and the young man was so thankful for it that he held his own loss in light estimation. It had been his fault, throughout, his thoughtlessness and disregard of the lessons he had been taught, that had done this thing, and he alone was to suffer for it. It was right, quite right that it should be so.

It was getting near morning and what with the cold and hunger and disappointments that came upon him, Anderson was well nigh exhausted. He went into an eating house near by where the firemen were being refreshed, and partook of a sandwich and cup of coffee. The men rose as he entered and gave three cheers for their entertainer, to which he responded. "Thank you, boys; you have worked hard and deserve better compensation than this." Then, the quadroon being ready for him at the door, he bid them a good morning, and was driven to the house he had made into a place of beauty. Pearl street, 114.

Dismissing the boy as usual, Anderson entered the door, and passed up stairs to his room—and hers. The stillness was unbroken by a sound save his own steps on the stair-cases and along the halls. He reached the door and entered it softly, lest he should wake her whom he left there lest night with his kiss upon her lips. Perhaps she is worse! He hopes not! There is that love within his heart for her that gives a pang at the thought of her suffering. He goes quietly into the room, and turns up the dimly-burning lamp. 'What!'

The bed is empty.

An icy chillness that he never knew came upon the young man, and a fear so horrible as to cut him to his inmost heart came sweeping over him. But he steadied himself a moment, and then hurried down stairs to the room of Ella's maid.

"Nanette," he called. "Nanette! Nanette!"

"Yes, sir."

"Come to my room as quickly as possible," said he, his voice in a tremor. "There's something wrong."

"Yes, sir, I will come directly."

In a few moments the maid came up, and he questioned her about her mistress, with such a steady look, and close attention, that she was almost afraid of him.

"Where is Miss Ella?" he demanded.

"Why sir, indeed, I thought her in her room," said the maid, in a frightened tone.

"When did you see her last?"

"Not since morning, sir; she said she would call if she wanted me, and I have not heard from her since."

Such a look of despondency as came over his face. "Call up the whole house," he said, choking with his fears; "call up everybody and see if we can find where she has gone."

Everybody in the house was aroused, and each solemnly declared they had not seen their mistress since the morning before. Albert's worst fears were confirmed; she must have gone of her own will, without a word of warning to any one. "Gone! But where? O God! how could she have left him, when she was his only life and happiness?"

He had too much of that pride which always held to him to show the depth of his grief before the servants, and he told them to go below stairs and wait until he wanted them again. Even after he was alone and the door was locked upon him he did not rave and tear his hair. That would have been the natural way, but who ever knew Albert Anderson to do as other men?

Now was the time for action, if it was ever to be taken, and the weight of his sorrow could not bear him down so low as to make him forget this. There was one person more about the premises who had not been notified of the fact that Ella was missing, and he must be called directly. The bell wire leading to the stables was pulled, notifying the quadroon that he was wanted at the house. Hardly had this been done when a knock at his door announced the housemaid.

"Here is a letter, sir," said she, "that was left here just now by a man, who wanted it delivered in haste. I thought it might be possible ——"

He tore the letter from her hand, and opened it quickly. He had never seen the writing before, and the momentary hope that it might be from Ella died within him. He looked for the signature. There was none. Then he read over the contents of the letter, which ran as follows:

—

To Mr. Anderson, 114 *Pearl street, City:*— If this letter, coming from a sorrowing woman, can assist in any way to undo the great wrong she has helped to accomplish, she will be very glad. Your ward, Miss Ella, left your house at 9 last evening, and took a carriage to Homer's Station on the Western Railroad. From there she took the midnight train west. I can tell you no more. You may find her by following at once. Do so, I pray you, and thus help to take from me the great sin I have committed. I have written truly and honestly, as there is a Heaven above!

Yours,

—

As Anderson finished the letter. Sam, the quadroon entered the door. Albert glanced at his watch anxiously, and then turned to his faithful servant.

"There is yet time," said he, "if you make haste, Sam. Ella is gone and I must take the next western train. Have the horses saddled immediately—it will take less time than to harness,— and we will gallop to the depot. No questions, now, but hurry."

The boy comprehended and ran down stairs with all speed, and his master was but a minute behind him. The horses were made ready, and hard riding brought them none too soon to the railroad station.

"If I am not home in a day or two," called Anderson, as he sprang for the train, "I will write you what to do." He said something more, but the increasing clatter of the train drowned his voice, and he took a seat in the car. Now came the first moment of rest since the great shock, and a flood of memories, like a mountain torrent, swept over him, and made him giddy with their rushing. He bent his head until it rested on the seat before him, and tried to hush the voices that whispered in his ear.

Whispered such dreadful things, too. Whispered of Hope, that had left him. Of Love, that had proved faithless. Of Trust that had decived him. And then of Hate, and Passions, and Revenge, and Death. It was a dreadful vision indeed that crowded his fair young head as he let it lie there while the train went rushing on. And it left him weak and tired when the locomotive shrieked for Homer's Station, and ran with its infernal noise into the little depot. But he had work to do here, and he nerved himself to his task. He went into the depot waiting room, and inquired for the depot-master of a girl who stood at the counter.

"He is busy among the baggage, now, sir," said the girl, "but he will be in soon. I am his daughter, and if it's any thing in the station you want, I can get it for you."

Anderson looked at the girl earnestly. "Were you here when the midnight train went out last night," he said.

"Yes, sir."

"Hah!" he cried nervously. "Did you see a young lady, with golden hair and blue eyes, —take the train?"

"Yes, sir, I did. She came in a carriage from the city. There was a gentleman here inquiring for her a few hours ago, and I believe——"

"A gentleman," cried Anderson.

"Yes, sir, a dark gentleman, with very dark eyes and hair, and felt hat. He was very anxious to know whether she took the train, as he said——"

"What? what did he say?" cried the young man, holding hard to the counter for support.

"Why, sir," replied the girl, astonished at the effect her words were having. "He said she was his wife, and——"

"*His wife!*" Albert Anderson's head dropped into his hands as if it had been severed from the body.

"Well,"—looking up again—"what else?"

"That she had—why, how pale you are — that she — that she was his wife, and had eloped with another man. He gave me a half eagle, and was quite excited about her loss."

Anderson put his hand in his pocket and drew a handful of gold and silver coins. Laying them on the counter he said, earnestly, "If it is money you want, girl, you shall be paid your own price. But if you know anything more, tell me for GOD's sake.

The girl looked at the money and then at the white face before her.

"I know nothing more sir," she said, "or I would gladly tell you. Was she a relative of yours, sir?"

"A relative! My God! She was my all."

"Perhaps you know the gentleman that was here before you, sir," said the girl — the dark gentleman I spoke of. A man with black hair and eyes and a felt hat. He was in here a few minutes ago and must have gone aboard the train. He said he should follow the young lady this morning." The depot-master's daughter was determined to earn her wages if possible.

The bell rang and Anderson staggered on board the train. Seating himself in one of the forward cars he gave himself up to thought for a few moments. Who could this dark gentleman be that had come out to find Ella, and even said that she was his wife? He knew no one with whom he could connect the description. Then he remembered what else the girl had said. This gentleman was probably on the train somewhere. He would go and find him.

Several cars were passd through, and then he came to the last one. A moment more, and his man stood before him. "A dark gentleman, with black hair and eyes, and a felt hat." That must be him. And more! As the man rose and recognized him in his terror, Albert saw the face that had looked into his last night on Commercial street, and accused the boy Harry. The face that he had marked, when the flames of the burning warehouse lit up its darkness, and the face he had seen before. With every bad passion centered to convulse his brain, he shouted, "I have you now," and sprang after him in the extremity of his madness, from the swiftly moving train, after his enemy.

The young man must have been mad indeed to risk such a leap. The chances were ten to one he would be taken up with broken limbs, even if he escaped with his life, as the penalty of his rashness. But he thought of nothing but the man before him, and when he found himself, half stunned, with his garments sadly soiled by the soft earth, but otherwise unhurt, his first thought was strong upon him again, and he started up and looked about him.

Away in the distance sped the train, and he saw the clouds of smoke that came from the engine blowing away over the tree-tops. Directly after, he heard a sharp whistle, which he well knew meant "down brakes." He felt that they must be stopping the train to back down to look for him and his enemy.

Where was his enemy? The train had been going so swiftly that he was far behind, and undoubtedly safe enough by this time. The young man saw it would not do to remain until the train arrived, and be taken aboard and compelled to answer the questions of the passengers. With his passions considerably cooled by his concussion with the ground, he hurried away from the place. The woods were thick about him and he did not know where he was, but by keeping along in a straight course he came to a travelled road, and walked along upon it, meaning to inquire his way definitely when he came to a house. Pretty soon he began to see that the road looked natural, and when he remembered when he had been there, it gave him a start that quite unmanned him.

There! under the shade of those overhanging elms, he had asked her that day to call him "Bert," because his father who loved him had called him so! There she had said, "I will call you what you like, Mr. Anderson!" and the new era had commenced. There she had submitted to his clasps and had made him happy by innocent ways and affectionate utterances. There he had taken his first steps out of the solitary road he had so long trodden, with her for his new companion. And was it all to end thus? Had he reached the end of the new path, and was he to find henceforth only thorns, where there had been roses, and sorrow, where there had been joy? Must he cast her image aside hereafter, as he had done those of other false friends? As each new thought crowded upon him, he groaned inwardly and clenched his hands in pain.

Of but one thing was he sure, and that was that she must be found if it was within the power of man to find her.

Coming to a little tavern by the roadside, Anderson engaged a carriage and driver to take him back to Homer's station. With his brain racked to indescribable suffering by the contest going on within him, he lay back in the covered carriage and tried to collect his thoughts, while he was being swiftly driven over the country. He penciled a brief note to Mr. Jenkins, telling him to take charge of his affairs while he should be absent, which might be longer or shorter according to circumstances. Arriving at last at the depot, he alighted and sat down to await the train. While sitting in the parlor of the little hotel near by, he saw from the window some men coming toward the house, bearing between them a still form on a stretcher. Walking out into the passage-way as the procession came in, Anderson asked one of the men what was the matter.

"Nothing serious, sir, I guess," replied the man, politely. "Only a broken leg or so. This chap was just foolish enough to jump from a train up here awhile ago, and did well to get off so easily, I think. There was two of 'em went off together, but t'other one hasn't been found yet. This one crawled more'n half a mile to where some laborers were fixing the track, and they helped bring him down. That's all, sir."

It was well Anderson had taught himself to control the exhibition of his feelings.

"Poor fellow!" he exclaimed. "Let me see his face."

There was a smell of ether in the room to which they led him, and two surgeons were busy with a white limb belonging to the form that had been brought in on the stretcher. The young man turned a shade paler as he recognized the features which the anæsthetic had rendered immobile and quiet. It was the face of Hawley, the dark gentleman.

One of the surgeons turned, and caught the expression of Anderson's face as he recognized the features on the bed.

"Ah!" he exclaimed. "The unfortunate gentleman is a relative of yours, is he not, sir?

"A relative!" cried the young man, recoiling. "He! That man of my kin? No, thank God! He is not!"

"And yet, pursued the surgeon, looking first at one and then at the other, "he is very like you, sir, in feature."

"What!" cried Anderson, startled.

"Yes, sir, it is so. He is dark and you are fair, but otherwise, baring the difference in age, you might be brothers."

"You have a strange view," said Anderson, contemptuously, "to pair such a man as he with one so precisely opposite. If I thought there was one feature similar between us," he added wrathfully, "I would cut it off, so help me Heaven!"

"Will you be able to save the limb, sir?" asked a bystander, of the surgeon.

"We may with care," was the reply. "But the gentleman must be kept quiet, and I would advise all to leave the room before he becomes conscious."

The spectators took the hint and gradually went out. Shortly after, the western-bound train came up, and Anderson started again on his journey. There was no dark gentleman on the train this time to disturb him, and he rode quietly on, mile after mile, always thinking and planning over the best course for him to pursue. He could lay out no definite plan to be followed, nor could he even determine positively what was to be done if his search should be crowned with success. Only one thing was sure, and that he never let fall from his mind an instant. Ella had left him without a clue to her whereabouts, and —she must be found if it was in the power of man to find her.

BOOK THE SECOND.

CHAPTER I.

AFTER THE STORM.

In one of the rooms of the Pearl street mansion—not the Tower Room! never there now! Albert Anderson sits by a well-filled grate. All has proved futile, all his endeavors to get trace of his ward, and he has come back to this place disheartened, tired and ill. Ill in body. For he has been idle in mind for days, and serious consequences have threatened from the dreadful strain upon his brain by the events of the past month. Physicians have come and gone, shaking their heads sagely in response to anxious inquiries from the domestics below stairs. They have poured out their doses of medicine, which he has swallowed unquestioningly. They have recommended courses of treatment, which he has quietly submitted to. And still the medical gentlemen shake their heads in a wise sort of way, and murmur among themselves that "he may survive the shock, but——."

The quadroon boy is troubled at his master's distress, and drops in often to see if there is not something he can do for him. The housekeeper issues instructions to her subordinates not to make unnecessary noise, and in their universal love for the young master, the house is kept so quiet, that he can hear from his room the ticking of the hall clock, down the stairs. The news-boys cry their papers less loudly as they approach the house, and the letter-carrier rings the muffled bell softly and goes down the steps on tiptoe. The business men on the street stop to inquire of each other about "young Anderson," and fear his heart was too much bound up in his lovely ward to allow him to rally again. Reporters from the newspapers interview the quadroon daily, and announce to their readers each morning that "Mr. Anderson is no worse than yesterday." Jacob Jenkins, Esq., thinks of the "poor boy" as he works upon his client's affairs, under a full power of attorney, and tells his good wife in confidence that there will be a will settled soon that will astonish people, he will warrant. More than one representative of the Meek and Lowly One, is deliberating sagely within himself as to whether, on the whole, he had better offer his services at the funeral of so great a sinner as Albert Anderson. And everybody else who has ever seen the fair-faced young man, with the long brown hair, and especially those who have seen him with his beautiful ward, talk over the affair, and have their own opinions and theories.

They all thought he was crushed by the weight that had come down upon him. But they did not know him. The blow had been hard, very hard, but he was not crushed yet. Only a little stunned, and bruised, and badly hurt.

After coming back from his western journey, convinced that further search in that direction was useless, Anderson had proceeded immediately to his lawyer for advice. Between them, they had decided to advertise in the New York, Boston, Baltimore and New Orleans papers, thinking it possible that some one of them might reach Ella and call forth an answer that might give a clue to her whereabouts. A notice was accordingly sent out, worded as follows:

"If Miss E. H. A., who has until recently resided in —— city, will send her address to Beach & Essex, bankers, New York, she will be furnished regularly with enough money to supply her needs; and no attempt will be made to induce her to return home against her wishes."

They had thought best that the New York firm should be designated, as the notice would attract less attention from people who knew Anderson, and also because Ella would be more likely to answer it if she believed it would not bring her face to face with her guardian. The young man determined that she should never come to want if he could help it, whether she was to return or not. He could not bear that she should be brought to suffering in any case, after the years of luxury she had passed under his roof.

"You say you have no possible clue to trace this 'dark gentleman,'" said Mr. Jenkins, when they were discussing the matter.

"No," said Anderson, bitterly. "Curse his black face! And I saw him lying on a bed drugged with ether, too, and the surgeons trying to put his ugly leg in shape. I wish I had been one of them. I'd have twisted it off and burned it in a furnace. The devil take his leg and him!"

"At Homer's Station," said the lawyer, musing. "You might have put a detective after him then, and found for certain whether he knew where Miss Ella was, or had only pretended so to the depot master's girl. You ought to have done that, Mr. Anderson."

"Ought to have done it!" cried the young man, savagely. "I ought to have wrung his neck, if it comes to that, or cut his throat before them all, before he does more harm. Who could have induced Ella to leave me but him or his accomplices? But make the will as I have said. Better risk his getting it, than her suffering. Meanwhile we will try to make the mystery clearer, and if I do find it has come to the worst, — I will not promise what I may do to him."

"Had the young mistress no lady friends?" asked the lawyer.

"None. That is — only one, a very fine appearing lady who called but a few times. But why do you ask?"

"I will show you presently," said the lawyer. "Has this friend called since this unfortunate affair took place?"

"Why, no, she has not. But you surely do not imagine—"

"In a moment. Do you know her residence?"

"Certainly. It is the brown house at the upper end of the city, that was deserted for so many years."

"Ah, I know. Now, not to leave a stone unturned, we must call on this lady, and get what information she possesses about Miss Ella. Shall we go now?"

"At once!" cried Anderson, catching at this straw with all his ardor returning. Half an hour later they drove up to the Mysterious House. There was an air of greater mystery that ever about it now, and not a sign of life upon the premises. The two men examined the house on every side, but were met only by shutters and locks. There was clearly not one living thing within the estate.

They were leaving the place, when a man met them at the gates, and asked what they desired. On being informed that thay wished to see the lady of the house, he said the family had moved he knew not where, some time before. In proof of his statements he took out a bunch of keys and let them into the house. They went with him all over the interior, treading the costly carpets, seeing their reflected forms in the foreign mirrors, and finding everywhere the marks of prodigal luxuriousness. The home had evidently been left without an article being removed, and also, it seemed, at short notice. The stables held the horses and carriages of the missing family, and the man showed him a letter directing him to take charge of the place until further orders. No name was signed to this letter, and he could only say that he had known the occupants of the mysteri-rions house since they had taken the place, being a near neighbor, and was promised full pay for his trouble. And that was all he knew about the matter.

"Can you describe the gentleman of the house, my good man?" asked Mr. Jenkins.

"Well, yes, sir, in a general way, I can. He was rather above the medium height, and would have been good looking but for his very swarthy complexion. So much was this noticed, in fact, that among the people here, he was known, in want of any other name, as 'The dark gentleman.'"

Anderson cried out suddenly. "A dark gentleman, did you say? With black curling hair?"

"Yes, sir."

"It is he," said the young man, moodily, turning to the lawyer. "The man I met on the train. There was a pair of them, then, and they were partners; curse him! And her! I wish I had them here."

The lawyer sighed. "There is one more chance," said he. "We will go to the banks and see whether they remember him."

Three banks did not remember him, and the fourth teller had answered likewise, when a messenger boy came forward, and informed his superior that a gentleman answering that description had been there to draw his money several weeks previous. Thus reminded, the teller turned to his books, while Anderson excitedly slipped a gold piece into the boy's hand. The date was found, and the name given.

"Mr. Fred Hawley, gentleman, drew out $1,000 this day, being the whole of his deposits."

"Mr. Fred Hawley," repeated An-derson, between his teeth.

The lawyer noted the name carefully and wrote it in his book.

"You had better put it down, Mr. Anderson," said he. "You may forget it if you do not."

The young man laughed derisively, with an ugly look.

"When I forget that name," he said, "I shall be past all need of it or anything else."

After a little further conversation, they left the bank, and drove to Homer's Station. With feelings most difficult to master, Anderson stepped into the little hotel again, and saw the stairs up which they had carried that form which had crawled so far by the railroad track before it reached a fellow-creature. He had a well-formed wish in his heart that moment, that the iron wheels of the engine had crushed it to a shapeless mass, and flung it to the crows and unclean beasts, ere it had been taken up and brought among men.

The hotel keeper told them all he knew about the gentleman that had been brought there with a broken leg. He had remained but two days, and would have left even sooner, had his surgeon permitted him. He was taken away in a carriage brought for the purpose ; and that was the last he had heard of him.

So, his last hope being gone, except the sole one of the advertisement, and as nothing could be done further, Albert Anderson came home to his house, and brooded day after day, in his chamber. He went once to the tower room for a few necessary articles and carried them himself down the stairs. He took the great painting that showed what had been when he and her were happiest, and brought that down also. Then he turned the key in the door, and carried it away with him.

"If she ever comes back," he said in his heart, with an inward sob of pain, "I will show her the dear, old room again, as it was on that dreadful night when she kissed, me, and went out into the world alone."

One day, while rocking silently as was his wont, and thinking — as he always did — of his ward, there came a little, timid tap at the door, and he called out to enter. It was a female form that opened the door, and a veil was thrown up that showed a face he had known well. When the face saw his face — so white and worn and sorrowful, a flood of tears came over it, and the woman ran up to him and threw her arms around his neck.

"Why, Mrs. Haynes ! Is it indeed you ? "

"Yes, Mr. Anderson, it is. I did not know how you would receive me, but I felt I must come. I only heard of your trouble last week, in another State, and I came on with all haste possible, " sobbed Mrs. Haynes.

"I am really glad to see you, " said Albert, but in such a voice that she was almost frightened. "I should have sent for you had I known your address. "

"Oh ! would you really ? " cried Mrs. Haynes, delighted. " Well, I shall not leave you again, after that ! You will let me stay all the time, now ? "

"I shall be thankful, " said the young man, in reply, " if you can overlook the past, to have you resume your former position in my household. Matters have gone ill about the place, since you left us. "

Mrs. Haynes kissed him again, and then blushed for having done it.

"You are a dear good man, Mr. Anderson, " cried she, " and I will stay as you desire." Then remembering Ella, she burst into crying afresh.

"Oh ! My poor girl, Albert. Have you any news of her ? "

"None. " He told her this with a choking in his throat, and then waited.

"And you have given her up entirely? You cannot forgive her for what she has done ? "

He raised his head and eyed her reprovingly.

"One who can say that has no conception of my character, " said he. "When I adopted Miss Ella, I considered well what I was doing. I made suitable provision for her, and it is hers still. Mr. Jenkins and yourself were witnesses to it, and you will see my wishes carried out as there expressed. "

" See your wishes carried out, Mr. Anderson! The provisions of your will? You do not speak of dying, surely? "

" Dying? ha! ha! " The choking in his throat was gone as he uttered this cry. He seemed roused from his lethargy by the word "Dying?" "No! No! Mrs. Haynes, that it too silly! What! Die because my hopes have been dashed to the ground! I should have to die often at that rate, " he added bitterly.

Mrs. Haynes heard him pityingly.

"I see I did not understand you, " she explained. " And yet you looked so pale and ill I was a little frightened to hear you speak so. You will not lose heart then on account of your last misfortune ? "

Albert Anderson raised himself in his chair, and threw back his proud head in majesty. Mrs. Haynes had never seen such an expression of conscious power to overcome, as beamed in his face that instant.

" No, " he cried, " I will not. No real man ever lost heart for a woman's sake, even though she was truest of the true. And I? I lived before I met her, and I shall live after she has gone from me. She came to my roof of her own choice; she has gone in like manner. I never compelled her to come; neither shall I insist upon her returning after she has chosen to leave me. It has been a shock, I freely admit, but I can bear it, and shall live it down. I thank you, Mrs. Haynes, for having roused me to a sense of my duty. I have been dreaming too long, and now I am well awake, I will go away where new scenes shall fill my mind, and when I return, it will be with a heart less heavy than I must confess I now carry. "

Laura Haynes was never so proud of the young man as at that moment. She had always held the belief that he had not a peer in the whole world, but now, as she saw the will which came to the surface when its power was questioned, she was filled with the deepest admiration. She took him by she hand, and said she was very glad to hear him speak so hopefully. It was clearly the best thing for him to do, — to go away for a time, and the less delay the better.

When the worthy Doctors of Medicine came in the next day, with muffled tread and glum faces the young man was found at his desk, writing business letters and examining accounts. When asked in surprise what he had done with his easy-chair, he said he had kicked it out of the room. Apparently fearful lest in his altered state they might be treated in a similar manner, the worthy gentlemen beat a hasty retreat. Their pills and potions shared the fate of the sick-chair. Anderson rode out daily; first in his carriage, and later in the saddle. He began to get better rapidly. And those who loved him rejoiced to see the roses coming again upon his cheek, and then sighed to think of Her who had gone away, and could not see them !

CHAPTER II.

A MELTING ICEBERG.

A month of good exercise and energy wrought wonders upon the health of Anderson. He began to feel his old interest in business matters, and surprised his friends by the sudden improvement in his looks and manner.

The physicians sent in their long bills by their boys, and were paid their several amounts, with a brief note stating the writer's surprise at the fact of his own recovery after learning to what extent he had been doctored. The newsboys doffed their hats again as they met the young man in the street, and the letter-carrier pocketed his fees with unusual politeness. The clergymen whose minds had been so greatly exercised about their duty in respect to his funeral, gave utterance to the belief that he was a hardened wretch, anyway, and no good would come of him. His time and money were, to be sure, always at the service of the needy; he forgave the quarter's rent of many a poor family, and had put more than one outcast upon his feet, when others passed him by. But what was this? He never gave anything to their church, never showed any reverence for their doctrines, and they feared he would live and die an unregenerate man. Poor Anderson!

There was business to be done, and Anderson went about it with nearly his old spirit. There were houses that needed repairs, bills that wanted his approval, land that had lain idle long enough and must be built upon; lumber, brick, stone, iron; carpenters, masons and laborers; all to be seen to as the spring advanced. His quick business faculties, so long blunted by unuse, were revived, and he saw clearly each move, and made it in a determined manner. Thus keeping his mind busy with planning and executing the young man did the best thing for himself in every sense. Mr. Jenkins marvelled anew at the spirit of his client, and spent much of his own time with him arranging his affairs. So that, in the course of a few months, the lawyer was made to understand every portion of the complicated business that had extended itself in three years into so many speculations and experiments. He was given full power to act for Anderson in his absence, and the whole matter was then placed unreservedly in his hands.

"I am trusting you," said Albert, one day, "as I have often resolved never to trust any one again. But what can I do? I cannot go through life without trusting some one, and I have selected this time a man universally believed to be upright, upon whose head the gray has begun to show itself. Well, Mr. Jenkins, if you prove false, I have, at least, one recourse left. There is a little broken-down log-cabin where I was born, standing yet in Texas; I can go there again and find a shelter, if in no other place."

Tears came into the good lawyer's eyes. "You may never doubt me, Mr. Anderson," he replied. "I would rather lose my right arm than see you defrauded."

"I believe you, sir," said Anderson, pressing his hand. "And when this storm has entirely blown over, and the sky is quite clear again, I may be able to do something for you that shall partially repay you for your faithfulness."

"When do you intend to go away, sir?" asked the lawyer.

"Very soon, now. There seems to be nothing further to remain for."

"There is one matter you have chosen not to mention, sir," said Mr. Jenkins. "It might be necessary to give me some instructions how to proceed in case—the — lad, came back."

Anderson had divined his thoughts before.

"Ah!" he exclaimed, "Harry?"

"Yes, sir."

"Little danger of your seeing him,

I guess," said Albert, grimly. "He'll not be likely to return after what has happened. But if he does," and Anderson smiled strangely — "you may use him as any other criminal — lock him up and have him tried for incendiarism. If he is innocent, a jury will surely find him so. If he is not, he must suffer the penalty of his crime according to our righteous laws."

"I will do so, sir," said the lawyer.

"Good-by," said Anderson.

"Good-by."

"Ah, wait a moment. Have you heard anything from the advertisement?"

"Nothing."

"If you should hear, you know, you will spare no pains nor money to bring Ella home again."

"I will do all I can."

"And if she will not come, at least you will keep track of her, and see that she does not suffer." Anderson bit his trembling lips.

"I will, Mr. Anderson."

Still he waited.

"If I thought you would fail me, I would remain here. But I will trust you."

"You may be sure of me, Mr. Anderson."

"Good-by, then."

"Good-by."

They shook hands earnestly at parting, and the young man's eyes met the lawyer's full and square. Then he mounted his horse and rode home.

Mrs. Haynes met him at the door. He was paler than she had seen him of late.

"No bad news, I hope?" she questioned.

"Bad! It's all bad. What could be worse than this uncertainty?"

"Then you think nothing of hope?"

"Hope is set in the skies. I never look in that direction, now."

"Oh, Albert! Have faith that all will come out right. Have faith through everything, as I do." The good woman's tears came to her aid, and she wept.

Albert Anderson, like a huge iceberg, had floated about unmoved by weathers until now. He had been driven before many a gale, but had withstood every shock. He was destined to be melted, however, and this was the beginning of the work. He took the housekeeper gently by the hand and led her to a sofa.

"My dear Mrs. Haynes," he began, "I believe your affection for me is sincere. Am I right?"

"Albert, you are indeed. I have loved both you and Ella, honestly and truly."

"I think you have, Mrs. Haynes, and I will tell you openly what I never meant to breathe to a mortal. I can rely upon you can I not?"

She pressed his hand in answer.

"You remember it all," he proceeded, "since that cold December day when I brought her to your door — forsaken, ragged and untaught; when, in the kindness of your heart, you consented to act the part of a mother to her. You remember how I paid her brutal employer to forego all further claims, and took out myself the papers of adoption. You remember this, do you not?"

She pressed his hand again.

"You will remember also that I took a great interest in her from that time; that I found leisure from business cares which had weighed heavily upon me, to call often at Giles's Row, to see the little girl, transforming so rapidly into a lovely young woman;

that I was ever anxious she should be provided with everything she could need, and always urged you to spare no expense when her benefit was in question. Is it not true, what I have been saying?"

"It is, Mr. Anderson, every word."

"She grew lovelier day after day, and acquired knowledge very fast. The next season she left us for the seminary at Claremont, I believe. Only a child still. Only fifteen years of age, if I remember rightly?"

His companion bowed, still pressing his hand. Anderson proceeded calmly, but his voice trembled a little.

"That year, I think, I went to Texas, and passed the winter. In the spring I travelled over the northwest. In the autumn I came home. One day she came in and surprised me, as I sat in my parlor at Giles's Row. You remember all this, no doubt?"

"All of it, Mr. Anderson."

"If she had been beautiful when I left her at Claremont, what could express her loveliness now. Her manners greatly changed by her contact with gentility, and her temper and disposition unapproachable. She came back into our house like a bright beam from the sun, and won our hearts before we had time to consider whether we should let them go. If I am not right you will correct me."

"You are quite right, Mr. Anderson. It was indeed so."

"Realizing that the house in Giles's Row was not a fit abode for such a jewel, I came here and set artisans and furnishers to work to make a place where she could find only pleasure, and have every wish supplied. They did their parts well. She came with us to this house, and I may ask you, Mrs. Haynes, whether she was not overjoyed at her new home?"

The lady bowed in acquiescence.

"What came next? I, who cared nothing for women, and had always prided myself on the fact, fell down, ay! on my knees, before this idol I had set up, and worshiped it as a god. She, inexperienced and so young, offered no discouragement. I fell in love, madly in love, as I will show you. I gave over my business affairs to others, and devoted myself wholly to my new study. There was but one thought in my mind, believe me, and that was, her happiness."

"I do believe you, Albert. I never once thought otherwise."

"I thank you for that, Mrs. Haynes. I am making a long story of this, and will hasten. It is like tearing my life out to confess what I must, but it will be done if I die for it."

He was choking and stopped to loosen his neckcloth. Mrs. Haynes was breathing hard also, and he paused in fright to see how pale she had suddenly become. He would have taken her hand again, but she held it from him, and rose with a dreadful look, to leave the room.

"Why, Mrs. Haynes!" he exclaimed. "You are ill! My story has been too long for you. Let me get some water."

She lifted a hand to stay him.

"I know the rest of your shameful story now," she said, hoarsely. "I had hoped before, it had not come to *that*. But go on and finish what you were saying. Confess it all! *You have been her ruin*, and may GOD forgive you!"

He was thoroughly alarmed at her terrible calmness.

"May he forgive me, indeed, Mrs.

Haynes," said Anderson, reverently. "But how this has affected you !"

"Cannot you guess why ?" replied the woman quickly, trembling like an aspen. "I will tell you. It has been a secret in my own breast too many years already. Look at me, Mr. Anderson, and believe it is GOD's truth when I tell you *Ella was my own child !*"

With a cry that rung In her ears for many months, Albert Anderson ran from the room. Whither he neither knew nor cared. Away, anywhere beyond the sight of that dreadful figure accusing him of her child's ruin ! A vessel was to sail at nine. It must be nearly that now. He ran to the wharves, and went aboard. He wrote a note to Mr. Jenkins saying simply that he had gone on his journey, and would be back in the summer, probably. The anchor was weighed, the sails were run up the sheets, a fresh wind sped him away upon the ocean's track. The sea-birds fluttered by in the darkness, the city's lights faded away, and the waters of the bay leaped about the vessel's side. But through all and over all, there was before him a pitiable figure, pointing him out and saying "He had been the ruin of her child, and might GOD forgive him !"

CHAPTER III.

A CHAPTER OF CONSEQUENCES.

It was indeed a hard lesson young Albert Anderson was learning.

Speeding out of the bay that night, with Mrs. Haynes's accusation ever before him, he passed hours that seemed like years, so fearfully was his mind distracted. It was daylight before he sought his berth, and later yet ere sleep came. In that struggle with himself he came to see many things more clearly, and before his eyes closed he was satisfied that he had been wrong in his views in more than one case. This was a great concession for him to make, and it cost him an effort ; but he made it. His months of mental suffering had not been with out avail. The Iceberg was melting away by degrees. Melting slowly, to be sure, but—melting away.

Toward evening on the second day, for he had somehow feared the light, he came from his state-room, and resumed his position upon the deck. The vessel dashed bravely forward under the impetus given by her huge clanking machinery, and a score or more of the passengers were out enjoying the beauties of the blue scenery and the bracing air. Anderson sat apart from the others, his arms upon the railing and his head resting upon his arms, thinking earnestly of what had been, and speculating over the probable results that were to come. Where was this to end ? Was he to be hunted down by the fates for his crime, for such he now felt it to be ? Was he to expiate his wrong with his life at last ? It seemed as though a shadow of what was to come rose before him out of the dancing waves ! The white caps rose and fell tauntingly as the vessel sped by them, telling each other who he was and what he had done. And, sometimes, scowling and dashing up their spray into his face savagely ; as if moved to indignation they could not suppress to think that he,—*he* whom they despised—should be riding in safety over their heads.

A young man, walking about the deck, espied the solitary figure sitting there so lonely, and being himself a stranger to the people on board the vessel, concluded to make his acquaintance. Being of an easy disposition, he made no ceremony about an introduction, but simply presented himself with the remark—

"It's a pleasant evening, my friend."

Anderson glanced up at the intruder, and waited for him to proceed.

"I remarked that it was a pleasant evening."

"Ah! yes. I did not think of it before."

"You must have been very busy with your thoughts."

"I was ; very busy."

"Perhaps I have disturbed you," said the other, apologetically. "You will excuse me if I have. I am a stranger upon the ship and as you seemed the same, I ventured to accost you. The young man was retiring politely.

"You are a stranger upon the ship?" said Anderson. "Stay then, I beg you. I am also a stranger upon the ship."

The new-comer reconsidered his intention and drew a chair to his companion's side.

"Were you studying the waves?" he asked presently.

Anderson replied in the affirmative.

"It is a great study, my friend," said the new-comer. "One that has no end of knowledge in it. I love to study them, myself, sometimes, but not as they are now. Give me the wild, roaring storm for my lesson. Ah! It is admirable, magnificent then !"

Anderson began to be interested.

"Before we proceed farther," said he, "we had ought to be better

acquainted. Here is my card. Please favor me with your own."

Anderson took his companion's card, reading the plain words, "F. L. Smith," and Mr. Smith glanced by the reflected moonlight at the card he had taken.

"Indeed!" he exclaimed, as he noted the name. "Have I the pleasure of meeting Mr . Anderson! I should have known you, sir, by your appearance, had the thought once entered my head you could possibly be here. Your works are placed among my most cherished books, and I have long desired to meet their author."

Anderson smiled. "Well," said he, "as you know my profession, now pray inform me of your own. We may meet again ashore."

"My profession? I am a lawyer. politician, and independent gentleman of leisure combined," said Mr. Smith, laughing. "As well as a sort of philosopher and looker into human nature. The latter study is my preference, however."

"And do you find much human nature in the waves?" asked Anderson lightly.

"O, yes. Plenty of it, I assure you. Anger and hatred and scorn and fury in the storms. Peace and quiet, and love and rest, in the calm. There is plenty of human nature to be studied on the sea, if we only appreciate its varying moods. A great study, Mr. Anderson, a great study."

Anderson became graver. "Do you find anything there that speaks of false friends, and of trifling with the deepest feelings of the heart? " he asked.

"Yes, I think I do," was the sober reply. "The waves are often called treacherous, and he who lies down to sleep in the most perfect calm, may awake with the waters sweeping over him."

"You are indeed a philosopher?" cried Anderson, grasping his hand.

"I am proud to hear you say so," replied Mr. Smith. "But I could not presume to teach you in these matters, for almost at your feet I have learned many of them. Your writings have often met with echoes in my heart that have showed me truth where there was no light before."

"You do me too much honor," replied Albert. "I can yet learn much from others, and am trying every day to unravel new mysteries. I am but twenty-five years of age yet — a very young man, you see — and what I have written can be of little consequence. I thank you the same, though, for your kind words."

"Speaking of the sea," resumed Mr. Smith, in a moment, "did you ever give thought to its dangers, and the number of men lying in its depths? Think of our situation at this minute, with only a plank between us and death. There is another illustration of the parallel we were speaking of."

"Yes, I have often thought of it," replied Anderson, "but never with feelings of fear. I cannot imagine a man in his right mind who has a fear of death, when he knows it must come to all. It is natural, to be sure, for us to cling to life while there is hope remaining in our breasts. But there is something, Mr. Smith, that is better than Life."

The speaker paused and fixed his eyes upon his companion.

"A life," resumed Anderson, "is nothing, compared with a principle. If the death of a man establishes a principle, it cannot be counted a loss.

There was a Man who lived once in Judea, whose whole life was spent in inculcating great principles into his disciples. His death established those principles, so they shall endure forever. We have called him the Master. For earth never saw his like."

There was a pause for a moment, and then Anderson resumed.

"I have read of a captain or some other officer who, when his vessel was sinking, called his men upon deck and ordered them to present arms. Then quietly, in true military style, they sank together. What were their deaths compared to the glory of that deed! It was worth a thousand deaths to give the great principle to mankind that death had no terrors to that noble company!"

Mr. Smith looked at his companion with admiration. "Think you," he asked, "that you would meet your death as they did, were it to come upon you in a like violent manner?"

"I would, indeed!" cried Anderson, throwing back his head, around which the breeze was blowing his long, brown hair. "It is no vain boast, I assure you, sir, when I say I would meet my death as a true man should, face to face, promptly and willingly, without a sign of fear. This is the result of long thought and study. My rule would be, 'Whatever must be, should be met firmly.' If I am ever brought to the test, I will show that I have not spoken vainly."

Anderson's eyes sparkled with his excitement, and as he raised his arm to emphasize his words, his face glowed under the moon's light until he seemed half transfigured. The soul was speaking through the man, and lent its own beauty to his face. His companion saw he was in deep earnest, and felt his bosom stirred by contact with this wonderful nature.

"Since you care so little for life," ventured Mr. Smith, presently, "I would be pleased to hear your opinion of the Death Penalty." .

"You shall have it, sir. I regard capital punishment in times of peace as one of the greatest blots upon the history of the world. In war, when the sternest necessity has forced it upon a people, the taking of a life to save a thousand, may be justified. But never during a tranquil peace can the law be right in dragging forth misguided men to death upon the scaffold. The influence is wrong, the deed is wrong, and the principle is wrong. If I write another book this curse shall find condemnation in its pages."

"Do you lay the death of a hanged man upon the officers of the law?"

"No. It comes further back than them, upon the system which gives them their power. It comes upon the people, who in their blindness allow such laws upon their statute books."

"If you were in authority," asked Mr. Smith, "and the power of commuting the death sentence of a man lay in your hands, would you carry out the law, or favor the side of mercy?"

"It would be a hard case for me to decide," replied Anderson after a moment's thought. "I believe fully in justice being done to the transgressor of our laws, and should in all possible cases favor a full punishment for crime. But I hardly think I could sign the death warrant of a fellow being. It would seem as if his blood was on my head."

"But society must be protected," urged Mr. Smith, apparently dissenting from his companion's views.

"Not by punishing one crime with another and a worse one," said Anderson. "However, this subject is a deep one and has many sides to it. My opinion remains the same as ever, and it will be useless for us to argue further. You have my views in brief, and if I live a year more, you may find them in full upon paper. For the present, if you please, we will drop the discussion.

The two men continued their conversation for some time upon other subjects, and parted for the night with friendly words and grasps of the hand. Mr. Smith was much impressed with his companion's theories, and was highly pleased at the chance which had brought them together. Anderson was always willing to speak with one interested in the questions he himself studied, and had enjoyed his friend's company very much. Early in the morning the vessel reached her destination and Anderson bid his friend a final farewell as they took trains bound in opposite directions.

"We may meet again, remember," said Mr. Smith. "And if I can serve you in any way you may be sure I shall do so."

"Thank you," replied Albert. "Do not forget what we were speaking of last evening, and if I am ever put to the test recall the words I told you then."

When the young man had rushed so confusedly from the presence of the housekeeper, he had had no idea where he should go. He had taken passage on the vessel because it would bear him away from the woman he had wronged, the quickest. As the sea-breezes cooled his hot brain, he had time to consider and decide upon his best course, and had concluded to take the railroad at the first port and proceed to Texas. There were several months to be passed before he intended to return home, and this plan was as good as any. He wrote letters to his lawyer informing him of his address, and to Mrs. Haynes expressing his deep sorrow at the estrangement between them, and hoping it would be only temporary. He told her no effort must be spared in finding Ella, now, and that she should be given up to her mother as soon as any trace could be obtained of her. He said neither Mrs. Haynes nor her daughter should ever want for anything he could procure, and in every possible way expressed his desire to atone for his sin. It was such a letter as the good woman would never have believed him capable of writing — it was so penitent and sad. The Iceberg was melting faster than ever.

Anderson reached Catherine town in a fortnight more, having to travel part of the way on horseback, and this change of scene wrought improvement in his looks. He rode much, and tried to keep his thoughts from the object which was always rising before them. He partially succeeded in this, and became nearly his old self by the time he had settled upon to return North. And one day in July, with the sun's hottest beams falling upon his head, he mounted his horse again and left Catherine behind him.

He came home by the same route as he had left, and came riding into the lower bay of the harbor about two o'clock one morning. By his request he had been called at one o'clock by the steward, for he intended to go, immediately upon the vessel's landing, to Mr. Jenkins's house, and see whether there was any news of Ella.

For some reason unexplainable to him, he had thought more than usual about the girl for the past two days, and felt sure she must be near him. As the vessel came nearer and nearer to the city, he became more and more excited, and had passed a nearly sleepless night. At the steward's call he hurried on deck, and looked about the sea.

The noble ship was plowing her way bravely through the waters, and the machinery clanked heavily as the great wheels were turned round and round. In the distance could be seen beams from the lighthouses and ships, the latter standing both in and out of the harbor. The city's lights were just visible ahead, and his heart leaped as he thought he would soon tread her streets again. Ella must be near — he felt it as though some supernatural agency had whispered it to him.

He sat down by the railing and thought of Her. The smouldering fires of love were blown into flames again by the breezes which were wafting him to her side. He knew he loved her and without her, — ay! theorist though he might be — life was a blank that was but worthless to him!

What was it that brought the old choking into his throat? That made him gasp for breath as he had done when he found her bed empty, and realized that she had gone from him, perhaps forever! He saw her lying once more in a bed; but so pale and sick his heart was moved to the deepest compassion. The form was there before him as plainly as if it was a reality, and he half suspected he was dreaming. But no! He was wide awake there on the vessel's side. The form vanished from view as it had come, fading out of sight into the sea! And he heard in its place a stifled wail, and those words which had impressed him so strongly before, when the deed was signed in the lawyer's office:

"Her heirs forever — her heirs forever."

It must remain a mystery to all men how these visions arise, but they do come. Albert Anderson heard as plainly as he could have heard those words repeated in his ear:

"Her and her heirs forever — her heirs forever!"

A hand touched him on the shoulder. He started, to see a well-known face looking into his. It was that of the quadroon formerly in his employ.

"Hush!" said the boy in a low tone, as Anderson was about to speak. "Your life is in danger, and I have come to save you."

"My life in danger, Sam? How?"

"I do not know it all," said the boy, "but there are certainly officers waiting at the docks to arrest you. It is a serious matter, Mr. Anderson, and you must come with me."

"Where?" asked the young man, almost stupefied by the rush of strange incidents which had come upon him.

"To St. George's. We are near there, and my boat is moored alongside. I rowed down to meet you. Come! we must not lose a moment. Where is your stateroom?"

Hardly knowing what he did, Anderson pointed out the room. Sam seized the baggage instantly, and called to his master to follow. .The deck was clear of people, and they reached the boat unobserved. Into this they stepped, and the fastening was cut off. In a minute more, the quadroon was pulling with all his might upon the oars, and the boat dashed forward at a good rate of speed toward St. George's Island.

"What were they to arrest me for?" asked Anderson, as soon as he could collect his scattered thoughts.

"I do not like to tell you now, sir. Wait till we are ashore."

"Tell me, I command you, this instant!"

"Well, sir, if you must know, it was — MURDER!"

CHAPTER IV.

A NEW LIFE FOR ELLA.

The town of Walden nestled in a valley formed by slopes of the Alleghanies one January morning. It was a little town and the people in it were mostly poor in this world's goods, and strict in their opinions upon morality and religion. The great house of the rich man of the place could be seen upon the rising ground to the eastward, contrasting strongly with the unpretentious cottages at the base. The rich man was a large land proprietor and owned at least a quarter of the property in town. His name was Henry Walden, Esq., and his family consisted of two daughters of fourteen and sixteen, and one son twenty-two years of age. The son was known as Mr. Walden, Jr., and was a young gentleman of upright character, handsome, and kind to all. He was a graduate of a law and scientific school in the State, and claimed the title of LL.D. There were essential points of difference in the characters of Mr. Walden, Sen. and Mr. Walden, Jr. For instance, the former was bigoted and austere; the latter unprejudiced and frank. The former a believer in the most rigid school of religion, the latter inclining to the liberal faith. The former, in short, holding to the doctrine of "an eye for an eye" and the latter believing in the sublime injunction, "Whatsoever ye would that men should do unto you, do ye even so to them."

The good people of Walden were divided in their opinions between the faiths of the father and son, though the majority were strongly in favor of the views held by the elder gentleman. The worthy pastor of this flock was often known to hurl his denunciations at Liberalism upon the devoted head of Walden, Jr., of a Sabbath, while pretending to address the rest of the congregation. On such occasions, Mr. Walden, Sen., would assume an expression of Christian resignation that was truly affecting, and called forth mute glances of sympathy from the villagers who sat near him ; while Mr. Walden, Jr., seemed as little impressed by the affair as though he had been made of stone, and generally fixed his handsome eyes as steadily upon the minister as though they, too, were chiseled out of rock. People then said that young Mr. Walden was coming to some evil end, as all would who persisted in holding such erroneous views as he did. Not a word could be said against his morals or his good intentions. But he was certainly wrong in persisting to believe in these new-fangled notions against his father's wishes.

In this village, as in hundreds of others of like size, the daily stagecoach was looked upon as one of the most important events of the twenty-four hours. And on this morning in January, there was assembled as usual, a motley crowd of men, women and boys, upon the walk near the hotel, as the stage drove up. It was a coach with six horses and a ruddy faced driver. The latter personage announced his coming while yet some way down the road, by sounding a tin horn, and on arriving at the hotel sprang from his box to open the stage-door with great alacrity.

The people who were in the habit of visiting Walden by the stage were principally merchants and business men, with a few persons who came in from the back districts for the purpose of trading at the village stores. The expectant crowd, therefore, looked for such a company to alight, when the driver hastened to open the door. But they were disappointed, for the official, after commanding in a stern voice that the boys should cease crowding, handed out with the greatest delicacy a young woman of petite figure and modest appearance, with a few loose curls escaping from her net, and a face that was hidden by a blue vail. This was so different from what the crowd had expected that they drew back without further orders, and contented themselves with staring hard at the new-comer as she was shown into the hotel, and passing various wondering remarks upon her probable business in Walden.

Just as the young woman alighted, a young man, on some errand to the hotel, walked up the steps, and as he did so his eyes fell upon her. He was interested immediately, and observed her carefully for a few moments. She walked to the office-counter and in a trembling voice asked for a room. On being requested to register her name, she took the pen offered her, and in a delicate little hand wrote the words, after some hesitation, " Ella Hastings."

Mr. Walden, Jr. — for it was he — looked earnestly at the girl's face as she put up her vail to see the page better. As she finished, she inadvertantly looked up at him; and then, finding that he was regarding her so closely, she blushed, dropped her vail and turned away.

The landlord's daughter came out to show her to her room, and she followed immediately, seeming very glad to escape the presence of so many strange gentlemen. Walden, Jr., glanced at the register, read the name, drew a long breath and left the house.

On leaving Ella at her room, the landlord's daughter, Carrie Hudson, asked her how long she should remain, and Ella answered perhaps a long time, she could not tell. The girl then went away, and Ella was left alone. She turned the key in the door, and slowly removed her traveling wrappings. Alone indeed! Among strangers with no one to trust with her great secret. She resolved never to reveal her identity, whatever came, and then, tired out, she sat down on the bed and cried.

Poor girl! she was satisfied she had done right in leaving Anderson, but how bitter was the cup she was called upon to taste! What a sacrifice she had made in leaving him whom she loved above all else, to come here where none knew or cared for her. No wonder the hot tears came as she thought. She was so young and inexperienced, and the trial was very hard.

After a time her grief became controllable, and she began to reason with herself. This would never do. She had her own way to mark out hereafter and must not waste her time in idle tears. She resolved to be brave. Rising, she bathed the sad face, and tried to smile, but it was a very unsuccessful attempt. The poor face looked woe-begone enough. She left the glass, and sitting down again, tried to collect her thoughts.

She had come a long way, and Albert could never find her here. Of that she was almost sure. She had some money that would support her for a while. How much? She took the purse from her pocket, and told out the bank notes, the gold and silver pieces, upon her lap. This had been His money, and she almost felt like a guilty thing as she saw it lying there in her possession. How much was there? One, two, three, four, five, eight hundred dollars. How often had he spent more money for some article of jewelry she fancied! There were bracelets on her arms, now, and a chain on her neck, and a pin on her bosom, and a watch in her belt, that had cost more than double, treble this sum. He had never asked the price of anything she wanted. "Dear, loving Bert. Have I not done wrong in taking this when I left you? It was all mine, surely, but you never thought I would leave you when you gave it. Well, there is no help now. I can spend it for his child by-and-by. Perhaps that will be some atonement. Heaven knows I would do no wrong to you, my dearest love."

The tears were coming again, but she stayed them by a strong effort.

She took off the jewelry she wore and put it away in the bottom of a trunk. It might raise questions were she to appear in the village with such costly ornaments. She donned a plain black dress and a common linen collar, and fastened her hair with the net she wore while travelling. Thus dressed, she looked as unpretending as could be, and felt a gleam of satisfaction as she glanced in the glass once more.

"I don't think even Bert would

recognize me in this plain dress, " she said, smiling sadly. "There, stay in there, you curls, and don't spoil the effect. How he used to love you, and pass you through his hands! But those days are over, and must be thought of no more. "

A knock at the door recalled her to herself, and she opened it to admit the landlord's daughter.

"Dinner is ready, if you please, Miss, " said the girl, staring in a surprised manner, as she noted the change in Ella's dress.

"You see I have donned a plainer garment, " said Ella, noticeing her manner, and divining her thoughts. "It will do just as well, I think, while I stay in your village, and I prefer to wear it here. "

"It is a black dress, " said Carrie curiously. "Are you in mourning, Miss ? "

"I am not in mourning, " replied Ella. "But I have lost a very dear friend, lately, and prefer to dress in a quiet shade. "

"A friend ? " the inquisitive girl asked. "A gentleman or lady friend ? "

"It was " — said Ella, biting her lips, "It was — a — gentleman friend. "

"Your lover, perhaps ? "

Ella felt disposed to give a sharp reply to the girl, for continuing her inquiries so long, but seeing she spoke from sympathy, she answered,

"Perhaps. "

"Did you live far from here, Miss? "

"A long way. "

"Do you come from the North ? "

"No; from the South. "

"You do not look as if you were used to labor, " continued the girl kindly, looking at Ella's hands.

"I am not. "

"Have you come to Walden to stay long ? "

"I do not know, " replied Ella sadly.

"Are you — are you very poor, Miss ? " asked Carrie.

"I shall be obliged to make my own living. "

"You have met with misfortune, then ? "

"I have, " replied Ella, wiping her wet eyes.

"Can I do anything for you ? " asked the kind-hearted girl, seeing Ella's eyes begin to fill with tears again.

"Perhaps so, my good girl. You are very kind to feel so much interest in my affairs, " said Ella. "If I might be of service here in the house for a while, I should much prefer it to anything else. If I might, for instance, help you and your mother — you have a mother, have you not ? "

The girl assented.

"Thank God that you have ! " said Ella, earnestly. "If I could help you, " she continued, "so as to partially pay for my support, I have some money and should get along very well. I cannot bear the thought of going into a shop among strangers. "

Carrie readily promised to see what could be done, and at Ella's earnest request, she was given a seat at dinner at the family table, away from the public dining hall. The landlord and his wife were both very favorably impressed with their new guest, and it was settled that there was to be nothing said about her board for the present, at least. In the meantime she might assist as she chose in the lighter duties of the hotel.

So ! The hands that but a month ago ran, sparkling with jewels, over the ivory keys of the piano, and did no heavier labor than to ring for servants who came to supply every wish ;

the hands that He had pressed within his own, many and many a time, admiring their beauty, and kissing them playfully as she ran up to him as he entered her room ; the hands that he would have given worlds, now, to find clasped about his neck ; were to be employed after this in ordinary household work. And the feet that had stepped so long on the softest carpets, were to run up and down stairs until they were tired, helping to earn her living.

In the evening of the first day Ella came to the village, Mr. Walden, Jr., called at the hotel, and stepped inside the kitchen door-way, as one who was on easy terms with the family. Carrie was standing at the table ironing, with her sleeves rolled up, and Ella sat near by with some sewing in her lap. The young man quietly addressed Carrie, as he removed his hat, and then stood waiting by the door.

"Good-evening, Miss Hudson."

"How do you do, Mr. Walden?" said Carrie, handing him a chair. "This is my friend, Miss Hastings. Miss Hastings, Mr. Walden."

Rising, Ella bowed to Mr. Walden, without lifting up her eyes, and he took the seat offered him in silence. She had caught a glimpse of the young man as he entered, and recognized at once the face that had met hers when she stood that morning in the office. She knew he had been watching her keenly then, and she did not care to encounter his eyes again.

"You are quite a stranger to our house, Mr. Walden," said Carrie.

"Somewhat so," replied Mr. Walden. "I have been away from the town, more or less, for the past month."

"Travelling on business matters, I suppose?"

"Yes."

"Which way do you come from now; from the North?"

"No ; from the South."

"Indeed! Our friend, Miss Hastings, also arrived from the South to-day."

Mr. Walden, Jr., looked at Our Friend, Miss Hastings, to mark the effect upon her of Carrie's words. She did not look up, but bent her attention even closer to her sewing ; he fancied, however, that she was listening carefully, and had an interest in the conversation deeper than she cared to show.

"I met with a young gentleman as I was returning home," continued Mr. Walden, after a pause, and never taking his gaze from Ella one moment, "who was in deep distress from the loss of a very dear friend. He was enquiring at every station, of the conductors, whether she had been seen in their neighborhoods. He looked careworn and sleepless, and I really pitied him."

Ella drew in her breath as he proceeded, and her work dropped unheeded to the floor. But she did not look up. She dared not.

"Did he succeed in his search?" asked Carrie, becoming interested.

"He had made little progress when I left him. I think he must have become discouraged and gone home, before this time."

Ella drew a sigh of relief that was not lost on the narrator.

"Was he a handsome young man?" asked Carrie."

"A woman's question," said Walden, smiling. "Yes, I believe he was what you call handsome. A tall, straight form, clear, open face, and beautiful long, brown hair, hanging about his neck. Such a man as I should think any woman might fall in love with. Yes. He was handsome without doubt."

Ella bowed softly to herself several times, as if in confirmation of his statements. Albert — it must have been him — there was no other such being on earth. So he had not hated her, and left her willingly to perish. Poor, dear Bert! Might Heaven bless him!"

"Is that all your story?" said Carrie, seeing that he paused.

"Yes, nearly all. Are you interested in the narrative?"

Carrie said yes, and Ella appealed to him to continue, by her silence and close attention.

"Well, this young man," continued Walden, "was also from the South, and was evidently rich as well as handsome. He seemed to have held a deep love for this girl, and I understood he had offered large rewards to detectives to find her. He resided in one of the coast cities, where he owns large amounts of property. It seems strange that a woman should leave him and such a home, does it not?"

"It does," said Carrie. "There must have been more of the story than you heard, if that is all."

Mr. Walden looked at Ella, who was taking up her neglected work from the floor, where it had fallen, and saw that he had said enough. So he answered, like an echo:

"That is all."

Carrie took up an armfull of the newly-ironed clothes, and begged to be excused a few moments, while she laid them away up stairs. And Henry Walden, Jr., and Miss Ella Hastings were left alone together.

Mr. Walden bent forward in his chair and addressed his companion.

"You were interested in my story," he observed.

Ella started, and trembled like a leaf in the wind. "Yes, sir," she said. "It was a strange account."

"True," said Walden, Jr., watching her narrowly. "Why should this young lady have left her lover in that way?"

"Why," said Ella, covering her face with her hands, and speaking in a frightened whisper, "why, but that she loved him too much to remain."

"Indeed! How could that be?"

"Might she not have seen," said Ella, taking her hands from her face, and commencing to wring them in anguish, "that he was giving up his bright future as a rising author to his love for one so unworthy as she was? Might she not have decided in sorrow such as few can know, that her only course for his best good was to leave him to his books again? Might she not have thrown all selfish considerations to the winds, and gone out actuated solely by the deepest love for him? O, Mr. Walden, might it not be so?"

"My God!" he cried, "is there such love in woman as this?"

"Ay!" she said. "There is no limit to real love. He may never know that this woman gave up everything for his sake, but some day when she hears his fame proclaimed among the great, she shall have in it a reward worthy of her sacrifice!

"Miss Hastings," cried Walden, "I honor this woman more than I can tell you. Should her secret fall in my hands, I swear it shall be safe. Should she come in my way, I hope I may have the pleasure of giving her assistance should she need it. She should ever find a friend, who would spare no pains to help her in her noble resolution."

She looked up now and saw his honest, earnest eyes bent upon her. She read there truth, honor and manliness, and held out her hand for him to take.

"Mr. Walden," she stammered, "I have known you but a few moments, and yet I am impelled to trust you. I have no need of present assistance, but I shall want counsel and advice, which you may be able to give. I thank you from my heart for your generous offer."

"As you will remain here," said Mr. Walden, deeply impressed by her confidence, "I shall see you often. You may safely trust me, and I beg you not to make any new move without letting me know of your intentions. I have more experience with the world than you have, and shall be very happy to help you in any way."

The arrangement was but just concluded, when the landlord's daughter returned, and after a few minutes more of conversation on other topics Mr. Walden withdrew, and the two girls were left together again.

"Isn't he a splendid fellow?" said Carrie, the minute the door was shut. "There isn't such a fine young man in the village, I'm sure."

"He is a very fine young man indeed," Ella acknowledged, thinking with the deepest gratitude of his kind words to her.

"What! You're not in love with him?" cried Carrie, roguishly.

"Hardly," said Ella, smiling. "But I like him very well for all that."

"I noticed he watched you pretty closely," said Carrie, determined to have a little more fun out of the affair.

"Did he?" said Ella, quietly. "I was occupied with my sewing and did not notice."

And Carrie was obliged to drop the subject.

Henry Walden, Jr., walking to his home, thought seriously of the revelations of the evening.

"She is a wonderful woman," he mused, "a wonderful woman to love in that way. What! I am not in love with her myself, am I? Oh, no, no, only deeply interested, that's all."

CHAPTER V.

ANDERSON AN OUTLAW.

St George's Island, August 12th. — *Mrs. Haynes*: The bearer of this note will inform you of my position. If you still have faith in me, come with him to this place, to-night.

Yours Faithfully,

James Albert Anderson.

Thus wrote Anderson in the quadroon's cabin, gave the note to his faithful attendant, saw him row away toward the city, and then — waited.

Would she come? He was by no means sure she would. She was as likely to desert him in his trouble as others, for all he knew. Those swift visions of last night, supplemented by the boy's fearful answer in the boat, had unsettled his mind to a marked degree. He watched Luna, the dark-faced mistress of the house, as she went singing about her labors. She was the quadroon's wife. They were joined in holy wedlock, and were happy. But was this enough? Was happiness the only goal that man should strive for? This couple knew nothing of high theories, of deep philosophies, of broad conceptions of the Unseen! Happiness — bah! A dog is happy when he has a bone to gnaw.

This could not be all; Albert Anderson had not sunk so low as this.

In waiting and watching by the cottage window, the day passed. Albert ate a few morsels from the dishes tendered him kindly by Luna, but he had no appetite for them. When it grew dark, he would not leave the window, but sat there still, gazing into the blackness, and — waited.

As time passed on he began to feel sure she would not come, and said so to the octoroon girl. But she reminded him that Sam would not think of starting before it was quite dark, and it was a long pull from the wharves to the Island. Her predictions were fully verified shortly after, for steps were heard approaching, and on the door being opened there entered both the quadroon and Laura Haynes.

"My dear boy!" cried the widow, falling impulsively on Albert's neck, the moment she saw him. "How sick and pale you are looking. Oh, dear! dear! What an amount of trouble we do find in this world. Come, cheer up, pray, and try to look more hopeful."

"Have I your forgiveness?" he whispered.

"Oh, yes! yes!" she cried. "I was so sorry you went away as you did. I was very wrong to speak so, and I repented it in a minute after you left."

"I am much relieved to hear you say so," said Albert in a low tone. "I am beginning to understand many things of which I have been ignorant. I have now *your* forgiveness, and I only desire one thing more — that is, *hers*. But we will say nothing about this, now. There is a more pressing subject to be considered. Sam, my boy, please draw up here, and we will hear your story first. You said something about a murder, I think."

"Yes, sir," said the quadroon, doing as he was requested. "I was at one of the wharves yesterday, and overheard a conversation between some gentlemen there. They were talking very earnestly, and the first thing that drew my attention was the mention of your name. Then I took more notice of them, and saw two men that I did not know, and one that I did. The latter was the well-known detective, Fred Steel."

"Can you describe the two other men?" interrupted Anderson, quietly.

"One of them was a flashy-looking fellow of middle height, and the other —— "

"Was a tall, curly-haired, dark gentleman!" cried Anderson. "So he's on my track again."

"You are right," said the quadroon. "Do you know him?"

"I have seen him," replied Anderson, grinding his teeth. "Go on."

"Well, the first thing I heard the men say was that Anderson had taken passage in the steamer due that evening, and as she stopped nowhere on her route, he must come in on her that night. Then I listened, lying down behind some bales near them, and heard this dark gentlemen tell Steel he should be well paid if he put you under lock and key where you would be out of mischief for a while. Steel then took something from his pocket which must have been a warrant, and said your eyes should have a look at that the minute the vessel touched. The other men laughed at this, and one of them said you might prove a tough customer to handle for a single man. At this Steel took out a pair of hand-cuffs, and spoke about those being the things for fellows who resisted. The dark gentleman laughed again, and said your white hands would look fine in those bracelets, and then they all went away."

The "white hands" worked nervously as the boy continued.

"Oh!" cried Anderson, "why didn't I spring on him then and there, and choke him to death while he lay drugged." '

Mrs. Haynes was terrified at his passion, but she did not speak, and Sam resumed his story.

"I followed the men from the wharf to an office up-town, where they went in together. The name over the door was 'Richard Tovin, Esq., Counsellor at Law.' This must have been the smallest man of the party. I found a closet at the head of the stairs, and went into it, where I could hear all they said. They commenced to talk about you directly. The first words I heard were Steel's : 'What could have induced Anderson to murder him?" said he.

"*Him!*" cried Anderson, throwing up his hands. "*Him!* Then it was not *Her* that they would accuse me of murdering."

"It was for killing Harry, sir ; that is what they said."

It is wonderful to think of a man having cause for thankfulness when he hears that he is accused of murder in any shape. But Albert was so overcome to find it was not Ella, as he had supposed, that he felt quite happy for a moment.

"Thank God !" he cried. "I have no fears now. I never thought of Harry, but I see it all. It was not my darling girl, then, that they would accuse me of murdering. Thank God ! Thank God !" He wiped the first tears from his eyes that had been seen there in years. Mrs. Haynes, who had been crying all the time, burst out anew when she witnessed this unwonted sight, and there was silence for some minutes.

"I could learn nothing of the grounds for the charge," continued the quadroon, after a time, "but was sure you were to be arrested for murder when the steamer came in. This I was bound to prevent if I could, and I laid my plans then to row out and bring you off when you were coming into the Bay. After the men had gone out of the office I waited awhile and then went down to the street. Who should I find standing by the doorway, but that same dark gentleman !"

"Did he know you ?" asked Anderson.

"Yes, he knew me at once. 'Upon my soul,' said he, 'here is that boy of his now.' 'What boy ?' said I, pretending ignorance. 'Aren't you Anderson's boy ?' said he. 'O, no, not since last winter,' I said. 'Sure enough,' said he, as if remembering, 'I had forgotten that. Well, he won't need any boy long.' 'Why, he isn't going to die, is he !' said I, opening my eyes. He laughed, and said that depended on the toughness of his neck. Then I came away, glad to get rid of him, and hurried home as fast as I could."

Those "white hands" began to work again, and after a moment's pause, Sam continued :

"You know the rest," said he. "I rowed away from here at midnight, and found you eight miles away, dreaming, on deck. I hurried you off before you could resist, and here we are."

"You shall lose nothing by your faithfulness," Anderson replied. "Though I do not know but I would have done better to have gone in and faced the charge, instead of doing as I have, and appearing guilty by running away from it. I have a little temper of my own, however, and would prefer to give myself up, if necessary, rather than to be handcuffed and dragged to jail like a dog. If that man Steel, or Iron, or Brass, or whatever name it is, had tried that game, I fear there would have been two charges against me instead of one, before I left him."

"I knew how it would be," said Sam, smiling, and brought you off to avoid the possibility of such an event happening."

"What is to be done now?" asked Mrs. Haynes, nervously. "What would prevent them coming here to take you, Albert, should they find out where you are?"

"Nothing," said he, calmly, "unless I should take a fancy to resist. Then, I cannot answer for the end."

"Then you will not let them take you?" she cried in admiration.

"I think not," replied Anderson. "But we can tell better when they come. I am sorry for your sake that there is such a danger. If they should come, Luna will go up stairs with you, and stay till the question is settled below."

"Oh, Albert," cried Mrs. Haynes, "you must not run any danger of your life, promise me that. It is for Her sake I ask you. She would die were she to return and find you dead."

He was moved.

"I will try and think of what you say," he answered. "As a good citizen I ought to submit peaceably to the officers of the law, and I will try to do so. But, if they should attempt too much — I have a villainous temper — and should be apt to forget myself.

They have not come yet, though, and we should not anticipate evil."

"If they do come," whispered the quadroon, "you will find a boat in that direction" — pointing with his finger — "and can make for it should you desire. There is no disgrace, you know, in running from superior numbers. But I am quite sure they will not be here to-night, and we might as well go to sleep and rest."

A knock at the door gave him the lie, and the women hurried up stairs, while Anderson stepped into the next room. The silence of the next ten seconds was oppressive, when the knocking was repeated.

"Who is there?" asked the quadroon.

"Open the door," was the answer, the voice being that of Mr. Fred Steel.

"We have retired," said the quadroon, "and shall not open again to-night. So you might as well go."

"You cannot play with me," continued Steel. "You know who I am and what I want. I command you, therefore, in the name of the law, to give me admittance."

Matters were becoming grave. It was a high crime to refuse admission to an officer after such a summons, and Anderson did not wish to bring more trouble on the head of his devoted servant.

"Come away, Sam," he whispered, "I will see the men myself."

"You want a gentleman named Anderson, don't you?" he called to the men outside. "Well, that is my name, and I am at your service, provided you conduct yourself properly. Wait a moment, and I will admit you." He had his hand on the door-bolt to draw it back, when a scream from above stayed him.

"Ah!" he exclaimed. "Is that their game?"

Followed by the quadroon, he ran up stairs, and took in the situation there at a glance. While Steel had been parleying at the lower door, those valiant gentlemen, his companions, being no less then the dark gentleman and a friend of his connected with the law, Mr. Dick Tovin, had placed a ladder, and entered the upper story. It was their sudden advent that had called forth the scream referred to.

The appearance of Anderson's head above the stairway was the signal for Dick Tovin to make an ignominious and hasty retreat down the ladder from which he was just alighting. The dark gentleman, however, in his exultation at having, as he thought, got Anderson now safely in hand, and being under the partial influence of several glasses of champaigne, had evidently misunderstood the situation entirely. For his first act on getting inside the window was to seize the arm of the pretty octoroon, and commence to cover her face with kisses, to her intense disgust; Mrs. Haynes looking on in the meantime with an expression of horror, and both ladies giving utterance to scream after scream with surprising volubility.

In the height of passion, some men seem to be endowed with the strength of a dozen ordinary persons. Anderson was one of these. With a bound he was at Hawley's side, and in an instant he had him spinning across the room as though a hurricane had struck him. The dark gentleman would have made a struggle had he been given time, but he had none. Catching him up as though he had been an infant, Anderson walked to the open window, and without a thought of the distance from the ground, tossed him out like a piece of wood.

All this occupied less than a minute, but before he had time to take breath, a new foe was upon him. Steel had been informed by Tovin of the turn affairs were taking, and came springing up the ladder. Anderson had no wish to show further fight, and he only cried "Good-by!" rushed down stairs, out of the house, and ran for the boat.

Steel was an active man and as brave as a lion. He was accounted the best officer on the force, and had been detailed for this duty on that very account. He never had a partner in a case, preferring to reap his honors alone, and had refused proffered assistance from his brothers that evening. He comprehended that his man had determined on flight, and started after him at full speed. As Anderson left the house, the Detective was but a few rods behind him, and the race was closely contested from that time.

There was something repugnant in the idea of running from his pursuer, and Anderson had half a mind to stop and end the question of strength at once. He was thinking of this when Steel called out, breathless with running——

"Stop, or as I live, I'll fire on you!

The Detective's injunction was obeyed sooner than he expected, for Anderson, bringing to use his long-forgotten tricks of Indian-fighting, halted with a jerk, and stooped down to the ground. The next minute, the Detective, unable to stop himself in his flight, was lying half-stunned, with Anderson's fingers on his throat. The revolver he had carried was thrown whizzing into the sea, and the hand-cuffs he had designed for his prisoner were locked tightly on his own wrists.

Anderson had not accomplished this without putting forth much strength. Indeed, it was a question at first who would come off victorious. But he had been roused to a frenzy of anger, and when his blood was up he was a match for any man.

The boat was lying there within ten feet of the men. Anderson dragged Steel to the boat and lifted him in, still keeping that fearful clasp on his throat. A cord attached to one end of the boat served to lash about the Detective's legs and feet, and the young man pushed off before either had uttered a word. Steel was the first to speak.

"Do you realize what you are doing, Mr. Anderson?" he asked, breathing heavily.

"I think I do," was the quiet reply.

"Don't you see," continued Steel, "That such resistance cannot last forever! The law cannot be trifled with in this way. You had better release me, and give yourself up peaceably. You ought to have a better appreciation of the duties of a good citizen, Mr. Anderson."

"It seems to me you have an unusually good opinion of *murderers*," said Anderson, ironically, bending himself to his oars. "Death is the penalty of my crime, I believe, when I am found guilty. Think you I would give up peaceably to that fate?"

"But you claim you are innocent, of course," ventured Steel, hardly knowing what to say.

"Why 'of course,' my friend? Besides, even if I am innocent, where are my proofs? I understand I am accused of killing Harry, my clerk. It is not likely I can produce him, and how else can I make a defence? No one is anxious for death, I believe. *You* aren't, now, I dare say."

Believing firmly that he was dealing with a man whose hands were already imbrued in human blood, the Detective looked up uneasily as he heard this question.

"What! You do not mean to drown me?" he cried.

"I don't know about that," said Anderson. "It might do some good to drop you overboard, and a man can hang but once, they say. You have been seeking my life, to-night, why should I not take yours? Nothing could be easier. Many a man has been murdered and thrown over here, I have no doubt."

The Detective thought a moment.

"Well," he said at length, "I am in your hands. If you choose to kill me I have no remedy. There is a wife and children at home who will miss me, but I shall not beg my life."

Anderson put his up oars for a moment, and kneeled by the side of the prostrate man.

"Come," said he, "enough of this silly talk. I admire you, Steel, and have given your bravery a good test. I am half disposed now to give myself up, lest you be laughed at for allowing a prisoner to escape; but I hardly think I can afford to do that. I will put you ashore where you can be easily found, and say good-by to you for the present. You are a brave man, and at some future day, after this plot against me is cleared up, we may meet on better terms. It is no disgrace to be vanquished by Albert Anderson, and your chief will tell you so. Next time you go after me take other company than blacklegs and scoundrels, and you will have better luck."

Taking up the oars again, Anderson rowed quietly but swiftly to the nearest shore. It was some miles from the docks, and he rowed upon the sand unobserved. He pulled the boat up high on the shore, and covered the Detective with a mat which lay in the bottom.

"There!" he said, as he left him, "you will be quite comfortable till daybreak, which can't be far off. There will be plenty of passers then whom you can call to. If I dared I would take off your bonds, but that you could hardly expect. Good-by, my brave fellow, till we meet again."

Anderson walked very fast after he left the Detective, and studied deeply on what course he had better take next. When he had labored most at his books, he had hailed adventures of any sort with delight. Experiments, however dangerous, were ever welcome. Experiments in Love and Literature he had in full abundance. Now here was a great experiment in Law. Yes. He determined to make the most of it, trusting in fate for his proofs of innocence. Thus thinking, he walked swiftly on toward where the lights of the outer city were looming into view.

CHAPTER VI.

HENRY WALDEN MAKES A MISTAKE.

A God-send had come to Walden in the shape of a piece of gossip, and the good people hailed its advent with unusual delight. It was whispered about first, and then spoken of openly, and then finally became the talk of the town. Why had Walden, Jr., taken to visiting the hotel so much of late? Why had he become so thoughtful and abstracted in his ways? Why did he confound the terms good-evening and good-morning when he was accosted by his friends upon the street? Why was he changed within a few weeks from a lively, careless young man, to a sober, steady, thoughtful one? Why, reasoned the old ladies and the young ladies and the rest of Walden, but that he had fallen desperately in love with the pretty stranger at the Hudson House.

That is — they were not all agreed on the word *pretty*; by no means. Some said she might have been were there more color in her cheeks, or if she were a little taller; or if some other *if* were different from what it was. The village girls began all at once to remember that they had not called on Carrie Hudson for a long time, and to make up for their negligence immediately. For several weeks the little parlor used by the family was turned into a public reception room. Ella could not help noticing the close attention which was given her, but she only thought it the usual curiosity to make the acquaintance of a stranger. She was uniformly pleasant and courteous to all who called, but made no particular friends among them. It would do no good, she said, when she was to remain in Walden but so short a time.

The young misses who called first to obtain a view of Ella were immediately exalted to the posts of informers-in-general to the rest of the community. The young men of the village began to take an interest in the matter, and their sweethearts were obliged to use their most persuasive arts to keep them within bounds.

At last, when the rumor began to circulate that Walden, Jr., was already the favored one, he became at once the target for scores of envious eyes, every time he made his appearance upon the street. Exactly why this jealous feeling should have arisen in the hearts of these young men, is a difficult problem to solve. For not more than half a dozen of them had ever seen Miss Hastings, and but one — a butcher's boy with a red head and freckled face, whom nobody would have thought of calling a rival — had been admitted to her presence ; and he testified on the same evening that the event took place, to having been so completely overcome by finding her in the kitchen when he entered, that he was constrained to cast down his eyes directly, and never once raised them until he was out of the house again. But the young men were determined to be jealous, and persevered in their scowls at Walden, Jr. ; who, very happily for himself, was totally ignorant of the fact, on account of the abstracted state of mind into which he had fallen.

It was no wonder that Henry Walden, Jr., had fallen into a state of mental abstraction. From the evening when he first met Ella Hastings, he constituted himself her protector and advisor. He became deeply interested in her unfriended condition, and strove to make her way as pleasant as he could. He brought books to solace her leisure hours. He bought new music for her to play on Carrie's ancient piano. He came often to see her, and she always looked the better and brighter after his visits, he was so engaging and pleasant in his ways. He came after a time with his carriage, and with some hesitation she accepted his invitation to take short rides, with himself and Carrie. She knew he would prefer that the third person were left out of the party,

but she was firm when he hinted his wish ; and they rode together when she went at all.

When Mr. Walden, Sen.'s venerable ears began to hear the tidings of his son's infatuation, he revolved the matter in his virtuous heart, and decided the thing must be brought to a stop then and there. And he took occasion to broach the subject at their next meeting.

"What is this I hear, Henry, about you and the young woman down at Hudson's ?" he inquired, addressing Walden, Jr.

"Sir !" stammered Henry, startled out of a deep reverie by the question.

Mr. Walden, Sen., repeated his interrgation.

"That depends on what it is you hear,' replied Henry after consideration.

"Well, sir, I hear that you are extremely attentive in that direction, and have even taken the young woman out to ride. How is that ?" Mr. Walden, the elder, sat back in his chair and waited, with the air of a man who had already decided the question in his own mind, and was constituting himself judge and jury, simply as a matter of form.

"I did take Miss Hastings to ride, certainly," stammered Henry.

"Then I must say you have done wrong, my boy—quite wrong," said Mr. Walden. "It is a bad beginning and shall be discontinued at once."

"Why !" exclaimed Henry, looking at his father. "What can you have against such a very estimable young lady as Miss Hastings !"

"Ah, nothing in particular *against* her, " replied Mr. Walden, musing, "though, by-the-way, I think she has not been out to church since she came here. "

"Ah, but she is in a strange place," said Henry, eagerly, "and of course did not like to go out at first among so many new people."

"No excuse at all," said Mr. Walden, decidedly. "She should think too much of her duty to let such considerations come in the way. I always go to church no matter where I am on Sunday."

There was no difference between a burly man of sixty and this little shrinking creature of eighteen!

"Is that the only reason you have for not liking Miss Hastings?" Henry asked, after a pause.

"I haven't said I did not *like* her," corrected Mr. Walden; "only that I did not wish you to continue to—visit her so much. You must understand what I mean, Henry. I don't wish you to make a love affair out of the case, and your only safety is in giving up going to see the girl altogether."

"Oh, father!" cried Henry, "you do not mean that. Surely you would not seek to influence me in such matters at my age. I cannot allow it, at any rate. You are asking too much, and I must decline to obey such a very strange request."

"Indeed!" said Mr. Walden, severely. "Then you acknowledge yourself in love with this girl, do you?"

"I acknowledge nothing, sir. Miss Hastings is one of the best young ladies I have ever seen, and is well educated and accomplished. Her only fault is in being poor, and that is nothing in my eyes. Were I, as you say, in love with her, it is extremely doubtful whether my suit would be successful. She is proud, as she may well be, with her beauty and graces, and can marry whom she will."

"Proud!" repeated the old gentleman, with surprise. "Did you say she might be too proud to marry *you?* What! Too proud!"—he stopped as if unable to comprehend the idea— "too proud to marry *my* son! Well, I never heard the like!"

"I wish I knew she was not, father," said Henry with a sigh.

"Too proud!" continued Mr. Walden, amazed with the thought. "Does she know who you are, and who your family is? Does she know there are no people in the State who stand higher than we? Does she know how much you will be worth, when I am — dead? Too proud, indeed!"

"Perhaps, father," ventured Henry, "she would not care for all these things, if she knew them. Perhaps she thinks an honest heart of more value than money. Perhaps—I say —she would not reckon your wealth at all in weighing out my account, were I to ask her to-morrow to be my bride."

This view of the subject was so wholly out of the power of Mr. Walden's mind to understand, that he left it and took another tack.

"How far has this matter gone?" he asked.

"Only so far that I have learned to esteem Miss Hastings very highly, and, I believe, to love her sincerely. I have never uttered a word to her on the subject, however."

"Then you had better not," said the old gentleman, persuasively. "Of course, you do not mean to marry against my will, and I should never give my consent to this union. You must marry nearer your station, Henry, and had better give up this attachment without further delay."

But this Henry Walden, Jr., refused to do, and the father left his son in a passion, giving him to understand that if he persisted in his intention, he need expect nothing more from him. The young man was too much excited to trust himself to make a reply just then, and so the matter remained.

The ways in which news spreads over a small village are past finding out, but the medium rivals the telegraph in activity. It is probable that one of Mr. Walden's servants overheard the above conversation, and casually narrated it anew to her friend who lived with somebody else; that the friend took occasion to repeat it with embellishments to another friend, who happened to mention it in conversation with an employe of the Hudson House; and that the latter personage told it to Carrie, knowing that Mr. Walden, Jr., was in the habit of calling at the hotel. Be this as it may, Miss Hudson certainly knew of the affair before a dozen hours had elapsed, and for want of better means of passing her time, went directly and told the whole story to Ella.

If Mr. Walden, Sen., had only seen the way in which Miss Hastings received this information, he might have rubbed his hands in glee, and given up all further fears of his son's marrying " below his station."

And if Mr. Walden, Jr., had seen it, he might have found there a rock on which all his wild hopes were drifting, there to be wrecked and shivered to atoms.

When Harry came that evening, Ella asked him to tell her without equivocation, whether it was true that he had spoken thus of her with his father. He replied with an earnest protestation of love, but she stayed him.

"Mr. Walden," she said, "please do not say more. It can never be, and you will understand why, some day. You would pain me deeply by such an avowal as you were designing to make. I shall soon leave this village and perhaps never see you afterwards. I am very sorry if I have ever led you to suppose that I regarded you in any other light than that of a very kind friend, whom I shall always respect and bless. Our acquaintance has been very pleasant to me and I shall remember it with feelings of happiness. But further than this, I do assure you, there must be nothing."

"I will say no more, as you request it," said Walden, Jr., deeply disappointed by her reply. "But you will not take from me my other position—that of trusted friend? You will still give me leave to advise and assist you, Miss Ella?"

"I will say yes, provided you take care not to mention this forbidden subject again," said Ella, after thinking a few moments. "I have a purpose in life that you only have an ink'ing of and it cannot be set aside. Within a short time I must leave Walden, perhaps never to return. It will be useless to try to dissuade me. When I am ready to go I will send for you to say farewell."

"Your conditions are hard," he pleaded.

"Mr. Walden," she cried, desperately, "you think you love me, now. What if I were to tell you that you one day would hate yourself for having spoken to one so low? It is well you were warned in time!" Ella's face became flushed with shame as she spoke.

"What can you mean?" he cried, shocked by her words. "You are trying to make me dislike you by falsely accusing yourself, but it is useless. I shall ever believe you the purest and best of women, come what may to cast stains upon you. Miss Hastings, if you are resolved to abide by to-night's decision, I will be the last one to recall the memory, in your presence, of this hope that was in my heart. But do not try to make me hate you, for that I cannot do."

"We will still continue friends," said Ella, giving him her hand as he rose to go.

"Ever and always friends," he repeated.

"You will forgive me the pain I have unintentionally caused you?" asked Ella.

"*Ah, God!* Ten thousand times — yes!"

"Good-night," he said, kissing her hand.

"Good-night," she answered, huskily, as she closed the door.

Then she went to her room and prayed God to bless Harry Walden. To make the blow she had cast on his head a light one. To give him some day a loving woman, worthy of him, for his wife. To keep him from hating *her*, when her full guilt was brought to his ears. And to reward him for his kindness to her — a stranger.

She could not pray for Albert in set words. But she had in her breast a prayer for him always, and who can say it did not rise as high toward heaven as any spoken from the lips.

"Poor Bert! Dear, darling Bert!" She had never regretted her great sacrifice, for she was sure he must be now on the highway to fame and greatness. Before he knew her, he was a steady worker at his pen, and now he must have gone back to his old occupation. Had she known, alas! that he was at that moment under a ban as a taker of human life, who can say what might have been the consequences?

There was another prayer that now ascended hourly from her breast — a prayer for his unborn babe! A prayer that she might live through her trial to see its face, and cherish it for his dear sake.

Time passed on, and Ella began to make her preparations for removing. Her condition was not suspected by any one as yet, but she dared not remain longer. Her small store of money had suffered but little under the kind roof of the Hudsons, and she stood in no fear of present want. Her few articles of dress were packed ready for going, and she began the work of saying farewell to her good friends. Walden, Jr., came among the rest, and Ella gave him her hand with tears in her eyes. He begged her never to forget her promise to send for him could he ever be of service to her. She promised again to do so, and he left her.

The Hudsons were much attached to Ella, and were very sorry to have her leave them. They had never learned from whence she came to them, and she declined to say in which direction she was going. They asked her to write, and to come and live with them again should she ever wish to do so. But she replied, while thanking them kindly for their offer, that promises were liable to be broken, and would not bind herself to anything. When the stage-coach came, the same ruddy-faced driver who had opened his door with such great officiousness to help her out four months before, handed her in with a touch of his former gallantry, and amid a general waving of handkerchiefs from the hotel, she was driven away.

As she rode out of the village, a gentleman appeared by the roadside, and signalled to the driver to stop. It was Henry Walden, Jr.

"I am going with you as far as the railroad," he said, entering the coach. "It is a shame that you should leave us unattended, in this manner."

She thanked him for his thoughtfulness, and they rode on silently together. When the town in which was the station drew near, she broke the stillness.

"Mr. Walden," she said, "I know you will never appreciate the deep regard I have for you, and I cannot expect that you should. My present conduct is inexplicable, I have no doubt, but no choice is left me. Will you be kind enough to accept this ring?"—taking one from her finger—"and keep it in remembrance of those days when you knew only good of Ella Hastings."

He took the ring from her as if it were a priceless treasure. It was an amethyst set in gold, but he did not care for its value. It had been on *her* finger, and he told her on this account he should prize it above everything he possessed. She smiled a little at this and reminded him that such thoughts were forbidden. Then, at the station, they parted again.

"Did you wish to go North or South?" asked the obliging ticket master, as she drew forth her portemonnaie.

She did not know at first, and thought over it a moment. She might die in the trial that was before her. The North was cold, and she could not think of being buried there. She would take a ticket for the South, if he pleased.

She took passage on the next train for a large city to the Southward, and from there she proceeded, after some inquiry, to a small town on the hills, fifty miles further on. There was another stage-ride before she reached her journey's end. Then she was welcomed by a rosy-cheeked girl of little more than her own age, who appeared to be the mistress of the house. She was shown a room, and made her first equivocation as she wrote her name on the register — "*Mrs.* Ella Hastings."

CHAPTER VII.

A NEW PROBLEM OF LIFE.

Five months more have gone, and are reckoned with the past. September is here with its heat, and the sickle of the reaper cuts down the ripened grain that stretches for miles over the hills and valleys. The orchard boughs hang loaded with luscious fruit, and the birds flit among them, singing to each other. The cattle stand at mid-day under the shade-trees, panting, with the hot sun's rays upon them. The sheaves of wheat stand in even rows upon the dry stubble where they sprang to life. The old farm house tavern, shaded by its massive elms, is the coolest place to be seen upon the landscape. In one of its large, airy chambers, there are gathered a little company of three, two ladies and one gentleman, who stand with sober looks about a bed. On the bed there lies a young woman — only eighteen — unconscious; and by her side an infant sleeps.

"How is she getting along, Doctor?" asks the elder of the two ladies, in a whisper.

"Oh, so-so," says the Doctor, declining to commit himself. "It is a close case if she lives, though, Mrs. Langdon. A close case if she lives, in my opinion."

"Is it as bad as that?" asked the younger lady, in dismay.

"I fear so," replied the physician, gravely. "There is trouble here that I cannot remedy, Miss Slader. Trouble with the mind, I mean. There is more to the young woman's story than you have heard, depend upon it. If she is to be saved, it must be by setting her mind at rest, when she recovers consciousness. We can do nothing but that, except what has been done."

"What was the poor child's story," asked Mrs. Langdon, pityingly.

"She came here early in May," said Sallie Slader, "and registered her name as Mrs. Hastings. She has always avoided company, and has kept her room a great deal, even taking her meals there. She has been very quiet and pleasant to everybody, and we have all liked her very much. I attempted to ask her about herself, once or twice, but seeing that she avoided the subject, I did not press it. She always paid her bills promptly, and there are handsome dresses and jewelry in her trunks that show she has been well provided for. When she first became sick, I asked her what I was to do, and she told me to stay by her until she was well again, which I promised. Then she said 'If I die and the child dies, you must bury us both together. If I die and the child lives, sell my jewelry and get it a home somewhere.' I asked her if her husband was living, and she cried out 'O, no, no! Dead long ago! Believe me, he is dead, and it will be useless to look for him.' She clung to me so as she said this, that I had to comfort her by saying I did believe her. That was all she ever said to me about it."

The doctor looked very grave.

"It is a sad matter," said he, shaking his head, "and one that is too common, I fear. Well, if women will be fools, who's going to be able to stop them?" He looked around as if expecting an answer to the question from his hearers; but as they were unable, very strangely, to account for a fact which has puzzled mankind for six thousand years, they said nothing.

The infant awoke and commenced to cry. Mrs. Langdon took it up in a motherly way and soon quieted it. The babe was nearly two months old, and was in a much more hopeful state than his young mother, who had suddenly relapsed into a sinking condition, and could not be roused sufficiently to understand that her child was in danger of starvation if she did not care for it. Had it not been for the fortunate presence in the neighborhood of the wet nurse, Mrs Langdon, it is not impossible that such an end might have come to the young cause of all this trouble.

Not that the Cause was in any sense to blame for the trouble he *had caused*, which is, to be sure, a strange statement to throw upon the public. The poor baby was happily unaware of the fact that he was in imminent danger of being left motherless, or even that he had any mother to lose. He could not know that his father was flying from the officers of the law, and that a high reward was set over his head. He had no knowledge of the fact that he was liable to be thrown in his helplessness upon a cold, cruel world. Well, it was better so.

Mrs. Langdon rocked with the child in a low chair near the window, while the Doctor and Sallie sat by quietly talking. The Doctor was a young man, of five-and-thirty perhaps, and a bachellor. He had often revolved a certain idea in his mind, as he entered his lonely lodgings of a night, and the same idea was in his mind now. He wondered if this idea ever entered Sallie Slader's head, and determined to find out definitely one of these days. He was, therefore, very sociable, and was trying with all his powers to make a good impression on the girl.

Suddenly there came a sound from the lips of the young woman in the bed. They looked in surprise to see her sitting upright, with eyes wide open, brows knit, hair streaming, and her white robe seeming like a shroud, as she held forth her hands toward the nurse.

"*Give me my child!*" she cried.

Mrs. Langdon looked at the Doctor for instructions. That gentleman rose, and walked to the bed. He was not certain his patient was in her right mind, and indeed she was not. But he saw only abstraction in her face — there was no danger there. And he said pleasantly, that she should have the child, oh, yes! And whispering to the nurse to watch the mother carefully, he took the babe and laid it in her outstretched arms.

For a moment she clasped the little form close to her breast, gazing into the face with a troubled look that showed her mind to be disordered. Then, looking up again, she viewed the Doctor with distrust in her features, and assuming an imperative tone, exclaimed briefly,

"Who are you?"

He replied in a soothing tone that he was the Doctor. Did she not remember that he had been there before when she was sick?

"What were you doing with my baby?"

"Why, bless her heart, nothing, but feeding it. That was all."

"*Feeding it!*" She looked at him in supreme contempt. But the words did have a meaning in her mind, though it was clouded, and she placed the child at her breast, where it might find its natural sustenance.

"Don't you think I can feed my own baby?" she said, haughtily, and rocked in the bed slowly, lovingly hushing the child to rest. It was a sight that might have melted any heart — this beautiful young mother holding her babe so jealously; and being but human, Mrs. Langdon cried; and Sallie cried; and the Doctor hemmed softly to himself, as he walked to one of the open windows.

"Ah!" cried Ella, perceiving it. "You may as well cry, all of you. It will do you good. But you can't have my baby; no indeed!" She lifted the child up, and looked at its face again. "Yes," she continued, "it's mine. I was afraid you had changed it for another." She looked suspiciously at the doctor and the nurse and then her eyes fell on Sallie.

"You—girl!" she cried, addressing her in a whisper, "I know you. Come here. I am not afraid of you." Sallie came and sat down on the bed. Ella looked at her sharply with those troubled eyes, and becoming reassured, took her into confidence. "Those people are plotting against me all the time, Sallie. See! They are whispering now about my baby. *My* baby! *Bert's* baby!"

Bert's baby! thére was a clue for the Doctor, and he resolved to try it.

"Bert?" he asked, "Who is *Bert?*"

Ella regarded him steadily for a moment, and then began to comprehend his question. "Oh, no," she cried. "You will never get that secret from me. Never! Never! This is his baby, but he must not know it. He does not dream of his baby's existence. Poor, darling Bert?"

"If you should die," urged the doctor, persuasively, "would you not want Bert to know, so he could take the child, and care for it?"

"He — Bert — take the baby! Ah, no. It would ruin all I have tried to do, for him were people to know of this. If I die, baby will die, too, and they will make one grave for us both."

She was firm about this, and the Doctor's arguments were of no avail. She would appeal so touchingly to Sallie, that the kind-hearted girl could do little but cry, and assure her no one wanted to do her harm. At length she become tired out, and consented to lie down, with the child close to her bosom. Sallie watched her carefully, lest her mood might change, but she continued to lie very still, and finally fell into a quiet slumber. The Doctor left some powders to be given by-and-by, and went away, promising to call around once more in the evening. Sallie took a book and tried to read a little while her charges were sleeping, but in a few minutes she was startled and chilled by a dreadful, unearthly cry. She sprang up, and calling to Mrs. Langdon, who was in another room, threw her whole strength upon the crazed girl in the bed. The nurse came running in, caught the child up and laid it in a cradle, and then lent her assistance to Sallie, who, strong as she was, had undertaken a task above her powers. A boy was despatched for Mr. Slader, and when the landlord arrived, the lad was ordered to go in all haste for the doctor.

Samuel Slader was a strong man, but he had his match in the delicate little creature lying in that bed. It was only by the strongest exertions that he was able to control her, in the convulsions which lent her an unnatural strength. Every minute she would utter those paralyzing cries, and spring with fury at some haunting phantom.

The Doctor came in haste, and when he saw his patient, he looked graver than ever. A quieting preparation was produced, and Ella's lips were forced open to compel her to swallow it. When this began to operate, the struggles became less violent, and when it had done its full work, she lay quite still on the bed.

The Doctor sat by the bed-side, and heard the moans of the sick girl with a darkened brow.

"It is very bad, Miss Slader," he whispered, in reply to an inquiry from Sallie. "If we could only quiet her mind, she might recover. But while she is possessed of this fear, she can make no progress." So the evening wore on. Not daring to give any more of the opiate, unless it should prove imperative, the Doctor and Sallie sat gloomily watching for the sick girl to awake.

It was past the midnight hour when she first began to show consciousness. The Doctor had been quite satisfied with his vigil, as long as the pretty object of his love was with him, and had heard contentedly the solemn ticking of the eight-day clock, and the tolling of the hours from the church steeples. The round moon shed its light softly over the old tavern, and a whip-poor-will's note broke the stillness at intervals. The poor girl lay there in the hushed room, with her spirit hovering between this world and the next. Where was he — where was the man who should have been at her side in this hour? Alas, that they should have been separated by the babe, whose very existence should have joined them more closely together!

When Ella first gave signs of life, she asked in a troubled voice where she was, and then where was her baby. Being shown the child in its cradle, sleeping peacefully, she asked to take it. They dared not refuse her in her weak condition, and the child was placed in her arms. Passing a hand carefully over its face, and listened to its breathing in a doubting way, and placing an ear close to its heart, satisfied her, and she gave it back to them, murmuring that it was not dead, as she had feared. Then she looked up, and recognized the Doctor. This was a favorable sign.

"O, you are the Physician," said she.

"Yes, yes," he said, smiling. "I am doing all I can for you, Mrs. Hastings. You must be very still, now, and we will bring you through all right."

"Am I very sick?"

"You have been, but we trust you are recovering. If you would only let us send word to the baby's father, now," said he, insinuatingly, "you would be in no further danger."

A shadow passed over her features.

"No," she replied, firmly. "I can die, if it comes to that, but I will not give up to that request."

She grew weaker as morning drew near, and the Doctor began to feel his old fears.

"If she continues in this way," he remarked aside to the ladies, "she will be but a short time for this world. Had you not better send for a minister to talk with her about death, and prepare her soul for the change, if it is to come?"

It could do no harm, at any rate, they said, and perhaps a clergyman might have more influence than they could. A boy was sent accordingly to the nearest parsonage, and returned in about an hour with an old gentleman, who had the appearance of being almost wholly concealed by a pair of spectacles which he wore on his nose. He always looked *over* the spectacles when he wanted to see anything, and retired behind them as though they were a fortress, when he chose to make himself invisible. He had a sleepy appearance, and carried a ponderous Bible, which in his grasp looked more murderous than did ever a surgeon's knife. With this book he had come prepared to probe the patient's spiritual wounds if she remained quiet, or to subject her to vivisection should she resist. It was bad enough to be woke up, and compelled to leave his bed at that hour of the night, but now he *was* up, he proposed to occupy the time to advantage. Here was a human soul drifting to perdition, and, by the account of the other physician, very near its journey's end. Hell was already yawning for its prey! He, as a minister of the Church, must plunge in and save her.

"Who are you, sir?" asked Ella, uneasily, as she saw the clergyman standing by her bed-side.

"'I am the Resurrection and the Life,'" read the Minister, from the book in his hands, as though he were replying. His strange manner puzzled the sick girl, and her mind began to wander again. But what mattered this? her soul was going to perdition all the same. He read on for a while, although he could see that she did not understand a word.

"My young friend," said he, as he closed the Holy Book, "will you accept Christ as your Saviour?"

An affirmative answer would have relieved him of all responsibility, and he could have gone home satisfied that his duty had been performed. But the reply she did give startled and shocked him:

"*I had rather have Bert!*"

"What does she mean?" inquired the clergyman, turning to the Doctor.

"She refers to the child's father," said the Doctor. "That is the only name she has ever called him by in our presence."

"Yes," said Ella, catching the idea, though her mind was wandering again. "The child's father. My Bert, my darling Bert. The only name I know him by."

This was shocking.

"Don't you love the Saviour, my child?" asked the minister, after a doubtful pause.

"Love!" she knew that word. "Ah yes, I love *him*, — Bert. Love him! My Bert! I shall always love him."

The minister nodded gloomily to the group, as if to say, "This soul is lost without doubt, but I shall try once more to save it from perdition."

"My young friend," he began, "Do you know that Jesus died for you?"

"Jesus? Jesus? Oh, yes. As we used to sing in the school:

"Jesus, lover of my soul,
   Let me to Thy bosom fly!"

She sang the words in a low tone, and the clergyman was constrained to think she was improving. She was so strange in her answers, and sang so sweetly, that the ladies' handkerchiefs came out and were assigned to duty at their eyes again.

"Then you accept Jesus as your Saviour?" said the minister, interrog-atively. The point must turn in the former question now.

"No," she replied promptly. "Bert said there was no Saviour, and I know he is always right. I do not believe it."

Poor girl! She had Anderson's theological views sadly confused to come to that conclusion.

"Doesn't your Bert believe in the Bible?" cried the clergyman, aghast.

Ella laughed softly to herself, and bowed abstractly.

"He believes one text," she replied. "Shall I tell you what one? It is very easy to remember when you try; and so very short:

'*Love one another.*'"

The minister came out from behind his spectacles and spoke:

"I will say, my good people," he said, "that in all my contact with sinners, I never met with so hardened a case as this girl. It is a waste of time to speak with her. I fear she is a lost soul. Good-night.

Although the minister had chosen to say "I *fear* she is a lost soul," his tone indicated a stronger feeling in the matter. And after he had been shown down stairs, Mrs. Langdon was moved to state that if it placed her reputation as a Christian at stake, she would say that she thought a man in his position, should know more than to try and frighten a poor, weak lamb in that way. And that, in her opinion, the poor, dear lamb was just as good, and just as likely to go to heaven, as he was.

This rank heresy was seconded by Sallie and the Doctor, and the latter declared that the poor lamb should die in peace, if she must die, and not be pestered by any more glum-faced ministers.

The morning light peeped in at the windows, and Ella was pronounced much better. She began from that time to grow stronger, and passed her time caring for her child, when she was able to sit up in a chair. But her kind friends saw with pain that her mind was still confused, and often she would find much difficulty in comprehending what was said to her. She was always mild and gentle, but her recovery was by no means perfect. Her world seemed, as it were, narrowed by her illness to three persons, " Bert, baby and I."

The child grew finely, and was as well as an infant could be. Ella gave the love she had in store for Albert, to his baby. She loved to think — when she thought intelligently at all --- that the baby was going to look like Bert when he became a man. Then she should see Bert always in the person of his baby. But it was so many, many years to wait !

On warm days she began to take a fancy to go out of doors, and find some sunny slope where she could sit, and spread a blanket on the grass for baby. It was a pretty picture to see them together there, and many a traveller felt his heart softened as his glance fell on them, while riding by in the highway. Samuel Slader — the avaricious — saw them often, from the windows of his shop, but his only interest in them was to see that the weekly account was squared of a Saturday. Ella always took out her portemonnaie when the day came, and handed a bill to Sallie, putting back the change, if there was any, without any idea, except that it was a proceeding made necessary in some way she could not understand.

One day, while sitting in her room, for it was getting colder, she saw the figure of an old man enter the yard, and walk slowly toward the house. She was sure she had never seen the man before, but for some reason her heart rose into her throat, and she trembled at sight of him. The old man happened to glance at the window as she sprang up and hurriedly retired to the other end of the room. He started violently, and almost fell to the ground with the shock it gave him. He stood gazing at the window, but the sight he had seen was gone.

"Strange!" he muttered, drawing breath, as he passed into the tavern. "How these visions do come to perplex one!"

The vision he thought he saw was of a beautiful girl, holding a babe at the window; the light of the setting sun shining calmly on the pair, and mellowing into golden lustre the rich, wavy hair which hung from the fairest of heads. A beautiful face he thought he had known, and then, it had vanished, to be seen no more.

Wiping the clammy sweat which rose to his forehead, the old man entered the low doorway, and sat down in one of the small stalls provided for travellers who desired lunches. The other stalls were occupied by young men of the neighborhood, who had dropped in toward evening to indulge in a glass of liquor or a game of cards. The old man was greeted with a stare by these young men, but he paid no attention to them, and quietly called for his supper.

He was a travel stained old man, with dusty coat, dusty hat, dusty shoes, and dusty face and hands. He wore a long gray beard, that might have once been red, and his hair was of a grizzled shade. He ate his meal in silence, and when he had finished, paid the bill, and went away. As he passed out of the door a young man entered it, meeting him squarely, and looked in surprised recognition at his face. But the old man avoided his gaze, and hurried down the street. As the other entered the bar-room, the young men sitting at the tables sprang up and gave him a hearty welcome.

"Hallo, Charlie! When did you get home?" was the cry.

"Only last night," said Charlie, shaking hands all around. "How are you, Mr. Slader? Now, boys, you know there's nothing suits me like a bet, and if you like, I'll make you one right off. What say you?"

"Yes! Yes! Give us the bet," cried all.

"Well, you saw the old man who just went out of here."

"Yes! Yes! What of him?"

"I will bet you what you like that he was not an old man at all."

"Not an old man!" cried the party in surprise.

"I will bet he is not an old man, but a young man in disguise."

A paltry sum was staked, and Charlie proceeded:

"There is a man living in a city not a thousand miles from here," began Charlie, "who took a notion once to disguise himself and go about the country, to see life in various phases. For instance, he would go as a beggar, or whatever trade he wanted to learn about. He was rich enough without work, and only did this for pleasure. It seems he has begun the thing again, though he pretended to give it up several years ago. That was the man whom I met in the doorway. He was pretty well disguised, but I knew him, though he tried not to have me see his face. Who do you think it was?"

"Tell us," cried the young men.

"It was no one less than the talented author—James Albert Anderson!"

Samuel Slader sprang over the counter with an oath, and caught the boy by the shoulder.

"Are you insane, or are you telling the truth?" he cried, almost foaming at the mouth. "Albert Anderson, the author! Look you, at that bill there! Do you see? Heavens and earth! *Five thousand dollars Reward!* Are you *sure* it was Anderson?"

"*Sure?* As I am of my life."

Samuel Slader waited to hear no more. With a cry more like that of a wild beast than a human being, he rushed madly down the steet. The rest of the company followed at full speed, as soon as they could collect their scattered wits. The whole pack of them ran like so many wolves, down the road—up another hill—and down into the valley again—ran until they were breathless, and dirty and tired out; spurred on by those talismanic words—*five thousand dollars*. But there was not a sign to be seen of their prey. No one had noticed him, and in an hour they came back, Slader at the'r head, swearing like a madman. Harnessing a horse, he drove at a break-neck speed to the city and gave in his story, hoping to get some portion of the reward, when the Detectives should find their man; and cursing his ill luck to let such a sum of money slip, almost literally, through his fingers.

The Detectives came out and beat through every bush for miles and miles. They searched in every shed and barn for leagues. But they found no old man with a long, gray beard, and went home with only their labor for their pains.

CHAPTER VIII.

DARKER DAYS FOR ANDERSON.

"It is very dangerous for you to remain here, Albert. The officers have been watching the house night and day for weeks, and I fear every moment they have discovered your hiding place. Do go, Albert, and find peace in some more distant place, where you can stay unmolested until we get news of Harry. You must come out all right at last, but now, when here is a reward offered for you, and appearances are so heavily against you, I think you ought to try and save yourself while there is time."

It was Mrs. Haynes who spoke, and as she uttered the words, her hand was placed affectionately upon the shoulder of a young man, dressed in a rough cloak and cap, and with a short beard upon his face. Besides this young man, there were present in the room the quadroon boy Sam and and a stranger. The latter gentleman was a man of middle age, and might as well be introduced at once: Reuben Harvard, Esq., of the Bar — a gentleman well known as a lawyer of ability; at the present engaged on the case of James Albert Anderson, accused of the murder of his partner, Harry Johnson. The meeting between the parties is being held in a retired room at Pearl Street, 114.

"The danger of arrest is no longer a trouble to me," replied the young man. "I have fully decided to give myself up, and risk acquittal before a jury of my peers."

Mrs. Haynes started. "Give yourself up and be tried! O, Albert!"

"Yes," he repeated, closing his lips firmly. "I have done unwisely in evading the law at all, I fear. I can never be in a condition to enjoy myself while this accusation is suffered to remain unmet. I will give myself up, stand trial, and abide the consequences. If I am acquitted, I can once more face my fellow beings uprightly. If I am not found innocent, and proved so before all men, life will be without pleasure to me, and I will be quite willing to yield it up."

"You forget Ella," murmured the widow, in a low tone, while the ever ready tears began to fill her sympathizing eyes.

"No, I do not forget her," replied the young man, knitting his forehead, as a spasm of pain crossed it. "I never forget her in anything, now, Mrs. Haynes. But I would not have her cast her lot with a man branded as a murderer. It would bring her young life down lower than it has been, which God forbid should happen! I am decided, and it is useless to attempt to dissuade me. Mr. Harvard agrees that it will be best, and he has had more experience in such matters than we have.

Mr. Harvard bowed in acknowledgement of the truth of the statement, and the widow could say no more. If it was for the best good of Albert she had nothing to say against it. The young man turned to the quadroon.

"Sam, my boy, how did that party get along after I left them the night I arrested the Detective?" he asked.

"Ah, that was a famous trick you played him, Mr. Anderson," said the boy, showing all his teeth with laughter. "We were expecting every minute to hear him fire and see you drop, and you may believe we were glad to see you throw him in that way. As soon as you were off in the boat, I went down stairs to see how our other friends were getting along. Mr. Tovin was helping the dark gentleman to their boat and they were swearing like troopers over the failure. When I came out I heard the dark gentleman say his leg was dislocated again where it was broken when he fell from the train, and I could see he was not able to use it. When Tovin saw me, he hurried his man into the boat and pushed off. The other man was groaning terribly, and said he would be well revenged on you. He wanted to come back and burn down my house, but Tovin persuaded him to keep quiet and wait for a better time. I told them if they ever touched foot on the island again, I should treat them as trespassers, and I have not seen them since."

"How came the fellow's leg broken?" asked the young man, looking at the narrator.

"Why, I suppose it was done when you threw him from the window. I should think it might have broken even if it was entirely sound before."

"Did I do that?" inquired the man, smiling strangely. "Gracious! what a dangerous man I am getting to be. The sooner I am under lock and key the better for society, I think. Is it not so, Mr. Harvard?"

Mr. Harvard laughed at this sally, and the quadroon laughed, and even Mrs. Haynes was obliged to smile a little through her tears. Then the young man said he must bid them good-by for the present, but they must be sure to come and visit him in prison. He bent tenderly down to kiss Mrs. Haynes before he left, as though she were a mother to him. Once, he would have been ashamed to do this, but he was learning, now.

"Good-by, Albert, good-by," sobbed the good woman. "Will you have to stay in prison until your trial comes off? Can't you get bail in such a case? I should think you might."

"No," replied the young man, gloomily. "I could give bail in half a million if they would accept it, but they will not. Money has no value before the law compared with a life. I must lie in jail, I suppose, until the next term of court. Ugh! It is a hard thought, by my soul! for one so used to liberty. Well, good-by. Come, Mr. Harvard."

Passing out of doors, they entered the lawyer's carriage and drove away towards the office of Chief Police. Mr. Harvard and his companion entered the building. The lawyer requested to see the Chief, and was told to sit down and wait until he was at liberty. Long ago, before this trouble came to Anderson, he came into this very room one day, and when they had told *Him* to wait the pleasure of the Chief, he had haughtily shown a card, and the name had proved an open sesame instantly. This was past now. The name on that card was of an advertised felon, and he was in no hurry to see the Chief this time. So they sat down and waited.

It must have been an hour before His Royal Highness, the Chief, chose to send word by one of his satellites that the two might be ushered into his august presence. There was really no reason for such a delay, but that His Excellency desired to impress the "two men" with a proper appreciation of the magnitude of his position. He had known Mr. Harvard as the lawyer who had brow-beaten his officers on the witness stand many a time, and not unfrequently had secured verdicts in the prisoners' favor after all his trouble in catching them. The person with him was nothing but a common laborer, anyway, and his wishes were of small account. So he had chosen to keep them waiting an hour, while he rested his imperial feet on the mantel-piece of his private office, and puffed a cigar from a box presented him by the last dealer who had had his shop broken open ; not as a bribe, oh, no! but merely in order to secure a more earnest effort to secure the robbers. When the two men entered his room he pretended to be very busily occupied with writing, and kept them waiting about fifteen minutes more in this way. He expected they would say something against such treatment, and intended to reply that they were at liberty to go if they were not satisfied. Finding at last that they were contrary, and would not get angry at the delay, he got very angry himself, and turning upon them suddenly, with the air of a tiger, advised them that if they came there to prefer some trumped-up charge against any one, they had better go at once ; and that, if they did not, and had anything to say, they had better say it, and be quick about it.

Albert Anderson had a lesson in human nature then, that was worth much to him. He had not forgotten the fawning way this same Chief of Police had received him when he came before, and it is to be doubted if he ever imagined until that moment that a man could be capable of such a variety of moods.

"Come," said the Chief, instantly, without giving them time to reply, "say what you want and go ; we have no time for fooling here." He glared at them after the manner of an Eastern despot.

"I came to see you about the young man Anderson," began Mr. Harvard, speaking as by a previous arrange-ment. "There is a reward of five thousand dollars offered for him, I believe."

"Yes," replied the Chief, wonderingly ; adding mentally, "What is the fellow coming at, I'd like to know."

"Well, sir, I thought I would bring him here, and claim the reward, if there was no objection." said Mr. Harvard, seriously.

"What ! You bring Anderson here!" cried the Chief. "Where is he ?"

"There will be no trouble about the reward, I suppose ?" said Mr. Harvard.

"N-no. If you've got the right man. But I think there must be some mistake. I—really ! Upon my soul !"

He might well stammer, and then turn pale with shame and wonder. For Mr. Harvard's companion — the common laborer he had kept waiting nearly two hours, when he might have left at any time — rose, and slowly removed his long cloak; kicked off an unwieldly pair of overshoes ; threw down his workman's cap; tore off his moustache, whiskers and wig. Then, wiping his face with a handkerchief, stood ready to substantiate his companion's claim to the reward.

There could be no mistake. There was never a man who looked so nearly like another as did this stranger like Albert Anderson. There was never such a handsome, firm mouth, or such beautiful brown hair as that which fell about his neck, when the black wig was torn away. It must be he. And though the Chief saw it was so strange, so incomprehensible, so very unaccountable, that a man should come and give himself up to die for the sake of a reward, and he a rich man too — though he could not understand it at all, and was almost sure he must be dreaming, he had the presence of mind to spring between the two men and the door, and to call loudly for his clerk to send officers there immediately.

Anderson laughed scornfully at the Chief's excitement, and sat quietly down with Mr. Harvard to await the coming of the officers.' He had to wait some time, for there were no officers below, and the clerk was obliged to run out of doors to hunt for one. Meantime, the valiant Chief kept his position by the door with a cocked pistol in his hand.

It so happened that while the clerk ran one way, an officer approached from another, and sauntering carelessly into the station, was about to take up a newspaper, when he heard his name called, and looking up, saw the Chief motioning to him excitedly.

"Mr. Steel — Mr. Steel — come here — Quick! I have got him, safe — the man, you know — Anderson! Hurry, or he may escape."

The Detective needed not a second invitation. He sprang up the stairs and passed into the room, expecting to find the young man held at bay by the Chief, and making the most frantic struggles to regain his liberty. His surprise cannot be imagined when he found only a quiet, smiling young gentleman, sitting with his lawyer, and appearing as cool and collected as though he were holding a reception in his own private parlors. He was talking to Mr. Harvard, when the Detective entered, and, looking up with a smiling, "Good-evening, Mr. Steel," went on with his conversation as though nothing had happened.

"There's your man, Steel!" cried the Chief. I have kept him here half an hour already, waiting for some one to come. Take him down stairs and lock him up in the strongest cell. You had better handcuff him, I think, or he may be up to some trick. We do not want to lose him again, you know."

The Detective's hand was wandering in the direction of his pocket as the Chief spoke. On the wrist of that hand there was left a plain red mark where those same handcuffs had been linked half a dozen hours a month ago. He had been too proud to tell his captor they were hurting him, but had borne the pain in silence. Hearing the Chief's advice, Anderson gave him a contemptuous glance, and then, throwing up his hands together, fixed his steady gaze on the Detective.

"If Mr. Steel is *afraid* of me," he said, slowly, keeping his eyes still in that same steady gaze, "he is at liberty to put on those irons in his pocket."

Not caring to say that he *was*, Mr. Steel immediately said that he was *not* afraid. Anderson then asked that he be permitted to say a few words more to Mr. Harvard, and Steel was pleased to grant this request also. After which Albert put his arm in a friendly way through that of the Detective, and bidding the lawyer good-by until the morrow, followed the officer down stairs.

The cell to which he was taken was indeed the strongest one in the station. The young man thought, as he entered its gloomy portals, how entirely it could shut out a man from his fellows, and how hopeless would be his chances of escape. The cell was a narrow one, very small, with only one chair and a berth. All around was stone, except the heavy iron-barred door, and it would have served as well for a lion's cage as for the safe-keeping of one unarmed man.

" I trust you will be comfortable to-night, Mr. Anderson," said Steel, as he turned the key.

Anderson looked up to see whether the Detective was in earnest or not. Then putting his hand through the bars he grasped that of the man.

" Mr. Steel," said he, feelingly, " what you have done has been only your duty, and I hold no spirit of ill-will to you for it. You will, perhaps, believe me, also, when I say that if I could, with safety to myself, have avoided the necessity of leaving you bound on the beach that night, I would have done so."

The Detective replied, assuring him of his belief that this was true, and they parted friends, shaking hands again through the bars.

When the young man was alone, the feelings he had suppressed until then began to rise. The shame of his position; the way people were bandying his name about; the knowledge that he must be led, jealously guarded like a slave, before a police Judge in the morning, with a crowd of vaga-bonds waiting there as he had seen them in other cases — waiting eagerly for a look at the prisoner in the dock; the horror of long days and nights behind such bars as these, and the possible finding at the end of all, a noose and a drop to tell the world he had died there; the living death for months to so active a disposition, of being held in custody by miserable men, so far below him in every sense; ordered about by them, guarded by them, fed by them, locked in by them. Oh God! It was too much!

His pride came to his aid before he quite broke down, and he assumed his old manner again. When one of the watchmen came in, soon after, there was not a sign of the struggle he had

passed through. The watchman informed him that there was a press reporter outside who would like to speak with him, but Anderson declined to hold any conversation. And the reporter, after taking a brief look at the caged prisoner, went away sullenly and wrote out a long account of the strange manner of the arrest, ending with the statement, "We took a look at the murderer in his cell, but he declined to communicate. He is ferocious looking enough, and seems fully capable of committing the dreadful crime with which he is charged."

It was well for Anderson, had he known it, that he had been placed in the Murderers' Cell. For here he had at least the advantage of cleanli ness, as murderers were not caught often enough to interfere with the semi- annual cleaning out of the cells. He lay down on the rough mattrass, but found it difficult to sleep; not because the bed was hard, but because the watchman's steady tramp disturbed him, and the place was so strange a bedroom; because he could only lie awake and think all night of his position, and of the way it would affect Ella. Where was she now? He would have willingly served months, years if need be, of imprisonment in such a cell, to know that she was well and safe, and would come back to him again.

How slowly the watchman walks his beat. How steadily he measures his paces; how his feet clank on the paved floor. He is ringing out a metre to which come set in the young man's mind the old, old song, so sad and strange :

—"Her heirs forever — her heirs forever!"

The night was very long, but it passed at length, and early in the morning Anderson's cell-door was opened to admit Mr. Harvard. The lawyer ordered a fine breakfast, which prisoners are allowed to have if they pay for it, and Anderson ate it, quite unconscious that his fellow-unfortunates were allowed only bread and water, and told they ought to be thankful for that. It seems odd that in our great country, an arrested man is used harder and fares worse in every sense before he is convicted of any crime than after. But such is the case.

Anderson and the lawyer occupied the time previous to the opening of the court, by making arrangements as to how they should proceed. It was decided to waive an examination and let the case take its course to a higher court before bringing in any evidence.

"Meantime, Mr. Harvard," said Albert, "you must exert yourself in every possible way to find Harry and bring him here. That would be enough to clear me without doubt. You must advertise immediately in the newspapers, far and wide, without regard to expense. Some of them must reach him, and he will not refuse to come when my life depends upon it."

The crowd assembled in the court-room, waiting impatiently the disposal of the smaller offenders against the law, until at last the chief of them all, the Murderer, was ushered into the room, between two officers. Then there was such a rush for good positions that the Honorable Court called upon the sheriff to clear the court-room unless order was maintained. This had the intended effect, and quiet reigned while Mr. Harvard rose, and in a low tone stated that his client was a man of well-known good standing in the community, of high talents and large property; that his client wished, although he did not enter it at this time as a plea, that the public would continue to believe him innocent until there was more than a mere accusation brought against him; that his client, being a gentleman of great interests pecuniarily in the city would not be likely to run away from a trial, especially as he had of his own accord delivered himself up to the officers; he asked that the Honorable Court would consider whether, in view of all these facts, bail in such sum as might be determined upon, should not be allowed in this case; as his client was fully convinced that the accusation was a plot of enemies which he could unravel were he given his liberty to do so; and Mr. Harvard hoped the Honorable Court would think seriously before he placed an innocent man's life in jeopardy on any flimsy pretext.

The waiting crowd listened with evident dissatisfaction to his speech-fearing that the murderer would be let loose upon the community. But they were relieved instantly by the appearance of a tall gentleman, with a fierce, black mustache, who arose and took off his long cloak in a manner highly impressive to all beholders. He was the honorable District Attorney of Prince County, and was there for the express purpose of alleviating the fears of the good people before mentioned.

"Your Honor," he began, bowing low to the desk behind which the Judge was sitting, "It seems to me that there can be no bail accepted in such a case as this without extreme injustice. That the defendent is rich, is no reason why he should escape the full penalty of his crime. [Cries of "that's so," from the crowd, which were instantly suppressed by the sheriff.] "He gave himself up to the officers, to be sure, after he found out that they must take him anyway. But who was it that so severely assaulted the Detective who first attempted his arrest" — the Attorney looked around for Steel, and on discovering that gentleman, pointed his finger at him in a manner that made him wish he was miles away — "and nearly made himself a double murderer, by leaving him exposed to the mercy of the winds and tides?" [Mr. Attorney knew that this was a fiction, but it sounded well.] "Who was it that kept half our police force hunting over the hills for six weeks, while he was eluding them by various disguises? It is clear, your Honor, that the defendant did all he could to evade the law, and because he gave himself up when he could no longer hold out, is that a reason why he should be set free again? I ask your Honor that the prisoner be fully committed, without bail, to await the action of the Grand Jury at their next term."

The Judge, who was a half-blind and wholly deaf octogenarian, pretended that he had heard the able arguments presented by the counsel before him, and said that he felt it his duty to commit the prisoner to jail, without bail, until the Grand Jury could investigate the case. This conclusion he stated in a quavering voice and with much difficulty, rousing himself from a deep lethargy for the purpose, and relapsing again the minute he had finished. It is said that His Honor, some fifty years previous, had the misfortune to have a prisoner forfeit his bail by fleeing to foreign parts, and the rule he had set down then, never to give bail if he could help it, was still strong on his mind. He was a half-foolish old Judge, who let his clerk manage affairs pretty

much after a regularly prescribed code, giving, like a Doctor's potions— ten dollars and costs for one offence, five dollars and costs .for another, sixty days for another, and so on. And it is safe to say that, year in and year out, there was not a blackleg in the State who caused as much needless misery and suffering, or created as many permanent violaters of the law as this Judge did. He has been dead a dozen years, but there are his living prototypes in our courts to-day, who are doing a similar work, and we blindly looking on without a word of protest.

The decision of His Honor was received with renewed cheers from the crowd, and the sheriff made another pretence of clearing the courtroom. Anderson cast a look of disgust around the room, which the newspaper reporters present set down as "another proof of the hardened condition of the prisoner." Then, surrounded by sheriffs, the young man was conveyed into a close carriage at one end of the Courthouse.

The crowd outside was very dense, and all struggled hard for the sight of the Murderer. Men were there who should have been at their work; boys who were truants from school that day; women, who held up their little children to see the Dreadful Man who had killed poor Harry! The officers hurried Anderson into the coach, and he was driven away as fast as the horses could go. But in that brief minute his cheeks were flushed and his lips more tightly compressed as he heard the crowd shouting, "Hang the villain!" "Lynch him!" followed by a volley of stones, one of which crashed into the carriage and struck a sheriff on the arm.

He was learning another lesson —

that men and women have a wolfish nature at the bottom of their hearts, and will show it on occasion as a tiger shows the claws muffled beneath the velvety fur. They tell us there was a time when the early men used to saunter in bands over the forests of Europe with clubs in their hands, and after striking down the black bear and beating out his brains, they would kneel around his body and with sharp stones cut out great pieces from the still quivering flesh, and hold a fearful banquet together. How can we feel, without the deepest shame, that the nature of those men is in us yet!

Prince County Jail! There it is, a great stone-and-iron cage, four stories high, surrounded by a wall with iron gates at the entrances. Anderson has seen it before, often; he has driven by it with Ella, when she expressed so much pity for the poor men inside. But going through its gates now, and feeling them jar after him, he has a sensation of a new character. He begins to realize how powerful is this thing they call Law, and how helpless is the man who gets within its clutches. His own money helped to pay these very men to guard him, but it cannot pay them to let him go. He is caught, bound, enveloped within the folds of the monster Law, and the repast is about to commence.

He walked curiously through the yard, and mounted the stone steps leading into the prison, giving to every object the keen, searching look he always had for new sights. He entered the massive prison door, and stood in a large, airy, pleasant looking office. What made it look so pleasant? The windows were very large and — yes, that was it — they were filled with flowers in pots and baskets: vines running luxuriantly over their cords, and flowers of all colors blending in beauty together. The jailor's wife came in while they were standing there, with a little basket on her arm, and commenced to cut off some of the flowers to fill it. She was a pretty little woman of five or six-and-thirty, and looked like a very humming bird as she flew from one flower to another. Curious to know what she was going to do with so many flowers, Anderson asked her politely.

"Do with them?" she repeated, smiling and turning toward the speaker. "O, they are for the prisoners, sir. I always cut some for them every day. It makes their cells a little more cheerful-like. Were you wishing to see my husband, sir?"

"Not exactly," said the young man, smiling. "He is wishing to see me, though, I believe. I came with these gentlemen," he added, more soberly, pointing to the sheriffs.

"What!" cried the little woman, putting her finger to her mouth. "You! Surely you are not a prisoner!"

"My name," said he, slowly, "is to go upon your books. I am James Albert Anderson."

"Bless me!" cried the little woman, again, "*you* can be no murderer. No, gentlemen. Don't tell me. I have seen men come here for all crimes since I was a child and my father was jailor. This young gentleman is innocent, and I predict he will be proved so. Poor boy!" She cast a pitying look at Anderson, and then said "Ah, here is my husband, gentlemen," and left the room with her basket.

The jailor was a man of business. He had no opinion to express about a man's innocence or guilt; that was for others to determine. It was for him to take a man delivered to his custody and keep him until he was told to let him go. He sat down and took out his books, ink and pen. Then he turned to Anderson, and asked the usual questions in a business-like tone :

"Your name ? "

" James Albert Anderson."

" Residence ? "

" Pearl street, 114."

" Occupation ? "

" Author."

" Age ? "

" Twenty-six years."

" Where were you born ? "

" In Catherine, Texas."

" Your religion ? "

" Protestant."

The jailor arose and took down a bunch of keys. He led Anderson across the long guard-room, up a flight of iron steps, along the corridor, and they stopped before a door over which were the figures "37." "This is your cell," said the jailor, and the young man went in, Mr. Harvard remaining outside. They shook hands, and the door was closed and locked between them.

"Bring me my books and papers and I shall do very well," said Albert, trying to look cheerful. "Tell Mrs. Haynes I shall be quite comfortable, and don't let her worry about me."

"I will," replied the lawyer. "Good-by."

"Good-by."

"Ah!" soliloquized the jailor. "The young gentleman is cheerful enough now, and in good spirits enough, but a few months breaks them down! I've seen them enough to know. It uses all alike."

And it must be said the jailor told the truth.

CHAPTER IX.

GOING INTO THE LION'S DEN.

The clouded mind of Ella Hastings had yet enough of perception in it to cause her no little agitation and fear over the discovery of the old man with a gray beard whom she had seen enter the tavern yard that day in October. She hurried from the window at the time and sat down trembling with her child in another part of the room, trying to think where she had seen the old man, and why his appearance should affect her so strangely. The real truth never once flashed upon her, but she was sure her agitation was in some way connected with the fear lest Bert should find her, and on no other subject could she have been so thoroughly alarmed. The baby fell asleep in her lap, little dreaming what fears distracted its mother. Looking down, Ella noticed that it slept, and put the child gently into its cradle. Then, hardly knowing why, she proceeded to bring out her clothing and her child's clothing, to arrange it ready for packing away. Each article was folded carefully and laid upon the bed, and after all were brought out, she began to separate the pieces from each other, and to place them in her trunks. While occupied in this manner, Sallie Slader came in.

"Why, what are you doing, Mrs. Hastings ? " asked Sallie, surprised.

Ella stopped in the midst of her packing, and looked up. She had an unnatural expression in her eyes, as if she had some trouble she could not understand, and Sallie was full of pity instantly.

"I am going away," said Ella,

slowly. "A great way from here. I am afraid to stay any longer."

"Going away!" echoed Sallie. "Surely you do not mean what you say. What can you be afraid of here? No one can hurt you."

"I am afraid to stay," said Ella, shaking her head," And I *must* go. I am afraid for His sake."

"For the baby's sake!" cried Sallie, seeing her glance at the cradle.

"O, no!" replied Ella, smiling through her troubled face, "Not for the baby's sake. Baby and I will do well enough. But I mean for His sake—for Bert's sake you know. I am going away for Bert's sake."

She spoke the word "Bert" as tenderly as if she were soothing a child to sleep. When Sallie heard her, and saw the depth of love in her bosom for baby's father, she could not help weeping a little, with her apron to her eyes.

"Don't cry," said Ella, in a tone of distress, perceiving it. "I am so sorry to leave you. But I must go. I am afraid Bert will find me here, and that — oh!— that would not do at all!"

The look on her face now was of genuine fright. Her bosom heaved rapidly, and she caught her breath fast.

"I must go away, I tell you. A long way off, where Bert can never find me, or — or the baby!" she cried. "I can work, and dress poorly, and eat little if it comes to that, but Bert must not know where I am. See how much money there is there"—handing Sallie her purse. "Count it for me and see how long it will last."

Sallie counted the money through her fast falling tears. She told Ella there was more than four hundred dollars!

"Four hundred dollars?" repeated Ella, pressing one hand on her forehead. "I don't know how much it is by that — tell me how much it will do — how much it is good for — how long it will last baby and I."

It would last a year or more, Sallie told her, if she was careful of it.

"A year, oh, yes; that's a long time, isn't it? The money will last a year. Yes. And then," — meditating hard — "I have some other things I can sell — this jewelry." She lifted out a little box, and showed the rings, pins, ear-rings, and chains, "This I can sell by-and-by for more money. Bert paid ever so much money when he bought them for me."

The jewelry seemed to carry her mind back to the days when she first wore it, and she showed it to Sallie, with the same half-awakened look.

"When my Bert bought these, you know," she continued slowly, thinking hard, with her hand to her forehead, "I was going away from him — somewhere. Somewhere? — oh, yes, to school. I was going to school. That was the first time I ever left him. That was long ago, you know, before I knew Carrie Hudson, or Mr. Walden, or you, or — before there was any baby, or — anything. Long ago."

She looked so troubled, and so sad, and so very pretty in her strange way, that Sallie could not help sitting down by her on the sofa, and kissing her with both plump arms around her neck. Ella looked a little surprised at this, but gently disengaged herself and smiled. Then, taking out the comb she now used to fasten back her hair, she commenced to smooth out its golden tresses, and to talk again.

"Did you know how Bert first got acquainted with me?" she asked, pulling the comb through the bright hair.

"Well, I will tell you, though you mustn't repeat it." She enjoined secrecy by raising a finger in caution. "I was a poor girl, you know, selling candy, when he found me. And he took me home and made a young lady of me. Wasn't he kind?" She smiled with the brightest eyes she had shown yet, and then added, "But then he was always that."

"Well, after that I went to school, you know," continued Ella, in a frank way, "and after I came back, Bert — he fell in love with me. Yes, he did. I was in love with him all the time, you see; and then he fell in love with me."

"Why did you leave him," asked Sallie, seeking to draw her out, "If he loved you and you loved him?"

"O," said Ella, putting her hand on the girl's shoulder, and looking very sad, "Bert was so good to me, and had so many friends, I could not stay there and bring trouble to him. He does not know he has a boy, does not imagine it even. I ran away from him to keep him from shame, and I shall keep it from him to the last."

The glow that lit up her face as she made this declaration made it as bright as the hair which enwreathed it. She might have been a young martyr, giving in her final decision to hold to her faith, just as the torch was applied to the wood about her.

"Yes," she repeated presently. "I will keep shame from Bert to the last. He would have done anything for me — I will do this for him. But I am getting tired, and must finish packing up. I cannot stay much longer with you, and had better go as soon as possible."

It was nearly dark, and Ella went to the window to raise the curtain higher. Hearing loud voices, she stopped to listen. Sallie had just left the room to attend to her duties below stairs, and all was silent about the desolate girl-mother when these voices broke in upon the stillness. She raised a window and looked out. A dozen men were coming up the road. As they drew nearer, she could see they were tired, hot and dusty. They had evidently been on a chase. But for what? They had no weapons with them. They looked and acted highly excited. From the dining-room door Sallie was issuing, attracted by the noise, to ask what was the matter. One of the party is telling her. Ella hears what he says, but cannot put the sentences together rightly. Her brain only comprehends a part of the story. "Mr. Slader is going to the city to warn the police." "The old man who came in an hour ago, dusty, with the long, gray beard." The little figure is now thoroughly startled, and sinks down by the window exhausted. What! What does he say now? "The talented author — James Albert Anderson."

James! Albert! Anderson! Bert! And Mr. Slader is going to the city to warn the detectives. To that clouded mind there by the open window there is but one meaning to all this: She sees that some one must have come to find her. Some one must have offered a reward for her, and Mr. Slader will give her up to the police, and Bert will be ruined!

This must not be! She will fly from the place at once with her baby. Thus spring the ideas into her mind. She will not delay longer, for while here she is in constant fear of discovery. Her excitement almost clears, for the moment, the cloud that hangs over her intellect. The work of packing is resumed, and by the time Sallie comes to say supper is ready, there is little left to be done.

She ate but little, and was so preoccupied with her thoughts that Sallie asked if anything unusual was the matter. She started on being addressed, and asked suddenly:

"Where has your father gone?"

"He has gone to the city."

"When will he return?"

"To-morrow noon, I expect. Why?"

"Not before that time?" asked Ella earnestly.

"I think not. He has gone with the buggy, and the roads are bad."

Ella thought a moment more.

"When does the next stage leave here?" she asked in a moment.

"Early in the morning," said Sallie. "But you must not think of going so soon. Stay a few days longer at least, before you leave us, if you must leave us at all."

"O, no," said Ella, firmly. "I have decided to go by the first coach. If you will come up stairs and help me get ready when you can, I will thank you. O, yes, I must go on the first coach."

"Which way are you going?" asked Sallie, seeing that expostulations would be in vain.

"O, I don't know," cried Ella, a little frightened. "I can tell when I get to the railroad. It makes but little difference so it takes me a long way from Bert. Yes, I must go in the morning."

After a while Sallie came up stairs and tried to reason with Ella; to induce her to remain until she had some definite plan of further proceedings in view. She reminded her that the time would come when her means must be exhausted, and asked her what she would do then among strangers. She tried in every possible way to show her the dangers of her present course. But in vain. There was but one answer ready for it all, and that was evidently sufficient to Ella's mind: "It would be best for Bert, and that was enough." Finding her arguments useless, Sallie helped in the packing, though with an aching heart, and insisted on giving Ella her address in full, and in extracting a partial promise that she would write to her if she ever needed assistance. It was late before the trunks were strapped and locked, and the valises placed ready to be fastened in the morning. But at last the work was done, and the young girl-mother lay down with her child to take the last night's rest she ever expected to have under that farmhouse roof.

Before sunrise the next morning, Ella was dressing and making her last preparations for leaving the tavern. The baby was awakened from a sound, healthy sleep, to receive its nourishment before starting on the journey. The stage-driver came up and carried her baggage down stairs; a slight meal was partaken of, and she was ready for the coach.

"Now I will pay you what there is due," said Ella.

Sallie would have left the small sum unpaid rather than mention it, but as Ella desired to settle the bill, she named the amount.

"Do I owe any one else here!" asked Ella, after handing over the money.

"No," replied Sallie. "It has all been paid."

"The Doctor—was he paid for everything?"

"Yes, dear."

"And the nurse?"

"Yes, dear."

Ella paused a moment to think, fearful lest she might forget something.

"You are quite sure it is all paid?" she asked, presently.

"Quite sure. It is all right."

Ella waited a few minutes more, trying to think if there was anything forgotten.

"O," she exclaimed, "You! I had nearly forgotten to thank you for your kindness to me since I have been here. God will reward you, my dear girl, though I never can. Here. You will please take this and wear it to remember me by when I am gone."

Ella handed her a ring as she spoke.

"O, no," replied Sallie, trying to smile. " Keep the ring, yourself."

Ella did not understand her motive, and looked a little troubled as she took back the jewel.

"Isn't the ring good enough?" she asked, opening her reticule, and taking out the box in which the others were laid. "Well, there. I don't believe there is a better one, but you can have your choice. The one I gave you first was a diamond. I tried to pick out the best one for you."

"You mistake me," said Sallie, looking very sad at the construction put upon her reply. "I only thought you might need it some time more than I do. But if you wish it, I will take the ring, certainly, and wear it for your sake. There. It fits my finger perfectly.

Ella was satisfied with this, and the two girls sat together, talking on various subjects, until the coach drove up to the door. Then Sallie, who had become greatly attached to the young mother and child, and had borne up with difficulty thus far, began to cry, and the baby's face she had been holding was wet with tears when she had kissed it and placed it in Ella's arms. Through the coach window the warm-hearted girl kissed Ella affectionately, and in the act partially awoke her to a sense of the truth. She gazed sorrowfully at the tearful face of her friend, and imprinted one kiss on her pure forehead. Here, she saw, was some one who loved her, and was sorry to have her go away. As the driver mounted his seat, Ella answered Sallie's "Goodby," with an earnest "God bless you!" and the stage coach rolled away toward the station.

Toward evening Ella alighted from a railroad train in the town of Kingston, several hundred miles from Hillsdale. She had selected this destination at random, from a guide-book, thinking it would do as well as any, so that it only carried her a long way from Bert. Here she ran the guantlet of several scores of eyes belonging to people congregated at the depot, all surprised at the sight of such a beautiful young mother with such a little child, traveling alone. But Ella did not notice them. She rode, unconscious of the attention she had attracted, to one of the hotels, and at the first opportunity inquired for a suitable private boarding house where she could go with her child. The obliging landlord exerted himself to find such a place, and was soon successful. He reported that a Mrs. Wilson, a widow lady, living alone, would be pleased to add one or two members to her family, consisting at present of herself and juvenile son. Mrs. Wilson was accordingly introduced to "Mrs. Hastings," and an arrangement was entered into between them. This was an easy thing to do, inasmuch as Ella accepted the woman's terms without a word, and agreed to pay each week in advance. Mrs. Wilson took great care to explain that she was in perfectly independent circumstances and had no need to increase her income in this manner. And after listening to her discourse for awhile, Ella really came to feel that the lady was very kind indeed, and had almost made a sacrifice of herself for her benefit; when the truth was that the accommodations were extremely limited, the prices high, and the lady's disposition exactly the opposite of amiable.

Installed at Mr. Wilson's, Ella found herself in possession of a couple of rooms on the second floor, overlooking the busiest street of the town. Here she stayed quietly by herself, for it was getting too cold to take baby out, and she would have trusted it to a famished tiger as soon as to Mrs. Wilson. Not that she ever thought of such a thing — the landlady was not partial to children, and never offered to touch Ella's — but if she had, it is sure the mother would have excused herself in some way, and gone away frightened with the child. She only saw the landlady at meal times, when little conversation passed between them. She was never molested in the quiet of her own chambers, where she used to sit, caring for baby and sewing most of the time; or gazing idly with folded hands into space, trying to recollect, to organize the chaos in her mind; to unravel the complications which clouded everything of late; to explain away numberless Whys and Hows and Whens; to understand something — something which was now a mystery.

As to who Ella was, where she came from, or anything of the sort, Mrs. Wilson seemed to care nothing, as she never asked a question bearing upon any of these points. This satisfied Ella. All she wanted was to be let alone, with baby. And so matters passed for the first month.

About the end of the first month, a very unusual circumstance occured at Mrs. Wilson's. On coming down to dinner, one day, carrying the child, for she never left it alone an instant, Ella found a strange gentleman occupying one of the seats at the little table. The landlady introduced him as her friend, but Ella was so excited over the matter that she did not hear the gentleman's name. During the meal he tried to carry on a conversation with her, but her short replies made the attempt a failure. Mrs. Wilson paid no attention to either of them, and when, after a constrained silence, the meal was finished, Ella departed for her own room, with a feeling of intense relief at leaving the presence of the strange gentleman.

Hardly was Ella out of hearing when the strange gentleman turned rapturously and addressed Mrs. Wilson.

"By George, ma'am!" cried he, "you are a perfect Angel!"

"Am I?" growled that amiable woman.

"You are, by all that's human! She is the very girl, there can be no doubt. If she is, and this affair comes out all right, you may set your bill at what you please, and I'll warrant it'll be paid without a murmur.

After delivering this extraordinary statement to the lady whose income was already large enough, and who only took lodgers for company and accommodation, the strange gentleman sat down at a table in the parlor, and wrote, with some difficulty, the following letter:

"KINGSTON, Oct. 27, 1854.

"To MR. FRED HAWLEY, care of RICHARD TOVIN, ESQ., City, Prince County:

Dear Sir: I have found her at last, as I fully believe, after so long a period of searching. She is in this town stopping with a Mrs. Wilson, under the name of MRS. ELLA HASTINGS. I had the pleasure (only think of that !) of dining with her to-day, and I must pronounce her the chief princess of fairy women. She answers the description perfectly, and you will have to be pardoned for your infatuation with such a very captivating creature.

"But there is one thing, and deuced important too, that I came near forgetting to mention. Now, don't start and say it can't be her. What I was going to say is, that she has a child four months old, which must belong to that fellow she ran away from, Anderson. She looks all the lovelier, though, for this, and really almost breaks a man's heart with her beauty when she lifts the baby in her arms. But what is the use of my trying to write it on paper! You must come and see for yourself, and if you don't agree with me in every particular, I'll throw my bill for services into the first fireplace I come to. You will find me at the Kingston House. Come at once.

Yours Faithfully,
FELIX McCABE, Ex-Detective, etc.

FRED HAWLEY, ESQ.

Mr. Fred Hawley received this letter the second day after it was written, and feeling that he could now leave the Masterpiece in the hands of Mr. Tovin and the Law, he set off at once for Kingston, in the best of spirits. Certainly fortune seemed to be smiling on him once more. Anderson lay in jail, securely fastened where he could do no harm, and now the Pleasure, so much sweeter after the Pain, loomed up before him. He had fallen desperately in love with Ella, and the thought of seeing her again made him almost forget the broken limb he had risked to gain her. When he did think of it, it was with set teeth, and a bitter determination that Anderson should suffer to the death for his

haste. But as he slowly limped from the train at Kingston to meet his employed detective, he sunk his hate our of sight for a while in the depths of his deeper passion.

"Felix, my lad," said Hawley, grasping the detective's hand, "you have done well, and shall be well paid for your work."

"Ah, but I had a long hunt, sir," said the man.

"Never mind that, so you found her at last. But take me to the house at once. I am dying to see the beauty after such a delay. How does she appear? Lonesome and quiet, or happy and jovial."

"Ah, sir, she is lonesome enough, I should think. She hardly ever speaks a word, but spends all her time in her room with the child. Mrs. Wilson says she never goes out of doors, and is always as quiet as she was the day I dined there."

"She'll get over that quick enough, once I get her acquaintance," said Hawley, laughing. "I'll have her out behind a pair of fast horses within a week, and that's what'll put color in her face. Never fear for me, Felix. I know women pretty well, I calculate, and few can resist a man when he is in earnest. I'll make our pretty friend Mrs. Hawley, before three months have gone over, now remember what I tell you."

McCabe did not reply to this boast, and may have had his doubts on the subject so well settled in Mr. Hawley's mind. The two men rode on to the hotel, and then procuring a carriage they drove to Mrs. Wilson's house. They were talking about the matter in hand as they came in sight of Ella's window, when McCabe called his companion's attention to it.

"There you are !" he cried.

"Mother and child together. Ah, Fred, wasn't I right, wasn't I right, my boy?"

His reply was pictured in Mr. Hawley's face. That gentleman's eyes were riveted on the pair in the window, while with one hand he tightened the reins of the horses and jerked them suddenly into a walking pace. Ella was sitting with the baby in her lap, watching the passers in the street, with her beautiful crown of golden hair hanging over her shoulders, and half hiding the child from view. Hawley held his breath an instant in sheer admiration.

"Yes, it is her," he murmured, more to himself than to his companion. "It is Ella, without doubt, but ten times more beautiful than ever. She might answer for a Madonna in point of beauty. Such a prize is worth more than I have suffered to obtain it."

The walking horses soon carried the men out of sight of the window, and when the young girl could no longer be seen, Hawley ordered McCabe to drive back to the house door. A ring at the bell brought Mrs. Wilson, to whom Mr. Hawley was introduced as the gentleman she had been told of. She received him graciously, and all three of the party adjourned to one of the parlors immediately.

"You understand, I suppose, the terms on which I have consented to receive you into my house," said Mrs. Wilson to Hawley, as soon as they were seated in the parlor.

"Yes, madam," replied that gentleman, politely. "I believe Mr. McCabe mentioned the arrangement to me on the way here. It is quite satisfactory to me ; quite so, madam."

"There must be no mistake, mark you both," said the landlady, impressively. "Whatever your business may be in Kingston — in my house, with a certain person whom we need not name, or in any other way — *I* know nothing about it. You understand me, gentlemen ?"

"I think so," said Hawly, smiling.

"Perfectly ?"

"I think so."

"Then it is all right. My terms are, payment in advance for each month's rent. You understand that, I suppose ?"

"Yes, madam. And here is your money. If my plan succeeds well with Miss — ha ! ha ! I should say — with a *certain person* — you shall have more than this sum and welcome."

Mrs. Wilson inclined her head, and intimated that such an act on the part of Mr. Hawley might take place if he choose to have it ; but it must be remembered that of everything beyond the letting of the rooms to the gentlemen, *she* should insist on knowing nothing. If this was perfectly understood, she had no more to say, and would withdraw. As no one had any objections to this course, she withdrew accordingly.

Mr. Hawley and his companion devoted the succeeding hour to closing their accounts up to that date. The crafty McCabe saw full well that there was no better time to settle with his employer than when he was in such spirits over his expected success. The sum that he asked and received was a generous one, and he was as well satisfied as his principal when he put the money away in his pockets. He had formerly been a member of the regular detective force of a large city, but was discharged on account of being discovered in irregular practices with the rogues he caught. Since that time he had been in various occupations, and was not unfrequently employed at private detecting, as he had been in the present instance. As he folded up the money, he remarked to Hawley that he might need his services again some time ; if so, he knew where to find him.

"Yes," said Hawley, "I know where to find you. But as to needing you again, I — I think not. I feel perfectly confident that I am now near the end of my troubles, and I — think — it unlikely that I shall have to call on one of your persuasion again.".

"Well, however that may be," said McCabe, "I wish you luck, any way."

Hawley thanked him, and limping on his crutches to the hall door, closed it after him. As he turned to re-enter his rooms, the babe and mother were coming down stairs. Ella had the child clasped in her arms firmly, as if in fear she should let it fall, and the lame gentleman thought how she looked, for all the world, like a large child hugging its favorite doll. The girl looked up as the door was shut, and seeing the stranger, stopped, hesitating.

"Why, surely you are not afraid of a poor lame gentleman, my child," said Hawley, smiling.

"No — I — am — not— afraid," replied the girl, disliking to show fear. She came on down the stairs, one step at a time, slowly and carefully, hugging the doll tighter than ever.

"Your baby is heavy, isn't it ?"

"No, sir — not — very." One step a time. Now she passes him.

"Shall I open the door ?" He springs to do it. And with an, "O, no, thank you sir, I can do it myself, very well !" she passes into the dining-room, out of his sight, leaving him in a fever of excitement.

CHAPTER X.

GUILTY OF MURDER IN THE FIRST DEGREE.

It was in October that the young man gave himself up to the Law, and being a slow and cumbrous body that high and mighty institution sat at its ease, so far as he was concerned, and left him safely under lock and key until December. The Grand Jury then sat patiently on his case, and finally returned a true bill, as it was called, against him, for murder in the first degree. The next week the Supreme Court convened for the purpose of testing the Grand Jury's veracity, and their open sessions were greeted with crowded galleries. The Sheriff was kept in a state of continual surprise to find he had so very many friends, and was driven to the verge of distraction when he saw that he could give admission tickets to only about one in a hundred. There was a phenomenon also in connection with this: The Sheriff noticed that those of his dear friends who were successful in obtaining tickets took them quite as a matter of course, while those who were necessarily refused were instantly transformed into implacable enemies. And the worthy functionary had occasion more than once to devoutly wish that some other person held the power to grant admission ; the ratio of enemies made to friends gained being in such outrageous proportion.

The Supreme Courtroom of Prince County was in the darkest, dirtiest and most miserable portion of a dark, dirty and miserable building. The efforts, often repeated, of the better class of Legislators, had failed to impress the rest of their body with the idea that this Courthouse was an abomination, and an insult to the goddess to whom it was supposed to be dedicated. The majority of the men in whose hands the sovereign people had placed their lives, limbs and general happiness, could not be prevailed upon to believe that they were wasranted in spending the public monies to build (as they expressed it), "A Palace for thieves and murderers." Honest men, they reasoned, were suffering by the hundreds for want of the necessaries of life, and they were not going to use criminals better than these. So the old Courthouse had stood year after year, until it was rank and rotten. Moss had grown in its chinks outside, and rats abounded in the basement, where the unfortunate victims of the monster Law were locked up over night during the courts' sessions. A smell that might have reached to heaven was always emanating from this underground dungeon, so much so that every committee appointed to investigate the grounds of complaint from petitioners against the nuisance, were fain to hurry this part of their duty through in quick time. For the moment they would be almost persuaded that reform was needed in the Courthouse, but a sprinkling of cologne from the nearest apothecary's, and a dinner at the county's expense, would invariably drive such an idea from their heads. And they were often known to remark jocosely over their wine that the dungeon might be a good thing after all, for there were undoubtedly plenty of rogues who caught fatal fevers and colds there, by which they were removed at no expense to the State beyond the jurisdiction of Prince County.

Into this miserable, ugly den of a Courtroom, Albert Anderson was ushered, one miserable, ugly day in December. It was the darkest, dampest day in the year, and every unfortunate who had been summoned as a witness seemed to realize that his position was one put upon him out of personal malice by the monster Law. Each and every one of them was afflicted with a fearful cold. So were the two Judges who occupied the bench. So was the clerk. So were the sheriff and deputy sheriffs. So were each and every one of the spectators who had been successful in obtaining admission tickets. The building itself had a cold; a cold contracted years before, which was leading it fast down into the valley of consumption. It was so damp that everybody commenced to sneeze directly they entered the Courtroom. One of the Judges soon noticed this fact, and at first attributed it to a lack of respect on the part of the spectators. He therefore became highly indignant, and was just about to order the sheriff to clear the room, when he sneezed himself, and gave up the idea. Into this miserable, damp and dirty room Anderson was led by the sheriff, and assigned a seat in a chair behind an iron railing. The sheriffs then turned the key upon him, and took chairs themselves close by. Being thus formally placed at the bar for trial, the proud young man lifted his eyes unflinchingly, and looked about him.

Directly in front sat the two Judges watching him earnestly. Below them sat the clerk. Nearer yet—the rows of seats were filled with legal gentlemen, young law students mostly, who had come in to see how trials were carried on. Nearer yet, and so near, that he could have shaken hands with any one of them (or clutched them by the throat!) were a half dozen newspaper reporters sitting at a table, ready to impale him on the points of their pencils, which they were sharpening for the purpose. Over to his left, opposite to the Judges, were seats for the twelve good and true men to be selected to try his case. Next to them the sheriff sat in his magnificence, high at a desk of his own, gazing complacently at the audience who were there by his kind permission. The said audience were straining their precious necks to an alarming degree in the gallery above, to get a sight of the prisoner; they, as well as many other persons in the Courtroom, watching Anderson with earnestness as he sat in his box. Had he been the greatest king on earth, and the box been a private box at some fashionable theatre, he could not have attracted more profound attention. He half thought, as he looked around and saw the close gaze of the multitude; caring nothing for them or what they could do to him; caring nothing, in his independent fearlessness, for the Jurymen, the Judges, or even that august personage, the Sheriff: That it was a wonderful sight for him to see, one but few men were permitted to have before them, and that it was really the best play he had ever witnessed. The reporters saw the fearless gaze, and hastened to write down the words: "The prisoner still continues to preserve a hardened demeanor, and will evidently abide the result of his trial with the same stoical fortitude he has thus far evinced."

At last the monster Law was ready to begin his repast, and his attentive waiter, the Clerk of the Court, announced the fact. For a minute, the array of eyes were turned from Anderson, and directed upon this individual; who seemed to take a sort of pride in his position.

"James Albert Anderson," said the clerk, in a slow, solemn and awful voice, "You are set at the bar to be tried, and these good men whom I shall call are to pass between the State and you on your trial. If you would object to any of them you must do it as they are called, and before they are sworn. You have a right to challenge twenty-two peremptorily, and as many more as you can show cause."

Anderson would have challenged no one, had he not been warned by his lawyer against the danger of such a course, and now as the names mere called, he objected only as Mr. Harvard directed him. A dozen men were challenged by the prisoner, and an equal number by the District Attorney. The witnesses were then excluded from the room until they should be called to testify, and after the remaining jurors were excused from further duty, that lengthy document, the indictment, was read by the Clerk.

By this indictment, Anderson was made to appear a very monster in human form. He was charged with having caused the death of Henry Johnson, clerk, by knocking him down with a club, and then throwing him into the Bay; by choking him to death; by choking him until he was insensible, and leaving him to perish in the fire set to cover all traces of the deed; and (as if not content with with having committed these heinous crimes) it alleged that he had killed Johnson in some other manner, to the jurors unknown. Anderson was almost too much startled when he heard the full extent of his supposed villainy to answer the clerk's question, "Are you guilty or not guilty?" But seeing what was required, he replied quietly, "Not guilty, most certainly," and the clerk continued : "Gentlemen of the Jury, the prisoner pleads not guilty to this indictment, and for his trial has put himself upon his country, which country you are. You are now sworn to try the issue. If he is guilty, you are to say so ; if he is not guilty, you are to say so, and no more. Good men and true, stand together and hearken to the evidence."

The gentlemen of the jury bowed, and, as they had been told to stand together, complied by immediately sitting down. These gentlemen did not escape the general tendency to catch cold, and it was several minutes before they had done sneezing. Finally, however, they became quiet, and the Honorable District Attorney rose, dropped his long cloak, twisted his fierce black moustache, and commenced to open the case for the government in due form.

The speech of the District Attorney lasted over two hours, when an adjournment was had for dinner. On re-assembling, the same dense crowd was found in the galleries, and on the floor of the Courtroom. Becoming more accustomed to his position, Anderson looked closer at the better portion of the crowd and saw many faces which were familiar, as men with whom he had been acquainted in the city. But he recognized no one by a nod or look, feeling it better that he should wait the verdict of those twelve men in the jury box. Only one face in the Courtroom attracted him enough to keep his eyes upon it long, and that was of a young girl of rare beauty, who sat in a chair not far from his. She was evidently in the higher walks of life, to judge by her jewelry and dress, and there was something about her sad, sweet face, with its dark eyes and luxuriant black hair, that charmed the young man instantly. He watched her for a few moments, until he became aware that she was returning his gaze with interest, when a sense of propriety compelled him to look away. Often, though, after that, he turned to see her again, and always found those sweet, sad eyes, intently regarding him with a pitying look, which began to almost disturb him. In other days of the trial he looked, to find her in the same place, watching him as before. He asked Mr. Harvard once who she was, and after inquiring he brought word that she was a Miss Le Moyne, an orphan from New Orleans, stopping in the city with an aunt. After that the first thing the young man did on entering the Court-room, was to look instantly to the beautiful girl's chair ; and he always found her there, with the same expression, day after day.

On this afternoon of the trial, Anderson was called to bear his first great shock. The first witness was called, and, contrary to usual custom, (though Heaven knows why!) a chair was placed for him on the witness-stand. The door was opened and a man came limping in with the help of a pair of crutches, and took the chair placed for him. Then, as he lifted his head and waited, the prisoner sprang to his feet and would have leaped the railing of his pen, but for the quick action of the Sheriffs who forced him to sit down again. There was a momentary flutter in the court-room, the Judge began to say something, the crowd to grow noisy, and the Sheriff to rap fiercely on his desk with his gavel. When order was restored, the man in the witness chair, who had caused such a sensation in the mind of the prisoner, held up his right hand and swore to tell the truth, the whole truth and nothing but the truth. It was the dark gentleman with the broken leg. There was hate enough in his face as he looked at Anderson's struggle with the sheriffs to have blighted its object in a less appropriate place than this; and the young man felt, as he saw the satisfaction with which the dark gentleman beheld the officers holding him down, that he would stop at nothing now to perfect the plot he had formed.

The witness testified that his name was Frederick Hawley; that he was a gentleman of property and leisure. He had known the young clerk Harry, for some months previous to his murder. Found him a pleasant and agreeable companion, and was much in his company. On the evening in question he was on his way to the warehouse to visit Harry, and paused on the outside of the building as he heard loud voices indoors. The first words he heard were from the prisoner: "I am in earnest and you had better not trifle with me!" Then a voice which he recognized as Harry's, replied, "I shall go when I choose, and no one can prevent me." After that, the prisoner spoke very loud and fast to the poor boy, in an angry tone, and witness heard a falling noise. Immediately after, the — the prisoner — came out looking very agitated, and started up street in his carriage, locking the warehouse door after him. Witness then went away. In a few minutes he heard the alarm of fire given, and on ascertaining where it was, rushed back to save the boy, but it was too late.

"But why," asked Mr. Harvard, "was it that you did not make these facts known until six months or more had passed?"

"Sure enough," said the District Attorney, as though he had just thought of it. "Why?"

Then it came out, and had its designed effect with the twelve good and true men. The witness had been attacked within a dozen hours of the fire by this same man — the prisoner — and to escape him had been compelled to spring from a flying railroad train, in which act his leg was broken. Being in mortal fear of the — prisoner — witness had waited in a hiding place until it was known he had left the city, when he came in and informed the authorities directly.

"But why," asked the District Attorney, marking the effect of the witness's story on the twelve good and true men. "Why has your leg been a year in getting well? Is not that an unusual length of time?"

Ah, to be sure it was, and witness had suffered more with it than he could tell. When he had nearly recovered, he went with his friend and Detective Steel to arrest the — prisoner — on St. George's Island. The — prisoner — showed fight, and being in a weak condition, witness was thrown from an upper window. At which the leg was again dislocated, and it was doubtful if it would ever be quite strong again. Witness looked at the member as he spoke, in a sad way, that drew much sympathy from beholders.

Thus was thrown upon the jury the masterpiece of the Masterpiece, and as they glanced from the unfortunate dark gentleman to the cause of his injury, glowering like a caged panther in the dock, they saw there exactly what the District Attorney wanted them to see: A young man of violent passions, who would scruple at nothing to carry out his wishes. It needed not the testimony of Mr. Jenkins, forced upon the stand against his will, to say that Anderson had told him there was little danger of Harry's coming back; it needed not the evidence of several persons who had heard a disturbance in the warehouse at Brown's Wharf on the night in question; it needed not that Fred Steel should be compelled to rehearse the usage he had received at Anderson's hand; and the other links of the chain of circumstantial evidence: to convince the jury that the prisoner was a most dangerous man to have at large in a community, and had without a doubt killed his partner in a fit of fierce anger. The plea of the District Attorney expatiated on this probability, and fixed more firmly their opinion. Mr. Harvard's evidence regarding the prisoner's position in society and the improbability of his committing the high crime with which he was charged was well brought in, and his argument was one of wonderful conception. But in the jury's ears there were ever ringing the remembrance of Anderson's strange actions after the fire; his low spirits, and sudden departure for Texas. Mr. Harvard would have explained the reasons for what followed Ella's loss, but Anderson forbade it. He saw it would make matters look no better, and preferred to bury his secret in his own aching heart, to live there if he lived, or die with him if he died.

So the trial lasted until the evening of the fourth day. The young man saw as it proceeded that he had little to hope, and was greatly astonished to see the circumstances of Harry's disappearance arraigned in such compact order against him. The continued closeness of the confinement, in a crowded unventilated room — though, thank Heaven! he was spared the horror of spending nights in the dungeon below — with the excitement he underwent on the appearance of each new clue, wore on him to a marked degree. It was breaking him down. But he held up to the last, watching with the deepest interest, until the evidence and pleas were all in.

This was, as has been said, on the fourth day. At the conclusion of the District Attorney's argument, one of the presiding judges arose, and delivered his charge to the jury. It was a long speech he made, but the substance was that usual in such cases —"If you think he is guilty, say so; if you do not, say he is not." Then those twelve good and true men marched out of the court-room, and a recess was had until they should announce their verdict.

This stay of proceedings enabled Anderson to rouse himself for a while, and was so far highly beneficial to him. He was taken by the officers to a private room, where Mr. Harvard did his best to raise his spirits, though he knew there was little to be said in favor of a probable acquittal. Anderson said little, but busied himself before a small glass in arranging his attire, washing the dull look from his eyes, and combing out that hair which was of itself a mantle of purity upon his young shoulders. He resolved to receive the jury's verdict, whichever way it was decided, in a perfectly unmoved manner, as he would, were it against him, walk by-and-by to the scaffold they would raise for him.

Soon the Sheriffs announced that

he was to resume his seat in the dock, and nerving himself to meet the shock which was was to come, Albert Anderson walked, almost smiling, into the court-room. One by one the twelve good and true men filed into their places, and the court-room was as silent as the graves of the men who had gone out of it, time after time, to their deaths.

The name of each juryman was called, and each answered " Yes."

" James Albert Anderson ? "

" Yes," — in a firm voice.

" Mr. Foreman, have you agreed upon your verdict ? "

" We have."

How the court-room clock ticked then !

" Is the prisoner at the bar guilty or not guilty ? "

" *Guilty of murder in the first degree !* "

The worst was over to Anderson now that the suspense was gone ; and he sat there without moving a muscle, still almost smiling.

" James Albert Anderson, have you anything to say why the sentence of death should not be passed upon you ? "

Now is your time, lovers of the sensational !

The young man has risen in his pen and raised his white hand.

" I have *this* to say, Your Honor," said the firm voice, while the raised arm might have grasped a thunderbolt as he held it on high, " that I have entered in truth my plea of not guilty to the terrible charge against me, and that it will stand on your records, a black witness against you, after I have been sentenced and executed ! I have *this* to say, that I have been found guilty without one atom of proof, and

if I die it will be with the firm belief that these gentlemen will yet repent most bitterly their unrighteous verdict. I believe Harry Johnson to be alive somewhere, and that he will sooner or later appear to show you the careful way in which you should receive circumstantial evidence. I am not afraid to die, and if my death has the effect to induce a revision of your criminal code in this respect, my life will be well yielded up ! "

Calmly the Judge arose. Calmly he advised the young man that protestations of innocence were too late now, and counselled him to prepare for the death which awaited him at the hands of the Law he had outraged. Calmly he dwelt on the fearful crime of which the prisoner stood convicted, and impressed his hearers with a sense of the power of that Law which protested against such acts. Then, calmly as ever, he uttered the sentence of death :

" The sentence of the Court is that you be taken from this place to the Common Jail of the County of Prince, there to remain until, on such day as shall be fixed by the Executive Government of the State, you be thence removed to the place of execution, there to be hanged by the neck until you are dead. And may God have mercy on your soul ! "

The young man bowed to the sentence, still almost smiling. The reporters drew their own conclusions from his demeanor. The gazing crowds in the gallery waited · to get the last look at the prisoner. The sheriffs waited by until the floor should better cleared for his pasaage. The twelve good and true men went away, doubting in their hearts whether they had done right by giving in such a verdict. The High Sheriff looked unconcerned and wise, as if to say, "O, I am so used to these matters, you know!" The clerk of the court busied himself among his papers as quietly as though they did not mark a fellow creature out for death. The witnesses asserted their importance by going out to mingle with the crowd and become temporary lions—all but one of them.

All but one! A dark gentleman with black, curling hair, came out of the witness seats on a pair of crutches, and limped into the aisle, waiting the passage of the prisoner.

Mr. Harvard came with tears in his eyes to comfort his client, but he did not need it. He was calm as had been the Judge when he read his doom, and received the lawyer as he had the sentence, almost smiling. While they were speaking, a noise attracted their attention in one of the spectators' seats, and they looked, to see officers carrying out a female form, insensible, with black hair streaming over the men's arms. It was the young woman who had sat near the prisoner through all the trial.

"Poor girl!" said one. "She fainted dead away when she heard the sentence."

Anderson was looking pityingly after the quiet form, when he was called to go with the sheriffs. As he turned, the dark gentleman with the broken leg confronted him.

"Ah!" he hissed, "Where are you now?"

It was too much to bear at that time, and springing from the officers, Anderson struck the man a fearful blow which felled him to the floor. The sheriffs caught their prisoner and hurried him away, but not until a voice had called out:

"Very well, you have had your way, once more. But I have your Ella, and, shall have her after you are dead!"

The officers lifted Anderson then like a dead weight, for he had fainted. At last! At last, he was broken down.

CHAPTER XI.

VALLEY OF THE SHADOW.

The sentence of death, or the prospective horror of a public execution could never have broken Albert Anderson down. It required those taunting words of the dark gentleman to give that twinge to his heart which had thrown him lifeless upon the Sheriff's officers. It required that spasm of pain which came from probing causelessly a wound which was already deep enough. Ella and he had been separated for this world, finally and irrevocably, by the results of the day. And when there was added to this the thought that after his death, she would live to bless such a man as Hawley, who had used such base means to obtain her—then his brain whirled, his strength failed him—he was broken down.

For a week afterward he knew nothing of what passed. He lay unconscious in his prison bed, with nothing before his mental vision but one horrid blank. Physicians came and went; friends from among the few there were left him; the Jailor's wife, with her boquets; Mr. Harvard, Sam, Mrs. Haynes; all came often to look on his still face, but he did not know it. Anxious representatives of the daily press came to the prison office to learn the condemned man's condition, and startled the public by expressing fears that "Anderson would yet cheat the gallows." This horrible fear induced the jailor to caution the prison physicians lest some secret poison might be given the young man in his medicines. Let all the world be cheated, if you will, but the gallows must have its due!

One day a young lady entered the Jailor's office whom he had never seen before. She walked trembling up to the Jailor's desk, and there waited to make her mission known. She was evidently in a strange place, and somewhat confused by the circumstance.

"Did you wish to speak to me?" inquired the Jailor, rising.

"Are you the — the prison-keeper, sir?" stammered the young lady.

"Yes, I am Jailor here. Take this chair and compose yourself. You are not used to such places as this, I imagine."

"O, no, sir! I was never in a prison before in my life. It must be dreadful, sir, to live here. There is one gentleman here, isn't there, who is very wealthy and highly educated? The one who was convicted recently of — killing."

"Mr. Anderson? Ah, yes."

"Does he, does Mr. — Anderson — live in a stone room, like these about us?"

"Yes, only a little stronger built. He has been convicted, you know, and after that we always put them in the murderers' cells."

If the Jailor had known what a stab he gave her, he would not have said these words so lightly.

"Do you think they will — hang him, sir?"

He might have heard her heart beat as she awaited his answer.

"There is little doubt of it, I guess."

"I see by the papers that he has been very ill since he was sentenced."

"Yes. He is lying sick in his cell, now. He has not spoken or recognized any one for a week. Would you like to see his cell?"

The girl held back a moment, and then said, "Yes, she should like to see it very much."

The Jailor proceeded up the iron steps, along the corridor, and stopped at the first in the row of murderers' cells. Mr. Harvard and a physician were sitting by Anderson's bed, but rose to welcome the Jailor and his companion. The lawyer looked surprised to see the girl, when the Jailor explained that she was only making a tour of the prison. As Mr. Harvard glanced at the young lady, her eyes met his and the recognition was mutual. The Janitor stepped inside the cell to speak with the physician, and the two were left alone together a minute.

"You are the young lady who sat near our poor boy at his trial, I believe," said Mr. Harvard.

"And you are the gentleman who tried so hard to save him," she replied, taking his hand. "O, is there yet no hope?"

"There is always hope while life lasts," said Mr. Harvard, gravely. "Albert has experienced a shock since the trial, which has laid him where he is, but he is getting better fast. We are hoping to hear from Harry every day, and if we do not hear before the day appointed for the execution, I think I can prevail with the Governor to grant a respite of a few weeks more."

"The gentlemen are coming out," said the girl, nervously. "I must talk longer with you, sir. Won't they leave us here a little while if you ask them ? Tell them you will show me to the office."

Mr. Harvard was interested in the fair girl, and at once willingly complied with her request. The Jailor was informed that the lady was an acquaintance, and they would be down soon together. No objection was made to this, and as the others went away, the girl and her new friend entered the cell. Albert was still in that fitful sleep, and their conversation could not awake him. The girl was trembling like a leaf when Mr. Harvard offered her a chair.

"I came here to-day," she began, "afraid and uncertain. I took a great interest in Mr. Anderson, the first day I saw him, which was long ago, and when I heard of this dreadful thing I got a ticket for the trial. The close Courtroom affected me, I think, or something, for when the Judge said the sentence, I fainted clear away."

"I noticed you every day," said Mr. Harvard, seeing that she hesitated. "So did Albert. He asked who you was once, and I inquired until I learned your name. He was quite concerned when he saw you had swooned, but the officers were ready for him, and he could do nothing."

The girl's eyes brightened, and she continued :

"You know my name then, Mabel Le Moyne. Yours is Mr. Harvard, I believe. I am stopping in this city with my aunt, Mrs. Davis. She is my guardian, and I have lived with her nearly all my life. I have always had my own way, and when I wanted to go to the trial she talked a little while and then let me go ; and when I told her this morning that I was coming here, she objected but little. I

heard Mr. Anderson was sick, and thought — perhaps — I could help, someway, about taking care of him."

Seeing that Mr. Harvard looked a little doubtful, she added :

"I am willing to do anything, sir, to help. When I thought of such a nice gentleman, so used to comfort, sick in prison, I could not help coming to see if there was not something I could do."

She was actually pleading with him now, and the lawyer's heart melted a little before her earnest face.

"I am sure," said he, "that Albert will appreciate your kindness, for I will tell him of your offer when he becomes conscious. But, really, whether the regulations of the prison, or whether you could do anything more than we can do, I don't know—"

"O, Mr. Harvard, try and arrange it in some way!" cried Mabel. "I am a splendid nurse ; I am, really. When my uncle was sick with the fever in New Orleans, I took almost all the care of him for five weeks. I came here to-day in this plain dress, so that I could make them think I was poor, and wanted a situation to take care of a sick person. Then I was going to ask that I be sent to Mr. Anderson's room. But when I saw you, I waited."

The lawyer smiled to hear of her ingenious device.

"I am afraid your intention would not have succeeded, Miss Le Moyne," said he. "Still, as you are so kind, I will see whether the Jailor will let you come here to watch with Albert a part of the time. There is little else needed to be done, except what the Doctor can do himself. I will call a turnkey, and we will go down to the office."

The Jailor was in his usual seat, while his little wife stood near by, cutting off roses for the prisoners.

"My friend, Miss Woods," said the lawyer, improvising the first name which occurred to him. The Jailor's wife bowed and smiled. "My friend," continued the lawyer, "has had some experience at nursing the sick, and if it is consonant with your rules, I would much like that she should be allowed to have partial charge of Mr. Anderson for a while. She can come in the morning, and relieve your physician of a part of his work, making it pleasanter all around."

"Yes," said Miss Woods, seeing that the Jailor looked to her for a confirmation. " Mr. Harvard was kind enough to mention the matter to me, and I should like to come very much."

The Jailor meditated a little while, and said the case was so unusual, he didn't know what he ought to reply. But if he did not, his little wife did, and stopped in the midst of her flowery kingdom to say so. "Of course the poor sick boy could have a nurse if Mr. Harvard wanted him to, the dear boy that never was guilty of the crime he was accused of. She should think he might be made comfortable for the little while he had to live, without anybody's fretting over rules and regulations." So earnestly did she argue her points, that the Jailor was quite taken by storm, and began to feel that he was acting very cruelly to make any words about the matter. "O, yes," he said, "certainly; there was no objection whatever."

Mabel thanked him with a glad look, and then left the office with Mr. Harvard, who insisted on seeing her home in his carriage before he would leave her. The girl was in high spirits over the results of her strategy, and her flushed cheek told the lawyer as he assisted her to alight before her aunt's mansion, that she was quite pleased and happy. Had Mr. Harvard been permitted to take a look into the future, and seen whither the day's work, which appeared to him so harmless, would ultimately lead, he might have hesitated ere the fictitious Miss Woods found creation in his mind. But as he could not, Mabel's life was interwoven with the rest of them.

The following morning found Albert's new nurse at her place. The prison physician and the Jailor were present to give her instructions, which she was told to observe very particularly. Remembering the newspaper rumor, the Jailor hinted to Miss Woods that if Anderson should be given any poison by her, she would be held for the crime of murder, as much as he was now. The expression of horror which came into her face when she comprehended his meaning, was genuine enough to have convinced a less careful man that he had nothing to fear in that direction. When the men went away and left her alone with the sick gentleman, she thought how dreadful the suspicion was, and knew she would sooner risk her life to save, than to destroy him.

Reared tenderly as she had been, Mabel LeMoyne accepted the trust before her without a fear. The shrinking, frightened girl, who until yesterday never saw the inside of a jail, could sit down quietly behind iron bars, and think nothing of the stone wall which encompassed her. Her infatuation with the young prisoner, strengthened by sympathy during his trial, had grown so strong now that beside it she knew no equal. As long as she could be near him, doing him good, she nothing for the lonesome jail, the close cell, or her own comfort.

Mabel had watched with Albert nearly two weeks, when one afternoon, being alone with him, he sat up in bed and asked for water. It was the first sign of consciousness he had shown, and the girl sprang joyously to obey the request. Her young heart beat hard and fast as she held the goblet to his lips, and saw that he watched her closely as he drank the cooling liquid. She blushed deeply before his searching eyes, and stood, uncertain how to act, by the bedside.

"How long have I been sick?" asked Anderson, in a feeble voice.

"Three weeks, sir," replied Mabel, timidly. She felt her courage going now that her patient had found his voice.

"So long! Where is Mr. Harvard?"

"He is away now, but will return soon. He comes to see you very often, and so does Mrs. Haynes and all of your friends. You must lie down and be quiet, sir. Those were the physician's orders."

The sick man laughed a little.

"Pray who are you?" he asked, pleasantly, "that come here to give me physician's orders, or anybody else's orders, for that matter. Reveal yourself, and explain your presence in this prison."

"Mr. Harvard engaged me to take care of you, sir, after you were taken ill. That is all."

"And you, then, are —— By Heaven! Where did I see you before? Are you not the young lady I saw in the Courtroom?"

"Please don't get excited, sir," she pleaded, casting down her eyes, "or you will be ill again. Yes, I—was in — the — Courtroom."

"And why; tell me truly; why did you come here?" asked Anderson, gently.

"O, sir, you were so ill, with only men to care for you! I could do no less than offer to watch with you part of the time. I pitied you so, sir."

The dimmest possible shadow of the truth came into the young man's mind.

"You were very kind," he said, "but let me warn you to be careful and be content with *pitying* me!" Then he added, bitterly, "For to those who care more for me than this there comes only sorrow and disgrace."

The labor of speaking was tiring him. He lay down for a few minutes, and then, rousing himself again, asked about Mrs. Haynes. Mabel told him she came often, but the doctors said her health would be jeopardized by remaining long in the jail, and she had yielded to her friends' persuasions.

"What was it," he suddenly asked, after a period of quiet, "What was it that made me sick? I saw you faint away, and then I turned to go with the officers, and then — oh, yes! I remember. It was what *he* said. O, the pain, the pain!"

Anderson pressed his hand to his heart, and a cloud came into his face. After that he did not speak again until it began to grow dark, when he looked up to see his nurse putting on her shawl and hood, as if to leave the cell.

"Where are you going?"

"Home, sir, as soon as Mr. Harvard returns."

"And you will come back to-morrow?"

"O, yes, to-morrow."

"Your name?"

"Mabel Le Moyne."

"I remember it now," said the sick man. "Please sit closer to me. There. Let me take your hand."

She yielded it to him bashfully, and when he took it, how her heart did beat!

"You reside with your aunt, I believe?"

"Yes, sir," she assented. "Mrs. Davis."

"Is she perfectly willing you should come here?" said Anderson.

"O, yes. She never opposes my wishes when I decide upon anything."

"Indeed! She has great confidence in you, then?"

A step was heard at the farther end of the corridor, which brought the blood to Mabel's cheek.

"Mr. Harvard is coming," said the girl.

Anderson looked up brightly.

"You will be back to-morrow?"

"To-morrow."

The steps became louder, and Mabel sat back a little from the bed. Mr. Harvard looked very much pleased to see the progress Anderson had made, and said cheerily:

"My dear boy, you are looking quite finely! Really, now, you will be on your feet in a day or two."

"Thank you," said Albert. "I hope so surely. I have to thank you for my good nurse, also, I understand."

Mabel blushed and said she must be going. She was quite well used to the walks of the jail by this time, and after saying good-night, she departed for home.

"Now," said Albert to the lawyer, when Mabel had gone, "sit down, and tell me everything."

Ought I not to wait a few days till you are better?" asked Mr. Harvard, hesitating.

"No, or I shall die of uncertainty. Tell me all, now, good or bad. I can bear it as well as I ever can."

"There is little to tell," said the lawyer, after a pause, "but you shall have what there is. In the first place, not a word has been received from Harry. The exceptions which I drew up the Supreme Court were overruled, though as for that for I built no hopes on their success. Tovin and Hawley are off and on about the city, and keep their affairs too close to enable us to get a word from them. My hopes now must lie on Harry's turning up at last, which he may do any day, you know, or in a commutation from the Government. I shall argue your case before the Council this week."

"Has the day for the execution been set?" asked Albert.

"Yes, but that is a mere matter of form, and will have no influence upon the case. The day has been set—11th of April. Three long months yet to work, Mr. Anderson. We should have much to hope from that."

Anderson smiled bitterly.

"Hope on as long as you can," he said. "I count but little on commutations or pardons. They are bound to hang me, innocent or guilty, and I think it will have to be done. But for one thing they might go ahead and welcome. You heard what that villain said when I fainted in the Courtroom?"

"The dark gentleman? Yes. He seems determined to make your life miserable to the last. But," said Mr. Harvard," I do not place any confidence in what he insinuated there. Not the least, I assure you. I thought you had more faith in Ella, Albert, than to heed such a story."

"My dear friend," said Anderson, "I hope you are right. I have indeed great faith in Ella, even though she left me as she did. I am willing to believe that she was led away by false representations, and not from any wish to do me wrong. Still we must consider that the same influence which was strong enough to induce her to leave me — and that all points to the dark gentleman — would very likely be strong enough to mould her to his other wishes. Poor Ella! She is to be pitied if her destiny has fallen into such hands as that man's. And to think that I must lie here and do nothing — it is horrible beyond description!"

The lawyer could say but little to comfort him, and as he was becoming weaker they parted for the night.

From that hour, Albert Anderson grew calmer, surprising his friends daily by his demeanor. He would lie for hours without speaking a word, watching Mabel at her sewing or reading, and then sometimes would change as suddenly and become very talkative, keeping the girl busy with his questions. At such times he always insisted on holding her hand in his, and her heart never got over that habit of beating fiercely when she was near him. Every morning he would welcome her with a glad look, which invariably sent the blood to her cheeks. And every evening he would say, holding her hand:

"You will be back to-morrow?"

And she would answer with her heart in a fluttter:

"To-morrow, Mr. Anderson."

It was not long before the sick man was pronounced able to sit up in an easy chair brought from Pearl street. The Jailor was careful now to have the cell door locked after visitors went in and out, lest the prisoner should attempt an escape. Had An-derson reached the yard, there were guards and high walls which he could not have passed, but the Jailor was jealous of the credit of his institution, and was unwilling to run the slightest risk. Somebody whispered, too, that Miss Woods' services could be spared, now that Anderson was so far recovered, but the young man himself would not hear of it. So Mabel came as before, every day, and as Anderson grew stronger she became more of a companion than nurse. They read books together, and talked of authors both were familiar with, making many a long day pass quickly and pleasantly. Every hour the chains which bound Mabel to Albert were riveted stronger and stronger. *He* never thought of *love* in connection with her, but only of the pleasure it was to have an entertaining companion, who would come to visit him in that dark cell. *She* thought of nothing but love in connection with him, and believed that if he should ever be proven innocent, he could do no less than repay her fidelity by marriage. She had heard of his love for Ella, but thought as did many others, that as she had deserted him his heart was again free. Each in their blindness was piling up suffering for the other with an unsparing hand.

The weeks flew by, but no new hope came to the prisoner. The Governor and Council reported that they could not grant either a respite or a commutation. No news came of the lost boy, Harry. All their hearts began to fail them. Mrs. Haynes was nearly wild with grief, and Mr. Harvard relapsed into melancholy he could not wholly conceal, for he had become strongly attached to his client. The rest of them felt severely the blows as each prop gave way, though none showed their feelings so little as Mabel. She resolved to be a comfort to Albert to the end, whether it were to be on a hangman's scaffold, or in the free, open air she hoped and prayed for. Anderson gave up all expectation of life long before April came, and busied himself in arranging his affairs with Mr. Jenkins. Several important changes were made in the will, and Anderson placed his signature to the document with a bold, steady hand. He wrote much of the time as April drew near, finishing several works which had been neglected, and closing up every duty he could think of. One day, while engaged in this manner, with Mabel sitting near by, reading, a sound struck on their ears which startled both.

It was the noise of a carpenter's saw driving through timber. Mabel did not need his whisper, " *The gallows,*" to know the dreadful import of the sound ; and losing all control of her feelings, she burst into tears.

Anderson reproved her mildly.

"My dear girl," he said, "you must be calm. This is only the beginning, and if you fail now, what can I expect in the future. The carpenters are only making the bed where I shall go to sleep soon. Pray do not cry. I thought you were braver than this."

" I will not cry," gasped Mabel, recovering herself. "It was only the first shock that affected me. I will not show my grief again."

"Now, you are truly a brave girl," said Albert, passing his arm about her waist. "You deserve a better reward than to be a condemned man's friend."

"Her fluttering heart heard him, and beat faster than ever. "O!" she thought, "if his life is spared will he remember that?"

The gallows was finished at last, and soon after the High Sheriff came to the jail to speak with the prisoner. He was surprised to be received with a grasp of the hand, and was obliged to mutter something about its being only his duty, you know, and he couldn't help it. To which Anderson replied that he had no doubt the execution would be very painful to the Sheriff, and he only wished to ask one favor. Being in a very nervous condition by this time, the Sheriff begged him to name it and it should be done if within the bonds of possibility.

"It is a very slight favor," said Anderson, "for you to grant; but it is much to me. I wish to be allowed some day, when no one is present, to go with you upon the scaffold, and have the whole thing explained to me. So that I can be ready on the day of execution to walk to my place unhesitatingly, unappalled by any new horror in the scene."

The Sheriff granted this wish, though he declared it a very strange one, and on the succeeding day he came to fulfil his promise. At one end of the yard the great instrument of death stood black and gaunt against the prison wall. Anderson walked up to it with the Sheriff, ascended the stairs, stood on the drop, saw the beam above his head where the rope was to hang, examined curiously the greased bolt that would be drawn by a pressure of the foot to send him into eternity, and then walked back to his cell satisfied that he could finish his part in the drama with credit. It seems very simple to him now. Only to walk up those steps, go through a few formalities, on with the rope, down with the black cap, six feet of sudden fall, a momentary flash of pain—and all would be over! The young man actually gained strength by settling in his mind the exact amount of horror there was in the decree—"hanged by the neck until you be dead!"

The days passed swiftly. Everything was ready for the final act in the long, long drama. As evening drew near on the 10th day of April, one after another of Anderson's friends took their farewell of him tearfully. He alone stood unmoved to bid them "good-by," and to beg them to remember that the day must come when his memory should be vindicated. To Mrs. Haynes he said, God would bless her child, and find her friends after he was gone. Anderson had previously received full proofs of Ella's relationship to the widow, and left them rich by his last testament. When all were gone but Mabel and Mr. Harvard, Albert stood by his little barred window, looking out on the harbor, a part of which was plainly visible, thinking of the Great Sea he should sail out upon to-morrow! Oh! was there no ship on this lower sea, coming in to bring him a rescue!

It was almost dark when Mabel, who had stayed till the very last moment, rose sadly to put on her shawl and bonnet. As she came to the door trying to look cheerful so that he should see her brave to the end, he turned. From very force of habit the words came, as they had every night for weeks:

"You will come to-morrow?"

She could not answer, and the turnkey swung the door which closed between her and Anderson. She staggered giddily down stairs, and fell fainting on the guard-room floor.

Here she found her. The Jailor's little wife bathed her hot head, and brought her to consciousness. The poor girl had borne up so long, but she could do it no longer. The first words which fell from her lips as she came to life were of utter desolation and despair:

"*To-morrow! My God! To-morrow!*"

BOOK THE THIRD.

CHAPTER I.

SCENES OF THE SCAFFOLD.

If the High Sheriff had been beset with friends when the trial commenced, what shall be said of the deep affection which he found existing for him when the day of the execution drew near? Everybody who had ever known him, or whose friends had ever known him; all of the police, city, County and State officers, with their friends; every doctor, coroner or undertaker, who might be supposed to have an interest in dead bodies; dozens of school teachers and clergymen, who wished to impress this lesson on their pupils and congregations; every newspaper reporter, correspondent and editor within a hundred miles; lawyers, young and old; with scores of other people who wished to be warned of the fearful consequences of Murder; came, personally and by letter, to the High Sheriff, and asked admission tickets to Prince County Jail Yard, for April 11, from 9 to 12 A. M., in the sacred name of Friendship. The Sheriff could not admit all, and finally adopted the sagacious plan of giving out a certain number of tickets until they were exhausted, and then declining to admit any one else on any pretex. This plan was a very simple one, but it enlarged the army of enemies to the worthy official in an alarming degree. In fact, it was broadly hinted by more than one outraged citizen, that Mr. Sheriff would not get his vote at the next election — not if he knew himself.

One of the prison officers came to the door to say that there were two clergymen waiting below who desired to talk and pray with the prisoner, and prepare him to meet the doom that was coming.

"Tell them I have no need of their services," said Anderson, "but thank them heartily for their kindness. I should only be excited and irritated by them," he explained to Mr. Harvard, "and they can do me no good. As for preparation, I am ready at any time."

"There is one thing that I have waited to the last to speak about," said Mr. Harvard. "Would you leave word what disposition we are to make of your — body?"

"Well, well," mused Anderson, smiling a little, and not in the least discomposed. "I thought I had remembered everything, but there I was wrong. There *will* be a body left, won't there?" He thought a few moments. "Well, it makes little difference, but if you will be so kind, it might be placed by my parents' grave in Catherine. My agent there will attend to the interment."

Mr. Harvard promised that this should be done.

"Does Mrs. Haynes take this much to heart?" Anderson asked after a pause.

"Very much, Albert. She loves you deeply."

"Yes," replied Anderson, bowing his head, "I suppose she does."

"Is there anything more you wish done that has not been attended to?" asked the lawyer.

"No. Not for myself. Sam will have St. George's Island to pay for his faithfulness. There hasn't been a truer friend at all times than that same boy."

"The public bequests I have tried to give judiciously. Mrs. Haynes and Ella will have enough to keep them always from poverty. Miss LeMoyne must take her share for my sake, though she does not really need it. Those of my tenants who are to be given their houses are all sober, honest men. Really, Mr. Harvard, there will be more joy than sorrow at my funeral."

"O, no," the lawyer replied. "He was sure there would not. They had all loved him, every one of them."

"I don't know why they should," said Anderson, still watching the sky. "I was hasty and rather hard with some of them at times, I fear. I hope they will all forgive me, now, as I would them under the same circumstances."

Mr. Harvard said he was sure they would, only there was nothing to forgive.

"I feel so at rest with all the world this morning," continued Anderson, "that I forgive everybody all the evil they have ever done me. There is a charm in such a spring day as this, when nature is waking in beauty all about us. I forgive all—even—the dark gentleman."

Mr. Harvard murmured a little at this. "But for the dark gentleman," he said, "you would be standing unfettered outside of these walls this instant. It would require more forgiveness than I could muster, to forgive that man!"

The still rising sun overtopped the window-sill and cast a glory of light on Albert at this moment. It lit up his face and shed such a lustre upon his fair head, that the lawyer marvelled.

"In a few hours," cried the young man, rapturously, "I shall be even as you have said. I shall stand unfettered outside of these walls, beyond the reach of bonds or hangman's rope! O, Mr. Harvard! I can scarcely wait that hour!"

He paused a moment, lost in the rapture of the thought, and then continued:

"Think of the crowd that will come here to-day, and *pity me* as I stand on the drop before them. Men of every religion, who would give their all to know what lies beyond the narrow river of death! And they will pity me! I, who shall know, before the sun is evenly above their heads, more than has been written by the wisest saint or prophet they are following." ·

"I understand," he added, a moment after, "how men may cling to life and look with terror on a painful and ignominious death. But when one is as near the other side as I am, he becomes impatient at delay."

There was no false religious enthusiasm in his tone. It was merely the outburst of a thoughtful mind, which loved no pursuit so well as that of knowledge.

About 9 o'clock Anderson could see from the window, spectators entering the yard by the gates, and one in particular called his close attention. It was a man on crutches, with black, curling hair, and dark complexion. This figure limped up the steps and into the office. "So," thought Anderson, "he is determined to pursue me to the last."

The Sheriff came up with the Jailor soon after, and he took farewell of Mr. Harvard in the cell, saying good-by as calmly as if he was only going for a short time. At the foot of the stairs the Jailor's little wife came, with weeping eyes, to see him. He was still as calm as ever, and suffered her in her violent grief to kiss his cheek without a sign. The Jailor also parted from him here, saying in a broken voice:

"Good-by, my boy, good-by. It was my duty to put on the rope, but O Lord! I couldn't do it for you. Good-by."

Out in the jail yard four hundred and fifty men are waiting for the condemned. They are ranged about on both sides of the yard, leaving an open passageway for the prisoner to reach the gallows between them. All are talking in low whispers, of the act which is to come. Newspaper reporters occupy tables near the gallows, and sit with their watches open, ready to write down the exact minute when each part of the piece takes place. Some of them have never attended an execution before, and sit a little uneasy, wishing they were away. Others have seen several, and are talking among themselves about them.

"The fall is full six feet, " says one, "and he will hang forty minutes. I hear the reason for this is that the last man this Sheriff executed didn't hang long enough. They sent his body to a college for dissection, I believe, and when the students took out the heart, they found it still pulsating. I asked the Sheriff if he thought the man could have been dead, and he replied, " Well, he was before they had done with him.""

The sarcasm of the Sheriff is fully appreciated, when a whisper goes round, "He is coming," and Albert Anderson walks, unsupported by the officers who accompany him, with a firm tread, calmly as ever, through the crowd, up the stairs, and takes his seat in the chair on the drop. Now! Attention everybody to the ceremonies which end with a drawn bolt, a clang, a tightened rope, and a human soul gone out by violent means from among you! This is the carnival of the Monster Law!

If there are several hundred men here who are very uneasy at this moment, there are certainly two others whose excitement rises to a pitch unequalled by their fellows. They are neither of them the High Sheriff; he goes about his work as he has about half a dozen executions before it; he is not responsible for this act — that belongs to the Governor, whose name is signed to the warrant in his hand which says, " *We therefore command you.* " They are neither of them the deputy sheriffs, who occupy their time during the reading of the warrant by buckling straps tightly about the condemned man's limbs, lest he should struggle for his life. Neither is one of them Anderson, who is the least ruffled of all that audience, and looks calmly as ever about the crowd to take his last glimpse of them in the body. But one of them is the lame gentleman, who at this moment would give worlds to undo his crime, so terrow-stricken has his conscience made him. And the other is a fine-looking, youngish man, who walks up and down nervously, with his right hand in his left breast-pocket.

Quiet, gentlemen! The High Sheriff will read the death warrant.

For when he is called—as he may be —to give an account of this at a Higher Bar, he will wish to point to the Detectives, the Judges, the Jurymen, the Governor and Council, and say, "The sin is their's, if there be sin. I am guiltless." What if the Detectives, the Judges, the Jurymen, the Governor and Council should plead in like manner, and lay the sin on his shoulders! Never mind now. Quiet, and let the reading proceed.

" *To the High Sheriff of our County of Prince, Greeting:*

"Whereas, at a term of our Supreme Judicial Court, holden at this City, within and for the County of Prince, on the 18th day of December, in the year one thousand, eight hundred and fifty-six, JAMES ALBERT ANDERSON of this City, in said County, was convicted of the crime of murder in the first degree : —

"And whereas, at a term of our said Court begun and holden at this City, in this County, on the 18th day of December, in the year one thousand, eight hundred and fifty-six, the said James Albert Anderson was, by our said Court, then and there sentenced for said crime to suffer the pains of death, by being hanged by the neck until he shall be dead; all of which, by an exemplification of the record of said Court, which we have caused to be hereunto annexed, doth to us fully appear : —

"WE THEREFORE COMMAND YOU, that upon Friday, the 11th day of April, in the year one thousand, eight hundred and fifty-seven, between the hours of 9 and 12 o'clock before noon of the same day, within the walls of the prison of said County, or wi·hin the enclosed yard of the prison of said County of Prince, agreeably to the provisions of the General Statutes, you cause execution of the said sentence of our said Court in all respects to be done and performed upon him, the said James Albert Anderson, for which this shall be your sufficient warrant.

"Whereof fail not at your peril, and make return of this warrant, with your doings thereon, into our Secretary's office, within twenty days after you shall have executed the same.

"Witness, His Excellency, Franklin L. Smith, our Governor, with the advice and consent of our Council, and our seal hereunto affixed, at this City, the third day of March, in the year one thousand, eight hundred and fifty-seven, and in the eighty-first year of the Independence of the United States of America.

"By His Excellency the Governor. With the advice and consent of the Council.

"ROBERT HAWKINS,
"Secretary of the State."

In a steady, solemn tone, the High Sheriff reads this warrant, while everybody present feels that the yard is a very close place, and wonders what has become of the air which vanished so suddenly. They stand uneasily watching each other, and nervously watching Him — the condemned man on the scaffold before them. His very calmness adds to their oppressed feelings, and they question in their hearts whether, after all, this is the best use that handsome form and finely-wrought mind can be put to. Each is sure of one thing — that he would not stand in the High Sheriff's place to-day for any worldly consideration which could be named.

One of the under sheriffs takes the hanging rope and fits it tightly around Anderson's neck. Better hurt him a little more now, that it may be easier by-and-by, says the Sheriff to himself. Anderson never winces under the trying ordeal, but merely looks up and says, smiling, "That will do very well." You may say he did not realize his position. I tell you he did, fully, more than most men would ; and had prepared himself to meet it !

When that rope was placed thus tightly around the prisoner's neck, the youngish looking man who was walking nervously about with his right hand in his left breast-pocket, stopped, breathing hard, and seemed to wrestle with himself a moment. When each strap was buckled around the prisoner's arms or legs, this man would stop again, with the perspiration gathering in beads on his face, and watching the proceedings with intense anxiety. He would always recommence his walking immediately after; but he did not get at any time more than a few yards from the scaffold.

The dark gentleman is striving desperately to look composed, though the feelings raging in his breast almost suffice to overpower him. He has hated this Anderson — hated him for years — hated him more and more as time went by — hates him now ! But he is not quite prepared for this. It is so much more horrible than he expected. The blood which is to be shed here is innocent blood, and is to be offered up by his own wicked perjury. It is true he has never felt at ease when this man was free, and would tremble at this moment, were he to step down from the scaffold with his limbs unshackled. But still, when that rope is fitted to his enemy's neck, the dark gentleman feels as if his own hands were doing the murder, and shudders at the horror of the deed.

The Sheriff reads the closing words, "Robert Hawkins, Secretary of the State," and folds up his document circumstantially. The prisoner is requested to rise. Everybody's heart is in his mouth. Anderson stands as quiet as ever. The under sheriff who placed the rope takes the black cap, and comes to put it over the young man's face.

Thank you ! Oh ! thank you, for

that, Mr. Sheriff! Our dear boy has done bravely, and is ready to die as he has borne the trial thus far—calmly and quietly—but when he shall feel the pain of the tightened rope about his fair young neck, and the death throes are on him, he may unconsciously contract his features in the agony. Thank you, then, for your black cap; for when it goes over his face, those who saw him will only remember the smile—the brightness, which covered it. Thank you, thank you, Mr. Sheriff.

There are only a score of words more to be said: "And now, by virtue of this warrant, I proceed to execute the sentence of the law." But before they have been uttered, the youngish looking man's excitement becomes too much for him to bear. He rushes up the scaffold stairs, and catching the High Sheriff's arm, draws him back from the fatal spring which his foot was about to touch. His right hand comes out of the left breast pocket, and in it is a legal document which the High Sheriff scans intently. Then that officer steps to the front of the platform to address the' excited throng.

" *The execution will not proceed.*"

" *Why?*"—from a hundred throats.

" *The man is pardoned.*"

" *Pardoned ?*"

" YES, AND PROVED INNOCENT !"

There is a moment of stupid wonder, and then the cheers break forth. The youngish looking man goes forward and addresses a few words to the crowd. As he closes, some one cries "Three cheers for Franklin L. Smith, our Govenor," and they are given with a will.

Albert Anderson sits down again in his chair, moved now a little off of that trap door, through which he was to fall into the other world. The sheriffs take off the rough rope and smooth down, almost tenderly, the long, brown hair which had come so near covering a dead man's head. Anderson was strong enough before, but he is faint, now. The rush of thought is overpowering him.

The Governor comes and bends over him.

"Mr. Anderson, do you know me ? "

"Yes," replies Albert, under his breath. "You were my companion on that Southern voyage."

"Did you know I was the Governor ? "

"No," is the reply. "I never thought of it." ·

"Well, it so happens that we are brought together again," replied the Governor, not yet over his excitement. "What will you do now, Mr. Anderson. My carriage is waiting outside, and I should be pleased to place it at your service."

Albert hears him, but it is so strange. Shall he ride in the carriage of this man, over whose signature he heard read ten minutes since, "We therefore command you that you cause execution of the said sentence in all respects to be done and performed upon him, the said James Albert Anderson ? "

"Am I free ? " he asks.

"Free as the air."

"Yes, then," he replies. "I will go with you."

Even in this hour of confused thought, he does not forget those who are suffering sorrow for his sake. Messengers are called to take to Mr. Harvard, to Mabel and the rest, the words, "Anderson is pardoned, but needs quiet for a day or two. He will see you all as soon as he is quite well again."

Through the dense throng that crowded the street outside of the Jail yard, Anderson made his way to the carriage. Men surrounded him in this time of his vindication, cheering him for his release, who had yelled for his blood when he rode in that other carriage guarded by the officers, the day he first entered Prince County Jail. These men were earnest then, and they are earnest now. And just here is one of the strangest lessons of this strange life of ours.

As the multitude surrounded the carriage, Anderson's name was called over and over again, until he was obliged to step out a moment where all could see him. The cheers were then renewed, to which he responded only by a "Thank you, my friends," and then re-entered the carriage. After they had driven away from the crowd, the Governor began an explanation.

"You will remember, Mr. Anderson, the conversation we had on the ship when we met that night on the ocean, about the death penalty and the fear of death. Your opinion interested me greatly, and when you were arrested last fall for this crime, I waited with great interest to see how you would carry out the principles you detailed to me at that time. In November I was elected Governor, and after that your life lay in my hands. The jury had found you guilty of murder, the Judge had pronounced your sentence, and much as I desired personally to save you, I could not, in my official capacity, give up to those feelings. I heard from day to day of your condition, and was led to believe that you would die as bravely as you had borne your trial and imprisonment. Last night a letter was brought me at a late hour, which, as it seemed unimportant, I laid aside till morning. When I came to read it, my surprise may be imagined, to see in it the means of saving your life honorably. It was signed by Henry Johnson, who lay in his berth on board of a Cuban vessel, and begged me to pardon you if it were not too late. Losing no time I rode to the wharves, went aboard the ship, saw the boy ——"

"Then he is alive!" gasped Anderson.

"Alive, and will come ashore to-day, though rather ill from his long sea voyage."

The young man breathed a heartfelt "Thank God."

"Saw the boy, as I was saying," continued the Governor, " received full proofs of his identity, and rode with all speed to the Jail. My first thought was to send in your pardon at once. But when I remembered our talk on the ship, I resolved to try your courage to the last, and stood ready at the gallows-foot to interfere before you were quite swung off. I endured the most intense suffering during the whole affair, but your sublime courage has well repaid me. Mr. Anderson, I know I have done wrong, and I ask your forgiveness. But promise me you will say nothing about this to any one, and only remember it as "The Governor's Experiment.""

Anderson was in no mood to censure his companion, though he felt he had trifled too far with a human life. And he said simply:

"I forgive you, Mr. Smith, from the bottom of my heart."

By this time the carriage had arrived at Pearl street. Anderson sprang out and ran up the steps and into the house without delay.

One of the servants saw him coming, and hurried away screaming to inform the others "that the Master's ghost had come, sure, with his dark brown hair all hanging down his shoulders!" The young man hastened to Mrs. Haynes's room, and rushed in. The widow was sitting in her chair, rocking backward and forward, and crying to herself, when the apparition entered. She heard the well-known voice cry, "It is I, mother, free and innocent;" then she fell, unable to bear the shock, and fainted away.

But joy does not kill, and soon the good woman was able to listen to the wonderful story of the pardon when the rope was round her boy's neck. She was able to clasp him in her arms again, and bless Heaven for having saved his life. He was quite weak and tired yet, however, and it was thought best by all that he should keep in the quiet of his room for a few days

After these few days were past, Albert sent messages to all of his true friends to come and see him at Pearl street.

Mr. Harvard came, and nearly made a woman of himself — to use his own expression — by crying over his saved client. The quadroon and and his wife came, nearly frantic with joy at Anderson's pardon ; Mr. Jenkins came, with his bandana, and renewed his statements that he never did — he was sure he never did. And then there came another, the last but not the least true friend — Mabel Le Moyne.

Anderson was glad to see Mabel, very glad to see her. If he had known as much as the Jailor's little wife surmised when she lifted the poor girl from the guardroom floor that evening, he might have appreciated her devotion to him even more that he did. They passed an afternoon pleasantly together, and when it came time for Mabel to go, Albert said in the old way :

"You will come to-morrow?"

She smiled and said they were not in prison now.

"No," he replied, "but you must come often just the same, and I shall ask leave to visit you, also."

"Ah!" thought Mabel as she rode home, "If he were only mine forever, there would be no 'to-morrow' then."

CHAPTER II.

HIS SIN COMES HOME TO HIM.

So Harry Johnson was not dead, after all. He did come back, though both Anderson and the dark gentleman predicted he would not. The great ship Anderson noticed tacking about in the bay, the night before his execution was to take place, bore into the harbor the freight which saved him from the doom prepared by the monster Law. The jury was proved to be wrong, the Governor and Council wrong, even the great agent of popular opinion,—the newspaper, all wrong. People were heard to remark that they had doubted all the while whether Anderson was really guilty, and were rejoiced to find their opinions correct. But one thing remained true. They had been wrong, all wrong,, and had nearly sacrificed a life of more than ordinary value before they were set right. They were wrong, as they have been fifty-thousand times before, and probably will be again and again. Human wisdom is exceedingly fallible, and such things must go on until we all accept the injunction of the Master, "Judge not, that ye be not judged!"

How came Harry alive, and how

did it happen that his bones were not lying under the wreck of the ship Tuscarora, as Mr. Hawley believed when he inaugurated his plot against Anderson's life? The answer comes plainly enough. When the ship to which the dark gentleman had consigned him, went down in the storm which overtook her, Harry clung to a floating mast until he was rescued by a Cuban vessel. Proceeding to Havana, he obtained employment as book-keeper in an American house, where he remained until he saw the advertisements calling on him to return home.

Although Harry's return had been the means of saving Anderson's life, the lad was yet averse to meeting his former partner after what had passed; and as soon as he was considered well enough to leave the ship, he took lodgings at an obscure hotel, where he intended to remain until he could decide what course he should take next. After a few days of rest, he concluded to pay a visit to Hillsdale, his former home, he having been a tavern-boy at the Hillsdale House years before, and entertained the closest feelings of love for the landlord's daughter. He was in some doubt as to how he would be received by Mr. Slader or his daughter, after the disgrace into which he had fallen. He was set at ease at once, however, when Sallie ran to meet him with expressions of glad welcome, and he saw that to her, he was only a very dear friend brought to life after months of loss. His faults were forgotten in the joy that he was still among the living. Harry's heart was warmed with new love for the girl, who seemed to him the only friend he could claim on earth. While he was recounting his adventures and narrow

escape from death, his eye caught a gleam reflected from the hand he held, which attracted him at once.

"What, Sallie!" said he, "Have you become engaged to another since I have been away?"

"No indeed, Harry! What do you mean?" said Sallie, in astonishment.

"The ring on your finger—whose present was that?"

She comprehended, and answered his blank looks with a merry laugh.

"O, you jealous boy, that was given me by a lady who stopped here at the hotel last autumn." And here she proceeded to narrate the strange story, giving a description of the lady and her child. As she proceeded, Harry grew deeply interested, asking so many questions that Sallie was much surprised.

It was all plain to Harry then. With this news he could get an interview with Anderson. As soon as possible he rang the Pearl street bell, and though abashed in manner, and halting in speech, he met his former partner, and told him what he had learned. In return Anderson took him kindly by the hand, and offered unconditionally to restore him to his old place in the new warehouse. "With the lessons of the past for a guide," said Albert, "we may always succeed better in the future. Shall it be as I have said, Harry?"

Harry was completely overcome at this generous proposal, and gathered courage to deny in formal terms that he had been guilty of the incendiarism, stating his belief that Fred Hawley, the dark gentleman, had done the deed. Anderson recognized the description of the plotter, and told Harry how he could not fix the man in his memory, though he was sure he had met him before. The reunited partners in the house of J. A. Anderson & Co. puzzled over this problem for some time, and then, with brighter hearts than they had known of late, bade adieu to each other for the time.

Early the next morning, after a nearly sleepless night, Anderson set out for Hillsdale. Disdaining, as he had often before, a carriage of any kind, he sprang into the saddle, which was upon the back of a strong roadster, and after assuring Mrs. Haynes that he would write soon the result of his researches, and cautioning her not to build too strong hopes on his success, he sat off on his long ride. He was not in the mood to spare his horse, and a few hours' hard riding brought him in sight of the Hillsdale House. There was the window in which he had seen the apparition of a woman with golden curls, holding a baby in her lap. It must have been Ella, with one of the neighbor's children. There was the yard where he walked into the house, so tired and dusty, with his old clothes and gray beard. There was the barn in which he hid while the landlord and his crew were chasing up and down the road like devils to find him; from which he had gone out after dark in a new disguise, and helped the detectives in their search the next day. As he looked at the open window where his darling had been seen, Albert knew well that had he believed it possible she were really there, and that the vision was not unreal like the one he saw in the ocean, he would have rushed to her room and revealed himself, regardless of the price set on his head. Then Samuel Slader would have been richer by five thousand dollars! But Anderson would have had

a month more of imprisonment, and he had had quite enough as it was.

Sallie Slader did not need Mr. Anderson's introduction of himself to know it was he. She had been too often the pleased listener to Harry's enthusiastic portraits of his friend to doubt that the handsome, open-faced young man with dark brown hair was any other than the young author. She received him, therefore, with the utmost cordiality, and they were soon seated in the old-fashioned parlor and engaged in conversation about the matter which brought them together. After introducing the subject, Sallie proceeded to relate what she knew of Ella during her stay.

"She came here on the railroad coach one evening in May," said the girl, "and gave the name of Mrs. Ella Hastings. She kept to her room nearly all the time, and we used to take our meals alone together, as she was very careful to avoid company. Thus she lived with us quietly, paying her board from a sum of money she brought with her, and which she often spoke of as having been given her at different times by "Bert." That was the only name I could ever make her apply to you. On the second day of August, her baby was born."

If she had laid on his bare flesh an iron rod, red from the furnace, he could not have writhed under it more than he did under those words. He gasped for breath until she was alarmed for his life. He clasped his hands over the heart which almost ceased to beat. He pressed his forehead, and covered his eyes with his hands to shut out the horrible sight which came to his bewildered brain. The agony of keen remorse was on him now. The vision of the girl which rose out of the sea, and those ringing words "Her and her heirs forever," came crushing upon his brain like some heavy beam, stupefying and blinding him with excruciating pain. He clenched his hands in his hair and tore it out in bunches. Such an exhibition of ungovernable feeling, the girl had never seen before.

When he was a little recovered, he suddenly turned upon her and grasped her arm so tightly that it made her scream.

"What was it you said?" he articulated. "Was it that — a — child — was — born?"

"Why, sir, I supposed Harry told you that. Did he say nothing about it?" said Sallie, becoming frightened.

"*Then it is true! O, God! it is true!*"

Back came the crushing weight on his brain, crushing and blinding him as before.

Again was the red hot iron laid on him, and again he writhed under the torment.

"Did she ever curse me?" he asked, shutting his teeth tightly together.

"O, no, sir! Never. She always blessed you. She often spoke of you as 'darling' or 'dear Bert.' She loved you, sir, as few men are loved."

Unconsciously the girl had heated the iron ten times hotter than before. Feeling his wrong to Ella as Albert Anderson did, it would have been a relief to know she had cursed him. But she loved him through all! O! The iron burned fiercely, then!

"Was she very ill?" he asked after a long pause.

"Ah, yes sir, we feared at one time she was dying. It was two months before she was able to have the care of the child."

Albert caught his breath at the word "dying." Had he, then, come so near losing her?

"The child lived, then?"

"Yes. It was very well all of the time they remained here. It must be eleven months old now. A very fine boy indeed."

"Hah! A boy? Did Ella name it?"

"She had not formally given it a name when she left here, but always called it 'Bert's baby.' She lavished all her time and love on the child, which was a sweet little thing, well worth her attention."

Sallie proceeded from this to give Anderson a history of all Ella's stay in the hotel; how she had kept his name secret through everything lest he should be disgraced; how she had hurried away in the stagecoach the morning after he was seen in Hillsdale; what she had said regarding her love for Bert, and of her past life with him; and how she had declared her willingness to live and die in poverty if need be, so that he come not to evil. When she finished, Anderson asked, in a hushed voice, whether Ella left anything at the hotel which he could have to take with him.

"Only this ring," said Sallie. "It was by this that Harry learned the story. He saw it on my finger, and his jealousy was aroused at once."

Albert took the ring and put it on his own finger. He told the girl she should have one in place of it, double its value, but this one he must keep for himself. He kissed it lovingly as he said this. "Did you say Harry was jealous of the ring?" asked Anderson, in a moment. "Ah," he continued, seeing her blushes, "He loves you, then?"

"We are very good friends, sir" Sallie stammered. "We have known each other for many years."

"Yes," replied Anderson, "and you are in love, too. And you shall be married. I will talk with Harry of this. He is now once more my partner, and I shall have some influence with him. Harry is a good boy and I believe you will make a wife worthy of him."

"Have you really forgiven Harry, sir?"

"Forgiven him? yes, and restored him to his old position as manager of the business."

"What words can I find to thank you!" cried Sallie, with warmth.

"No words are necessary," said Anderson. "Make him a good wife, and that will be enough. And if you are ever tempted to evil, look at me, broken down under the weight of one sin, suffering more this day than when standing upon the gallows waiting for death, and rather put your right hand into the fire than yield to it!"

They went out to the gate where the young man remounted his horse. Sallie tried to persuade him to partake of some refreshment, but he said he could eat nothing. Waiving a sad good by, he rode out of her sight, toward the railroad station.

Why should we follow him through those two weeks of search which brought forth nothing? Why need we detail the numberless times he fancied he had really found a clue, only to prove it wrong on investigation? Women with children in their arms were not so scarce as to excite the attention of everybody. There were scores of golden-haired girls in every county, who rode upon the railroad trains with their children. But he always found them at last, gathered round their own firesides, with husbands to love and bless them. The one girl he was searching for was wanting.

Coming back to the city, he recounted the failure of his mission to Mrs. Haynes, in as brave a manner as he could command. He told her also of the child's birth, which news she received much more calmly than he had expected. The widow saw the great change which had come over the young man, and resolved to give up to her sorrows as little as possible in her presence.

One evening, as she was sitting with Albert in his study-room, a servant brought up a card on which was written the name, strange to both of them, "Felix McCabe."

Anderson went down to the parlor to see Mr. McCabe, and begged him to state his business with him. Mc-Cabe proceeded to do so, accordingly, with his usual politeness.

"You are wishing to learn the whereabouts of a young lady, Miss Ella Hastings, I believe?"

"I am, indeed," said Anderson. "What do you know of her?"

"Everything, Your Honor, everything," replied Mr. McCabe. "But it is best to be business-like, as you, who have been in business know very well. I naturally have no personal interest in coming here to give you information. No, sir, I came here to earn some money, and if you want my information you must pay for it. My terms are one hundred dollars down, and another hundred if you find the lady."

"No tricks, with me, my friend," said Anderson, counting out the sum asked for. "Say what you have to say, and I will give you your price when you have done."

"Fair enough," said Felix. "Well,

then, I saw Miss Ella in February at the house of a Mrs. Wilson, on the high street in Kingston. I will tell you who was with her there, if you will agree not to mention my name in the matter. For that would get me into trouble."

Anderson willingly promised, and Felix continued:

"She was riding out with a man named Hawley——"

"The dark gentleman again! Well, go on."

"She had her child in her arms. I inquired about her, and from what I heard I think he is trying to induce her to marry him, but has little prospect of success.

"You are sure they are not married already?"

"I am sure they were not at that time. But this Hawley is a persistent fellow, and will try hard to carry his ends."

"Is this all you have to tell me?"

"Yes, sir, that is all," said McCabe; and he soon after withdrew. As he passed down the steps, he muttered:

"Ah, Mr. Fred Hawley, I'll be even with you now for treating me like a dog after I had finished your dirty work."

So there was a motive beside making money which actuated Felix McCabe. And thus it came about that he was able to strike one of the first blows which were to stagger the dark gentleman.

The next morning Anderson took an early train for Kingston. On reflection he had decided to conceal his mission from Mrs. Haynes, until he was sure it would prove successful. This was, without doubt, the wisest course, as there is nothing so painful as hope awakened, only to be dashed again to the earth.

At Kingston, Anderson soon obtained directions how to find Mrs. Wilson's house. As he approached it, he looked longingly up to the windows lest a familiar face might appear there, but he saw none. The hard-visaged landlady answered his ring, and knew the instant her eyes fell on the young man, who he was and what he wanted.

"Is Miss Hastings living with you now?" Anderson asked, and waited in suspense for her answer. It came to carry him again beyond hope.

"She left more than a month ago."

"I am her guardian. Can you tell me in which direction she went."

"I cannot," said Mrs. Wilson, composedly. "She went away one night in what *I* call a highly improper manner, stealing out quietly with her child, when we were asleep. I have never seen or heard from her since, and if she is the sort of person I have reason to fear, I have no wish to see her or anyone belonging to her. Is there anything more you want, sir?"

"No, I thank you." Anderson turned away from the door faintly. His sun had gone behind a cloud once more. At the depot he renewed his inquiries, and along the railroad line. But he could learn nothing, and heartsick, he again gave up the search. After leaving Kingston he went to the Hillsdale station, and procuring a horse, started for home by the road which led by the Hillsdale house. There he stopped several hours to rest, and informed Sallie how he had failed again in his search for Ella. The girl said what she could to comfort him, and after a while he set off for the city.

Everybody knows that the long hill just after you leave Hillsdale, going to the city, is one of the longest and most tedious hills in the county. Down its steep descent, Anderson rode slowly, fearing to hasten his horse lest he should stumble. On either side of the rode the new mown hay gave forth a sweet scent, while the sun, waning into the west, threw its hot beams over the face of Nature, lulling her to sleep. Men, working in the fields, looked up with curious glances at the young rider who had not to toil like them for his bread. An old farmer and his wife sat on one porch in the shade, resting from the heat, and saluted Anderson with a pleasant "Good-morrow," as he passed. After this he rode through the valley between the hills, where the cool woods covered both sides of the way, and the babbling brooks ran sparkling over the stones. A rustling in the branches drew his attention, and the figure of a young woman came out; with a basket on her arm; with straw hat hanging by a ribbon down her back; with black hair negligently lying about her shoulders; with large, dark eyes that looked up suddenly, stood trembling in their orbits a minute, at sight of Anderson, until their owner cried out in fear, and ran back into the woods as fast as she could run.

Anderson stood transfixed.

Who was she?

In an instant, though she was somewhat changed, he knew she was the dark lady who had beguiled Ella from him!

CHAPTER THREE.

FATE, GOD OR CHANCE IS DRAWING HIM.

At his books, or riding about the city and suburbs, Anderson spent the rest of that summer. Among the few people on whom he called was Mabel Le Moyne and her aunt, Mrs. Davis. When one pleasant autumn day was nearing its close, he sat with Mabel on the broad piazza of the Davis Mansion, carrying on a brisk conversation.

"What are you doing all these days, Mr. Anderson," she inquired, "when I never see you for so long a time together?"

"Writing. Writing most of the time," Anderson replied. "I am pretty busy just now, trying to make up for the days I lost when I lay sick in the jail."

Mabel frowned prettily and shook her head.

"So you consider those days as loss, Mr. Anderson?"

"Loss in one sense," he explained, seeing the construction she had put upon his words. "But gain in another and better sense, which much more than equals the first. I lost a little time, which might have been used in work, and I gained a friend whom I prize highly. There. Does that satisfy you, Miss Faultfinder?"

She laughed merrily.

"Yes, that will do very well indeed. But I have a proposal to make, which you must hear this evening, and as I see you glancing toward your horse, impatient to leave me, I will proceed at once. I (and my aunt), have concluded that you are working too hard, and ought to take a vacation, a rest, a few weeks of change and recreation. And we have fixed a plan between us, which will suit your case nicely."

"Indeed!" said Anderson. "You have it all arranged then, and I am to be allowed no word in the matter whatever? Well, let us hear your plan, and know our fate at once. This suspense is dreadful."

Mabel laughed again, and put her

little hand over his mouth to stop him.

"How dare you make fun of my plans?" she asked, with mock seriousness. "You are a bad boy to interrupt when *older* people are talking to you. Now be quiet and hear me out. Every winter, you know, my aunt and I go out to our Louisiana home at Longwood, where my papa used to live. It is a beautiful place, with plenty of shade and fishing — and — all such things, you know, that young gentlemen are fond of. We intend to start from here in a few weeks now, and must insist——"

He was about to make some reply, when the little hand was clapped over his mouth again.

"Must *insist* on your accompanying us, either for the entire winter, or, if that is impossible, for as long a time as you can spare. You need the rest and the change of scene — I know you do — and there the case is decided. I am judge and jury, you are tried and sentenced, and from this decision there is no appeal."

As Mabel finished, she removed the little hand from Albert's mouth, when he took it up gallantly, and kissed it.

"My dear Miss Mabel, I fear I cannot accept of your kind invitation. My writing is imperative, and cannot be put by at my liking, as you seem to think."

"Well, then, if you must write, I will so far commute your sentence, as to allow you to take it with you, and devote part of your time to it while you are gone."

Mabel was so earnest, and waited his reply so anxiously, that Albert could hardly bring himself to give a direct refusal.

"I am afraid I should do very little writing with your bright eyes watching near by," he said, shaking his head.

"O, if that is all, I will give you a room to yourself, and I promise not to disturb you when you are at work. Now are you satisfied, I wonder."

Her arguments were irresistable, but lest they should be wanting in effect, she continued to pour into his ears details of the loveliness of Longwood. The beauty of its scenery, the healthfulness of its climate, and other inducements without limit.

"You will not be obliged to stay one precious minute after you become tired of Longwood, Mr. Anderson. So you will run very little risk indeed. You really require a change of scene, —you may laugh, but it is true—and I wish you to go very much ; that is, I think it will be the best thing for you. Come, now ! Promise me."

The young man considered briefly.

"After such an imperative demand as you make, Miss Mabel," he said, "I hardly see how I could escape compliance with your request, were I so disposed. Perhaps you are right. I think, myself that a few days——"

"*Weeks*, Mr. Anderson ! Weeks, or months ! "

"Very well, then, weeks," said Albert, doubtfully. "A few weeks of change could do me no harm. Since you are so kind to invite me to spend them in Longwood, I — don't — know — but I will accept."

"O, then you will go!" cried Mabel," in a tone which showed how happy his answer had made her. "Ah, there is my aunt ! Mrs. Davis! Mrs. Davis ! Mr. Anderson is here. Please come in a minute."

Mrs. Davis rustled her black silk into the room, and received Anderson as cordially as her reserved nature would allow her to receive anybody. He was Mabel's friend, Mabel wanted him there, Mabel had said she wished him to accompany them South, and the matter was settled, of · course. Mrs. Davis had gradually become, during her later years, a sort of echo to Mabel's desires and opinions. What Mabel wanted, must be right. What Mabel thought must be true. Mrs. Davis was fully prepared on all occasions to express her approbation of Mabel's acts in advance, and learn what they were afterwards.

"Auntie," said Mabel, "Mr. Anderson has accepted our invitation, and will go with us to Longwood."

" I trust you will enjoy your visit to the South," murmured Mrs. Davis, "and return better fitted for the discharge of your multiplied duties."

This was an unusual long speech for her to make, and Mabel looked at her in some astonishment. Anderson thanked the lady, and expressed a similar hope. After which, her conversational powers being exhausted, Mrs. Davis graciously bowed herself out of the room. And soon after, Anderson departed for Pearl street, leaving a very happy girl behind him, watching his retiring figure, until, as he turned a bend in the road, he stood in his stirrups and lifted his cap to her. Mabel answered with her hand-kerchief, and stood leaning on the gate, looking in the direction he had gone, a long time. She finally became aware that rain drops were falling on her, and that she was standing alone under a very black sky, with no light to be seen except that which streamed from the parlor windows. Before Albert went, she was sure the sky had been clear enough. While he was by her, there was no darkness near. How it all changed, when he disap-

peared around the road turning ! She walked back into the house, with her heart beating as of old. Ah, Mabel, Mabel !

When Anderson informed Mrs. Haynes that he should leave the city on a short vacation, she was glad for his sake ; and when he told her where he was going, and with whom — she acquiesced without outward sign of dislike. But within her heart the good woman would have wished it otherwise. She thought she saw here a possible rival to Ella, and loving her daughter so deeply, she feared the consequences which might ensue from a too close friendship between Anderson and Mabel. Still she said nothing, feeling that it would be inadvisable to do so, and tried to watch and wait patiently. That Mabel loved Albert was but too evident, but that he could so far forget his duty to Ella as to yield to a new love, Mrs. Haynes would not believe. She only hoped and prayed for a speedy restoration of her long-lost child to the arms from which a hard fate had taken her, to give both a dearly-bought lesson of life. Thus she lived on, and waited.

Just as the approaching winter began to shadow its coming by throwing a chill into the evenings, Anderson departed for Longwood with Mrs. Davis and Mabel. The climate of the section was almost exactly the same as that of his birth-place, Catherine, and Albert enjoyed his change from the first. A new color came into his cheek, a new buoyancy into his step, and he was forced to acknowledge that Mabel's prophecy was a true one.

He rode horseback over the estates and adjacent roads, every evening, and Mabel, being a supurb horse-woman, kept at his side, even at the fastest gallop he could spur his animal to undertake. There is no sport the superior of this to give a quick motion to the blood, and throw a healthy vigor over the frame; none the less so either, when races are frequent between the riders, with the accompanying jollity and excitement. One evening, when they were riding thus, Anderson said:

"Few women can ride a horse as you can, Miss Mabel. You seem to have no fear, whatever."

"Why should I?" she answered, laughing. "I am as much at home in this saddle as if I were sitting on the house veranda."

"You must have had considerable experience, Miss Mabel."

"Yes, indeed! When I was hardly tall enough to reach a pony's head with my hand, papa used to put me on their backs, and teach me how to ride. When I was seven years old, I could ride with any of them. I should not know how to pass an evening now, without a ride."

"And when I was less than seven," said Anderson, "my father used to take me to ride with him, on a horse as large as his own. How long ago that seems! How little of life I knew then, and for years after! Twenty years ago, Mabel——"

He stopped because she laid her gloved hand on his arm. The action was impulsive, and the hand was taken away as quickly as it came there. He knew what it meant, and was sorry; for he had awakened a new hope in her heart which he had not meant to do. He had never called her "Mabel," before.

Without finishing his sentence, Anderson proposed that they ride back to the house, and they walked their horses along under the trees together. Each knew that a chord had been struck in the other's heart which awakened old remembrances too precious to be disturbed. At the house the negro servants took the horses, and the riders sought their own chambers.

Mabel had been true to her promise not to disturb Albert at his hours of labor, for nearly a week, when one day she came to his room, and asked admission. He looked a little surprised as he opened the door, to see her there, and asked her if she would come in a while.

"O yes, Mr. Anderson," said she. "I am lonesome enough to die down stairs. Auntie has gone away in the carriage to call on some of her friends, and if you will let me come in, and sit down here, I will be very quiet, and not disturb you a bit."

"Very well," he said, "you shall come in, but I must hold you to your word. You may take a seat where you please, and I will go on with my writing as though you were not here."

This satisfied Mabel, and she took a seat by one of the windows, where she could see Anderson at his writing. How handsome she thought him, in his dressing gown and slippers, with his clear, earnest eyes, finely cut features, and long, brown hair, hanging in such heavy masses over the page he was working upon! How like lightning his pen flew over the page, leaving its track of characters behind it in those odd black lines! What could he be writing about to-day? How much she would like to know!

Her woman's curiosity would allow her no rest after this until she did know what he was writing about. She waited until he came to the end of a paragraph, and held his pen poised, fresh-dipped in the ink, for another commencement.

"Mr. Anderson?"

He looked up, with a curious smile playing about his mouth, as if to say "I thought as much," but only answered:

"Well?"

"If you would tell me what you are writing about, I should not be so lonesome. I could think about it then, as well as you."

"I am writing the Second Part of my Story of the Prisoner."

"It is based on your own experience, isn't it?"

"Partly."

"How far have you written, now?"

"To where he was lying sick in his cell," replied Anderson, soberly.

"Did he have a nurse to care for him?" faltered Mabel, feeling that she was treading on dangerous ground.

"He did," said Albert, "and a very good one."

"A young lady?"

"A young lady."

He answered her so calmly, that Mabel felt a new strength coming, and she proceeded to ask yet more. How she ever gained courage to do it was a mystery, but it came.

"Have you the rest of the book fully planned in your mind?" she asked.

"Nearly so," said Albert, laying down his pen and turning his chair towards her.

"And this prisoner," said Mabel, averting her gaze from his face, and looking out of the open window, "was he hung upon the gallows?"

"No, he was pardoned at the last moment, and proved innocent."

"And did he ever remember his nurse, after he was released?"

"O, yes, they lived the best of friends."

Mabel's courage was going, but she found courage to ask desperately:

"Never more than that, never more more than friends?"

"*Never!*" cried Albert. "Why should they?"

"I fear you are a poor novelist, Mr. Anderson," stammered Mabel, faintly. "Did not this girl love this prisoner?"

"He did not believe it, Miss Mabel. It was only sympathy for him, and not love, which she felt."

Mabel drew a long breath.

"Don't you believe it, Mr. Anderson. The girl loved him truly."

Albert looked astonished.

"If that be so," said he, "it is a pity, and I am heartily sorry for both of them. The prisoner told his kind nurse a few chapters back to be content with sympathy, for more than that would bring evil upon them. The nurse should have remembered this."

"It may be too late for that, now," said Mabel. "You can alter the plot enough to change this part, I should think. That would be very easy, would it not, Mr. Anderson?"

Mabel bit her lips to keep back the tears which came into her eyes, but one of them rolled down her cheek in spite of her. Anderson began to feel how hard a task she was laying on him.

"Miss Mabel," he said, slowly, "if the Prisoner should find that the nurse had loved him, he would deeply regret that she did not let him suffer alone, instead of brightening his cell with her presence. He would try to explain to her that he could not return her *love*, though his friendship would be eternal. He would say to her, 'My dear girl, give up these thoughts, and be brave enough to outlive them.' That is what the Prisoner would say, and if the girl were as brave as I think her, she would hearken to his advice."

Her rebellious heart throbbed fiercely against her bosom.

"But you have not told me why you cannot change the plot of the story in this particular, Mr, Anderson. If the girl loves him devotedly, (and I can imagine how she may!) why should he not love her in return?"

Anderson was more than ever surprised at her persistency.

"What if there were Another," he said, soberly, "who had a prior claim?"

"Whoever she was," said Mabel, "she could not love him better than the nurse did."

"Perhaps not," he said; "but her claim is prior, nevertheless. I am writing the Second Part of my novel now. The First has gone out into the world, and that world will demand the ending I have given them reason to expect."

Mabel was not to be put off in this way.

"O!" she cried, "stop the printers of the First Part; search the bookstores and private libraries; call in the whole edition, and burn it in one bonfire. Is it not better than to break a woman's heart, as you will by continuing the story as you have begun?"

"The woman's heart will not be broken," said Albert, kindly, drawing his chair nearer to her, and taking her hand in his. "I have drawn her character as that of a brave girl, who will not succumb to such a small trial. She will continue to live the Prisoner's friend, and some day, she will find a better man than he is for her husband."

His touch was magnetic, and she suffered him to stroke her hair for some moments without a word. Then she said:

"Mr. Anderson, tell me truly, is there no possibility that this may be changed as I have asked?"

"No, Miss Mabel. None. It cannot be."

The girl drew herself a little away from him, and there came into her face something of the look she had shown when he reproved her for weeping over the gallows-building, and she had promised not to do so again. A look of a new resolve, which lit up her face with a sort of grandeur.

"Then," she said firmly, "the nurse will overcome her love for the Prisoner. Not all at once, may be, but gradually, if she is, as you say, a brave girl. She can do this, and she *shall* do it! Now are you pleased, Mr. Anderson?"

He *was* pleased, and in his admiration would have grasped her hand again, but she sprang up to leave the room.

"No," she said, "I cannot bear it now. My bravery is new-found, and I am afraid to trust it. Good-bye for a little while. God bless you!"

She threw a meaning into that last invocation that told him it was no light work she had undertaken, when she promised to give up him — the Prisoner. He thought how, perhaps, if there never had been any Ella, he might have loved such a woman as Mabel. But since there *had* been an Ella, and such a devoted Ella, who held his whole heart and soul, and would, he believed, some day, be restored to him again, he could not think of any other — no, not while life lasted!

It was coming on evening, and as he did not wish to ride with Mabel that night, he went out for a stroll, and wandered down by where the deep, dark river flowed by the plantation, with its ceaseless murmur of running waters.

CHAPTER IV.

LOST AND FOUND AGAIN.

"Where is your husband, girl? You should be at home with him, and not wandering upon the road in this manner."

It was a woman who spoke. At least she bore the appearance of being a woman. She was past the middle age, and had daughters of her own. And she might have spoken kinder, one would think, to the poor child who stopped by her door to ask leave to rest there an hour or two.

"Dear lady," said the girl addressed, "I am so tired, and the child is so tired, and his father is many miles from here. It is such a little favor I ask you, lady. We are very far from any city, and we must rest somewhere."

"No doubt," said the woman, ironically. "You strolling people always have excuses enough. But you can't stay here. It shan't be said I encouraged any of ye. Come, now, go along, or I will call the dogs, and then I reckon ye'll start quick enough."

The girl lifted her child upon her shoulder, with a disheartened look, and went down upon the road again. It was such a dusty road, so hot that she almost fainted under the burning sun. The child was heavy, and the mother small and weak. It seemed as if she must give up under her burden.

Struggling along the hot road for another mile, the wanderer found shade at last under a little clump of trees off from the roadside, and sank down there almost exhausted. The child slept soundly, and she spread out her shawl for a bed, and laid him on it. He was a remarkably pretty child, with hazel eyes, and brown, curly hair. A heavy burden to his tired mother, but a precious one.

"Ah, little Bertie," said the mother, "if I could lie down and sleep like you, I should be happy. But we have a long journey to go yet, and I must keep awake till nightfall."

The speaker started at a near footstep, and grasped the shawl on which her child lay. How could she know but what the step was that of a wild beast, or of some man worse than a wild beast. She soon discovered it to be neither, however. It was an old negro woman with a basket on her arm.

The old woman stopped on seeing the girl, and signalled to her to have no fear. She came up and asked whether the girl was hungry, and on being answered yes, took some hoe-cake from her basket, and gave it to her. The food was homely, but the gift was kindly meant. The old woman sat down on the ground, and looked at the sleeping child. Then she looked from the child to the mother, and back again.

"Yours, honey?"

"Yes." The girl opened her lips, and made the form of the word, but no sound came forth.

"Tired, honey?"

Again the lips opened, but there was no sound.

"Goin' far, honey?"

"Yes." The girl pointed over the tree tops, to indicate in which direction.

The old woman bent over the child in compassion a few moments. She shook her head and murmured her sorrow.

"It's allus de same, honey, in dis here worl'. Suff'rin', suff'rin' all de time. Wish I could do somethin' fur yer, but I'se only an old nigger woman, and I aint got nuthin' to give. "

The girl heard her, and felt ashamed that this poor creature should think she wanted charity from *her*. She put her hand in her pocket, and drew out a purse. It was light, now—a good deal lighter than it had once been—but there was money there yet. The old woman looked amazed to see the girl pour it out in her hand and hold it up. The girl took out a piece, and motioned that she should pay for the hoecake she had eaten, but the woman would not touch it.

"Keep it, chile," she said. "Yer'll need it yerself, bimeby." Then she went away muttering.

The girl waited until the woman was out of sight, and then went down to a little brook which ran near by, to wash the dust from her hands and her face. The child awoke and she dipped her handkerchief into the water to wash its hands and its face. After this, the pair sat down on the bank of the little brook, the mother trying to collect her thoughts, and the child munching a piece of hoe-cake contentedly.

Her and her heirs forever! Ella Hastings Anderson, and her child. Tramping over the hot roads to get away, farther and farther, from those she loved, and those she feared. And yet, it is certain, that loving Albert as her life, and fearing Hawley as she would death, Ella would rather have met the dark gentleman at any time than Anderson. For to meet the lame gentleman could only harm herself, while to meet Albert, would harm him, whom she loved more than herself.

Her mind was clouded still, but this one thought was dominant—Whatever happened, Bert must not be disgraced. No matter if she had to rise in the night-time and steal away from places with baby, and always be on the watch for some one who knew her, or had heard of her, lest they carry back the tidings to Anderson. And as if this fear was not enough, she had now another one to watch for—the lame gentleman with the broken leg.

She tried to remember, as she sat there with her child on the bank of the little brook, all that had passed since she first saw the lame gentleman at Mrs. Wilson's house. How kind he had been at first, bringing her oranges, and little presents for the baby. How he used to praise the child, and pet it when he came in to see her. She even rode out with him once, when he urged that her health was suffering by her long confinement in the house. Then, when they were in the outskirts of the town, he asked her if she would marry him, and go to his home miles away, where she should always be happy, and the child should never come to want anything. With what earnestness he pleaded she remembered well. But she thought of Bert, and could not answer him as he wished. When she refused him as kindly as she could, how suddenly his love turned to anger! It frightened her now to think of it. He told her she had better marry him, or he would denounce her as Anderson's paramour wherever she might go. He foamed in his wrath until the white froth came down the sides of his mouth. Still she told him it could not be. Then he had grown terribly angry, and said that if she ever expected to marry that brown-haired devil, she might give that up at once, for he would be hung on the gallows before many weeks ! But she did not believe it. Innocent men were never hung, she reasoned, and Bert was not one to commit a crime worthy of death. So she clung to the child, and tried not to mind the lame gentleman, and in this way they rode back to Mrs. Wilson's. At the door stood waiting the man who had eaten dinner with her before the lame gentleman came there. As she passed up the stairs she heard the man say to Hawley, laughing, "She'll be too many for you, Fred," and Hawley answered, "I wish you'd mind your business, Felix McCabe."

The little Bertie had eaten all his hoe-cake, and the mother rose to give him another piece. The child received the coarse food graciously, and the mother was left again to her reflections.

"I wish you'd mind your business, Felix McCabe." Yes, that was what the lame gentleman said, in a very angry tone. And afterwards, "Do I owe you anything, or why do you come around me after your work is done, when you know I hate the sight of you?" The men's voices were loud, and she heard the man answer: "Yes, Mr. Hawley, you *do* owe me something for those words of yours, and I'll have my pay, too, before I am through with you." Then she heard the word "Anderson," and was so affrighted that she ran into her room, and locked the door.

That night she gathered a few articles of clothing in a bundle, and stole quietly out of doors when Mrs. Wilson was asleep. The night was a very bright one, and she was afraid until she was gone several miles from the house. A team overtook her, and the driver kindly asked if she would like to ride. Thinking only of getting away, away from the lame gentleman, Ella thankfully accepted this offer, and climbed into the wagon with the baby. Ten miles of riding, and the team drew up before a railroad station. It might as well be that way as any, she thought. Which way did the train go? Toward the South, they told her. Well, she would take a ticket for the South; a long, long way south, as far as the railroad would take her. The train came at last, and she went aboard with the baby. A day's ride brought her to the end of the railroad. She left the train, and found herself and little Bertie in a strange land. New rooms were found, and she lived in them some months, as economically as she could, for her money was going fast. She obtained a little sewing from the lady who owned the house, and one day, being in her parlor, she asked leave to play a little on the piano. This request being granted, the lady found that Ella was an excellent pianist, and engaged her to teach music to her young daughter. From this, several other ladies brought their daughters to her, and she taught quite a little class of them. She was very quiet and reserved, but the ladies liked her all the better for this, and they had paid her well. Bertie was growing finely, and the girls all loved him and used to play with him. Thus the sunshine spread over the young mother. But one day the shadow came, and darkened all.

It was such a little shadow, but she was afraid of it as much as though it had covered the whole earth.

Sitting at her window, sewing, one afternoon, she saw the lame gentleman, walking with a cane, limping down the street near the house. He did not see her, but she had no peace after that. She feared he might find her, and denounce her before her friends as he had threatened, and she resolved on flight.

The lame gentleman seemed always to be found in cities. To escape him she must go into the country. She did not dare to go to the great railroad stations, lest he might be among them; she did not even dare to go in the daytime, but waited until darkness covered the earth. Then she left a note for her kind landlady, begging her not to think evil of her for her sudden departure, for she must go, and then, taking Bertie, she wandered away.

Daylight found her near a poor man's cabin. The poor man saw her, and told her to come in and rest, and she would be right welcome. The poor man's wife gave her breakfast, but would take no money from her. The poor man's little boy volunteered to show her a short cut to the highroad, for she insisted that she must be going; and they all said "God speed you!" when she left them. The child could not walk, and though she was very tired, she had to carry it in her arms. There was no rest for her. She felt she must be going on, on, until she could be sure she was beyond the reach of the lame gentleman who had been so angry because she would not marry him.

The little Bertie had eaten his cake, and gone to sleep again. Ella took the child in her arms, and pillowed his head on her shoulder. The bright hair of the mother mingled with that of the little one. How few the years since she first laid her girlish head on the other Bert's shoulder, in their night passage to Claremont

Seminary! "Dear Bert," sobbed Ella, "If he knew *this*, he would believe truly that I loved him; but he must never know!"

Then she resumed her thoughts of the journey. After leaving the poor man's family she walked on until she came to a village. There was a little factory in the village, like the factories she had seen in the towns further north, and she came to it just as the factory girls were coming out to dinner. Some of the girls were black and some were white, but they all looked merry, she thought, and the wanderer stopped to inquire for the Superintendent, to ask him to employ her. Then the white and black girls gathered around her and her baby, laughing, and the Superintendent came out. He was an ugly brute, with no pity about him. As soon as he heard Ella's request for work, he turned to the laughing girls, and said:

"Do you want such people as this to work with you, girls?"

And they all shouted with one voice:

"No! No! We don't want her here."

"Why?" asked Ella, surprised. And then the girls laughed again, and pointed to the child, and the Superintendent said, brutally:

"Honest women don't travel the roads with children. You must go elsewhere than here if you want work. Come, now! Be going."

This was her first lesson in the ways of the world toward the unfortunate, but there were more to follow. One woman farther on offered to hire her as a house-servant, if she would give her child away to an asylum.

"I will say nothing about the strangeness of your having a child at all, travelling with you on the road," said the woman. " I overlook that entirely, which is what few people would do. But if you wish to take my situation, you must send him away and never ask to go to visit him again."

Ella returned a shocked look to the woman's proposition.

"Give up little Bertie, ma'am? O, no, I couldn't do that! We will live together or die together."

Then she went on again; on, on, but always meeting with rebuffs for Bertie's sake, and refusals to employ her with the child.

"Oh, Bertie, Bertie!" cried Ella as the child lay in her arms, "Why do they hate you so? Why do they turn me away on your account. You are a good baby, and they need not be ashamed of you. Oh, my poor Bertie!"

It would have brought tears to your eyes, if there is one particle of God's spirit in you, to have seen the young mother pondering in anguish over this great social problem. The sun.was already out of sight when Ella took the child once more on her shoulder, and resumed the travelled road. It was cooler to walk then than it had been when she had sought the grove, and she intended to make the most of the night-time. She was not as afraid of the lonely, desolate road as of the men who gazed curiously at her as she met them. They were often gruff, bad-looking men, but they generally accosted her with a pleasant ' evenin' miss," and made no attempt to detain her. So she walked on, on, till she grew so tired she could scarcely proceed a step farther. She had been alone with the child for several hours, when toiling along the road, its numerous windings brought her a companion—the River.

The River was not very wide, but it was deep, dark and swift. It was rushing on toward its mouth, where it joined the Father of Waters, twenty miles away. The sound of the River struck sweetly on the tired girl's ear, and she sat down to rest on its banks.

Little by little the River sung to her a song which made her start in horror at first, and then clasp her hands together in indecision. Father in Heaven! Must it come to that!

The River told her—"You are tired, you are weary, you and your child will starve together. No one will employ you while the baby is with you. To save both your lives there is but one thing to be done. Search my banks until you find a boat. Wrap Bertie in your shawl, and lay him in it while he sleeps. Push out the boat upon my bosom; I will carry it down by the towns, the cities, the villages and the plantations. Such an object as a boat floating alone will soon be noticed, and some one will row out to capture the prize. He will find the child, and bring it to the shore. Some good family will adopt it, and it will grow up happy. You will then be left free. You will find every avenue opened which closed against you yesterday. Both your life and the child's can be saved if you heed my proposal.

The little golden-haired figure kissed the baby passionately, and listened again to the siren voice of the River.

If you do not heed me, you have no choice but to go, meeting rebuffs everywhere, until you go, tired out, into some quiet place to die. If you die, the child must die, too. Do as I have said, and both of you shall live."

Thus the River seemed to whisper, as it flowed by her, deep, dark and swift.

Ella Hastings was tired; she was weary; she was discouraged. What suffering it had taken to bring her to listen to the River's voice, judge ye who know something of her misfortunes. If the River had only whispered of her own good, she would not have listened a moment, but when it spoke of this being to save Bertie, she caught every word eagerly. She listened afterward to hear some new sound in the waters, but they only repeated the same words: "If you die, the child must die too — the child must die too. Do as I have said, and both of you shall live."

The young mother caught up the baby and hurried along the shore. She soon found a boat pulled up on the bank, and with much difficulty she pushed it into the water. She worked fast, fearing that her courage would forsake her before the deed was done. She wrapped the sleeping child in her only shawl and laid him in the bottom of his little ark. She took a pencil and a leaf of paper from her pocket, and wrote a few words to place with the child to be read by his discoverers. She lifted a little gold chain with a ring attached, from her own neck, passed the note through the ring, and hung it on the child's neck. She kneeled on the sand, and prayed God to bless her baby — Bert's baby —and find him friends. She bent over the boat and kissed the little sleeper gently, lest he should wake, and by his crying divert her from her purpose. Then with another prayer in her heart for the child's safety, she turned her face away from the boat, and with one hand pushed it out upon the River's bosom, which took it up in its current and carried it along.

Half-blinded and shocked at what she had done, Ella ran from the place, as fast as she could go. In her haste she fell several times, and her hands were torn and scratched by the bushes. She regained the road and ran on. As the daylight became visible in the east, an early market wagon overtook her, and she asked leave to ride to the nearest railroad. The boy who drove the wagon kindly gave her a seat, and once more she entered a depot, with only one desire, to flee as far as possible from her troubles. A ticket was procured, which left a woeful little sum of money in Ella's purse. Again she rode away over the iron track, behind the snorting engine which had become her best friend in times of fear and danger. And as the rapidly turning wheels carried her farther and farther from her child, she prayed :

"God be merciful to me if I have done wrong to thee, oh, my baby !"

* * * * *

Albert Anderson walked up and down on the banks of the stream which washed the shores of Longwood, that night after his conference with Mabel, trying to quiet his troubled breast. Those newly awakened remembrances of Ella weighing on his spirits, and he fell to dreaming of her as he walked. He stepped into a boat which lay moored at the little pier, and taking up the oars, pulled across the stream, and cast anchor where there could come no sound to disturb his thoughts. Here he sat for hours, his head bowed in his hands ; calling it all to memory, from the day he first saw his girl, to the present time. If he had been able to live those years over again, he would have shaped his course very differently. Thus taught experience, and how stern a teacher that was, he knew well. He had passed through many Dangerous Experiments to arrive at some truths. Perhaps they were even worth the sorrow he had undergone, but this seemed almost doubtful.

He stopped in his reverie, thinking he heard a sound upon the water.

Not hearing it repeated, he relapsed into the reverie again.

And yet, no matter how much *he* had suffered, Ella had suffered more. The revelations of Sallie Slader and Felix McCabe showed what a noble, true, loving heart beat in her breast for him. Poor Ella! At that moment she might be wandering somewhere with her child——

Was that a cry he heard coming from out on the river?

The night was very dark, and Anderson could see but a short distance before him. He strained his eyes to pierce the blackness, and listened intently.

It *was* a cry which he heard. And as he listened, it was repeated. He caught up his oars and pulled with all speed into the current. The cries became more frequent, and served to guide him toward the spot from whence the sound came. Pausing to look ahead of his boat, he discovered another boat, floating at the river's will, and the cries seemed to come from the bottom of the latter craft. A few more strokes brought the young man alongside, and, throwing up his oars, he caught the boat, and pulled it toward him.

"Good Heavens!" he exclaimed, "It is a child!"

The child ceased crying as it saw the new face, and raised its little arms to be taken up. The young man attached the child's boat to the stern of his own, and guided both crafts toward the shore, where they soon grounded on the sand ; then he took the infant in his arms, and brushed the tears from its face with his handkerchief.

It was the first time the baby had ever seen its new protector, but it nestled to his breast as if it had found a natural home there. The young man searched, both in the boat and about the child's clothing, for some clue to the parties who abandoned it, for this seemed the most probable conclusion to arrive at.

"Who could have been so cruel as to desert you in this manner?" mused Anderson. "Some evil mother, I fear, who had no love for you. Ah! What is this?"

It was a fine gold ring and chain. In the ring was thrust a tightly folded piece of white paper. Anderson struck a match and opened the paper. He started, looked at the chain, started more than before, looked at the ring, and turned very pale. His trembling fingers managed to press a catch in the ring, and as it opened, he saw a little cluster of hair lying inside. Frenzied by the sight, he tore a bunch from his own head and compared them. They were alike beyond the power of mistaking. As he was trying to comprehend the letter, his match went out and left him in utter darkness.

The baby, who had lifted up its head to watch the bright light, laid down again as it vanished, and Anderson knew as it pressed his arm that it was the child of his darling.

Trembling violently, yet striving hard to be calm, the young man lit another match, and read. The letter was written in a straggling way, and he could only decipher it with difficulty:

"Kind People,
      "Who may discover my child, care for him, and may God bless you. He will be two years old on the second day of August ——"

The match went out once more, though that was not strange when his hand shook so hard. He lit another and read on:

"The second day of August next. He is a good child, but I am poor, and no one will give me work"— a mist came before his eyes as he read — "while I have the baby with me. I shall fly to some place far from here, and no one can find me after that. The last thing I write is — Be good to my child."

The ring was Ella's and the young man felt the hot tears rising to remember how she had begged a little lock of his hair to place in it, so long ago. The chain he had put on her neck one evening, and told her it was to be a symbol of their love, — without an end. The writing was Ella's, and the child must be theirs.

Anderson pulled the boats to Longwood Pier, and after tying them there, took his child in his arms and walked to the house. The occupants had long been abed, and his ring at the bell brought out an astonished negro, who was surprised to see the young man there at all, at that hour, and still more so to see the child he carried in his arms.

" Goodness gracious, Massa Anderson !" he exclaimed, " What under de sun you got dere ? "

" A little child which I found floating in a boat, Cæsar," replied Anderson, " I wish you would call up Miss Mabel and Aunt Dinah. They will know how to care for it better than I. "

Cæsar scrambled up stairs to do as he was bid, and soon spread the tidings that " Massa Anderson had found a pickanninny floating in de water, fur sho !" Nearly all the house was aroused by the strange news, and faces of all complexions began to peep in upon the young man as he sat in the sitting-room, holding the child. Presently Mabel came in, blushingly excusing her white wrapper and loose hair, and Cæsar ordered everybody else out of the room in haste.

"Dear me, Mr. Anderson," said Mabel, "What a pretty child it is. Where did you find it ? "

The young man detailed the facts, excepting the discovery of the chain, ring and letter.

" Have you found anything which gives a clue to the people who abandoned the poor little fellow ?"

"I have not looked very carefully," he replied, evasively. "Perhaps you may discover some clue hereafter."

"Let me take him," said Mabel, holding out her arms for the boy. The child looked first at Anderson, and then fell laughingly into Mabel's embrace.

"You are fond of children," said Anderson, are you not ?"

"Well, rather, said Mabel, blushing again. "When they are good, you know. And I am sure this one must be."

"Why ?" asked Albert Anderson.

" Because," she replied, " he is so handsome. He has such a sweetly formed face, such lovely eyes, and such beautiful brown hair. He cannot help being good, Mr. Anderson."

The earnest face which looked up at the young man, met a photograph of the very features she had described.

Mabel noticed it for the first time, and exclaimed :

"Why, the child looks enough like you, Mr. Anderson, to be — your younger brother !"

Mrs. Davis came in at this moment, having risen with great labor, curious to see what had aroused the attention of the whole house at that hour of the night. While dressing she had been constantly receiving exaggerated re- ports concerning the affair, some stat- ing that Anderson had the sitting-room full of babies, and others contending that there were only five or six. The stately lady glanced around the room as she entered, as if expecting to step upon some of the new children unless she exercised considerable care. See- ing only the one child which Mabel held to her bosom, Mrs. Davis be- came reassured, and closed the door with a bang.

"O, Auntie !" cried Mabel. "Do come and see this lovely boy which Mr. Anderson has found.

Mrs. Davis came nearer and in- spected the child as though it were some new specimen of one of the lower animals.

"What are you going to do with it?" she asked, stepping back a little.

Anderson noticed her manner, and it annoyed him.

"I am intending to adopt it, and rear it as my own !" he answered.

"O, Mr. Anderson ! You cannot mean it ! Why, it is probably the child of some low people, or it would not have been abandoned in this way."

Anderson frowned, darkly.

"Is it only low people, then, who may become too poor to care for their offspring? Might not a mother give up her child in this way from poverty, who is as good as you or I ?"

"O, well," said Mrs. Davis, lan- guidly. "I do not care to argue the matter. Of course you will do as you like."

"Of course I shall," said Ander- son, severely. "What do *you* say, Miss Mabel? Will you help me in the work, if I adopt the child ?"

Mabel promised with bright eyes, and took the little one away then to her room, where she undressed it, and laid it on her own pillow for the night. How much his eyes and hair were like Mr. Anderson's ! She kissed the face on the pillow as she had kissed the prisoner's when he lay sick in the cell. And as she did so, her rebel- lious heart forgot the resolution she had made, and throbbed against her bosom, fiercely !

CHAPTER V.

THE BEGINNING OF THE END.

Albert Anderson's latest freak fur- nished gossip for hundreds of good people, when it became known that he had actually adopted a child which he found floating, Moses-like, upon the water. Some people were kind enough to state that they supposed he had a right to do as he pleased with his own money, but the majority considered this a dangerous degree of liberty to allow him, and steadfastly persisted in objec- ting to it as liable to form a bad pre- cedent. Others wanted to know why we were taxed to build asylums and almshouses, if children who naturally came under these institutions were to be regarded as better than respectable people's, and raised above their heads in this way. Still others suggested that if Anderson was going into the adoption business, why didn't he take this child as that one they knew of, whose parents had died of hard work, after building fortunes for such men as him. Now, these last mentioned children must grow up to eat the bread of labor, while this waif, whom nobody knew the history of, would be reared in velvet and satin. So the gossiping crowd grumbled. As they always will grumble over what does not concern them. And, as usual, Albert Anderson paid as little attention to what they said as to the buzz of any other flies which came about him.

If he had only loved the child for Ella's sake at first, he could not help loving it for its own sake as time went by. Mabel's assertion that it must be a good child, showed her to be an unusually acute judge of character. He was a very quiet little fellow, who made scarcely any trouble, and could amuse himself by the hour with any new plaything that was given him. Of all the things he preferred, however, a woolly-headed little negro, who would lie down and let him pull his hair, seemed to afford him the greatest delight. He soon became fond of stepping out of doors and walking slowly about the lawn, picking himself up after each fall with a good deal of philosophy, but never asking help or giving up to tears.

Mabel, too, had undertaken Bertie's charge as a labor of love for Mr. Anderson, but learned immediately to love the child for its own sake. She liked nothing better than to dress and feed the boy, or sit on the veranda, and watch him running about, or to have him come up to her with his arms extended for her to lift him from the ground. It was a pretty sight to see Mabel of an evening, sitting upon the veranda, in her white wrapper, and taking baby in her lap, stroke his curls and talk to him about the river

and the moon he saw reflected in the river. It was a pretty sight, but it struck home to Anderson's heart with a sort of chill, as he came upon them sitting thus, one pleasant evening.

"O, Mr. Anderson!" cried Mabel, "I am very glad you have come."

It seemed to him she was always glad when he came, and he wished in his heart it were otherwise. He took a seat near the pair, and looked at them gravely. He was grown very sober since that night when he found such freight floating down to him on the river. As he looked at the pretty sight, he was chilled again.

"I hope Bertie is not a trouble to you, Miss Mabel," he said.

They had named the child after Albert, and called it Bertie as Ella had done.

"No indeed," said Mabel. "He is a treasure, aren't you, Bertie? I love him too well for him to be a trouble to me."

Mabel kissed the boy as she finished, and Albert Anderson winced.

"I hope, Miss Mabel," he said, "that you will be careful not to—love—the child—too much."

"Love him too much! Why, Mr. Anderson, what can you mean?"

"It is not well in this world," said Anderson," to give up our whole hearts to any idol, or we may reap a reward of bitter sorrow afterward. This child has probably a mother living, who may come some day to claim it. If she comes, I cannot hold the boy against her wishes. Therefore I say, Be careful not to love the boy too much. I hope you understand me, Miss Mabel."

"I think so," replied Mabel, softly. "Have you heard any news of Bertie's mother, Mr. Anderson."

"Only a little," said the young man

taking off his hat, and wiping the perspiration from his forehead. "She was seen in the village opposite us by several people, but after she left the river the trail is lost."

"Was she a young woman?"

"Ah, yes. A mere girl, they tell me."

Mabel sighed. "What a pity, Mr. Anderson."

"Yes, a great pity, Miss Mabel."

"Did you learn her name, Mr. Anderson?"

"She told it to no one," replied Anderson, evasively. "She had little conversation, I understand with the people she met. One old negress I saw, who gave her some hoe-cake as she sat with the baby under a shade, and I rewarded the old woman with enough to buy her finery for years to come.

"You seem very much interested in the girl, whoever she is," said Mabel, looking at the young man suspiciously.

"Well," said Anderson, suddenly. "What if I am?"

"O, nothing," replied Mabel casting down her eyes.

"Is it possible," said Anderson, reprovingly, "that you blame me for wishing to know where Bertie's mother is? Or is it possible that you wonder because I chose to reward the old negress's kindness to her?"

"I did not mean to convey either of those impressions," said Mabel, pressing the baby against her bosom. "I only meant—that is—I don't know what I did mean."

Anderson sat looking at Mabel for a long time, without speaking. What a strange girl Mabel was! How she seemed to love the child! What a motherly look she had with her white wrapper and evening shawl. He was afraid of this new affection between Mabel and Bertie. And he said, at last, as he arose to get into the house:

"You will remember what I said about loving baby too much, Miss Mabel?"

"I will try," said Mabel, in a low tone.

"Then you will certainly succeed" replied Anderson. "Let me kiss the boy good-night!"

Albert kissed the child in Mabel's very arms, and as he finished she put the baby lips to her own, and kissed it, too. He must have been less observant than he was not to notice the way she did this, and as his eyes encountered her's again, she blushed deeply to see how he read her like an open book.

"Good-night, Miss Mabel," said Anderson, extending his hand toward her.

"Good-night," she replied, without accepting the hand he proffered. And he left her there in the moonlight, in her white wrapper and evening shawl, and in her lap the child he had cautioned her not to love too much.

Mrs. Haynes was notified by a long letter from Albert, of the discovery he had made, and the proofs that he had indeed found Ella's child. The good woman was induced to make the southern journey, and Albert met her at New Orleans on her way to Longwood. Mrs. Haynes was glad to receive even this token that Ella was still living, and she comforted Albert by assurances that she would yet be found and restored to her child and him. On seeing Bertie, Mrs. Haynes could hardly restrain her feelings, but having been previously cautioned by Anderson, she managed to keep some control of them. She remained at Longwood only a few weeks, when finding that the hot climate was seriously affecting her, she was obliged to return North. She was as kind in her manner to Albert as if he had been her own child, and, indeed, since Ella went away, he had acted the part toward her well. His roof was her home, his servants was at her disposal, and in every way did he try to show her how much he regarded her as a very dear friend. For her part, she had never held in her heart one particle of evil feeling against the young man since that day when she had felt the weight of his great confession crush in upon her spirit so that she cried, "May God forgive you!" The horror that he manifested then taught her that he was as sorry for his sin as she could be, and she did well in hesitating before she added to the suffering that was already deep enough.

Another summer passed away, and when autumn came Anderson concluded to go North for a time to arrange business matters. The climate of Longwood seemed peculiarly suited to Bertie's constitution, and it was thought best to have him stay there during the coming winter. Mabel had endured the heat for his sake, and Mrs. Davis, feeling that she would be lost without her niece, had also spent the summer at Longwood. But, as autumn drew near, she grew anxious to attend to some matters at home, and Anderson agreed to act as her companion on the journey at the same time that he made his own trip. On the evening before they were intending to go, Anderson took his child from Mabel's arms, and kissed him tenderly.

"You will care for the child while I am gone, Miss Mabel?"

"Yes," replied Mabel, struggling with her heart. "And I will be careful not to love him—too much, Mr. Anderson."

Anderson looked at the girl strangely, and kissed his child again. Mabel would have given more than life to have him kiss her in that manner. But he never did! And she could not help showing a little bitterness.

"The child loves you, Miss Mabel," said Anderson, as he observed the readiness with which Bertie nestled in her arms.

"Yes, sir," faltered the girl.

"You have been almost a mother to him," said Anderson, gently.

"I have tried to be, sir."

"I am afraid you have been overtasking yourself, Mis Mabel, with Bertie's care. I should advise you to procure the services of some good girl to assist you while we are away."

"Very well, sir."

He began to notice her short replies, and to wonder at their cause.

"Miss Mabel," said he, "have I said or done anything which displeases you? If I have, I am truly sorry."

He added the last words when she put down the child and bowed her face in her hands.

"You have been very kind to me, Miss Mabel, and to my—the child. I am pained if anything has gone wrong with you in relation to us two."

The girl bit her lips but would not answer.

"Miss Mabel—" began Anderson, again.

"Don't call me that name!" cried the girl. "Don't call me *Miss* again! I hate the word. Why cannot you call me *Mabel* as the others do?"

"Very well, I will call you *Mabel*,"

said Anderson, surprised at her excitement. "Now tell me what displeases you, Mabel."

"Many things," replied the girl. "I am giving no certainties to found my hopes and plans upon in life. Those I love are liable to be taken from me at any time, and my voice would have no influence in the matter. I have let my heart wind around this child, and yet you can take him away at any hour. I have loved *you* —you know it well, Mr. Anderson—and what will be my reward? I will tell you what it will be — Desolation and a broken heart!"

"Mabel!" said Anderson, very tenderly, "Have I not warned you twice before, that these thoughts were idle, and should be banished from your brain. Once under this very roof, and once in my cell at Prince County Jail?"

"Yes, you have!" said Mabel, commencing to weep bitterly. "And you have gone on, letting me love you just the same. You have brought here this boy, through whom I ·have only loved you the more. I wish," said the girl, passionately, "that those days when the nurse watched by the prisoner, had been without an end. They were sad enough, I know, but they were heaven compared with this!"

Albert Anderson listened, feeling that Mabel's nature was deeply stirred to bring her to such a confession. As usual, he determimed what to do, quickly.

"My dear girl," he said, "the past cannot be recalled, but my duty for the future seems plain. I must take Bertie with me to the North, and you must try to forget us both. This is a sad matter, and should be ended at once."

Nothing could have affected Mabel more than such a proposition as this. She was so troubled by the fear that he would really take the child away that she promised to say no more on the subject. She urged that the boy must at least stay till spring, as the northern winter would be dangerous for him. And at last, Anderson consented that he should stay, and that he would return himself for a while after finishing his business matters at home. Mabel stilled her heart as well as she was able, and when Anderson left her for his chamber, she was apparently calm and unruffled.

But when the morning came, and they all arose before sunrise, that the travellers might reach an early train, Mabel's resolutions broke down again. It was when he asked to see Bertie once more, and she led the way·to her own room, where the beautiful child was lying on her own pillow. It was when he paused to admire the sleeping boy, and put back the curly hair to kiss his forehead gently. It was then that Mabel, unable to control her. self, caught him by the arm and cried:

"O! Kiss me, too, Mr. Anderson! Kiss me once before you go, or I shall die."

The young man passed his arm about her, and kissed her, exactly as he had kissed his child.

"There, Mabel," he said, "God bless you. Be good to Bertie, and I will return in a few days. Now, good·by."

Not till he had kissed her once, twice more, did she release him. Then, as his retreating footsteps were heard in the hall, she fainted, as she had done at the jail, and lay as one dead on her chamber floor.

After Albert was gone, Mabel soon recovered enough to be about her duties, but having now the care of the whole establishment on her shoulders, she thought well of the young man's advice in relation to engaging a nurse for Bertie, and began to inquire among her friends to see if they knew of a suitable person for the place. There were colored girls by the hundred whom she could procure, but she had seen Anderson's dislike when they were holding the boy, too much to think he would be satisfied with one of these. It was clearly a white girl that he would have her engage. Such nurses were found to be very scarce in the vicinity, and Mabel had almost despaired of obtaining one, when one day word was brought her that a girl was at the door who wished to app'y for the situation.

"Ask her if she will please step up to my room," said Mabel.

Mabel Le Moyne heard her door open, and being engaged with some work at the time, merely asked the newcomer to be seated, without looking up. The child's nurse took a chair as requested, and sat down, nervously clasping her hands. In a few moments Mabel put down her work, and turned to address the girl. Her vision met a creature so very different from what she had expected, that she started in surprise.

A sweet, girlish figure, perhaps nineteen or twenty years of age, with eyes of deepest blue, a mouth around which nature seemed to have set its most beautiful expression, but where time and suffering had added a touch of sadness; hair a queen might have envied for its golden magnificence, hanging in simple braids about her neck, and in one shining band above her forehead; a simple dress, with few ribbons, and but little jewelry. A figure that might have served well for an artist's model, except that he could never hope to reproduce it on his canvas. Is it a wonder that Mabel started in surprise, as this vision first met her eye?

"I beg your pardon, lady," said the girl's voice, apologetically, as she noticed the look with which she was met. "I hear you wish a girl to care for a child. I came to apply for the situation."

"Ah!" smiled Mabel, recovering herself, and still regarding the girl with deep interest. "Do you reside in the neighborhood?"

"No, Madam. I came from a place some way to the north of here."

"Did you ever have the care of a child?" asked Mabel, wonderingly.

"O, yes, madam. I had the care of one for more than a year. I love children, and I know I could suit you."

"No doubt of that," said Mabel, quickly. "But — excuse me if I am too inquisitive — were you always obliged to work for your living, Miss?"

The girl saw that it was more a heartfelt interest than idle curiosity which prompted this question, and she answered it in the spirit with which it was asked.

"No, madam, only for a few years past. I was left to earn my own bread · after being used to better things. But I assure you, I never think of that now. I am satisfied to work at any respectable employment, and consider it no disgrace so long as I give satisfaction."

"You are quite right, my girl," rejoined Mabel. "I have had considerable trouble in searching for a nurse, and will be glad to engage you at once, if you will stay." She named the wages she was willing to pay, which proved quite satisfactory, and the matter was settled immediately.

"Could I see the child now, madam?" asked the girl directly.

"He has gone out to ride with some of the men," Mabel replied. "I am expecting him soon."

It was getting late in the afternoon, and the evening was well advanced when Uncle Cæsar came up the stairs with Master Bertie. The boy was looking rosy enough to have attracted any nurse, and the newly engaged girl received him smilingly. Mabel kissed the little fellow lovingly, and on learning that he had already eaten his supper, and was tired enough to go to bed, introduced him at once to his new nurse, and told him he must be a good boy and give her very little trouble indeed.

"I believe I have not heard your name yet," said Mabel to the nurse.

"Emma Harding," answered the girl, quietly.

"Well, Emma, you may put the boy to bed now and then come down again. Cæsar, show Miss Harding the child's room. Now, come here and kiss me good-night, Bertie."

"Good-night," said the boy, kissing her.

"You will be a good boy to Emma, Bertie?"

· "Yes, mamma."

Cæsar showed Emma Harding the child's room, and she entered and closed the door. That she was excited, was shown by the changing color of her cheek. And why? Simply by that one word which fell from her mistress's lips — "Bertie."

"Are you sleepy, darling?" asked the nurse, kindly, as she took the boy in her lap, to undress him.

"Yes, awful sleepy," lisped the child, drowsily.

The nurse went on in the process of undressing, when suddenly she cried out:

"Bertie! What is this you wear on your neck?"

"My chain and ring," said the child, opening his eyes. "I always wear it."

The nurse began to behave very strangely after that. She lifted the chain from Bertie's neck, and in some manner her trembling fingers opened the catch in the ring. She looked in, as Anderson had done in the boat, and saw the shining hair curled away there. She pressed it to her lips a moment, and raised her eyes and heart to Heaven in mute thanksgiving. If she had spoken, she would have said:

"My God, I thank thee that my child still lives!"

Was it indeed her child? Is this the one, Mabel, that has the prior right to the man you love? Is this the girl he has loved, when for you he has only friendship? Is this her on whose faithfulness the First Part of the Prisoner's Story was founded, and the Second Part depends? And you, Mabel, have taken her under your roof!

The boy lay asleep in the arms of his nurse. Gently she removed his clothing, and substituted his little night-dress. Holding him to her breast, the first time in many months, she thought of another child who, after being placed in a boat and pushed out into the stream, had been rescued by a Princess, and its own mother sent for to nurse it. She thanked God once more in her heart for having directed her steps toward this house, where another Princess had taken her child in like manner, and given it into its mother's hands.

Then, fearing that her mistress would wonder at her long absence, the nurse kissed the child again, laid him tenderly in his bed, and went down stairs.

The Princess was sewing, and the nurse asked leave to assist her, wishing to be where she could learn the later history of the child she had just left. The Princess complied, and the two women, so strangely brought together, each knowing nothing of what filled the other's heart, sewed their seams together in one room, quietly.

"Did you leave Bertie asleep?" asked the Princess, looking up from her work to address the new nurse.

"Yes, madam. He went to sleep at once."

"He was pretty tired," said the Princess.

"Yes, madam, he seemed to be. How old is the boy, madam?"

"Over two years," said the Princess.

"It is strange he has such fair hair when you are so dark, is it not madam?"

"O," said the Princess, blushing, "Bertie is not my own child. I am not married, Emma."

"Indeed!" said the nurse, counterfeiting surprise. "Whose child, then, if not yours?"

It might have been the nurse's child, if such an idea were not quite preposterous. Or it might have been Albert Anderson's child, or both. The nurse need not have expressed such wonder, but that she feared to commit herself otherwise. But she was very anxious to hear the rest of the story, and paused to allow the Princess to proceed.

"It is the adopted child of a gentleman who has spent the past year here at Longwood," said the Princess. "There is quite a strange history connected with the child. This gentleman being out in a boat one night, heard a cry, and on investigating its cause, found Bertie in another boat floating down the River. This was in October last. All the tokens of the child's ownership which were found, were a brief note stating that he would be two years old on the second day of the following August, and a chain and ring about his neck. The chain and ring he has always worn since. You saw it, I suppose, when you undressed him?"

Yes, the nurse had noticed it. The history was indeed a strange one. And the Princess continued:

"The gentleman who found the child was wealthy, and after trying in vain to discover its parents, he adopted it, giving it the name of Bertie. The gentleman left him in my care, and I have learned to love him very much. You noticed, perhaps, that he called me Mamma?"

Yes, the nurse had noticed it, and she said so. How much it cut her to the heart to remember it, knowing that she had a better right to the name but could not claim it, she did not say.

"Where is the gentleman now?"

"He is at the North on business matters but will return before many weeks," replied the Princess; and fearing to excite suspicion by asking lengthy questions, the nurse said no more about the matter then.

Days passed on, and Emma Harding, as she was called, cared for her own child under the roof of strangers, eating of their bread and taking their money for the service. The cloud upon her mind was only partially lifted, and she continued the same sweet, quiet girl who had left weeping friends at Hillsdale House, and had aroused such fierce passion in the breast of the lame gentleman. Quietly she performed her daily duties, speaking kindly to all, but saying little at any time. Everyone who saw the girl loved her, and remarked upon her sweet, sad beauty. Little Bertie loved her as well as the rest, and she became almost contented in her new home.

Saying as little as the girl did to the people around her, it is not strange that she never came to hear spoken the name of the wealthy gentleman who had adopted Bertie. One sound of the word Anderson would have caused her to fly from Longwood and her child instantly. But she never heard the name mentioned, and indeed, as she supposed, the name of Bertie's adopted father had no peculiar significance to her.

It was in this state of things that Mabel received a letter from Anderson one day, stating that Mrs. Davis had been taken ill at her residence, and wanted her niece to come there at once, if possible. He advised that she leave the child at Longwood if she could find a suitable nurse for it, and obey her aunt's wishes. He stated that he would return to the South directly, and meet her at one of the cities on her route, if she would come.

Mabel was not long in deciding. She despatched a message stating where she would meet Anderson, and hurriedly made preparations for her journey to her sick aunt's bedside.

"Emma," said she to the nurse, while dressing for her journey, "I have just received word that my aunt is very ill, and I must go without delay to her home. You will take care of Bertie until I return, which will be before long, I hope. The gentleman I spoke to you about, who adopted Bertie, will be here in a few days, and take charge of affairs. Till that time, I leave all to you."

Emma assented quietly, and assisted Mabel in getting ready for her departure.

"Be very careful of Bertie. We should all die if he should come to hurt. You will, won't you, Emma?"

"I will, indeed," replied the nurse with truth, and Mabel hurried into her carriage and was driven away by the coachman.

The third day after this, a boy was sent with saddled horses to the station for the coming gentleman. In a few hours he came — galloping up the road at full speed, with his servant far behind, and the hoofs of his horse struck fire out of the Longwood avenues. The negroes took off their hats, and cried:

"Massa's come!" And Albert Anderson himself rode smiling up to the house, until, looking up at one of the chamber windows, he reined in his horse so hard as to throw him on his hind feet.

"*Will these visions never cease?*" he gasped, lifting his cap to brush the long, brown hair from his perspiring forehead.

But was it a vision?

He was in doubt of this even, and giving his rein to one of the men, he hurried into the house and up stairs to the room where he had seen the vision. It was still there by the window, and he staggered into the room and cried:

"Ella! Ella, my darling! if it is you, speak to me!"

"It is I, Bert," replied the nurse, faintly.

"And what do you here?" cried Albert, the old choking rising in his throat.

"*You see.*" She lifted the child, and turned her sad blue eyes upon the man.

"Our boy, Ella!"

"Our boy, Bert."

"Then you are the nurse they have engaged for him?"

"Yes, and you must be the gentleman who adopted him? Believe me, Bert," cried Ella, "if I had imagined it possible that this was so, I would have been miles from here this hour. Believe me, Bert, I would have drowned myself, rather!"

"*Ella!*" He dropped on one knee beside her.

"Believe me, Bert, I never meant to do this! Believe me, I have tried hard to keep disgrace from you! Believe me, oh, Bert!

The tired girl could utter no more. She sank lifeless into the arms opened to receive her. Albert Anderson held her there, on one knee, kissing her face over and over again. While the little Bertie, who could not understand the matter at all, came and laid his infant cheek to the nurse's wonderingly, and watched the pair with his baby eyes.

CHAPTER VI.

EXPLANATIONS.

When the news reached Mabel LeMoyne that Anderson had found his love in her late servant-maid, her mind was so overcome by the shock as to deprave her temporarily of her reason. Added to the thoughts of losing Albert forever, was that of losing Bertie, to whom Mabel was devotedly attached. When Anderson and Ella returned to the city where Mabel lived, the latter sought every opportunity to witness the united cou-ple's happiness, and giving up her life to the one thought of her wrong, her brain became fired and beyond control. At last, one day, she managed to decoy the boy into a secluded place, and calling a carriage, rode to the nearest station, and without any preparation, took a train to the northward. When Anderson found his boy missing, he called in the services of Steel, the detective, and they were soon on the right track. Mabel had gone but a few score of miles by rail, and then taken to the highway. They traced her some distance into the country, her appearance having attracted general attention, and finally, in the the midst of a fearful snow-storm, came upon them the runaways by the roadside, and rescued them, though with considerable difficulty, as Mabel fought her captors like a tigress. She was at last overcome, however, and brought to Anderson's house in the city, where she was not long in recovering under the kind care of Ella. In a short time she was able to recognize those about her. The poor girl was overwhelmed with grief when she learned the narrow escape Bertie's life had in the snow storm, and it was quite evident that Mabel was not sane after she took the boy from the city. She had no recollection of anything from the time when she left her aunt's house till she found herself in a sickbed at Anderson's with her rival in love attending to her wants. At first she shrank from Ella's touch, not being able to conceal the light in which she regarded her, but it was only necessary for Albert to say reprovingly, "Mabel!" to change her in a moment. Afterward she altered completely, received Ella with embraces, and seemed really to repent the passion which had carried her beyond the control of reason. Mrs. Davis had been kept in ignorance of her flight until she was again in safe hands, when she was summoned from Longwood, and came in haste. On her return, Mabel left Anderson's house for her own home, a changed girl in many respects. She continued the fast friend of Ella, and came often to visit her and her child.

Fred Steel, the Detective, was often closeted with Anderson at this time, and people wondered what business the two could have together, which seemed to be of so much interest to both. For several months, Steel worked on, until, one evening, he informed his employer that he was ready to make clear the matters which had seemed so strange to all for these many years.

"Can you clear up all the strange things which have perplexed me?" asked Anderson. "If you can, I shall consider you a genuine wizard."

"Patience," said the Detective, "and I will promise to do even that —to clear up every dark place, and make it all plain as the day."

Steel was as good as his word. Before many weeks he had his train of powder laid, and stood with match in hand, ready to fire it. He planned a little party at Pearl street, to which were invited Anderson and Ella, Mabel Le Moyne, Mrs. Davis, Mr. Harvard, Mr. Jenkins, Mrs. Haynes, Harry Johnson, Mr. and Mrs. Samuel Harrison, and a few more tried friends, when the Detective assumed the role of wizard with great success.

"Ladies and Gentlemen," said he, "let me first introduce to you, Mr. John Raymond, of San Joaquilla, South America."

The folding doors opened, and two officers entered with a handcuffed man between them. There was an exclamation of surprise. The new comer was a tall gentleman with clustering auburn hair and a scowling countenance. There was some mystery here, as all knew in a moment. For every one in the room who had seen Hawley, the dark gentleman, knew it was he and no one else, that stood before them now.

"John Raymond," said the wizard, "be seated while you case is attended to!"

"You have done bravely, you Steel, to bring me here, and address me by a false name," answered the other. "But if it is any pleasure to you, go on, by all means. I am handcuffed you see, and cannot prevent you."

The wizard turned quietly to the quadroon. "Sam," he said, "call Annie Andrews."

Even the well-trained mind of the prisoner was not proof against an exhibition of a severe shock when that name was pronounced. And when, a moment later, a modest appearing girl, with dark hair and eyes, and a sweet expression of face, entered the room timidly, supported by Harry Johnson, he fairly turned white with dismay.

"Was it not enough," cried the prisoner, bitterly, "that these hordes of liars should be hired to come here and abuse me, but you must join with them! Do you want me murdered by these hounds, or why have you come here?"

"O, John!" cried the girl, weeping. "I would do you no harm for the world."

"No, I suppose not," returned he, mockingly. "Gentlemen, you have done bravely in bringing this woman here. Do you know what she is? and has been? Look at her shrink and cover her face! Bah! For years, good people, this woman was my mistress!"

"Hold!" cried Harry, coming forward. "Say another word and I will strike you to the floor. Are you so much of a coward that you would blame that poor girl for being what you made her? If she has done wrong, what name shall we apply to your crime?"

"It is for you to threaten, when you are a dozen against one," said Sherman, contemptuously. "But we waste time. Put your fine woman on the stand and let us see whether she is as good at invention as the rest of you."

Still weeping, Annie came forward.

"Do you know the prisoner, Miss Annie?"

"Yes, sir."

"Where did you make his acquaintance?"

"In Hillsdale, five years ago."

"Will you give us the particulars?"

"Yes, sir. He came from the city into Hillsdale for a rest during part of the summer, and after we became acquainted, he asked me to marry him. He had just fallen heir through his father's death to a large property in South America, and asked me to marry him and go with him to his new home. Knowing that my parents would object, he persuaded me to go secretly, saying that I could write soon and obtain their forgiveness. Trusting him implicitly, I did so. On getting me into his power, however, he refused to fulfil his word. If there is any disgrace upon me now," said Annie, sobbing, "he is to blame for it and not I."

"We went South, and in San Joaquilla, his home, we were quite happy for a while. Then a desire seized him to come North, and getting control of part of the property, most of which was not to be sold, he took me to this city again. For reasons of his own, not wishing to be recognized by his former friends, he procured a preparation for darkening the hair and skin, which soon changed us both beyond recognition. By using the preparation often, we were enabled to keep up the disguise and remain unknown."

"This is the way," explained the wizard, "that our friend became known as the 'dark gentleman.'"

"By too great a love for this man," continued Annie, "I was led to assist him in one of his schemes which proved to be the ruin of us all. It seems that before he knew me, he had been in the poorest circumstances, and had been making a living in any way which presented itself, principally, I fear, by dishonest means. I am certain of one thing, that he obtained work in Mr. Anderson's warehouse for the purpose of robbing it, where he succeeded in taking some two hundred dollars from the safe, and laying the appearance of the evil deed upon the book-keeper, Mr. Fogg, who fled the country when he found he was suspected. At another time, when disguised as an old man, he attacked Mr. Anderson in his own house, now torn down on Pearl street, and would have taken his life had he not been prevented by the timely entrance of his servant. When we came back to the North, he vowed to bring Mr. Anderson down to the dust, and in my wickedness and blindness, I assisted him."

Annie paused, being overcome with a fit of weeping. Raymond looked savagely at her, and gnashed his teeth in impotent rage. After a moment the witness continued:

"The plan he proposed was to ruin

Mr. Anderson completely at one blow. He wanted me to induce Miss Ella to leave Mr. Anderson, while he got Harry Johnson into his power, and destroyed the warehouse business. I confess to my share of the work with sorrow. By representing to Miss Ella that Mr. Anderson would be disgraced by her remaining with him, and that she could best show her love by leaving him, I persuaded her to fly with me one evening in a closed carriage and take a western train at Homer's Station. On returning I became convinced that John had more than one motive in view — in short that he designed to leave me for Miss Ella if he could win her for himself. I accused him of it when I returned, and his conduct convinced me that my suspicions were correct. In his anger he cast me from him, and left the house. From that day to this I have never met him face to face, or had any communication with him whatever until to-night."

Raymond was about to speak again, when he looked up, and his eyes met a sight which stopped the words on his lips. Albert Anderson, till now invisible, stood leaning on a table by the doorway, regarding him attentively. The dark-brown hair of the young man was brushed carefully from his high forehead, his clear eyes were sweeping over the assembly, and his head was inclined a little to one side in sober thought. Ella stood by his side, with one hand caressingly placed on his shoulder, while on her other arm was held the child, clinging about her neck, and mingling his tresses with her own. The prisoner looked, and noted the trio, and said nothing.

The wizard turned to the quad-roon again. "Call Henry Johnson," said he. When Harry had taken his stand, the Detective commenced to examine him. It seemed as if the wizard took delight in asking his questions in a legal style, as though he were no wizard at all, but the High Prosecuting Attorney of the State.

"This man," said Harry, "made my acquaintance at the warehouse when I was on the high road to prosperity, and by his arts induced me to forsake my business, and to drink and gamble with him. At last he got me wholly into his power by lending me money to play away, and then persuaded me to take the amount from the safe. On the night the warehouse was burned, he induced me to leave America by saying that I would be accused of setting the fire if I remained. I believe the prisoner set the fire with his own hand to complete his ruinous work."

"Do you know whether he is the same man who passed for John Raymond in Hillsdale?"

"He is, sir. I recognize him now, though I did not when he was disguised by the darkness of his complexion."

"Do you know Miss Andrews?"

"I had seen her, sir, in Hillsdale, before she went with the prisoner. But her dark complexion deceived me the same as in his case."

The wizard turned to his prisoner: "How do you like the investigation as it proceeds?" he asked.

"Very much, indeed," said Raymond, carelessly. "I had no idea any man could be capable of such wonderful acts as I hear ascribed to myself here. Really, Steel, it is almost fabulous."

"We have not finished yet," said the Wizard. "Mr. Anderson, we will trouble you next, if you please."

The prisoner was uneasy enough as Anderson stepped forward to testify. He dreaded to have that form too near, and was almost stifled by the thoughts which came with him. How everything he had labored to do against him had failed! How every shaft he had launched at him had turned and entered his own body! As Anderson ran his fingers through his hair to throw it from his forehead, and turned upon him, the prisoner could scarcely draw his breath.

"Do you know the prisoner, Mr. Anderson?"

The young man was fresh from the side of the girl he loved, and her whispered petition that he be not too hard upon his enemy still rung in his ears. So he simply answered:

"I do know him, sir."

"Please state what you know of him."

"Carrying my memory back, now," said the young man, "I see him first at my warehouse, where I cautioned Mr. Fogg to be watchful of him, as I had heard his reputation was bad. After the warehouse was robbed, I remember the fight I had with him at the old house in Pearl street. The night the warehouse burned, I see him on Commercial Street accusing Harry of the crime. Later he prefers charges of murder against me which he knows are false, and attempts to assist in arresting me. Again, he is on the stand in court, solemnly swearing my life away, and later yet, as I sit on the scaffold, I see him in the crowd awaiting my death. That is all, Mr. Steel."

Raymond breathed easier as the witness retired, and assumed his old air of bravado. As the testimony thickened around him he grew more reckless, and had clearly made up his mind to take whatever came in a bold spirit, knowing there was no help for it.

"Miss Ella," said the wizard, "A word from you, if you please."

Giving Bertie to Anderson, Ella came forward.

"I wish to say nothing against this poor gentleman, sir," said she. "He has already been punished enough for what he has done. He never harmed me, sir, and only tried to have me marry him. I would not consent to that, of course, but I could not blame him for loving me."

Ella paused and blushed as she closed the sentence.

"That will do, then," said the wizard, kindly. "You may retire, Miss Ella."

The wizard then announced that the main evidence was all in, and with a flourish of a legal appearance asked if any person was present who would defend the prisoner. A fine looking young gentleman, to whom Ella and Albert were speaking, and who was unknown to others present, except the wizard himself, the latter having, by his magic arts, brought him there, arose and said he would volunteer for the defence.

"Perhaps the ladies and gentlemen present would like to hear your name," suggested the wizard, smiling.

"Certainly, said the young gentleman. "I am Henry Walden, Jr., of the Bar, an acquaintance and, I trust, a friend of Miss Ella Anderson."

The prisoner, who had watched the young gentleman narrowly, now became convinced that he was only designing to make a pretence of defending him, and objected strongly.

"Come, Steel," he pleaded, "this is shameful. This farce has gone on quite long enough. I shall bring this affair into court if I am compelled to submit to the imposition any longer."

"I do not think you will," said the wizard, quietly. "I will assign Mr. Walden as your counsel, and you had better say nothing until we hear what kind of a defence he can make out of so hard a case as yours seems to be."

As he could do nothing else, Raymond assented with an ill grace, and Walden, Jr. commenced his plea.

To begin with, he said, he would not attempt to impeach the testimony of any witness present, but would merely endeavor to show just how much there was proved against his client. As to the greatest charge — attempted murder, that was years ago, and if the attempt was made, it had certainly proved a failure. The prisoner was charged with falsely swearing the life of another man away, but that man, too, had been almost miracculously saved, and here again the prosecution failed. The young lawyer followed down the successive charges, disposing of them as best he could. As he finished, Anderson came forward and took his place.　.

"My friends," he said, "I believe it is common in law in some cases for a court to consider an acknowledgment of satisfaction from the party aggrieved, as sufficient reason for the discharge of a prisoner. I was going to make a proposition. We are all friends together, I believe, and what transpires here will be held secret by all."

The audience acquiesced, wondering what was coming next. Mr. Jen-kins sat by Mr. Harvard, and the two lawyers conversed in whispers of the case as it proceeded. Mr. Jenkins had just whispered that Anderson was "*the* strangest young man," when Albert continued:

"I think, my friends, that it will be plain to all of you that I and mine have suffered more than any one from this man's evil passions. But I remember that for many years I had no more control over my hates and dislikes than he had of his. Long trial, and many hard lessons have taught me reason. Yet I cannot but think that perhaps but for circumstances differing in our experience, I might have been as bad, or even worse, than the prisoner. Thinking of this, and thinking too, of how in various ways he had his emnity to me increased by my own violent and hasty acts, I wish before you all to say he has my full forgiveness for what he has injured me or mine. And that, so far as my influence goes, no hand shall be further lifted against him."

Anderson's remarks were received with a tumult of applause that shook the mansion from end to end. Ella threw her arms about his neck, sobbing and thanking him through her tears. The good Mrs. Haynes, Mrs. Davis, Harry and the others joined in the cheering. Mabel looked admiringly at the young man, and cheered too. Mr. Jenkins, thunderstruck, informed Mr. Harvard, privately, for the hundredth time, that "he never did, — he was positive he never did —." Mr. Harvard joined the group that crowded round Anderson, and called him his dear boy. John Raymond, the prisoner, grew more uneasy than before, and looked vacantly at Steel for an explanation, till Annie Andrews came up to him crying and told how

Mr. Anderson had agreed beforehand that he should not be harmed, or she never would have come in to testify as she did.

Then the prisoner took the girl gently on his knee and sheltered her poor head, where it had lain so often before, on his own bosom. When the assemblage turned to resume their seats they were thrilled to see a tear in his eye, and knew then that there was still left in him some element of goodness. Anderson, looking up, saw Raymond, with Annie in his lap, and was so overcome with joy at the success of his experiment, that he could not proceed for a moment. Seeing their leader so deeply affected, the others began to cry again. And when they had done so, they all felt the better for it.

When all was quiet again, the wizard turned to Anderson, and addressed him in low tones.

"My part of this affair should be about ended," said he, pleasantly.

"You have acted it well," said Anderson, in reply. "But you must remain until it is all settled."

"Very well," said Steel. "By the way, there is one matter I had nearly forgotten. In looking up this case I have discovered another fact which I decided not to make known to you until you had announced your intention to avoid prosecuting our prisoner. Did you ever notice a resemblance between you and Raymond in feature!"

Anderson was perplexed.

"Others have noticed it," he said musingly, "but I regarded the idea as absurd."

"I have noticed it," said the Detective, "even when the prisoner wore his dark complexion. Now that is gone, the resemblance is striking."

"Well, what has this to do with me?"

"Slowly, if you please, Mr. Anderson. What was your mother's maiden name?"

The young man started, and looked almost frightened.

"Catherine Raymond."

"My dear fellow," said Steel, placing his hand on Albert's arm, "I believe this young man to be her younger brother. In fact — I know it to be the case."

"How do you know it!" asked Albert.

"Because his father was Alexander Raymond of San Joaquilla. Miss Andrews will tell you that it was in that country they lived in South America. I purposely kept you from the room while she was testifying that everything might go smoothly. There is no doubt, Mr. Anderson, that this is the truth."

The young man paused a momsnt to think. "Does *he* know it?" he asked finally.

"No," replied Steel, "nor any one but you and I. It can be kept from him, if you choose, altogether."

"I will speak with Ella about it," said Anderson, soberly. "Then I will let you know what I will do."

In a few minutes he came back with a brighter face.

"The dear girl says I shall own him, by all means. It may make a man of him, she thinks. Ask the people to excuse us, and we will step into one of the other rooms."

Raymond wondered what was to be done next; when he entered the room with Annie, and found there waiting Anderson, Ella, Mrs. Haynes and Mabel. But he took the chair assigned him, and Annie drew hers to his side quietly.

"Mr. Raymond," began Anderson, earnestly, "Had you ever a sister?"

The question was a simple one, but it brought tears to Raymond's eyes.

"Yes sir, a good girl, some years older than myself, whom my father disinherited for marrying against his will. She was my only protection from his wrath, and when she left home, I soon followed."

"Do you know the name of the man she married?"

"No, sir," replied Raymond, "I asked once, and was told never to mention the subject again. I only know he was a miner, and that they afterwards moved to the north."

"Her name was Catherine, was it not?" asked Anderson, with a trembling voice.

"How did you know?" said Raymond, looking up in surprise.

"I will tell you," said Anderson, biting his lips. "I am the child of that miner and his wife."

"You!" It was all the astonished man could articulate.

"Yes, *I*. We have both had our share of the passionate nature of Alexander Raymond developed in us, and we now find it springs from the same source. Whatever we may have been to each other, the same blood is in our veins."

The prisoner was perplexed how to act.

"This is too much to bear in one evening," he said. "I hardly know what to say."

Ella left Albert, and coming to Raymond, put her hand on his shoulder tenderly.

"Say you will harbor no more enmity against us," she said. "Say you will do all in your power to remedy what wrong you may have done. Say you will be a better man from this night forth."

Standing by the man's side, the girl might have been an angel pointing him to the path of right. He saw the path and stepped into it.

"I do say it," he replied. "A harsh father threw me upon a bad world when I was young, and I have let it drift me at will these years. For all I have done against you, I ask your pardon, every one of you."

This was more than they had expected. Anderson was emboldened to proceed still further.

"We intend to make no prosecution against you, Mr. Raymond," he said. "You will be at liberty to go when and where you choose. But one thing I would ask. There is a true woman by you who deserves your hand. Do not forget her devotion, whatever you do."

Raymond took Annie gently by the hand and pressed her to his bosom.

"I suppose you think, all you people," he stammered, "that there is no good in me, and you may well think so from what I have done. But if you will call a justice, I would like to be married now, if Annie is willing to take me after all this time."

Anderson joyfully sprang up and opened the door. The first person he saw was Henry Walden.

"Are you a Justice of the Peace?" he asked, smiling.

"I am," said Walden, Jr.

"We wish to have a marriage ceremony performed," said Anderson. "Throw open the doors, and oblige us by repeating the service."

Raymond took Walden's hand warmly, and said he was glad he had come to finish the defence, which would now be complete. In five minutes more there was a blushing bride to be kissed, and the sober details of a criminal trial made way to admit a bridal party.

Supper, which had waited till now, was served, and at a very late hour the party dispersed. Some of them congratulated Anderson on the success of the evening's work, but he gave all the credit to the wizard, and was quite satisfied to leave it in that way. Being pressed to remain, Mr. and Mrs. John Raymond passed the night under the Pearl street roof. Henry Walden, also, who had been sent for quietly by Ella and the Detective, remained at Anderson's house. Mabel went home in her aunt's carriage, bidding her friends good-night shyly and modestly, for she still felt constrained in their presence.

Walden, Jr., asked so many questions about Mabel the next day that Anderson agreed to go over to the Davis mansion with him that he might become better acquainted with her. Walden praised her beauty to the skies, and Albert told him aside she was just the sort of woman he needed for a wife. The young lawyer received this intimation slightingly, but continued to visit Mabel, nevertheless, even after he was obliged to go to her house alone. And before many months Madame Rumor — but, then who can believe her? — was heard to say on all sides, that Cupid had won another victory.

CHAPTER VII.

PARTING WORDS.

What better time to bring my story to a close than when the Dark Gentleman has resolved to take an upright position among the fellowmen he has held his hand against since the cradle? What better than when James Albert Anderson finds rest in a true wife's love, after his most Dangerous Experiments in Love, Law, and Literature? What better than when Ella Haynes finds her unparalleled sacrifice repaid by a mother, child, and the man for whom she was willing to give up them all! What better time to close my story than when all of its characters are marvelling at the course pointed out by the finger of God, to bring each one to his proper knowledge and appreciation of the better natures of the others!

I know of no better time. For the years since these characters acted their parts, there might be much to say. But at the climax of the work which has drawn them into companship, they shall be left before your eyes.

One evening, when Mrs. Haynes was sitting in one of the Pearl street parlors with Albert and Ella, she explained the manner in which she had discovered that Ella was her daughter.

"When I was left a widow, nearly twenty years ago, I went to New York to live with my child. I understood dressmaking, and readily obtained employment in a large establishment, where I earned enough to support myself and Ella. After I had been there two years, however, I was attacked by a violent fever, and lay unconscious for many weeks. When I recovered I was told that my child had died with the same disease, and been buried some time before by the authorities. Too weak to doubt what was told me, I lay in my bed some days longer, selling everything, almost, to pay for my room and physician.

When I was well, at last, I went back to my work with a heavy heart, feeling that I was indeed alone ; and having no care, now, for anything but my business, I worked very hard. After a few years, I opened a shop of my own, which I kept until I became ill again, and was advised to come to this city for my health. Here I took one of Mr. Anderson's tenements at Giles's Row, and lived quietly under my maiden name of Haynes, which I had borne since I left my early home.

" As to my taking charge of the little ragged girl Mr. Anderson brought to me"—Mrs. Haynes smiled lovingly at Ella—" You already know. Albert laughs now to remember how I said that Cross street was such a bad neighborhood, and hesitated at first about taking Ella at all. Afterwards, as her appearance was improved, I began to love her for the resemblance she bore to the little girl I had lost. Thus matters went on, until I came with Albert and Ella to Pearl street, and then left there again to go to New York once more. At the latter city I espied, one evening, an advertisement in one of the daily papers which attracted my attention. It said that if Mrs. Laura Haynes, who formerly kept a dress-making shop on Broadway, would communicate with the signer she would learn something to her advantage. I immediately answered the advertisement, and the next day received a note asking me to call at a certain number in one of the lowest streets of the city. Procuring a carriage, I drove to the place. In a miserable room I found lying the woman who had tended me when I had the fever. She was very sick, and could only tell me that Ella was not dead, but had been sent to an orphan asylum, when it was believed I could not live. She did not know to what asylum, and was much troubled in mind over her sin, in concealing the truth from me so long. I did what I could for the poor creature, and then went about the hard task of finding my long-lost girl.

" After going through more than a dozen different asylums, I found the right one, and learned that Ella had been taken by a Mrs. Jones, living on Cross street, in the very city I had left. At this time I received word that Ella had gone from Albert, and hastened back with an aching heart to find that I had recovered a daughter only to lose her again. Albert will remember that I asked him one day particularly about the woman who had adopted Ella before him, and his replies convinced me that my dear girl was the same one I had been caring for for his sake. Now she is restored to me, never to be lost again.

Mrs. Haynes clasped Ella in her arms as she concluded her recital, and Anderson looked on with a tear in his eye. What a good, motherly woman she was !

Harry Mitchell, while attending to his duties at Brown's Wharf, could always find time some day in the week to ride to Hillsdale, and pay a visit to Miss Sallie Slader at the Hillsdale House. It came to be an acknowledged fact before long that a wedding was contemplated between the young people, and Sallie received blushingly the congratulations of her friends when the news spread over the village. Samuel Slader, the avaricious, satisfied himself that Harry was doing well in business, and likely to have money enough, before he gave his consent to the proposed marriage. Even then he lamented the fact that the hotel would have to be cared for by hired help, and the matter wore hard upon his miserly mind. And one day, when he did not appear at dinner at his usual time, a search made by one of the men servants revealed a limp and lifeless body hanging to one of the rafters in the old, tumble-down barn.

Sallie cried, of course, for her father's death, though he had never merited love from her. But a young bride's sorrow is of short duration, and in her husband Sallie found a friend which more than took the place her father had held in her heart. The newly married couple lived in one of the houses in Giles's Row for a time. Anderson soon disposed of his share of the warehouse to Harry, and the sign was changed to H. Johnson & Co. Under the new title the business prospered finely, and is, in fact, leading all competitors to the present day.

When children came to brighten Harry's home, he removed his family to Hillsdale, where the old farm house, after some needed alterations, served as a healthful and pleasant place of residence. A new railroad carried the young husband to and from his work, and the advantage of the clear air of the hills could not be over-estimated for the little ones. With a faithful, loving wife, good children and a pleasant home, Harry lives, the happiest man within many miles.

John Raymond. What of *him?* A change, greater in his case than in any of the others, was wrought. Wishing to leave the place where he had been known only in evil acts, he set out with his wife Annie for Australia. Farmer Andrews and his good wife died before this occurred, happy in the affection of the daughter they had mourned as lost so long. In Australia, Raymond found a good field for his adventurous habits, and

liking the country well, he bought out the estates he had taken charge of, and became an extensive land proprietor. His family was increased by a son and daughter, and his beautiful home became the abode of peace and contentment. Annie never had occasion to regret the day she testified at the wizard's mock trial. Her life was given much to works of charity, and especially was she noted for her kindness and sympathy for the unfortunate of her own sex. Many a poor girl, who might otherwise have been permanently lost, rejoices in her deliverance and ascribes her happy fireside to Annie Raymond's assistance. May it not be that He who guides us through this world had planned this from the hour she left her parents' home with her promised husband?

Mabel Le Moyne became, in time, entirely cured of her passion for Anderson, and when Henry Walden, Jr., asked her hand, she gave it to him with her whole heart. He felt how much the prize was worth, and she appreciated fully the noble nature of the young attorney. Walden, Sen., was graciously pleased to give his consent to this union, as it was clearly not below his son's station. As the town of Walden furnished little business for a gentleman of his profession, Henry built a fine residence in the city, near Pearl street, where he went with his young bride. As the years passed he obtained a good practice, and was always noted for his high minded and upright ways. Mabel had afterwards children of her own, which she could not "love too much." She was a frequent visitor at Pearl street, and both Ella and Albert were always glad to see her enter their doorway. Mrs. Davis stayed with her niece after marriage, and they often used to laugh at the old lady in a pleasant way, remembering how averse she was to having Anderson adopt his own child the day he found him floating in the river.

Of the other steadfast friends a few words must suffice. Mr. Harvard and Mr. Jenkins continued to have the charge of Anderson's property, while the young author gave his attention principally to literary work. The quadroon, Sam, stayed with his wife Luna, on St. George's Island, raising wonderful crops, and never tiring of telling how he had rowed out to save Anderson when he came up the Bay, and how the young man had vanquished the Detective, when he was running for the boat that night. Fred Steel received the present of a pretty cottage house in the city, for his share in the work of unveiling the mysteries which per plexed them all so long. By certain representations made to Governor Smith by friends, Steel received the position of Chief of Police, in place of the unaccomodating man who held the office before him. His fame as a diligent and efficient officer has never decreased.

And last, O, Albert Anderson! Thou whom I have loved for thy independent, noble, manly spirit! Thou whom I have pitied in the midst of thy Dangerous Experiments in the search after truth! Thou who hast been led through difficult places unto the perfect realizing of so many problems! Thou, who hast stumbled so many times, and hast struggled so hard to regain thy feet! Thou who hast taught us that life is nought and principle is eternal. Thou, who yielded so willingly to the teachings of experience, even when they were diametrically opposed to thy theories, long cherished and loved! Thou who hast come, through all, to a right understanding of that great problem, Life. What of *thee?*

A private wedding joined him to the truest and best woman who ever lived. A woman who had once given him up for very love, and would have refused to marry him to the last from very love, had he not whispered, "Darling, for baby's sake." When the ceremony was over, he took his bride on his arm, and led the way up the stairs to the long-forsaken Tower Room.

A great painting hung there, representing a beautiful girl sitting in the lap of a handsome lover. Books lay there they had read together. Numberless articles were there that recalled the first days of their love. A little roll of lozengers lay in a basket on the table. The roll he had picked up when he found his girl that freezing day by the lake. He pointed it out to Ella, and when it started a bright tear from her blue eyes, he bent tenderly and kissed it away.

The next autumn, Albert and Ella left the city and crossed the seas to England. From England they travelled over much of southern Europe with their child until the spring, when they visited the countries farther north. Since their marriage, they had become more inseparable than ever, and Anderson was convinced that in this state only could he look for perfect happiness. After three years of living abroad, they came home with another little Ella for Bertie to love. Filled with new ideas, Albert wrote much, and his little wife grew prouder of him every day. The world, or at least the best and worthiest part of it, smiled on the productions of his pen, and all was well. Secure in his loving family, James Albert Anderson asks for nothing more.

And Ella, truest of women! You "who gave up everything for your idol, *even the idol itself!*" Are you not well repaid for your sacrifice?

THE END.

FOR ONE INSTANT, ONE INSTANT ONLY, FORTUNE FELT SURE, QUITE SURE, THAT IN SOME WAY OR OTHER SHE WAS VERY DEAR TO ROBERT ROY. [*Page* 22.

THE LAUREL BUSH.

An Old-fashioned Love Story.

BY THE AUTHOR OF

"JOHN HALIFAX, GENTLEMAN," &c.

MONTREAL:
DAWSON BROTHERS, PUBLISHERS.
1876.

THE LAUREL BUSH.

CHAPTER I.

It was a very ugly bush indeed; that is, so far as any thing in nature can be really ugly. It was lopsided—having on the one hand a stunted stump or two, while on the other a huge heavy branch swept down to the gravel-walk. It had a crooked gnarled trunk or stem, hollow enough to entice any weak-minded bird to build a nest there —only it was so near to the ground, and also to the garden gate. Besides, the owners of the garden, evidently of practical mind, had made use of it to place between a fork in its branches a sort of letter-box— not the government regulation one, for twenty years ago this had not been thought of, but a rough receptacle, where, the house being a good way off, letters might be deposited, instead of, as hitherto, in a hole in the trunk—near the foot of the tree, and under shelter of its mass of evergreen leaves.

This letter-box, made by the boys of the family at the instigation and with the assistance of their tutor, had proved so attractive to some exceedingly incautious sparrow that during the intervals of the post she had begun a nest there, which was found by the boys. Exceedingly wild boys they were, and a great trouble to their old grandmother, with whom they were staying the summer, and their young governess— "Misfortune," as they called her, her real name being Miss Williams—Fortune Williams. The nickname was a little too near the truth, as a keener observer than mischievous boys would have read in her quiet, sometimes sad, face; and it had been stopped rather severely by the tutor of the elder boys, a young man whom the grandmother had been forced to get, to "keep them in order." He was a Mr. Robert Roy, once a student, now a teacher of the "humanities," from the neighboring town—I beg its pardon—city; and a lovely old city it is!—of St. Andrews. Thence he was in the habit of coming to them three and often four days in the week, teaching of mornings and walking of afternoons. They had expected him this afternoon, but their grandmother had carried them off on some pleasure excursion; and being a lady of inexact habits—one, too, to whom tutors were tutors and nothing more—she had merely said to Miss Williams, as the carriage drove away, "When Mr. Roy comes, tell him he is not wanted till to-morrow."

And so Miss Williams had waited at the gate, not wishing him to have the additional trouble of walking up to the house, for she knew every minute of his time was precious. The poor and the hard-working can understand and sympathize with one another. Only a tutor, and only a governess: Mrs. Dalziel drove away and never thought of them again. They were mere machines —servants to whom she paid their wages, and so that they did sufficient service to deserve these wages, she never interfered with them, nor, indeed, wasted a moment's consideration upon them or their concerns.

Consequently they were in the somewhat rare and peculiar position of a young man and young woman (perhaps Mrs. Dalziel would have taken exception to the words "young lady and young gentleman") thrown together day after day, week after week—nay, it had now become month after month—to all intents and purposes quite alone, except for the children. They taught together, there being but one school-room; walked out together, for the two younger boys refused to be separated from their elder brothers; and, in short, spent two-thirds of their existence together, without let or hinderance, comment or observation, from any mortal soul.

I do not wish to make any mystery in this story. A young woman of twenty-five and a young man of thirty, both perfectly alone in the world—orphans, without brother or sister—having to earn their own bread, and earn it hardly, and being placed in circumstances where they had every opportunity of intimate friendship, sympathy, whatever you like to call it: who could doubt what would happen? The more so, as there was no one to suggest that it might happen; no one to watch them or warn them, or waken them with worldly-minded hints; or else to rise up, after the fashion of so many wise parents and guardians and well-intentioned friends, and indignantly shut the stable door *after* the steed is stolen.

No. That something which was so sure to happen had happened; you might have seen it in their eyes, have heard it in the very tone of their voices, though they still talked in a very commonplace way, and still called each other "Miss Williams" and "Mr. Roy." In fact, their whole demeanor to one another was characterized by the grave and even formal decorum which was natural to very reserved people, just trembling on the verge of that discovery which will unlock the heart of each to the other, and annihilate reserve forever between the two whom Heaven has designed and meant to become one; a completed existence. If by any mischance this does not come about, each may lead a very creditable and not unhappy life; but it will be a locked-up life, one to which no third person is ever likely to find the key.

Whether such natures are to be envied or pitied is more than I can say; but at least they are more to be respected than the people who wear their hearts upon their sleeves for daws to peck at, and very often are all the prouder the more they are pecked at, and the more elegantly they bleed; which was not likely to be the case with either of these young folks, young as they were.

They were young, and youth is always interesting and even comely; but beyond that there was nothing remarkable about either. He was Scotch; she English, or rather Welsh. She had the clear blue Welsh eye, the funny *retroussé* Welsh nose; but with the prettiest little mouth underneath it—firm, close, and sweet; full of sensitiveness, but a sensitiveness that was controlled and guided by that best possession to either man or woman, a good strong will. No one could doubt that the young governess had, what was a very useful thing to a governess, "a will of her own;" but not a domineering or obnoxious will, which indeed is seldom will at all, but merely obstinacy.

For the rest, Miss Williams was a little woman, or gave the impression of being so, from her slight figure and delicate hands and feet. I doubt if any one would have called her pretty, until he or she had learned to love her. For there are two distinct kinds of love, one in which the eye instructs the heart, and the other in which the heart informs and guides the eye. There have been men who, seeing an unknown beautiful face, have felt sure it implied the most beautiful soul in the world, pursued it, worshiped it, wooed and won it, found the fancy true, and loved the woman forever. Other men there are who would simply say, "I don't know if such a one is handsome or not; I only know she is herself—and mine." Both loves are good; nay, it is difficult to say which is best. But the latter would be the most likely to any one who became attached to Fortune Williams.

Also, perhaps, to Robert Roy, though no one expects good looks in his sex; indeed, they are mostly rather objectionable. Women do not usually care for a very handsome man; and men are prone to set him down as conceited. No one could lay either charge to Mr. Roy. He was only an honest-looking Scotchman, tall and strong and manly. Not "red," in spite of his name, but dark-skinned and dark-haired; in no way resembling his great namesake, Rob Roy Macgregor, as the boys sometimes called him behind his back —never to his face. Gentle as the young man was, there was something about him which effectually prevented any one's taking the smallest liberty with him. Though he had been a teacher of boys ever since he was seventeen—and I have heard one of the fraternity confess that it is almost impossible to be a school-master for ten years without becoming a tyrant—still it was a pleasant and sweet-tempered face. Very far from a weak face, though: when Mr. Roy said a thing must be done, every one of his boys knew it *must* be done, and there was no use saying any more about it.

He had unquestionably that rare gift, the power of authority; though this did not necessarily imply self-control; for some people can rule every body except themselves. But Robert Roy's clear, calm, rather sad eye, and a certain patient expression about the mouth, implied that he too had had enough of the hard training of life to be able to govern himself. And that is more difficult to a man than to a woman.

> "All thy passions, matched with mine,
> Are as moonlight unto sunlight, and as water unto
> wine."

A truth which even Fortune's tender heart did not fully take in, deep as was her sympathy for him; for his toilsome, lonely life, lived more in shadow than in sunshine, and with every temptation to the selfishness which is so apt to follow self-dependence, and the bitterness that to a proud spirit so often makes the sting of poverty. Yet he was neither selfish nor bitter; only a little

reserved, silent, and—except with children —rather grave.

She stood watching him now, for she could see him a long way off across the level Links, and noticed that he stopped more than once to look at the golf-players. He was a capital golfer himself, but had never any time to play. Between his own studies and the teaching by which he earned the money to prosecute them, every hour was filled up. So he turned his back on the pleasant pastime, which seems to have such an extraordinary fascination for those who pursue it, and came on to his daily work, with that resolute deliberate step, bent on going direct to his point and turning aside for nothing.

Fortune knew it well by this time; had learned to distinguish it from all others in the world. There are some footsteps which, by a pardonable poetical license, we say "we should hear in our graves," and though this girl did not think of that, for death looked far off, and she was scarcely a poetical person, still, many a morning, when, sitting at her school-room window, she heard Mr. Roy coming steadily down the gravel-walk, she was conscious of—something which people can not feel twice in a lifetime.

And now, when he approached with that kind smile of his, which brightened into double pleasure when he saw who was waiting for him, she was aware of a wild heart-beat, a sense of exceeding joy, and then of relief and rest. He was "comfortable" to her. She could express it in no other way. At sight of his face and at sound of his voice all worldly cares and troubles, of which she had a good many, seemed to fall off. To be with him was like having an arm to lean on, a light to walk by; and she had walked alone so long.

"Good-afternoon, Miss Williams."

"Good-afternoon, Mr. Roy."

They said no more than that, but the stupidest person in the world might have seen that they were glad to meet, glad to be together. Though neither they nor any one else could have explained the mysterious fact, the foundation of all love stories in books or in life—and which the present author owns, after having written many books and seen a great deal of life, is to her also as great a mystery as ever—Why do certain people like to be together? What is the inexplicable attraction which makes them seek one another, suit one another, put up with one another's weaknesses, condone one another's faults (when neither are too great to lessen love), and to the last day of life find a charm in one another's society which extends to no other human being? Happy love or lost love, a full world or an empty world, life with joy or life without it—that is all the difference. Which some people think very small, and that it does not matter; and perhaps it does not—to many people. But it does to some, and I incline to put among that category Miss Williams and Mr. Roy.

They stood by the laurel bush, having just shaken hands rather more hastily than they usually did; but the absence of the children, and the very unusual fact of their being quite alone, gave to both a certain shyness, and she had drawn her hand away, saying, with a slight blush:

"Mrs. Dalziel desired me to meet you and tell you that you might have a holiday to-day. She has taken the boys with her to Elie. I dare say you will not be sorry to gain an hour or two for yourself; though I am sorry you should have the trouble of the walk for nothing."

"For nothing?"—with the least shadow of a smile, not of annoyance, certainly.

"Indeed, I would have let you know if I could, but she decided at the very last minute; and if I had proposed that a messenger should have been sent to stop you, I am afraid—it would not have answered."

"Of course not;" and they interchanged an amused look—these fellow-victims to the well-known ways of the household—which, however, neither grumbled at; it was merely an outside thing, this treatment of both as mere tutor and governess. After all (as he sometimes said, when some special rudeness—not to himself, but to her—vexed him), they were tutor and governess; but they were something else besides; something which, the instant their chains were lifted off, made them feel free and young and strong, and comforted them with a comfort unspeakable.

"She bade me apologize. No, I am afraid, if I tell the absolute truth, she did *not* bid me, but I do apologize."

"What for, Miss Williams?"

"For your having been brought out all this way just to go back again."

"I do not mind it, I assure you."

"And as for the lost lesson—"

"The boys will not mourn over it, I dare say. In fact, their term with me is so soon coming to an end that it does not signify much. They told me they are going back to England to school next week. Do you go back too?"

"Not just yet—not till next Christmas. Mrs. Dalziel talks of wintering in London; but she is so vague in her plans that I am never sure from one week to another what she will do."

"And what are your plans? *You* always know what you intend to do."

"Yes, I think so," answered Miss Williams, smiling. "One of the few things I remember of my mother was hearing her say of me, that 'her little girl was a little girl who always knew her own mind.' I think I do. I may not be always able to carry it out, but I think I know it."

"Of course," said Mr. Roy, absently and somewhat vaguely, as he stood beside the laurel bush, pulling one of its shiny leaves to pieces, and looking right ahead, across the sunshiny Links, the long shore of yellow sands, where the mermaids might well delight to come and "take hands"—to the smooth, dazzling, far-away sea. No sea is more beautiful than that at St. Andrews.

Its sleepy glitter seemed to have lulled Robert Roy into a sudden meditation, from which no word of his companion came to rouse him. In truth, she, never given much to talking, simply stood, as she often did, silently beside him, quite satisfied with the mere comfort of his presence.

I am afraid this Fortune Williams will be considered a very weak-minded young woman. She was not a bit of a coquette, she had not the slightest wish to flirt with any man. Nor was she a proud beauty desirous to subjugate the other sex, and drag them triumphantly at her chariot wheels. She did not see the credit, or the use, or the pleasure of any such proceeding. She was a self-contained, self-dependent woman. Thoroughly a woman; not indifferent at all to womanhood's best blessing; still, she could live without it if necessary, as she could have lived without any thing which it had pleased God to deny her. She was not a creature likely to die for love, or do wrong for love, which some people think the only test of love's strength, instead of being its utmost weakness; but that she was capable of love, for all her composure and quietness, capable of it, and ready for it, in its intensest, most passionate, and most enduring form, the God who made her knew, if no one else did.

Her time would come; indeed, had come already. She had too much self-respect to let him guess it, but I am afraid she was very fond of—or, if that is a foolish phrase, deeply attached to—Robert Roy. He had been so good to her, at once strong and tender, chivalrous, respectful, and kind; and she had no father, no brother, no other man at all to judge him by, except the accidental men whom she had met in society, creatures on two legs who wore coats and trowsers, who had been civil to her, as she to them, but who had never interested her in the smallest degree, perhaps because she knew so little of them. But no; it would have been just the same had she known them a thousand years. She was not "a man's woman," that is, one of those women who feel interested in any thing in the shape of a man, and make men interested in them accordingly, for the root of much masculine affection is pure vanity. That celebrated Scotch song,

"Come deaf, or come blind, or come cripple,
　O come, ony ane o' them a'!
Far better be married to something,
　Than no to be married ava,"

was a rhyme that would never have touched the stony heart of Fortune Williams. And yet, let me own it once more, she was very, very fond of Robert Roy. He had never spoken to her one word of love, actual love, no more than he spoke now, as they stood side by side, looking with the same eyes upon the same scene. I say the same eyes, for they were exceedingly alike in their tastes. There was no need ever to go into long explanations about this or that; a glance sufficed, or a word, to show each what the other enjoyed; and both had the quiet conviction that they were enjoying it together. Now as that sweet, still, sunshiny view met their mutual gaze, they fell into no poetical raptures, but just stood and looked, taking it all in with exceeding pleasure, as they had done many and many a time, but never, it seemed, so perfectly as now.

"What a lovely afternoon!" she said at last.

"Yes. It is a pity to waste it. Have you any thing special to do? What did you mean to employ yourself with, now your birds are flown?"

"Oh, I can always find something to do."

"But need you find it? We both work so hard. If we could only now and then have a little bit of pleasure!"

He put it so simply, yet almost with a sigh. This poor girl's heart responded to it suddenly, wildly. She was only twenty-five, yet sometimes she felt quite old, or rather as if she had never been young. The constant teaching, teaching of rough boys, too—for she had had the whole four till Mr. Roy took the two older off her hands—the necessity of grinding hard out of school hours to keep herself up in Latin, Euclid, and other branches which do not usually form part of a feminine education, only having a great natural love of work, she had taught herself—all these things combined to make her life a dull life, a hard life, till Robert Roy came into it. And sometimes even now the desperate craving to enjoy—not only to endure, but to enjoy

—to take a little of the natural pleasures of her age — came to the poor governess very sorely, especially on days such as this, when all the outward world looked so gay, so idle, and she worked so hard.

So did Robert Roy. Life was not easier to him than to herself; she knew that; and when he said, half joking, as if he wanted to feel his way, "Let us imitate our boys, and take a half holiday," she only laughed, but did not refuse.

How could she refuse? There were the long smooth sands on either side the Eden, stretching away into indefinite distance, with not a human being upon them to break their loneliness, or, if there was, he or she looked a mere dot, not human at all. Even if these two had been afraid of being seen walking together—which they hardly were, being too unimportant for any one to care whether they were friends or lovers, or what not—there was nobody to see them, except in the character of two black dots on the yellow sands.

"It is low water; suppose we go and look for sea-anemones. One of my pupils wants some, and I promised to try and find one the first spare hour I had."

"But we shall not find anemones on the sands."

"Shells, then, you practical woman! We'll gather shells. It will be all the same to that poor invalid boy—and to me," added he, with that involuntary sigh which she had noticed more than once, and which had begun to strike on her ears not quite painfully. Sighs, when we are young, mean differently to what they do in after-years. "I don't care very much where I go, or what I do; I only want—well, to be happy for an hour, if Providence will let me."

"Why should not Providence let you?" said Fortune, gently. "Few people deserve it more."

"You are kind to think so; but you are always kind to every body."

By this time they had left their position by the laurel bush, and were walking along side by side, according as he had suggested. This silent, instinctive acquiescence in what he wished done—it had happened once or twice before, startling her a little at herself; for, as I have said, Miss Williams was not at all the kind of person to do every thing that every body asked her, without considering whether it was right or wrong. She could obey, but it would depend entirely upon whom she had to obey, which, indeed, makes the sole difference between loving disciples and slavish fools.

It was a lovely day, one of those serene autumn days peculiar to Scotland—I was going to say to St. Andrews; and any one who knows the ancient city will know exactly how it looks in the still, strongly spiritualized light of such an afternoon, with the ruins, the castle, cathedral, and St. Regulus's tower standing out sharply against the intensely blue sky, and on the other side—on both sides—the yellow sweep of sand curving away into distance, and melting into the sunshiny sea.

Many a time, in their prescribed walks with their young tribe, Miss Williams and Mr. Roy had taken this stroll across the Links and round by the sands to the mouth of the Eden, leaving behind them a long and sinuous track of many footsteps, little and large; but now there were only two lines—"foot-prints on the sands of Time," as he jestingly called them, turning round and pointing to the marks of the dainty feet that walked so steadily and straightly beside his own.

"They seem made to go together, those two tracks," said he.

Why did he say it? Was he the kind of man to talk thus without meaning it? If so, alas! she was not exactly the woman to be thus talked to. Nothing fell on her lightly. Perhaps it was her misfortune, perhaps even her fault, but so it was.

Robert Roy did not "make love;" not at all. Possibly he never could have done it in the ordinary way. Sweet things, polite things, were very difficult to him either to do or to say. Even the tenderness that was in him came out as if by accident; but, oh! how infinitely tender he could be! Enough to make any one who loved him die easily.

SHE WENT ALONG THE SHINING SANDS IN A DREAM OF PERFECT CONTENT.

[*Page* 17.

quietly, contentedly, if only just holding his hand.

There is an incident in Dickens's touching *Tale of Two Cities*, where a young man going innocent to the guillotine, and riding on the death-cart with a young girl whom he had never before seen, is able to sustain and comfort her, even to the last awful moment, by the look of his face and the clasp of his hand. That man, I have often thought, must have been something not unlike Robert Roy.

Such men are rare, but they do exist; and it was Fortune's lot, or she believed it was, to have found one. That was enough. She went along the shining sands in a dream of perfect content, perfect happiness, thinking—and was it strange or wrong that she should so think?—that if it were God's will she should thus walk through life, the thorniest path would seem smooth, the hardest road easy. She had no fear of life, if lived beside him; or of death—love is stronger than death; at least this sort of love, of which only strong natures are capable, and out of which are made, not the lyrics, perhaps, but the epics, the psalms, or the tragedies of our mortal existence.

I have explained thus much about these two friends—lovers that may be, or might have been—because they never would have done it themselves. Neither was given to much speaking. Indeed, I fear their conversation this day, if recorded, would have been of the most feeble kind—brief, fragmentary, mere comments on the things about them, or abstract remarks not particularly clever or brilliant. They were neither of them what you would call brilliant people; yet they were happy, and the hours flew by like a few minutes, until they found themselves back again beside the laurel bush at the gate, when Mr. Roy suddenly said:

"Do not go in yet. I mean, need you go in? It is scarcely past sunset; the boys will not be home for an hour yet; they don't want you, and I—I want you so. In your English sense," he added, with a laugh, referring to one of their many arguments, scholastic or otherwise, wherein she had insisted

that to want meant, *Anglicè*, to wish or to crave, whereas in Scotland it was always used like the French *manquer*, to miss or to need.

"Shall we begin that fight over again?" asked she, smiling; for every thing, even fighting, seemed pleasant to-day.

"No, I have no wish to fight; I want to consult you seriously on a purely personal matter, if you would not mind taking that trouble."

Fortune looked sorry. That was one of the bad things in him (the best men alive have their bad things), the pride which apes humility, the self-distrust which often wounds another so keenly. Her answer was given with a grave and simple sincerity that ought to have been reproach enough.

"Mr. Roy, I would not mind any amount of trouble if I could be of use to you; you know that."

"Forgive me! Yes, I do know it. I believe in you and your goodness to the very bottom of my heart."

She tried to say, "Thank you," but her lips refused to utter a word. It was so difficult to go on talking like ordinary friends, when she knew, and he must know she knew, that one word more would make them—not friends at all—something infinitely better, closer, dearer; but that word was his to speak, not hers. There are women who will "help a man on"—propose to him, marry him indeed—while he is under the pleasing delusion that he does it all himself; but Fortune Williams was not one of these. She remained silent and passive, waiting for the next thing he should say. It came: something the shock of which she never forgot as long as she lived; and he said it with his eyes on her face, so that, if it killed her, she must keep quiet and composed, as she did.

"You know the boys' lessons end next week. The week after I go—that is, I have almost decided to go—to India."

"To India!"

"Yes. For which, no doubt, you think me very changeable, having said so often that I meant to keep to a scholar's life, and be a professor one day, perhaps, if by any means I could get salt to my porridge. Well, now I am not satisfied with salt to my porridge; I wish to get rich."

She did not say, "Why?" She thought she had not looked it; but he answered: "Never mind why. I do wish it, and I will be rich yet, if I can. Are you very much surprised?"

Surprised she certainly was; but she answered, honestly, "Indeed, you are the last person I should suspect of being worldly-minded."

"Thank you; that is kind. No, just; merely just. One ought to have faith in people; it does one good. I am afraid my own deficiency is want of faith. It takes so much to make me believe for a moment that any one cares for me."

How hard it was to be silent—harder still to speak! But she did speak.

"I can understand that; I have often felt the same. It is the natural consequence of a very lonely life. If you and I had had fathers and mothers and brothers and sisters, we might have been different."

"Perhaps so. But about India. For a long time—that is, for many weeks—I have been casting about in my mind how to change my way of life, to look out for something that would help me to earn money, and quickly, but there seemed no chance whatever. Until suddenly one has opened."

And then he explained how the father of one of his pupils, grateful for certain benefits, which Mr. Roy did not specify, and noticing certain business qualities in him— "which I suppose I have, though I didn't know it," added he, with a smile—had offered him a situation in a merchant's office at Calcutta: a position of great trust and responsibility, for three years certain, with the option of then giving it up or continuing it.

"And continuing means making a fortune. Even three years means making something, with my 'stingy' habits. Only I must go at once. Nor is there any time left me for my decision; it must be yes or no. Which shall it be?"

The sudden appeal—made, too, as if he thought it was nothing—that terrible yes or no, which to her made all the difference of living or only half living, of feeling the sun in or out of the world. What could she answer? Trembling violently, she yet answered, in a steady voice, "You must decide for yourself. A woman can not understand a man."

"Nor a man a woman, thoroughly. There is only one thing which helps both to comprehend one another"

One thing! she knew what it was. Surely so did he. But that strange distrustfulness of which he had spoken, or the hesitation which the strongest and bravest men have at times, came between.

"Oh, the little more, and how much it is!
Oh, the little less, and what worlds away!"

If, instead of looking vaguely out upon the sea, he had looked into this poor girl's face; if, instead of keeping silence, he had only spoken one word! But he neither looked nor spoke, and the moment passed by. And there are moments which people would sometimes give a whole lifetime to recall and use differently; but in vain.

"My engagement is only for three years," he resumed; "and then, if alive, I mean to come back. Dead or alive, I was going to say, but you would not care to see my ghost, I presume? I beg your pardon: I ought not to make a joke of such serious things."

"No, you ought not."

She felt herself almost speechless, that in another minute she might burst into sobs. He saw it—at least he saw a very little of it, and misinterpreted the rest.

"I have tired you. Take my arm. You will soon be at home now." Then, after a pause, "You will not be displeased at any thing I have said? We part friends? No, we do not part; I shall see you every day for a week, and be able to tell you all particulars of my journey, if you care to hear."

"Thank you, yes—I do care."

They stood together, arm in arm. The dews were falling; a sweet, soft, lilac haze had begun to creep over the sea—the solemn, far-away sea that he was so soon to cross. Involuntarily she clung to his arm. So near, yet so apart! Why must it be? She could have borne his going away, if it was for his good, if he wished it; and something whispered to her that this sudden desire to get rich was not for himself alone. But, oh! if he would only speak! One word —one little word! After that, any thing might come—the separation of life, the bitterness of death. To the two hearts that had once opened each to each, in the full recognition of mutual love, there could never more be any real parting.

But that one word he did not say. He only took the little hand that lay on his arm, pressed it, and held it—years after, the feeling of that clasp was as fresh on her fingers as yesterday—then, hearing the foot of some accidental passer-by, he let it go, and did not take it again.

Just at this moment the sound of distant carriage wheels was heard.

"That must be Mrs. Dalziel and the boys."

"Then I had better go. Good-by."

The day-dream was over. It had all come back again—the forlorn, dreary, hard-working world.

"Good-by, Mr. Roy." And they shook hands.

"One word," he said, hastily. "I shall write to you—you will allow me?—and I shall see you several times, a good many times, before I go?"

"I hope so."

"Then, for the present, good-by. That means," he added, earnestly, "'God be with you!' And I know He always will."

In another minute Fortune found herself standing beside the laurel bush, alone, listening to the sound of Mr. Roy's footsteps down the road—listening, listening, as if, with the exceeding tension, her brain would burst.

The carriage came, passed; it was not Mrs. Dalziel's, after all. She thought he might discover this, and come back again; so she waited a little—five minutes, ten— beside the laurel bush. But he did not come. No footstep, no voice; nothing but the faint, far-away sound of the long waves washing in upon the sands.

It was not the brain that felt like to burst now, but the heart. She clasped her hands above her head. It did not matter; there was no creature to see or hear that appeal —was it to man or God?—that wild, broken sob, so contrary to her usual self-controlled and self-contained nature. And then she leaned her forehead against the gate, just where Robert Roy had accidentally laid his hand in opening it, and wept bitterly.

CHAPTER II.

The "every day" on which Mr. Roy had reckoned for seeing his friend, or whatsoever else he considered Miss Williams to be, proved a failure. Her youngest pupil fell ill, and she was kept beside him, and away from the school-room, until the doctor could decide whether the illness was infectious or not. It turned out to be very trifling—a most trivial thing altogether, yet weighted with a pain most difficult to bear, a sense of fatality that almost overwhelmed one person at least. What the other felt she did not know. He came daily as usual; she watched him come and go, and sometimes he turned and they exchanged a greeting from the window. But beyond that, she had to take all passively. What could she, only a woman, do or say or plan? Nothing. Women's business is to sit down and endure.

She had counted these days—Tuesday, Wednesday, Thursday, Friday, Saturday—as if they had been years. And now they were all gone, had fled like minutes, fled emptily away. A few fragmentary facts she had had to feed on, communicated by the boys in their rough talk.

"Mr. Roy was rather cross to-day."

"Not cross, Dick—only dull."

"Mr. Roy asked why David did not come in to lessons, and said he hoped he would be better by Saturday."

"Mr. Roy said good-by to us all, and gave us each something to remember him by when he was out in India. Did Miss Williams know he was going out to India? Oh, how jolly!"

"Yes, and he sails next week, and the name of his ship is the *Queen of the South,* and he goes by Liverpool instead of Southampton, because it costs less; and he leaves St. Andrews on Monday morning."

"Are you sure he said Monday morning?" For that was Saturday night.

"Certain, because he has to get his outfit still. Oh, what fun it must be!"

And the boys went on, greatly excited, repeating every thing Mr. Roy had told them —for he had made them fond of him, even in those few months—expatiating with delight on his future career, as a merchant or something, they did not quite know what; but no doubt it would be far nicer and more amusing than stopping at home and grinding forever over horrid books. Didn't Miss Williams think so?

Miss Williams only smiled. She knew how all his life he had loved "those horrid books," preferring them to pleasure, recreation, almost to daily bread; how he had lived on the hope that one day he—born only a farmer's son—might do something, write something. "I also am of Arcadia." He might have done it or not—the genius may or may not have been there; but the ambition certainly was. Could he have thrown it all aside? And why?

Not for mere love of money; she knew him too well for that. He was a thorough bookworm, simple in all his tastes and habits—simple almost to penuriousness; but it was a penuriousness born of hard fortunes, and he never allowed it to affect any body but himself. Still, there was no doubt he did not care for money, or luxury, or worldly position—any of the things that lesser men count large enough to work and struggle and die for. To give up the pursuits he loved, deliberately to choose others, to change his whole life thus, and expatriate himself, as it were, for years—perhaps for always—why did he do it, or for whom?

Was it for a woman? Was it for her? If ever, in those long empty days and wakeful nights, this last thought entered Fortune's mind, she stifled it as something which, once to have fully believed and then disbelieved, would have killed her.

That she should have done the like for him—that or any thing else involving any amount of heroism or self-sacrifice—well, it was natural, right; but that he should do it for her? That he should change his whole purpose of life that he might be able to marry quickly, to shelter in his bosom a poor girl who was not able to fight the world as a man could, the thing—not so very impossible, after all—seemed to her almost incredible! And yet (I am telling a mere love story, remember—a foolish, innocent love story, without apologizing for either the folly or the innocence) sometimes she was so far "left to herself," as the Scotch say, that she did believe it: in the still twilights, in the wakeful nights, in the one solitary half hour of intense relief, when, all her boys being safe in bed, she rushed out into the garden under the silent stars to sob, to moan, to speak out loud words which nobody could possibly hear.

"He is going away, and I shall never see him again. And I love him—love him better than any thing in all this world. I couldn't help it—he couldn't help it. But, oh! it's hard—hard!"

And then, altogether breaking down, she would begin to cry like a child. She missed him so, even this week, after having for weeks and months been with him every day; but it was less like a girl missing her lover —who was, after all, not her lover—than a child mourning helplessly for the familiar voice, the guiding, helpful hand. With all the rest of the world Fortune Williams was an independent, energetic woman, self-contained, brave, and strong, as a solitary governess had need to be; but beside Robert Roy she felt like a child, and she cried for him like a child,

"And with no language but a cry."

So the week ended and Sunday came, kept at Mrs. Dalziel's like the Scotch Sundays of twenty years ago. No visitor ever entered the house, wherein all the meals were cold and the blinds drawn down, as if for a funeral. The family went to church for the entire day, St. Andrews being too far off for any return home "between sermons." Usually one servant was left in charge, turn and turn about; but this Sunday Mrs. Dalziel, having put the governess in the nurse's place beside the ailing child, thought shrewdly she might as well put her in the servant's place too, and let her take charge of the kitchen fire as well as of little David. Being English, Miss Williams was not so exact about "ordinances" as a Scotchwoman would have been; so Mrs. Dalziel had no hesitation in asking her to remain at home alone the whole day in charge of her pupil.

Thus faded, Fortune thought, her last hope of seeing Robert Roy again, either at church—where he usually sat in the Dalziel pew, by the old lady's request, to make the boys "behave"—or walking down the street, where he sometimes took the two eldest to eat their "piece" at his lodgings. All was now ended; yet on the hope—or dread—of this last Sunday she had hung, she now felt with what intensity, till it was gone.

Fortune was the kind of woman who, were it given her to fight, could fight to the death, against fate or circumstances; but when her part was simply passive, she could also endure. Not, as some do, with angry grief or futile resistance, but with a quiet patience so complete that only a very quick eye would have found out she was suffering at all.

Little David did not, certainly. When, hour after hour, she sat by his sofa, interesting him as best she could in the dull "good" books which alone were allowed of Sundays, and then passing into word-of-mouth stories—the beautiful Bible stories over which her own voice trembled while she told them—Ruth, with her piteous cry, "Whither thou goest, I will go; where thou diest, I will die, and there will I be buried;" Jonathan, whose soul "clave to the soul of David, and Jonathan loved him as his own soul"—all those histories of passionate fidelity and agonized parting—for every sort of love is essentially the same—how they went to her very heart!

Oh, the awful quietness of that Sunday, that Sabbath which was not rest, in which the hours crawled on in sunshiny stillness, neither voices nor steps nor sounds of any kind breaking the death-like hush of every thing. At length the boy fell asleep; and then Fortune seemed to wake up for the first time to the full consciousness of what was and what was about to be.

All of a sudden she heard steps on the gravel below; then the hall bell rang through the silent house. She knew who it was even before she opened the door and saw him standing there.

"May I come in? They told me you were keeping house alone, and I said I should just walk over to bid you and Davie good-by."

Roy's manner was grave and matter-of-fact—a little constrained, perhaps, but not much—and he looked so exceedingly pale and tired that, without any hesitation, she took him into the school-room, where they were sitting, and gave him the arm-chair by Davie's sofa.

"Yes, I own to being rather overdone; I have had so much to arrange, for I must leave here to-morrow, as I think you know."

"The boys told me."

"I thought they would. I should have done it myself, but every day I hoped to see you. It was this little fellow's fault, I suppose," patting Davie's head. "He seems quite well now, and as jolly as possible. You don't know what it is to say 'Good-by,' David, my son."

Mr. Roy, who always got on well with children, had a trick of calling his younger pupils "My son."

"Why do you say 'Good-by' at all, then?" asked the child, a mischievous but winning young scamp of six or seven, who had as many tricks as a monkey or a magpie. In fact, in chattering and hiding things he was nearly as bad as a magpie, and the torment of his governess's life; yet she was fond of him. "Why do you bid us good-by, Mr. Roy? Why don't you stay always with Miss Williams and me?"

"I wish to God I could."

She heard that, heard it distinctly, though it was spoken beneath his breath; and she felt the look, turned for one moment upon her as she stood by the window. She never forgot either—never, as long as she lived. Some words, some looks, can deceive, perhaps quite unconsciously, by being either more demonstrative than was meant, or the exaggeration of coldness to hide its opposite; but sometimes a glance, a tone, betrays, or rather reveals, the real truth in a manner that nothing afterward can ever falsify. For one instant, one instant only, Fortune felt sure, quite sure, that in some way or other she was very dear to Robert Roy. If the next minute he had taken her into his arms, and said or looked the words which, to an earnest-minded, sincere man like him, constitute a pledge for life, never to be disannulled or denied, she could hardly have felt more completely his own.

But he did not say them; he said nothing at all; sat leaning his head on his hand, with an expression so weary, so sad, that all the coaxing ways of little Davie could hardly win from him more than a faint smile. He looked so old, too, and he was but just thirty. Only thirty—only twenty-five; and yet these two were bearing, seemed to have borne for years, the burden of life, feeling all its hardships and none of its sweetnesses. Would things ever change? Would he have the courage (it was his part, not hers) to make them change, at least in one way, by bringing about that heart-union which to all pure and true natures is consolation for every human woe?

"I wonder," he said, sitting down and taking David on his knee—"I wonder if it is best to bear things one's self, or to let another share the burden?"

Easily—oh, how easily!—could Fortune have answered this—have told him that, whether he wished it or not, two did really bear his burdens, and perhaps the one who bore it secretly and silently had not the lightest share. But she did not speak: it was not possible.

"How shall I hear of you, Miss Williams?" he said, after a long silence. "You are not likely to leave the Dalziel family?"

"No," she answered; "and if I did, I could always be heard of, the Dalziels are so well known hereabouts. Still, a poor wandering governess easily drops out of people's memory."

"And a poor wandering tutor too. But I am not a tutor any more, and I hope I shall not be poor long. Friends can not lose one another; such friends as you and I have been. I will take care we shall not do it, that is, if— But never mind that. You have been very good to me, and I have often bothered you very much, I fear. You will be almost glad to get rid of me."

She might have turned upon him eyes swimming with tears—woman's tears—that engine of power which they say no man can ever resist; but I think, if so, a woman like Fortune would have scorned to use it. Those poor weary eyes, which could weep oceans alone under the stars, were perfectly dry now—dry, and fastened on the ground, as she replied, in a grave steady voice,

"You do not really believe that, else you would never have said it."

Her composure must have surprised him, for he looked suddenly up, then begged her pardon. "I did not hurt you, surely? We must not part with the least shadow of unkindness between us."

"No." She offered her hand, and he took it—gently, affectionately, but only affectionately. The one step beyond affection, which leads into another world, another life, he seemed determined not to pass.

For at least half an hour he sat there with David on his knee, or rising up restlessly to pace the room with David on his shoulder; but apparently not desiring the child's absence, rather wishing to keep him as a sort of barrier. Against what?—himself? And so minute after minute slipped by; and Miss Williams, sitting in her place by the window, already saw, dotting the Links, group after group of the afternoon church-goers wandering quietly home—so quietly, so happily, fathers and mothers and children, companions and friends—for whom was no parting and no pain.

Mr. Roy suddenly took out his watch. "I must go now; I see I have spent all but my last five minutes. Good-by, David, my lad; you'll be a big man, maybe, when I see you again. Miss Williams" (standing before her with an expression on his face such as she had never seen before), "before I go there was a question I had determined to ask you—a purely ethical question which a friend of mine has been putting to me, and I could not answer; that is, I could, from the man's side, the worldly side. A woman might think differently."

"What is it?"

"Simply this. If a man has not a halfpenny, ought he to ask a woman to share it? Rather an Irish way of putting the matter," with a laugh, not without bitterness, "but you understand. Ought he not to wait till he has at least something to offer besides himself? Is it not mean, selfish, cowardly, to bind a woman to all the chances or mischances of his lot, instead of fighting it out alone like a man? My friend thinks so, and I—I agree with him."

"Then why did you ask me?"

The words, though low and clear, were cold and sharp—sharp with almost unbearable pain. Every atom of pride in her was roused. Whether he loved her and would not tell her so, or loved some other woman and wished her to know it, it was all the same. He was evidently determined to go away free and leave her free; and perhaps many sensible men or women would say he was right in so doing.

"I beg your pardon," he said, almost humbly. "I ought not to have spoken of this at all. I ought just to have said 'Good-by,' and nothing more." And he took her hand.

There was on it one ring, not very valuable, but she always liked to wear it, as it had belonged to her mother. Robert Roy drew it off, and put it deliberately into his pocket.

"Give me this; you shall have it back again when I am dead, or you are married, whichever happens first. Do you understand?"

Putting David aside (indeed, he seemed for the first time to forget the boy's presence), he took her by the two hands and looked down into her face. Apparently he read something there, something which startled him, almost shocked him.

"God forgive me!" he muttered, and stood irresolute.

Irresolution, alas! too late; for just then all the three Dalziel boys rushed into the house and the school-room, followed by their grandmother. The old lady looked a good deal surprised, perhaps a little displeased, from one to the other.

Mr. Roy perceived it, and recovered himself in an instant, letting go Fortune's hands and placing himself in front of her, between her and Mrs. Dalziel. Long afterward she remembered that trivial act—remembered it with the tender gratitude of the protected toward the protector, if nothing more.

"You see, I came, as I told you I should, if possible, to bid Miss Williams good-by, and wee Davie. They both kindly admitted me, and we have had half an hour's merry chat, have we not, Davie? Now, my man, good-by." He took up the little fellow and kissed him, and then extended his hand. "Good-by, Miss Williams. I hope your little pupils will value you as you deserve."

Then, with a courteous and formal farewell to the old lady, and a most uproarious one from the boys, he went to the door, but turned round, saying to the eldest boy, distinctly and clearly — though she

was at the farther end of the room, she heard, and was sure he meant her to hear, every word:

"By-the-bye, Archy, there is something I was about to explain to Miss Williams. Tell her I will write it. She is quite sure to have a letter from me to-morrow—no, on Tuesday morning."

And so he went away, bravely and cheerily, the boys accompanying him to the gate, and shouting and waving their hats to him as he crossed the Links, until their grandmother reprovingly suggested that it was Sunday.

"But Mr. Roy does not go off to India every Sunday. Hurrah! I wish we were all going too. Three cheers for Mr. Roy."

"Mr. Roy is a very fine fellow, and I hope he will do well," said Mrs. Dalziel, touched by their enthusiasm; also by some old memories, for, like many St. Andrews folk, she was strongly linked with India, and had sent off one-half of her numerous family to live or die there. There was something like a tear in her old eyes, though not for the young tutor; but it effectually kept her from either looking at or thinking of the governess. And she forgot them both immediately. They were merely the tutor and the governess.

As for the boys, they chattered vehemently all tea-time about Mr. Roy, and their envy of the "jolly" life he was going to; then their minds turned to their own affairs, and there was silence.

The kind of silence, most of us know it, when any one belonging to a household, or very familiar there, goes away on a long indefinite absence. At first there is little consciousness of absence at all; we are so constantly expecting the door to be opened for the customary presence that we scarcely even miss the known voice, or face, or hand. By-and-by, however, we do miss it, and there comes a general, loud, shallow lamentation, which soon cures itself, and implies an easy and comfortable forgetfulness before long. Except with some, or possibly only one, who is, most likely, the one who has never been heard to utter a word of regret, or seen to shed a single tear.

Miss Williams, now left sole mistress in the school-room, gave her lessons as usual there that Monday morning, and walked with all the four boys on the Links all afternoon. It was a very bright day, as beautiful as Sunday had been, and they communicated to her the interesting facts, learned at golfing that morning, that Mr. Roy and his portmanteau had been seen at Leuchars on the way to Burntisland, and that he would likely have a good crossing, as the sea was very calm. There had lately been some equinoctial gales, which had interested the boys amazingly, and they calculated with ingenious pertinacity whether such gales were likely to occur again when Mr. Roy was in the Bay of Biscay, and, if his ship were wrecked, what he would be supposed to do. They were quite sure he would conduct himself with great heroism, perhaps escape on a single plank, or a raft made by his own hands, and they consulted Miss Williams, who of course was a peripatetic cyclopedia of all scholastic information, as to which port in France or Spain he was likely to be drifted to, supposing this exciting event did happen.

She answered their questions with her usual ready kindliness. She felt like a person in a dream, yet a not unhappy dream, for she still heard the voice, still felt the clasp of the strong, tender, sustaining hands. And to-morrow would be Tuesday.

Tuesday was a wet morning. The bright days were done. Soon after dawn Fortune had woke up and watched the sunrise, till a chill fog crept over the sea and blotted it out; then gradually blotted out the land also, the Links, the town, every thing. A regular St. Andrews "haar;" and St. Andrews people know what that is. Miss Williams had seen it once or twice before, but never so bad as this—blighting, penetrating, and so dense that you could hardly see your hand before you.

But Fortune scarcely felt it. She said to herself, "To-day is Tuesday," which meant nothing to any one else, every thing to her. For she knew the absolute faithfulness, the careful accuracy, in great things and small, with which she had to do. If Robert Roy said, "I will write on such a day," he was as sure to write as that the day would dawn; that is, so far as his own will went; and will, not circumstance, is the strongest agent in this world.

Therefore she waited quietly for the postman's horn. It sounded at last.

"I'll go," cried Archy. "Just look at the haar! I shall have to grope my way to the gate."

He came back, after what seemed an almost endless time, rubbing his head and declaring he had nearly blinded himself by running right into the laurel bush.

"I couldn't see for the fog. I only hope I've left none of the letters behind. No, no; all right. Such a lot! It's the Indian mail. There's for you, and you, boys." He dealt them out with a merry, careless hand.

There was no letter for Miss Williams—a circumstance so usual that nobody noticed it or her, as she sat silent in her corner, while the children read noisily and gayly the letters from their far-away parents.

Her letter—what had befallen it? Had he forgotten to write? But Robert Roy never forgot any thing. Nor did he delay any thing that he could possibly do at the time he promised. He was one of the very few people in this world who in small things as in great are absolutely reliable. It seemed so impossible to believe he had not written, when he said he would, that, as a last hope, she stole out with a plaid over her head and crept through the side walks of the garden, almost groping her way through the fog, and, like Archy, stumbling over the low boughs of the laurel bush to the letter-box it held. Her trembling hands felt in every corner, but no letter was there.

She went wearily back; weary at heart, but patient still. A love like hers, self-existent and sufficient to itself, is very patient, quite unlike the other and more common form of the passion; not love, but a diseased craving to be loved, which creates a thousand imaginary miseries and wrongs. Sharp was her pain, poor girl; but she was not angry, and after her first stab of disappointment her courage rose. All was well with him; he had been seen cheerily starting for Edinburgh; and her own temporary suffering was a comparatively small thing. It could not last: the letter would come to-morrow.

But it did not, nor the next day, nor the next. On the fourth day her heart felt like to break.

I think, of all pangs not mortal, few are worse than this small silent agony of waiting for the post; letting all the day's hope climax upon a single minute, which passes by, and the hope with it, and then comes another day of dumb endurance, if not despair. This even with ordinary letters upon which any thing of moment depends. With others, such as this letter of Robert Roy's— let us not speak of it. Some may imagine, others may have known, a similar suspense. They will understand why, long years afterward, Fortune Williams was heard to say, with a quiver of the lip that could have told its bitter tale, "No; when I have a letter to write, I never put off writing it for a single day."

As these days wore on—these cruel days, never remembered without a shiver of pain, and of wonder that she could have lived through them at all—the whole fabric of reasons, arguments, excuses, that she had built up, tried so eagerly to build up, for him and herself, gradually crumbled away. Had she altogether misapprehended the purport of his promised letter? Was it just some ordinary note, about her boys and their studies perhaps, which, after all, he had not thought it worth while to write? Yet surely it was worth while, if only to send a kindly and courteous farewell to a friend, after so close an intimacy and in face of so indefinite a separation.

A friend? Only a friend? Words may deceive, eyes seldom can. And there had been love in his eyes. Not mere liking, but actual love. She had seen it, felt it, with that almost unerring instinct that women have, whether they return the love or not. In the latter case, they seldom doubt it; in the former, they often do.

"Could I have been mistaken?" she thought, with a burning pang of shame. "Oh, why did he not speak—just one word? After that, I could have borne any thing."

But he had not spoken, he had not written. He had let himself drop out of her life as completely as a falling star drops out of the sky, a ship sinks down in mid-ocean, or—any other poetical simile, used under such circumstances by romantic people.

Fortune Williams was not romantic; at least, what romance was in her lay deep down, and came out in act rather than word. She neither wept nor raved nor cultivated any external signs of a breaking heart. A little paler she grew, a little quieter, but nobody observed this: indeed, it came to be one of her deepest causes of thankfulness that there was nobody to observe any thing —that she had no living soul belonging to her, neither father, mother, brother, nor sister, to pity her or to blame him; since to think him either blamable or blamed would have been the sharpest torture she could have known.

She was saved that and some few other things by being only a governess, instead of one of Fate's cherished darlings, nestled in a family home. She had no time to grieve, except in the dead of night, when "the rain was on the roof." It so happened that, after the haar, there set in a season of continuous, sullen, depressing rain. But at night-time, and for the ten minutes between post hour and lesson hour—which she generally passed in her own room—if her mother, who died when she was ten years old, could have seen her, she would have said, "My poor child!"

Robert Roy had once involuntarily called her so, when by accident one of her rough boys hurt her hand, and he himself bound it up, with the indescribable tenderness which the strong only know how to show or feel. Well she remembered this; indeed, almost every thing he had said or done came back upon her now—vividly, as we recall the words and looks of the dead—mingled with such a hungering pain, such a cruel "miss" of him, daily and hourly, his companionship, help, counsel, every thing she had lacked all her life, and never found but with him and from him. And he was gone, had broken his promise, had left her without a single farewell word.

That he had cared for her, in some sort of way, she was certain; for he was one of those who never say a word too large—nay, he usually said much less than he felt. Whatever he had felt for her —whether friendship, affection, love—must have been true. There was in his nature intense reserve, but no falseness, no insincerity, not an atom of pretense of any kind.

If he did love her, why not tell her so? What was there to hinder him? Nothing, except that strange notion of the "dishonorableness" of asking a woman's love when one has nothing but love to give her in return. This, even, he had seemed at the last to have set aside, as if he could not go away without speaking. And yet he did it.

Perhaps he thought she did not care for him? He had once said a man ought to feel quite sure of a woman before he asked her. Also, that he should never ask twice, since, if she did not know her own mind then, she never would know it, and such a woman was the worst possible bargain a man could make in marriage.

Not know her own mind! Alas, poor soul, Fortune knew it only too well. In that dreadful fortnight it was "borne in upon her," as pious people say, that though she felt kindly to all human beings, the one human being who was necessary to her— without whom her life might be busy, indeed, and useful, but never perfect, an endurance instead of a joy—was this young man, as solitary as herself, as poor, as hardworking; good, gentle, brave Robert Roy.

Oh, why had they not come together, heart to heart—just they two, so alone in the world —and ever after belonged to one another, helping, comforting, and strengthening one another, even though it had been years and years before they were married?

"If only he had loved me, and told me so!" was her bitter cry. "I could have waited for him all my life long, earned my bread ever so hardly, and quite alone, if only I might have had a right to him, and been his comfort, as he was mine. But now—now—"

Yet still she waited, looking forward daily to that dreadful post hour; and when it had gone by, nerving herself to endure until to-morrow. At last hope, slowly dying, was killed outright.

One day at tea-time the boys blurted out, with happy carelessness, their short-lived regrets for him being quite over, the news that Mr. Roy had sailed.

"Not for Calcutta, but Shanghai, a much longer voyage. He can't be heard of for a year at least, and it will be many years before he comes back. I wonder if he will come back rich. They say he will: quite a nabob, perhaps, and take a place in the Highlands, and invite us all—you too, Miss Williams. I once asked him, and he said, 'Of course.' Stop, you are pouring my tea over into the saucer."

This was the only error she made, but went on filling the cups with a steady hand, smiling and speaking mechanically, as people can sometimes. When tea was quite over, she slipped away into her room, and was missing for a long time.

So all was over. No more waiting for that vague "something to happen." Nothing could happen now. He was far away across the seas, and she must just go back to her old monotonous life, as if it had never been any different—as if she had never seen his face nor heard his voice, never known the blessing of his companionship, friendship, love, whatever it was, or whatever he had meant it to be. No, he could not have loved her; or to have gone away would have been—she did not realize whether right or wrong—but simply impossible.

Once, wearying herself with helpless conjectures, a thought, sudden and sharp as steel, went through her heart. He was nearly thirty; few lives are thus long without some sort of love in them. Perhaps he was already bound to some other woman, and finding himself drifting into too pleasant intimacy with herself, wished to draw back in time. Such things had happened, sometimes almost blamelessly, though most miserably to all parties. But with him it was not likely to happen. He was too clear-sighted, strong, and honest. He would never "drift" into any .thing. What he did would be done with a calm deliberate will, incapable of the slightest deception either toward others or himself. Besides, he had at different times told her the whole story of his life, and there was no love in it; only work, hard work, poverty, courage, and endurance, like her own.

"No, he could never have deceived me, neither me nor any one else," she often said to herself, almost joyfully, though the tears were running down. "Whatever it was, it was not that. I am glad—glad. I had far rather believe he never loved me than that he had been false to another woman for my sake. And I believe in him still; I shall always believe in him. He is perfectly good, perfectly true. And so it does not much matter about me."

I am afraid those young ladies who like plenty of lovers, who expect to be adored, and are vexed when they are not adored, and most nobly indignant when forsaken, will think very meanly of my poor Fortune Williams. They may console themselves by thinking she was not a young lady at all—only a woman. Such women are not too common, but they exist occasionally. And they bear their cross and dree their weird; but their lot, at any rate, only concerns themselves, and has one advantage, that it in no way injures the happiness of other people.

Humble as she was, she had her pride. If she wept, it was out of sight. If she wished herself dead, and a happy ghost, that by any means she might get near him, know where he was, and what he was doing, these dreams came only when her work was done, her boys asleep. Day never betrayed the secrets of the night. She set to work every morning at her daily labors with a dogged persistence, never allowing herself a minute's idleness wherein to sit down and mourn. And when, despite her will, she could not quite conquer the fits of nervous irritability that came over her at times—when the children's innocent voices used to pierce her like needles, and their incessant questions and perpetual company were almost more than she could bear—still, even then, all she did was to run away and hide herself for a little, coming back with a pleasant face and a smooth temper. Why should she scold them, poor lambs? They were all she had to love, or that loved her. And they did love her, with all their boyish hearts.

One day, however—the day before they all left St. Andrews for England, the two elder to go to school, and the younger ones to return with her to their maternal grandmother to London—David said something which wounded her, vexed her, made her almost thankful to be going away.

She was standing by the laurel bush, which somehow had for her a strange fascination, and her hand was on the letter-box which the boys and Mr. Roy had made. There was a childish pleasure in touching it or any thing he had touched.

"I hope grandmamma won't take away that box," said Archy. "She ought to keep it in memory of us and of Mr. Roy. How cleverly he made it! Wasn't he clever, now, Miss Williams?"

"Yes," she answered, and no more.

"I've got a better letter-box than yours," said little Davie, mysteriously. "Shall I show it to you, Miss Williams? And perhaps," with a knowing look—the mischievous lad! and yet he was more loving and lovable than all the rest, Mr. Roy's favorite, and hers—"perhaps you might even find a letter in it. Cook says she has seen you many a time watching for a letter from your sweetheart. Who is he?"

"I have none. Tell cook she should not talk such nonsense to little boys," said the governess, gravely.　But she felt hot from head to foot, and turning, walked slowly in-doors.　She did not go near the laurel bush again.

After that, she was almost glad to get away, among strange people and strange places, where Robert Roy's name had never been heard.　The familiar places—hallowed as no other spot in this world could ever be—passed out of sight, and in another week her six months' happy life at St. Andrews had vanished, "like a dream when one awaketh."

Had she awaked?　Or was her daily, outside life to be henceforward the dream, and this the reality?

CHAPTER III.

WHAT is a "wrecked" life? One which the waves of inexorable fate have beaten to pieces, or one that, like an unseaworthy ship, is ready to go down in any waters? What most destroy us? the things we might well blame ourselves for, only we seldom do, our follies, blunders, errors, not counting actual sins? or the things for which we can blame nobody but Providence—if we dared—such as our losses and griefs, our sicknesses of body and mind, all those afflictions which we call "the visitation of God?" Ay, and so they are, but not sent in wrath, or for ultimate evil. No amount of sorrow need make any human life harmful to man or unholy before God, as a discontented, unhappy life must needs be unholy in the sight of Him who in the mysterious economy of the universe seems to have one absolute law—He wastes nothing. He modifies, transmutes, substitutes, re-applies material to new uses; but apparently by Him nothing is ever really lost, nothing thrown away.

Therefore I incline to believe, when I hear people talking of a "wrecked" existence, that whosoever is to blame, it is not Providence.

Nobody could have applied the term to Fortune Williams, looking at her as she sat in the drawing-room window of a house at Brighton, just where the gray of the Esplanade meets the green of the Downs—a ladies' boarding-school, where she had in her charge two pupils, left behind for the holidays, while the mistress took a few weeks' repose. She sat watching the sea, which was very beautiful, as even the Brighton sea can be sometimes. Her eyes were soft and calm; her hands were folded on her black silk dress, her pretty little tender-looking hands, unringed, for she was still Miss Williams, still a governess.

But even at thirty-five—and she had now reached that age, nay, passed it—she was not what you would call "old-maidish." Perhaps because the motherly instinct, naturally very strong in her, had developed more and more. She was one of those governesses—the only sort who ought ever to attempt to be governesses—who really love children, ay, despite their naughtinesses and mischievousnesses and worrying ways; who feel that, after all, these little ones are "of the kingdom of heaven," and that the task of educating them for that kingdom somehow often brings us nearer to it ourselves.

Her heart, always tender to children, had gone out to them more and more every year, especially after that fatal year when a man took it and broke it. No, not broke it, but threw it carelessly away, wounding it so sorely that it never could be quite itself again. But it was a true and warm and womanly heart still.

She had never heard of him—Robert Roy—never once, in any way, since that Sunday afternoon when he said, "I will write to-morrow," and did not write, but let her drop from him altogether like a worthless thing. Cruel, somewhat, even to a mere acquaintance—but to her?

Well, all was past and gone, and the tide of years had flowed over it. Whatever it was, a mistake, a misfortune, or a wrong, nobody knew any thing about it. And the wound even was healed, in a sort of a way, and chiefly by the unconscious hands of these little "ministering angels," who were angels that never hurt her, except by blotting their copy-books or not learning their lessons.

I know it may sound a ridiculous thing that a forlorn governess should be comforted for a lost love by the love of children; but it is true to nature. Women's lives have successive phases, each following the other in natural gradation—maidenhood, wifehood, motherhood: in not one of which, ordinarily, we regret the one before it, to which it is nevertheless impossible to go back. But Fortune's life had had none of these, excepting, perhaps, her one six months' dream of love and spring. That being over, she fell back upon autumn days and autumn pleasures—which are very real pleasures, after all.

As she sat with the two little girls leaning against her lap—they were Indian children, unaccustomed to tenderness, and had already grown very fond of her—there was a look in her face, not at all like an ancient maiden or a governess, but almost motherly. You see the like in the faces of the Virgin Mary, as the old monks used to paint her, quaint, and not always lovely, but never common or coarse, and spiritualized by a look of mingled tenderness and sorrow into something beyond all beauty.

This woman's face had it, so that people who had known Miss Williams as a girl were astonished to find her, as a middle-aged woman, grown "so good-looking." To which one of her pupils once answered, naïvely, "It is because she looks so good."

But this was after ten years and more. Of the first half of those years the less that is said, the better. She did not live; she merely endured life. Monotony without, a constant aching within—a restless gnawing want, a perpetual expectation, half hope, half fear; no human being could bear all this without being the worse for it, or the better. But the betterness came afterward, not at first.

Sometimes her craving to hear the smallest tidings of him, only if he were alive or dead, grew into such an agony that, had it not been for her entire helplessness in the matter, she might have tried some means of gaining information. But, from his sudden change of plans, she was ignorant even of the name of the ship he had sailed by, the firm he had gone to. She could do absolutely nothing, and learn nothing. Hers was something like the "Affliction of Margaret," that poem of Wordsworth's which, when her little pupils recited it—as they often did—made her ready to sob out loud from the pang of its piteous reality:

> "I look for ghosts, but none will force
> Their way to me: 'tis falsely said
> That there was ever intercourse
> Betwixt the living and the dead:
> For surely then I should have sight
> Of him I wait for day and night
> With love and longings infinite."

Still, in the depth of her heart she did not believe Robert Roy was dead; for her finger was still empty of that ring—her mother's ring—which he had drawn off, promising its return "when he was dead or she was married" This implied that he never meant to lose sight of her. Nor, indeed, had he wished it, would it have been very difficult to find her, these ten years having been spent entirely in one place, an obscure village in the south of England, where she had lived as governess—first in the squire's family, then the rector's.

From the Dalziel family, where, as she had said to Mr. Roy, she hoped to remain for years, she had drifted away almost immediately; within a few months. At Christmas old Mrs. Dalziel had suddenly died; her son had returned home, sent his four boys to school in Germany, and gone back again to India. There was now, for the first time for half a century, not a single Dalziel left in St. Andrews.

But though all ties were broken connecting her with the dear old city, her boys still wrote to her now and then, and she to them, with a persistency for which her conscience smote her sometimes, knowing it was not wholly for their sakes. But they had never been near her, and she had little expectation of seeing any of them ever again, since by this time she had lived long enough to find out how easily people do drift asunder, and lose all clew to one another, unless some strong firm will or unconquerable habit of fidelity exists on one side or the other.

Since the Dalziels she had only lived in the two families before named, and had been lately driven from the last one by a catastrophe, if it may be called so, which had been the bitterest drop in her cup since the time she left St. Andrews.

The rector—a widower, and a feeble, gentle invalid, to whom naturally she had been kind and tender, regarding him with much the same sort of motherly feeling as she had regarded his children—suddenly asked her to become their mother in reality.

It was a great shock and pang: almost a temptation; for they all loved her, and wished to keep her. She would have been such a blessing, such a brightness, in that dreary home. And to a woman no longer young, who had seen her youth pass without any brightness in it, God knows what an allurement it is to feel she has still the power of brightening other lives. If Fortune had yielded—if she had said yes, and married the rector—it would have been hardly wonderful, scarcely blamable. Nor would it have been the first time that a good, conscientious, tender-hearted woman has married a man for pure tenderness.

But she did not do it; not even when they clung around her—those forlorn, half-educated, but affectionate girls—entreating her to "marry papa, and make us all happy." She could not—how could she? She felt very kindly to him. He had her sincere respect, almost affection; but when she looked into her own heart, she found there was not in it one atom of love, never had been, for any man alive except Robert Roy. While he was unmarried, for her to marry would be impossible.

And so she had the wisdom and courage to say to herself, and to them all, "This can not be;" to put aside the cup of attainable happiness, which might never have proved real happiness, because founded on an insincerity.

But the pain this cost was so great, the wrench of parting from her poor girls so cruel, that after it Miss Williams had a sharp illness, the first serious illness of her life. She struggled through it, quietly and alone, in one of those excellent "Governesses' Homes," where every body was very kind to her—some more than kind, affectionate. It was strange, she often thought, what an endless amount of affection followed her wherever she went. She was by no means one of those women who go about the world moaning that nobody loves them. Every body loved her, and she knew it—every body whose love was worth having—except Robert Roy.

Still her mind never changed; not even when, in the weakness of illness, there would come vague dreams of that peaceful rectory, with its quiet rooms and green garden; of the gentle, kindly hearted father, and the two loving girls whom she could have made so happy, and perhaps won happiness herself in the doing of it.

"I am a great fool, some people would say," thought she, with a sad smile; "perhaps rather worse. Perhaps I am acting absolutely wrong in throwing away my chance of doing good. But I can not help it—I can not help it."

So she kept to her resolution, writing the occasional notes she had promised to write to her poor forsaken girls, without saying a word of her illness; and when she grew better, though not strong enough to undertake a new situation, finding her money slipping away—though, with her good salaries and small wants, she was not poor, and had already begun to lay up for a lonely old age —she accepted this temporary home at Miss Maclachlan's, at Brighton. Was it— so strange are the under-currents which guide one's outward life—was it because she had found a curious charm in the old lady's Scotch tongue, unheard for years? that the two little pupils were Indian children, and that the house was at the sea-side?—and she had never seen the sea since she left St. Andrews.

It was like going back to the days of her youth to sit, as now, watching the sunshine glitter on the far-away ocean. The very smell of the sea-weed, the lap-lap of the little waves, brought back old recollections so vividly—old thoughts, some bitter, some sweet, but the sweetness generally overcoming the bitterness.

"I have had all the joy that the world could bestow;
  I have lived—I have loved."

So sings the poet, and truly. Though to this woman love had brought not joy, but sorrow, still she had loved, and it had been the main-stay and stronghold of her life, even though to outsiders it might have appeared little better than a delusion, a dream. Once, and by one only, her whole nature had been drawn out, her ideal of moral right entirely satisfied. And nothing had ever shattered this ideal. She clung to it, as we cling to the memory of our dead children, who are children forever.

With a passionate fidelity she remembered all Robert Roy's goodness, his rare and noble qualities, resolutely shutting her eyes to what she might have judged severely, had it happened to another person—his total, unexplained, and inexplicable desertion of herself. It was utterly irreconcilable with all she had ever known of him; and being powerless to unravel it, she left it, just as we have to leave many a mystery in heaven and earth, with the humble cry, "I can not understand—I love."

She loved him, that was all; and sometimes even yet, across that desert of despair, stretching before and behind her, came a wild hope, almost a conviction, that she should meet him again, somewhere, somehow. This day, even, when, after an hour's delicious idleness, she roused herself to take her little girls down to the beach, and sat on the shingle while they played, the sound and sights of the sea brought old times so vividly back that she could almost have fancied coming behind her the familiar step, the pleasant voice, as when Mr. Roy and his boys used to overtake her on the St. An-

C

drews shore—Robert Roy, a young man, with his life all before him, as was hers. Now she was middle-aged, and he—he must be over forty by this time. How strange!

Stranger still that there had never occurred to her one possibility—that he "was not," that God had taken him. But this her heart absolutely refused to accept. So long as he was in it, the world would never be quite empty to her. Afterward— But, as I said, there are some things which can not be faced, and this was one of them.

All else she had faced long ago. She did not grieve now. As she walked with her children, listening to their endless talk with that patient sympathy which made all children love her, and which she often found was a better help to their education than dozens of lessons, there was on her face that peaceful expression which is the greatest preservative of youth, the greatest antidote to change. And so it was no wonder that a tall lad, passing and repassing on the Esplanade with another youth, looked at her more than once with great curiosity, and at last advanced with hesitating politeness.

"I beg your pardon, ma'am, if I mistake; but you are so like a lady I once knew, and am now looking for. Are you Miss Williams?"

"My name is Williams, certainly; and you"—something in the curly light hair, the mischievous twinkle of the eye, struck her—"you can not be, it is scarcely possible—David Dalziel?"

"But I am, though," cried the lad, shaking her hand as if he would shake it off. "And I call myself very clever to have remembered you, though I was such a little fellow when you left us, and I have only seen your photograph since. But you are not a bit altered—not one bit. And as I knew by your last letter to Archy that you were at Brighton, I thought I'd risk it and speak. Hurra! how very jolly!"

He had grown a handsome lad, the pretty wee Davie, an honest-looking lad too, apparently, and she was glad to see him. From the dignity of his eighteen years and five feet ten of height, he looked down upon the governess, and patronized her quite tenderly—dismissing his friend and walking home with her, telling her on the way all his affairs and that of his family with the volubility of little David Dalziel at St. Andrews.

"No, I've not forgotten St. Andrews one bit, though I was so small. I remember poor old grannie, and her cottage, and the garden, and the Links, and the golfing, and Mr. Roy. By-the-bye, what has become of Mr. Roy?"

The suddenness of the question, nay, the very sound of a name totally silent for so many years, made Fortune's heart throb till its beating was actual pain. Then came a sudden desperate hope, as she answered:

"I can not tell. I have never heard any thing of him. Have you?"

"No—yet, let me see. I think Archy once got a letter from him, a year or so after he went away; but we lost it somehow, and never answered it. We have never heard any thing since."

Miss Williams sat down on one of the benches facing the sea, with a murmured excuse of being "tired." One of her little girls crept beside her, stealing a hand in hers. She held it fast, her own shook so; but gradually she grew quite herself again. "I have been ill," she explained, "and can not walk far. Let us sit down here a little. You were speaking about Mr. Roy, David?"

"Yes. What a good fellow he was! We called him Rob Roy, I remember, but only behind his back. He was strict, but he was a jolly old soul for all that. I believe I should know him again any day, as I did you. But perhaps he is dead; people die pretty fast abroad, and ten years is a long time, isn't it?"

"A long time. And you never got any more letters?"

"No; or if they did come, they were lost, being directed probably to the care of poor old grannie, as ours was. We thought it so odd, after she was dead, you know."

Thus the boy chattered on—his tongue had not shortened with his increasing inch-es—and every idle word sank down deep in his old governess's heart.

Then it was only her whom Robert Roy had forsaken. He had written to his boys, probably would have gone on writing had they answered his letter. He was neither faithless nor forgetful. With an ingenuity that might have brought to any listener a smile or a tear, Miss Williams led the conversation round again till she could easily ask more concerning that one letter; but David remembered little or nothing, except that it was dated from Shanghai, for his brothers had had a discussion whether Shanghai was in China or Japan. Then, boy-like, they had forgotten the whole matter.

"Yes, by this time every body has forgotten him," thought Fortune to herself, when, having bidden David good-by at her door and arranged to, meet him again—he was on a visit at Brighton before matriculating at Oxford next term—she sat down in her own room, with a strangely bewildered feeling. "Mine, all mine," she said, and her heart closed itself over him, her old friend at least, if nothing more, with a tenacity of tenderness as silent as it was strong.

From that day, though she saw, and was determined henceforward to see, as much as she could of young David Dalziel, she never once spoke to him of Mr. Roy.

Still, to have the lad coming about her was a pleasure, a fond link with the past, and to talk to him about his future was a pleasure too. He was the one of all the four—Mr. Roy always said so—who had "brains' enough to become a real student; and instead of following the others to India, he was to go to Oxford and do his best there. His German education had left him few English friends. He was an affectionate, simple-hearted lad, and now that his mischievous days were done, was taking to thorough hard work. He attached himself to his old governess with an enthusiasm that a lad in his teens often conceives for a woman still young enough to be sympathetic, and intelligent enough to guide without ruling the errant fancy of that age. She, too, soon grew very fond of him. It made her strangely happy, this sudden rift of sunshine out of the never-forgotten heaven of her youth, now almost as far off as heaven itself.

I have said she never spoke to David about Mr. Roy, nor did she; but sometimes he spoke, and then she listened. It seemed to cheer her for hours, only to hear that name. She grew stronger, gayer, younger. Every body said how much good the sea was doing her, and so it was; but not exactly in the way people thought. The spell of silence upon her life had been broken, and though she knew all sensible persons would esteem her in this, as in that other matter, a great "fool," still she could not stifle a vague hope that some time or other her blank life might change. Every little wave that swept in from the mysterious ocean, the ocean that lay between them two, seemed to carry a whispering message and lay it at her feet, "Wait and be patient, wait and be patient."

She did wait, and the message came at last.

One day David Dalziel called, on one of his favorite daily rides, and threw a newspaper down at her door, where she was standing.

"An Indian paper my mother has just sent. There's something in it that will interest you, and—"

His horse galloped off with the unfinished sentence; and supposing it was something concerning his family, she put the paper in her pocket to read at leisure while she sat on the beach. She had almost forgotten it, as she watched the waves, full of that pleasant idleness and dreamy peace so new in her life, and which the sound of the sea so often brings to peaceful hearts, who have no dislike to its monotony, no dread of those solemn thoughts of infinitude, time and eternity, God and death and love, which it unconsciously gives, and which I think is the secret why some people say they have "such a horror of the sea-side."

She had none; she loved it, for its sights and sounds were mixed up with all the happiness of her young days. She could have sat all this sunshiny morning on the beach doing absolutely nothing, had she not remembered David's newspaper; which, just to please him, she must look through. She did so, and in the corner, among the brief list of names in the obituary, she saw that of "Roy." Not himself, as she soon found, as soon as she could see to read, in the sudden blindness that came over her. Not himself. Only his child.

"On Christmas-day, at Shanghai, aged three and a half years, Isabella, the only and beloved daughter of Robert and Isabella Roy."

He was alive, then. That was her first thought, almost a joyful one, showing how deep had been her secret dread of the contrary. And he was married. His "only and beloved daughter!" Oh! how beloved she could well understand. Married, and a father; and his child was dead.

Many may think it strange (it would be in most women, but it was not in this woman) that the torrent of tears which burst forth, after her first few minutes of dry-eyed anguish, was less for herself, because he was married and she had lost him, than for him, because he had had a child and lost it—he who was so tender of heart, so fond of children. The thought of his grief brought such a consecration with it, that her grief—the grief most women might be expected to feel on reading suddenly in a newspaper that the man they loved was married to another—did not come. At least not at once. It did not burst upon her, as sorrow does sometimes, like a wild beast out of a jungle, slaying and devouring. She was not slain, not even stunned. After a few minutes it seemed to her as if it had happened long ago—as if she had always known it must happen, and was not astonished.

His "only and beloved daughter!" The words sung themselves in and out of her brain, to the murmur of the sea. How he must have loved the child! She could almost see him with the little one in his arms, or watching over her bed, or standing beside her small coffin. Three years and a half old! Then he must have been married a good while—long and long after she had gone on thinking of him as no righteous woman ever can go on thinking of another woman's husband.

One burning blush, one shiver from head to foot of mingled agony and shame, one cry of piteous despair, which nobody heard but God—and she was not afraid of His hearing—and the struggle was over. She saw Robert Roy, with his child in his arms, with his wife by his side, the same and yet a totally different man.

She, too, when she rose up and tried to walk, tried to feel that it was the same sea, the same shore, the same earth and sky, was a totally different woman. Something was lost, something never to be retrieved on this side the grave, but also something was found.

"He is alive," she said to herself, with the same strange joy; for now she knew where he was, and what had happened to him. The silence of all these years was broken, the dead had come to life again, and the lost, in a sense, was found.

Fortune Williams rose up and walked, in more senses than one; went round to fetch her little girls, as she had promised, from that newly opened delight of children, the Brighton Aquarium; staid a little with them, admiring the fishes; and when she reached home, and found David Dalziel in the drawing-room, met him and thanked him for bringing her the newspaper.

"I suppose it was on account of that obituary notice of Mr. Roy's child," said she, calmly naming the name now. "What a sad thing! But still I am glad to know he is alive and well. So will you be. Shall you write to him?"

"Well, I don't know," answered the lad, carelessly crumpling up the newspaper and throwing it on the fire. Miss Williams made a faint movement to snatch it out, then disguised the gesture in some way, and silently watched it burn. "I don't quite see the use of writing. He's a family man now, and must have forgotten all about his old friends. Don't you think so?"

"Perhaps; only he was not the sort of person easily to forget."

She could defend him now; she could speak of him, and did speak more than once afterward, when David referred to the matter. And then the lad quitted Brighton for Oxford, and she was left in her old loneliness.

A loneliness which I will not speak of. She herself never referred to that time. After it, she roused herself to begin her life anew in a fresh home, to work hard, not only for daily bread but for that humble independence which she was determined to win before the dark hour when the most helpful become helpless, and the most independent are driven to fall a piteous burden into the charitable hands of friends or strangers—a thing to her so terrible that to save herself from the possibility of it, she who had never leaned upon any body, never had any body to lean on, became her one almost morbid desire.

She had no dread of a solitary old age, but an old age beholden to either public or private charity was to her intolerable; and she had now few years left her to work in —a governess's life wears women out very fast. She determined to begin to work again immediately, laying by as much as possible yearly against the days when she could work no more; consulted Miss Maclachlan, who was most kind; and then sought, and was just about going to, another situation, with the highest salary she had yet earned, when an utterly unexpected change altered every thing.

CHAPTER IV.

THE fly was already at the door, and Miss Williams, with her small luggage, would in five minutes have departed, followed by the good wishes of all the household, from Miss Maclachlan's school to her new situation, when the postman passed and left a letter for her.

"I will put it in my pocket and read it in the train," she said, with a slight change of color. For she recognized the handwriting of that good man who had loved her, and whom she could not love.

"Better read it now. No time like the present," observed Miss Maclachlan.

Miss Williams did so. As soon as she was fairly started and alone in the fly, she opened it, with hands slightly trembling, for she was touched by the persistence of the good rector, and his faithfulness to her, a poor governess, when he might have married, as they said in his neighborhood, "any body." He would never marry any body now—he was dying.

"I have come to feel how wrong I was," he wrote, "in ever trying to change our happy relations together. I have suffered for this—so have we all. But it is now too late for regret. My time has come. Do not grieve yourself by imagining it has come the faster through any decision of yours, but by slow, inevitable disease, which the doctors have only lately discovered. Nothing could have saved me. Be satisfied that there is no cause for you to give yourself one moment's pain." (How she sobbed over those shaky lines, more even than over the newspaper lines which she had read that sunshiny morning on the shore!) "Remember only that you made me very happy—me and all mine—for years; that I loved you, as even at my age a man can love; as I shall love you to the end, which can not be very far off now. Would you dislike coming to see me just once again? My girls will be so very glad, and nobody will remark it, for nobody knows any thing. Besides, what matter? I am dying. Come, if you can, within a week or so; they tell me I may last thus long. And I want to consult with you about my children. Therefore I will not say good-by now, only good-night, and God bless you."

But it was good-by, after all. Though she did not wait the week; indeed, she waited for nothing, considered nothing, except her gratitude to this good man—the only man who had loved her—and her affection for the two girls, who would soon be fatherless; though she sent a telegram from Brighton to say she was coming, and arrived within twenty-four hours, still—she came too late.

When she reached the village she heard that his sufferings were all over; and a few yards from his garden wall, in the shade of the church-yard lime-tree, the old sexton was busy re-opening, after fourteen years, the family grave, where he was to be laid beside his wife the day after to-morrow. His two daughters, sitting alone together in the melancholy house, heard Miss Williams enter, and ran to meet her. With a feeling of nearness and tenderness such as she had scarcely ever felt for any human being, she clasped them close, and let them weep their hearts out in her motherly arms.

Thus the current of her whole life was

changed; for when Mr. Moseley's will was opened, it was found that, besides leaving Miss Williams a handsome legacy, carefully explained as being given "in gratitude for her care of his children," he had chosen her as their guardian, until they came of age or married, entreating her to reside with them, and desiring them to pay her all the respect due to "a near and dear relative." The tenderness with which he had arranged every thing, down to the minutest points, for them and herself, even amidst all his bodily sufferings, and in face of the supreme hour—which he had met, his daughters said, with a marvelous calmness, even joy—touched Fortune as perhaps nothing had ever touched her in all her life before. When she stood with her two poor orphans beside their father's grave, and returned with them to the desolate house, vowing within herself to be to them, all but in name, the mother he had wished her to be, this sense of duty—the strange new duty which had suddenly come to fill her empty life—was so strong, that she forgot every thing else—even Robert Roy.

And for months afterward—months of anxious business, involving the leaving of the Rectory, and the taking of a temporary house in the village, until they could decide where finally to settle—Miss Williams had scarcely a moment or a thought to spare for any beyond the vivid present. Past and future faded away together, except so far as concerned her girls.

"Whatsoever thy hand findeth to do, do it with thy might," were words which had helped her through many a dark time. Now, with all her might, she did her motherly duty to the orphan girls; and as she did so, by-and-by she began strangely to enjoy it, and to find also not a little of motherly pride and pleasure in them. She had no time to think of herself at all, or of the great blow which had fallen, the great change which had come, rendering it impossible for her to let herself feel as she had used to feel, dream as she used to dream, for years and years past. That one pathetic line

"I darena think o' Jamie, for that wad be a sin,"

burned itself into her heart, and needed nothing more.

"My children! I must only love my children now," was her continual thought, and she believed she did so.

It was not until spring came, healing the girls' grief as naturally as it covered their father's grave with violets and primroses, and making them cling a little less to home and her, a little more to the returning pleasures of their youth, for they were two pretty girls, well-born, with tolerable fortunes, and likely to be much sought after—not until the spring days left her much alone, did Fortune's mind recur to an idea which had struck her once, and then been set aside—to write to Robert Roy. Why should she not? Just a few friendly lines, telling him how, after long years, she had seen his name in the papers; how sorry she was, and yet glad —glad to think he was alive and well, and married; how she sent all kindly wishes to his wife and himself, and so on. In short, the sort of letter that any body might write or receive, whatever had been the previous link between them.

And she wrote it on an April day, one of those first days of spring which make young hearts throb with a vague delight, a nameless hope; and older ones—but is there any age when hope is quite dead? I think not, even to those who know that the only spring that will ever come to them will dawn in the world everlasting.

When her girls, entering, offered to post her letter, and Miss Williams answered gently that she would rather post it herself, as it required a foreign stamp, how little they guessed all that lay underneath, and how, over the first few lines, her hand had shaken so that she had to copy it three times. But the address, "Robert Roy, Esquire, Shanghai"—all she could put, but she had little doubt it would find him—was written with that firm, clear hand which he had so often admired, saying he wished she could teach his boys to write as well. Would he recognize it? Would he be glad or sorry, or only indifferent? Had the world changed him? or, if she could look at him now, would he be the same Robert Roy—simple, true, sincere, and brave—every inch a man and a gentleman!

For the instant the old misery came back; the sharp, sharp pain; but she smothered it down. His dead child, his living, unknown wife, came between, with their soft ghostly hands. He was still himself; she hoped absolutely unchanged; but he was hers no more. Yet that strange yearning, the same which had impelled Mr. Moseley to write and say, "Come and see me before I die," seemed impelling her to stretch a hand out across the seas—"Have you forgotten me? I have never forgotten you." As she passed through the church-yard on her way to the village, and saw the rector's grave lie smiling in the evening sunshine, Fortune thought what a strange lot hers had been. The man who had loved her, the man whom she had loved, were equally lost to her; equally dead and buried. And yet she lived still—her busy, active, and not unhappy life. It was God's will, all; and it was best.

Another six months went by, and she still remained in the same place, though talking daily of leaving. They began to go into society again, she and her girls, and to receive visitors now and then: among the rest, David Dalziel, who had preserved his affectionate fidelity even when he went back to college, and had begun to discover somehow that the direct road from Oxford to every where was through this secluded village. I am afraid Miss Williams was not as alive as she ought to have been to this fact, and to the other fact that Helen and Janetta were not quite children now; but she let the young people be happy, and was happy with them, after her fashion. Still, hers was less happiness than peace; the deep peace which a storm-tossed vessel finds when kindly fate has towed it into harbor; with torn sails and broken masts, maybe, but still safe, never needing to go to sea any more.

She had come to that point in life when we cease to be "afraid of evil tidings," since nothing is likely to happen to us beyond what has happened. She told herself that she did not look forward to the answer from Shanghai, if indeed any came; nevertheless, she had ascertained what time the return mail would be likely to bring it. And, almost punctual to the day, a letter arrived with the postmark, "Shanghai." Not his letter, nor his handwriting at all. And, besides, it was addressed to "*Mrs. Williams.*"

A shudder of fear, the only fear which could strike her now—that he might be dead—made Fortune stand irresolute a moment, then go up to her own room before she opened it.

"MADAM,—I beg to apologize for having read nearly through your letter before comprehending that it was not meant for me, but probably for another Mr. Robert *Roy*, who left this place not long after I came here, and between whom and myself some confusion arose, till we became intimate, and discovered that we were most likely distant, very distant cousins. He came from St. Andrews, and was head clerk in a firm here, doing a very good business in tea and silk, until they mixed themselves up in the opium trade, which Mr. Roy, with one or two more of our community here, thought so objectionable that at last he threw up his situation and determined to seek his fortunes in Australia. It was a pity, for he was in a good way to get on rapidly; but every body who knew him agreed it was just the sort of thing he was sure to do, and some respected him highly for doing it. He was indeed what we Scotch call ' weel respeckit' wherever he went. But he was a reserved man; made few intimate friends, though those he did make were warmly attached to him. My family were; and though it is now five years since we have heard any thing of or from him, we remember him still."

Five years! The letter dropped from her hands. Lost and found, yet found and lost. What might not have happened to him in five years? But she read on, dry-eyed: women do not weep very much or very easily at her age.

"I will do my utmost, madam, that your

letter shall reach the hands for which I am sure it was intended; but that may take some time, my only clew to Mr. Roy's whereabouts being the chance that he has left his address with our branch house at Melbourne. I can not think he is dead, because such tidings pass rapidly from one to another in our colonial communities, and he was too much beloved for his death to excite no concern.

"I make this long explanation because it strikes me you may be a lady, a friend or relative of Mr. Roy's, concerning whom he employed me to make some inquiries, only you say so very little—absolutely nothing —of yourself in your letter, that I can not be at all certain if you are the same person. She was a governess in a family named Dalziel, living at St. Andrews. He said he had written to that family repeatedly, but got no answer, and then asked me, if any thing resulted from my inquiries, to write to him to the care of our Melbourne house. But no news ever came, and I never wrote to him, for which my wife still blames me exceedingly. She thanks you, dear madam, for the kind things you say about our poor child, though meant for another person. We have seven boys, but little Bell was our youngest, and our hearts' delight. She died after six hours' illness.

"Again begging you to pardon my unconscious offense in reading a stranger's letter, and the length of this one, I remain your very obedient servant,   R. Roy.

"P.S.—I ought to say that this Mr. Robert Roy seemed between thirty-five and forty, tall, dark-haired, walked with a slight stoop. He had, I believe, no near relatives whatever, and I never heard of his having been married."

Unquestionably Miss Williams did well in retiring to her chamber and locking the door before she opened the letter. It is a mistake to suppose that at thirty-five or forty—or what age?—women cease to feel. I once was walking with an old maiden lady, talking of a character in a book. "He reminded me," she said, "of the very best man I ever knew, whom I saw a good deal of when I was a girl." And to the natural question, was he alive, she answered, "No; he died while he was still young." Her voice kept its ordinary tone, but there came a slight flush on the cheek, a sudden quiver over the whole withered face—she was some years past seventy—and I felt I could not say another word.

Nor shall I say a word now of Fortune Williams, when she had read through and wholly taken in the contents of this letter.

Life began for her again—life on a new and yet on the old basis; for it was still waiting, waiting—she seemed to be among those whose lot it is to "stand and wait" all their days. But it was not now in that absolute darkness and silence which it used to be. She knew that in all human probability Robert Roy was alive still somewhere, and hope never could wholly die out of the world so long as he was in it. His career, too, if not prosperous in worldly things, had been one to make any heart that loved him content—content and proud. For if he had failed in his fortunes, was it not from doing what she would most have wished him to do—the right, at all costs? Nor had he quite forgotten her, since even so late as five years back he had been making inquiries about her. Also, he was then unmarried.

But human nature is weak, and human hearts are so hungry sometimes.

"Oh, if he had only loved me, and told me so!" she said, sometimes, as piteously as fifteen years ago. But the tears which followed were not, as then, a storm of passionate despair—only a quiet, sorrowful rain.

For what could she do? Nothing. Now, as ever, her part seemed just to fold her hands and endure. If alive, he might be found some day; but now she could not find him—oh, if she could! Had she been the man and he the woman—nay, had she been still herself, a poor lonely governess, having to earn every crumb of her own bitter bread, yet knowing that he loved her, might not things have been different? Had she belonged to him, they would never have lost one another. She would have sought him, as Evangeline sought Gabriel, half the world over.

And little did her two girls imagine, as they called her down stairs that night, secretly wondering what important business could make "Auntie" keep tea waiting fully five minutes, and set her after tea to read some of the "pretty poetry," especially Longfellow's, which they had a fancy for—little did they think, those two happy creatures, listening to their middle-aged governess, who read so well that sometimes her voice actually faltered over the lines, how there was being transacted under their very eyes a story which in its "constant anguish of patience" was scarcely less pathetic than that of Acadia.

For nearly a year after that letter came the little family of which Miss Williams was the head went on in its innocent quiet way, always planning, yet never making a change, until at last fate drove them to it.

Neither Helen nor Janetta were very healthy girls, and at last a London doctor gave as his absolute fiat that they must cease to live in their warm inland village, and migrate, for some years at any rate, to a bracing sea-side place.

Whereupon David Dalziel, who had somehow established himself as the one masculine adviser of the family, suggested St. Andrews. Bracing enough it was, at any rate: he remembered the winds used almost to cut his nose off. And it was such a nice place too, so pretty, with such excellent society. He was sure the young ladies would find it delightful. Did Miss Williams remember the walk by the shore, and the golfing across the Links?

"Quite as well as you could have done, at the early age of seven," she suggested, smiling. "Why are you so very anxious we should go to live at St. Andrews?"

The young fellow blushed all over his kindly eager face, and then frankly owned he had a motive. His grandmother's cottage, which she had left to him, the youngest and her pet always, was now unlet. He meant, perhaps, to go and live at it him-

self when—when he was of age and could afford it; but in the mean time he was a poor solitary bachelor, and—and—

"And you would like us to keep your nest warm for you till you can claim it? You want us for your tenants, eh, Davie?"

"Just that. You've hit it. Couldn't wish better. In fact, I have already written to my trustees to drive the hardest bargain possible."

Which was an ingenious modification of the truth, as she afterward found; but evidently the lad had set his heart upon the thing. And she?

At first she had shrunk back from the plan with a shiver almost of fear. It was like having to meet face to face something —some one—long dead. To walk among the old familiar places, to see the old familiar sea and shore, nay, to live in the very same house, haunted, as houses are sometimes, every room and every nook, with ghosts—yet with such innocent ghosts— Could she bear it?

There are some people who have an actual terror of the past—who the moment a thing ceases to be pleasurable fly from it, would willingly bury it out of sight forever. But others have no fear of their harmless dead—dead hopes, memories, loves—can sit by a grave-side, or look behind them at a dim spectral shape, without grief, without dread, only with tenderness. This woman could.

After a long wakeful night, spent in very serious thought for every one's good, not excluding her own—since there is a certain point beyond which one has no right to forget one's self, and perpetual martyrs rarely make very pleasant heads of families—she said to her girls next morning that she thought David Dalziel's brilliant idea had a great deal of sense in it; St. Andrews was a very nice place, and the cottage there would exactly suit their finances, while the tenure upon which he proposed they should hold it (from term to term) would also fit in with their undecided future; because, as all knew, whenever Helen or Janetta married, each would just take her fortune and go, leaving Miss Williams with her little legacy, above want certainly, but not exactly a millionaire.

These and other points she set before them in her practical fashion, just as if her heart did not leap—sometimes with pleasure, sometimes with pain—at the very thought of St. Andrews, and as if to see herself sit daily and hourly face to face with her old self, the ghost of her own youth, would be a quite easy thing.

The girls were delighted. They left all to Auntie, as was their habit to do. Burdens naturally fall upon the shoulders fitted for them, and which seem even to have a faculty for drawing them down there. Miss Williams's new duties had developed in her a whole range of new qualities, dormant during her governess life. Nobody knew better than she how to manage a house and guide a family. The girls soon felt that Auntie might have been a mother all her days, she was so thoroughly motherly, and they gave up every thing into her hands.

So the whole matter was settled, David rejoicing exceedingly, and considering it "jolly fun," and quite like a bit out of a play, that his former governess should come back as his tenant, and inhabit the old familiar cottage.

"And I'll take a run over to see you as soon as the long vacation begins, just to teach the young ladies golfing. Mr. Roy taught all us boys, you know; and we'll take that very walk he used to take us, across the Links and along the sands to the Eden. Wasn't it the river Eden, Miss Williams? I am sure I remember it. I think I am very good at remembering."

"Very."

Other people were also "good at remembering." During the first few weeks after they settled down at St. Andrews the girls noticed that Auntie became excessively pale, and was sometimes quite "distrait" and bewildered-looking, which was little wonder, considering all she had to do and to arrange. But she got better in time. The cottage was so sweet, the sea so fresh, the whole place so charming. Slowly Miss Williams's ordinary looks returned—the "good" looks

which her girls so energetically protested she had now, if never before. They never allowed her to confess herself old by caps or shawls, or any of those pretty temporary hinderances to the march of Time. She resisted not; she let them dress her as they pleased, in a reasonable way, for she felt they loved her; and as to her age, why, *she* knew it, and knew that nothing could alter it, so what did it matter? She smiled, and tried to look as nice and as young as she could for her girls' sake.

I suppose there are such things as broken or breaking hearts, even at St. Andrews, but it is certainly not a likely place for them. They have little chance against the fresh, exhilarating air, strong as new wine; the wild sea waves, the soothing sands, giving with health of body wholesomeness of mind. By-and-by the busy world recovered its old face to Fortune Williams—not the world as she once dreamed of it, but the real world, as she had fought through it all these years.

"I was ever a fighter, so one fight more!" as she read sometimes in the "pretty" poetry her girls were always asking for—read steadily, even when she came to the last verse in that passionate "Prospice:"

"Till, sudden, the worst turns the best to the brave,
    The black minute's at end:
And the elements rage, the fiend voices that rave
    Shall dwindle, shall blend,
Shall change, shall become first a peace, then a joy,
    Then a light—then thy breast,
O thou soul of my soul! I shall clasp thee again,
    And with God be the rest!"

To that life to come, during all the burden and heat of the day (no, the afternoon, a time, faded, yet hot and busy still, which is often a very trying bit of woman's life) she now often began yearningly to look. To meet him again, even in old age, or with death between, was her only desire. Yet she did her duty still, and enjoyed all she could, knowing that one by one the years were hurrying onward, and the night coming, "in which no man can work."

Faithful to his promise, about the middle of July David Dalziel appeared, in overflowing spirits, having done very well at college. He was such a boy still, in character and behavior; though—as he carefully informed the family—now twenty-one and a man, expecting to be treated as such. He was their landlord too, and drew up the agreement in his own name, meaning to be a lawyer, and having enough to live on—something better than bread and salt—"till I can earn a fortune, as I certainly mean to do some day."

And he looked at Janetta, who looked down on the parlor carpet—as young people will. Alas! I fear that the eyes of her anxious friend and governess were not half wide enough open to the fact that these young folk were no longer boy and girls, and that things might happen—in fact, were almost certain to happen—which had happened to herself in her youth—making life not quite easy to her, as it seemed to be to these two bright girls.

Yet they were so bright, and their relations with David Dalziel were so frank and free—in fact, the young fellow himself was such a thoroughly good fellow, so very difficult to shut her door against, even if she had thought of so doing. But she did not. She let him come and go, "miserable bachelor" as he proclaimed himself, with all his kith and kin across the seas, and cast not a thought to the future, or to the sad necessity which sometimes occurs to parents and guardians—of shutting the stable door *after* the steed is stolen.

Especially as, not long after David appeared, there happened a certain thing—a very small thing to all but her, and yet to her it was, for the time being, utterly overwhelming. It absorbed all her thoughts into one maddened channel, where they writhed and raved and dashed themselves blindly against inevitable fate. For the first time in her life this patient woman felt as if endurance were *not* the right thing; as if wild shrieks of pain, bitter outcries against Providence, would be somehow easier, better: might reach His throne, so that even now He might listen and hear.

The thing was this. One day, waiting for some one beside the laurel bush at her gate —the old familiar bush, though it had grown and grown till its branches, which used to drag on the gravel, now covered the path entirely—she overheard David explaining to Janetta how he and his brothers and Mr. Roy had made the wooden letter-box, which actually existed still, though in very ruinous condition.

"And no wonder, after fifteen years and more. It is fully that old, isn't it, Miss Williams? You will have to superannuate it shortly, and return to the old original letter-box—my letter-box, which I remember so well. I do believe I could find it still."

Kneeling down, he thrust his hand through the thick barricade of leaves into the very heart of the tree.

"I've found it; I declare I've found it; the identical hole in the trunk where I used to put all my treasures—my 'magpie's nest,' as they called it, where I hid every thing I could find. What a mischievous young scamp I was!"

"Very," said Miss Williams, affectionately, laying a gentle hand on his curls—"pretty" still, though cropped down to the frightful modern fashion. Secretly she was rather proud of him, this tall young fellow, whom she had had on her lap many a time.

"Curious! it all comes back to me—even to the very last thing I hid here, the day before we left, which was a letter."

"A letter!"—Miss Williams slightly started—"what letter?"

"One I found lying under the laurel bush, quite hidden by its leaves. It was all soaked with rain. I dried it in the sun, and then put it in my letter-box, telling nobody, for I meant to deliver it myself at the hall door with a loud ring—an English postman's ring. Our Scotch one used to blow his horn, you remember?"

"Yes," said Miss Williams. She was leaning against the fatal bush, pale to the very lips, but her veil was down—nobody saw. "What sort of a letter was it, David? Who was it to? Did you notice the handwriting?"

"Why, I was such a little fellow," and he looked up in wonder and slight concern, "how could I remember? Some letter that somebody had dropped, perhaps, in taking the rest out of the box. It could not matter—certainly not now. You would not bring my youthful misdeeds up against me, would you?" And he turned up a half-comical, half-pitiful face.

Fortune's first impulse—what was it? She hardly knew. But her second was that safest, easiest thing—now grown into the habit and refuge of her whole life—silence.

"No, it certainly does not matter now."

A deadly sickness came over her. What if this letter were Robert Roy's, asking her that question which he said no man ought ever to ask a woman twice? And she had never seen it—never answered it. So, of course, he went away. Her whole life—nay, two whole lives—had been destroyed, and by a mere accident, the aimless mischief of a child's innocent hand. She could never prove it, but it might have been so. And, alas! alas! God, the merciful God, had allowed it to be so.

Which is the worst, to wake up suddenly and find that our life has been wrecked by our own folly, mistake, or sin, or that it has been done for us either directly by the hand of Providence, or indirectly through some innocent—nay, possibly not innocent, but intentional—hand? In both cases the agony is equally sharp—the sharper because irremediable.

All these thoughts, vivid as lightning, and as rapid, darted through poor Fortune's brain during the few moments that she stood with her hand on David's shoulder, while he drew from his magpie's nest a heterogeneous mass of rubbish—pebbles, snail shells, bits of glass and china, fragments even of broken toys.

"Just look there. What ghosts of my childhood, as people would say! Dead and buried, though." And he laughed merrily —he in the full tide and glory of his youth.

Fortune Williams looked down on his happy face. This lad that really loved her would not have hurt her for the world, and her determination was made. He should never know any thing. Nobody should ever know any thing. The "dead and buried" of fifteen years ago must be dead and buried forever.

"David," she said, "just out of curiosity, put your hand down to the very bottom of that hole, and see if you can fish up the mysterious letter."

Then she waited, just as one would wait at the edge of some long-closed grave to see if the dead could possibly be claimed as our dead, even if but a handful of unhonored bones.

No, it was not possible. Nobody could expect it after such a lapse of time. Something David pulled out—it might be paper it might be rags. It was too dry to be moss or earth, but no one could have recognized it as a letter.

"Give it me," said Miss Williams, holding out her hand.

David put the little heap of "rubbish" therein. She regarded it a moment, and then scattered it on the gravel—"dust to dust," as we say in our funeral service. But she said nothing.

At that moment the young people they were waiting for came to the other side of the gate, clubs in hand. David and the two Miss Moseleys had by this time become perfectly mad for golf, as is the fashion of the place. They proceeded across the Links, Miss Williams accompanying them, as in duty bound. But she said she was "rather tired," and leaving them in charge of another chaperon—if chaperons are ever wanted or needed in those merry Links of St. Andrews—came home alone.

CHAPTER V.

"Shall sharpest pathos blight us, doing no wrong?"

So writes our greatest living poet, in one of the noblest poems he ever penned. And he speaks truth. The real canker of human existence is not misery, but sin.

After the first cruel pang, the bitter wail after her lost life—and we have here but one life to lose!—her lost happiness, for she knew now that though she might be very peaceful, very content, no real happiness ever had come, ever could come to her in this world, except Robert Roy's love—after this, Fortune sat down, folded her hands, and bowed her head to the waves of sorrow that kept sweeping over her, not for one day or two days, but for many days and weeks—the anguish, not of patience, but regret—sharp, stinging, helpless regret. They came rolling in, those remorseless billows, just like the long breakers on the sands of St. Andrews. Hopeless to resist, she could only crouch down and let them pass. "All Thy waves have gone over me."

Of course this is spoken metaphorically. Outwardly, Miss Williams neither sat still nor folded her hands. She was seen everywhere as usual, her own proper self, as the world knew it; but underneath all that was the self that she knew, and God knew. No one else. No one ever could have known, except Robert Roy, had things been different from what they were—from what God had apparently willed them to be.

A sense of inevitable fate came over her. It was now nearly two years since that letter from Mr. Roy of Shanghai, and no more tidings had reached her. She began to think none ever would reach her now. She ceased to hope or to fear, but let herself drift on, accepting the small pale pleasures of every day, and never omitting one of its duties. One only thought remained; which, contrasted with the darkness of all else, often gleamed out as an actual joy.

If the lost letter really was Robert Roy's—and though she had no positive proof, she had the strongest conviction, remembering the thick fog of that Tuesday morning, how easily Archy might have dropped it out of his hand, and how, during those days of soaking rain, it might have lain, unobserved by any one, under the laurel branches, till the child picked it up and hid it as he said—if Robert Roy had written to her, written in any way, he was at least not faithless. And he might have loved her then. Afterward, he might have married, or died; she might never find him again in this world, or if she found him, he might be totally changed: still, whatever happened, he had loved her. The fact remained. No power in earth or heaven could alter it.

And sometimes, even yet, a half-superstitious feeling came over her that all this was not for nothing—the impulse which had impelled her to write to Shanghai, the other impulse, or concatenation of circumstances, which had floated her, after so many changes, back to the old place, the old life. It looked like chance, but was it? Is any thing chance? Does not our own will, soon or late, accomplish for us what we desire? That is, when we try to reconcile it to the will of God.

She had accepted His will all these years, seeing no reason for it; often feeling it very hard and cruel, but still accepting it. And now?

I am writing no sensational story. In it are no grand dramatic points; no *Deus ex machinâ* appears to make all smooth; every event—if it can boast of aught so large as an event—follows the other in perfectly natural succession. For I have always noticed that in life there are rarely any startling "effects," but gradual evolutions. Nothing happens by accident; and, the premises once granted, nothing happens but what was quite sure to happen, following those premises. We novelists do not "make up" our stories; they make themselves. Nor do human beings invent their own lives; they do but use up the materials given to them—some well, some ill; some wisely, some foolishly; but, in the main, the dictum of the Preacher is not far from the truth, "All things come alike to all."

A whole winter had passed by, and the spring twilights were beginning to lengthen, tempting Miss Williams and her girls to linger another half hour before they lit the lamp for the evening. They were doing so, cozily chatting over the fire, after the fashion of a purely feminine household, when there was a sudden announcement that a gentleman, with two little boys, wanted to see Miss Williams. He declined to give his name, and said he would not detain her more than a few minutes.

"Let him come in here," Fortune was just about to say, when she reflected that it might be some law business which concerned her girls, whom she had grown so tenderly anxious to save from any trouble and protect from every care. "No, I will go and speak to him myself."

She rose and walked quietly into the parlor, already shadowed into twilight: a neat, compact little person, dressed in soft gray homespun, with a pale pink bow on her throat, and another in her cap—a pretty little fabric of lace and cambric, which, being now the fashion, her girls had at last condescended to let her wear. She had on a black silk apron, with pockets, into one of which she had hastily thrust her work, and

her thimble was yet on her finger. This was the figure on which the eyes of the gentleman rested as he turned round.

Miss Williams lifted her eyes inquiringly to his face—a bearded face, thin and dark.

"I beg your pardon, I have not the pleasure of knowing you; I—"

She suddenly stopped. Something in the height, the turn of the head, the crisp dark hair, in which were not more than a few threads of gray, while hers had so many now, reminded her of—some one, the bare thought of whom made her feel dizzy and blind.

"No," he said, "I did not expect you would know me; and indeed, until I saw you, I was not sure you were the right Miss Williams. Possibly you may remember my name—Roy, Robert Roy."

Faces alter, manners, gestures; but the one thing which never changes is a voice. Had Fortune heard this one—ay, at her last dying hour, when all worldly sounds were fading away—she would have recognized it at once.

The room being full of shadow, no one could see any thing distinctly; and it was as well.

In another minute she had risen, and held out her hand.

"I am very glad to see you, Mr. Roy. How long have you been in England? Are these your little boys?"

Without answering, he took her hand—a quiet friendly grasp, just as it used to be. And so, without another word, the gulf of fifteen — seventeen years was overleaped, and Robert Roy and Fortune Williams had met once more.

If any body had told her when she rose that morning what would happen before night, and happen so naturally, too, she would have said it was impossible. That, after a very few minutes, she could have sat there, talking to him as to any ordinary acquaintance, seemed incredible, yet it was truly so.

"I was in great doubts whether the Miss Williams who, they told me, lived here was yourself or some other lady; but I thought I would take the chance. Because, were it yourself, I thought, for the sake of old times, you might be willing to advise me concerning my two little boys, whom I have brought to St. Andrews for their education."

"Your sons, are they?"

"No. I am not married."

There was a pause, and then he told the little fellows to go and look out of the window, while he talked with Miss Williams. He spoke to them in a fatherly tone; there was nothing whatever of the young man left in him now. His voice was sweet, his manner grave, his whole appearance unquestionably "middle-aged."

"They are orphans. Their name is Roy, though they are not my relatives, or so distant that it matters nothing. But their father was a very good friend of mine, which matters a great deal. He died suddenly, and his wife soon after, leaving their affairs in great confusion. Hearing this, far up in the Australian bush, where I have been a sheep-farmer for some years, I came round by Shanghai, but too late to do more than take these younger boys and bring them home. The rest of the family are disposed of. These two will be henceforward mine. That is all."

A very little "all," and wholly about other people; scarcely a word about himself. Yet he seemed to think it sufficient, and as if she had no possible interest in hearing more.

Cursorily he mentioned having received her letter, which was "friendly and kind;" that it had followed him to Australia, and then back to Shanghai. But his return home seemed to have been entirely without reference to it—or to her.

So she let all pass, and accepted things as they were. It was enough. When a shipwrecked man sees land—ever so barren a land, ever so desolate a shore—he does not argue within himself, "Is this my haven?" he simply puts into it, and lets himself be drifted ashore.

It took but a few minutes more to explain further what Mr. Roy wanted—a home for his two "poor little fellows."

"They are so young still—and they have lost their mother. They would do very well in their classes here, if some kind woman would take them and look after them. I felt, if the Miss Williams I heard of were really the Miss Williams I used to know, I could trust them to her, more than to any woman I ever knew."

"Thank you." And then she explained that she had already two girls in charge. She could say nothing till she had consulted them. In the mean time—

Just then the tea bell sounded. The world was going on just as usual—this strange, commonplace, busy, regardless world!

"I beg your pardon for intruding on your time so long," said Mr. Roy, rising. "I will leave you to consider the question, and you will let me know as soon as you can. I am staying at the hotel here, and shall remain until I can leave my boys settled. Good-evening."

Again she felt the grasp of the hand: that ghostly touch, so vivid in dreams for all these years, and now a warm living reality. It was too much. She could not bear it.

"If you would care to stay," she said— and though it was too dark to see her, he must have heard the faint tremble in her voice—"our tea is ready. Let me introduce you to my girls, and they can make friends with your little boys."

The matter was soon settled, and the little party ushered into the bright warm parlor, glittering with all the appendages of that pleasant meal—essentially feminine— a "hungry" tea. Robert Roy put his hand over his eyes as if the light dazzled him, and then sat down in the arm-chair which Miss Williams brought forward, turning as he did so to look up at her—right in her face—with his grave, soft, earnest eyes.

"Thank you. How like that was to your old ways! How very little you are changed!"

This was the only reference he made, in the slightest degree, to former times.

And she?

She went out of the room, ostensibly to get a pot of guava jelly for the boys—found it after some search, and then sat down.

Only in her store closet, with her house-keeping things all about her. But it was a quiet place, and the door was shut.

There is, in one of those infinitely pathetic Old Testament stories, a sentence—"And he sought where to weep: and he entered into his chamber and wept there."

She did not weep, this woman, not a young woman now: she only tried during her few minutes of solitude to gather up her thoughts, to realize what had happened to her, and who it was that sat in the next room—under her roof—at her very fireside. Then she clasped her hands with a sudden sob, wild as any of the emotions of her girl-hood.

"Oh, my love, my love, the love of all my life! Thank God!"

The evening passed, not very merrily, but peacefully; the girls, who had heard a good deal of Mr. Roy from David Dalziel, doing their best to be courteous to him, and to amuse his shy little boys. He did not stay long, evidently having a morbid dread of "intruding," and his manner was exceedingly reserved, almost awkward sometimes, of which he seemed painfully conscious, apologizing for being "unaccustomed to civilization and to ladies' society," having during his life in the bush sometimes passed months at a time without ever seeing a woman's face.

"And women are your only civilizers," said he. "That is why I wish my mother-less lads to be taken into this household of yours, Miss Williams, which looks so—so comfortable," and he glanced round the pretty parlor with something very like a sigh. "I hope you will consider the matter, and let me know as soon as you have made up your mind."

"Which I shall do very soon," she answered.

"Yes, I know you will. And your decision once made, you never change."

"Very seldom. I am not one of those who are 'given to change.'"

"Nor I."

He stood a moment, lingering in the pleasant, lightsome warmth, as if loath to quit it, then took his little boys in either hand and went away.

There was a grand consultation that night, for Miss Williams never did any thing with-out speaking to her girls; but still it was merely nominal. They always left the decision to her. And her heart yearned over the two little Roys, orphans, yet children still; while Helen and Janetta were grow-ing up and needing very little from her ex-cept a general motherly supervision. Be-sides, *he* asked it. He had said distinctly that she was the only woman to whom he could thoroughly trust his boys. So—she took them.

After a few days the new state of things grew so familiar that it seemed as if it had lasted for months, the young Roys going to and fro to their classes and their golf-play-ing, just as the young Dalziels had done; and Mr. Roy coming about the house, almost daily, exactly as Robert Roy had used to do of old. Sometimes it was to Fortune Williams the strangest reflex of former times; only—with a difference.

Unquestionably he was very much changed. In outward appearance more even than the time accounted for. No man can knock about the world, in different lands and climates, for seventeen years, without bearing the marks of it. Though still un-der fifty, he had all the air of an "elderly" man, and had grown a little "peculiar" in his ways, his modes of thought and speech—except that he spoke so very little. He ac-counted for this by his long lonely life in Australia, which had produced, he said, an almost unconquerable habit of silence. Al-together, he was far more of an old bachelor than she was of an old maid, and Fortune felt this: felt, too, that in spite of her gray hairs she was in reality quite as young as he—nay, sometimes younger; for her in-nocent, simple, shut-up life had kept her young.

And he, what had his life been, in so far as he gradually betrayed it? Restless, strug-gling; a perpetual battle with the world; having to hold his own, and fight his way inch by inch—he who was naturally a born student, to whom the whirl of a business career was especially obnoxious. What had made him choose it? Once chosen, probably he could not help himself; besides, he was not one to put his shoulder to the wheel and then draw back. Evidently, with the grain or against the grain, he had gone on with it; this sad, strange, wandering life, until he had "made his fortune," for he told her so. But he said no more; whether he meant to stay at home and spend it, or go out again to the antipodes (and he spoke of those far lands without any distaste, even with a lingering kindliness, for indeed he seemed to have no unkindly thought of any place or person in all the world), his friend did not know.

His friend. That was the word. No other. After her first outburst of uncontrollable emotion, to call Robert Roy her "love," even in fancy, or to expect that he would deport himself in any lover-like way, became ridiculous, pathetically ridiculous. She was sure of that. Evidently no idea of the kind entered his mind. She was Miss Williams, and he was Mr. Roy—two middle-aged people, each with their different responsibilities, their altogether separate lives; and, hard as her own had been, it seemed as if his had been the harder of the two—ay, though he was now a rich man, and she still little better than a poor governess.

She did not think very much of worldly things, but still she was aware of this fact —that he was rich and she was poor. She did not suffer herself to dwell upon it, but the consciousness was there, sustained with a certain feeling called "proper pride." The conviction was forced upon her in the very first days of Mr. Roy's return—that to go back to the days of their youth was as impossible as to find primroses in September.

If, indeed, there were any thing to go back to. Sometimes she felt, if she could only have found out that, all the rest would be easy, painless. If she could only have said to him, "Did you write me the letter you promised? Did you *ever* love me?" But that one question was, of course, utterly impossible. He made no reference whatever

to old things, but seemed resolved to take up the present—a very peaceful and happy present it soon grew to be—just as if there were no past at all. So perforce did she.

But, as I think I have said once before, human nature is weak, and there were days when the leaves were budding, and the birds singing in the trees, when the sun was shining and the waves rolling in upon the sands, just as they rolled in that morning over those two lines of foot-marks, which might have walked together through life; and who knows what mutual strength, help, and comfort this might have proved to both?—then it was, for one at least, rather hard.

Especially when, bit by bit, strange ghostly fragments of his old self began to re-appear in Robert Roy: his keen delight in nature, his love of botanical or geological excursions. Often he would go wandering down the familiar shore for hours in search of marine animals for the girls' aquarium, and then would come and sit down at their tea-table, reading or talking, so like the Robert Roy of old that one of the little group, who always crept in the background, felt dizzy and strange, as if all her later years had been a dream, and she were living her youth over again, only with the difference aforesaid: a difference sharp as that between death and life—yet with something of the peace of death in it.

Sometimes, when they met at the innocent little tea parties which St. Andrews began to give—for of course in that small community every body knew every body, and all their affairs to boot, often a good deal better than they did themselves, so that there was great excitement and no end of speculation over Mr. Roy—sometimes meeting, as they were sure to do, and walking home together, with the moonlight shining down the empty streets, and the stars out by myriads over the silent distant sea, while the nearer tide came washing in upon the sands—all was so like, so frightfully like, old times that it was very sore to bear.

But, as I have said, Miss Williams was Miss Williams, and Mr. Roy Mr. Roy, and there were her two girls always besides them; also his two boys, who soon took to "Auntie" as naturally as if they were really hers, or she theirs.

"I think they had better call you so, as the others do," said Mr. Roy one day. "Are these young ladies really related to you?"

"No; but I promised their father on his death-bed to take charge of them. That is all."

"He is dead, then. Was he a great friend of yours?"

She felt the blood flushing all over her face, but she answered, steadily: "Not a very intimate friend, but I respected him exceedingly. He was a good man. His daughters had a heavy loss when he died, and I am glad to be a comfort to them so long as they need me."

"I have no doubt of it."

This was the only question he ever asked her concerning her past life, though, by slow degrees, he told her a good deal of his own. Enough to make her quite certain, even if her keen feminine instinct had not already divined the fact, that whatever there might have been in it of suffering, there was nothing in the smallest degree either to be ashamed of or to hide. What Robert Roy of Shanghai had written about him had continued true. As he said one day to her, "We never stand still. We either grow better or worse. You have not grown worse."

Nor had he. All that was good in him had developed, all his little faults had toned down. The Robert Roy of to-day was slightly different from, but in no wise inferior to, the Robert Roy of her youth. She saw it, and rejoiced in the seeing.

What he saw in her she could not tell. He seemed determined to rest wholly in the present, and take out of it all the peace and pleasantness that he could. In the old days, when the Dalziel boys were naughty, and Mrs. Dalziel tiresome, and work was hard, and holidays were few, and life was altogether the rough road that it often seems to the young, he had once called her "Pleasantness and Peace." He never said so now; but sometimes he looked it.

Many an evening he came and sat by her fireside, in the arm-chair, which seemed by right to have devolved upon him; never staying very long, for he was still nervously sensitive about being "in the way," but making himself and them all very cheerful and happy while he did stay. Only sometimes, when Fortune's eyes stole to his face —not a young man's face now—she fancied she could trace, besides the wrinkles, a sadness, approaching to hardness, that never used to be. But again, when interested in some book or other (he said it was delicious to take to reading again, after the long fast of years), he would look round to her for sympathy, or utter one of his dry drolleries, the old likeness, the old manner and tone, would come back so vividly that she started, hardly knowing whether the feeling it gave her was pleasure or pain.

But beneath both, lying so deep down that neither he nor any one could ever suspect its presence, was something else. Can many waters quench love? Can the deep sea drown it? What years of silence can wither it? What frost of age can freeze it down? God only knows.

Hers was not like a girl's love. Those two girls sitting by her day after day would have smiled at it, and at its object. Between themselves they considered Mr. Roy somewhat of an "old fogy;" were very glad to make use of him now and then, in the great dearth of gentlemen at St. Andrews, and equally glad afterward to turn him over to Auntie, who was always kind to him. Auntie was so kind to every body.

Kind! Of course she was, and above all when he looked worn and tired. He did so sometimes: as if life had ceased to be all pleasure, and the constant mirth of these young folks was just a little too much for him. Then she ingeniously used to save him from it and them for a while. They never knew—there was no need for them to know—how tenfold deeper than all the passion of youth is the tenderness with which a woman cleaves to the man she loves when she sees him growing old.

Thus the days went by till Easter came,

announced by the sudden apparition, one evening, of David Dalziel.

That young man, when, the very first day of his holidays, he walked in upon his friends at St. Andrews, and found sitting at their tea-table a strange gentleman, did not like it at all—scarcely even when he found out that the intruder was his old friend, Mr. Roy.

"And you never told me a word about this," said he, reproachfully, to Miss Williams. "Indeed, you have not written to me for weeks; you have forgotten all about me."

She winced at the accusation, for it was true. Beyond her daily domestic life, which she still carefully fulfilled, she had in truth forgotten every thing. Outside people were ceasing to affect her at all. What *he* liked, what *he* wanted to do, day by day—whether he looked ill or well, happy or unhappy, only he rarely looked either—this was slowly growing to be once more her whole world. With a sting of compunction, and another, half of fear, save that there was nothing to dread, nothing that could affect any body beyond herself—Miss Williams roused herself to give young Dalziel an especially hearty welcome, and to make his little visit as happy as possible.

Small need of that; he was bent on taking all things pleasantly. Coming now near the end of a very creditable college career, being of age and independent, with the cozy little fortune that his old grandmother had left him, the young fellow was disposed to see every thing *couleur de rose,* and this feeling communicated itself to all his friends.

It was a pleasant time. Often in years to come did that little knot of friends, old and young, look back upon it as upon one of those rare bright bits in life when the outside current of things moves smoothly on, while underneath it there may or may not be, but generally there is, a secret or two which turns the most trivial events into sweet and dear remembrances forever.

David's days being few enough, they took pains not to lose one, but planned excursions here, there, and every where—to Dun-

dee, to Perth, to Elie, to Balcarras—all together, children, young folks, and elders: that admirable *melange* which generally makes such expeditions "go off" well. Theirs did, especially the last one, to the old house of Balcarras, where they got admission to the lovely quaint garden, and Janetta sang "Auld Robin Gray" on the spot where it was written.

She had a sweet voice, and there seemed to have come into it a pathos which Fortune had never remarked before. The touching, ever old, ever new story made the young people quite quiet for a few minutes; and then they all wandered away together, Helen promising to look after the two wild young Roys, to see that they did not kill themselves in some unforeseen way, as, aided and abetted by David and Janetta, they went on a scramble up Balcarras Hill.

"Will you go too?" said Fortune to Robert Roy. "I have the provisions to see to; besides, I can not scramble as well as the rest. I am not quite so young as I used to be."

"Nor I," he answered, as, taking her basket, he walked silently on beside her.

It was a curious feeling, and all to come out of a foolish song; but if ever she felt thankful to God from the bottom of her heart that she had said "No," at once and decisively, to the good man who slept at peace beneath the church-yard elms, it was at that moment. But the feeling and the moment passed by immediately. Mr. Roy took up the thread of conversation where he had left it off—it was some bookish or ethical argument, such as he would go on with for hours; so she listened to him in silence. They walked on, the larks singing and the primroses blowing. All the world was saying to itself, "I am young; I am happy;" but she said nothing at all.

People grow used to pain; it dies down at intervals, and becomes quite bearable, especially when no one sees it or guesses at it.

They had a very merry picnic on the hill-top, enjoying those mundane consolations of food and drink which Auntie was expected always to have forth-coming, and which those young people did by no means despise, nor Mr. Roy neither. He made himself so very pleasant with them all, looking thoroughly happy, and baring his head to the spring breeze with the eagerness of a boy.

"Oh, this is delicious! It makes me feel young again. There's nothing like home. One thing I am determined upon: I will never quit bonnie Scotland more."

It was the first clear intimation he had given of his intentious regarding the future, but it thrilled her with measureless content. If only he would not go abroad again, if she might have him within reach for the rest of her days—able to see him, to talk to him, to know where he was and what he was doing, instead of being cut off from him by those terrible dividing seas—it was enough! Nothing could be so bitter as what had been; and whatever was the mystery of their youth, which it was impossible to unravel now—whether he had ever loved her, or loved her and crushed it down and forgotten it, or only felt very kindly and cordially to her, as he did now, the past was—well, only the past!—and the future lay still before her, not unsweet. When we are young, we insist on having every thing or nothing; when we are older, we learn that "every thing" is an impossible and "nothing" a somewhat bitter word. We are able to stoop meekly and pick up the fragments of the children's bread, without feeling ourselves to be altogether "dogs."

Fortune went home that night with a not unhappy, almost a satisfied, heart. She sat back in the carriage, close beside that other heart which she believed to be the truest in all the world, though it had never been hers. There was a tremendous clatter of talking and laughing and fun of all sorts, between David Dalziel and the little Roys on the box, and the Misses Moseley sitting just below them, as they had insisted on doing, no doubt finding the other two members of the party a little "slow."

Nevertheless Mr. Roy and Miss Williams took their part in laughing with their young people, and trying to keep them in order; though after a while both relapsed into silence. One did at least, for it had been a long day and she was tired, being, as she had said, "not so young as she had been." But if any of these lively young people had asked her the question whether she was happy, or at least contented, she would have never hesitated about her reply. Young, gay, and prosperous as they were, I doubt if Fortune Williams would have changed lots with any one of them all.

CHAPTER VI.

As it befell, that day at Balcarras was the last of the bright days, in every sense, for the time being. Wet weather set in, as even the most partial witness must allow does occasionally happen in Scotland, and the domestic barometer seemed to go down accordingly. The girls grumbled at being kept in-doors, and would willingly have gone out golfing under umbrellas, but Auntie was remorseless. They were delicate girls at best, so that her watch over them was never-ceasing, and her patience inexhaustible.

David Dalziel also was in a very troublesome mood, quite unusual for him. He came and went, complained bitterly that the girls were not allowed to go out with him; abused the place, the climate, and did all those sort of bearish things which young gentlemen are sometimes in the habit of doing, when—when that wicked little boy whom they read about at school and college makes himself known to them as a pleasant, or unpleasant, reality.

Miss Williams, who, I am afraid, was far too simple a woman for the new generation, which has become so extraordinarily wise and wide-awake, opened her eyes and wondered why David was so unlike his usual self. Mr. Roy, too, to whom he behaved worse than to any one else, only the elder man quietly ignored it all, and was very patient and gentle with the restless, ill-tempered boy—Mr. Roy even remarked that he thought David would be happier at his work again; idling was a bad thing for young fellows at his age, or any age.

At last it all came out, the bitterness which rankled in the poor lad's breast; with another secret, which, foolish woman that she was, Miss Williams had never in the smallest degree suspected. Very odd that she had not, but so it was. We all find it difficult to realize the moment when our children cease to be children. Still more difficult is it for very serious and earnest natures to recognize that there are other natures who take things in a totally different way, and yet it may be the right and natural way for them. Such is the fact; we must learn it, and the sooner we learn it, the better.

One day, when the rain had a little abated, David appeared, greatly disappointed to find the girls had gone out, down to the West Sands with Mr. Roy.

"Always Mr. Roy! I am sick of his very name," muttered David, and then caught Miss Williams by the dress as she was rising. She had a gentle but rather dignified way with her of repressing bad manners in young people, either by perfect silence, or by putting the door between her and them. "Don't go! One never can get a quiet word with you, you are always so preternaturally busy."

It was true. To be always busy was her only shield against — certain things which the young man was never likely to know, and would not understand if he did know.

"Do sit down, if you ever can sit down, for a minute," said he, imploringly; "I want to speak to you seriously, very seriously."

She sat down, a little uneasy. The young fellow was such a good fellow; and yet he might have got into a scrape of some sort. Debt, perhaps, for he was a trifle extravagant; but then life had been all roses to him. He had never known a want since he was born.

"Speak, then, David; I am listening. Nothing very wrong, I hope?" said she, with a smile.

"Nothing at all wrong, only— When is Mr. Roy going away?"

The question was so unexpected that she felt her color changing a little; not much, she was too old for that.

"Mr. Roy leaving St. Andrews, you mean? How can I tell? He has never told me. Why do you ask?"

"Because until he is gone, I stay," said the young man, doggedly. "I'm not going back to Oxford leaving him master of the field. I have stood him as long as I possibly can, and I'll not stand him any longer."

"David! you forget yourself."

"There—now you are offended; I know you are, when you draw yourself up in that way, my dear little anntie. But just hear me. You are such an innocent woman, you don't know the world as we men do. Can't you see—no, of course you can't—that very soon all St. Andrews will be talking about you?"

"About me?"

"Not about you exactly, but about the family. A single man—a marrying man, as all the world says he is, or ought to be, with his money—can not go in and out, like a tame cat, in a household of women, without having, or being supposed to have—ahem!— intentions. I assure you"—and he swung himself on the arm of her chair, and looked into her face with an angry earnestness quite unmistakable—"I assure you, I never go into the club without being asked, twenty times a day, which of the Miss Moseleys Mr. Roy is going to marry."

"Which of the Miss Moseleys Mr. Roy is going to marry?"

She repeated the words, as if to gain time and to be certain she heard them rightly. No fear of her blushing now; every pulse in her heart stood dead still; and then she nerved herself to meet the necessity of the occasion.

"David, you surely do not consider what you are saying. This is a most extraordinary idea."

"It is a most extraordinary idea; in fact, I call it ridiculous, monstrous: an old, battered fellow like him, who has knocked about the world, Heaven knows where, all these years, to come home, and, because he has got a lot of money, think to go and marry one of these nice, pretty girls. They wouldn't have him, I believe that; but nobody else believes it; and every body seems to think it the most natural thing possible. What do you say?"

"I?"

"Surely you don't think it right, or even possible? But, Auntie, it might turn out a rather awkward affair, and you ought to take my advice, and stop it in time."

"How?"

"Why, by stopping him out of the house. You and he are great friends: if he had any notion of marrying, I suppose he would mention it to you—he ought. It would be a cowardly trick to come and steal one of your chickens from under your wing. Wouldn't it? Do say something, instead of merely echoing what I say. It really is a serious matter, though you don't think so."

"Yes, I do think so," said Miss Williams, at last; "and I would stop it if I thought I had any right. But Mr. Roy is quite able to manage his own affairs; and he is not so very old—not more than five-and-twenty years older than—Helen."

"Bother Helen! I beg her pardon, she is a dear good girl. But do you think any man would look at Helen when there was Janetta?"

It was out now, out with a burning blush over all the lad's honest face, and the sudden crick-crack of a pretty Indian paper-cutter he unfortunately was twiddling in his fingers. Miss Williams must have been blind indeed not to have guessed the state of the case.

"What! Janetta? Oh, David!" was all she said.

He nodded. "Yes, that's it, just it. I thought you must have found it out long ago : though I kept myself to myself pretty close, still you might have guessed."

"I never did. I had not the remotest idea. Oh, how remiss I have been! It is all my fault."

"Excuse me, I can not see that it is any body's fault, or any body's misfortune, either," said the young fellow, with a not unbecoming pride. "I hope I should not be a bad husband to any girl, when it comes to that. But it has not come; I have never said a single word to her. I wanted to be quite clear of Oxford, and in a way to win my own position first. And really we are so very jolly together as it is. What are you smiling for ?"

She could not help it. There was something so funny in the whole affair. They seemed such babies, playing at love ; and their love-making, if such it was, had been carried on in such an exceedingly open and lively way, not a bit of tragedy about it, rather genteel comedy, bordering on farce. It was such a contrast to — certain other love stories that she had known, quite buried out of sight now.

Gentle "Auntie"—the grave maiden lady, the old hen with all these young ducklings who would take to the water so soon—held out her hand to the impetuous David.

"I don't know what to say to you, my boy: you really are little more than a boy, and to be taking upon yourself the responsibilities of life so soon! Still, I am glad you have said nothing to her about it yet. She is a mere child, only eighteen."

"Quite old enough to marry, and to marry Mr. Roy even, the St. Andrews folks think. But I won't stand it. I won't tamely sit by and see her sacrificed. He might persuade her ; he has a very winning way with him sometimes. Auntie, I have not spoken, but I won't promise not to speak. It is all very well for you ; you are old, and your blood runs cold, as you said to us one day—no, I don't mean that ; you are a real brick still, and you'll never be old to us, but you are not in love, and you can't understand what it is to a young fellow like me to see an old fellow like Roy coming in

and just walking over the course. But he sha'n't do it! Long ago, when I was quite a lad, I made up my mind to get her; and get her I will, spite of Mr. Roy or any body."

Fortune was touched. That strong will which she too had had, able, like faith, to "remove mountains," sympathized involuntarily with the lad. It was just what she would have said and done, had she been a man and loved a woman. She gave David's hand a warm clasp, which he returned.

"Forgive me," said he, affectionately. "I did not mean to bother you ; but as things stand, the matter is better out than in. I hate underhandedness. I may have made an awful fool of myself, but at least I have not made a fool of her. I have been as careful as possible not to compromise her in any way ; for I know how people do talk, and a man has no right to let the girl he loves be talked about. The more he loves her, the more he ought to take care of her. Don't you think so ?"

"Yes."

"I'd cut myself up into little pieces for Janetta's sake," he went on, "and I'd do a deal for Helen too, the sisters are so fond of one another She shall always have a home with us, when we are married."

"Then," said Miss Williams, hardly able again to resist a smile, "you are quite certain you will be married ? You have no doubt about her caring for you ?"

David pulled his whiskers, not very voluminous yet, looked conscious, and yet humble.

"Well, I don't exactly say that. I know I'm not half good enough for her. Still, I thought, when I had taken my degree and fairly settled myself at the bar, I'd try. I have a tolerably good income of my own too, though of course I am not as well off as that confounded old Roy. There he is at this minute meandering up and down the West Sands with those two girls, setting every body's tongue going! I can't stand it. I declare to you I won't stand it another day."

"Stop a moment," and she caught hold of

David as he started up. "What are you going to do?"

"I don't know and I don't care, only I won't have my girl talked about—my pretty, merry, innocent girl. He ought to know better, a shrewd old fellow like him. It is silly, selfish, mean."

This was more than Miss Williams could bear. She stood up, pale to the lips, but speaking strongly, almost fiercely:

"*You* ought to know better, David Dalziel. You ought to know that Mr. Roy has not an atom of selfishness or meanness in him—that he would be the last man in the world to compromise any girl. If he chooses to marry Janetta, or any one else, he has a perfect right to do it, and I for one will not try to hinder him."

"Then you'll not stand by me any more?"

"Not if you are blind and unfair. You may die of love, though I don't think you will; people don't do it nowadays" (there was a slightly bitter jar in the voice); "but love ought to make you all the more honorable, clear-sighted, and just. And as to Mr. Roy—"

She might have talked to the winds, for David was not listening. He had heard the click of the garden gate, and turned round with blazing eyes.

"There he is again! I can't stand it, Miss Williams. I give you fair warning I can't stand it. He has walked home with them, and is waiting about at the laurel bush, mooning after them. Oh, hang him!"

Before she had time to speak, the young man was gone. But she had no fear of any very tragic consequences when she saw the whole party standing together—David talking to Janetta, Mr. Roy to Helen, who looked so fresh, so young, so pretty, almost as pretty as Janetta. Nor did Mr. Roy, pleased and animated, look so very old.

That strange clear-sightedness, that absolute justice, of which Fortune had just spoken, were qualities she herself possessed to a remarkable, almost a painful, degree. She could not deceive herself, even if she tried. The more cruel the sight, the clearer she saw it; even as now she perceived a cer-

tain naturalness in the fact that a middle-aged man so often chooses a young girl in preference to those of his own generation, for she brings him that which he has not; she reminds him of what he used to have; she is to him like the freshness of spring, the warmth of summer, in his cheerless autumn days. Sometimes these marriages are not unhappy—far from it; and Robert Roy might ere long make such a marriage. Despite poor David's jealous contempt, he was neither old nor ugly, and then he was rich.

The thing, either as regarded Helen, or some other girl of Helen's standing, appeared more than possible—probable; and if so, what then?

Fortune looked out once, and saw that the little group at the laurel bush were still talking; then she slipped up stairs into her own room and bolted the door.

The first thing she did was to go straight up and look at her own face in the glass—her poor old face, which had never been beautiful, which she had never wished beautiful, except that it might be pleasant in one man's eyes. Sweet it was still, but the sweetness lay in its expression, pure and placid, and innocent as a young girl's. But she saw not that; she saw only its lost youth, its faded bloom. She covered it over with both her hands, as if she would fain bury it out of sight; knelt down by her bedside, and prayed.

"Mr. Roy is waiting below, ma'am—has been waiting some time; but he says if you are busy he will not disturb you; he will come to-morrow instead."

"Tell him I shall be very glad to see him to-morrow."

She spoke through the locked door, too feeble to rise and open it; and then lying down on her bed and turning her face to the wall, from sheer exhaustion fell fast asleep.

People dream strangely sometimes. The dream she dreamt was so inexpressibly soothing and peaceful, so entirely out of keeping with the reality of things, that it almost seemed to have been what in ancient times would be called a vision.

First, she thought that she and Robert

Roy were little children—mere girl and boy together, as they might have been from the few years' difference in their ages—running hand in hand about the sands of St. Andrews, and so fond of one another—so very fond! with that innocent love a big boy often has for a little girl, and a little girl returns with the tenderest fidelity. So she did; and she was so happy—they were both so happy. In the second part of the dream she was happy still, but somehow she knew she was dead —had been dead and in paradise for a long time, and was waiting for him to come there. He was coming now; she felt him coming, and held out her hands, but he took and clasped her in his arms; and she heard a voice saying those mysterious words: "In heaven they neither marry nor are given in marriage, but are as the angels of God."

It was very strange, all was very strange, but it comforted her. She rose up, and in the twilight of the soft spring evening she washed her face and combed her hair, and went down, like King David after his child was dead, to "eat bread."

Her young people were not there. They had gone out again, she heard, with Mr. Dalziel, not Mr. Roy, who had sat reading in the parlor alone for upward of an hour. They were supposed to be golfing, but they staid out till long after it was possible to see balls or holes; and Miss Williams was beginning to be a little uneasy, when they all three walked in, David and Janetta with a rather sheepish air, and Helen beaming all over with mysterious delight.

How the young man had managed it—to propose to two sisters at once, at any rate to make love to one sister while the other was by—remained among the wonderful feats which David Dalziel, who had not too small an opinion of himself, was always ready for, and generally succeeded in; and if he did wear his heart somewhat "on his sleeve," why, it was a very honest heart, and they must have been ill-natured "daws" indeed who took pleasure in "pecking at it."

"Wish me joy, Auntie!" he cried, coming forward, beaming all over, the instant the girls had disappeared to take their hats off.

"I've been and gone and done it, and it's all right. I didn't intend it just yet, but he drove me to it, for which I'm rather obliged to him. He can't get her now. Janetta's mine!"

There was a boyish triumph in his air; in fact, his whole conduct was exceedingly juvenile, but so simple, frank, and sincere as to be quite irresistible.

I fear Miss Williams was a very weak-minded woman, or would be so considered by a great part of the world—the exceedingly wise and prudent and worldly-minded "world." Here were two young people, one twenty-two, the other eighteen, with — it could hardly be said "not a half-penny," but still a very small quantity of half-pennies, between them—and they had not only fallen in love, but engaged themselves to be married! She ought to have been horrified, to have severely reproached them for their imprudence, used all her influence and, if needs be, her authority, to stop the whole thing; advising David not to bind himself to any girl till he was much older, and his prospects secured; and reasoning with Janetta on the extreme folly of a long engagement, and how very much better it would be for her to pause, and make some "good" marriage with a man of wealth and position, who could keep her comfortably.

All this, no doubt, was what a prudent and far-seeing mother or friend ought to have said and done. Miss Williams did no such thing, and said not a single word. She only kissed her "children" — Helen too, whose innocent delight was the prettiest thing to behold—then sat down and made tea for them all, as if nothing had happened.

But such events do not happen without making a slight stir in a family, especially such a quiet family as that at the cottage. Besides, the lovers were too childishly happy to be at all reticent over their felicity. Before David was turned away that night to the hotel which he and Mr. Roy both inhabited, every body in the house knew quite well that Mr. Dalziel and Miss Janetta were going to be married.

And every body had of course suspected it long ago, and was not in the least surprised, so that the mistress of the household herself was half ashamed to confess how very much surprised *she* had been. However, as every body seemed delighted, for most people have a "sneaking kindness" toward young lovers, she kept her own counsel; smiled blandly over her old cook's half-pathetic congratulations to the young couple, who were "like the young bears, with all their troubles before them," and laughed at the sympathetic forebodings of the girls' faithful maid, a rather elderly person, who was supposed to have been once "disappointed," and who "hoped Mr. Dalziel was not too young to know his own mind." Still, in spite of all, the family were very much delighted, and not a little proud.

David walked in, master of the position now, directly after breakfast, and took the sisters out for a walk, both of them, declaring he was as much encumbered as if he were going to marry two young ladies at once, but bearing his lot with great equanimity. His love-making indeed was so extraordinarily open and undisguised that it did not much matter who was by. And Helen was of that sweet negative nature that seemed made for the express purpose of playing "gooseberry."

Directly they had departed, Mr. Roy came in.

He might have been a far less acute observer than he was not to detect at once that "something had happened" in the little family. Miss Williams kept him waiting several minutes, and when she did come in her manner was nervous and agitated. They spoke about the weather and one or two trivial things, but more than once Fortune felt him looking at her with that keen, kindly observation which had been sometimes, during all these weeks now running into months, of almost daily meeting, and of the closest intimacy — a very difficult thing to bear.

He was exceedingly kind to her always; there was no question of that. Without making any show of it, he seemed always to know where she was and what she was doing. Nothing ever lessened his silent care of her. If ever she wanted help, there he was to give it. And in all their excursions she had a quiet conviction that whoever forgot her or her comfort, he never would. But then it was his way. Some men have eyes and ears for only one woman, and that merely while they happen to be in love with her; whereas Robert Roy was courteous and considerate to every woman, even as he was kind to every weak or helpless creature that crossed his path.

Evidently he perceived that all was not right; and, though he said nothing, there was a tenderness in his manner which went to her heart.

"You are not looking well to-day; should you not go out?" he said. "I met all your young people walking off to the sands: they seemed extraordinarily happy."

Fortune was much perplexed. She did not like not to tell him the news—him, who had so completely established himself as a friend of the family. And yet to tell him was not exactly her place; besides, he might not care to hear. Old maid as she was, or thought herself, Miss Williams knew enough of men not to fall into the feminine error of fancying they feel as we do—that their world is our world, and their interests our interests. To most men, a leader in the *Times*, an article in the *Quarterly*, or a fall in the money market is of far more importance than any love affair in the world, unless it happens to be their own.

Why should I tell him? she thought, convinced that he noticed the anxiety in her eyes, the weariness at her heart. She had passed an almost sleepless night, pondering over the affairs of these young people, who never thought of any thing beyond their own new-born happiness. And she had perplexed herself with wondering whether in consenting to this engagement she was really doing her duty by her girls, who had no one but her, and whom she was so tender of, for their dead father's sake. But what good was it to say any thing? She must bear her own burden. And yet—

Robert Roy looked at her with his kind, half-amused smile.

"You had better tell me all about it; for, indeed, I know already."

"What! did you guess?"

"Perhaps. But Dalziel came to my room last night and poured out every thing. He is a candid youth. Well, and am I to congratulate?"

Greatly relieved, Fortune looked up.

"That's right," he said; "I like to see you smile. A minute or two ago you seemed as if you had the cares of all the world on your shoulders. Now, that is not exactly the truth. Always meet the truth face to face, and don't be frightened at it."

Ah, no! If she had had that strong heart to lean on, that tender hand to help her through the world, she never would have been "frightened" at any thing.

"I know I am very foolish," she said; "but there are many things which these children of mine don't see, and I can't help seeing."

"Certainly; they are young, and we are —well, never mind. Sit down here, and let you and me talk the matter quietly over. On the whole, are you glad or sorry?"

"Both, I think. David is able to take care of himself; but poor little Janetta— my Janetta—what if he should bring her to poverty? He is a little reckless about money, and has only a very small certain income. Worse; suppose being so young, he should by-and-by get tired of her, and neglect her, and break her heart?"

"Or twenty other things which may happen, or may not, and of which they must take the chance, like their neighbors. You do not believe very much in men, I see, and perhaps you are right. We are a bad lot— a bad lot. But David Dalziel is as good as most of us, that I can assure you."

She could hardly tell whether he was in jest or earnest; but this was certain, he meant to cheer and comfort her, and she took the comfort, and was thankful.

"Now to the point," continued Mr. Roy. "You feel that, in a worldly point of view, these two have done a very foolish thing, and you have aided and abetted them in doing it?"

"Not so," she cried, laughing; "I had no idea of such a thing till David told me yesterday morning of his intentions."

"Yes, and he explained to me why he told you, and why he dared not wait any longer. He blurts out every thing, the foolish boy! But he has made friends with me now. They do seem such children, do they not, compared with old folks like you and me?"

What was it in the tone or the words which made her feel not in the least vexed, nor once attempt to rebut the charge of being "old?"

"I'll tell you what it is," said Robert Roy, with one of his sage smiles, "you must not go and vex yourself needlessly about trifles. We should not judge other people by ourselves. Every body is so different. Dalziel may make his way all the better for having that pretty creature for a wife, not but what some other pretty creature might soon have done just as well. Very few men have tenacity of nature enough, if they can not get the one woman they love, to do without any other to the end of their days. But don't be distressing yourself about your girl. David will make her a very good husband. They will be happy enough, even though not very rich."

"Does that matter much?"

"I used to think so. I had so sore a lesson of poverty in my youth, that it gave me an almost morbid terror of it, not for myself, but for any woman I cared for. Once I would not have done as Dalziel has for the world. Now I have changed my mind. At any rate, David will not have one misfortune to contend with. He has a thoroughly good opinion of himself, poor fellow! He will not suffer from that horrible self-distrust which makes some men let themselves drift on and on with the tide, instead of taking the rudder into their own hands and steering straight on — direct for the haven where they would be. Oh, that I had done it!"

He spoke passionately, and then sat silent. At last, muttering something about "begging her pardon," and "taking a liberty," he changed the conversation into another channel, by asking whether this marriage, when it happened—which, of course, could not be just immediately—would make any difference to her circumstances.

Some difference, she explained, because the girls would receive their little fortunes whenever they came of age or married, and the sisters would not like to be parted; besides, Helen's money would help the establishment. · Probably, whenever David married, he would take them both away; indeed, he had said as much.

"And then shall you stay on here?"

"I may, for I have a small income of my own; besides, there are your two little boys, and I might find two or three more. But I do not trouble myself much about the future. One thing is certain, I need never work as hard as I have done all my life."

"Have you worked so very hard, then, my poor—"

He left the sentence unfinished; his hand, half extended, was drawn back, for the three young people were seen coming down the garden, followed by the two boys, returning from their classes. It was nearly dinner-time, and people must dine, even though in love; and boys must be kept to their school work, and all the daily duties of life must be done. Well, perhaps, for many of us, that such should be! I think it was as well for poor Fortune Williams.

The girls had come in wet through, with one of those sudden "haars" which are not uncommon at St. Andrews in spring, and it seemed likely to last all day. Mr. Roy looked out of the window at it with a slightly dolorous air.

"I suppose I am rather *de trop* here, but really I wish you would not turn me out. In weather like this our hotel coffee-room is just a trifle dull, isn't it, Dalziel? And, Miss Williams, your parlor looks so comfortable. Will you let me stay?"

He made the request with a simplicity quite pathetic. One of the most lovable things about this man—is it not in all men?

—was, that with all his shrewdness and cleverness, and his having been knocked up and down the world for so many years, he still kept a directness and simpleness of character almost child-like.

To refuse would have been unkind, impossible; so Miss Williams told him he should certainly stay if he could make himself comfortable. And to that end she soon succeeded in turning off her two turtle-doves into a room by themselves, for the use of which they had already bargained, in order to "read together, and improve their minds." Meanwhile she and Helen tried to help the two little boys to spend a dull holiday indoors—if they were ever dull beside Uncle Robert, who had not lost his old influence with boys, and to those boys was already a father in all but the name.

Often had Fortune watched them, sitting upon his chair, hanging about him as he walked, coming to him for sympathy in every thing. Yes, every body loved him, for there was such an amount of love in him toward every mortal creature, except—

She looked at him and his boys, then turned away. What was to be had been, and always would be. That which we fight against in our youth as being human will, human error, in our age we take humbly, knowing it to be the will of God.

By-and-by in the little household the gas was lighted, the curtains drawn, and the two lovers fetched in for tea, to behave themselves as much as they could like ordinary mortals, in general society, for the rest of the evening. A very pleasant evening it was, spite of this new element; which was got rid of as much as possible by means of the window recess, where Janetta and David encamped composedly, a little aloof from the rest.

"I hope they don't mind me," said Mr. Roy, casting an amused glance in their direction, and then adroitly manœuvring with the back of his chair so as to interfere as little as possible with the young couple's felicity.

"Oh no, they don't mind you at all," answered Helen, always affectionate, if not always wise. "Besides, I dare say you yourself were young once, Mr. Roy."

Evidently Helen had no idea of the plans for her future which were being talked about in St. Andrews. Had he? No one could even speculate with such an exceedingly reserved person. He retired behind his newspaper, and said not a single word.

Nevertheless, there was no cloud in the atmosphere. Every body was used to Mr. Roy's silence in company. And he never troubled any body, not even the children, with either a gloomy look or a harsh word. He was so comfortable to live with, so unfailingly sweet and kind.

Altogether there was a strange atmosphere of peace in the cottage that evening, though nobody seemed to do any thing or say very much. Now and then Mr. Roy read aloud bits out of his endless newspapers—he had a truly masculine mania for newspapers, and used to draw one after another out of his pockets, as endless as a conjurer's pocket-handkerchiefs. And he liked to share their contents with any body that would listen; though I am afraid nobody did listen much to-night except Miss Williams, who sat beside him at her sewing, in order to get the benefit of the same lamp. And between his readings he often turned and looked at her, her bent head, her smooth soft hair, her busy hands.

Especially after one sentence, out of the "Varieties" of some Fife newspaper. He had begun to read it, then stopped suddenly, but finished it. It consisted only of a few words: "'Young love is passionate, old love is faithful; but the very tenderest thing in all this world is a love revived.' That is true."

He said only those three words, in a very low, quiet voice, but Fortune heard. His look she did not see, but she felt it—even as a person long kept in darkness might feel a sunbeam strike along the wall, making it seem possible that there might be somewhere in the earth such a thing as day.

About nine P.M. the lovers in the window recess discovered that the haar was all gone, and that it was a most beautiful moonlight night; full moon, the very night they had planned to go in a body to the top of St. Regulus tower.

"I suppose they must," said Mr. Roy to Miss Williams; adding, "Let the young folks make the most of their youth; it never will come again."

"No."

"And you and I must go too. It will be more *comme il faut*, as people say."

So, with a half-regretful look at the cozy fire, Mr. Roy marshaled the lively party, Janetta and David, Helen and the two boys; engaging to get them the key of that silent garden of graves over which St. Regulus tower keeps stately watch. How beautiful it looked, with the clear sky shining through its open arch, and the brilliant moonlight, bright as day almost, but softer, flooding every alley of that peaceful spot! It quieted even the noisy party who were bent on climbing the tower, to catch a view, such as is rarely equaled, of the picturesque old city and its beautiful bay.

"A 'comfortable place to sleep in,' as some one once said to me in a Melbourne churchyard. But 'east or west, home is best.'...... I think, Bob, I shall leave it in my will that you are to bury me at St. Andrews."

"Nonsense, Uncle Robert! You are not to talk of dying. And you are to come with us up to the top of the tower. Miss Williams, will you come too?"

"No, I think she had better not," said Uncle Robert, decisively. "She will stay here, and I will keep her company."

So the young people all vanished up the tower, and the two elders walked silently side by side by the quiet graves—by the hearts which had ceased beating, the hands which, however close they lay, would never clasp one another any more.

"Yes, St. Andrews is a pleasant place," said Robert Roy at last. "I spoke in jest, but I meant in earnest; I have no wish to leave it again. And you," he added, seeing that she answered nothing—"what plans have you? Shall you stay on at the cottage till these young people are married?"

"Most likely. We are all fond of the little house."

"No wonder. They say a wandering life after a certain number of years unsettles a man forever; he rests nowhere, but goes on wandering to the end. But I feel just the contrary. I think I shall stay permanently at St. Andrews. You will let me come about your cottage, 'like a tame cat,' as that foolish fellow owned he had called me—will you not?"

"Certainly."

But at the same time she felt there was a strain beyond which she could not bear. To be so near, yet so far; so much to him, and yet so little. She was conscious of a wild desire to run away somewhere—run away and escape it all; of a longing to be dead and buried, deep in the sea, up away among the stars.

"Will those young people be very long, do you think?"

At the sound of her voice he turned to look at her, and saw that she was deadly pale, and shivering from head to foot.

"This will never do. You must 'come under my plaidie,' as the children say, and I will take you home at once. Boys!" he called out to the figures now appearing like jackdaws at the top of the tower, "we are going straight home. Follow as soon as you like. Yes, it must be so," he answered to the slight resistance she made. "They must all take care of themselves. I mean to take care of you."

Which he did, wrapping her well in the half of his plaid, drawing her hand under his arm and holding it there—holding it close and warm at his heart all the way along the Scores and across the Links, scarcely speaking a single word until they reached the garden gate. Even there he held it still.

"I see your girls coming, so I shall leave you. You are warm now, are you not?"

"Quite warm."

"Good-night, then. Stay. Tell me"—he spoke rapidly, and with much agitation—"tell me just one thing, and I will never trouble you again. Why did you not answer a letter I wrote to you seventeen years ago?"

"I never got any letter. I never had one word from you after the Sunday you bade me good-by, promising to write."

"And I did write," cried he, passionately. "I posted it with my own hands. You should have got it on the Tuesday morning."

She leaned against the laurel bush, that fatal laurel bush, and in a few breathless words told him what David had said about the hidden letter.

"It must have been my letter. Why did you not tell me this before?"

"How could I? I never knew you had written. You never said a word. In all these years you have never said a single word."

Bitterly, bitterly he turned away. The groan that escaped him—a man's groan over his lost life—lost, not wholly through fate alone—was such as she, the woman whose portion had been sorrow, passive sorrow only, never forgot in all her days.

"Don't mind it," she whispered—"don't mind it. It is so long past now."

He made no immediate answer, then said, "Have you no idea what was in the letter?"

"No."

"It was to ask you a question, which I had determined not to ask just then, but I changed my mind. The answer, I told you, I should wait for in Edinburgh seven days; after that, I should conclude you meant No, and sail. No answer came, and I sailed."

He was silent. So was she. A sense of cruel fatality came over her. Alas! those lost years, that might have been such happy years! At length she said, faintly, "Forget it. It was not your fault."

"It was my fault. If not mine, you were still yourself—I ought never to have let you go. I ought to have asked again; to have sought through the whole world till I found you again. And now that I have found you—"

"Hush! the girls are here."

They came along laughing, that merry group—with whom life was at its spring —who had lost nothing, knew not what it was to lose!

"Good-night," said Mr. Roy, hastily. "But—to-morrow morning?"

"Yes."

"There never is night to which comes no morn," says the proverb. Which is not always true, at least as to this world; but it is true sometimes.

That April morning Fortune Williams rose with a sense of strange solemnity—neither sorrow nor joy. Both had gone by; but they had left behind them a deep peace.

After her young people had walked themselves off, which they did immediately after breakfast, she attended to all her household duties, neither few nor small, and then sat down with her needle-work beside the open window. It was a lovely day; the birds were singing, the leaves budding, a few early flowers making all the air to smell like spring. And she—with her it was autumn now. She knew it, but still she did not grieve. . .

Presently, walking down the garden walk, almost with the same firm step of years ago —how well she remembered it!—Robert Roy came; but it was still a few minutes before she could go into the little parlor to meet him. At last she did, entering softly, her hand extended as usual. He took it, also as usual, and then looked down into her face, as he had done that Sunday. "Do you remember this? I have kept it for seventeen years."

It was her mother's ring. She looked up with a dumb inquiry.

"My love, did you think I did not love you?—you always, and only you?"

So saying, he opened his arms; she felt them close round her, just as in her dream. Only they were warm, living arms; and it was this world, not the next. All those seventeen bitter years seemed swept away, annihilated in a moment; she laid her head on his shoulder and wept out her happy heart there.

*   *   *   *   *   *

The little world of St. Andrews was very much astonished when it learned that Mr. Roy was going to marry, not one of the pretty Miss Moseleys, but their friend and former governess, a lady, not by any means young, and remarkable for nothing except great sweetness and good sense, which made everybody respect and like her; though nobody was much excited concerning her. Now people had been excited about Mr. Roy, and some were rather sorry for him; thought perhaps he had been taken in, till some story got wind of its having been an "old attachment," which interested them of course; still, the good folks were half angry with him. To go and marry an old maid when he might have had his choice of half a dozen young ones! when, with his fortune and character, he might, as people say—as they had said of that other good man, Mr. Moseley — "have married any body!"

They forgot that Mr. Roy happened to be one of those men who have no particular desire to marry "any body;" to whom *the* woman, whether found early or late—alas! in this case found early and won late—is the one woman in the world forever. Poor Fortune — rich Fortune! she need not be afraid of her fading cheek, her silvering hair; he would never see either. The things he loved her for were quite apart from any thing that youth could either give or take away. As he said once, when she lamented hers, "Never mind, let it go. You will always be yourself—and mine."

This was enough. He loved her. He had always loved her: she had no fear but that he would love her faithfully to the end.

Theirs was a very quiet wedding, and a speedy one. "Why should they wait? they had waited too long already," he said, with some bitterness. But she felt none. With her all was peace.

Mr. Roy did another very foolish thing, which I can not conscientiously recommend to any middle-aged bachelor. Besides marrying his wife, he married her whole family. There was no other way out of the difficulty, and neither of them was inclined to be content with happiness, leaving duty unfulfilled. So he took the largest house in St. Andrews, and brought to it Janetta and Helen, till David Dalziel could claim them; likewise his own two orphan boys, .

until they went to Oxford; for he meant to send them there, and bring them up in every way like his own sons.

Meantime, it was rather a heterogeneous family; but the two heads of it bore their burden with great equanimity, nay, cheerfulness; saying sometimes, with a smile which had the faintest shadow of pathos in it, "that they liked to have young life about them."

And by degrees they grew younger themselves; less of the old bachelor and old maid, and more of the happy middle-aged couple to whom Heaven gave, in their decline, a St. Martin's summer almost as sweet as spring. They were both too wise to poison the present by regretting the past—a past which, if not wholly, was partly, at least, owing to that strange fatality which governs so many lives, only some have the will to conquer it, others not. And there are two sides to every thing: Robert Roy, who alone knew how hard his own life had been, sometimes felt a stern joy in thinking no one had shared it.

Still, for a long time there lay at the bottom of that strong, gentle heart of his a kind of remorseful tenderness, which showed itself in heaping his wife with every luxury that his wealth could bring; better than all, in surrounding her with that unceasing care which love alone teaches, never allowing the wind to blow on her too roughly—his "poor lamb," as he sometimes called her, who had suffered so much.

They are sure, humanly speaking, to "live very happy to the end of their days." And I almost fancy sometimes, if I were to go to St. Andrews, as I hope to do many a time, for I am as fond of the Aged City as they are, that I should see those two, made one at last after all those cruel divided years, wandering together along the sunshiny sands, or standing to watch the gay golfing parties; nay, I am not sure that Robert Roy would not be visible sometimes in his red coat, club in hand, crossing the Links, a victim to the universal insanity of St. Andrews, yet enjoying himself, as golfers always seem to do, with the enjoyment of a very boy.

She is not a girl, far from it; but there will be a girlish sweetness in her faded face till its last smile. And to see her sitting beside her husband on the green slopes of the pretty garden—knitting, perhaps, while he reads his eternal newspapers—is a perfect picture. They do not talk very much; indeed, they were neither of them ever great talkers. But each knows the other is close at hand, ready for any needful word, and always ready with that silent sympathy which is so mysterious a thing, the rarest thing to find in all human lives. These have found it, and are satisfied. And day by day truer grows the truth of that sentence which Mrs. Roy once discovered in her husband's pocket-book, cut out of a newspaper—she read and replaced it without a word, but with something between a smile and a tear—"*Young love is passionate, old love is faithful; but the very tenderest thing in all this world is a love revived.*"